The Way of Thorn and Thunder

D1452663

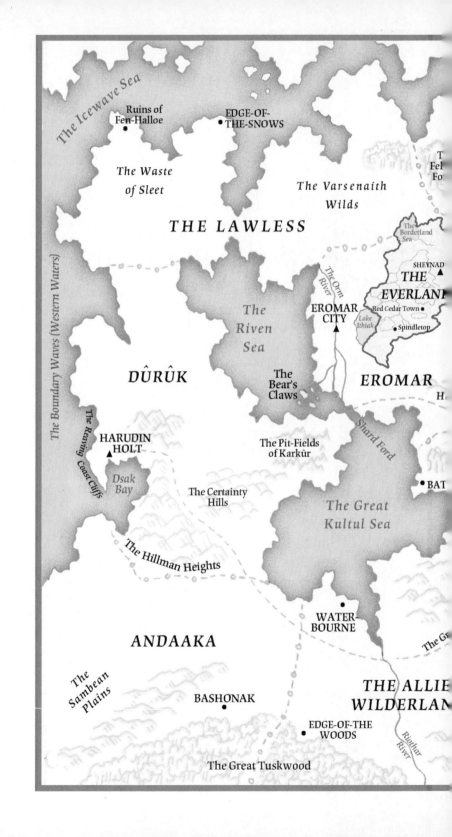

MAP OF THE MELDED WORLD

N

The
Borderland
Sea

Delvholme

The Wild

←Wildwater River

THE
ELDARVIAN
WOODS

SHEYNADWIIN
Dardath
Vale

THE
SUNRISE
FOREST

Thornholt

Lake
Ravanak

Meshiwiik
Forest

Birchbark
Hollow

The Panther River

Red Cedar
Town

Harvesthome

Thistlewood

The Kraagen Mountains

Edgewood
Spindletop

The
Downlands

Blackfly
Fen

THE EVERLAND

The
Way
of
Thorn
and
Thunder

>»||‹·<

The Kynship Chronicles

NEW HANOVER COUNTY
PUBLIC LIBRARY
201 CHESTNUT STREET
WILMINGTON, NC 28401

Daniel Heath Justice

UNIVERSITY OF NEW MEXICO PRESS

ALBUQUERQUE

© 2011 by the University of New Mexico by arrangement with Kegedonce Press
All rights reserved. Published 2011
Printed in the United States of America
15 14 13 12 11   1 2 3 4 5

Library of Congress Cataloging-in-Publication Data
Justice, Daniel Heath.
  The way of thorn and thunder : the Kynship chronicles / Daniel Heath Justice.
      p. cm.
  "... a revised and expanded omnibus edition of The way of thorn and thunder
trilogy (individual titles Kynship, Wyrwood, and Dreyd) published by Kegedonce
Press ..."–T.p. verso.
  ISBN 978-0-8263-5012-1 (pbk. : alk. paper)
  I. Justice, Daniel Heath. Kynship. II. Justice, Daniel Heath. Wyrwood. III. Justice,
Daniel Heath. Dreyd. IV. Title.
  PR9199.4.J87W39 2011
  813'.6—dc22
      2010038343

This is a work of imaginative fiction. Names, characters, places, relationships, beliefs, and
incidents are either the product of the author's imagination or are used fictitiously; rituals
and ceremonial practices are fictitious and do not reflect those of contemporary or historical
communities. Any resemblance to actual human or other-than-human persons (living, dead, or
otherwise), events, lifeways, or locales is entirely coincidental. The Way of Thorn and Thunder:
The Kynship Chronicles is a revised and expanded omnibus edition of The Way of Thorn and
Thunder trilogy (individual titles Kynship, Wyrwood, and Dreyd) published by Kegedonce Press,
with illustrations by Steve Sanderson.

To Kent—the dream, the journey, and the destination

Contents

Acknowledgments

MANY PEOPLE HAVE GIVEN their support, advice, and patient assistance in seeing this story through its various manifestations. In addition to the still-relevant acknowledgments in the trilogy editions, I'd like to extend particular appreciation to the following: all the fine and fabulous folks who made this University of New Mexico Press edition a beautiful reality, particularly the extraordinary Beth Hadas, as well as Elizabeth Albright, Sheila Berg, Karen Mazur, and Mina Yamashita; from Kegedonce Press, the two people who first took a chance on this story and have been steadfast supporters ever since, Kateri Akiwenzie-Damm and Renee Abram; good readers and thoughtful critics Jim Cox, Sophie Mayer, Sam McKegney, Michelle St. John, Richard Van Camp, and Craig Womack. Numerous people have taught the trilogy in classrooms all over North America and elsewhere in the world, and I've had the wonderful privilege of chatting or corresponding with them and their students about this story; this omnibus edition reflects some of their suggestions, and it's better as a result of their engaged responses. In particular, I'd like to thank Ellen Arnold, Qwo-Li Driskill, Keavy Martin, Mareike Neuhaus, Angeline O'Neill, Deanna Reder, Lisa Tatonetti, Christopher Teuton, Kyle Wyatt and Jim and Sam again, as well as their wonderful students. My apologies and belated thanks to anyone I might have forgotten in this list.

My parents, Kathy and Jim Justice, remain my inspiration; whatever honor inhabits this story is because of their loving example. Mom in particular has journeyed with these characters longer than anyone else, and she's both the toughest and the best reader I've known; her good guidance is made manifest throughout the tale. My mother-in-law, Murielle Dunn, has put up with all the weirdness that accompanies living with a writer, and she's done so with good humor and grace. Though we speak different languages and inhabit different understandings, my four-footed friends Raven and Bambam have had to put up with far fewer walks and less playtime as a result of my distraction at the keyboard, as did the much-missed Otis and Ivy before them, but they've all shown me limitless love beyond the deserving of any human being.

My greatest appreciation, as always, is to my husband, Kent Dunn. I've known no better friend, no finer man, no kinder heart. Thank you, my love.

This Is Their Story: Major Characters

The Tree-Born Kyn

Tarsa'deshae, the Redthorn Wielder
Unahi Sam'sheyda, the Wielder of Thistlewood
Garyn Mendiir, the Governor
Neranda Ak'shaar, the Lawmaker
Daladir Tre'shein, the Ambassador
Jitani Al'daar, the Mercenary
Averyn, the Spirit-Mender

The Beast-Clan Tetawi

Tobhi Burrows, the Leafspeaker
Quill Meadowgood, the Dolltender
Molli Rose, the Spirit-talker
Jago Chaak, the Toymaker

Other Folk of the Everland and Beyond

Denarra Syrene, the Strangeling Wielder
Blackwick, the Ubbetuk Chancellor
Padwacket, the Valet
Guaandak, the Emperor Triumphant
Biggiabba, the Gvaerg Wielder
Myrkash the Unbroken, the Beast-Chief
Smudge, the Little Deer

The Sons and Daughters of Man

Lojar Vald, the Reaver and Dreydmaster of Eromar
Vergis Thane, the Seeker
Merrimyn Hurlbuck, the Binder
Qualla'am Kaer, the Reachwarden
Meggie Mar, the House Matron
Klaus, the Guardian

Cycle One
Aspenglow

I want to tell a story.

This story has many beginnings, like the great Wildwater that runs in a roaring rush through the narrow canyons and high peaks of the Old Everland, its voice loud with the knowing ways of uncountable years. Some of these beginnings are swift and wild, with unseen dangers, shards and shadows, while others are slow and gentle, a lover's tender touch over the land, giving a spirit some time to ponder the deep, restless ways of the water. It's sometimes hard to tell which of these beginnings give it life. Maybe it isn't one way at all. Maybe it's all of them, each giving a true and necessary part to the whole.

The memory of the world is short, and death rides hard in the forgetting, so I hold these teachings and share them, mindful that only the stories weave our past into our future. The memories of those days are clear, though the pain sometimes gives shape to the joy. But I suppose that all the important stories are like that, if they're told truthfully. Everything that endures seems so much more precious when you've suffered thorn and thunder to keep it.

So I hold to these teachings, and I tell these stories, with the hope that they're true to what we fought for, and what so many died for. This isn't my story alone, but this is my knowing of the story, and this is my understanding of its beginnings.

1

Stone and Spear

WEARS-STONES-FOR-SKIN STALKED with an easy grace through the canyon toward Red Cedar Town. His was the steady walk of one to whom fear was barely the itch of a memory. He was in no hurry. Only the rumbling in his stomach, like two river rocks grinding against each other, gave any indication of his purpose, for he hungered this day, as he always hungered. He knew that he would feed well at his destination, even if the Kyn fled at his approach. He would sniff out all their hiding places, from the forest canopy to the root-tangled caves; his untiring pace was more dependable than their panic. They would run, they would tire, and then, they would die.

He stopped and looked with some satisfaction at the fly-swarmed elk skin he pulled along behind him, piled high with swollen and rotting Kyn bodies. He bent and tore a large bite from a leg severed roughly at the hip, the bone gleaming in the leaf-shadowed sunlight. Days-thickened blood slid down his cobbled chin as he chewed in distraction. Old meat was tasty, but it was empty of spirit; he much preferred his food warm and screaming.

Three towns were behind him—Nine Oaks, Downbriar, and High Marching—and perhaps two dozen more lay ahead in the deep clefts and wooded valleys of this end of the Kraagen Mountains. Wears-Stones-for-Skin had fed well in the weeks since he fled his

3

own rocky ridge up north. While Kyn were not his favorite meat—he particularly enjoyed the rare and savory deep-rock Gvaergs, as their struggles were most deliciously desperate—he could hardly remember a time when he was so sated. Of course, the Kyn had fought back valiantly with all manner of weapons: stout stone and copper blades, strong wood and bright fire, pitfalls, spiked rams that dropped from trees, and even more ingenious traps. But he was a Feaster, one of the Eaters of old, and his skin was thick with thousands of jagged stones that protected him from most wounds. Those wisdom-keepers who had once challenged him and his kind were rare these days, driven from these lowlands by their own people, and their teachings now lay hidden in dark, secret places, leaving his ravenous path clear.

His chewing slowed slightly. No, it wasn't just those wise ones of the elder times who could have driven him away. Now there were others—bright-eyed, hairy creatures with sharp, fire-forged iron and a hunger almost as great as his own, and it was their unyielding persistence that had sent him fleeing southward from his high mountain cave to these ancient wooded valleys. Those strange pain-bringers made him an exile, and he hated them even more than he hated the blazing light of the sister suns, now mercifully shrouded by the thickly crowded pines lining the canyon.

He pulled a resistant tendon from his teeth and tossed it into the ferny undergrowth, and his pebbled brows narrowed in memory of his desperate escape. There were some who could hurt him. Their cruel shining weapons burned through stony flesh, and the wounds ached for days. But there was no smell of Humans in these valleys. Those creatures were far away, and he was safe. Nothing worried him here.

Wears-Stones-for-Skin grunted and moved forward again, carelessly dragging the skin behind. His path led up a steep slope, along a dry riverbed that cut a deep gorge through the mountain. The way was littered with river stones and larger rocks, but there was a manageable trail to follow.

As he shifted his massive frame between two smooth boulders, he sniffed the air deeply. His fat lips parted, and dozens of broken brown teeth clacked in amusement as he inhaled again, deeper this time: he-Kyn waited for him on the canyon walls above. Wears-Stones-for-Skin slowly swung his head back and forth, catching the different scents, each lingering for a moment on his mottled tongue as he counted the distinctive odors of eleven warriors with freshly uprooted stones ready to toss down; he tasted the soil's sharp tang, mingled with the softer sweetness of fear. His smile stretched wider. The feeding was always better when he could play a bit.

Feigning ignorance of their presence, Wears-Stones-for-Skin strode forward again, his heart thundering in eager anticipation. The canyon narrowed. Despite his massive bulk that dwarfed all but the largest boulders along the way, he passed smoothly through the gap, walking with the slow, easy certainty of a patient hunter. The smells of the he-Kyn were stronger now, and Wears-Stones-for-Skin could barely conceal the laugh that rattled in his belly as he continued up the slope to a level path ahead.

The Feaster sniffed at the air for a moment and nodded with satisfaction. The he-Kyn were at the upper rim of the gorge, only about fifty strides ahead. He would let them throw down their rocks; he might even pretend to be wounded, crying out in pain and fear like those Kyn and other Folk he'd so eagerly hunted in the earlier towns. And then, when these proud warriors were sure of their success and curious about their defeated quarry, he would end the game, for he was famished.

As he rounded another large boulder in the path, Wears-Stones-for-Skin staggered to a halt. His yellow eyes narrowed. Not far ahead, a lone she-Kyn stood in the path to block his way. She was small— not quite half his height—but there were powerful muscles under the green flesh, and she promised to fight with far more enthusiasm than had been demonstrated by the spindly oldsters and squalling fat babies of his former feasts. Her turquoise eyes were hard with cold anger.

As odd as it was to encounter a Redthorn she-warrior among the fighters, Wears-Stones-for-Skin was more intrigued than worried. Though the war-hardy Redthorns were courageous opponents, they were rare—the Feaster had seen none of their kind in the earlier towns he'd raided, and very few in the ages before that. They, like the wisdom-bearing Wielders, belonged more to memory than to the living age. Like most Kyn, this Redthorn was solid, her body's curves round and full, her arms and legs tightly muscled but not bulky. She held only one weapon in her three-fingered hands: a long, black-bladed spear. It was a pathetic defense against one such as him.

The Feaster now let his mocking laughter fly free, and the sound rattled the canyon walls. Wears-Stones-for-Skin licked the air; though the she-Kyn stood firm, he could feel the fear roll off of the he-Kyn above. It was as it should be. He was an elemental power who had existed since the elder times—he'd always fed on the Folk of the Everland, and their flesh and fear would continue to amuse and nourish him well in the limitless ages to come. These quivering creatures were little more than gristle and bone; they would soon come to understand how inconsequential they truly were, and he would give the memorable lesson. With a gleeful roar and clenching claws extended, he loped forward in slavering anticipation.

The she-Kyn stood pale but unwavering, her spear held ready, even as the wave of corpse stench boiled over her, even as his howl pierced her mind and set her muscles trembling. She stood in his path, defiant.

Wears-Stones-for-Skin opened his mouth to bellow again in murderous triumph, but he suddenly slid to a stop, sending a spray of dust and gravel flying. Something was wrong. It wasn't the Redthorn's determined stance that unnerved him. It was something else that fluttered, moth-like, around his thoughts, elusive but vital.

Then he knew, and the knowledge chilled his heart: he'd never smelled her.

He smelled the fear and anticipation of the he-Kyn above, perceived each individual's salty tang as clearly as he could sense his own gnarled hands before him. He smelled the stones at his feet, the chickadees and ravens nesting in the thick, scrubby pines, the deer and squirrels and bobcats in the forest undergrowth. He even smelled the Kyn in the town beyond and those he'd left dead, wounded, and grieving in the ravaged towns, but he couldn't smell *her*.

Now he knew why, and for the first time since leaving his beloved mountain sanctuary, he was frightened. He knew terror here, and the freezing sensation rolled off his body like the new spring run-off from the high peaks.

Wears-Stones-for-Skin swung around to flee back down the gorge to safety, but he recoiled as six other she-Kyn closed the gap he'd just passed through. Two wore Redthorn leggings and loincloths, with wooden breastplates and copper bracers. The other four wore simple woven skirts, blouses, and short boots. And all were in their moon-time, like the solitary spear-bearer who now stood at his back. Unlike the four town matrons who also walked toward the cringing Feaster, the Redthorn warriors were fully trained in blood and battle. But this cyclical power made *all* the she-Kyn doubly powerful. Wears-Stones-for-Skin's ancient might, the bindings that kept his spirit whole, were scattered to the winds by their strength. He was death's shadow—they burned with life's fire.

It was all they needed to unmake him.

He stumbled away. As deadly and strong as this hunter had been during his ageless life, the she-Kyn were stronger still. Their blood-time was power beyond bearing for a creature of pain, and he knew terror now as he never had, even when the iron blades and thundering fire-sticks of Men bit through his stony flesh. He tried to flee, but the strength dropped from his legs, and he crashed against the dry riverbed with the squeals of a suckling bear cub. The seven she-Kyn moved forward. The lone warrior stopped just beyond the Feaster's reach, spear held aloft.

Unable to bear the torment of their presence, Wears-Stones-for-Skin thrashed onto his back, vomiting a rolling black plume into the air. Stones burned and cracked where the slime struck earth. The creature writhed and screamed, and the six other she-Kyn halted their forward advance.

The spear-bearer whistled then, and rocks fell from above. The he-Kyn had moved up from their earlier position; they were far better prepared than the ancient one had thought. Boulders and smaller stones, some no bigger than a Kyn's fist, others larger than the Feaster's head, smashed into the invader's body with furious precision. Wears-Stones-for-Skin's screams rose to a wordless howl as bones shattered beneath cracking skin, as his weakened body snapped and sagged like a stick-pierced waterskin. So much pain—so much fear. For all the death he had brought to others in his long existence, this was the first time he'd tasted its bitterness himself, and he found it far from his liking.

As quickly as the assault had begun, the rocks stopped falling, and all was quiet except for the rasping groans of the creature on the canyon floor. The spear-wielding Redthorn came toward him again. Wears-Stones-for-Skin lay on his back, the broken remnants of his face pointed toward the pine-rimmed sky. One milky eye watched her movements with wild terror; the other lay crushed in its socket.

She stood above the once-terrible Feaster, her face impassive. Her presence alone filled him with agony, but he couldn't escape. He could only writhe helplessly before this small, green-skinned creature, his throbbing heart a death-drum in his chest.

There was no hope, only desperation. *Go away—she must go away. If they would all leave me, I could heal—I could survive. Maybe they think me already dead.*

He was wrong. As though sensing his frantic thoughts, the she-Kyn lifted her weapon, and Wears-Stones-for-Skin's gurgling shriek betrayed him. His death had come, for the spear's shaft was of wyrwood, blood-bane to the Eaters and their kind. Like spring lightning from the Upper Place, the obsidian blade flashed in the sunlight and drove down into the Feaster's chest, past the fragments of his rock-lined flesh, deeper through soft, creamy tissues into his bursting heart. The she-Kyn plunged the spear into the creature with such force that the shaft shattered in two. The other warriors rushed forward and rammed long wyrwood spikes into his belly and throat, pinning him to the riverbed, spattering his burning blood across the rocks.

Wears-Stones-for-Skin screamed again, this time with a torment so great that the ground buckled. The Kyn fell to their knees and covered their oak-leaf ears in anguish. Not even the bindings wrapping the sensory stalks on their temples could muffle the creature's death agonies, and a few of them collapsed from the sudden shock. The cry rang through the rocky canyon, ripping through the sky, driving birds and other Beasts from their rest, sending sprouts in Red Cedar Town wailing to their mothers and aunties. The sound became a shredding whirlwind that rose louder and louder, drowning out all thought, all feeling but pain.

Then the screams ended, and the world was quiet again.

The Stoneskin lay unmoving in a stinking, steaming black pool. Faces pale and drawn, the she-Kyn looked at one another and back to their long-anticipated quarry. Their attention moved upward as a trill of victory erupted from the he-Kyn warriors on the gorge's rim, who scrambled hurriedly down to the riverbed.

The spear-bearer felt her knees buckle, and she sagged, shaking, to the earth. Her heart throbbed wildly, and her eyes were bright with tears of relief and delayed fear. "We've bested him," she whispered. Oda'hea, the eldest she-Kyn warrior of the group, knelt down beside her.

"Yes, young 'thorn," Oda'hea smiled. "Red Cedar Town is safe. We'll send a runner to tell the others, and then we'll burn him, though clean fire is too good for this murderous filth."

The younger Redthorn stood shakily. "Where did he come from?"

One of the unarmed matrons shook her head. "We've never had a Stoneskin down this far before. I've only ever heard of them in the upper mountains."

"Another bad sign to add to the rest. Well, whatever his reasons for being here may have been," Oda'hea growled as she drove more wyrwood spikes into the creature's broken flesh, "he won't be going back."

A messenger sprinted through the forest toward Red Cedar Town, and the battle party, eighteen in all, gathered together to burn the body of the Stoneskin before his poisonous blood corrupted the much-traveled path. The he-Kyn stood apart from the moon-time females and praised their bravery from a safe distance, and all recounted the experience with awe. The spear-bearer shared their joyful mood, but the emotions of the day still sent her head and heart pounding. Aside from a few raids against Human squatters in the valley, this was her first great excursion as a fully trained Redthorn warrior. She'd faced a powerful foe and she still lived. She even had a new name now, one given to her by her fellow Redthorns: Tarsa'deshae—She-Breaks-the-Spear. It was the honored name of a warrior, of the battle-strength-ened she-Kyn who was no longer the youngling Namshéké.

Tarsa still held the broken spear shaft. She looked at it from time to time in amazement; everything seemed somehow unreal, as though she stood halfway between the waking world and a dream. But she stood tall beside the other she-Kyn, her body sore with tension and training, her heartbeat only now slowing from the surge of excitement and fear. Her thick gold-brown hair, the color of old honey, was woven into a single tight braid that was swept away from her forehead and ears by a plain copper headband. Her serpentine sensory stalks, two on each temple, were now unwrapped and moved gently in the open air, free from the bindings that protected them from harm and dulled their sensitivity to the emotions and pain of battle. Fresh honor marks scored her cheeks, joining the other simple blue tattoos that tracked the green skin of her face, arms, and legs. The blouse, leggings, supple boots, and breechcloth she wore had been chosen for comfort, not protection, for there was no armor in Red Cedar Town that could have withstood the fury of the Stoneskin's claws.

Tarsa's stomach clenched at the thought, but her rising nervousness was broken as the zhe-Kyn, pox-scarred Fa'alik, stepped toward the Stoneskin's body with a burning cedar branch. The zhe-Kyn straddled the male and female worlds in all things, garbed in blouse and skirt, head tattooed and shaved but for a braided topknot, moving between the blood of war and the blood of the moon without fear. Fa'alik drew the group together and, singing a song of healing and reconciliation, drove the flames into the monster's chest.

The Stoneskin's blood caught fire instantly, and within moments the body was ablaze, the sweet scent of cedar wafting through the air, the smoke cleansing their thoughts of death and destruction while easing the creature's journey into the Spirit World. Each group went separately to a nearby creek to wash the blood from their bodies and purge the death-taint from their spirits with the help of bitter herbs, prayers, and cold water. When they were finished, Fa'alik gathered them together and shared stories from the time of the Ancestrals, when it was told that a Stoneskin, though brutal and bloodthirsty, was also one of the wise ones of long ago, and that with his death came great knowledge. But there were none here who knew what that knowledge would be, as none of them, even the eldest of the Redthorns, had ever challenged a Feaster and lived. Those who might have once been able to tell them no longer lived in Red Cedar Town, where the Redthorns and Fa'alik were the last adherents of the Deep Green.

Tarsa stood away from the burning body. She felt strangely distanced from her celebrating companions. She couldn't feel the fire's heat or hear Fa'alik's voice. Her head still pounded, but it was like a deep beating drum, a rhythm that moved in cadence with her heart. The smoke swirled and danced to the drumbeat, turning grey, sometimes firelight-red, as it drifted around her and then rose into the star-strewn sky. And as she watched the Stoneskin's body crumble into glittering ash, she felt a voice singing to the drum inside her head and heart. It was the voice of the Stoneskin, but there was no rage, no pain or hunger. It was an ancient song that twisted into her blood, diving deep, calling down to sing into being the secrets that pulsed there. The drums beat faster; the voice rose higher; the flames filled her vision and pulled her into the burning rhythm.

Tarsa stumbled dizzily out of the circle. She couldn't breathe, couldn't think beyond the pounding surge that filled her consciousness. The world slipped away—the dark sky and red soil shifted places and spun in wild confusion. The earth was no longer beneath her feet—she barely felt her body pitch forward, toward the Stoneskin's smoking remains. She struck the ground with a cry, and a shroud of darkness fell across her mind.

2

Red Cedar Town

LIKE THE WARMING MONTHS OF SPRING, Unahi came slowly to the inner valleys of the ice-mantled mountains, and the old Wielder's arrival was as certain as that of the blossom-bearing season. She usually waited until the first leaves budded on the aspens before leaving the deep shadows of Thistlewood on her spring rounds, traveling to most of the towns and isolated settlements within a two-week walk of the cluttered but comfortable cabin that she had called home for many years. She enjoyed little rest until the aspen leaves turned a brilliant gold at the first bitter touch of winter. By that time, the grey-green Wielder would have assisted in a few dozen births, numerous marriages and love-bondings, the removal of a handful of minor curses and harmful medicine chants from quarrelsome gossips and vindictive conjurors, the proper observation of a wide range of rituals and ceremonies to ensure good harvests and harmonious relationships with neighboring towns and, sadly, in recent years, far too many funerals.

The old Wielder was bent and wrinkled like a wind-worn cypress, and though she walked with the strength of a warrior, her spirit carried a heavy burden. That morning she'd finished the lengthy rites of mourning and purification at Downbriar Town after its decimation by a Stoneskin a few days before. Unahi's fourth day of isolation was over; the death-taint of the bodies would no longer follow her. She was relieved that the creature had been stopped before it reached Red Cedar Town, yet it also grieved her that such an aged spirit was now lost to the world. It was unusual for those Feasters to leave their rocky homes in the high mountains. Many things were changing these days, and few for the better.

Unahi stopped to lean on Dibadjiibé, the wyrwood staff that had long been her companion, protector, and, increasingly, her support. Callused fingers absently tapped the red-veined chunk of amber embedded in the smooth golden wood at the tip as she anticipated the path ahead. She'd walked this trail many times in her youth, more years past than she cared to remember. She knew the placement of every bearded pine, each sheltered hollow, the brush-hidden game trails, and the clear, cold creeks that tumbled down hidden pathways through the tangled mountains. It wasn't just the voices of the *wyr* that gave the Wielder this knowledge, although at this time of her life it was sometimes difficult to tell where that spirit-language ended and her own understandings began. Her memory was still strong, her flowing head-stalks still sensitive to the pulse of green life around her, her wyrweave boots still thin enough to let her feet feel the heartbeat of the soil. In other days, these things would have been enough to sweep the shadows from her mind.

Unahi breathed deeply, taking in the earthy spice of the pine and aspen slopes around her. There was even the slightest sweet hint of willow from the streambed below. But there was also pain in the air. It was nothing like the hurt of Downbriar or High Marching Town, which had a tangible source and a clear reason for their ache. The Kyn of those towns had already been sorely wounded by the latest wave of wasting fever that arrived with last year's snows. The cold months had cost them much that they had treasured, particularly their sprouts and elders. Now, after the Stoneskin's bloody visit, only a handful of the young ones remained, and two of them would never walk again. Unahi hadn't yet been to Nine Oaks, but she feared that its survivors would share similar stories.

No, the pain that Unahi felt now was something different. She could sense it all the way up the valley, a gnawing deep in the bones, scattering across the world like crows in a tempest. She couldn't fully identify the feeling yet, but she knew its source, and that was now her destination. The Kyn of Red Cedar Town were not as friendly to Wielders these days as they had once been. Her Branchfolk would be bound by kinship and still-strong traditions of hospitality to give her a pallet and a meal during her visit, but that would be the most she could expect. Besides, even though she would have sought the pulsing pain on her own, curiosity and duty compelling her forward, she'd received a soft summons from someone in the town just two nights before, a blue clay bead delivered deep in the night by a skittish bat who clearly longed to be elsewhere. Blue was the color of the north, a portent of despair and fear. She could hardly ignore that call.

The Wielder moved forward again with a stronger stride. Her heart's reluctance didn't match her will's weathered determination, though she would almost rather face the Stoneskin herself than what awaited her in Red Cedar Town.

Her sisters had long and unforgiving memories.

"Sit down, Unahi, but let's not pretend that you're welcome here," Ivida scowled at the Wielder as she handed out steaming wooden bowls of pumpkin soup. Unahi nodded silently as she accepted the bowl and leaned back against the wall, her staff beside her, a long-stemmed clay pipe jutting from her lips.

The five sisters sat on the floor together in a small, octagonal cabin, the four she-Kyn of the town eyeing their long-absent sibling warily. Unahi was silent as she sipped the spiced liquid and looked around. The cabin was well built and insulated, a testament to the high status of the Cedar Branch-mothers. A fire pit in the center sent playful shadows skipping around the seated figures, oblivious to the tension that hung heavy with the pine smoke. The walls were coated with a thick clay glaze and adorned with black and grey-blue images, generally meek sky and star scenes. Aside from these modest designs and the flickering fire, the cabin was sparsely furnished, a far cry from her long-ago sapling days, when the Kyn of Red Cedar Town had celebrated the *wyr*-rich world around them with bright tapestries of color, intricate swirls and serpentine patterns that shimmered with a life of their own. Every dwelling, no matter how humble, would have been boldly painted, with ribbons, baskets, wyrweave banners, bits of bright rock, and chunks of river-worn driftwood in strange shapes scattered everywhere. Even now, her own little cabin in Thistlewood, a worn assemblage of log, stone, and living pine that splayed comfort-ably against the base of a rocky outcropping, was pleasing to the eyes and welcoming to the spirit. Her sisters' Branch-house was a symbol, and not an inviting one; it was far from being a home.

Vansaaya, the eldest of the five, placed her bowl beside her crossed legs and leaned forward. Her hair was silver like that of the Wielder, but its sheen was steel-cold in the dim firelight. "Why are you here, Unahi? Red Cedar Town has long been Celestial."

The others exchanged smug smiles as the real business of their meeting began.

The Wielder followed Vansaaya's movements and spoke. "I haven't forgotten. For twenty-six years I've avoided this valley as you demanded. In spite of my vow to Lan'delar, and even after Kiyda died, I stayed away from here, no matter how much my heart ached to share the burden of my family's grief. But something has hap-pened; someone has called me here." She held out her hand to reveal the blue bead to her sisters, locking Vansaaya's gaze. "And I mean to find out why."

"Witchery!" Ivida hissed through clenched teeth. With Lan'delar long dead, Ivida was the youngest, and she enjoyed the freedom that role provided, even now that she was six times a grandmother and her black-green hair was streaking grey. "Your ways will bring noth-ing but pain and suffering to us again, to the entire town. Just look at yourself, Unahi. Your back is bent, your face worn by age and marred by those wicked marks on your flesh. You're a rag-and-bone ghost of what you could have been. And you'll determine conditions for *us?*" She snorted scornfully.

Unahi shook her head. "No, sister. As I told you those long years past, I have no intention of challenging your decision, even if it's ignorant and spiteful." Ivida's face darkened, but the Wielder contin-ued, her eyes narrowing to hard slits as she spoke. "I'm not here to stay. I am here, however, to find out why I was called here to help. I was summoned for a reason."

The others looked to Vansaaya, whose expression remained mild and detached. Geth, the oldest aside from Unahi and Vansaaya, ladled more soup into her sisters' bowls, her left hand shaking, fin-gers knobby and curled from the ache that had long burned into her joints. Her eyes glanced quickly at the Wielder and scanned the others, as if in silent debate. All was silent except for the gentle slosh of the steaming pot. With the barest intake of breath, she mumbled, "No more, sisters . . . please. I sent for her."

The others turned on her. Sathi'in, a recent widow who generally preferred to follow Vansaaya's lead, spat, "Be silent! You'll only make it worse!"

Wearily, Geth shook her head. "How? We can't help the sapling; Luran knows we've tried. Not even the Shield knows what's wrong. Maybe Unahi can help. If we just stand back, if we don't try something, Tarsa might die."

"Better that," Ivida said, her voice dripping with malice, "than be corrupted by the Green!"

"Enough!" Vansaaya stood abruptly. Though older than Unahi, her body was straight and proud, unbent by the passing of the years. She turned toward Ivida. "Whatever else we may be, we are not kith-killers. We do not cut healthy fruit from our Branch if we can avoid doing so. She is our niece, the only surviving child of our youngest sister. We are obliged to help her by whatever means are available." She cast a dark glance at Unahi. "No matter how distasteful those means might be."

The others stood up, although Geth wavered a bit as she tried to stand without putting pressure on her left arm. Vansaaya turned to her. "As you brought her here, she is your responsibility. Take her to the sapling." Her lips tightened. "We will speak about this later. Come, sisters." She walked out the door without another glance at the Wielder, followed silently by Ivida and Sathi'in, ever dutiful in their obedience.

Geth's eyes filled with tears, and she rushed to embrace Unahi, who held her gently, careful not to jar her sister's curled hand. "I knew you'd come," Geth whispered as they walked together out of the Branch-house. "I knew you wouldn't forget your promise."

As she looked around at the site of her birth and of much of her early life, Unahi noted that Red Cedar Town hadn't changed as much as she'd feared it might. The cabins were much like her own, and they still stood scattered in roughly circular rows around the central clearing. They were short and widely round, like oversized mushroom caps, with mud-and-thatch or wood-tiled roofs and solid stone chimneys rising from the center of each structure to send plumes of smoke and shimmering sparks into the night sky. Warm light filtered through thick wyrweave curtains hanging in the circular windows. Small, unfenced gardens surrounded each house, and rich reddish soil lay piled in mounds around wooden stakes driven deeply into the earth. Two- and three-story drying houses stood on stilts throughout the town. Beneath them were the underground store-houses that preserved the dried corn, squash, beans, nuts, herbs, and other foodstuffs.

Beyond the central settlement, just outside the protective log palisade, were the community growing fields, which mirrored the home gardens but on a larger scale. The watch pillars could still be seen in the moonlight beyond the palisade, tall tree trunks with rough seats atop them, scattered throughout the fields to provide sharp-eyed scouts with an unobstructed view. From time to time Unahi would see other Kyn walking past on errands of their own. It was dark, and the shadows obscured her tattoos, so that none seemed to know that a Wielder was in their midst. They smiled at Geth and tipped their chins pleasantly to Unahi as they continued on their way. She recognized some of the eldest among them, and homesick-ness washed over her.

But as she and her sister moved closer to the central ceremonial clearing, the changes from the years gradually grew more apparent, and hopeful nostalgia gave way to sad resignation. Even here Time held sway, the embracing circle giving way to the unyielding line. The houses, once adorned with beautiful carvings of plant- and Beast-people, or of the hidden spirit creatures who shared the Everland along with the Kyn and their Folk kith, were now lifeless. There were no guardian masks hanging on the doors, no shell or copper chimes hanging from the eaves, no doublewoven splint baskets piled high with drying herbs dangling from the roof beams. She was shocked to see dried deer haunches, plucked sage grouse and turkeys, and various fish strung up on tall poles leaned against the cabin walls. In earlier days, the soil had provided all the necessary food for the Kyn, without one of their animal neighbors paying a blood price for the meal. Hunting was practiced only against creatures who threatened the towns and their fields, and even that action required the Kyn sensory stalks to be bound against the death-pains of the hunted.

The little gardens, so promising in the distance, were now revealed to be strictly separated from one another. The sisters halted as Unahi reached into a mound and closed her eyes, drawing on the *wyr* that pulsed there like the land's heartbeat. Unlike her own garden and those of other Greenwalking Kyn, the gardens of the Celestials were segregated with ruthless precision—reflecting the Celestial insistence on one way, one truth, one perspective, only one type of bean grew in this mound, unnourished by the rich possibilities of many different seeds sharing their *wyr* with one another. This food might provide health for the body, but it would never provide true nourishment for the spirit, not like those foods that were planted together to help one another grow strong.

"A solitary seed is vulnerable and weak," she whispered to herself as she reflected on the reality of her own isolation, but it was only a passing worry. True, she lived without other Kyn nearby, but she was never alone; Dibadjiibé was always at her side, and she was part of a larger community that extended far beyond the little cabin in Thistlewood. It was an understanding of communal duty and kinship that her sisters would never be able to comprehend in their safe Branch-house at the top of the valley.

Unahi stood, shaking her head and wiping her hands on her skirt. She'd never expected to return to Red Cedar Town; if she didn't look too closely, she could almost feel like she belonged here again with her sisters and Branch-kith. Any lingering hope of connection crumbled, however, when she turned toward the clearing.

She'd known it would happen when she left—they told her as much as she was driven away from the valley—but the physical reality of the change still shook the heartwood of her being. Tsijehu, the magnificent cedar who once stood rooted so solidly in the center of Red Cedar Town, his bristling branches bedecked with bright wyrweave ribbons and lanterns aglow with fragrant beeswax candles, was now gone. Even his roots were absent, torn away years before. Only the memory of the great tree remained, and even that was fading. There was no one left here who mourned his passing. Now, instead of the green-headed uncle who had been ancient even when the Kyn had first built their cabins around his sheltering branches, there stood an arch of white stone, hard and cold in the moonlight. Geth looked around nervously but followed Unahi's slow pace to the arch.

It stretched high above them, as imposing in height as in its heavy weight on the red earth. Where the stone had come from, Unahi couldn't tell, but it was clear that it been brought a long distance, for it did not belong to this place; there was no spirit, no voice, no memory to be found in the structure. It stood mute but not harmless. The blocks of stone were polished to an unforgiving white shine, and each segment was joined to the others by thick bands of reddening iron, mortal poison to the Kyn and many other Folk. The Wielder was amazed that here, in the heart of a Kyn town, were two dozen or more coils of the toxic metal, each as wide around as her fist. She turned to Geth, who placed her finger over her lips.

Unahi's eyes scanned the rest of the arch. Strange markings scored its entire length, all sharp angles and deep gouges, roughly cut to resemble stars, the sister suns, and the moon. The night sky was starless through the opening. It was a Celestial shrine, raised here to remind everyone in Red Cedar Town that the Greenwalker ways were no longer welcome: Zhaia, the Tree-Mother of the Kyn, and the other spirit-beings of the green earth were abandoned; the he-moon, Pearl-in-Darkness, had been overthrown, and Luran, the Virgin Moon, singular, cold, and remote, more suited to the world of Men than the Everland, took his place. Those who disagreed, like Unahi, were given a simple choice: to leave, or to die. For some, it had been no choice at all, and their moss-painted bones could still be found scattered throughout the mountains in sheltered hollows or lonely grave sites. Though scarred in body and in dreams, Unahi was one of the lucky ones.

Geth tugged at the Wielder's shawl, leading her toward the tree-lined shadows to the north of the clearing. "You didn't need to look at that," she whispered.

"Of course I did," Unahi said in a normal tone, unwilling to keep her voice low. "I had to see what happened after I left. I just didn't expect it to be so . . . final." She kept her face fixed forward, but the fluttering ache in her chest was the start of a building grief that she didn't dare acknowledge, not yet. She had a difficult task ahead that required her focus. There would be time enough to grieve old Tsijehu, and all that once was and might have been.

Geth was silent as they moved into the woods. They were immersed in a fragrant hush of heavy green timber. The aspens and pines teased the sisters' senses and drew them up the slope. But beneath the whispering welcome of the shaggy old forest, Unahi could feel an unease gingerly tugging at her consciousness. Her sensory stalks grew tense in warning. She stopped and looked quizzically at her sister.

The younger she-Kyn lowered her eyes. "It's been this way since the troubles started. Everyone can feel it, even the Shield. They all try to explain it away. But I didn't forget the old teachings, Unahi. I always remembered. I shared the stories with her all her life. That's why she became a Redthorn. That's why she faced down the Stoneskin. And that . . . that's why we—they—brought her here." She pointed to a thin, nearly overgrown trail that disappeared up the slope into the deeper darkness of the trees, barely discernible in the moonlight.

"But what's—?" The Wielder stopped, understanding at last. The memories flooded back, and with them came a nearly blinding rage. She grabbed her sister's good arm and hissed, "What have you done to her? She's our niece!"

Geth stumbled away. "We didn't have any choice, Unahi," she whispered, her eyes filled with hurt and sudden tears. "She was mad with the pain. Things were happening, awful things. One of the warriors who brought her back was almost torn apart by thorns that grew out of her skin, dagger-sharp and as long as a spear-point. He very nearly died. Tarsa couldn't help herself—she didn't know what was happening. She was a witched thing. Every time someone came near to help, she'd unleash some new horror. It was either this, or . . ." She went silent, but the meaning was clear. An Awakening was agonizing even in the best of circumstances, but the young she-Kyn—once a bright-eyed sapling named Namshéké, now called by her warrior's name, Tarsa'deshae—had Awakened alone and unguided. Tarsa was older than most who'd had the benefit of a Wielder to lead them safely through their transformation, the opening of the self to the primal powers of the Deep Green. Given the lingering hostility of the Purging that had decimated the ranks of the Wielders not so many years past, Unahi was surprised that the young Redthorn warrior was given even this reprieve.

It was likely due to the very fact that Tarsa was a member of that honored company that she still survived. Redthorns were the only traditionalist Kyn who still remained generally unmolested by the Celestials and their followers, more out of a need for the Redthorns' unrivaled skills in battle and defensive strategy than from any sentimental attachment to kinship with Greenwalkers.

All those who had been Purged were family to those who walked the Celestial path, but they'd been cut away in spite of that kinship—Tarsa's earlier good fortune was as rare as it was brief, and it was swiftly fading. The young warrior was strong, but only death would ease her pain without an experienced Wielder's guidance. Unahi tore through the pine boughs, ignoring the bite of their needles on her skin and Geth's rasping breath as the latter tried to keep up. The aspen leaves whispered frantically at their passing. The evening chill disappeared as they moved through the underbrush, thin moonlight turning the slight path to deep-night silver. They hurried on.

There were dangers in the Burning Mouth that no degree of Redthorn courage could overcome.

A Redthorn warrior stands strong.

Tarsa could feel the fire pulse through her blood. Each muscle, each span of her body ached from within. She desperately wanted a release that would not come. If she could have detached her spirit from flesh, she would have seen herself curled into a corner of the pit, hair matted with blood, mud, and filth, skin bruised and torn. She would have seen a creature possessed, thrashing outward, then contracting again into a tense, quivering ball. But she was trapped inside herself, and there was no escape, no freedom of removed observation.

And the pain. It was nearly beyond bearing.

A Redthorn warrior is a stranger to pain.

The Stoneskin's bloodsong rose up again. It pushed at the limits of her skin, drawing the *wyr* through her body, pushing her senses to the dull edge of sanity, and then fell back again, recoiling from the poisonous iron veins that stretched like spiderwebs across the walls and floor of the pit. But each crest of the *wyr* reached higher than the next. There would soon be a flood, and her spirit would rush away forever, leaving the body to rot in the stinking darkness.

It hadn't always been this way. Once, not so long ago, when she was still Namshéké, she'd been powerfully alive, strength certain, courage vibrant. The memory of the night she'd passed the Redthorn blooding ceremony and joined the ranks of that honored fellowship was etched deeper in her spirit than the Stoneskin's song could reach, and it was the calm center to which she desperately clung. The Greatmoon had been bright and full, and the light from his scarred, smiling face painted the mountains a shimmering silver. After months of trials that tested her body's limits and her spirit's endurance, she'd come that night with Oda'hea and the others to the ceremonial grounds, where they painted her skin red and black and shaved the sides of her head. When they'd finished, Fa'alik emerged from the whispering aspens and evergreens with a basket of long thorns and leaf-covered shells. Zhe sang an honor song as zhe etched her flesh with pigments of bright blue and dull black from the shells, until Namshéké's face, shoulders, arms, and thighs were slick with sweat, paint, and blood.

She'd known pain that night, but it had been fleeting, and she hadn't been alone—the Redthorns had been with her, and she understood that they'd each shared the same emotions, the same fears, the same exhilaration as Fa'alik smiled broadly, helped her stand, and presented her to the group as one of their own. It was the first time that she'd ever *belonged*. There her presence had been not just welcome, but essential; her skills made the Redthorns more than they'd been before, and they recognized the qualities she brought to them. Their numbers were few and fading, but with such gifts as she possessed, they had a chance against a world that was increasingly turning down newer, untested paths. Every moment of that night—from the body marking, the dancing, and the feasting to the tender lovemaking with Fa'alik that followed—was woven through her memory like the graceful patterns on the zhe-Kyn's chanting-sash, and every moment had been a reminder of all that was perfect and beautiful and balanced in the world. They'd all known who they were, and she was one of them—they belonged to these tree-covered mountains. That night had been warm, the Redthorns had rejoiced, and she'd been fully, vibrantly, alive.

But now Tarsa'deshae was dying. The knowledge was growing more certain with every convulsion. And she knew, too, that in this struggle she was utterly alone. The loneliness made the rising pain so much harder to resist. Not even facing the Stoneskin had been this frightening.

Before she could drift fully into surrender, she was surprised to sense something new now pushing against the burning tide. Tarsa responded instantly, every fiber of her agonized consciousness reaching out to any chance of hope. She didn't recognize the presence, but it had a hint of familiarity, like a lingering taste on the tongue of something she'd once known and treasured. She drifted on the pain, no longer submerged within it but floating in the middle place between consciousness and oblivion. There was a voice, one she might recognize if she could calm the throbbing beneath her flesh. With what little strength remained to her, she pushed her thoughts forward, drawing her spirit up through the jagged slice of the bloodsong, back to the cold wetness of the pit, back to the heavy ache of her battered body.

"Tarsa, niece, hurry!" It was Geth's voice, but it sounded strange—touched by an energy that Tarsa had never heard from this meek shadow of an aunt. The stench of her own waste swept over her when she tried to move her head and shake the thick fog from her mind. *How long have I been here?* Her temples and sensory stalks throbbed violently, and she slid back into the mud, her body convulsing with nausea and sick, sudden shame.

"Tarsa, listen to me." A new voice, powerful yet strangely familiar, firmly rooted in the green growing world. The Redthorn's pain diminished slightly as the bloodsong stilled. She sobbed with relief, then with rising fear, for she could feel another wave cresting, threatening to overflow.

The voice continued. "You must listen to my words very carefully, Tarsa. We can't come down there—there's too much iron. We've thrown a rope near you. All you have to do is wrap the loop around yourself, and we'll pull you up. You must be strong, and you must hurry."

The Redthorn warrior tried to speak, but her throat was raw from days and nights of frenzied screaming. Shaking her head, she pushed herself toward the rope, but the effort was too much. Her hands slipped in the mud, and she collapsed again with a groan.

"What are we going to do?" Geth wept.

Unahi moved to the edge of the pit but backed away, her face pale. It wasn't very deep, only about three times her height, and a stout wooden ladder rested beside the hole—it should have been an easy rescue. But the powerful natural iron that coursed through these stones was almost as toxic to the Wielder as forge-strengthened steel. "There's nothing I can do from here. The wild *wyr* is the only thing keeping her alive. If I try to go in there, I'll be almost as sick as she is, and then we'd both be dying."

"Interesting." A shape materialized out of the darkness behind them. Vansaaya. She walked toward her sisters with a small wrapped bundle in her hands. Looking impassively into the pit, she said, "There was a time, Unahi, that I would have welcomed that knowledge."

The Wielder's eyes never left the hole. "It shouldn't be a surprise. You were here when I was in her place."

"Yes. I was here." Vansaaya turned to Unahi. To her sad surprise, Unahi saw regret in her sister's eyes. "I remember your Awakening, and your agony. I said then that I would have gladly taken your place. But you were the one who had been chosen. There was nothing I could do, nothing anyone here could do to help you. And after we sent for one of the few remaining Wielders to still your blood and draw you back from your pain, I knew that you were lost to us forever."

Vansaaya's face grew hard again. "For all these years, you have trodden the Deep Green path, turning your eyes from the immortal heavens towards the dying wilds of this twice-cursed world. And when you were held here in the Burning Mouth, given the choice to surrender to something greater than yourself, to join the Shields in readying the world for the Realignment, to turn from the darkness of our past and seek the possibilities of illumination, you chose to remain behind. Your weakness shamed our family, a blight of honor that I have spent my life working to erase." Her voice broke in aching frustration. "And now you are here again, drawn back from the wilderness, a tattered old carrion bird still proud, still clinging to the world of the Ancestrals that is destined to perish. And yet you are the only hope that this young one has."

She dropped the bundle at her sister's feet. Unahi bent, placed her staff gently on the ground, and unwrapped the cloth, her hands struggling for a moment with the cord, to find inside a stone necklace. It was a chunky, unwieldy thing, slate grey, with weighty, interlocking chains of wood interspersed between dull stones that made her fingers tingle and seemed to absorb the moonlight.

Vansaaya answered her sister's unspoken question. "An iron-ward. Our Shield wears it when he trades with Humans, to avoid the possibility of deceit should they slip the base metal into his presence. This will help you—both of you."

Unahi nodded. She slid the clinking stones over her head and let them rest heavily on her chest. Without hesitation, she and Geth maneuvered the wide-bottomed ladder to the pit's edge as Vansaaya stood to the side. After testing the ladder's stability, the Wielder descended swiftly into darkness.

Vansaaya and Geth stood waiting with ill-disguised impatience and listened for sounds in the pit. There was nothing. An oppressive silence descended on them, and the air grew heavy. Even the whispers of the aspens were silent. The only movement in the sky was a stream of clouds that slid noiselessly across the greater moon, Pearl-in-Darkness, and his two shattered brothers, who gleamed like silver dust among the stars.

Geth turned to speak to her elder sister, but Vansaaya held up her hand. A noise drifted up from the darkness of the Burning Mouth. They watched as Unahi heaved herself onto the ladder and back over the edge of the pit, one end of the rope she'd tied around Tarsa firmly in hand. Vansaaya stepped up and grabbed the rope, tugging it hard around a stout aspen trunk for leverage, and she and the Wielder pulled steadily on the long fiber braid as Geth guided the rope with her good arm. A ragged tangle of dark, mud-caked hair soon appeared, and Tarsa lay on the grass, her body heaving with sobs.

Eyes warm with worry, Geth moved toward her weeping niece. Unahi grabbed her sister's shoulder. "Let her be."

Vansaaya opened her mouth to protest, but Tarsa's body, now freed from the toxic effects of the iron-lined pit, began to thrash. A violent wind rushed through the clearing. Dust and debris swept against the sisters, blinding them with its sudden ferocity. The Redthorn's back arched, her hands clawed into the earth, and her eyes rolled back. A low, wild howl erupted from her throat.

"Leave her!" Unahi shouted through the choking wind. Geth stepped away from her niece, but not quickly enough to avoid the thick green vines that burst from the soil and whipped around her legs. They curled and twisted, climbing higher with each of the convulsing warrior's feral cries.

A tendril wrapped around Geth's crippled arm. Sharp pain flared, and she screamed as she crumpled to her knees. Dozens of vines burst upward from the soil with impossible speed, twisting around her body, pulling her relentlessly against the hard earth. Small, sharp thorns erupted along the edge of each tendril and tore into her flesh. Geth, too terrified to scream, simply gaped at the twisting shapes that roiled and writhed around her. She tried to turn, to look behind her, but there was no escape. The vines were everywhere. A dagger-like thorn, growing long and wickedly sharp before her eyes, slashed into the soft flesh of her cheek, sending a gleaming spray of blood into the moonlight. Geth covered her face with her right arm and finally found her voice. Her desperate screams echoed Tarsa's own.

And then, as quickly as it had arisen, the wind was gone. Geth heard the gentle rustle of leaves and pine boughs, and felt the burning tightness around her body begin to loosen. She opened her eyes, distracted for a moment by the dull amber glow that pulsed from Dibadjiibé, which stood upright at the end of the clearing, its base driven deeply into the earth.

Unahi knelt over Tarsa. The old Wielder was covered in mud and fresh cuts of her own. Her clenched left hand moved back and forth over the young warrior, while her other hand traced the woven threads of the ragged sash she wore around her waist. She muttered low and rhythmically, as she reached into a pocket of her dress and removed seven white beads. These she dropped on the ground in a circle around Tarsa's unconscious body. The beads quivered for a moment as they darkened, shifting from white to pink, red, purple, and finally black. Unahi waited only a few heartbeats before she gathered them up again and tossed them into the Burning Mouth.

Tarsa lay still, her chest rising and falling steadily in sleep. Geth stood, shaking and pale, while Vansaaya wiped blood away from a series of thin gashes on her legs and watched the last of the tendrils slide back into the ground. Nothing remained of the thorny plants but hundreds of small dark holes in the red soil.

Unahi pulled her shawl from her shoulders and draped it across Tarsa's sleeping form. She then removed the iron-ward and handed it back to Vansaaya. The elder sister nodded once and turned wordlessly back down the trail that led to Red Cedar Town. When she had passed into the shadows, the mountain slope seemed to find its balance again, and the aspens took up a whispering chorus on the rising breeze.

Geth, though hesitant at first, knelt beside her niece and softly brushed the matted hair away from her face, tracing the recent tattoos that celebrated the young warrior's victory over the Stoneskin. "We won't see each other again, will we?" Geth asked.

Unahi sighed and turned her gaze back toward Red Cedar Town. It was lost beyond the trees, but she could smell its familiar hearth fires burning. The deep spice of pine was heavy in the air. She was a stranger here, or would be again in the morning. It was still spring in the mountains, and, though she hadn't noticed it before, she could now feel the coldness wrap around her old body. "We should bathe her, and gather some of her things for the journey. We'll leave before sunrise. There will be fewer questions that way." Geth nodded, her fingers still softly caressing the Redthorn's matted hair.

Unahi placed a strong hand on her sister's shoulder. "I don't know if she'll be back, Geth; that's out of my knowing. But I swear that I'll look after her as best I can. I can promise that, at least." Geth reached up and grasped Unahi's hand, but she kept her soft gaze lingering on Tarsa's sleeping face, so gentle now in the moonlight. They remained by the young warrior's side in the cold night, watching over her sleep.

It was a long goodbye.

3

Uprooted

AN EXCERPT FROM CHAPTER 12 of the classic *Reach-wide Journeyer's Gazetteer*, written by the Learnèd Doctor Abrosian Dellarius of the People's Academy of Alchaemical and Mechanical Arts in Chalimor, titled "On the Matter of the Forever-land":

> *This fertile, untamed territory, known to its aboriginal inhabitants by the roughly translated "Forever-land," remains the last great enclave of lawlessness in the Reach. The goodly justice of the Reachwarden's authority does not extend into those dark forests and jagged mountains, wherein bandit, robber, thief, and all manner of outlaw find refuge among the feral remnants of the once-proud Unhuman tribes. Traders and explorers who have braved the interior of this "Forever-land" tell of savagery run rampant, of Human decency given way to Unhuman license and ignorance. Yet travelers tell, too, of great bounty, for there is a fierce beauty in these lands: woods that promise both timber of magnificent quality and great tame herds of deer not unlike those that once roamed the Allied Wilderlands; blue-cold rivers teeming with strange but succulent fishes; and skies darkened with the passage of bright-plumaged birds as appealing on the lady's cap as in the stew-pot. . . .*

There can be no remaining doubt that there will be much virtue in bringing this "Forever-land" fully under the authority of the Assembly of Reach-States. Law, order, and civil society must always stand firmly against the corrosive chaos of barbarism. Provincial and territorial administrators have repeatedly called upon the Reachwarden to cultivate this weed-choked garden, to girdle rank trees and fill miasmic marshes for the benefit of all Men of the Reach and their descendants, a call that is increasingly heard in the marbled halls of Chalimor. It is the destiny of all lands to be tamed by Men of virtue and strength, without fear of the difficulties of such an undertaking. The plowshares and mercantile virtues of Human civilization will long endure and bring credit to their cultivators. Not so the fragile trees and hunted beasts of the Unhuman wilderness, whose much-diminished wanderings are moving ever swiftly toward sunset, where they will inhabit hearthside stories and memories of our great nation's heroic days of old.

Unahi and Tarsa passed their first day out of Red Cedar Town without speaking. The second morning dawned with a cold drizzle, a steady drenching that drained the walking warmth from their bodies and pulled their spirits mudward. Even the thickly clustered pines and firs seemed bedraggled and gloomy. Still weak from her imprisonment, Tarsa leaned on Unahi's staff and silently mourned her sudden banishment, while the elder Wielder's thoughts often lingered on a past she'd thought safely put to rest.

They returned back down the stream-fed valley that the elder Kyn had traveled just two days before, a path largely ignored by most Folk who sought Red Cedar Town. Only root-gatherers and keen hunters spent much time on this trail, and both she-Kyn were relieved that the rain kept questioning eyes away. Tarsa noticed that the rain increased to a raging downpour the few times they encountered another traveler, forcing everyone to hurry forward with heads bowed and nothing more than polite chin-nods of acknowledgment, then faded away to a lighter misty patter once the strangers had passed. Immediately afterward, Unahi would untie the colorful sash from around her waist and sprinkle a few pinches of cedar shavings over it before wrapping it back again, her mouth moving with the words of a noiseless prayer, and continue on as though nothing was amiss. Tarsa eyed the bent old she-Kyn warily but remained silent.

Her thoughts were otherwise occupied, her misery complete. Fewer than five days past, she'd been the most honored warrior in Red Cedar Town, and her new name reflected that status. Then it all changed, and the same warriors who'd stood by her side over the Stoneskin's broken body had carried her to the darkness of the Burning Mouth, terror in their eyes, as the wild *wyr* drove her toward madness. No one understood what had happened to her, but there was nothing they could do beyond abandoning her in that pain-making maw at the town's margins. There was no expectation of a healing; she'd been left to die. If not for Unahi . . .

Tarsa swallowed against the grief knotting in her throat. She'd become an unwanted exile, driven from her home, sent into the unknown forests far from Red Cedar Town with a Wielder she'd only heard about in furtive whispers and scornful asides. She'd been raised with Geth's stories of the Old Ways, even experienced them as a sprout, and she'd always treated them with respect, but for most of her family these philosophies were nothing more than unwanted remembrances of a rejected past. Her other aunts were firm Celestials, and their unyielding dictates gave the greater form and substance to her world. Even when she'd joined the traditionalist Redthorns, she'd found it hard to walk the thorny ground between both paths.

And that uneasy balance was suddenly gone, hidden in the mournful mountains at her back, and it was Unahi, ragged and aloof, who walked beside her now.

Midday came but brought no warmth, just a brief rest under the wide-spreading boughs of a giant spruce and a meal of dried fruit and cornbread that Geth had given them for their journey. Unahi passed a small water-skin to her niece, who accepted it wordlessly before walking to the trailside stream to refill it. They gathered their goods and continued on in silence, Unahi carrying much of Tarsa's share.

The rain lasted into the late afternoon of their second day of travel, and by that time they'd emerged from the sharp alpine valley into the heavy scrub oak and black willow of the higher hill country. Red Cedar Town was the first Kyn settlement of twenty

or so that crept up the sheer canyons into the soaring heights of the
Kraagen Mountains. The she-Kyn were still in the embrace of the
mountains—the peaks rose over the land for days to the east and
west, and for the full length of the Everland to the north and south—
but the tall hills before them lost their snowy crowns as the summer
grew near, whereas the higher summits of the Kraagens never knew
the warmth of the sun. Here, tall jumbles of red sandstone stood
scattered across the landscape, some reaching up hundreds of feet in
strange flowing shapes, looping into bridged arches or stony spears
jutting skyward. The valley beneath the hills was blanketed with a
spread of thick green growth, a bewildering mix of stunted oaks and
long-needled pines on the dry sandstone ridges and dense willows in
the boggy stretches.

Tarsa had never been so far down the western valley; most of her
travels were to the east, where trade and conflict were more common. This might have been a lovely sight, but she was too miserable
in flesh and spirit to appreciate their surroundings. Unahi rested
for a while, allowing the younger she-Kyn to stretch out her tired
muscles and breathe in the fragrant air, and motioned to a noticeably
large outcropping to the northwest. "We'll stay there tonight. There
are some dry overhangs at the top of the ridge where we can rest
without more drenching. These old bones need a fire, and I'm sure
your young ones do, too."

The Redthorn nodded, then winced. Her head had been pounding since early afternoon, and it seemed that every muscle in her
body had twisted and tightened during the night. Her moon-time
had passed, but she hurt too much everywhere else to be pleased
at the loss of those pains. For most of the day she'd concentrated
on keeping one foot following the other down the seemingly endless valley trail. A few times she'd felt the terrifying tension bubble
beneath her skin again, but Unahi, sensing her rising panic, had
rested a callused hand on her back as the heat rose, and the tightness
faded back to the familiar dull throb.

The trail narrowed as they drew closer to the thick scrub. They
moved down the slope toward the marshy bottomland, and all they
could see were slender grey-gold willows crowded in upon one
another, a tangle of leaf and bough so dense that little of the fading
light could be seen through their shaggy branches. The violet hush of

twilight would soon fall, but there was little chance that they would see it in the unending drizzle. They hadn't seen the sister suns all day, and it was hardly likely they would see the Greatmoon or the farther spheres and stars in the night sky.

Unahi stopped at a small tussock at the base of a massive old willow and motioned for Tarsa to kneel in the wet grass beside her. "An Awakening shocks the body out of its understanding of itself, and there's much left to be done for a healing. You've survived the worst of it already. It's past time for survival. Now you've got to *understand* what your survival means." Unahi smiled. "You've been given a powerful gift, niece."

Tarsa flushed. "It's no gift to me," she corrected. "It's a curse. I don't want it."

"Want it or not, it's yours, and you have to decide what to do with it. You can either let it destroy you, or you can learn to understand it."

"I'm not interested in witchery."

The old Wielder's eyes narrowed to cold slate slits. "You're a Wielder now, Tarsa, or will be soon enough, and it ill-serves a Wielder to be a fool." Her voice went hard. "There's no going back to who and what you were before."

Tarsa knelt in stony silence and stared into the distance. Unahi lowered her palms to the damp ground, and a hush descended on the approaching night. The Redthorn's heart began pounding hard, a heavy rhythm that seemed to reverberate in the circle of willow branches that now rose up and reached tentatively toward them. She felt a sudden surge of fear, but Unahi reached out a calming hand. Tarsa stiffened at the touch, but she didn't move away.

Heartbeat. The trees swayed in time with her heart's rhythm— she was captivated in spite of her fear. All the world seemed to flow toward them, each movement drifting on the throbbing drum in her chest. Without conscious thought, Tarsa felt herself slide back into the bloodsong, down into the steady scarlet rush beneath the skin, deeper than the terror that clung, sharp and clear, to the back of her memory. She heard the Shield of Red Cedar Town rail against the Deep Green, but his voice was weak compared to this elemental drumbeat. With every liquid beat, with every slow and steady rumble of that inner drum, she felt the green world open up to her again, heard the

Stoneskin's song draw the rhythm from her blood, knew herself to be connected to this place, this land and its peoples, far more deeply than ever before. She drifted down into the warmth of her belly, then to her knees and two-toed feet, into the very earth itself, no longer cold, wet, and worn-down with pain and grief, no longer terrified of the steady song that flowed within, nor ashamed of that fear.

Opening her eyes, she saw the filmy curtain between the forested valley and the Spirit World pull back. Her eyes grew wide, her body rooted in the soil, sensory stalks tense and pulsing in the moist air, and she watched through a green-blue haze as the mind-fog dissolved to reveal the pale, curious faces of the tree's willow-spirits. She didn't see faces as she'd always expected them to be; she couldn't explain how she knew them to be faces, but they were. Their collective gaze was ageless and deep, utterly alien to her understanding but warmly familiar through the connective *wyr* that coursed through her. The willow-folk reached toward her, their sinuous spirit-fingers stretching out like slender branches in a breeze.

It was too much. Tarsa cried out and cupped her face in her hands, silencing the beating drum, forcing the bloodsong back into familiar courses and established currents. When she looked up again, the curtain between worlds had dropped across her perception, and the spirits were gone; the tree's quivering branches were the only evidence that they'd been there. Her awareness of the chill drizzle returned slowly. For a moment her body trembled, but Unahi stood and pulled the Redthorn firmly to her feet.

"Come now. We'd better get these clothes to drying by a fire. We're in for quite a rain tonight, I think." Leaning alternately on the old Wielder and the wyrwood staff, Tarsa followed Unahi's guidance as they moved into the dense twilight of the hill country willows.

They found a sizable supply of dry firewood in the back corner of the overhang, which the elder Wielder stacked in the fire pit, while Tarsa spread their wet clothes on the ground. The rocks were streaked with soot from unknown numbers of past visitors. On clear days, the view of the steep valley and mountains must have been remarkable, but all they saw was darkness, and the occasional burst of lightning in the rainy night.

Flames rose up crackling through the wood, but Tarsa's thoughts were elsewhere; she was as quiet and sullen as she'd been from the first day out of the pit. Unahi watched the young warrior with interest, thinking about the conversation with Geth as Tarsa had slept during their last night in Red Cedar Town. The old Wielder was only now realizing how much a stranger she was to her niece; Tarsa had already experienced a whole lifetime of joys and pains before Unahi arrived. The elder she-Kyn had rarely seen so young a Redthorn before, but Tarsa's tight muscles and proud silence gave hints as to why she'd accomplished so much so quickly, and why Unahi had failed to sense her Wielding potential earlier.

There had been inklings, surely, when Tarsa was a strong-willed seedling named Namshéké: Storm-in-Her-Eyes. Unahi had even spoken to Lan'delar about the possibility. And in those days, even though the Purging was still going strong, her youngest sister was pleased to hear the news. Wielders tended to run in families, and it was a great honor among those who followed the Deep Green to say that one's Branch bore wild fruit.

But then came the feverish pox, and the blisters that boiled through the skin, and Lan'delar was dead. Unahi could do nothing to help her sister; this sickness came from outside the Everland, from the beyonder lands where Men fed upon each other and the land suffered in unceasing torment. She'd hoped to have another opportunity to see her infant niece then, but the Shields followed the fever, whipping terror of the unknown plague into hatred of the Wielders, and Unahi no longer found welcome in Red Cedar Town.

For all these years, Tarsa grew up in a world where the *wyr* was something to be scorned and cast away, where the many spirit people of the forests and mountains were enemies to be overcome rather than wisdom-bearers to be understood. Geth had shared her own lingering loyalty to the Old Ways with the sapling, but it was a thin memory generously mixed with romantic nostalgia that was as distant from the heart of the Deep Green as were the lies spread by the Shields. Geth was thus utterly unprepared when the young Namshéké fell into dazed states for whole days, emerging to tell her aunt about the voices she heard and the spirits she saw—visions shared by no one else around her. This was nothing like Geth's stories of gentle forest spirits help-ing lost sprouts find their way back to home or hearth, or the noble mountain ghosts who gave riches and glory to beautiful and virtuous she-Kyn maidens. The unnerving reality was far closer to the menacing tales of the Shields than to her own sentimental imaginings, and the terrified old she-Kyn did the only thing she could think of to help her dead sister's daughter: she thrashed Namshéké into fearful silence.

This was another new gift of the Celestials.

So Namshéké hid her growing awareness of strange voices that beckoned in her sleep. For a while it seemed that those hidden voices had given way to the more immediate surprises of the body, especially after she reached her first moon-time and was initiated into adulthood by the elder aunts of Cedar Branch. The voices faded further as she became more aware of a different kind of fever that followed a run with the young he-Kyn of the town, or when she escaped her lessons and splashed in a hidden mountain pool with a few shapely she-Kyn. They all intrigued her, and she quickly learned from both what delightful mysteries could be found in the flesh.

These new understandings drowned out the subtle but ever-present drumbeat in Namshéké's blood. These things she understood: the thrill of rushing through the mountains, sweat hot on the skin, in pursuit of a greedy bear who thought to take an easy meal from one of their storehouses; the release of smashing the traplines of Human trespassers in the Everland and driving them back to their own blasted lands; or the fiery joy of sliding beneath a doeskin blanket and feeling the moist lips of a lover or two on her soft green flesh. These things she knew. These were all she wanted.

Then the Stoneskin came to the valley. And now the young warrior called Tarsa didn't understand anything anymore.

Unahi nodded slightly to herself as she chewed on a freshly roasted acorn, its bitter tang lifting a bit of the night's deepening gloom. She was old, but she still remembered her own Awakening and how swiftly it had thrown her world into turmoil. Tarsa still stared into the darkness. Lightning illuminated the tattoos on the Redthorn's face—a good sign. Shields and their followers never tattooed themselves anymore; only those who were given to the Deep Green continued those traditions. The Redthorn way was one enduring holdout in the few but growing Celestial towns, and Unahi was glad of their endurance. She'd known a couple of saplings who'd Awakened into Kyn families that were unflinchingly

Celestial, and although she'd eventually spirited them away from the brutal punishments of the shame-seeing Shields, she was never able to fully guide them into the Deep Green, and they were ultimately consumed by the *wyr*-fire within. Such happenings were fortunately rare. There were still enough Wild families within the Branches to give guidance to those who were yet to Awaken.

She noticed Tarsa's shining turquoise eyes on her. It was time for truths to be told. "Things will be different for you now. If you ever return to Red Cedar Town, don't expect to find the friends you once knew. You might find the necessities of Branch hospitality, but nothing else."

The Redthorn shrugged. "There's nothing for me in Red Cedar Town."

Unahi sighed. Tarsa had lost many things in her short life—her mother, friends, lovers, and now the only place she'd ever known as home. Grief still hung heavily on the young she-Kyn; it was likely that this helped to start her Awakening, as great emotion sometimes opened a sensitive spirit to the *wyr* in unexplained ways. She'd been so strong for such a long time. Yet as strong and stubborn as the Redthorn was, if she continued to reject the call of the Deep Green, she'd eventually lose this battle.

Unahi felt the gloom settle on her own bowed shoulders, and she fell again into troubled silence.

The night passed slowly. Warm now, they sat by the red embers, each lost in private reflection. Tarsa hesitated to speak; she didn't know how to say what she was thinking, but the silence was too oppressive. She couldn't go back to Red Cedar Town, not after revealing herself as a Wielder. Her family had already demonstrated that their fear of her overwhelmed any sense of kinship. And although she was no longer alone, one question in her mind was a wall that separated her from this strange old she-Kyn.

Tarsa was surprisingly comfortable around Unahi, in spite of the elder she-Kyn's curt manner. At least Tarsa knew what to expect; there were no secret grievances or suppressed emotions that required constant guesswork and nervous uncertainty to navigate. When Unahi was annoyed, she made it clear; when she was pleased, she smiled or laughed. It was a welcome change, one that reminded Tarsa of better times with her Redthorn companions. They were far away now, back in Red Cedar Town. Those few friends and lovers had ignored her strangeness and seemed to love her in spite of it, but that was before the Stoneskin came to the valley.

Everything changed then. She could still see their fear-maddened faces as they joined her family in driving her to the Burning Mouth, deaf to her pleas for help. For a moment her chest tightened, but she didn't cry—those memories belonged to another life. It was Namshéké's life, not hers. Namshéké was gone. Through blood, death, and fire she'd become Tarsa'deshae, and she'd now have to build a different understanding of herself. Unahi was the only one who could help her with that task.

But one question still kept her from embracing the old Wielder's presence and guidance. She took a deep breath. "Did you kill my mother?"

Unahi's mouth dropped open in shock. "Why would you ask such a thing?"

"Ivida told me once, when I was very young. She said that you were jealous of my mother, so you made her sick and then refused to heal her." Tarsa's eyes shimmered, but her full lips were drawn in a tight line of defiance.

She looks just like Lan'delar, Unahi thought sadly. She shook her head. "Not all elders are wise, Tarsa, remember that. A mean spirit sometimes just gets stronger with age, not smarter." The Wielder chose her words with care. "No. I never harmed your mother, except maybe in a sprout's game of tag-the-tree. But then, she usually hit me back twice as hard."

Tarsa smiled nervously, and Unahi continued. "I loved Lan'delar. We all did. She was the youngest, a little tree in a grove of tall saplings. No one thought our mother would be able to have any more sprouts; she'd suffered greatly when Ivida was born, and two seedlings were lost before your mother joined us. But though we all adored her, I was her favorite, and she was mine."

Unahi stood and walked to the edge of the firelight, rummaging around in her pack for a small cloth bag that she brought back to the fire with her. Her three digits drew a handful of leaves and twigs from the bag and tossed them into the fire. The air grew rich with the earthy scents of tobacco and juniper that cleared the mind and the eyes. She returned to her seat and looked back at her niece.

"The pox was a sudden one. I'd heard of it, of course; in those days, you usually heard about these sicknesses from traders and refugees, before death suddenly appeared in the town, usually in a sucking seedling or a weak old burl who couldn't leave his pallet. And this one was no different in that way. It struck the old and young without mercy. It ran like fire through dry leaves, burning all that it touched to ashes."

Her voice grew hoarse. "I was one of the first of Red Cedar Town who fell to the fever. All my understanding of the *wyr* was useless. This pestilence came from outside the Everland, like so many of our woes. I thought I would die alone. That's usually what happened when the blistering sickness hit a town; all who could leave did so, as quickly as they could, and they scattered, sometimes carrying the plague with them to other towns. So I lingered in a fever for I don't know how many days. And when I emerged, I saw your mother. She'd stayed with me through the worst of it, bathed my wounds, kept me from scarring too terribly." Unahi drew a mottled hand across her eyes. "She stayed with me until I recovered, but by then she'd already started to suffer herself. So I stayed by her side and cared for her as best as I could in my weakened state, but it wasn't enough."

Tarsa hugged her knees to her chest as she listened. The lightning had ceased, but the rain was heavy again. Occasionally, the eyes of small Beast-people glinted in the darkness beyond, their curiosity aroused by the two figures who sat on either side of the crackling fire.

The old Wielder cleared her throat. "When everyone returned, the Shield blamed me for the deaths. What defense did I have? No one was there to see what had happened; Lan'delar gave you into Geth's keeping before coming back to look after me, and in the end it was just the two of us in Red Cedar Town. I was the only survivor; I should have been dead, too, but instead it was Lan'delar who was gone. My sisters went mad with grief. Your mother's last words were for you, Tarsa, and I begged the others to let me share them with you, but they listened to the Shield and drove me away. Even Geth refused to speak to me. Most had turned away from the

Deep Green when two of our brothers—Greenwalkers to the heart, and Redthorns themselves, like you—fell to an ambush by a Human raiding party. My sisters believed the Shield when he said that the Old Ways were useless, that the only peace our brothers would have was in the arms of Luran. And they believed him when he said that I had brought Lan'delar to her death through jealousy and witchery. So I was beaten and sent from the only home I'd ever known, and I'd never returned until two nights ago, when I saw you for the first time since you were a swaddled sprout, twenty-six years past."

Unahi's face softened in a sad smile. Tarsa rocked in place for a while, listening to the rain fall off the stony shelf, and to the steam of the nuts roasting in the coals of the fire, watching as sparks popped and flew on smoke into the night. A nightbird cried mournfully in the distance. His shrill voice railed against the rain that would leave him drenched and hungry this night.

"Geth did believe you," Tarsa said at length, still watching the night shadows. "She told me that it wasn't your fault. She told me a lot of things, but there was a lot she didn't know. We stood at the arch with the others, but we weren't Celestial, not in our hearts. She never wanted to leave the Deep Green." She turned to her aunt. "Will you teach me?"

Unahi nodded. Tarsa remained silent for a moment more, then said, "My mother—you said her last words were for me?"

"Yes," the Wielder nodded, draping her still-damp shawl on the rocks beside the fire.

"What did she say?"

Unahi's eyes were warm. "Tell her to tend to her roots."

4

Visitations

ALTHOUGH JITANI GENERALLY THOUGHT THAT CATTLE were rank-smelling creatures of low intellect, she reserved some measure of admiration for oxen, if for no other reason than the slow and steady strength that they showed as they dragged their heavy carts. That admiration extended to the Human teamsters of the trading train, for there was a welcome gentleness in their regard for the hulking beasts under their care. A well-trained pair of oxen rarely required the whip, for they were eager to follow their Human guides if treated with kindness, and they'd patiently pull even the heaviest loads over these many miles of rough and rocky trade roads. It was only an incompetent teamster who lashed his charges in temper; as her employer had little patience for the lazy, foolish, or inept, such Men disappeared from the train in short order, to everyone's relief.

Of all of her jobs over the past ten years, this was one of the best, even though the bronze-skinned she-Kyn generally didn't like to work too closely with Humans—she'd been too much among them to trust them completely. But Sylas Gwydd paid her well for her blade skills on each of these trading trips, and his many years of respectful business in the Everland had brought him a reputation as an honest merchant who regarded the Folk as friends, not just customers or trade targets to exploit. It didn't hurt his reputation that he'd had a long, happy marriage to an Apple Branch she-Kyn, nor that their children were among the most promising young Kyn traders in Sheynadwiin. The name Gwydd was one of esteem in the Kyn peace-city and political capital, and Sylas defended that regard with utmost care.

The recent attacks on his mercantile trains were thus more than a business loss—they were a personal affront to his character. Two trains had been seized by Eromar authorities under the most absurd bureaucratic justifications, while another had simply been plundered and burned by Human bandits with ties to Eromar. Silas's eldest son had barely survived that attack. Traders in the past had generally been able to pass through Eromar from eastern Béashaad and the Allied Wilderlands to the south without much difficulty. But the newest agitations by Lojar Vald, the prefect of Eromar, were an ill omen for the future, as they were becoming increasingly aggressive, and often without any pretense of legality. Gwydd's business interests weren't the only ones suffering, but his high status among the small group of intermarried Humans made his own troubles very public. Now, at last, the Humans who lived among the Sheynadwiin Kyn were getting as worried as their Folk neighbors had been for some time.

Jitani's mood turned ugly at these thoughts, and she grimaced as she urged her pony forward toward the head of the train. Like most Kyn, she disliked binding animals to her service—she refused to use spurs, unlike her Human counterparts—and though she'd long since trained herself to tolerate the sensory backwash of the pony's bridle pain and saddle sores, it was an experience that she was eager to finish with when they reached their destination. She was tired of the incessant squealing of the wagon axles, tired now of the stinking, trundling oxen and their hunched and bearded keepers. And she wasn't the only one: most of the Folk kept to themselves at the back of the wagon train, rarely mingling among the Men. They all wanted to see green trees and blue sky, not the ass-end of Humanity and their cud-chewing beast-slaves.

Trust Men to wait until their own selfish interests are endangered before they look around and see the suffering of others. Folk had been dying in Human raids for months now, ever since Vald declared his intention to extend the political authority of Eromar over the Everland, but it was only when their own fortunes were threatened that Gwydd and the other Human merchants had started to pay attention and add their voices to the growing protest. Vald's proposal to levy a hefty tax on all Humans in the Everland who refused to declare their loyalty to Eromar certainly added to their newfound defiance.

Yet no matter how annoyed she might be, Jitani still had a job to do, and right now it was to protect Sylas Gwydd's shipment of housewares and bolts of fine cloth to its destination. They'd had a bit of trouble in Eromar just after the wagons were loaded, but they'd been out of the province's boundaries for nearly a week already and were well inside the Eldarvian Woods. Still, it was no small distance to Dardath Vale and the protective palisade around Sheynadwiin, and none of the sixteen Folk or ten Men felt much at ease, even this far into the Everland.

The she-Kyn heard some of the teamsters call out from the front of the train, bringing the wagons to a halt. She kicked the pony into a trot. When she reached the lead wagon, Sylas was already off his horse and deep in conversation with Ryn, an old Tetawa scout. Seeing the green-haired warrior, Sylas waved her forward.

"Problems ahead," he said in the Folk trade-tongue. He was stout, but with more muscle than fat. His bristling cheeks and forehead were always flushed, though they'd deepened to an angry red at Ryn's report. "Damn Vald and his drag-tailed lackeys! A toll-gate here, so close to Sheynadwiin?"

"A toll-gate?" She looked at the Tetawa.

"It's recent," he said, nodding. "Probably no more than a six-day at best. They have a rough cabin there, too, and a few horses—I counted five, but there could be more in the trees. They have logs blocking the road at three points: one at the gate and two just beyond."

Jitani nodded. "How many Men?"

"Four at the gate. I don't know how many in the cabin." Ryn frowned. "They've got steel swords, and muskets, too."

Sylas's cheeks paled slightly, though his nose and forehead remained bright pink. "Do they know we're coming?"

Jitani turned to look at the ten creaking wagons and twenty grunting oxen. "They probably knew we were coming ten miles back." She shrugged and turned to Sylas. "Well, we can't turn around. Go to the middle of the train and spread everyone throughout the wagons, from the front to the back. Most of the Folk are keeping to themselves at the rear. Have them come up to the front where they can keep a better eye on things, and tell them to have their weapons handy in case we need them. Ryn, go into the trees, and make sure that nobody's out there waiting to surprise us from behind. We'll keep going forward, and we'll see what happens when . . ."

A flintlock explosion and scream from the back of the train cut off her plans. Cursing herself for allowing the more keen-eyed Folk scouts and hunters to linger too much together at the rear of the train when they were so close to home, Jitani threw Sylas to the ground and dragged him under the head wagon as her pony whickered shrilly and galloped back down the road. Ryn lunged for cover in the under-brush, but a Man in soiled leathers stepped out of the trees in front of him. A blade flashed in the sunlight as it came down hard and fast on the scout's exposed neck. The Tetawa's head rolled wide-eyed into the rutted road, his body following with a sickening thump.

Ignoring the screams of Men and the rising panic of the oxen, and thankful that she kept her remaining sensory stalks tightly bound against unexpected trauma, Jitani slid her own sword from its scabbard and rolled out from under the wagon. The blade she held was a rare weapon, shaped from the heartwood of an ancient wyrwood tree and given strength and keen sharpness by a Wielder's patient skill. She'd hoped that she wouldn't need to use it on this trip; she'd grown tired of death and killing. But she had a duty, and now she had even more of a reason to fight, one that had nothing to do with protecting Sylas Gwydd's trinkets from destruction. It had everything to do with avenging the Folk who were watching their homeland disappear beneath them, stone by tree, who were dying all around her. It had to do with keeping her attacker's blade from spill-ing her own heart's blood, and with avenging the brave Tetawa scout whose grandchildren would weep at the news of his murder.

This wasn't the first time she'd felt the cold threat of a steel blade, but she was no longer a frightened sapling. She could defend herself now.

Jitani raised her voice in a war-song as she rushed forward, and the wyrwood sword tasted hot blood again.

The destruction of Nine Oaks Town was worse than either Unahi or Tarsa had expected. It was a smaller community than Red Cedar, but it was older and infinitely more defensible, with a wider range of protections, including rockfalls, hidden alcoves in the stone wall that provided cover for ambushes, and sheer cliffs without handholds. It sat in a jagged bowl of stout red granite, and could only be reached through a handful of tight clefts in the steep walls. Kyn scouts and warriors used arrows and spears to keep enemies at a distance, and if danger came too close, there were always obsidian-spiked war-clubs and wyrwood blades to help seal up the gap. But these defenses were only useful against conventional attackers, and the Stoneskin had been anything but that.

Unahi would have preferred that Tarsa not experience this side of a Wielder's duty so soon, especially as the young she-Kyn was still largely a stranger to the necessary teachings. The last few days had made painfully clear that most of Tarsa's early education about the Old Ways was actually a tangled mix of romantic sapling tales, naive fantasies, and superficial suppositions that had nothing to do with the long, often lonely work and painful transformations that the Way of Deep Green would demand of her. The Awakening was only the first great change she'd experience. Ordinarily, Unahi would have been rather discouraged by the young warrior's ignorance. But Tarsa had had wiser teachers than her meek aunt Geth—the Redthorn war-leader Oda'hea and the zhe-Kyn ceremony leader Fa'alik—and they'd started her toward a deeper understanding of the Way of Deep Green, their training interrupted only by her violent Awakening. Tarsa, to her credit, was a quick study; what she lacked in experience, she made up for in an almost desperate willingness to learn. And it was fortunate that she was so accommodating, because they couldn't delay with the purification rituals at Nine Oaks—Tarsa would just have to follow along, pay attention, and do the best she could. Neither she-Kyn imagined that it would be an easy task.

Tarsa shivered as they climbed the narrow path that led to the larger of the passes into the bowl, though the sister suns had long ago emerged from behind the morning clouds. No wagon could make it through this pass, so anything that entered into Nine Oaks came by foot or on pack animal. At least, that had been before the Stoneskin came. Now, the gap stood wide enough for three Kyn to walk side by side through it. Huge chunks of rubble littered the ground, even into the far distance. The normalcy of the scene unnerved the Redthorn warrior: the quiet whisper of a breeze through the pine needles, the warmth and brightness of sunlight as they neared what both knew to be a site of slaughter. The sides of the cleft were scored by claw marks. Blood stained the stones and rust-colored gravel through which unconcerned chickadees hopped and twittered in search of seeds and small insects.

Unahi stopped, her breathing labored. It was a steep climb up the ridge, and these last few days had given her little rest. Her grey eyes scanned the narrow gorge facing them. She was old; she'd felt old even when Tarsa was born, although she would never have admitted it in those days. As the only Wielder remaining to serve and protect the Folk in Thistlewood and its surrounding hills, Unahi had spent much of her life cleaning up after conflicts and accidents. She knew too well the sticky flow of blood over her callused hands; she'd bound innumerable wounds with those same six fingers. Sometimes she awoke in the night to an endless chorus of screams, the cries of all whose pain she'd watched and experienced. Sometimes she wondered if there would come a time when she would get used to the horrors of mortality, but she doubted it. If anything, her sensory stalks were increasingly sensitive to the emotions of the inspirited world around her. It wasn't always a bad thing. It was likely the reason she felt Tarsa's anguish from her own warm cabin far away in the woods. But it was ever more exhausting, and there were far too many nights without sleep.

Unahi turned to the Redthorn warrior. "Do you want to wait here? There's no reason that you should have to deal with this right now."

"No, I'll go with you." Tarsa cleared her throat and stood proudly. "After all, I'm the one who killed the monster." She didn't add that the empty silence of the world outside the rock ring held far more fear for her than anything they might find within it.

"Monster?" Unahi frowned. "I don't know what you mean by that word. He was a killer, that's certain. But he also belonged to the days of the Ancestrals, a spirit of the mountains given flesh and blood long before we came to this world. He knew the voices of the stones and snowy heights, sang the songs that traveled on thunder from the far reaches of the world. For that alone he deserves respect."

Tarsa stared at her aunt in sudden disgust, her stalks quivering. "Respect? He would have slaughtered everyone in Red Cedar Town if we hadn't stopped him. Look there." She pointed at the blood-stained rubble on either side of the rocky cleft. "I can't respect that."

Unahi grunted slightly as she started up the slope again. She leaned heavily on her staff for support, having retrieved it from Tarsa when the warrior was strong enough to walk on her own. She reached the wall without much difficulty and slid her hand across the claw marks in the stone. The gouges were thick, each as wide as her two large fingers together. The Stoneskin had ripped through the rock in a frenzy. His emotions still clung to the walls; she could feel his elation, his eager joy to tear through hard stone and feast on the town beyond. His weren't the only emotions here. So, too, were those of the handful of Kyn who were surprised on their watch; their death pain nearly drowned out all other sensations.

The Wielder's fingers drifted farther across the cold surface. Five Kyn died here. Four were he-Kyn. The fifth was a young she-Kyn, the sister of one of the warriors, there to visit and share a laugh with her brother and one of his handsome friends. She was the last of the five to die. Unahi's stomach tightened.

"No, Redthorn, I can't respect what he did either," she said. "His cruelty was well repaid. But he's still connected to us; he's still a voice in the song. Things are rarely as simple as we want them to be. Vengeance for its own sake, without concern for balance, is destructive in its way, too." She reached into one of the many small pouches around her waist and pulled out a handful of long cloth strips, handing a few to Tarsa. "Tie up your stalks. You're already sensing too much, and there's going to be much more pain and ugliness all too soon." Without another glance at her niece, Unahi slipped into the shadows of the cleft.

Tobhi tried to stretch the numbness from his legs, but it was a tough task from the back of an irritable deer. Whoever thought that deer were sweet and docile forest creatures had never met Smudge, a black-nosed, long-eared little brute with sharp teeth and even sharper antler buds. Rather than risk another nasty bite, the Tetawa pulled on the reins and dismounted. He dreaded to think what wounds he'd be risking when Smudge's fall antlers came in.

They were later getting to Nine Oaks Town than Tobhi liked, as night was approaching all too swiftly, and the stories he'd recently heard about the area didn't make him eager to camp in the open air. But Smudge had nearly reached the end of his brown-eyed patience with all this business. The deer shook himself vigorously. Without Tobhi's weight, the saddle and blanket slipped easily to the ground. Turning an exasperated eye toward the Tetawa, who stood stretching against a tree, Smudge tore huge clumps of spring grass from the roadside and munched on them in noisy spite.

Tobhi grinned and flopped to the ground, the tingle now gone from his limbs. "Not a bad notion. It's best not to show up with a grousin' belly; who knows if they even got anythin' good to eat." He reached over and grabbed the nearest fallen saddlebag, rummaged through it, and pulled out a stained canvas bag of crumbling corn cakes. Smudge ignored him.

It had been too long since Tobhi's last visit to the mountains. There was really nothing quite as wondrous as the sunset over blue peaks in the distance, unless it was sitting right in the middle of them when the last scarlet gold of day slid down over their shining crowns. He hadn't been in this area since he was nearing his age-naming, probably twelve years past or better, on one of his father's trading visits. He was pleasantly surprised that he still remembered the shortcut through the pass. Jekobi would be proud of him. "Wonder where Pepa would be right about now," Tobhi muttered softly, as much to his cranky companion as to himself. "Prob'ly nappin', if I know him. He's likely teasin' Mema, pretendin' to sleep instead of huskin' green corn for supper." He looked at the bag in his hands and sighed. "I reckon she's cookin' somethin' a sight better than gritty travel bread tonight."

He stood up and stretched again. The last leg of the day's journey was always the longest, and though he'd been traveling for weeks and should have been used to the pace, it seemed that every day dragged out longer than the one before. His eyes spotted a thick trail of smoke from the center of the rocky ring below. It wasn't quite as far away as he'd feared. "Maybe they got enough for us down there; it can't be no worse than what we got up here." Tobhi picked up the saddle and stepped toward Smudge, but the deer's glare stopped him.

"Now, now, Smudge," Tobhi cooed, moving forward slowly. Not for the first time he wished he knew deer speech; he'd have to settle on his round brown face sending what he hoped was an expression of deer-friendly benevolence. "Ye know I en't tryin' to hurt ye none. We're almost there. Just a little farther, and I'll give ye all the grain ye can eat. Maybe I'll even give ye a shiny green crabapple. I got one in m' pack, just for ye. Ye'd like that, wouldn't ye?" The deer stood staring; the only muscles that moved were the ones still working through a particularly large mouthful of grass.

Tobhi inched closer and reached out a hand to stroke the deer's back. Smudge bounded quickly to the side and trotted into the trees on the opposite side of the trail. The Tetawa, now unbalanced, fell heavily to the ground, his shapeless brown hat slipping over his eyes.

"Ye stinkin', mean-eyed drum skin!" Tobhi shouted. He pulled the hat up and glared at the deer, who now stood contentedly chewing in the trees about fifteen feet away, with what Tobhi could only interpret as a look of smug superiority. Another strategy was clearly necessary. With a dramatic flourish, Tobhi stood and wiped the dirt and pine needles from his green leggings, hefted the saddlebags over his shoulders, and walked toward the trail. "Well," he called behind him, "I guess I'll be eatin' that feast by m'self tonight. Sure will be sad, though, to throw all that good food away, 'cause there'll be more than I can eat by m' lonesome. 'Specially that apple. Ah, well. At least *I'll* get plenty to eat." With that, he strolled down the trail toward the stone-ringed town in the distance.

Smudge remained where he was, still chewing and watching the path that Tobhi had taken. Suddenly Tobhi raced back up the hill with lips puckered. "Ye'r more jackass than deer, ye know that?" He charged after his mount, who skipped just out of reach and turned to face the Tetawa. They squared off for a moment before Tobhi rushed again. This time, however, Smudge stood his ground, taking Tobhi off guard and his feet by planting his budding antlers into the thick leather vest over the Tetawa's belly and flinging him backward into the grass. Tobhi landed with a grunt but stood up again with a smile, a little breathless but unhurt. The deer shook himself and lowered his head again.

"All right, ye want to play that way, do ye?" Tobhi grinned and crouched. "Well, then, let's go—ye'r about three steps away from deer stew anyways." Smudge snorted and moved toward the little Tetawa but stopped as a large shadow moved over them. They looked up to see a scowling figure astride a stout horse.

<<By Luran's grace, what *are* you doing?>> The newcomer's voice dripped with exasperation and scorn.

Tobhi shrugged and playfully grabbed at one of Smudge's ears. <<Nothin' to worry y'self about,>> he said with a grin, following the visitor's lead by speaking in the Reach-tongue of Men. <<We're just havin' ourselves a bit of fun.>> With his other hand, Tobhi swung the saddle across the deer's back and cinched it tight, noting with some satisfaction that Smudge was more subdued—even dignified—in the presence of the mare. That knowledge made the cinching even more entertaining, as one particularly hard pull of the belt across the deer's belly brought forth a simultaneous grunt of displeasure and a loud blat from Smudge's hindquarters. Tobhi chuckled and swung himself into the saddle, pretending that he couldn't see the deer's reproachful glare.

<<I hardly think this is a time for levity. We have an important duty to fulfill, and the sooner we accomplish that, the sooner we will be able to get out of this wretched wilderness.>> The figure shook his head wearily and spurred his horse toward Nine Oaks Town. Smudge and his grinning companion trotted close behind.

5
A Cleansing Fire

NIGHT WAS THE FLOCK'S CHOSEN TIME to travel; the deeper shadows of the alpine forest were soothing to the creatures' nerves in this strange world. Even the thin light of the Greatmoon was painful to their senses—born as they were of the wrappings of shade and darkness, light gave form to the creatures but no comfort. The hidden springs and deep, fragrant hollows of mushroom and moss were more welcoming for their nighttime murk than for the rush of life that flourished there. These things held not even passing interest; something much more compelling drew the creatures on.

The air was pensive, as if all the hidden spirits of the timeless forest readied themselves to flee from an approaching storm. The creatures felt the tension and flapped their black wings in annoyance, but they were used to such a response, for they knew too well that they didn't belong here. Wherever the shadow-creatures had been, whatever their origins, the purpose of their belonging was lost far behind them, like a dying breath in the night. The past was gone; they had a different purpose now, one that had been delayed by unexpected frustrations. Occasionally, they squawked and gibbered their tangled fury on the wind. They'd never been this thwarted, and while the creatures had little idea of their age or history—little tangible memory of anything but hunger, and the unnamed compulsion that pushed them forward—they knew that they'd been on the hunt many times before this, and nothing so far had escaped their patient pursuit. The most maddening thing was that the hunters were *certain* that their quarry was unaware of the seeking shadows, yet it remained so elusive. Those who knew they were stalked tended to make stupid and ultimately fatal mistakes; this prey suffered no such weakness.

The shadow-creatures had first followed the scent into the deep forest, but the lichen-covered cabin was empty when they arrived. The hunters descended on the cabin like a sudden tempest, tearing at the logs and stones of the structure, smashing clay jars and shredding baskets and thick quilts, but it was useless: their frustration was vented, but they had lost very valuable time. The shadows rushed from that shattered forest cabin over marshes and hills and narrow canyon walls—sending wood-spirits and water-folk scrambling in mad desperation to avoid the unnatural otherness—up to the edge of a small settlement that stood proudly on a flat mountain ridge. Even as they crowded around and sniffed the palisade wall, the creatures knew that their quarry was gone again, but they couldn't sense the best direction to follow. Daylight was fast approaching, so the shadows glided up the hillside and found a dank pit on the edge of the settlement to lair in until darkness returned. The hole hummed with pain and fear, and this made it a surprisingly comfortable place for the flock to rest, in spite of its stink of iron. The metal irritated the creatures' senses but caused no lasting harm; not born of the *wyr,* they possessed none of the weaknesses that came with such an inheritance. The shadows spent two days there gathering strength and enjoying the residue of hurt that clung to the rocky walls, a memory that was strong enough to taste—and to nourish.

Now, after slipping again through mist, rain, mud, and forest, the creatures knew that the end of the hunt was growing near. Although the prey was still some distance away, the unwitting quarry had stopped again. This brief hesitation would be its last.

Choking clouds of ash and smoke billowed from the bonfire, and Tarsa wiped sweat from her forehead as she threw another armful of wood into the flames. It had been an achingly long day, and night promised to be even longer. As they'd walked in from afar, nothing looked amiss. Nine Oaks was a tiered town built into a hollow bowl against the eastern edge of a large sandstone butte, one of the many natural stone towers scattered through the hill country. A central meeting house, round and squat like that of Red Cedar Town, lay at the base of the stone wall, while the individual Branch-houses clung to the sides of the stone like brightly painted mushrooms growing from fissures in the rock. A series of tall wooden poles surrounded the meeting house, each draped with bright cloth banners and topped with the roughly carved image of one of the seven Kyn Branches: Oak, Willow, Thorn, Pine, Cedar, Ash, and Apple. The town fields were still only half-planted; abandoned wooden hoes and planting sticks were the first signs of wrongness.

It was only as they approached that the devastation became evident. Every dwelling was damaged in some way, mostly around the doors. The framing timbers were shattered, looking as splintered as if a massive boulder had smashed through the narrow entrances. Darkened splatters of blood were everywhere—even, to Tarsa's horror, staining the fluttering standards high atop the Branch-poles.

They were further surprised to find that the unconsumed bodies had already been wrapped and placed atop thirty makeshift scaffolds of various sizes. As per custom, Kyn were generally buried after a season or more of exposure to the elements: during this period, their flesh would feed the four-legged, crawling, and winged people who shared the land with them, and their spirits would have enough time to surrender their attachments to this place and travel westward to the ghostlands in the Lower Place, where they would return fully to the endless voices of the *wyr*. But these hastily built scaffolds were now abandoned, likely to remain untouched by Kyn for years, thus leaving incomplete the necessary rituals that would bring peace to the murdered dead.

This would be the legacy of Nine Oaks Town. Both she-Kyn wept at the terrible thought, and at the sight of so many seedlings and sprouts among the dead. Tarsa had expected to see carnage beyond imagining, bodies savaged and torn apart, but all she saw was a mournful emptiness, and this absence, the cold erasure of all that had been so vibrantly alive, was so much worse than her fears. Where the living had fled, they didn't know; likely to another town where they had

Branch-kith to take them in. Before leaving, the survivors had ful-filled as many of their duties to the dead as they could. But it wouldn't be enough. The spirits would remain in this place, until their bones were dust scattered on the wind or until they were at last buried deep in rich, red soil, to give strength to the growing world and the deep-rooted people again. And even then, their pain would remain.

Tarsa didn't realize how much was left undone until she removed her stalk-wrappings late in the day to cool her head in the pine-scented breeze. A sudden wave of anguish stripped her spirit bare, driving her gasping to the ground. Dozens of screaming and weep-ing voices battered her mind, to be swallowed up in the Stoneskin's gurgling laugh. The bloodsong took control again, so fast that she had no chance to fear its approach, and she released it into the world again, the unheard voices of the *wyr* flowing through the ground and up into the charred branches of the tall pines nearby. The first wave passed; as Unahi had taught her that day, she forced herself to push the burning song from her surface thoughts to drift back to muted currents. Tarsa lay sprawled on the ground for a few moments, chest heaving as she caught her breath and tried to push back against the gnawing ache that burrowed again deep into her consciousness.

She lifted her eyes to an unexpected and terrible sight: the pines were now twisted and malformed, contorted into nightmarish shapes. The branches of one tree curled like strangling ivy into those of the next, pulling them inescapably together into a tormented embrace. The thick bark gaped in places to reveal tender heartwood, now bleed-ing sweet red sap in the fruitless attempt to heal the sudden, deadly wounds. Tarsa watched, bile rising in her throat, as the trees' needles turned brown before her eyes, and her stomach clenched violently.

Unahi stood beneath the trees and coolly regarded her niece. Tarsa dropped her head in shame and horror. After the warrior was able to stand again, Unahi curtly directed her to gather up what-ever still remained in the dwellings—from furniture and clothing to corn-husk brooms and gourd dolls—and set them ablaze in the meeting house's fire pit. They couldn't leave these remnants to linger with the taint of death.

Neither looked at the tortured pines again that day.

Unahi stepped to Tarsa's side and threw a stout stool into the flames. Her eyes watered from the ashes and the acrid stink of hair that burned along with various clothes, brushes, and hide-rugs. "That's the last of it. We should eat a bit," she said, pointing to a stout log near the fire pit, where a clay pot bubbled with a thick stew that Unahi had put together from gatherings of their journey. After washing the grime from her skin and performing a brief cleansing prayer that Unahi had taught her, Tarsa sat down and stared into the fire. The flames were the only comfort she had in this ruined town. Even after all their work, the place looked no less ghastly. Directly opposite she could see, through the flames, the misshapen forms of the *wyr*-twisted pines. And beyond the trees, barely visible in the firelight, stood row after row of death-scaffolds. The possessions of the dead were now crumbling to clean ash, and with them the mortal long-ings that had made them precious. Though it wouldn't be enough to bring peace to the murdered, at least the spirits wouldn't be further hindered in their journey by the material desires of life.

"This town was built by nine members of Oak Branch, from Dropwater," Unahi said, filling two pitted bowls with the stew. "They came here during the Purging, in the hope that they could guard the Deep Green teachings until later generations would appre-ciate those ways. And they'd succeeded quite well—for a while, anyway. Kith from the other Branches, including ours, found sanc-tuary in this place. I was always welcome here." She frowned and shook her head in sorrow.

They continued eating. Unahi watched the flames dance in the night air, but Tarsa was now restless. She didn't want to be here. She didn't want to keep feeling all the emptiness and pain, or to know that, no matter how hard they worked this day, Nine Oaks Town would long remain a haunted place. Her eyes drifted back to the pines; she couldn't have avoided looking at them if she tried, and even though she had rewrapped her stalks immediately after regain-ing her strength, she could still almost hear their tortured screams.

"The *wyr* is the heart-fire of the Folk," Unahi said, interrupting Tarsa's uncomfortable reverie. The elder she-Kyn pulled out her pipe and filled the shallow bowl with sweet tobacco. "It's the language of creation, the voiced embodiment of the Ancestrals and their spirits. The words belong to another time and another world, but we continue to speak them, because they continually renew our world, our own life-fires. Without the *wyr*, the Folk are rootless, empty and alone in the darkness. It's what binds us to the world and each other."

As the cleansing pipe-smoke mingled with that from the fire pit, Tarsa clenched her fists. "I don't understand them . . . the voices. When I hear them, everything comes at me in a rush, and the words tumble all together in my head. It's awful. Every time I feel the words rise up, it's all I can do to keep from losing myself in them. And when everything clears away . . ." She glanced back toward the trees and flushed again with shame.

"Only those who walk in the Spirit World speak the living *wyr* with full grace," Unahi said, patting Tarsa's arm awkwardly. "The rest of us just have to try to keep up. It will come, with time. But you must be careful, niece, because words are very powerful, especially these words. They can hide or reveal truth with equal ease, and many people have Wielded the spirit-tongues without respect, and come to terrible grief because of it." She pointed at the long woven cloth wrapped around her own waist. "We'll make you a chanting-sash in the next few days; it'll root you better, help you focus your mind. You have a powerful tie to the *wyr*, Tarsa, but it demands much . . ."

A noise from the shadows—four figures stepped out of the darkness. Tarsa jumped to her feet, snatching a burning brand from the fire with one hand, the other straying to a throwing knife hidden in the back of her belt. She might have had very little confidence in her *wyr*-Wielding abilities, but she had no such hesitation about her Redthorn training.

When the shapes emerged into the light, Tarsa watched them closely, for they were unexpected in this grim place. The first was a stately he-Kyn leading a tall brown horse. He wore a high-collared coat with thick brass buttons that gleamed in the firelight. Beneath the knee-length coat she could see a red vest and white shirt with a flowery neck wrapping, each trimmed with golden thread. His breeches and high, trade-leather boots were red with dust from his travels, but there was no mistaking their fine quality. Around his neck hung a heavy medallion, an iron-ward not much different from that of the Shield of Red Cedar Town.

But the most surprising thing about this elegant he-Kyn was his face: his blue flesh was free of tattoos and honor-marks, his oak-leaf ears were unsplit and free of rings and other piercings. Even the most dedicated followers of the Celestial path in Red Cedar Town had at least some facial markings. Tarsa didn't know how to respond—he looked more than naked to her.

She was glad to turn her attention to the deer and his rider. While not often seen in the higher mountains, the Tetawi were occasional visitors, and this one looked very much like the others Tarsa had seen. He stood only about half her height, solid but not stout, with brown skin the color of ripe acorns and shining black hair that trailed to his waist in a single braid. Two small black eyes twinkled pleasantly, and two parallel tattoo trails of black circles crossed his wide cheeks and nose to mark his own people's adulthood rites. A floppy brown hat perched low on his head, with bright feathers woven into a red hatband; the hat may have once had a peak, but it, like the brim, dropped lazily to the side. The Tetawa's vest was mostly red, but green, black, and yellow beaded swirls danced like snakes across the heavy fabric. In one hand, as a walking stick, he held a long-handled hatchet with a dark stone blade; in his other hand, he tugged on the reins of a small mule deer, who glared at his companion with undisguised irritation.

The Tetawa walked to the elder she-Kyn and jerked his chin upward once in greeting. Unahi returned the gesture. The old Wielder still smoked her pipe as she sat on the downed tree, seemingly unsurprised by the new arrivals, but Tarsa stood with her flaming branch held slightly toward them. The he-Kyn watched her warily.

"*Hanahé*," the Tetawa greeted them in their own high-mountain Kyn-tongue. "What happened here?" His tone was friendlier than his suspicion-filled eyes. Tarsa suddenly realized how strange she and Unahi must look. Here were two she-Kyn, calmly eating and smoking together in the middle of a ruined town filled with death-scaffolds. She listened while Unahi briefly recounted the story of the Stoneskin's raid and eventual demise. The Tetawa nodded and let out a low whistle of awe as he looked around at the devastation, casting an appreciative glance toward Tarsa when Unahi came to the story of the creature's death. He turned back to the he-Kyn, and they walked away to speak.

Unahi sat unperturbed, but Tarsa clasped the brand tightly. They both watched, in the dim edge of firelight, as the smaller visitor drew something from a pouch on his belt. His hands gyrated slowly in a wide arc. The air tingled slightly, a tensing of the *wyr*. It was a Wielding, but one with a feel different from those Tarsa had experienced—it was tentative, a gentle, questioning probing of the *wyr*. The Redthorn's eyes widened, but Unahi shook her head. The moment passed, and the Tetawa turned with a smile. "*Hanahé*," he said again, this time without hesitation.

The elder Wielder smiled, motioning for him to sit beside her. He slipped the bridle from the deer's head, letting the creature roam freely through the town, and settled himself onto the log. "*Tsodoka*."

"You're welcome," Unahi said. Her eyes strayed to the deer. "You ride him all the way here?"

"As much as he'd let me," he laughed. He pulled up his left sleeve to show a nasty bruise on his forearm. "He en't been none too happy 'bout it, neither. This en't the only one I got, but it's the only one I can show without turnin' four shy shades of red!"

Unahi laughed, and Tarsa smiled hesitantly. The Tetawa seemed pleasant enough, but the he-Kyn's strangeness troubled her. Still, courtesy demanded that he be made welcome. "Have you eaten?" she asked.

The he-Kyn turned to the Tetawa with a quizzical look. The little deer-rider replied in a strange tongue, and the he-Kyn nodded curtly. Turning to Tarsa, the Tetawa said in Kyn, "He en't interested, but I'd be willin' to take somethin', if ye'r offerin'." Noting her glance at the he-Kyn, the Tetawa added, "He don't know the old Kyn-speech of these parts, but I'd be glad to tell him what ye want to say."

Unahi turned to Tarsa. "There are extra bowls in my pack. Bring them here, would you?" Her voice was gentle, but Tarsa could sense the tension in it. A Kyn who couldn't speak the People's tongue? He was more unusual than she'd guessed. Nodding once, Tarsa dropped the brand back into the fire and turned to the pack. Unahi and the Tetawa continued chatting, engaging in the customary introductory conversation that preceded formal discussion. When Tarsa returned, Unahi filled both bowls and handed them to each of the visitors. The Tetawa took his with a smile. "*Tsodoka*." The he-Kyn bowed stiffly but remained standing at the fire's edge. With an exasperated sigh, the Tetawa turned and said something in a sharp tone, which Tarsa now recognized with a jolt—it was a Mannish dialect, similar to that used by a couple of Human traders who'd married into Ash Branch in Red Cedar Town. With obvious discomfort, the he-Kyn accepted the bowl from Unahi's outstretched hand.

"Sorry 'bout him," the Tetawa muttered between mouthfuls of stew. "He en't the most sociable fellow I ever traveled with, nor none too polite about it. But he don't mean no harm; he just don't know any better."

He suddenly stopped and put his bowl down with a shake of his head. "Here I'm criticizin' his manners when I don't use m' own." He extended his hand palm up, which Unahi touched lightly in welcome. "I'm Tobhi Burrows, Badger Clan from Bristlecone Hollow, 'bout a ten-day ride northwest of here. That bruise-maker yonder is Smudge. It's a pleasure."

"I'm Unahi Sam'sheyda, Cedar Branch from Thistlewood, and this is my niece, the Redthorn warrior Tarsa'deshae, of Red Cedar Town." Both she-Kyn nodded at the Tetawa and turned their eyes to the other visitor.

Tobhi smiled at the he-Kyn and then turned back to Unahi. "This is Leith Fynon. He's a messenger from the Sevenfold Council at Sheynadwiin, and I guess ye'r the last one we been lookin' for."

Neranda Ak'shaar stood at the rostrum, her shimmering white robes flowing in pleated waves around her feet, and waited with dignified patience for the tumult to die down. It took some time. She calmly scanned the vast Gallery of Song where the other Lawmakers continued their heated debate. More Assembly members were listening than ever had before; she and her allies were still in the minority, but their righteous position had greater momentum now. The discussion had been going on for weeks; tempers were fraying on both sides, yet no one could deny the calming influence of the white-cloaked she-Kyn at the central dais—not even the Governor, who had bitterly denounced her in his private rooms that very morning. His words might have wounded her when she was younger, but a long absence from Sheynadwiin, followed by a few years in the contentious Assembly, had taught her much. She had come to realize that opinion and conviction were often two very different things.

Neranda could trust in her own certain convictions; his opinions were weak without similar determination.

She was now a powerful Lawmaker from a long line of respected political figures in the Nation, a fitting image of what the Kyn could become—a stately and formidable Shield in both body and mind. When many of the old Branch elders had surrendered the autonomy of their individual towns for a unified government that they believed better suited to face the threat of Human encroachment, her father's immediate Branch-kith—the Ak'shaar family, in particular—found themselves in a fortunate position. They were concerned less with Branch customs and the expectations of their extended families than with the fortunes of their direct line. In their philosophy, the Branches belonged to the past, while the more immediate concerns of the Ak'shaar family belonged to the inescapable reality of Man's growing influence over their world. And thus the Ak'shaars led the way. They'd long studied the ways of Humanity—even sent some of their sons and daughters, like Neranda, to be educated in the cities of Men and to learn the foundations of the Celestial Path from benevolent Human Proselytors—and were well prepared to advise the Assembly of Law and the Governor, who now led the combined Kyn Nation.

For the past three generations, at least one Ak'shaar was groomed to guide the Nation toward what the family believed was a more reasonable relationship with their Human neighbors, in spite of the unending intransigence of the traditional Wielders and their mountain-bred supporters. But as Neranda often noted, those old Wild ways were dwindling as surely as the ineffectual Branches, and soon the Celestials would find their path to a dignified state of grace that would be free of barbarity and the blind chains of the past. The days of the Greenwalkers were gone, no matter how much the Wielders wanted it to be otherwise. They must now find a way to exist in the world of Men, or else fade into oblivion.

Neranda, though by Branch tradition of her mother's line, embraced the new ways of her father's folk, becoming the first member of his Ak'shaar family to seek election, the others being content to lead from behind the Assembly's curtains, where influence was hidden and all the more powerful because of it. There were dangers to public life, to be sure, but Neranda knew that hidden influence depended entirely on having trustworthy allies to put your suggestions into practice, those confident enough in their beliefs to stand against unpopular opinion. Such allies were, unfortunately, entirely too rare, so Neranda took it upon herself to be the example of such virtue in the Assembly. If one strong voice was raised toward Truth, others would follow.

She became that voice.

When the shouting had diminished, she struck the brass tip of the speaker's staff against the granite circle in the dais, sending a sharp ring through the chamber to signal the conclusion of her speech. "Benevolent Lawmakers, friends and family, do not allow your fears to outweigh your good judgment. Do not let your uncertainty obscure your duty. This offer is more than generous, and shadows lengthen on the horizon. Will we continue to deny the inevitable, and thus leave our people to chaos and ruin in the coming storm? Will we abandon our responsibilities to lead our Nation into the future, even though we know too well how few of our unfortunate brethren truly understand the complexities we face? My kith, we were elected not as followers of public opinion but as leaders of the Kyn *Nation*. If we fulfill our duty, future generations will look upon us with both respect and love, as we will have been the steadfast champions who made an unhappy choice in dark times for the good of all. But if we fail to change, if we surrender to our fears and blind nostalgia, there will be no future reflection on us, for there will be no future for us or our descendants."

The hood of her cloak slid away to reveal a cascade of burnished copper hair that fell in shining streams down her back, secured in place by a web of bright silver netting. Hers was a cold beauty, but it seemed to warm with righteousness as she lifted the staff in the air. "We have two choices: resistance, or life." Her violet eyes flashed in the everlights that illuminated the chamber. "*I choose life!*" With that, she brought the speaker's staff down again, and its thundering peal was drowned in the overwhelming roar of applause that erupted from the Assembly. Voices cried out "Life!" in response. Any voices in opposition were lost in the chaos.

The Lawmaker bowed to the Assembly and stepped from the dais into a wave of enthusiastic supporters. It was the finest moment of her career, but it was only the first step of a difficult journey. She looked to the tall chair at the far end of the chamber, where the

Governor sat in his massive seat carved from wyrwood and precious stones into the shape of a butterfly in flight. His silver head was bowed. Neranda's elation faded, and her throat tightened in momentary sorrow: Garyn Mendiir, the great warrior and politician who had bravely led the Kyn for half her life, sat alone in the shadows, and she stood tall in the light.

Neranda's sadness vanished. All things changed—it was the way of the Melded world. The wisdom of those Wild ages no longer served in this time. It was inevitable, and she would be the one to show her people the new way—a stronger, wiser way.

All was as it should be. She smiled and returned her attention to her allies in the Assembly. The Governor's grief was quickly forgotten.

6

Shadow and Story

TOBHI TRANSLATED LEITH'S WORDS AGAIN. "The leaders of the seven Folk Nations are worried 'bout the raids and growin' pride of the Eromar Humans, so they've called a gatherin' to meet soon. The Kyn Assembly will host the Sevenfold Council in Sheynadwiin."

Unahi stared into the fire. When no questions were forthcoming from the elder she-Kyn, Tarsa asked one herself. "Why have you been looking for my aunt? She's no Assembly member." She knew a bit about the Assembly, as every Kyn town had a representative in Sheynadwiin to be their voice in National affairs, but beyond that the concerns of the Kyn capital had had little visible impact on Red Cedar Town. Sheynadwiin was a place shrouded by stories and a distant mystique, hardly the sort of place where old Unahi would be welcome, let alone summoned by formal messengers.

The he-Kyn waited for Tobhi to translate, but the latter replied directly to Tarsa's question. "She's a Wielder, and they's the most important part of the whole thing, 'cause they understand the Old Ways better than anyone. There's more to this mess than just politickin'. The Wielders is the only ones who can bring the Folk back to a sensible understandin' of things—the world is all out of balance right now. Them Kyn Shields is gettin' completely out of hand. They're even talkin' about givin' up the Everland and movin' away to some

62

forsaken place in the lands of Men. I'd say it was a joke, but there en't nothin' funny 'bout it. They're deadly serious."

Surrender the Everland? Tarsa wanted to laugh, too, but Tobhi's grim face silenced her. It was an absurd notion. Who would want to abandon their homeland? It was one of the few Thresholds of the Eld Green that had survived the Melding, when Men had shattered the barrier between the worlds and brought their world and that of the Folk together in catastrophe. Many of the 'Holds were destroyed then, others had been slowly stolen and fragmented in the thousand years since that devastating betrayal, but the Everland remained strong and resilient. Within its fertile borders, the Folk were truly alive; the *wyr* coursed unhindered through all that lived there. The innumerable spirits of creation were woven together in this world— from the leaf-headed standing people and the lichen-spotted stone people to the furred four-leggeds and the feathered folk who danced on wind and breeze—and they belonged to the land as much as the land belonged to them.

Leave the Everland? It was barely imaginable. Yet she believed him.

Unahi turned back to Tobhi and Leith. "Are other Wielders attending the Council?"

Tobhi interpreted, and Leith responded to him. "Yes. He's already talked with a few of 'em, and there's other messengers headin' throughout the Everland to show 'em the Governor's seal." Leith reached into an inner pocket of his coat and handed a flat clay disk to the Wielder. Tarsa saw the image of a butterfly on the disk, each wing a different color: red, black, blue, and white. Beneath it was a symbol she didn't recognize, an angled half-moon or bear's claw, with a small azure circle to its right, but Unahi seemed satisfied and handed it back to the messenger.

Tarsa watched Leith closely. "Why doesn't he speak to us himself?"

Tobhi shrugged. "He's on the One Moon Path, with his learnin' taken from Men most of his life, and he never learned to speak the Kyn Tongue. Why they sent him is beyond me, but with all the fightin' goin' on in the Assembly, he's prob'ly the only one who'd go, honor and glory and all that. There's lots of them types in Sheynadwiin these days. When the Council sent him out on this errand, m' Clan mothers asked me to help out as best I could, since I been speakin' both tongues, and a few others, all m' life; m' pepa's tradin' days among the Kyn have been comin' in useful. I been wantin' to come this way for a while, anyway—to remember over old times, ye know—so I saddled up this bow-legged deer, grabbed m' hat, and headed for the hills. Leith and I en't had too much to chat about, to be sure, but as he don't bother me much, we generally been gettin' along just fine."

He bent over and scooped another steaming batch of stew into his bowl. The old Wielder was quiet, her grey eyes lingering thoughtfully on Tarsa.

"We'll come," Unahi said at last. "My niece is a Wielder as well, although still very young and unsteady in her knowledge." Her eyes flickered to the twisted pines, and Tarsa's cheeks went hot. "In any event, she would need to meet with the Wielders' Circle before finishing her training. This might actually be better than I'd expected."

Tobhi repeated the elder she-Kyn's words to Leith, who smiled broadly and turned to secure his saddle. "That's all he needed to hear," Tobhi said, but he made no move to follow.

As the he-Kyn finished his preparations to leave, Unahi's long sensory tendrils twitched in agitation, and she raised her head. There was something strange in the air, but she was weary in body and spirit, and she couldn't place the feeling. It unnerved her. She walked over to Leith and rested a wrinkled hand on his arm.

"Wait until dawn," she said softly, her eyes slightly glazed from sending her thoughts into the distance. "There's no real hurry."

The he-Kyn looked at her quizzically and turned to Tobhi, who translated. Leith smiled and shook his head proudly, pulling a handmusket from a bag on his horse's saddle as a sign of his preparedness. Unahi stumbled away from the sudden taint of cold iron, and Tarsa jumped up to catch her.

The he-Kyn hurriedly returned the firearm to its case and said a few words to the Tetawa as he swung himself into the saddle.

"He en't worried," Tobhi said, clearly unconvinced. "Besides, he says he can't get no rest here, not in this place of death."

Without another glance at the trio, Leith spurred his horse toward the shadows, and soon the only sounds left were the crackling logs of the fire and the harsh caw of ravens in the dark night.

❧

The dolls were often a mystery, even to Quill, who had known the ways of their creation since before her granny traveled over to the Spirit World when she was still a cub. The dolls and the secrets of their creation passed down through Spider Clan from granny or mema to daughter, along with the soft tongue that would help the cub understand them. She learned much before and after Granny Pearl's death, but there was still much about the dolls that remained maddeningly outside her comprehension. She half suspected that the little apple-headed figures preferred it that way—they were every bit as cranky and mischievous as their squinting, wrinkled features indicated. They were also her closest family now, and she cared for them with as much kindness and care as her own mema had given her.

Quill loved the dolls deeply, but that didn't stop the frustration, especially at this time, when she really needed them to share what they knew. Many Tetawi came to her squat little cabin on the hilly acreage she shared with her uncle and maternal cousins, and each visitor hoped that the dolls could give wise counsel or offer hope for a problem or healing for a wound. Yet tonight it wasn't a love-medicinal for a pining young *fahr* that took Quill's attention, nor a soothing treatment for an elder's dull aches and unspoken loneliness. This was an entirely different, and desperately urgent, situation. Yet the dolls remained stubbornly silent.

The four cubs had disappeared the day before, and there had been no sign of them since then. Even the settlement's hunting hounds couldn't catch a trace of them. Bryn and his sisters were not likely to run away; ever since their eldest brother had been kidnapped by slaving Men, they were much too skittish to wander past the ravine that separated the moundhouse cabins of Spindletop from the wilder Edgewood. Everyone was trying to pretend that the cubs were just teasing, that they were crouched giggling in their mother's pantry, that they were anywhere in the Tetawi settlement and not *Out There*. But such imaginings didn't bring the cubs back.

The room was quiet in spite of the dozens of Tetawi who sat on cushions, benches, and thick braided rugs, or who stood, tense and grim-faced, when they couldn't find any room to sit. Quill sat in her doll-making chair, a high-backed seat of smoothed tree roots that her uncle had carved for her when she reached her age-name birthday.

It was here that she fashioned the dolls from dried crabapples, corn-cobs and corn husks, beads, feathers, shells, bits of colorful cloth, and other scavenged or hand-shaped accessories, each element combining to create another wizened figure who looked into the world's mysteries with polished-pebble eyes and sometimes came back with needed wisdom. Quill could often understand their speech, but just as often the dolls chattered away in a language that was completely their own, unintelligible to others, or they just kept quiet, unable or unwilling to share what was going on behind their shining eyes. To those without the gift of Dolltending, the figures simply stood, stiff and silent, on their shelves. Whatever it was that Quill saw and heard, it belonged to her alone.

The Tetawa's shoulders slumped, and she let out a long, ragged breath. Her tawny face, recently adorned with the three-claw mark of adulthood under her left eye, was pinched with exhaustion. She'd already tried to speak with six of the dolls, but they shared nothing. It wasn't that they were ignorant of the situation—far from it. The Moth Clan cubs were well known to both Quill and the dolls, largely because of Chadda, the youngest, who insisted on stopping in every time she was passing Quill's home to squeal with delight in anticipation of the dolls' patient conversation, to which the cub was already sensitive, even at her young age. The Dolltender had reminded the dolls of Chadda's loving ways, but even that sentimental appeal was useless. They stared at her without emotion in their dark eyes. She'd never known them to be so unyielding. Perhaps her granny could have moved past that barrier to wrest away the dolls' secrets, but Quill wasn't her granny, as she had to acknowledge once again. She was lost.

"Anything yet?" It was Meerda, the cubs' mother. She'd been beautiful once, with full round cheeks and luxurious dark hair, but the loss of her eldest son and his uncle—her dearest brother, who left to find the kidnapped cub and disappeared along with him—had ravaged her. And now this. A thick knot swelled in Quill's throat, and she shook her head as she reached for another doll.

Someone bumped into the table beside her tree-root seat, shifting the doll that she wanted out of her reach, and her brown fingers closed on another one. It was Hickory, one of the older dolls, and far from one of her favorites. Over the years his face had dried into an unpleasant grimace, in spite of all her efforts to mold it into something a little less gruesome, and she'd never quite gotten used to his scowl and narrow, suspicious bead eyes. A stiff shock of white thistledown stood up on his head, adding to his unpleasant strangeness. Quill had never destroyed one of her dolls—it was almost unthinkable to do so—but if any of the sixty or more dolls were to be the first, Hickory would be the one to feed the flames. Still, he was the nearest to her, so she pulled the frowning doll from the table and spoke to him.

She wasn't at all surprised that he was as silent as the rest; she'd expected nothing more from him—he'd never once spoken to her. His wizened face seemed to twist into an almost spiteful grimace, and his eyes rolled around to take in the gathered Tetawi. He watched them sit, hands clenched in fear and anticipation, some clinging tightly to one another in the dimly lit room, hope swallowed by a growing fear as a bone-deep cold enveloped them.

And then Hickory laughed.

It was a thin, piercing giggle that ripped through the terrified gathering. The Dolltender was dimly aware that the other Tetawi heard the awful sound, for she could hear their cries. The world seemed to darken, like a cold blanket dropped across their eyes. Quill gasped and tried to release the doll, but Hickory's twine and twig arms wrapped tightly around her hands, digging hard into the flesh. The puckered apple mouth rose and fell maliciously as the cackle grew louder, more biting. A shadow filled the frigid room. The Dolltender heard the others call out, but their voices were distant and removed, for she wasn't with them anymore. All that she could see was the doll in her bleeding hands, his contorted face growing more malevolent with each shrieking laugh. Her gaze fell into his burning eyes, shiny black stones no longer. She was drawn into their endlessness.

Then she saw the cubs, and she shouted to them. They couldn't hear her. They clung desperately to one another, eyes shut in terror, as a tall shadow approached them through the trees. Quill was sharing the shadow's view, could hear its gurgling laugh echoed by the doll in her hands. The children were torn and bloody, Bryn most of all. He pushed his sisters and brother behind him when the shadow drew near. Quill watched helplessly as two clawed white hands rose into view and slashed downward with uncanny speed. Bryn threw his hand up to protect himself, pulling it away to stare at the bloody stump that was once his arm. Slowly, the cub turned his eyes to the gaping hole in his chest and the heart that pumped, steaming still, in the pale talons.

Quill's own screams rang louder than those of the cubs, and the shadow slid over Bryn's still-warm body. She could almost feel its glee as it reached out again. A sudden rage filled her, and she felt her body become her own again, if only for a moment. In that brief flash, Quill threw herself into the table of dolls, knocking it over. The dolls tumbled over her body and across the floor. She slid back into that grim half-world, but this time noted with satisfaction that the shadow had stopped. The air was filled with a new sound that drowned out the weeping of the cubs and the hissing laughter of the shadow. *Shakka-shakka-shakka, shakka-shakka-shakka.* Dozens of small, bright-eyed figures emerged from the darkness in the trees, their corn-husk garments crackling softly, and made a ring around the younglings. *Shakka-shakka-shakka.* Beady stones stared defiantly at the shadow. *Shakka-shakka-shakka.* The laughter ended abruptly. *Shakka-shakka-shakka-shakka.* The dolls brought their circle closer around the cubs and withdrew with a soft shuffling whisper into the trees. *Shakka-shakka-shakka. Shakka-shakka-shakka.*

The tension in her hands loosened, and Quill opened her eyes to see Hickory's broken body crumbling into pieces in her fingers. The apple head was distorted into an expression of feral rage, the brows knotted in frustration, but he was silent now. She took a deep breath, and a couple of Tetawi helped her get shakily to her feet. Although the room was warm again, it was now in shambles. Many of her neighbors had fled, but a few still remained, including Meerda, who lay sobbing on the wooden floor. Whatever Quill had seen, all those present had shared the grisly experience.

Quill draped her arms around Meerda's shoulders and tightly held the grieving *firra*, while a few of the remaining Tetawi picked up the scattered furniture and tried to give some order to the room. Most of her dolls were gone, but they would be back with the surviving cubs, and she would prepare the dolls' meal of cedar and tobacco and thank them with the proper words. And after that, the Tetawi of Spindletop would prepare for Bryn's funeral.

She turned her attention to the remains of old Hickory, now broken and impotent on the worn wooden floor. Quill walked to the corner beside the fireplace and drew out a broom and thin-edged copper shovel. She was careful to gather all of the pieces, leaving not even the smallest shred of corn husk or chunk of apple behind, and when she was finished, Quill strode to the fireplace and drove the entire head of the shovel deep into the still-smoldering ashes. There was a rush of air and a crackle, followed by a blast of flame that flew up the chimney. She stepped back. The sweet smell of burnt apple filled the room . . . and something else with it, a sour bitterness that gathered thickly in the back of her throat. When she was sure that Hickory had been reduced to ashes, Quill washed her hands in a basin beside the fireplace, turned toward the door, and waited for the dolls to come home.

Leith wanted a quick escape from the ruins of Nine Oaks Town, but the mare stubbornly refused to match his desired pace; instead, she pulled back, snorting and shaking her head, her hooves digging deep trenches in the hard red soil. The he-Kyn snapped the reins and shouted, and she finally moved forward, but slowly, grunting and quivering with each hesitant step.

This mission was meant to be the first glorious step in a great career. He'd actively pursued the assignment when he overheard one of his mother's Assembly friends mention that a Sevenfold Council had been called. He was one of the finest riders of Sheynadwiin's Celestial families, widely admired for his grace in the saddle and his casual mastery of the temperamental beasts. When the call came for messengers, he was first in the queue, and he was the first to receive the Governor's seal and his instructions. He'd been more than a little disappointed that his guide would be a backcountry Brownie scribbler, but Leith was eager for the adventure, and he was confident that the journey would be a success in spite of its rather mundane beginning.

The journey was anything but the exciting adventure he'd antici-pated. In fact, it was a constant experience in humiliation. He didn't understand the Kyn of the Wild lands, either their customs or their language, and he found out quite quickly how unprepared he was for the rigors of the mission. He'd expected to ride along well-maintained roads, only to find that the only access to these places was along rough and rocky trails that left him battered and sore. Sleep was no better, as his bedroll was inadequate for the mix of terrain he slept on. His fine clothing was too thin for the cold nights; he'd forgotten an oil wrap, so rain often left him damp and sniffling for days.

And this was before he even encountered any of the Folk he was meant to speak with. Far from being the mysterious figures out of winter night stories, the Wielders turned out to be rather ordinary and uninspiring. Leith seemed to always cause offense when encountering them; he didn't know when to speak or be silent, when to eat or not eat, which direction to walk around the ceremonial fires, what he should or shouldn't offer as a gift. Tobhi told him to simply pay attention and follow his example, but the Brownie seemed to insist on indulging every superstition and backward custom they encountered, and whenever Leith tried to intervene with good Celestial teachings, he'd find his guide looking at him with lips pursed and eyebrow raised, as though the he-Kyn was an ignorant youngling. So Leith simply stood back, aloof, and waited with ever-growing impatience for the time when he could return home and get away from this strange world. He just didn't belong here. He was lonely, and frightened. Tobhi had seen his failure, and even though the Brownie had never used it against him, there was some small part of the he-Kyn that hated him for it.

And now the old Wielder and her niece had witnessed his inadequacy, too. It was more than he could bear. He had to get away from them all, and quickly.

Full of rage now, he finally slammed his heels into the mare's side, piercing her flesh with the spurs. She rose up with a bubbling scream and at last jerked forward down the road, just as a black shape streaked out of the darkness and swept past Leith's head. He barely had time to duck as a second shadow rushed toward him. His hand went to the flintlock at his side, but the horse twisted wildly, and the weapon fell, unfired, to the ground. The air was suddenly thick, and Leith gagged as the acrid stench surrounded him, burning his eyes and throat. He covered his mouth with his arm, but the oily foulness permeated everything.

The mare reared back again, her eyes rolling wide in stark terror. The he-Kyn cursed the beast and drove his spurs hard against her, heedless of her pain and his own stalks' sympathetic throb. Weaponless, and unwilling to return in frightened shame to Tobhi and the she-Kyn, Leith saw only one reasonable option: to ride far and fast.

Leith's mother had begged him to withdraw from this mission for the Sevenfold Council and its Speaker; she'd never approved of Garyn's sympathetic coddling of the Greenwalkers and their backward ways, and she certainly didn't approve of Leith's restless interest in the wild lands beyond Sheynadwiin's walls. But she was as indulgent of her eldest son as Garyn was of the Wielders, so in spite of her disapproving frowns, she nodded her reluctant assent when Leith kissed her forehead before he departed, his saddlebags slung carelessly across his back.

<<*You worry too much, Mother,*>> he'd laughed then, as if this journey would be nothing more than a brisk canter through the city's center green. <<*I have my musket, and I have a guide who is quite knowledgeable of the area. Do not worry about me—the most troubling events I am likely to encounter will be rain or saddle sores.*>>

<<*You might get fever from the rain, or skin-blight from the sores . . .*>> Leith had laughed again at her final appeal, waving farewell as he spurred the horse onward, not even bothering to look back as he called out to her, <<*I will return in glory, Mother.*>>

The words returned now, unbidden and unwelcome. They pierced his thoughts with their mocking irony. His mother was always wringing her hands in fear and worry, and always without good cause—so why should this night be any different? Why should she now be right, when she'd so often been wrong?

The answers never came. Blots of darkness streamed out of the forest, and Leith gasped in an agony too deep for screams as a talon raked across the surface of one of his sensory stalks. The tendril thrashed wildly, like a worm skewered on a fishhook. He couldn't breathe. He hurt too much even to be afraid. He didn't notice that his nerveless fingers had loosened their hold on the reins, or that the mare's frantic movements had tossed him from the saddle to writhe blindly on the rock-strewn earth.

Maddened by pain, Leith never saw the shadows darken in the trees above him, nor did he hear the sniggering mass of sharp-toothed figures descend in eager anticipation. He only became aware of their presence when they began to feed.

Tobhi found what little remained of Leith's mangled body the next morning, just outside the wall of Nine Oaks Town. The he-Kyn's horse was gone, but the musket lay broken in two on the ground next to his bloodstained iron-ward. Tobhi searched for tracks, but other than signs of the horse's frantic escape, there was nothing more than a handful of foul-smelling black feathers. The companions didn't speak about the night before, or the reason for the savage attack. It clearly wasn't random: the Governor's seal was conspicuously missing.

They carried what remained of Leith back to Nine Oaks Town, wrapped and prayed over his body and added it to the others on the scaffolds, and followed the ceremony with a cold purifying bath. There was no luxury of four days in purifying isolation—yet another breach of etiquette and ritual that grieved Unahi. Gathering up their own few belongings, the travelers left the silent shadows of Nine Oaks behind.

Of the three, Unahi was the most familiar with this region, so, after brief consultation with Tobhi, who'd spent much of his childhood on the trade routes in the area, she decided that the route east along the banks of the Wildwater would be best; it would lead them north for a few weeks through the lower Eldarvian Woods, then on to the city of Sheynadwiin within Dardath Vale. There were faster and more direct ways to Sheynadwiin, but the she-Kyn and Tetawa hesitated to travel in the full view of too many interested eyes, just in case whatever had killed Leith was waiting for those Wielders who had actually received his missive.

They finished out the night well beyond the rock ring that enclosed Nine Oaks, then left the region at dawn. Unahi estimated about seven days to the Wildwater, if they stuck to a steady pace and didn't encounter any unexpected delays. Though never mentioned by name, Leith was often in their thoughts.

It grieved the old Wielder to be taking Tarsa away from Thistlewood, where the younger she-Kyn could have received a full understanding of the *wyr* and its teachings in a calmer place that still sang with ancient spirits. Unahi had tended that land and its peoples for many years, and the relationship was strong. But the People needed them at the Council, and that was the higher duty now. Perhaps, when the gathering was over, they would return to the deep forest, and Tarsa's training could expand in peace. In the meantime,

Unahi would just have to do her best on the journey and hope that the young warrior could find ways to guide her emotions and frustration to healthier ends.

The Kraagen Mountains stood high and strong along the eastern horizon. Travel across the mighty, snow-peaked range was difficult at the best of times, unless one knew the passes that cut through the peaks. Tarsa was an utter stranger to this place; the jagged wall that loomed in the distance filled her with curiosity and—though she would have been too proud to acknowledge it—more than a little hesitation.

The Wildwater would be their first significant destination. The valley stretches that spanned either side of the raging river were some of the easier routes for travel in this rocky expanse. Few of the more communal Folk knew or cared about the inner valleys, as they tended to prefer the more temperate and crop-friendly slopes that stretched, lush and green, on either side of the mountains; what happened in the middle of the cold and brutal Kraagens was of little interest. The life-giving Wildwater was much beloved in the lowlands to the south of the Kraagens, as most of the river's fury had already been spent by the time it reached these gentle regions, and that broad, muddy stretch was the form in which the great water was best known to most of the Folk.

Yet there were hearty Folk—relatively few in number but not entirely rare—who treasured the fierce, mid-mountain river and the fertile grasslands that flanked it. Mineral-rich waters descended from the tall peaks, first in thin rivulets, then in thick streams that cascaded down five-thousand-foot cliffs, finally drawing together into a boiling flood of frigid whiteness that crashed and smashed its way through mountains, and fast on its way past Tangletop Forest at the southeastern edge of the Everland, where it disappeared between worlds, never reaching the lands of Men. Most who knew the river at its greatest strength were solitary wanderers, like the Stoneskin who ravaged the Kyn towns, but rock-spirits were everywhere, and some small communities of Gvaergs, Ubbetuk, Tetawi, and Feral Beast-Folk called the valleys home. Some of these were cautious but friendly with strangers; others preferred to kill interlopers as a matter of expedient principle, especially in these unsettled times.

The first full day's travel was slow and generally quiet, as both Tarsa and Unahi were exhausted from their earlier journey and their grim labor in Nine Oaks Town. It was a pleasant day, though, that combined the crispness of spring with the bright clarity of the approaching summer, and the gentle mood helped to lift the earlier one. Tobhi was thankful for the silence. He hadn't known Leith too well or even liked him much, but he was nevertheless shaken by the brutality of the he-Kyn's death.

They walked at an easy pace when possible, but the eastern side of the hill country was littered with steep, blocky cliffs that required careful planning to maneuver. Just when they were sure that they'd reached the end of a stretch of reaching stone, they'd find themselves on another one and spend much of their time searching for the faint game trails that led to the scrubby base of the bluff. They'd occasionally see a flight of great firebirds wheeling in the far distance, the creatures' multicolored plumage iridescent in the two suns' light, or encounter giant elk grazing calmly in the peace of rustling aspen groves, grumbling bears who lumbered past with no more than a glance of cursory interest at Smudge's panicked snorts, and once even an antlered greatwyrm sunning itself on a vast flat slab of red stone just a few miles away. They kept close to the bluffs to avoid agitating this latter creature but returned to their planned course when the pearly silver of an airborne stormdrake glinted in the late afternoon, sending the greatwyrm slithering swiftly back into its hidden lair.

They camped in a pine grove at the base of a tall, chunky mound of streaked sandstone, one of many that dotted the rising hills to the east, choosing the site largely because of a little spring-fed creek that wound its way down the slope. Tobhi took Smudge into the trees and returned with a few thick bundles of firewood lashed to the deer's back, while Tarsa swept a gravelly area free of pine needles and other debris and dug a pit, lining it with rocks and filling it with dead leaves. Unahi searched through the Tetawa's saddlebags and found dried marsh rice that she added to some of the root vegetables that she carried in her own traveling pack. These she placed in a clay pot of water that she nestled inside the ashes. The Wielder then mixed a few handfuls of ground nut flour with water and formed a sticky dough to bake on the fire-heated rocks.

Unahi ate quickly and excused herself early that night. After so much pain and death over the past few days, she was exhausted, and this was as safe a place as any in the Everland these days. She spoke briefly to a few of the pines, who agreed to shrug off some of their listlessness to watch over the travelers that night. Tobhi and Tarsa remained awake and began an unspoken contest to see who could eat the most food. Though just a little over half the she-Kyn's height, Tobhi maintained a respectable pace.

While working on her third bowl, Tarsa's glance fell on the thick pouch that the Tetawa kept tightly fastened next to his belly. "What were you looking at last night when you first talked with Leith?" she asked.

Tobhi's hand went defensively to his belt. "Did ye see it?" he mumbled through a mouthful of stew.

"No," she said, breaking off another piece of bread. "You were turned away from us, but I definitely *felt* something. Are you a Wielder?"

He chuckled. "A Wielder? Nah. Our Wielders en't often as easy to spot as yours; Tetawi Wielders are healers and shape-shifters, medicine-makers and spies. They're filled with animal spirit; sometimes they even become like their Clan animals, more spirit than flesh, I reckon. No, I en't one of them wisdom-bearers; I'm just a Leafspeaker."

The she-Kyn gave him a questioning glance. The Tetawa smiled. "Ye en't never heard of a Leafspeaker afore? Well, then, ye gotta see for ye'self." He finished his meal and glanced at the last bit remaining in the cooking pot, then sighed and slipped the pouch off of his belt. It was a beautifully crafted bag of hand-tooled leather, with a front pocket cunningly designed to look like the head of a bristle-cheeked badger, the symbol of Tobhi's maternal Clan. He lifted the badger's snout and pulled a bundle wrapped in red cloth from the pouch. Tarsa set her bowl aside and moved closer.

Tobhi's nimble fingers quickly unwrapped the cloth to reveal a stack of broad leaves of various shapes and colors, each at least half the size of the Tetawa's hand. "They're lore-leaves," he grinned, proud to be sharing his talent with someone so clearly interested. He lifted a single leaf into the air to reveal a dark sigil carved delicately into its surface. "Every leaf's got a name and a voice, each a different story to tell, and together they can tell ye pretty much any story ye might want to hear. The leaves talk to me, ye see. Stories 'bout the past, or stories 'bout what's comin' down the road."

"You can see the future with them?" Tarsa asked, her eyes bright. Her stalks, now unwrapped and pulsing slightly in the cool air, curled softly against her cheeks.

Tobhi shook his head. "Can't see it, no, but I can sometimes hear it; depends on what they tell me. Sometimes I can get a sense of what's comin', but the future's a tricky thing, and it's hard to get the full understandin' of the story. It's too easy to read what ye *want* to read instead of what the *true* story is. So I try to avoid seekin' them stories. They bring too much grief and misunderstandin'. I prefer the stories that brought us here, the stories that help us know where we come from and who we are. Them stories is generally more helpful for guidin' the future than tryin' to look ahead and seein' what's on the way. It's a knowin' circle, tellin' us that what's come afore can help us with what's comin' now."

He lifted the leaf into the air and pulled his hand away. The leaf remained in midair, floating as if pinned to an invisible wall. He followed with other leaves—oak, birch, aspen, maple, beech, dogwood, and others that Tarsa couldn't identify—each large and marked with its own distinctive symbol. Soon there were twenty leaves, then thirty-two, then forty, each hanging in the air, combining in a series of vertical spirals. Finally, satisfied with the number, Tobhi folded the remaining leaves into the cloth and returned them to the pouch.

His attention firmly fixed on the leaves, Tobhi said softly, "This en't a common gift among my people; I think m' pepa learned somethin' like it when he lived with the Kyn at Thornholt afore I was born, then put it to Tetawi uses, so ye might say it's a Kyn-gifted talent. Now," he jerked his chin toward the Redthorn, "think 'bout somethin' ye want to know more 'bout, somethin' that's important, somethin' that might help ye with decisions in yer life." He shifted the location of some of the leaves, but they maintained the same complex pattern of intersecting swirls.

Tarsa thought for a few moments. There were so many things that she wanted to know—too many, and most of them were about the future. She was at the start of a new life, and it was a frightening beginning. Yet it was also one that brought a strange sort of anticipation and excitement. It wasn't the life she had chosen or expected, but already there were opportunities she'd never imagined.

Her world had been completely remade in just a few days. Transformation and change—that was the story for this night. She knew the story she wanted to hear.

"Tell me about the Melding, Tobhi. Tell me what's in the leaves." She had heard the story many times, and by masterful Kyn storytellers, but Tobhi's gift promised to reveal something new.

The Tetawa nodded, his face grave. "I'll tell ye the truth as I know it, but there's lots of other stories that have the truth, too. I still en't that far past a cub m'self, so there's lots I don't know in the story. But the leaves tell me a little more each time, so I've got to listen to the stories over and over to really understand 'em. It en't a happy tale, that's certain, but it's an important one. All right now—time to dance." He lifted his hands into the air and closed his eyes.

The light of the Greatmoon and his shattered sky-brothers was brighter tonight; it was still some time before the greater sphere would be full, but the glow of the moon and the shimmering band of silver that cut across the night sky dimmed the stars and illuminated the little lore-keeper's outstretched hands. The sigils on each leaf suddenly flared into a reddish gold light. For a moment, Tarsa thought the fragile leaves would burst into flame, but their brightness only illuminated the shadows around them. Forty strange symbols flashed to life against the night. Tobhi's hands began to move, and the leaves followed the motion. The glowing shapes spun and wove together as they circled around in a rhythmic pattern that slipped from ages past to the present and back again. They moved so quickly that Tarsa lost track of the individual signs and soon saw only golden trails of twisting light. Tobhi's dark eyes tracked their movements, and he began to speak, his voice low and hollow, his attention fully focused on the swirling flashes of green, gold, and red in the darkness.

"This is the truth as I know it. This world en't always been what it is today, ye know. Our world was once our own—it was all the Eld Green. There wasn't any 'Holds, no Darkenin's, no Decay or Otherness. Everythin' was the *wyr*, and we was part of it. The hills spoke to us, told us stories, as did the trees, the rivers, the hollows, and the swamps. The Beasts had themselves councils in them days, and we all respected 'em as equals. The Tetawi still do, ye know, but we're the only ones, I think, 'cept for them other Folk who follow the Old Ways.

"There was no time back then, nothin' like there is now. Surely, there was death, but it was different. It weren't somethin' to be feared like it is today. It came to us when our time was done, after a long, full life, and our passin' was a cause for celebration of a life lived, not mournin' for a life lost. But now things is different, and too often the flower is cut down afore it blooms.

"In them days, we had all we needed for livin', and we made things of great beauty, things that spoke to our joys and our happiness. In them days, any grievances we had with one another were settled peaceable; if we couldn't do that, we talked in council with Granny Turtle, Ol' Jenna, first of my people and mother of all the Beasts. Granny Turtle would listen and talk with the other spirit-folk, then decide what was best, as was her duty as first Clan mother, and we'd generally live just fine together. If we couldn't, well—even in them days we fought with one another, truth to tell, but it was always somethin' we could manage, and it was for survival, not for conquerin' and power.

"Now, Granny Turtle had herself a few sisters. There was Zhaia, the True Tree, the mother of yer folk. There was Shobbok, the Winter Witch, who brought all kind of sufferin' and mean critters out of the stone and ice of the north country. There was Avialle, the river-mother, who gave life to all them swimmers and mud-divers. There was others, too, and some brothers among 'em, but the sisters was the first to come about, so they're the ones in this tellin' of the story.

"It was gentle, trustin' Avialle who first met up with the Man called Kaantor. He was a bad sort, but nobody could've known that at the time, 'cause they'd never seen themselves a Human afore. He was a tall, fine-lookin' Man, with long hair and a short bit of beard. He didn't come across the Canopy Veil by accident; he was sent here by some of his own kind who'd come across the Veil in their greedy reachin' for knowledge that twisted on itself, becomin' witchery and the like. He came across and saw green bounty and happiness like nothin' he'd ever seen afore. He saw trees so heavy with sweet fruit that their branches nearly dragged the ground. He saw the Folk, the tree-born and the river-born, Folk of air and mountain, hill and swampy-land, Folk of rocks and deep places, too, all livin' peaceable most of the time, side by side, and he wanted to be part of it. After a while, he forgot them that sent him.

"Our way is to trust folks 'til they give us reason not to, so there was no way of knowin' what was to come. The first one to meet up with this Man Kaantor was sweet Avialle, who soon fell in love with him. I suppose he fell in love with her, too, in his own manner of doin' things. So for a time they was pretty happy. They spent most of their time rollin' in the furs—natural, of course, but somethin' them Humans seem to have all kinds of trouble with, gettin' it wrapped up with shame and guilt and meanness and such. Avialle didn't know any of them ways, so she was happy, and she gave of herself freely. But Kaantor never intended to stay and be satisfied with what he had. He wanted more, and he'd betray the one that loved him as well as them that called 'emselves his masters.

"It didn't help matters none that Shobbok, that tricky ol' thing, had a bit of meanness in her heart for Avialle, too. Winter ain't a kind season to rivers, ye know, even now, freezin' 'em solid, cuttin' 'em into pieces even when the warmin' months come along. But even them big ice glaciers in the Waste of Sleet can't stop the rivers from flowin' through 'em, so I guess Avialle gives as good as she gets, eh? Anyway, Shobbok knew what was bubblin' up in that Man's heart, so she whispers to him that there's treasure across the Canopy Veil, and all he has to do is cut through with his iron sword to find the prom- ised riches, 'cause that's the only thing that'll do it.

"Now, I don't know what was goin' on in that ol' spirit's head to put such an idea out there; I en't entirely sure that she knew what she was doin', neither, but all Kaantor's greed and selfishness couldn't be held back, no matter how much Avialle loved him. So one mornin', while she was sleepin', he took up his iron sword and walked up to the Veil between the worlds. Avialle woke up sudden-like to find him missin' and a deep, groanin' ache in the world, a pain so deep and raw that all life in the Eld Green cried out. She rushed to the Canopy Veil only to find Kaantor standin' there, sword piercin' the curtain, his flesh withered and worn like a dried-up crabapple. The Veil had kept all that age and dyin' and Decay out of the land, but since he cut it up with killing iron, Decay flowed in like a poisoned river, reachin' its dry claws out to claim everythin' it had been denied. I reckon even ol' Shobbok didn't expect that.

"So there stood that dung-hearted Kaantor, now an old man made mad by greed and lust, and when he sees Avialle come up to him, he turns his iron sword on her, sayin' that she tricked him, that she denied him what was by rights his, that she was hidin' all the treasures that should'a gone to him. He said that she'd seduced him, that she was nothin' but a ruttin' whore, that she'd cursed him with her feminine ways. And then he attacked. Poor, gentle Avialle. She never knew that her love-mate would turn out this-a-way. It's an old story, sad to say. She had no way of knowin' how her trust would be repaid, but she weren't no weak flower—she had sharp thorns. She fought back. She called on all the *wyr* she could reach to drive Kaantor and his new master, Decay, back through the Veil. And even then, the *wyr* was stronger than Decay, at least in the Eld Green. All the spirits of the Eld Green came to help her, and soon Kaantor and Decay fell together into shadow. But Kaantor wasn't done yet. As he slid toward the Veil, Decay's burnin' hand clutchin' and witherin' his legs, the treacherous Man drove his sword into the Veil again, this time piercin' it from the inside, mixing the sword's poison with the last bit of bile his spirit could muster. And as he fell dead into the Darkenin' between the worlds, the Canopy Veil split completely, and the two worlds crashed together, destroyin' much of both and givin' Decay another chance at us.

"Never afore, and certain never since, was there such a terrible time as the Meldin'. It was a lot like two balls of soft mud smashed together—entire lands destroyed, their spirits lost in the shatterin'. Some parts of both worlds was only lightly touched, while others was broken and scattered like a seed pod in a storm. Mountains rose up from oceans, deserts took the place of ancient forests, rivers flowed into new cracks in the land that disappeared into nothin'ness, and everywhere there was death and devastation. The Greatmoon, ol' Pearl-in-Darkness, watched as his two brothers were shattered into shinin' dust, and he still bears the scars of the Meldin' on his pale round face and weeps for his lost family. Some entire lands was pushed into shadows, becomin' Darkenin' pockets where the spirits still go on, neither dead nor livin', always hungerin' for the warmth of the life they once had. Doors opened up into other worlds unknown to either the Folk or Men, bringin' monstrosities into the Melded world, and with 'em pain, sufferin', and unendin' turmoil. Them was bad days for everyone, but the Meldin' was worst for the Folk, as we was driven on and on into fragments of the world we once knew, brought down by diseases as much as by the Men who hungered for the *wyr*-rich 'Hold-lands we call home.

"So now, all these many years later, our world is different. This broken world en't just ours no more. Many of our 'Holds are strong, but them Humans is never satisfied, and they want more and more of what little we got left. They never suffered like we did, but still they want more, and they begrudge us them things that's always been ours anyway. But we keep fightin', hopin' one day that they'll listen to all their own high talk about goodness and justice and fairness and peace and not keep trying to take all of ours away. And maybe they will, one day."

Tobhi lowered his hands and whispered, "Thankee, m' friends— ye've given us a good gift this night." The bright lights faded away, leaving only dark marks on the leaves. He pulled the lore leaves from the air, wrapped them up, and placed the bundle back into his pouch. He and Tarsa finished eating, and the rest of the night passed quietly, the Greatmoon's scarred and mournful light blanketing their wounded world.

7

Determination

"ENTER, AND WELCOME TO YOU."

The sturdy oak door swung open slowly, as though hesitant to admit the visitor. Neranda looked up from her desk, laying her quill and wyrweave paper to one side and rubbing the exhaustion from her eyes. The room was illuminated by everlights, adding softness to the bright moonlight streaming in through the great windows that overlooked the Sheynadwiin falls. The Lawmaker generally disliked anything more than the gentlest lighting in her chambers at night, as this was the best aid for deep reflection and undistracted thought. But there was simply too much work to be done these days, and such time, once inviolate, was all too scarce now.

Her maidservant, Iseya, entered and bowed. "Forgive the interruption, my lady, but Desha'al Myyrd, Assembly Counsel to Captain Pradu Styke, has arrived."

Neranda smiled. "Of course, Iseya. Please show him in. And please bring us some wine. Ask Mandra to be at hand—you deserve a bit of rest. It has been a very long day for us all." Iseya returned the smile and dropped for an instant to one knee before leaving the room.

The Lawmaker stood. She was still dressed for visitors, although she would much rather have been retired for the night. She wore a violet gown that draped far past her slippered feet. It had been dyed specifically to match the hue of her striking eyes, all the more heightened by the stark white collar and ruffled sleeves of the dress. The only accessories that she permitted herself were a small silver Celestial medallion of the Greatmoon in crescent hanging from a chain around her neck and a slender silver diadem that held her thick copper locks from her face. Blue face powdered white; nails modestly painted and trimmed to a respectably fashionable length; only the subtlest silver embroidery along the hem of her dress. Neranda turned to the polished mirror mounted on the opposite wall and quickly scrutinized her appearance. Neither too ornate nor too simple— eminently suitable for tonight's business. Satisfied with the result, she returned to her desk. It was essential to be prepared, to find a balance of grace and strength, as this would not be a pleasant visit.

The door opened again to admit Myyrd, his thin face haughty but pleasant enough. In spite of herself, Neranda felt her face grow warm with stirrings of anger. Yet it took only a well-trained heart-beat for her to shift the emotion into the necessary energy to accomplish her task. She held her hand out, palm up, and Myyrd lightly touched her fingers in greeting.

"Lawmaker Ak'shaar. I was most pleased to receive your invitation. It is, I trust, in response to my own brief query, which I promised to expand upon in this meeting?"

Of course. No delay—the matter at hand immediately. There were few things Neranda missed about the old social etiquette, but one of them was the slow, considerate entrance into diplomatic discussions. In the old days, such a meeting would never have begun until each member of the gathering had engaged in conversation with the others. The process would sometimes take days, even weeks, but it was time well spent, as the representatives of all perspectives would come to know and respect one another's lives, strengths, and weaknesses. Any conflicts were minimized by the intimacy of familiarity; the alliances and agreements that emerged were strengthened by everyone's mutual regard for one another. Such basic courtesies were a lost art these days, among Kyn as much as anyone.

The councilor was taller than the Lawmaker, but his slight stoop made him seem her shadow. His sensory stalks were drawn severely back and tied, along with his thin hair, into a simple topknot. He wore the standard brown cloak and golden vest of Assembly councilor, but they were threadbare and worn, conspicuous details in spite of the dim lighting in the room. Ambition clung to the shabby he-Kyn like a rancid second skin.

She nodded and motioned him to a seat opposite her desk. "Why else would I invite you here at this late hour? Please sit down." Iseya entered and handed the Lawmaker a small tray bearing two unadorned silver goblets and a cut-glass decanter of jeng wine—a rare delicacy from the Human lands of Pei-Tai-Pesh, drawn from her family's private stock. The housemaid slid out of the room, drawing the door closed behind. Myyrd flashed Neranda what he surely thought was a charming smile, and she coolly returned the gesture. She handed him a goblet, filled one for herself, and returned to her seat at the desk. "How may I help you, Councilor Myyrd? Your letter was most . . . intriguing."

He sipped his wine slowly, savoring it, watching her with heavy-lidded brown eyes. When an awkward silence settled over the room, Myyrd drained the goblet and said, "I come on behalf of your old friend, Captain Styke, to remind you of an offer he made, a number of months past, that he believes would be of great service to you."

"And what would that be? Do remind me."

"The Captain is, at this very moment, heavily engaged with protecting the trading routes on the western border, but he has, to date, received very little Assembly support or compensation for his activities. It is in regard to this matter that he urgently requests your immediate attention."

Neranda lowered her goblet. "I see. What, Councilor, does Captain Styke believe to be a reasonable demonstration of support?"

He smirked. "One of your fellow Lawmakers, Braek the Younger, has introduced a Writ of Commerce into the Assembly Rolls that would, among other things, provide additional financial resources and a small stretch of land—almost insignificant—on the northern side of the road, to ensure the safe travel and responsible transport of trade goods to Eromar. We feel certain that the passage of this Writ would eliminate the unfortunate delays of the trading trains and would, in fact, provide the western center for safe commerce that Sheynadwiin so clearly requires, especially in these unsettled times. Such passage would not only increase the ability of Captain Styke to expand trade opportunities to the west, but it would also expand the influence of those families, like your own, that have strong familiarity with such commerce. It's entirely a winning proposition, for the Nation as well as for those families who most quickly take advantage of its possibilities." His smile stretched wider.

Neranda nodded as she pulled a detailed *wyr*bark map from her desk drawer. It showed the lands in question, and the Lawmaker scrutinized it closely. "A declaration like this would violate our most ancient laws on the distribution and possession of land, would it not? It would seem to give the good Captain a rather strategic stretch of land into his private keeping, land that is not under the full authority of the Kyn Nation. How might the Tetawi and Ferals of that area respond to such a law, given the fact that those particular lands are shared hunting and gathering grounds for various Folk, not reserved for Kyn alone?"

Myyrd waved his hand dismissively. "It has been Kyn blood that has kept the road open; they can hardly begrudge their protectors this tiny bit of land."

"Protec*tor*, I think you mean," Neranda said, her voice even. "And what do you make of the fact that, by law, no Kyn can be the sole master of any territory in all the Everland? These lands are held in common, not owned by one alone. This custom has kept our domain from being fragmented by petty rivalries and alienated by personal desires for enrichment."

The he-Kyn leaned forward and smiled again. "Yes, but as you've so often pointed out, the world as we know it is changing, and our laws and customs can and should change with it. The only way we'll ever be able to compete with Men is by understanding our lands as power. And power in the world of Men comes from ownership. This could be the beginning of a great new era for our people."

"With Captain Styke leading the way, it would seem. Do you think, Councilor, that my support of this Writ will significantly assist its passage?" She stood again and refilled their goblets, then returned to her seat. "I am, as you well realize, of a minority in the Assembly."

"Yes, but even your opposition has nothing but the greatest respect for you, Lawmaker. You are well regarded as a voice for reason and for . . . honesty. These are qualities that could well decide the fate of the Writ." He leaned forward eagerly.

Neranda stood by the window, looking at the Greatmoon beyond. "Yes, I suppose your assessment is correct in that regard. I have long prided myself on serving the truth and abiding by the laws of our Nation, no matter the consequences to myself. Sometimes we must suffer much to keep the truth and our honor unblemished. Is that not correct, Councilor?" She turned her strange gaze toward him, and the air went thick. Myyrd blinked twice and gurgled as his windpipe suddenly tightened. Neranda's eyes were as bright and cold as the moon.

The Lawmaker stood and walked over to the Councilor, who leaned back in the chair, wheezing in terror and pain. He was frozen, the air slowly, teasingly drawn from his burning lungs, as panic began to consume him. Neranda reached down and plucked the goblet from his nerveless fingers before its contents dropped to the floor and stained the carpet.

She leaned down. "You will not die, Councilor—not this day, and not here. But you will travel to Captain Styke, and you will share a message with him: Neranda Ak'shaar cannot be bought. I will not bring dishonor to my name or to that of the Kyn Nation. You may also tell him that, as a result of this treachery, I will personally see to it that the Writ is crushed in the Assembly, and that your maggot-bound hides are delivered to the most undesirable, beast-infested outpost in the Blackfly Fen, where you will spend the remainder of your serviceable days subsisting on bogworms and keeping a detailed log of the rates and consistency of the filth that the Eromar Humans are so fond of dumping in that swamp."

Myyrd slid to the floor, sobbing as the air returned to his spasming lungs. He lay face-down on the carpet, a stream of spittle pooling beneath his mouth. Neranda stood tall above him. "One more thing, Councilor, before my servants escort you from my home: your days as traitor and bribe-seeker are over. Prepare for a significant change of occupation—and pray that you find bogworm to your liking." A tinkling bell rang in the distance, and two well-muscled young he-Kyn, both dressed in high-collared white shirts and black vests, entered the room to drag the half-conscious councilor away.

Mandra, the younger maidservant, entered after, her eyes filled with concern. "My lady, are you . . ."

"No, do not concern yourself." Neranda gently patted Mandra's arm. "All is well. It is one of the inevitable but intolerable aspects of my position. There are many who believe themselves entitled to any number of privileges, generally because they are experienced thieves and bullies who have never been denied anything in their lives. Not one of them has a jot of self-respect or self-restraint, and each believes himself to be untouchable by the law." She returned to her desk. Mandra gathered the goblets onto the tray and left the room.

"But they are always wrong," the Shield continued to herself. "There are laws of the earth and laws of the heavens, and there are many ways to be a lawmaker." She smoothed the wrinkles from her dress and sat down, taking up her pen again as though the interruption had never occurred.

The old garden should never have been this warm. The trailing end of the winter cold still reigned at night. Spring was a reluctant visitor to Eromar City, hampered by the city's high steppe elevation and its proximity to the ice-shrouded lands of the Lawless to the north. The garden, untended for a generation or more, lay at the farthest western edge of Gorthac Hall's rambling grounds. Skeletal trees jutted like pale spears into the air, while all around their trunks, wrapped in a shroud of sooty snow, crouched the withered remnants of the garden's brief bounty. It stood open to the frigid night, the stars and slivered moon bright in what should have been chill air, but the binding and reaving of Fey-spirits shifted the surrounding reality, invoking the conditions of the spirits' Elsewhere home. The Dreydmaster had just as often suffered through crackling electric storms and shrieking blizzards as blistering heat waves. Yet, as with all things, he knew that this necessary stage, while disconcerting, would last only a moment. It would pass.

The reaving of spirits from their Otherworldly existence was a treacherous and often deadly business, and it was thus a profession suited to those without regard for their own lives or those with a will and mind honed sharp with merciless determination. Lojar Vald was of the latter group. His many years as a hard-eyed jurist had taught him about the depths of depravity to which both Humans and Unhumans could descend; he had learned too well that the only worthy aim of any dignified people was the reasoned application of consistent and unyielding law. It was the law of Men that had moved him up through the ranks of the judiciary and into the political arena, where survival required him to understand his enemies better even than they understood themselves.

And it was the greater law of the hidden Dreyd—those Human alchaemists who had long ago overthrown the Old Immortals of Men during the cataclysmic Great Ascension—that had shown him possibilities beyond the mortal realm. The only way that Vald's name and deeds would live beyond his death would be to reshape the world of Men, to guide it toward the principles of the Dreyd and their followers, by linking the profane and the sacred, the temporal and the eternal. He became a Dreydmaster, and the mandates of the Dreyd became the guiding laws of Eromar. Lojar Vald closed the shackles on the chaos of Men, and law ruled supreme.

The dangers of his new life didn't end with the reaving of Fey-spirits. Any entity drawn from afar and entrapped by a Binder—the second rank of the Dreydcaste and those who brought the spirits fully into the Reaver's control—would always hold unmitigated hatred for the Reaver, who became its master in slavery. Reaving required one's thoughts to be as unyielding as forge-hardened iron. A Fey-spirit might be fickle or furious, but it would always be dangerous, and it was only through brutal control that it surrendered to the Reaver's will, often being torn apart in the struggle and never lasting long even if it acquiesced. If the Binder's skill faltered, or if the alchaemical bindings themselves ever weakened, every spirit who was released would seek out not only the Binder but also the Reaver, even if decades had passed since the summoning-spell. And their vengeance was always gruesome, and inescapable.

Yet Reavers were needed by the Binders, for each served a purpose. So, too, did Reavers and Binders need the Seekers, who roamed the Reach of Men in patient search for those Human witches and Unhuman Fey-Folk who possessed spirit-given powers that could be put to use by the Binders and their Reaving superiors. That none of these sorcerous creatures had any interest in sharing their powers was of little concern to the Seekers; there were many ways to ensure cooperation, most rather painful.

It was all in a delicate balance: the Seekers found witches with particular talents, the Binders drew the captives' spirits and wrapped enchantments and magical chains around them, and Reavers bent the spirits to their will. All ranks of the Dreydcaste served and supported one another, each performing the tasks that the others could not.

The Binders of Eromar City were devoted to the Dreydmaster and his law; even now they were putting their thoughts firmly toward Vald's most ambitious goal, one that even the other Dreydmasters scattered across the Reach could barely imagine. Other people saw only that Vald had devoted years to returning Eromar to its former national glory, which was now eclipsed by the upstart petty politicians who pranced through the Reach's bloated, gilt-edged capital, Chalimor. Eromar had become one of the most powerful of the allied nations of the Reach, a position it claimed as much through aggressive expansion as through cunning political maneuvering. While not yet in any position to challenge the authority of Chalimor directly, Eromar would not be a subject state for much longer—through an iron fist and an unyielding will, Vald was fashioning a new order of things.

Yet that was only the surface of his plans. Mortal law was weak; it crumbled with time and the inevitable frailty of misdirected sympathies that undermined the convictions of Men. Vald's goal now was far greater, and it would be rooted in eternity. The will of the Dreyd, and thus that of Lojar Vald, would endure forever. This night's ceremony was yet one more step down the road to perpetual glory.

The sweltering heat had slowly drained away. The Crafting was complete. The trio of Binders beside the Dreydmaster moved backward, their eyes wide and bodies shaking in sudden terror, as they beheld what they had helped to create. Each held a massive, skin-bound book in one hand, which was shackled to a chain that led from bony wrist to book's spine. These were the snaring-tomes, the Binders' source of power—and their curse, for their own souls were wrapped within the mystical Craftings placed on the fearsome books. They spent their lives in service to the Reavers, unable to escape, for the snaring-tomes hungered for Fey-spirits or the souls of Men, and the Binders had no choice but to let their tomes feed. If they denied the snaring-tomes for too long, the books would begin to consume them, and such deaths were horrific beyond imagining. Theirs was a brutal existence, but such sacrifice gave worthwhile glory to the Dreyd.

Vald's dark brows lifted slightly as he looked upon the result of the evening's ceremonies, while the other Men in the garden swallowed in discomfort. In form as well as manner, the Dreydmaster was an imposing figure. He stood over six feet tall and rigidly straight, as though his spine was formed of forged steel. His grey hair rose away from his forehead in a sharp widow's peak, and bristling muttonchops flanked his gaunt face; thick brows met over dark, narrow eyes that absorbed the light but never reflected it. He wore the dark coat and maroon waistcoat of his office as jurist, with a stark white neck cloth knotted and pulled tight against his pale throat. The wide cuffs of his coat exposed just the slightest hint of white linen shirt sleeves, and his buckled black boots were polished bright from toe to knee. He was a Man on whom happiness looked unhealthy, even wrong. And yet, as he surveyed his Crafting, a thin smile crept across his tight lips.

Where once had stood a dead, weed-choked fountain, there was now a shimmering crack in the air, a pulsing wound that led to other, darker worlds. The rift stretched at first nearly seven feet high, sometimes expanding to a greater height, sometimes shifting and shrinking to three feet or less, but the longer Vald watched, the more constant the opening became. An iridescent glow oozed out of the gap, throbbing with an erratic beat that strengthened and became a regular throb as the portal's edges became stable.

It wasn't the first gate he'd opened in this garden; there had been another, one he'd used not long before to summon the raven-winged hunters he sent to the Everland. The creatures were spreading farther across the land every day—they were his eyes, ears, and claws far beyond the reach of his official authority. He now knew the Everland and its defenses better than did most of its own inhabitants. Soon, very soon, he would put that knowledge to use. Tonight's Crafting was one more move toward that purpose.

Dreydmaster Vald stood motionless, his sharp gaze taking in every edge of the portal, each snowbound weed beneath it, even the bright stars in the sky above, until he was certain that everything was as it should be. He stepped to a leafless sapling that quivered beside the portal and tied a small silver bell to one of its stouter branches with a yellow ribbon. After flicking the bell and listening to its shrill chime echo through the garden, he turned to the six militiamen who stood at the doorway leading into the Hall.

<<Captain,>> the Dreydmaster said, his deep voice harsh in the crisp air, <<you know your duty. Send for me at once when the messenger arrives; you should have adequate time to find me. There will be no unpleasant surprises if you precisely follow my commands.>>

Vald turned to one of the Binders, a pale-faced youth who seemed more unnerved by the Crafting than did his more experienced companions. He'd stumbled over a few of the words during the ritual, and, although the others compensated for his weakness, the risks were anything but minimal. Any hesitation, any slip, even now, could render the gate dangerously unstable. It was entirely unacceptable. The boy would have to be reminded of his responsibilities to the Dreydcaste—and to his Dreydmaster.

<<What is your name?>>

Fear radiated from him, but the youth licked his chapped lips and replied, <<Mmm . . . Merrimyn Hurlbuck, Authority.>>

Vald's eyes held no pity or warmth. <<Come with me, Merrimyn Hurlbuck. We shall discuss your incompetence this evening. Be warned: I am not in a generous mood.>> He walked away, and Merrimyn reluctantly followed behind.

From the darkness of a window that overlooked the garden, leaf-green eyes watched the Reaver and Binder disappear into the shadows of Gorthac Hall.

"How many survivors?"

Averyn wrapped a worn cloak around hir shoulders and hurried from the bedchamber to grab a heavy satchel from the woven-reed trunk by the door. The magpie swept through the house behind the healer, cawing harshly in response, and Averyn stopped short, hir eyes wide.

"So few?" The bird descended to a table and bobbed her head in affirmation. Averyn swallowed. Such a small number spoke of desperation, ferocity, or both; the injuries would be grievous, and likely beyond the zhe-Kyn's strength to heal; hir gifts belonged more to the mending of the spirit than the flesh. Although zhe could set broken bones, give balm to burns, and bind the common injuries of hearth and home, Averyn's true skills were with aching hearts and wounded minds. There would be plenty of such work with the survivors in the days to come, but that was a later consideration; what mattered most now was simple survival, and there were others in Sheynadwiin who were far better equipped for this task.

Averyn swung the bag across hir back and opened the door. "Find the she-Tetawa named Jynni Thistledown of Bristlecone Hollow. She's staying in the east quarter of their settlement. Tell her what you've told me. I'll meet her at the gathering ground in front of the main gate." Zhe took a deep breath. "Tell her to hurry—Jitani was a guard on that train."

The magpie let out a deep croak and shook her glossy feathers, but Averyn was already running up the red cobbled road toward the city gate by the time the bird took flight.

The destruction was terrible indeed. Averyn tried to blot out the coppery smell of old blood and the cries of the wounded and grieving, but even with hir sensory stalks tightly wrapped by thick *wyr-weave* cloths, the sharp tang of trauma bled through, and in a very short time zhe was dizzy and nauseated. Of the twenty-eight Folk and Men who left Sheynadwiin on this trading journey two months previously, only five now survived: the merchant Sylas Gwydd, a young Human teamster, two he-Kyn hunters, and, to Averyn's great relief, the sell-sword Jitani. Thanks almost entirely to Jitani's fighting skill, Gwydd would survive with little more than bruises and nightmares; the teamster and one of the hunters, on the other hand, would likely die in the night. Jitani's wounds were scarring but minor, at least in the flesh; the deeper effects would be more difficult to assess.

Averyn didn't know Jitani very well, but zhe was quite familiar with the she-Kyn's brother Sinovian, an angry and influential Greenwalker warrior who despised the presence of Humans in Sheynadwiin—anywhere in the Everland, in fact. Had Jitani died in Gwydd's service, nothing could have quenched Sinovian's fury, and every allied Human would have been targeted, even those adopted into a Branch and accepted as kith. The bonds of kinship were vulnerable these days, and not only through the actions of the Shields and their Man-gifted ways.

But Jitani had survived, so that confrontation wouldn't happen—not yet, anyway. The allied Humans still had a place among the Folk, albeit a tenuous one. Averyn looked at Gwydd, whose leg was being bathed and wrapped by one of the daughters of the Tetawa healer Jynni, while the silver-haired knitbone herself cared for the more grievously wounded. It didn't take an empathic Wielding to reveal what was in Gwydd's heart. The Man's gaze was hollow. His financial loss was great, but he'd lost something far more precious than trade goods in the attack: Sylas Gwydd had finally experienced for himself the carnage that the Folk dealt with every day, and all his Human rank and privilege hadn't protected him or his money. He'd been just a sword's thrust from death; never again would he have the illusion of safety, or impunity.

Good, thought Averyn in a sudden rush of bitterness. *Let him know what it's like to feel afraid in your own home, to be expendable to all the world. If he wants to live like one of us, let him know our fear.* They were uncharacteristic thoughts for the kindly Kyn, but these were unhappy days, and Averyn had already seen more pain than hir gentle spirit could absorb in one day.

Zhe turned away from the Man and moved toward Jitani, who sat beside a blanketed pallet, her sword in its belted scabbard lying nearby. The body beneath the bloodstained shroud was small and clearly mutilated—the head lolled to one side at a strange angle. This was one of the few bodies that had been recovered in the quick retreat; the others were still in the woods, unprotected and exposed to scavengers and the elements. There would be no burial rites. Until and unless they were recovered, they might be lost forever. Averyn's sensory stalks tensed, and bitter bile rose up in hir throat.

Jitani looked up as the zhe-Kyn approached. "*Hanahé*," Averyn whispered thickly, lifting hir chin in greeting.

The mercenary returned the gesture, but a long-simmering anger clouded the welcome in her eyes. "You'd better sit down before you fall down, healer."

"Yes," Averyn said, kneeling beside Jitani on the grass. "I knew it would be bad, but not like this." Zhe took a few deep breaths and closed hir eyes, descending into a focused awareness of the *wyr* until an unsteady calm drifted over hir thoughts. Zhe opened hir eyes, gave Jitani a weak smile, and pulled a bundle of thin linen strips from hir satchel, along with a lidded clay pot. "How deep are your wounds?"

"Not bad. I've had worse."

Averyn cast a furtive glance at the warrior's head. Jitani's hair was shaved along the sides in the old warrior's style, leaving a long green braid that stretched from brow to waist. This was unremarkable. What drew Averyn's attention were Jitani's temples, where the withered remnants of two sensory stalks jutted outward like rotting stumps in a fallow field. The other two stalks were well wrapped, but the damaged ones remained stark and exposed in the late-day sunlight.

Yes, indeed, Jitani had suffered worse injuries than these new cuts on her face and arms. The loss of a stalk through accident was a rare but devastating event that, more often than not, drove its bearer mad with both pain and the sudden deprivation of the sensory world's full intimacy. Averyn had heard it described as a heavy muffling of the senses, where the most precious tenderness of touch and connection was forever stripped away.

An accidental loss was one thing. But Jitani's injury had been far from the natural way of things. A Man with a steel sword had taken the two brow stalks years before. It was the sort of brutality that was becoming almost commonplace as Men grew bolder and celebrated their attacks on Kyn with the desire for a gruesome memento, or for evidence to ensure a lucrative bounty. Jitani hadn't been the first to lose her sensory stalks to such an assault, but she was the only one Averyn knew who'd survived it and remained sane.

Well, largely so, anyway. There was a coldness in the mercenary that signaled a deep wounding far beyond the skill of any healing *wyr* that Averyn could draw upon.

Suddenly aware that zhe was staring rudely at Jitani's old injury, the zhe-Kyn opened the jar and dipped the linen strips inside, coating them with a paste that smelled of mountain mint and goldenseal. "This will hasten the healing, though you'll likely still be scarred. The bandages will harden soon in the fresh air; in a few days they'll come loose, and you can go on as usual."

"*Tsodoka.*" Jitani's golden eyes turned to the remnants of the single wagon she'd managed to salvage after the attack, where weeping relatives of the slain and injured had gathered. Some of the Kyn were in Celestial mourning robes, and there was as much anger as grief in their faces.

Averyn followed her gaze. "It's going to get worse for us again."

Jitani nodded. "Just one more arrow for the Shields to feather us with. Each death adds to their strength. They'll play with these bodies like buzzards, and with less grace."

"But what about the traders? Surely they'll stand with us?"

The warrior gave a bitter bark of a laugh. "Not likely, now that they're targets. No, healer, Gwydd and his family have little to gain from supporting us, and much to lose. Their gain won't come through loyalty to the Folk." Her face darkened. "They're established in the Everland now. They know the trade-ways and hunting paths. They know how the planting and harvesting seasons differ here from those of the Reach; they know what will grow in our soils and what will wither. These Men and their families have valuable knowledge about the Everland. But they can't use it as long as there's chaos. They're going to push for peace at all costs—it's in their best interests to do so."

Averyn felt hir skin tingle with dread as zhe finished wrapping the last of the bandages around Jitani's sword arm. "How can you be so sure?"

The mercenary stood and pointed her chin toward Gwydd, who stared with empty eyes at the ravaged wagon. "Look at him, healer." Her tone was coldly efficient. "Everything about him says it. He's a broken Man now, and he's terrified." She grabbed her scabbard-belt and buckled it around her waist, where it hung snug and low on her hips. "I've spent enough time around Men to know one fundamental truth about them: when Men are scared, that's when they're most dangerous."

Nodding once more to the zhe-Kyn, Jitani walked stiffly away, leaving Averyn to sit alone beside the body of the he-Tetawa scout. It was a long time before the healer returned home to share the day's events with hir mate, as was each day's custom. Zhe generally tried to bring good news to hir beloved, to lessen his burdens with the mundane pleasures and simple joys of the people who depended upon his strength and wisdom, but Averyn couldn't keep these unpleasant tidings from Garyn—they were already spreading like pestilence through the city. The Governor would need to be prepared when the grief-maddened families came to his door.

Of all his remarkable qualities, it was Garyn's strength that Averyn loved most of all, but each day's news brought new weight to the Governor's already bent shoulders, and even the strongest tree couldn't stand forever under blistering winds. Garyn, Averyn, and their Greenwalker allies put much hope for the future in the Sevenfold Council and the Wielders, who could remind the Folk of their own strength again.

But the Shields were finding more support with every new outrage, and far fewer of the Wielders had responded to Garyn's appeal than they'd expected or hoped. Averyn sighed as hir lodge came into view. The always-fragile state of Kyn unity was unraveling, day by day and death by death.

And the Celestials were in the ascendant at last.

Cycle Two
The Eternity Tree

This is a story of the First Days, and the beginning of the Kyn.
This is a teaching.

In a birthing storm that made the Three Worlds tremble, the Seven Branches emerged from the loins of their deep-green mother, Zhaia, the True Tree: Oak, Pine, Willow, Thorn, Cedar, Apple, and Ash. Born of leafy-haired Zhaia and her green-skinned lover, Drohodu, Grandfather of the Mosses, the first Kyn danced to life in their new world, and they gave joy to their Mother and Father and to their world. Their roots drank deeply from the endless Eld Green, and they flowered in the sunshine and bounty of the unending heavens. The Kyn grew strong and flourished, and each family Branch brought different gifts to all the People.

The Kyn of Oak Branch were the chieftains of the deep forests, the voices of leadership and reason, orators and philosophers of old. Those of Pine Branch called the high mountains home. They were teachers, wisdom-bearers, the mystics of the People, and in their dreams sought the future and the knowledge of the past. Willow Branch was dedicated to the way of the wanderers, and Willow Kyn traveled the rivers and great waters, becoming great diplomats and traders, friends of other Folk in lands far away. Within rocky hills and brush-hidden caves lived the Thorn Kyn, and they were honored for their war-teachings and courage. They were the weapon-makers, the strength-finders, the warriors who rose against all enemies and led the People to victory. Cedar Branch was the line of the artists, singers, storytellers, and history-keepers of the Kyn. They wove the teachings into their songs and baskets, and it was in their paints and clay statues that the Old Ways were made manifest in physical form. Among the Apple Kyn were the earth-bearers, the planters and ground-gatherers, those who brought great bounty forth from the dark soil. They understood and honored the ways of the plant-people, who in return gave sustenance to all the Folk. It was left to the Ash Kyn to bring comfort to the People when death and pain brought down the green tree. They were the healers, the spirit-tenders and guides to the ghost-lands, where the People would endure in another form and return again, as the lightning-struck tree falls to earth and becomes new seedlings with the care of fresh rain and warm sunshine.

When all was in balance, the Branches grew strong and wise, and the People flourished. But there came a time when some of the restless ones—those who watched the stars and turned from the green world—lingered too long in the heavens and forgot about their deep roots. Their hold on the old earth began to wither and die, and they drifted, seeing nothing but the sky, even as they hungered, their mouths filling with cinders. They forgot the ancient language that all Creation shared; they forgot that the trees have long-reaching voices, that the clouds sing to heron and goshawk alike, that the river whispers to the swimming otter, the bullfrog, and the little water beetle. The balance unrav-eled, the soil weakened and crumbled away, and even those who held to the soil found themselves falling, washed away by the rain, scattered sunward by the blistering wind. Some of the People dug deeply in the earth and turned away from the sky, thinking to return to the balance, but they forgot the sunshine. Their leaves became dust, and their roots starved.

Those treading firmly on the Celestial Path called themselves Shields, for they saw themselves as guardians of a new way of being in the world, and they scorned the flesh and its joys and pains. Those holding fast to the Way of Deep Green were the Greenwalking Wielders, and they drew on the lifeblood language of the Eld Green, the wyr, *and ignored the gathering storm that, even then, threatened to uproot them without mercy.*

So it came to be that the Shields fell upon the Wielders, seeking to purge the People of the trees in their blood, the moss in their skin, the leaves in their hair. And though some Wielders survived, many died, their blood running like floodwaters through the Lower World. And the People suffered.

This is a teaching.

It is a reminder, and a remembrance.

8

Wrath

EVEN THOUGH THE BIRDS AND OTHER Beast-Folk of the forest had gone eerily silent, the attack came as a surprise, as the travelers had become careless in the afternoon's gentle warmth. The first blast shattered a branch above Tarsa's head. Splintered wood and sap exploded in the air, and she dove headfirst into the underbrush, dragging Unahi behind her. Tobhi frantically rushed Smudge to the road's edge and hurled himself on the deer's neck, pulling the squalling animal to the ground. They were all hidden by thick brambles and bushes, but the cover was neither effective nor comforting.

Tarsa tried to gauge where the attackers were hiding, but something blocked her senses. She shook her head dizzily. Her connection to the *wyr* was confused again, and now so were her thoughts. The small inklings of understanding that she'd developed from her aunt's teachings over the past few days scattered aimlessly. Her thoughts wrapped back into themselves in confusion.

"They have a *wyr*-ward," Unahi whispered to her niece. While iron-wards protected the Folk from the toxic taint of that cold metal, the *wyr*-wards of Men blocked the Folk from their most fundamental connection to the world. Crafted by Human witchery from the ensorcelled blood and pain of captive Folk, these implements were rare abominations suitable only for murder and torment. Both the elder and the younger she-Kyn found their Wielding disoriented by the *wyr*-stifling instrument, though the effect was more wearing on Tarsa, whose skills and defenses were less developed.

They were now in the High Timber, a region of mostly brown grass and dusty sage among gnarled pines, spruces, and cedars, with only smallish thickets of aspens and creek-bed willows to break the grey-green blanket surrounding them. They'd made good time in the last few days, far better than expected. Their route took them along one of the better dirt paths northward, and they occasionally encountered other travelers along the way, even stopping once or twice to share meals at homesteads near the path. They were always made welcome, and Tarsa had her first full taste of Tetawi hospitality, which was as warm and respectfully curious as Tobhi had promised it would be.

Only two weeks or so remained until they would reach Sheynadwiin, the valley home of the Kyn Nation. Earlier that morning, they'd crossed over a high, long slope, and, aside from this tree-strewn knob, the next few days on the road would take them on an even draw between gentle brown hillocks. Yet here the trees weren't as thick as they'd been during their first day in the Timber, and the travelers were far more vulnerable as a result. Their hiding place was a temporary respite at best; it wouldn't be defensible for long.

"Men, ten or more of 'em," Tobhi announced, after a quick scan of the area. The invaders were clearly unconcerned about being seen. "Why're they so far in the 'Hold?"

None of them liked the possibilities. Human traders weren't uncommon in the Everland, but they were generally integrated into specific Folk communities, and they rarely had the freedom to wander without an escort; they were safe from harm only if interwoven into the social web of kinship responsibilities and rights as defined by a particular Kyn Branch, Tetawi or Feral Clan, or Gvaerg House. The Men facing the Folk were different. Beyonder raiders on the periphery of the 'Hold were increasingly common these days, but neither Tobhi nor the she-Kyn had ever heard of Men bold enough to find their way so deeply into the Everland's interior. Bold indeed, and foolish.

But here they were, and as objectionable as their presence was, they held the advantage.

Another explosion shook the air. Pine needles and small branches rained down on the she-Kyn and Tetawa. In the distance, bird-people cried out in panic at the unfamiliar sound.

"They have muskets." Unahi had seen a few of the weapons before the encounter with Leith. The Kyn of Far-Meadows Town, near the upper fork of the Panther River to the west of her home in Thistlewood, had long maintained uneasy relations with Humans traveling upriver, a relationship that turned hostile when the Kyn discovered a large cache of strange instruments after driving a group of Human squatter families from the area. They'd found mostly swords and crossbows, all laced with cold iron, but there were some strange thundering smoke-sticks as well. The Wielder was summoned to help those who'd been wounded in the attack and saw firsthand the terrible damage caused by the weapons. "One of the he-Kyn I tended was struck by musket-fire," she whispered to Tarsa. "A hole in his belly the size of my fist; he didn't last the night." She puckered her lips. "I'd thought they were very rare."

"Not rare enough," Tarsa said, her voice thin and strained, and the air crackled with tension. Unahi looked at her in alarm. The *wyr*-ward was sapping the Redthorn's unsteady strength far more than it should have. Either the artifact was more powerful than most of its kind, which the old Wielder doubted, or Tarsa's hard-fought defenses against the rising bloodsong were weakening under the *wyr*-ward's influence. Either way, something unpleasant was building, and there was little Unahi could do as long as they remained trapped.

The Men weren't moving any closer, but they weren't retreating, either. Unahi's own quick glance confirmed Tobhi's estimate: there were at least ten invaders, males of varying heights and appearances but all wearing dirty knee-high boots, flared breeches, and thick linen shirts cinched around the waist with belts or twisted rope. A pile of canvas bags rested on the ground between them, and all the Men were armed—most had shovels and picks, but the silver-haired she-Kyn could see at least one firearm, held high and at the ready by a slack-jawed stripling.

"They're waiting for us to move," she hissed. Their bit of underbrush wasn't very substantial. With the Men on the upward slope, they wouldn't be able to get to a more defensible spot without exposing themselves to danger.

Tarsa groaned and slid face down into the dirt. Her resistance was dangerously low. Smudge jerked slightly as the air grew suddenly thicker, as though a heavy, unseen cloud had descended over the ridge. Though his own eyes were filled with growing concern, Tobhi kept pressure on the deer, smoothing his terrified friend's neck with gentle strokes. "They're well armed for squatters, don't ye think?" he whispered, his words muted in the strange air.

A couple of the Men shouted down the hill, and the others laughed gratingly. Unahi's face flushed with anger; she could understand some of their mocking speech, and their audacity annoyed her beyond her fear. Her temples and stalks burned. The chortling ended, and the world went unnaturally quiet again. She and Tobhi exchanged puzzled glances.

Tarsa's breathing went suddenly shallow—she'd been trying to draw on the *wyr*, and the exertion of pushing past the Men's addling iron instrument was almost beyond her abilities. She felt the world grow hazy, herself grow distant from the others. Without thinking, she reached out and grabbed her aunt's hand for support. Unahi's sensory stalks were rigid in response, both to the effect of the *wyr*-ward and to the Redthorn's burning touch, and in that moment a heated rush of *wyr* flowed from her, unhindered by will or flesh. Unahi collapsed, too surprised to cry out, in too much pain to scream. For an instant, she saw Tobhi straining to see past the undergrowth while keeping the poor shuddering deer from bolting, and the world went suddenly dark.

Then the earth erupted under the Men, and a hulking mass of tendrils, stones, leaves, and soil smashed into the screaming group. Shovels and picks were useless against this heaving aggregation of root, dirt, and mulch. Two Men disappeared into the earthy maw, their shrieks silenced by its grinding force. The musket-bearer and a few others fled, but some, knowing nothing else to do, lifted their weapons and swung desperately against the onrushing heap. Great arms of compacted soil burst out and struck the Men where they stood, pulling them screaming into the depths of the *wyr*-shaped monstrosity.

Unahi's vision cleared, and her breath returned with a gasp. For a moment, she couldn't understand what was happening. As she coughed and fought to orient herself to the raging turmoil, she dimly perceived a *wyr*-strengthened Tarsa bursting from their hiding place toward the writhing mass of earth. Smudge had bolted when the hill exploded, and now Tobhi, too, rushed from the undergrowth, though he followed after Tarsa, seemingly in pursuit of the young she-Kyn.

Unahi was alone on the hill. Dust and gunpowder smoke filled the air, and, even in their wrappings, her stalks were burning from the agonies of the wounded and dying Men.

The *wyr*-ward was gone, swallowed up by the great elemental force that still writhed on the hillock. Unahi's muscles trembled from Tarsa's unwitting *wyr*-drain, but the old Wielder forced herself to stand. Her staff was gone, still in Tarsa's hand, so it took Unahi a few false starts to find her footing and walk slowly back up to the road.

All was devastation. One of the great canvas bags lay split wide, its contents broken and spread across the area: brown and yellow Kyn skulls, dragged from their burial rest by fortune-seeking grave-robbers. Screams of pain roared in the old Kyn's ears, and the agony of the injured Men filled her stalks and mind. Her head pounded and her chest tightened, and a red-black curtain of pain dropped swiftly over her eyes. Unahi staggered and stumbled into the dirt as the roiling earth rose above her like a cresting wave ready to crash down.

She looked up, and her grey eyes flashed dangerously. "*ENOUGH!*" she thundered, and the heavens split apart. A driving blast of wind slammed against the surging earth and sent a tremor of confusion through its newly awakened consciousness.

She would have to be quick—the words and their order had to be chosen carefully for their desired effect, as though her intention had already come to pass. "*You have returned to your deep roots—you are sleeping again, as you were meant to do!*" the old Wielder shouted, her voice straining over the howling winds and bursts of thunder. One hand traced the patterns on her chanting-sash; the other was raised in a tight fist. Lightning crackled in blinding streaks all across the hill, and sudden rain fell hard and fast, turning the hard soil to thick, roiling mud.

The earthform shuddered in slow understanding as spirit-tongues of skyfire, wind, and water bore down hard against it. It tried to resist the Wielder's will, but her words created an irresistible reality, and the force of the other elemental voices were too strong to deny. A low, deep groan of surrender rumbled across the hill, and the *wyr*-summoned aberration collapsed in on itself.

The storm broke at that moment, and the soft glow of dusk returned to the road. The few surviving Men crouched quivering in lightning-formed holes along the muddy slope. The only things still standing on the hill were dozens of freshly torn and ravaged tree trunks, and a bent old she-Kyn spreading a thin dusting of cedar shavings and tobacco before each squelching step, her eyes hollow with exhaustion, and fear.

Tarsa didn't remember standing up or rushing after the Man with the musket. All she knew, when her mind cleared, was that she was still a Redthorn warrior, trained to challenge any threat to her people, no matter how chaotic the circumstances. She called out a high-pitched trill and rushed forward, Unahi's wyrwood staff suddenly in her hands as though it had been formed to belong there. The Man was badly injured, but desperation carried him quickly down the dirt trail. He didn't make it far enough to miss the howl that flew from the Redthorn's throat as she bore down on him. He turned to level his musket at her, but he'd underestimated her speed, and she spun like a whirlwind, the amber-topped staff smashing hard into his weapon, sending the barrel sideward. It roared in blinding smoke and fire, but Tarsa was too far into this strange, sudden battle-rage to be distracted by the noise. The Man recoiled as the staff swung down again. This time it caught the musket's stock and sent it flying down the path, bent almost double and now useless.

The Man screamed and turned to flee, but his injured leg twisted beneath him and he fell hard to the ground. Tarsa drove the end of the staff into the earth and howled, nearly mad from the sensory inundation. She still didn't know what the *wyr*-voices sang in the hot depths of her blood, and she didn't care—all she knew was that the voices were now free to live in the world, carried on the force of her rage. The staff twisted, its surface bubbling, as piercing thorns jutted out to shine in the orange light of the lowering suns.

She lifted the staff high above her head. "Defiler!" she hissed through clenched teeth. The grasses beneath the Man tangled themselves into scores of fibrous ropes and lashed across his limbs to pin him to the earth. He opened his mouth to scream, and a clump of vegetation crept across his lower face. Soon, only his terrified eyes remained free of the creeping plants that writhed beneath him, help-less to deny the she-Kyn's bidding.

Tarsa's body shook. In the brief moment between the shattering of the earth beneath the Men and her emergence from the roadside, she'd seen the freshly dug skulls roll free from one of the sacks, mat-ted grave-dirt still clinging to the bone. She'd barely suppressed the bloodsong after the pain and helplessness of Nine Oaks Town—this terrible sight sent her strength past the weak barriers of her waking consciousness.

"Grave-robber! Murderer!" The words rose free, tangled with grief and blinding rage. The spirits of the dead were now cursed to wander until returned to the green earth, but even if these bones were rebur-ied, it was likely that the disturbance had been too great to allow the spirits to make their way in peace to the ghostlands.

The enormity of the violation was too much. Tarsa brought the staff down on the Man's struggling body. He screamed, but it was the satisfying crack of bone and the meaty *splut* of pulverized muscle that burst through the raging haze in her mind. She looked down. The thorns glistened red and green; the remnants of the flailing grasses that bound the Man writhed in his blood. Pain pulsed through the green world, and she could feel the plant people and their roots ach-ing to get away from her. She stared at the dripping thorns, and the white-hot fire across her eyes faded as she looked at the gasping crea-ture and the crimson stain that spread across his upper body.

She returned the end of the staff to the earth. The thorns were the first to recede, then the grass tendrils and other vegetation unwound themselves from around the Man. He curled into a tight ball, in too much pain and far too frightened to try to escape.

The crackle of leaves caught Tarsa's attention, and she turned as a heavy fist smashed into the side of her face. She stumbled backward over the Man on the ground and rolled into the dirt. A hob-nailed boot caught her in the ribs. She cried out and spun helplessly into the coarse trunk of a bristlecone pine. Another foot lashed out, but this time she saw it coming. Though barely able to breathe, she jerked to the right, threw her arms outward, and grabbed the iron-shod boot, heedless of the cold burn that raced through her blistering hands.

It was another invader, a massive bear of a Man, whose hairy face was scarred and contorted with rage. Using his weight against him, she lunged to the right, throwing his balance off. As she twisted back to the left, he bellowed and plummeted hard to the ground. Such a fall would have stunned an ordinary Man, but this one seemed almost unhurt, though his face was torn and bloody.

Tarsa's chest ached from the blows. The rage had disappeared, and now pain pulsed all around her, unchecked by other emotions. Exhaustion began to seep in, and with it sudden fear. But she knew that to abandon herself to this churning sensory world would be her death. The second Man was regaining his feet, and the other might soon join him. In this weakened state, she was clearly vulnerable.

Tetawi, however, had no sensory stalks to bind them to the world's pain—Tobhi now stood beside the Redthorn warrior. He dropped Unahi's staff at her feet and spun his own hatchet menacingly into the air, its sharpened stone blade flashing in the failing light.

The first Man wouldn't be a problem now—he lay screaming on the ground as Smudge pawed the earth and lunged at him, velvet antler-buds as menacing as daggers, dirt flying in thick clouds. The performance was harmless, but it heightened the little deer's suddenly vicious demeanor.

The second Man howled and charged toward the swirling brown shape, but Tobhi was ready. The Tetawa twirled around, a diminutive and deadly dancer. He darted under the rushing Man, smashing the flat end of his hatchet into the Man's kneecap as he slid past. A splintering crunch split the air, and the Man shrieked and collapsed. Tobhi stood and turned, ready to face his opponent again, but the hulking shape lay shuddering on the ground.

Tobhi rushed over to Tarsa. She was weak now and leaned heavily on the staff, but her eyes were clear. "What about the others?" she asked wearily.

"They're mostly dead or wounded; these was the only ones to get away. That *wyr*-ward disappeared into the ground first thing, so I s'pose yer aunt was able to keep 'em out of the way." He took her wounded hand in his and frowned. "We'd best get ye looked at, or the iron sickness could set in." She nodded. They walked up to Smudge, who seemed to be thoroughly enjoying himself by repeatedly bumping the younger Man with his head and hooves.

"Enough of that," Tobhi muttered and pulled the deer away as thunder crashed upslope. They looked up to see a mass of black clouds and lightning suddenly rage on the hill. They heard a booming voice roll through the storm, and fear clutched at their hearts. "Unahi . . . ," Tarsa began, but a blast of debris-choked wind enveloped them, and they clung to one another, coughing and gasping for breath.

As swiftly as it had struck, the storm was over, and calm returned to the hillside. They wiped the dirt and rain from their faces and, ignoring the injured Men, hurried back up the slope toward the old she-Kyn, who stood stark on the hill against the day's last light.

"What happened?" Tarsa asked. "What attacked the Men?"

Tobhi glanced up at her in surprise. "Ye don't know?" he said, one eyebrow creased in disbelief.

"No . . ." She looked up to see Unahi picking through the wreckage on the slope, gathering up all the scattered Kyn bones and fragments that she could find. It was a delicate task, for many of the bones had been shattered beyond salvaging in the melee, and there were great pools of mud and dirty water everywhere.

The handful of surviving Men clustered together in a terrified mass at the base of the slope. Their weapons were missing, swallowed up by the now-still earth. They'd be set free—the Folk were in too big a hurry to keep the Men as prisoners for the next few weeks—but, without weapons for defense, the grave-robbers wouldn't likely last very long in the Everland, especially when word spread of their plundering. Scores of small trees had been uprooted or shattered in the frenzy, and the Redthorn could feel their death-pain trickle toward her as they drew nearer. All was silent, save for the groans of some of the injured Men and the soft call of a raven nearby.

She looked down at the Tetawa by her side, a cold awareness flowing over her. "I did this." Unahi looked wearily toward her niece and the surrounding destruction before returning to her search in the uprooted soil.

Tarsa's knees buckled. "I didn't know, Tobhi," she whispered. "I swear I didn't know."

Merrimyn lifted his sleep-addled head from the rag-strewn bench, eyes wide in alarm, but the darkness was complete, and he saw nothing but the now familiar flashing shadows that danced across his straining vision. The cell stank of death and excrement, and the terror of solitude returned like a crashing surge, swamping him, pulling him under until he crouched against the wall, his breath thin and labored.

He listened intently. There. He heard it again—a soft metallic scraping at the door. It wasn't the sound of a key, so it couldn't be the Dreydmaster or his Questioners. The Binder didn't know how much time had passed since he had been brought here, but he was long past hunger, so it didn't seem likely that food was on its way. He'd given up hope some time ago, when, in the darkness, his fumbling fingers made out the shape of a wet Human skull in a pile of rotting fabric.

After that, all was despair.

For a moment he thought the noise might be a rat, or something worse. Unseen creatures had slipped past his limbs as he struggled to sleep, and not all had resembled rodents. He'd long ago screamed himself hoarse, so his only defense was to retreat to the farthest corner and hide from whatever was creeping along by the door.

A light click echoed in the room, and the iron door swung open on screaming hinges. The Binder covered his head with his left arm, the noise and sudden light burning into his senses. It was a while before he heard a voice at his shoulder urging him to his feet. He opened his eyes, squinting tightly, and saw a dark silhouette against the lantern light that streamed from the hall.

<<Hurry, Man,>> the figure hissed, shaking him roughly. <<If you want to live, you must come with me!>>

Merrimyn wanted to ask a thousand questions, to learn what was happening, but the demands of survival took control and he lurched to his feet, stumbling out of the cell as the stranger pulled the iron door shut with a shudder. The pulse in the Binder's right wrist began to beat harder, and the snaring-tome on his right arm trembled with hunger. He stared at his rescuer with the shock of recognition.

<<You . . . you're Unhuman!>> he gasped, his voice little more than a croaking whisper.

The figure turned. It was one of the Snake-heads—"kiin" in their own strange tongue—the most dangerous of the Unhuman races, mockingly dressed in the manner of civilized Men. Somehow, the unnatural contrast wasn't entirely unpleasant; although the creature had two writhing tendrils draping from the sides of its head,

waist-long black hair woven into dozens of thin braids, dark tattoos on its yellow cheeks and chin, and split-lobed ears with trade-
silver rings, its velvet cassock and lacy sleeves, high-wrapped neck
scarf, long breeches, and high, buckled boots gave it a comfort-
ingly Human appearance. The Binder supposed the creature to be
a male of its race, but it was hard to tell. Those strange eyes—deep
green, without pupil or whites, and lit with the inner fire of a polished gem—filled him with new fear, for it was in those eyes that
Merrimyn saw the creature's Unhumanity. Even its rhythmic use of
the Mannish tongue wasn't enough to drive away the fear that now
pulsed through the young Binder's veins.

Merrimyn might have flung open his snaring-tome at that
moment, but Vald had ordered an iron band to be wrapped around
the book when the Binder was imprisoned, so he was denied even
this defense. Untrained in the ways of battle, weakened with fear
and exhaustion, and unable to protect himself with the only weapon
he knew, Merrimyn was helpless before the creature. He almost
preferred being locked away in the cell. Almost.

The Unhuman stared at him. <<Well, why are you waiting?>>

Merrimyn blinked. <<What? I don't . . .>>

<<You're free, fool. Now go, before Vald discovers what I've
done. It's both our lives if you're caught.>>

<<But where do I go?>> Merrimyn looked around. The tunnel
stretched into yawning darkness in both directions; the only light he
could see was the small, quivering lantern in the Unhuman's three-
fingered hand.

The creature sighed, turning its strange gaze on the Binder.
<<Follow me—for now. I'll help you to the stables; after that, you
go on alone.>>

Casting a nervous look down the hall, the Unhuman shuttered
the lantern until nothing but a thin stream of light guided their way,
and they hurried into the gloom. The Binder was weak, and he often
stumbled, but the Unhuman slipped a strong arm around the young
Man's waist, and it was enough to help Merrimyn get his footing.
Every little while they came to another tunnel, and Merrimyn's
strange guide looked around at the dirt, as though he'd lost something. After a few minutes, he moved forward again, sometimes
turning into the new tunnel, sometimes continuing down the old

one. Eventually they came to a rough stone stairway that stretched upward until it disappeared beyond the limit of the lantern's light.

<<Up there,>> the creature whispered. <<Those stairs lead to the back of the Hall. When you reach the top, go left, and you'll find your way to the stables.>> It began to move away, but Merrimyn caught its arm.

<<Wait a moment, please!>>

The Unhuman turned and looked at him again with those unnerving eyes. <<What is it?>>

The young Man swallowed in fear, but he had to know. <<Why did you do this?>>

An expression, something like sympathy, passed over the creature's face. <<My people don't believe in cages, Merrimyn, and I've seen far too many of both our kind disappear into the darkness beneath Gorthac Hall.>>

The lantern light suddenly vanished. Merrimyn felt a pressure on his arm and heard a crack. As the sliver of light returned, he looked down to see the iron lock on the snaring-tome fall to the ground. The book began to throb with sudden hunger, but Merrimyn held it in check—his will was still strong enough to deny it, for now. The Unhuman handed the lantern to the Binder and disappeared back into the darkened tunnels.

Merrimyn was nearly at the stables when he wondered how the Unhuman knew his name.

9

Owl and Dragonfly

"WHAT'S HAPPENING TO ME, UNAHI?"

They were gathered on the mossy bank of a small spring, a lengthy walk from the battle but still well within sight of the now treeless hilltop. It was deep night now. Tobhi sat at a respectful distance from the Wielders, brushing the dirt and grime from Smudge's smooth coat, his battle-tainted clothes freshly washed and drying on a flat rock beside the fire. Tarsa had been grimly unresponsive for a while; though she'd helped Tobhi and Unahi bury all the Kyn remains that they could find, even leading a prayer before their individual purifications to ease the spirits' pain and passing, she'd afterward fallen into a dark mood.

The Leafspeaker was worried about her. She had a good heart and a fiery spirit, two traits much honored by his people. Her *wyr*-rooted talents, however, were quickly becoming a crippling burden to her and a danger to everyone else, and Tobhi was afraid that she'd soon be overwhelmed by them. It was different with Tetawi *wyr*-workers—their strengths came from their connections to the Beast-people, not from the voices of the elements themselves. The thoughts of Beasts weren't all that different from those of Tetawi, so the understanding was easier; of all the Folk, Kyn suffered the most from their particular link to the *wyr*, because of the nearly alien minds of the spirits in wood, sky, and stream, and the deeper connection that they had to those entities through their mysterious sensory stalks.

He didn't much mind that Tarsa had used the *wyr* against the Men, but he could tell from Unahi's reaction that there was terrible danger in the Redthorn's actions. He thought about reading the lore-leaves, but decided against it. It wasn't his place to interfere. Not yet, anyway.

It was all very depressing.

Unahi sat away from the water. They'd washed the mud and blood from their skin and clothing, and had eaten a bland meal of trailbread, nuts, and dried fruit. The elder Wielder turned stiffly to her niece. The young she-Kyn beside her now was nothing like the *wyr*-maddened creature who'd drawn on Unahi's own life-spirit and created an abomination to wreak brutal vengeance on her enemies. Tarsa had come to the edge of a precipice, and Unahi wasn't sure whether the warrior would be able to step away before the fall. "Come here, seedling," she beckoned awkwardly, and Tarsa leaned into her aunt's arms, insensitive to the old she-Kyn's discomfort.

"I don't know what to do." The Redthorn's voice cracked. "What am I becoming? I used to know who I was, but now . . . nothing makes sense anymore." Her voice fell to a near whisper. "I've never been so afraid."

The old Wielder held her niece tightly, rocking her gently but saying nothing. There were no words of comfort that she could share this time: Unahi was frightened, too. Tarsa's Awakening had come late in life; she'd already survived more trauma than most Kyn who were similarly delayed in coming to such awareness. Latecomers to the *wyr*-ways were most often like falling stars, blazing briefly and then disappearing into darkness.

And Tarsa's power—Unahi had rarely seen such unbidden strength. It even rose up against the ensorcelled iron *wyr*-ward, which should have limited Tarsa's connection as it did her own. Unahi had trained other Wielders in her long life, but none possessed so much possibility—or so much potential for catastrophe—as the young she-Kyn warrior who was curled crying in her arms.

Unahi looked down at Tarsa. For a moment she saw Lan'delar in the near-sapling's face. The resemblance did nothing to ease the pain. But it did remind the Wielder of something.

"To be truthful, brown-hair, I don't know the full measure of what's happening to you. You're traveling a rocky path that's very different from the one I walked so long ago." Tarsa's sobs increased in intensity. "Hush, now. Just because our paths are different doesn't mean I can't help you understand your own. Do you remember your mother's last words for you? 'Tell her to tend to her roots.' What do you think she meant by that?"

Tarsa didn't look up, but her crying softened. "I don't know anymore."

"That's a bit too easy, isn't it?"

Tarsa's lips tightened. "My roots—the Old Ways, the Deep Green. But I'm already following those ways."

"Are you?" Unahi's pointed back down the trail, back to the battle site and beyond. "Doesn't look like it from here. You can draw on the *wyr*, that's certain, but what are you doing with it?"

The Redthorn pulled away. "I saved our lives, didn't I?"

"But at what cost?" Unahi grabbed her staff and held it under Tarsa's flushed face. The shard of amber was now lined with cracks, and the wood was gouged and pocked with the remnants of broken thorns. "A Wielder will often have to call upon the *wyr* to protect herself, but she never *forces* it to do anything. That's where you've crossed over, niece. The *wyr* is the spirit-language of kinship, a part of you, of all the Folk and our land, and that means we have to respect it and give it care, to honor its strengths and also its weaknesses. Words give shape to the world and our relationships, but they can poison as readily as they can heal. We must listen to what those voices tell us, not drown them out with our own wants."

Her voice hardened. "Through you, the language of the *wyr* has become twisted; you turn it against itself, against the green world that would gladly help you in its own way when your heart and mind are balanced. You're not there yet, not by any means. You've destroyed many tree-people, warped their spirits out of all recognition. You uprooted the little green ones, tangled them together into weapons, fed them with the poison of Man-blood. Forcing spirits to your will is Mannish witchery, Tarsa, *not* the way of a Wielder."

Tarsa stood up, but she didn't walk away. Her hands were clenched so tightly that the nails dug into her palms. Tobhi, seeing her anguish, turned back to Smudge. Unahi's expression shared the Tetawa's sorrow, yet it was mingled with anger as well.

"Until you stop fighting the bloodsong and give honor to the *wyr* that flows through you and through all the Eld Folk," said the old Wielder sharply, "you will always be a stranger to the Deep Green."

Tarsa looked at her aunt, turquoise eyes brimming with sudden tears, and fled into the darkness. Unahi sat for a while and stared at the bubbling spring. When she finally stood, her old joints creaking, she carried her bedroll to a thick blanket of pine needles at the flat base of an old wind-twisted pine and settled down for a troubled sleep. Tobhi waited until the Wielder's breathing became soft and even, set Smudge free to graze, then slipped into the shadows.

The grave-mounds were easy enough to find, for they radiated agony. Tarsa followed the dull throb, pulsing like a rotten tooth, into an old, hoary stand of stunted pines on the windswept side of a low ridge. The first mound was actually outside the trees, just barely distinguishable from the broken brown grass that carpeted the meadowlands of the High Timber. The soil was uprooted, gouged outward to leave a gaping blackness behind, and the heavy remnant tang of iron hung in the air. Chunks of rocks lay scattered all around, each oozing hurt from its wounded sides.

Tarsa stepped gingerly around the hole and looked in. Yellowed shards of bone lay scattered in the dirt, pieces too small to be of interest to the looters. She cupped her hands and refilled the hole as best she could but left her six digits deep in the soil. Closing her eyes, she pushed her thoughts into the dry brown ground, searching for the voices that lingered there, voices she felt but couldn't yet hear. There was no response at first; it seemed like nothing more than empty earth. But soon a furtive emotion reached out, and she recoiled in bitter understanding.

The land was afraid of her.

Shame, guilt, and anger twisted around her heart, but Unahi's words returned. She was a Redthorn warrior in name, but the society's guiding principles had slipped away since her Awakening. The *wyr*, once a gentle throb of life that constantly caressed her stalks, had become an overwhelming chorus of voices that nearly drove her mad, and she'd forgotten her duty to the Old Ways, to the Way of

Deep Green. She could play-act at Greenwalking all she wanted, but it wouldn't give her peace or help her understand what she'd become, and it wouldn't keep those around her safe.

I don't want any of this. How many times since the Stoneskin's death had she repeated those words to herself? Was she being punished? Unahi said it wasn't a curse, but if it was truly a gift, it was a terrible one. She wanted to be a Redthorn forever, to be a brave warrior and fight with spear, knife, and throwing axe until death-chants were sung in her memory. That was the life she'd planned to have. It was the life she *should* have had.

But that life was lost to her now. Now she had a very simple choice: she'd be a Wielder, or she'd die. She could show true Redthorn strength and take hold of her unwanted gift, or she could end up raving and broken. There were no other choices.

Tarsa pushed her thoughts away and opened herself to the *wyr* as it was given, not as she wanted it to be. She could almost hear the earth's spirits now, timid and uncertain but still present. Faintly, at first, they answered her soft query, sliding against her fingers and her thoughts. When satisfied and certain of her intent, the voices wrapped themselves around her flesh, their words weaving into her senses and her mind, drawing on her strength as she drew on their pain. They remained together for a long time, spirit on spirit and thoughts joined as one, until she felt the pain grow muted. It didn't disappear—it might never fully fade, as its echo was too firmly rooted in the earth around the violated mound—but the hurt no longer drowned out the voices.

Tarsa felt as though she'd stood up too quickly. Her muscles were weak, her head dizzy. The link had taken more concentration than she'd realized. Heaving a deep sigh, she pushed the hair away from her face to see Tobhi strolling through the meadow toward her. The thin glow of the Greatmoon danced on the Tetawa's shapeless brown hat, sometimes catching the reflective surface of the beaded band or his small black eyes that gleamed in the pale light.

"*Hanahé*," he said when he reached her, his face grim as he surveyed the ravaged grave. "What a hard-hearted mess."

The Redthorn nodded, her voice weak. "I haven't been to the other mounds yet; I'm not sure that I want to." She took his outstretched hand and stood up, brushing dirt and loose grasses from her leggings. "Why would they do something like this?"

"I couldn't begin to understand the ways of Men," the Tetawa shrugged. "They just don't make no sense at all. M' mema Nenyi traveled a lot afore she and m' pepa married; in them days she was part of a pretty well-known Tetawi singin' group that took her all over the Men's Reach. She went to Harudin Holt once, out on the far Western Waters. Pretty place, by her reckonin', but colder than she'd expected, and there was orphaned Human cubs ever'where— she couldn't turn 'round without seein' hungry younglin's reachin' out for a crumb or a smile.

"Anyways, she told me that she was troubled for a while by a well-to-do Man who wouldn't leave her alone over what he said was 'a most important business matter.' Said he was willin' to pay well for anythin' he could get a hold of that belonged to Folk, livin' or dead, 'specially bones and burial gifts. Mema was pure unnerved by him, and he just wouldn't let it go, but he weren't the only one like that— apparently there's a fairly flourishin' business in Human circles for all things that can make 'em believe that we're long dead and forgotten. I even heard once that some of their more learned types measure the bumps and dips of the skulls they dig up to tell how capable we are of thinkin'. Trust Men to come up with somethin' like that. Ye can figure we never rank too high 'gainst Humans by them standards. It's all just another way of provin' that Humans is better than everybody else. Ye'd think, with all the energy that they's always puttin' into these tests and laws and such things, they wouldn't be so worried all the time 'bout us havin' a little somethin' of our own, but I guess they just won't be satisfied 'til everythin' comes out the way they want it to." He pulled a thin shoot of grass from the ground and chewed thoughtfully on one end.

They walked together to the trees, where they found more than twenty freshly looted graves. Shards and splinters of bone littered the ground, as did the remnants of those burial items that the Men didn't think had immediate value, including the fragments of an unadorned brown clay bowl, some decomposing drinking gourds, and a few torn shreds of cloth. It was a gruesome and sobering sight. Even without sensory stalks, Tobhi could feel the wounded pall that ebbed through the soil, trees, and air in the grove.

"I'm too weak to do it again," Tarsa whispered. "I wish I could do more."

The Tetawa nodded turned back toward the moonlit meadow. "Ye did what ye could. No one's askin' ye to do no more." The young Wielder's brows narrowed. "Unahi is. She never said anything about what I did *right*—the only thing she talked about was what I did wrong." Her proud chin quivered. Turning away, her voice thick, she continued. "I know I'm a danger to you both . . . to everyone. I'm trying to learn how to control it. It's all I can do to hold it back when nothing is happening, but when things get dangerous I can't seem to stop myself. It just flows through me. I become part of the storm—or it becomes part of me. I don't know what to do." Her last words were soft, but they cut through the night. "No one can help me. I can't even help myself."

Tobhi looked at Tarsa again. She was so alone. Whatever family she'd once known was now far away. Without sisters or brothers to look after her, she'd drifted in isolation, and, though Unahi was kind in her way, the older Wielder was often distant and impatient. Tarsa needed a friend. More than that, she needed to feel like she *belonged* somewhere. She needed deep roots to keep from blowing away in this rising tempest.

The pain in the grove was heavier now with their intrusion, so they left the darkness of the trees and moved into the open air again, where they looked up to admire the world around them. To Tobhi, nowhere had the sky ever been so endlessly welcoming as it was this night, with stars and distant worlds shining like burning jewels on night's dark mantle. Pearl-in-Darkness seemed to understand the burdens of their day, for the silver softness of his light brought a calming peace to their spirits. The air was crisp—not enough to chill the body, but enough to charge the skin and clear the senses.

Morning was still some time away. They walked away from the graves and lay down on the ridge, where they watched the heavens and tried to forget the day's traumas. Occasionally, an owl or other night wanderer would call out, and they both shuddered, for among many of the Folk the owl was a traveler between the worlds, and its knowledge of the Spirit World gave it wisdom in all things, as well as the unmistakable taint of death and Decay.

Tobhi took off his hat and smoothed a small shell comb through his long hair. There were a few tangles, so he gently teased them out with the narrow edge. Tarsa lay on her back, arms crossed behind her head, and stared at the stars, her thoughts as distant as the sky.

The owl-song brought something to Tobhi's mind. "Have ye ever heard the story of Dragonfly and Owl?"

Tarsa rolled toward him and shook her head. "No. Is it a good one?"

He glowered in mock outrage. "'It's one of mine, en't it?!'"

"Well, in that case, tell it," she laughed. "Will you use your lore-leaves?" She was fascinated by the ways of the leaves, and she wanted to see them dance again in story.

He shook his head. "No, I only use 'em for special occasions, when I'm learnin' somethin' new, or when I'm addin' to the stories they tell. This one I can tell without 'em." Seeing the flash of disappointment on her face, he added, "But don't ye worry—I'll be sharin' lots more stories with ye, I promise."

"Anyways," he said, leaning back against the grass, "this story comes from the days of the Eld Green, when all the People could talk to one another. It weren't like today, ye know, where most folks don't know how to share words without losin' their understandin' of each other. In them days, Dragonfly—we call her Akjaadit, the Hummin'bird's granddaughter—was a small, almost insignificant nothin'. Well, she saw herself that way, anyways. She really weren't much to look at, to be truthful. In them days, she didn't have no pretty blue nor green nor gold on her wings. In fact, she didn't have no wings at all—she was just a pale little wormy thing in the water. There weren't no place for her in the way of things. After all, there was already worms around, and so she weren't much good for that job neither.

"So one day she decides that she's goin' to find ol' Strivix the Unseen, the first and most ancient Owl in the world, and ask that ol' night-seeker to just end her days and make a quick meal of her. At least that-a-way she could provide some nourishment and be of some use to somebody. Now Strivix, she weren't too set on doin' such things. She en't trusted by a lot of us, sometimes for good reasons, but at heart she really en't so bad; she's just been painted by the fact that she knows more than she oughta 'bout the end of things, 'specially life, and she en't too welcome when she comes to let us know 'bout it.

"Anyways, Strivix sees this poor ol' worm-thing weepin' all over her feathered claws, and she says, 'Now, listen here, Akjaadit, don't ye know nothin'? Ye en't a worm at all. Ye'r a Dragonfly.' Of course, there was no way Akjaadit could'a known that, as there'd never been no Dragonfly afore, but it sounded interestin'. So Akjaadit says to Strivix, 'I don't know how to be a Dragonfly,' and Strivix says, 'All ye got to do is tell yer people's story, and ye'll figure it out.'"

Tarsa's brows narrowed. "What story? How could she know a story about something that didn't exist before?"

Tobhi smiled and scratched his nose, nodding. "Well, to be perfectly truthful, there weren't no story to tell at all—at least as far as that ol' Owl was concerned. Strivix just said the first thing that came into her ol' feathered head. But she didn't let on none. She just kept sayin', 'Tell yer story.' So li'l ol' wormy Akjaadit crawls back home, and all the way there she's sayin' to herself, 'What's our story?' And as she's movin' and thinkin' 'bout her story, she starts to think back to her mema and the rest of the family, and the way they was always tellin' her how smart she was, how beautiful she was, how she was gonna be the prideful joy of the family, how with her speed and quick wits she and her kith was gonna find their way in the world and make it a sweeter place. So she's walkin'—well, since she's a worm, I s'pose she's crawlin' along—and she feels this itchin' on her back, so she turns and sees these pretty green and blue wings just a-shinin' in the sunlight. Then she looks down and sees that she's got herself six delicate li'l legs and a long, shimmerin' tail swishin' 'round behind her. It don't take her too long to figure out what them wings is for, and soon she's flyin' around her family and tellin' 'em all what happened. They laugh when they hear her, 'cause her story is theirs, too, and pretty soon they's all flyin' around, pretty as can be, dartin' here and there all over the world, tellin' everybody their story. And when they tell ol' Strivix, she just nods to herself with a wise look on her face, like she was expectin' that all along. And maybe she was."

"So," Tarsa said with a smile, "is this story supposed to be a teaching?"

The Tetawa shrugged his shoulders. "En't they all? Maybe it'll ease yer mind, and maybe it'll just rattle around in yer thoughts for a while 'til ye find what ye'r lookin' for. It could even just be an interestin' story 'bout how Dragonfly learnt to tell the story of her people to all the world." He stood up and stretched. "And maybe it was just a way to distract ye, to get you sleepy and relaxed so's I'd beat ye back to camp." Grinning, he sprinted down the hillside.

Tarsa laughed and jumped up to race across the meadow after him.

Vergis Thane nearly always worked alone; he preferred the solitude. He trusted himself and his own abilities, but he didn't have any control over the others he now traveled with. They were weak, easily turned from the seriousness of their mission toward frivolities that wasted time and tested his patience. He'd begrudgingly accepted this charge with the knowledge that, for a while at least, he'd be part of a larger group. He wouldn't make that mistake twice. Fortunately, this part of the journey was almost over. He'd be on his own again at dawn, and then he wouldn't have to deal with such weak-willed and low-minded fools again.

While his name was hated in certain circles, and fearfully admired in others, he wasn't a large or physically imposing man; those who didn't know him nearly always underestimated him, inevitably to their deep regret. He stood just a few inches under six feet in height, with thinning brown and grey hair, a ragged goatee flanked by a long, bristling mustache. One eye was covered with a dirty black patch, the lasting reminder of the one and only time he'd misjudged an opponent; the other eye, shocking blue, gleamed brightly under a bushy brow. He held no bitterness over the loss of the eye. He'd accepted it as a useful lesson that had kept him alive through many dangerous situations that otherwise would have been deadly.

Thane's clothing was as unimpressive as his physique: a wide-brimmed, water-stained leather hat and thick cloak, durable leather boots, drab breeches and tunic, and an open-sleeved traveler's coat. He looked like any one of a thousand Human wanderers, except for the frigid blue eye and the long knife and short sword that loosely hung in matching scabbards from his belt. They were modest and not particularly special weapons—no alchaemical formulas had been read over them to ensure a keen edge or unbreakable strength—but they served their purpose, and Thane cared for them well.

He lit his pipe—one of the few purely hedonistic pleasures he allowed himself—and settled back against the tree to watch the other

Men slip deeper into alcoholic imbecility. The Seeker had little use for drunkards at the best of times, but he saw no reason to intervene; the others already hated him, and even a Man well trained to survive a solitary life found it desirable to avoid agitating others when possible. The shattering of a wine jug on a rock near him, however, made it clear that he wouldn't be able to avoid it tonight.

Thane looked up. A pale-lipped young Man, thin and sickly, teetered unsteadily on the other side of the fire, his inebriated eyes filled with arrogance and anger. A couple of the Man's friends pulled at his arms, trying to drag him away, but he jerked out of their grasping hands and stumbled toward the Seeker. Thane drew easily on the stem of his pipe, his gaze never wavering.

The Man stopped just out of reach and leaned down, head bobbing awkwardly. <<Why don't you have a drink with ush?>> he slobbered.

Thane didn't move. <<I don't drink.>>

<<You heard that, didn't you?>> the young Man sneered, turning back to his friends. <<He shaid he don't drink. Know what that meansh? Meansh he don't drink with *ussssh*.>> The word hissed through his teeth like steam from a kettle. <<Ish that what you're shaying, you ugly bashtard?>>

<<I said, I don't drink. Go back to your companions.>>

<<What did you just shay t' me?>> He wobbled beside the fire and crouched down. The stink of cheap whiskey and brown teeth wafted through the pipe smoke toward the Seeker, but Thane showed no sign of his disgust.

<<I shaid, what did you shay? Are you ordering *me* around? Jusssht who do you think you are? You're jusssht shome dirty little witch-shniffer who don't show proper reshpect for hissh betterssh. Maybe I'll teach you a lesshon, how 'bout that?>> He lurched forward again, now with a burning stick from the fire in his hand, and shrugged off the restraining hands of his more sober friends.

<<You won't get another warning. You either walk back to your friends now, or they'll be burying you at dawn.>> Thane blew a smoke ring into the air.

<<We'll sshe who'sh gonna be buried,>> the Man bellowed, rushing at the Seeker. He never reached his target. Thane's leg shot out to catch the Man in the crotch and lift him forward in one fluid

movement. There was a bright crimson flash, and the Man slid to his knees, staring in drunken disbelief at the long, neat gash across his belly that slowly spread open. His intestines slipped steaming through the gap to the dirt. Thane, still smoking his pipe, drew a clean white cloth from an inner pocket of his jacket and wiped the long knife's blade as he tapped the Man's forehead with his boot. The body slumped limply into the dirt.

No one made a noise. When he'd finished cleaning his knife, Thane stood and walked away from the fire toward his hammock hanging between two large standing stones some distance from the others. He never looked back, but he could hear the whispers begin.

Good. They'd leave him alone now.

He swung himself into the hammock and pulled his hat down over his face. It had been a long day, and tomorrow looked about as tiresome. Still, it was a nice enough place to spend the night. The smell of burning cedar and pine was a comforting one, as it had been a common mixture in the fire pits of the hill country of his youth in southern Dûrûk. That particular smell brought back good memories. He was always amazed at the little joys that popped up unexpectedly on even the most routine mission.

Thane pulled the hat away from his eye and looked around again. The standing stones had been part of a large arch just half a day before. Each etched pillar was polished white and bound with rings of iron, which surprised the Seeker, given the natural aversion that most of the Snake-heads felt for the ore. The keystone of the arch, carved with symbols apparently meant to represent various heavenly bodies, had been one of the first things loaded into a cart. Those females who hadn't died in the initial attack, from stinking babe to crooked-armed crone, were chained and loaded into one of the iron-barred wagons; they would bring a good price, spoiled or not, at the market in the Dreydhold city of Chimiak in southern Eromar. Unless they were children, the surviving males were killed outright, as they wouldn't bring much gold in that slaving square.

He reached under his coat and pulled out the chunky stone necklace he'd taken that morning. A primitive ward against witchcraft—even these creatures feared the witches in their midst—and so precious to the Unhuman priest who held it that Thane had to kill him for it; an unnecessary waste of a life, but the creature wouldn't let go of the bauble. Although he'd skewered that babbling fool, Thane refrained from joining the brigands as they swept through the village; he had no stomach for useless torment and slaughter. Besides, his quarry wasn't there.

But Thane *was* on the right path, and he was patient. He'd find Fey-witches in these mountains. He had Fortune's favor. Even as skilled a Seeker as he was, Thane believed in the reality of luck as much as he trusted in the importance of a sharp mind and well-honed fighting skills. When the other Men were finished here, they'd return to Chimiak with their slaves and looted treasures, and Thane would take the strange Fey necklace with him into the mountains. It might be useful.

He slid the prize back into his coat, pulled his hat back over his face, and slipped into a dreamless sleep, the smoke of the ravaged remnants of Red Cedar Town wafting over him, reminding him of home.

10

Sheynadwiin

IF ANY PLACE COULD BE FAIRLY CONSIDERED the center of Kyn power and history in the Everland, it would be the venerable peace-city of Sheynadwiin, a populous settlement hidden deep within Dardath Vale, the ferny green home of the Kyn Nation. The verdant valley lay nestled in a region of sheer, vine-streaming cliffs, turbid rivers that crashed with abandon down mountainsides and rocky precipices, shadowed grottoes that had never known sunlight or starshine, and ancient emerald-green trees stretching hundreds of leafy feet into the air, mossy sentinels whose deep-rooted memories traveled back to times far outside the understandings of the walking world.

And if any place within the great valley could be considered the spirit of the Everland, the living essence of all it was to be woven into the *wyr* and the world, it would be the Eternity Tree, the pulsing heartbeat of the *wyr*, guarded by high-walled Sheynadwiin itself. The Tree was the embodied covenant between the Folk and the land, the law of reciprocity that both sides had honored in good faith since time immemorial. This was the home of antiquity, of ancestral memory and song.

Alone of all the remnant 'Holds, the Everland grew green and wild; many believed that this was due to the Eternity Tree, held by the Kyn as the living embodiment of Zhaia, the forest mother of their kind, from whose leafy body the seven Branches of the People had long ago emerged into an endless golden summer. Time held little power here. While other 'Holds fell to the grasping hand of Humanity, the Everland stood proud against the onslaught. Though it grew no larger in the Melded world, it surrendered nothing, and it continued on as it always had, its *wyr*-fed currents nourishing the old growth and protecting the new. Those Folk who called the Everland home were known throughout the Reach of Men as implacable foes who gave no quarter in defense of their lands; trespassers never escaped unscathed, and most who came with iron blade or burning brand were never seen again, as a warning to others who would dare intrude upon the Folk. Though wars of power and plunder carved a bloody swath through the lands of Humanity, the Everland had long remained untouched. Men had enough to worry about without risking the wrath of the Folk.

But those wars were largely over now—the Reachwarden of great Chalimor ruled supreme in the Reach, in name if not entirely in fact—and the eyes of Men turned once again to the deep forests and mist-shrouded mountains, eyes that saw only downed timber, gleaming gold, fine furs, endless meat, and hardy slaves for the market. And so they came, a few at first, but soon Men and Women began to build on the outskirts of the Everland in ever greater numbers, pushing farther inward, driving Folk deeper into the interior, a rising stream that threatened to become an overwhelming flood.

Much had already been lost. Word came to Sheynadwiin on the wings of bird, bat, and butterfly, on the swift cloven hooves of doe and the steady pads of bobcat and coyote, that the customs of Men ruled in places where once only the voices of Folk and their kith had echoed free. Kyn towns were burning to the south; Gvaerg-havens in the north echoed with the fresh ache of mourning songs; Tetawi moundhouses to the west lay in ruins, abandoned to scavengers on feathered wings, on four feet and two. Beast-Folk fled from warren, canopy, and copse, unable to withstand cold iron or hot flame. Even the implacably urbane Ubbetuk, called Goblins by Men, were surrendering their great learning-houses to the onrush of Humanity, taking to the safety of their distant sky-cities.

Yes, much had been lost, but not all. As messages came into Sheynadwiin, other messages went out. For only the fourth time in a thousand years, since the Melding that had forever severed the way to the Eld Green, a Sevenfold Council had been called. Representatives of the Seven Sisters, the first seven Folk of the Everland—Kyn, Tetawi, Gvaergs, and Ubbetuk, as well as the Wyrnach spider-people, the Beast-Folk, and the eldest of the half-animal Ferals, the Harpies—were asked to travel at great haste to Sheynadwiin, where together, it was hoped, they would discover a way to ensure the continued survival of the Everland.

For one thing was clear to all who called the Everland home: a great storm crouched on the borders of their home, and they would all soon know its fury.

"En't it a pretty sight?" Tobhi asked. Both she-Kyn nodded in awe-struck silence, neither having seen anything quite as beautiful as the great valley. Thin streams of mist rose here and there over the lush expanse, and on each side of the vale rose tall cliffs streaked grey, red, and green, their heights lost in the low-settled clouds. The trio stood on a packed-soil road that moved northward through the Vale toward their destination: Sheynadwiin, the gathering place of the Sevenfold Council. Day would soon fade to night, but they wanted to linger here, to try to absorb the vast reach of life that embraced them.

Tarsa suddenly felt very small and uncertain. This was a world entirely different from the one she had known in Red Cedar Town. Here great minds gathered to debate issues that would affect all the Folk throughout the Everland; it was no bickering town council chamber where, more often than not, petty jealousies and long-held grudges were the greatest concerns of the community leaders. Sheynadwiin was a place of heroes, of powerful speakers and war-leaders who knew the ways of their own world and of those beyond the misty edges of the Everland.

Tarsa wiped a layer away from her dirt-caked clothes and tried fruitlessly to untangle her long-matted braids. Unahi had given her an old, threadbare cloak to wear against the cold in the deeper mountains, and it looked far worse now, with its roughly sewn patches more prominent than the dull green fabric itself. Her copper arm-bands no longer shone in the sunlight, and cracks now snaked across her wooden bracers where well-oiled wood once gleamed.

The journey had been fairly uneventful after the battle with the grave-robbing Men, but even with easy travel and baths every sunrise, she looked bedraggled and unkempt; a quick glance at her similarly disheveled companions merely deepened her sudden melancholy. *Why would anyone listen to us?*

Neither Tobhi nor Unahi seemed to share her discomfort, so Tarsa kept her thoughts to herself and tried to absorb Dardath Vale's full grandeur. As Tobhi had said, it was a truly magnificent sight. The valley stretched for many miles to the east and west, fewer to the north and south, and was lined at the mountains' base, from edge to edge, with massive wyrwood trees. Wyrwood was native to the Everland but alien to the Human lands beyond; it was the most important of the standing-people to the Kyn, and precious to other Folk. Weapons made with the proper Wieldings and entreaties to both Zhaia and the tree-spirits were not only equal in strength and sharpness to Human steel, but they could also draw on the *wyr* to enhance the already considerable powers of those who carried them. Wyrwood armor and wyrweave clothing crafted from the naturally shed outer bark were largely impervious to the elements and could often be used to hide the wearer from unfriendly eyes; indeed, the power of wyrweave cloaks was enough to protect the sun-fearing he-Gvaergs from turning to stone in the daylight. Fallen branches or deadwood could become walking sticks, furniture, even canoe hulls; seed pod beads and leaves made their way into jewelry and delicate works of art. Even the sweet golden sap that the Kyn tapped from the reddish trunks in the fall was used for medicinals and to give great nourishment to a wide range of foods. Wyrwood clothed, nourished, protected, and healed the Kyn, and there was no question why that was the case: the great Eternity Tree was the first wyrwood tree, and each of its descendants carried on the covenant between Zhaia and her descendants.

The Redthorn warrior had never seen so many wyrwood trees in one place, nor any so imposing: even the smaller trees were as big around as the Red Cedar Town council house. The few wyrwoods remaining in the southern stretches of the Everland were deeply treasured by all of the Folk who lived nearby and were treated with utmost reverence. Tarsa's wyrwood bracers had been given to her at her marking when she'd passed the trials to join the ranks of the

Redthorns, and Oda'hea, her mentor and friend, made all too clear just how difficult those gifts had been to obtain.

Yet everywhere around the young warrior walked Folk bearing all manner of wyrwood decoration with an almost casual disregard. It was as common here along the road to Sheynadwiin as the knobby old pines in the hills around Nine Oaks Town. The only Folk unadorned with wyrwood were those wanderers like themselves from other areas far from Dardath Vale, and the Celestial Kyn who walked in tight groups, their chins high, silver jewelry jingling, eyes never straying from the path ahead of them.

Unahi waved her hand across the horizon. "Where will the Council meet?"

The Tetawa pointed ahead. "In the Gallery of Song, where the Kyn Nation's been debatin' for a long while 'bout the proposal to leave the Everland. Ye can't see the Gallery yet, but it won't be too long 'til we can look down on the city and see everythin'." Smudge trotted along, pulling at his bridle with the knowledge that he'd soon be back to enjoying life in a well-stocked stable along with other Tetawi riding companions: deer, goats, burros, even large dogs and the occasional stout wolf. This more congenial attitude pleased Tobhi enormously, as Smudge had grown more and more irritable on the journey until, in a fit of temper, he'd charged into Tarsa and had nearly been skewered by her quick knife. Since that incident, the deer had remained quite docile, although he refused to come anywhere near the Redthorn warrior.

As Tobhi had promised, the road soon crested on the high edge of a rocky outcropping, and the travelers looked down on the city of Sheynadwiin itself. Unahi gasped with long-awaited joy at the sight, but Tarsa's throat was too thick with emotion; all she could do was stare with brimming eyes.

Built inside a massive, river-swollen grotto at the jagged feet of the great Kraagen Mountains, the city seemed to shimmer in the rainbow light of sunset that gleamed through the river spray. The air was alive with light and laughter. Twisted into beautiful arches and swirling waves by the erosion of the river water, natural stone towers stood tall and proud throughout the city, the sharp, angular images of leaves, trees, and animals carved into their sides until each looked to be formed more by mindful intent than by the water-worn effort of ages. Bridges of stone, vine, wood, and rope spanned the city to link with dozens of stout wyrwood trees that each stretched at least five hundred feet into the sky. Brightly painted Kyn houses, taller than those of the south but still comfortably familiar, crowded both the ground below and the bustling canopy above, lining well-maintained streets that bustled with activity. With round stone and log bases and thatched or tiled roofs, some houses were multilevel like the city itself, with gardens growing untamed on each level. Their round doors and windows had few shutters against the clean air and the warm sun. Grocers, traders, merchants, singers, cane-flute players, storytellers, and others sold their wares to or shared their skills with appreciative passersby; from time to time a flock of birds with brilliant plumage would skim like winged arrows of fire through the treetops and dart among the people above and below. And there were the smells— sweet baking spices mingled delicately with the rich earthy musk of the forest—rising up in the air to welcome the new arrivals.

Tobhi pointed to a massive amphitheatre at the far northwest edge of the grotto. Though it was largely open to the sky, a wide half-dome extended outward beyond it, like the leading edge of a rolled seashell. "That's the Gallery. They sometimes draw that roof over the top of it, but most folks like to see the sky when they're debatin' with one another. Can't say as I blame 'em—there's nothin' quite like the stars above Sheynadwiin." Even in the last light of the fading day, Tarsa could tell that the night sky would be spectacular, as Pearl-in-Darkness and the various astral spheres were already bright beyond anything she remembered. The great ring that circled the world—remnants of the Greatmoon's shattered brothers— gleamed like a silver band in the sky, which seemed deeper here, more distinctly otherworldly. One could look into the heavens and see something new every time. Here the dense green world opened up to endlessness above.

On a low stone ridge to the northeast of the amphitheatre stood a massive stone and lashed-timber longhouse, four times as long as its fifty-foot height. Various designs resembling beaded weavings were painted onto large squares of colored mud plaster on the sides. At the apex of the front eave stood a massive carving of a bull elk's head, its wooden knot eyes turned eastward toward the rising suns. Well-tended vines wrapped themselves into the antlers and extended down the sides of the lodge to the ground. It was a sacred space, where ceremony adhered to the Deep Green, safe from winter snows and summer storms.

Yet here, perhaps more than anyplace else, Tarsa could see the impact of the Shields and the Celestial Path, for dozens of large stone-carved arches, like the one that stood over the memory of the old cedar in Red Cedar Town, had been erected in proud defiance throughout the city. Three of the arches crowded together around the Wielders' longhouse, as though to hem in its influence, to force Kyn through their stony embrace before they gained the freedom of the lodge. And yet here the arches seemed almost insignificant, a futile attempt to confine the laughing wind. The Deep Green still endured.

Tobhi led them down the road toward the city. They stopped at a rising series of four guarded walls, some built of ruddy stone and mortar, others formed from the living trees and earth by the still-strong Wielding of generations before. The warders looked at both Unahi and Tarsa without hostility, for Greenwalkers were not unwelcome in Sheynadwiin as they were in Red Cedar Town. After passing the fourth wall, the travelers headed toward the large city center, a grassy gathering place from which the red-stone cobbled roadways radiated like a spider web across the grotto. Kyn and other Folk gathered in the area, many purchasing provisions and goods from the various merchants wandering around, others locked in intense conversation.

Though the earlier sense of peace hadn't faded completely, the mood among the People was not as calm as the newcomers had assumed from afar. Here the very air seemed to ache. Some passersby cast dark looks at the Wielders and ignored Tobhi entirely. The Tetawa was surprised to see weapons hanging in plain view from belts and bandoliers, rather than being secured in the weapons-house by the gate militia before permission was granted to enter the peace-city, as was the long-standing tradition. Kyn warriors—both Greenwalker in dusty wyrweave garments and Celestial in pristine white and blue silks—walked through the crowd with lips pursed and eyes darting around in search of trouble; some seemed a bit too eager to find it. The few Human merchants in the city were given wide berth, even though most of them had long since demonstrated their loyalty to the Folk, and many were married into Folk families. Although the two she-Kyn Wielders couldn't understand all of the speech around them, it was clear that life was changing in Sheynadwiin.

It was not a comforting realization.

Darkness had, by this time, fallen in the valley, but when twilight deepened toward night the air erupted with the soft glow of ever-lights hanging on trees and atop tall wooden posts on the ground and in the canopy of trees. The lanterns were wrought to resemble pine-cones and apples, acorns, willow baskets, and other shapes in honor of the seven Kyn Branches. Their lights were soft, not so brilliant as to drive away the gentle hush of night, but bright enough to give shape to the shadows.

They stopped here to rest. Tobhi walked up to the wagon of an old he-Tetawa baker and chatted with him for a moment, then returned with a warm armful of plump pumpkin cakes and a steam-ing clay jar of apple cider to share. Hands sticky from the meal, the three gathered at the base of a good-sized wyrwood sapling on the edge of the green.

"Well, niece, we've finally found our way here," said Unahi, sipping from the cider jug. Tarsa nodded silently, her mouth too full with cake to speak. The elder Wielder turned to Tobhi. "What's next for you, Leafspeaker?"

He held a pumpkin cake out to Smudge, who nibbled content-edly at the snack, and shrugged. "I en't too sure, really. M' aunties might want me to take notes at the Council and add 'em to the stories in the lore-leaves; they're really interested in gettin' a good under-standin' of the proceedin's for future reflectin'. Until then, though, I s'pose I'm pretty well free to do whatever I like."

Unahi nodded. "And you, niece?"

"I'm going with you." Tarsa hesitated. "Aren't I?"

"Eventually, yes. But first I must meet with the other elder Wielders. We rarely meet in large numbers—not since the Purging—and we'll have plenty to talk about with one another for the next couple of weeks until the Council is fully under way. After we've cleared a path for the upcoming discussions, you and the other young Wielders will join us."

Seeing Tarsa's countenance fall in disappointment, Unahi reached out and gently patted the young she-Kyn's hand. This time there was no hesitation in her touch. "Tarsa, this has nothing to do with your

Wielding. Your strength and bravery are very much needed at this grim time. But, for now, rest and let your heart be light; you've had far too many burdens on your strong young shoulders lately, and I haven't been able to give you the kind of attention you deserve. I want you to see the city, to meet people, to understand all the many different ways it is to be Kyn, and to know our other kith among the Folk a little better." She smiled wearily, not adding that she hoped this brief respite would extend a calming influence over Tarsa's spirit as well. "This is the heart-home of our Nation, Tarsa, and one of us must be familiar with both the city and the many peoples who are here; that one must be you. I'm a stranger here, too, and I'll need you to be my eyes and ears outside the Wielders' Circle, to help me understand what's happening out there, to know who our friends are and who opposes us, to know fully what's at stake. Will you do that for me?"

Tarsa nodded, visibly relieved. It had been a long time since she'd felt truly needed—a lifetime ago, since she'd killed the Stoneskin. And, in truth, she did want to see more of Sheynadwiin, to immerse herself in the noise and energy of the city, which was so unlike anything she'd experienced before. So many different peoples were gathered together in this place as they'd done for countless ages; the deep and abiding spirit of Sheynadwiin was so clear to her senses that she could almost see it. If she could satisfy her rising curiosity and still be of help to Unahi and the other Wielders, she'd be content. For the first time since her banishment, her heart didn't ache for the familiar comforts of Red Cedar Town.

Tobhi's face erupted into a broad grin. "Ye know, if ye'r gonna be wanderin' all over the city, ye'll need y'self a guide." He winced. "This time, though, I en't takin' along that rump-bitin' Beast with me—I'm so bruised that I en't likely to sit down comfortable for at least a month!" Tarsa laughed, but Smudge ignored them, continuing to chew on a pumpkin cake.

News of Tobhi's arrival spread quickly. When he wasn't engaged in his daily explorations of the city with Tarsa, his aunties had him busy running errands between Tetawi Clans throughout Sheynadwiin. Unahi and Tarsa took up quarters with one of the elder she-Kyn's friends, an enormous Gvaerg Wielder named Biggiabba. Tarsa had seen a few Gvaergs in her patrols as a Redthorn warrior, but never so closely.

Even bent low in a perpetual stoop, Biggiabba stood well over twice the she-Kyn's height. Her thick skin was mottled and creased like the bark of an old spruce, and her coarse hair fell down in green cords around her broad, sloping brow. The old Gvaerg wore a rough brown robe that covered her vitals without constricting her movement; it was free of adornment, as Biggiabba had little use for vanity. The two she-Kyn slept in hammocks strung from the upper timbers of her open, two-story roundhouse, while the kindly old Gvaerg snored peacefully on a thick wyrweave mat on the floor below them.

Like Tobhi, they too soon had frequent visitors, and it was these first few days that gave Tarsa a clear sense of Unahi's true work. The handful of Wielders who called Sheynadwiin home had for some time been overwhelmed by the number of Folk seeking assistance during these dark days, so they were thrilled to be able to send the overflow to the various visiting Wielders throughout the city. Tarsa soon discovered that both Unahi and Biggiabba had good reputations that extended far from their respective home grounds, and every day brought with it a steady stream of Folk looking for guidance or comfort. Tarsa had a fast education as a result. From Unahi she learned a wide tange of medicinal and counter-witching formulas, while Biggiabba taught her to identify the spirits and personalities of dozens of different kinds of rocks and their surprisingly diverse healing gifts. She helped both of the elder Wielders to set broken bones, deliver seedlings, counsel the bereaved, guard the fertility of crops, drive out minor menacing spirits and curses, and perform other duties of greater and lesser significance. Tarsa learned from her aunt many of the Kyn ways of the *wyr*, and from Biggiabba she learned those teachings that were most appropriate for non-Gvaergs. Gvaerg Wielders zealously guarded their deeper knowledge from *rijjik*—"unbelievers"—for the Gvaergs were a deeply devout people, and they took few into their confidence.

Those weeks were a revelation. While in Red Cedar Town, Tarsa had always thought of Wielders as being strange and romantically menacing, appearing in times of great peril with powers out of legend, then disappearing again to their mysterious fog-guarded hollows. Her own Awakening had shattered that fanciful illusion while heightening her fear, yet it wasn't until she encountered Unahi's daily work that she lost much of that discomfort. Yes, the *wyr* demanded much, and she wasn't entirely sure that she was up to the task of being a Wielder, but she saw that Unahi filled a need in the lives of the Folk, and, while most of the work was rather mundane, its value was no less important in the lives of the Folk than Tarsa's own Redthorn war-craft. The Folk who visited were generally grateful for the help. Some were clearly more comfortable with Wielder wisdom than others, whose reluctance and occasional fear spoke to both their own desperation and the growing power of the Shields in the city. Yet no matter what their motivations or misgivings, each visitor brought a gift of food or cloth or other practical item for respectful exchange, and the house became so packed with these gifts that Unahi soon had Tobhi and a few of his cousins making regular distribution runs to the refugees who were arriving in the city in ever-growing numbers.

And each night, after the last visitor had gone home with a kind word and gentle touch, Tarsa would prepare the evening meal while Unahi and Biggiabba went through the day's teachings with her, encouraging questions and giving thoughtful answers that seemed to bind themselves firmly to the young she-Kyn's consciousness. She learned quickly, and she learned well. Unahi's gruffness hadn't vanished entirely, but Tarsa saw far more of her aunt's gentle spirit than in all the weeks before, and she treasured the gift.

Those lessons grew fewer after the first month, as the members of the Wielders' Circle began their discussions in their great longhouse beside the Gallery of Song and the older Wielders spent more time among their colleagues, leaving Tarsa more often in Tobhi's good company. As her elders focused their attention elsewhere, she became increasingly restless, even during the most intensive teachings. Neither Unahi nor Biggiabba ever mentioned her distraction, though their shared glances made clear that they noticed the change. Tarsa's walks with Tobhi through the city helped her to clear her thoughts, if only for a while. She felt as though something called to her at a great distance. Its voice was too soft to hear, and, as much as she tried, she couldn't make out the words.

While the Wielders were busied with the Circle, Tarsa found that her time with Tobhi brought its own learning opportunities. Of all the Folk, the Tetawi were the closest in habit and ceremony to the Kyn. Both peoples preferred to live in deep woods and wild places. They organized their communities on a similar structure that passed through the female line—Clans for the Tetawi, Branches for the Kyn—and both Folk were deeply committed to their immediate and extended families. Yet the Tetawi were far more sociable with others than were the Kyn. Many Tetawi traveled throughout the Everland and beyond as traders, scholars, writers, musicians, and performers, or as archers and scouts. Tobhi was far from unusual in his familiarity with other tongues and peoples, although his leaf-reading was certainly a rare gift.

Tetawi settlements tended to be widely dispersed; the one in Sheynadwiin was very small and compact by comparison. Their moundhouses—stocky timbered cabins with carved entry posts and arched roofs—were clustered in Clan groups and built around the base of a great earthen mound at the center of the settlement, where they buried their dead and performed their ceremonies. Every few years they hauled more dirt to the top and built it higher; the central mounds of older settlements were massive, some stretching three hundred feet or more into the sky. The one in the Sheynadwiin settlement was just over two hundred feet high, speaking to a lengthy Tetawi presence in the city.

Perhaps the most striking difference between the Kyn and the Tetawi was in their connection to the *wyr*. Both peoples loved and honored their wild world, and Tarsa found deep comfort in that. Whereas the Kyn found their greatest love for and connection to the green growing things of the land, the Tetawi followed the guidance of the animals of the earth and of the air, from Tobhi's own Badger Clan to others that honored Spider, Nuthatch, Lizard, Moth, Marmot, and more. Kyn Wielding linked to the spirits of the elements, but Tetawi Wielding linked minds with those creatures closest to the Wielder's Clan animal or, if a healer, with any blood-bearing creature in need.

"Some of us," Tobhi mentioned to her one day, "can even take the shape of their Clan animal—it seems to give 'em a deeper understandin' of the ways of Beasts, but it en't common at all, and we don't often talk 'bout it. It's a more intimate connection than most things we do, and so it en't much of a topic for heedless mouth-rattlin'." He continued with a story about the shadow-side of that connection, the cannibal Skeegers, those shape-shifting Tetawi who were exiled from their Clans due to unspeakable crimes and now wandered through the world and lingered on the outskirts of Tetawi settlements in search of warm-blooded prey.

"And then there's the Owl Clan," he began. "Nobody is born into that Clan of death; ye gotta be called to it—" It was still early afternoon, but a sudden chill in the air gave the Tetawa pause, and he quickly diverted their conversation to more benign topics. Their mood brightened when some of Tobhi's cousins arrived to play a vigorous game of Groundhog's keep-away, which involved a round clearing, a doublewoven basket, a ball of tanned bearskin, and stout wooden cudgels that smashed into toes and shins with surprising frequency. Tarsa watched the enthusiastic aggression for a while from the clearing's edge before joining in and receiving a few bruises of her own.

Skeegers and Owls were a distant menace. Most Tetawi were like Tobhi: open and generous, with a respectful curiosity that inquired but never demanded. Many spoke with Tobhi's same deep-woods bluntness, while others were more refined in their speech, but all were friendly. Tarsa ate well as Tobhi's friend and guest—huge feasts of thick-grained breads, rich gravies, corn, beans, squashes of varied flavors and forms, and a wide array of fruit, including a rich fermented strawberry drink that eased the body's tensions and gave comfort to her increasingly unsettled spirit. Out of respect to her own traditions, the Tetawi refrained from placing meat on the table, although they generally had no hesitation to eat animals that had fallen on the hunt. There were few visible tensions between Clans, although Tarsa noticed a great deal of good-natured rivalry between groups, notably between those who followed Buborru the Keeper, the old Badger-father of Tobhi's Clan, and those of Peccary Clan, who honored Mother Malluk as the protector of their family. It was a bit different from her own upbringing in Red Cedar Town, where the Willow Branch Kyn often clashed—sometimes violently—with Ash Branch Kyn.

She learned other things, too, more personal stories about Tobhi's family, his parents in the far-distant Edgewood, his older sister, and extended kin. And she learned about Tobhi's love of a sweet young she-Tetawa, a *firra*, who lived a few days from his birth-Clan's settlement. The story transformed him. His stories about his sandy-haired beloved burned with an honest fire that stripped away the shadows of those dark days. He planned to talk to her family when he returned from Sheynadwiin, as he had his own family's blessings for the marriage. Once the Sevenfold Council had finished its business, he'd head back to Spindletop with gifts and a wedding belt, and there begin the next great stage of his life. Such deep feeling filled Tarsa's own heart with longing.

Tobhi caught her pained expression. "Are ye all right, Tarsa? D'ye have someone of ye'r own back in Red Cedar Town waitin' for ye?"

"No, not anymore," she said quietly. "They always seemed to want . . . something more than I could ever give. That sounds ridiculous, doesn't it? But it's true. I guess I always knew that there was something dangerous inside me, something wrong." She smiled, but the ache bled through. "And I was right. With everything now—it's probably good that no one is waiting for me." They didn't talk much for the rest of that day, and Tobhi didn't return to the subject.

Tarsa enjoyed her visits with Tobhi's folk, but she couldn't always be with him, so she sometimes explored the city on her own. She'd linger at the center green and peruse the traders' stalls, or assess the difference in training styles between the city's Greenwalker and Celestial guardians. Sometimes she'd help with the building of temporary arbors for the ever-arriving refugees. Most often, though, she'd simply walk among the great wyrwood trees and take comfort in their stable rootedness. The bloodsong was calmest in these moments, but the respite was only temporary. When her wanderings were over, she inevitably found her way back to the house Tobhi shared with his aunt Jynni and a few cousins, and there she'd stay until late in the night, listening and watching as they ate and laughed together, quietly experiencing the kindly joys of Tetawi kinship. It was so different from the cold dignity of her rank-conscious aunts in Red Cedar Town, for whom any public frivolity was a danger to the Cedar Branch position. This new freedom—and acceptance—was wholly unexpected, and welcome beyond measure.

One afternoon, while Tobhi was busy writing a letter back to Birchbark Hollow for his aunts, Tarsa decided to explore the northern part of the city on her own. The Tetawi settlement and most of the trading center were in the southern half of the grotto, closer to the trees of the Eldarvian Woods than to the roots of the great

Kraagen Mountains, so she'd seen very little of this area, and she was drawn to the misty ridges of the high northern quarter. Unahi and Biggiabba had been in council for three full days and nights, leaving her alone in the Gvaerg's roundhouse, and that time had weighed heavily on her restless spirit. When she felt the pull toward the upper city, she didn't even try to resist. The call was too strong; she hungered for something she couldn't name.

A great waterfall rushed down the vine-choked northern cliff, plummeting hundreds of feet into a roaring pool below. White spray turned to thick silver mist at the base of the falls, absorbing the greater part of the noise. The effect was surprisingly soothing, as though the river's enthusiasm for life could ease the minds of those who heard him. The water glowed with a soft light of its own that wasn't lost in the brightness of the early afternoon.

A dozen spray-splashed stone benches sat around the pool, and Tarsa walked to one. It was a place to sit and listen to the river's voice, to watch the play of light through mist and deep water. Each bench was carved with odd faces of spirit-creatures, some rather comical, others grotesque and unpleasant. But they were silent, and she gave herself to the sounds of the water. Her thoughts drifted away. She was safer in this place than she'd been in a very long time. There was no tension in her blood, no pain, no fear of herself or her rage. She didn't know what brought such sudden peace to her mind and spirit, but her heart swelled with love of it.

An odd scraping noise caught her attention, and she turned to see a tall, russet-skinned he-Kyn approaching a bench not far from her. He was old but unbent, with a full head of bright silver hair that cascaded down to the middle of his back, matched by a silver mustache that draped past his chin. His grey eyes were large and heavy, but he smiled at her in friendly greeting. In one hand he held a slender walking stick that was smoothed and polished a deep red-brown.

"My apologies," he said gently. "I did not mean to frighten you." His voice had a pleasant roughness, like the creak of old oak.

She shook her head. "You didn't. I was just looking at the water."

"There are few places more suitable. May I join you?"

Tarsa dipped her chin. He sat on a nearby bench and watched the waterfall. She returned her own gaze to the pool, while at the same time casting furtive glances at the stranger. He looked to be a

Strangeling, the child of a Human female and a he-Kyn, born without Branch identity and thus something other than Kyn. His ancestry was clear from the dullness of his ear tines and sensory stalks, his height, and the thickness of his chest. Most of the Strangelings that she knew in Red Cedar Town were firm Celestials, occasionally even called upon to be the ceremonial Shields. In some ways he reminded her of the messenger Leith: his clothing was similar to the Celestial fashions she'd seen since coming to Sheynadwiin, complete with chin-high white cravat, layered jacket and forest green breeches, knee-high boots, and a cloak of fine satin. Yet he had none of Leith's aloofness. She stared off into the water again but turned to the newcomer in sudden surprise.

"You speak the Old Tongue!"

He smiled at her. "Yes. It is my language, too."

"Oh." She looked away. "I'm sorry to be rude. It's just that I haven't been able to speak with any of your kind since I've been here." Even the most Man-friendly Celestials in Red Cedar Town had spoken the old Kyn language, but here in Sheynadwiin, a number of Celestials—and nearly every Greenwalking Strangeling who'd visited Biggiabba's house—spoke nothing but Mannish.

"'Your kind'?" he asked with an eyebrow raised.

She shook her head again. They'd just met, and this was already going badly. "It's just . . . I didn't mean to offend you. You *are* a Strangeling, aren't you?"

"Ah." He smiled. "No, I am Pine Branch Kyn. True, my father was Human, but I am no Branchless Strangeling—my mother was Kyn. I belong to her people, and I wear my honor markings with pride." He lifted the hair away from his neck to reveal a series of intricate spiral- and cone-shaped tattoos that disappeared beneath his collar.

Tarsa cringed. She should have known the distinction—the Strangelings in Red Cedar Town were all born to Human Women, not to she-Kyn. The few seedlings born to she-Kyn and Human sires in that community were Kyn, no matter their appearance, and belonged there as much as any of the other Branch-born. "Please, forgive me. I'm almost a stranger to this place, and I'm still learning a great deal. I shouldn't have assumed anything."

The he-Kyn held up his hand. "You did not offend me; do not concern yourself about it any longer. As so much has lately changed in Sheynadwiin, you were not entirely wrong in your assessment; many born of two peoples follow the unbending Celestial Path. But not all two-roots follow the ways of Men, nor do all Strangelings follow the guidance of the Shields. Many here who speak Mannish or walk among Men are still dedicated Greenwalkers, and for that we are truly fortunate." He smiled. "I must admit that it is something of a pleasant surprise to be able to speak with one who knows of these things, especially considering your youth."

Tarsa's green skin darkened. "My elders have taught me well."

The he-Kyn held his hands up in mock surrender and laughed. "Now it is I who ask forgiveness! I did not intend offense. Indeed, age is no better a sign of one's path than is one's outer raiment, be it flesh or cloth." Tarsa nodded and smiled in spite of her embarrassment.

"Who is your family?" the he-Kyn asked.

"I am a daughter of Cedar Branch, Red Cedar Town, to the far south. My mother was Lan'delar Last-Born, my father Setharian Kills-Two-Men of Oak Branch. My mother named me Namshéké, but the name I share is my warrior-name, Tarsa'deshae, which I earned through blood and battle." Her voice trembled a bit toward the end, but she held her chin high as she claimed her Redthorn name.

The stranger nodded appreciatively. "Indeed, you were taught well. I am of Pine Branch, Thornholt Town, six days southwest of Sheynadwiin. My mother was Kei'shaad Mendiir, my father a Human merchant named Ramyd Thalsson. My mother named me Garyn, and that is the name I share with you." He held his hand out to Tarsa, palm upward, and she briefly rested her three digits on his own five-fingered Man's hand.

"I have heard of you before this," Garyn said. "You came here with Unahi, the Wielder of Thistlewood, and the Tetawa Leafspeaker." Tarsa nodded. "Then indeed, this is a rare and wonderful privilege. There are few Redthorn warriors in these lands, and none within memory who can tell of facing down a Stoneskin and surviving. Most impressive. Most impressive, indeed."

Garyn stood up. He favored his left leg, and Tarsa realized that the scraping she heard earlier was the he-Kyn's right foot, which curled inward slightly.

"I will not trouble you any longer, Tarsa'deshae. I have stayed away from my duties much too long as it is. I thank you for your conversation; you do not know how much you have lifted my spirits." He smiled as he bowed in farewell, but his gaze seemed to pass beyond her to take in the whole of Sheynadwiin. "Perhaps we will have a longer opportunity to talk of the Deep Green again. In the meantime, I must say farewell."

She stood and nodded to him, watching him go with a mingled sense of relief and curiosity. Before he disappeared up the stairs that led away from the pool, Garyn turned to her again. "Follow the path behind the waterfall if you would see the Eternity Tree. You will find it well worth the visit, I assure you. *Hanahé.*" He moved up the stairs and vanished into the mist.

Tarsa looked back to the waterfall. A narrow but well-worn path hugged the wet cliff face and disappeared behind the rushing water. She tried to look past the waterfall to see what lay beyond. For a moment, all that she could see was the silver-blue curtain, but as she peered deeper through the rushing waters she could see a bright spot in the darkness. It was the same light, the same soothing blue that flowed through the pool, and her spirit sang with sudden recognition as a deep peace washed over her body. She forgot about the he-Kyn stranger, her worries, her fears. All she saw and sensed lay beyond the river's roar. It called to her.

Tarsa didn't hesitate in answering. She hurried across the left-ward path, slipping slightly on the slick stones but never falling, and disappeared behind the waterfall.

11

Becoming

THE ROAR OF THE FALLS FADED in the distance as Garyn limped slowly through the grotto. His eyes, grey as old slate, held a heavy distance in their depths, as if his spirit looked out through a drizzling veil. He stopped on a high patch of ground that overlooked much of Sheynadwiin and took in the midday sunlight and crisp air. Here in the mountains even summer carried a bite. The ache in his leg was easier to bear on days like this, but he still mourned the old battle injury. The city was as beautiful now as it had been when he'd first stepped through the vine-wrapped gates as a Speaker to the Gathering, the ancient council-meet of Kyn town representatives from throughout the Everland.

Those days were long past, but he could still remember the happy arrogance of youth, the mingled fear and heady anticipation that had accompanied him on his first truly adult task. He'd served his town wisely and well—so well, in fact, that his Branch-mothers had sent him back to the Gathering the next year, and the year after, eventually gaining support from other Branches to choose him as the Firstkyn of Thornhold. The Gathering had slowly given way to the great Assembly, and still he'd spoken for Thornhold. Twenty years later, after the unification of the autonomous towns into the Kyn

Nation, the town elders chose Garyn as Governor and Voice of the Nation. For all these many years, he'd served his people as wisely and courageously as he could, and the Nation had endured.

Politics were less Garyn's pleasure than his duty, but he held no resentment; he was honored to have been chosen, time and time again, to speak for his people's interests and for their concerns. But he no longer burned with the fire of youth. The full, fresh lips that had once turned up in a winning grin now rarely found joy enough to smile. He still stood dignified and strong, was still a powerful figure with a commanding voice and compelling gaze, but his heart had somewhere lost its lightness.

The city that had once known only the joy of eternal summer now trembled under autumn's shadow. It was a time he'd never thought to see. Though his people went about their lives much as they always had, fear dogged their steps and darkened every task. Kyn sprouts no longer ran laughing together through the streets, dodging merchant wagons and their aunties' grasping hands. Now they sat, together or alone, and watched with too-old eyes as their elders trembled with each day's news.

And every day his own fear grew that he would have the grim honor of leading the Everland Kyn into their last days as a free people. The thought was like cold iron in his blood. He bowed his head and squeezed his eyes tight, but he pushed aside the desire to wish the new times away. Such wishes were fleeting solace at best; he could change nothing by ignoring the world. He looked up again. The cobbled streets were still clean; the windows remained open to the wind. Wyrweave flags and banners still fluttered atop the thatched and tiled houses, river-cane flutes and gourd-bodied fiddles still rang up from the mossy trunks of the lower tree-city, and from the branches above the Shields still sang their songs of penance with each new day's light. Life would continue much as it had for all time; normalcy was their greatest comfort. Sometimes the crouching fawn fell under the cougar's claws, but sometimes death passed by.

Sometimes.

Garyn listened to the melancholy music that danced down through the canopy. It was a fitting companion to his mood. He turned to walk down the road to the center green of the city but stopped to wait for a figure striding with purposeful ease up the wide street, a golden shawl wrapped tightly around her white-clad shoulders to keep out the chill. His mood soured further, but he didn't turn away.

"Health and long happiness, my Governor," Neranda said with a respectful nod, slightly winded from the climb.

"*Hanahé,*" Garyn replied.

The Lawmaker looked at him with one eyebrow raised at the old greeting. "You were not in your rooms when I came to speak with you."

"No. I wanted some peace; it is far too difficult to find it at the Gallery House. Too many voices, too much noise. I have much on my mind."

Neranda looked at the fog-shrouded path behind the Governor that led toward the waterfall. "It is not wise to linger in the past, Garyn."

"Perhaps not," he sighed, "but it may have more to teach us than you think. Why have you come here, Neranda?"

Thick strands of her dark red hair fluttered on the breeze, pulled free of the heavy silken mesh that draped backward from a silver circlet on her forehead. She pulled the shawl closer. "I know too well the burden that rests on your shoulders, Garyn, because that burden rests heavily on my own. Why must you insist on carrying that weight alone? It need not be so."

The Governor shook his head. It was a familiar and tiresome argument, and he was in no mood to continue it this day. "The same song, Neranda, if a different tune. Our burdens are *not* the same, although they could well be." He pointed to the city below. "Look at them. Listen. This is their home—*our* home. We cannot forsake them."

The first hint of emotion flashed in her violet eyes. "Forsake them? I suffer *with* them, as much as you do, if not more, as I can actually see the full measure of darkness that hovers on the horizon. You do not know the ways of Men as I do, and our people are stronger than you suppose, Garyn. They can make a life elsewhere . . . anywhere. You can make them see this. The People trust you as they trust no one else. They can rebuild, better and stronger, in a land that will always be ours, far from the grasping hand of Humanity."

"There is no such place."

She smiled. "There is. The offer is most generous. We would never have to deal with Men again unless we wanted to. In the new land, we could become a power unlike anything we are now. We could throw off the old shackles," she cast a glance toward the waterfall, "and the old superstitions. We could learn the best things that Men have to offer and, one day, become stronger even than they are. This is the legacy that we are offered, Garyn. Our names will be remembered for all time. We will be the ones to bridge the transformation from the dark past to the bright future. It is more than a great opportunity—it is a great obligation." Her powdered blue face glowed. Garyn had no doubt that she believed every word that she spoke, and her certainty chilled his marrow more than her words.

He gestured toward the heart of the city. "And what of their decision to remain? Would you dismiss it so readily?"

Neranda shrugged. "They do not understand all that is at stake. They are still held by barbarism's allure. The Celestial Path is a difficult and demanding way, and too many who applaud its virtues in public still dance with the Tree in their hearts. If they cannot be taught—and I am afraid that too many of our kindred have proven themselves uneducable—it is our responsibility to make these choices for their best benefit, much as a caring parent forces a sick but obstinate child to eat the bitter healing root. This is why we were chosen to lead. Some must follow."

"I place more trust in the good judgment of our people than you do, Neranda. We have survived well for untold ages trusting in the Deep Green. Besides, I do not have your faith in the good word of Men. They have proven themselves treacherous and faithless too often. Why should we trust them now?"

"Look around you, Garyn. We have no choice. This is the twilight of our kind. Men will never stop until they have claimed all that is ours. We can remain here with our eyes turned inward and fall to their unending numbers, or we can accept the inevitable and start again."

She reached out and placed a hand on his arm. They had been close once, not so long ago. That bond was strained, but it still endured.

"Garyn," she said softly, "we cannot stay here much longer. The longer we remain, the worse our fate shall be. The Dreydmaster's terms, while by no means generous, *are* satisfactory. Yet he is not a patient man. If we delay . . . well, you know the result as well as I."

The Governor looked at the shimmering valley in the far distance. "What terms, Neranda, are worth our homeland? If you will not look at the city, look at the world around us. It is not just land: it is our life-blood. Zhaia gave birth to us in this valley. She resides here still, giving us strength, weaving us into the pulse of life that beats through the Everland. We have kept faith with Her, and She has kept faith with us—this is the Law that we have always honored. We belong to this place; it is our source, everything we are. Many Humans understand this. For generations, we have signed pacts and oaths with Reachwardens and Assemblies of the Reach, each acknowledging, again and again, that this is our land by birthright and by right of existence, as is manifest in the Tree. What could Vald possibly offer us that would be worth sacri-ficing all that we are and all that we hold dear?"

"Our lives, dear uncle," she replied. She pulled away from him and strode toward the Gallery. Garyn watched her depart, his heart heavy, and walked slowly to the city's center green.

The Dreydmaster's expression was mild when Daladir entered the icy room. Other than a couple of hard, high-backed benches and an inadequate fire that crackled weakly in the gaping fireplace, the only furniture in the room was a small table, upon which sat a long wooden board with triangular ends, riddled with scores of small holes and mul-ticolored pegs. The soot-streaked drapes were pulled away from the windows, but drizzling clouds outside blanketed any sight of the after-noon sky. The he-Kyn was trembling, in spite of every ounce of inner strength he tried to muster. If Vald noticed, he didn't acknowledge it. Instead, the Man stood up and waved a hand to one of the seats, taking off his overcoat as he did so. Daladir nodded and sat down.

Vald's cold eyes swept over the he-Kyn, but his face seemed placid, almost pleasant. He pulled three smooth bone dice from his vest pocket and placed them on the table. Daladir removed his own ragged-edged coat, folded it over the back of his chair, and leaned forward to examine the board. The pegs were unmoved since the night before. He wasn't surprised; Vald had never once cheated in the many games they'd played since Daladir first arrived with the other diplomats from the Everland. And, although the he-Kyn rarely won a game, he knew that his failures came from his own slow skill with the pegs and dice, not from any subterfuge on the Dreydmaster's part.

Over those long late winter and cold spring months, the ranks of the diplomats had slowly thinned, one by one, and each night Vald summoned Daladir to this room in the north wing of the many-gabled Hall, where they would play trump-the-peg for a few hours and engage in banal conversation. And even after all this time, Daladir was no closer to understanding the Man than he had been when he first arrived. This, more than the disappearances and deaths, filled the he-Kyn with a waking terror, which he revisited every night when he scribbled in his daybook by tallow candlelight, chronicling his danger, trying to make sense of the shifting shadows, hoping to find courage in the scrawled words that left no room for doubt or uncertain memory. It was the way that he kept sane.

His mind was his only sanctuary in this cold place, but even that was beginning to break down. Trump-the-peg wasn't the only game being played in Gorthac Hall, and Daladir was painfully aware that he was losing at both of them.

They took up again where they'd ended the evening before. Daladir rolled the dice: three, one, four. His green eyes scanned the holes on the board—eighty-seven holes divided unevenly between six rows—and then at the colored pegs scattered across them. His pegs were blue; those of the Dreydmaster were red. Finally, he chose the third row and moved one of the pegs four spaces. He had other choices within the dice numbers, but this seemed a safe one.

Vald stroked his muttonchops thoughtfully as he watched the he-Kyn's move. <<What were we discussing last night before our game was interrupted?>> he asked, his voice a rumbling growl.

Daladir's jaw clenched. The "interruption" of the previous night had been a steward's hurried announcement that a member of the Kyn delegation, Fear-Takes-the-Fire, had been crushed against a wall by a raging stallion in the stables. When Daladir found the battered body of his friend, he found no evidence of a horse, but plenty of indications that the younger he-Kyn had been beaten to death somewhere else and his body dumped in the stable, just steps away from the door the young Binder had fled through a few nights earlier. This was the most blatant message thus far that Merrimyn's disappearance hadn't gone unnoticed.

Now only three members of the Kyn delegation remained.

Swallowing his anger and fear, Daladir responded in mannered Mannish, <<Your philosophy on trade, sir.>>

<<Of course.>> The Dreydmaster rolled the dice—six, six, and five—and surveyed the board. Doubles weren't good; he'd have to sacrifice one of the rolls. <<It is always a pleasure to share these thoughts with one who pays close attention to the world around him. You are quite observant, Daladir; I respect that. I am observant, too.>> The he-Kyn's heart skipped, but Vald continued smoothly. <<Trade, you see, is but one stream in the lifeblood of a nation, yet it is vital to every nation's continued health. A people can be virtuous, but if they are limited in their access to wealth, such virtue crumbles, and chaos erupts. The only solution is to lower those impediments to a nation's success, and the swiftest course is to start with the foundation of all wealth: land. At the heart of all is land. All Men must have land of their own, to use it as best they see fit. What else will a Man fight and die for if not for the soil under his feet, his measure of immortality. Otherwise, what can be the impetus for improvement? It is my understanding that the Fey-nations have no such belief?>>

<<Although I can't speak for all of the Folk, my own people don't believe that the land is something to be used as such, no. She belongs to us, just as we belong to Her. We owe our lives to the green world; we honor Her as kith, as family. Whatever She gives us belongs to all the People, not just to a few with rank and title to enjoy it.>>

Vald pursed his lips thoughtfully as he surrendered his turn, unable to move his chosen row further. <<Yes, but then what is the motivation for advancement?>>

Daladir rolled. Two, three, four—a good roll. When the numbers came up consecutively, a player could choose any row and move a maximum of six pegs forward to the highest number on the dice. He went with the third row and moved the pegs into place. <<We don't generally measure success as Men do, Dreydmaster. We are linked to one another, and to the rest of the world, by bonds of kinship and history. To follow my own desires at the unthinking expense of others would be an act of gradual suicide, for those actions would always come back again to me. It's a philosophy of responsibility to all things, not just unfettered freedom for oneself.>>

<<Interesting,>> Vald purred. <<So it is not so very different from our laws of accountability: all Men must be held responsible for their actions. If you blind your neighbor, you must lose your eye; if your tongue speaks untruths, it must be cut away to purify your

mouth.>> His voice took on a subtle hard edge. <<If you steal from your host, you must lose something you treasure as well.>>

Daladir felt a trickle of fear creep down his spine, but a long smoldering rush of anger moved against it. <<The comparison isn't entirely apt, sir. One must always think of the higher good and balance, as in all things. The sightless life of the first Man is in no way improved by the blinding of a second, nor is the harm of falsehood ended by tormenting the liar. Instead, the wrongdoer in both cases should give of his service to those he's harmed, until such time as the measured harm is repaid.>>

Vald's gaze never left the board as he rolled the dice, but Daladir could feel the room grow colder. <<And what of the thief?>>

<<In this case, we must look to see if the property belongs to the one who claims it. Perhaps it didn't belong to him at all. Perhaps the one called a thief is doing nothing worse than avenging an earlier theft.>>

The dice bounced on the board: one, five, six. The Man moved five of the pegs in the first row forward six spaces, bringing the first to the single hole at the triangular end of the board. Another win for the Dreydmaster.

<<There is a great deal of supposition in that hypothesis, Ambassador. We cannot look too far into the past, can we? If we did so, would anyone emerge untainted by guilt? No. The only true justice is swift, certain, and unclouded by irrelevant complications. We cannot look to the ghosts of history for justice.>> He pulled the pegs out, one by one, and returned them to the other end of the board. <<Shall we play another, or would you like to end this game?>>

Daladir smiled grimly. <<Let's play.>>

The first thing that Tarsa noticed when she crossed the curtain of water was the sudden, overwhelming silence. She looked back. The water still crashed down in roiling waves, but the only sounds that the young Wielder could hear were the slow and steady drip of water down the cavern's walls and the echo of her own ragged breath. The air nearly crackled with *wyr*-fed vitality.

Tarsa examined her strange surroundings. She stood in a wide tunnel that stretched into the far distance, its end unseen in the bright blue phosphorescence radiating toward her. A deep stream of the glowing water snaked down the center of the cavern's floor. The walls and roof were etched with strange sigils and shapes of curled, creeper-like tendrils and sharp-angled symbols, but the floor on either side of the tunnel was undecorated and worn smooth from ages of traffic. The flickering sunlight through the waterfall flashed like silver scales across the walls of the cavern, dazzling her eyes and making her slightly dizzy.

She thought of turning back for a moment, but the light beckoned her away from the silver-white radiance of the waterfall. There was nothing menacing here—of that fact she was absolutely certain—but fear still gnawed at her chest. Whatever lay beyond the end of the tunnel existed outside of anything she understood. There was a rising anticipation in the air that sang in chorus with the bloodsong throbbing again beneath her skin.

If she continued now, there would be no turning back; she would never be free of the touch of the *wyr*, not even in death.

This was the threshold. The Stoneskin's song had laid bare her spirit, but she'd never fully chosen this path: not when she followed Unahi and Tobhi into the mountains, not when she faced the ravaged results of her early Wieldings, not even when she'd slipped into the *wyr* currents and drew herself into the Spirit World and its ways. Unahi's teachings over the past few weeks had helped Tarsa learn to still the bloodsong enough so that it wouldn't completely overwhelm her; she had nearly finished her chanting-sash, which brought further calm. The ancient patterns of the wide woven band held stories and songs of great power, and when she recounted them in her mind, they shifted her consciousness away from herself to the voices of the world around her. They gave strength to her spirit.

She now had what she needed to survive, if not to thrive. She could always step away and return to the warrior's ways she knew and loved, the ways that had long been her refuge and her only dependable strength. If she continued on this path, the life she'd known would become something else entirely.

Tend to your roots. Tarsa stood at the mouth of the tunnel. She remembered very little of her mother, more feelings than images.

Even the stories that Geth and her other aunts had told her throughout her youngling days were indistinct, the trailing edge of memory
rather than any tangible remembrance. But when Unahi had spoken those four words and shared her own memories of Lan'delar,
Tarsa's heart had warmed with recognition, with the touch of light
and laughter. Her mother hadn't abandoned her through death. Those
roots ran far deeper than she'd thought.

*This is my choice now. It isn't given by force or someone's idea of destiny.
What I become is freely chosen.* Her thoughts returned to the sight of
her lifelong community as they threw her into the Burning Mouth,
visceral fear stark on their faces as the next wave of desperate power
flowed through her writhing body. It hadn't mattered whether they
were kith who'd watched her grow from shy seedling to strong warrior, or lovers who'd shared moist, warm pleasure with her in the welcoming darkness. To them, she was now a monster out of unwanted
stories, and they'd never see her in the same way again. As Unahi
had explained not so long ago, there would never again be a welcome
for Tarsa'deshae in Red Cedar Town, for, with her Awakening, the
youngling Namshéké had gone forever.

Tarsa cast one glance back at the waterfall, then at the azure starshine beyond. For a moment longer she hesitated, but it was only for
the space of a heartbeat.

"Yes, Mother—I go rootward." She stepped boldly down the
tunnel.

She walked on the left side of the swift stream, where the footing was firm and dry. The blue radiance bounced off the water and
walls to break into a thousand glimmering shards, but by this time
her eyes had adjusted, and she could see the tunnel's features more
clearly. The symbols on the walls continued on like a stone tapestry.
Tarsa recognized a few of the more common images, mostly those
doublewoven geometrical designs that were often beaded onto or
etched into ceremonial regalia, but most of the symbols were strange
to her. On occasion, a shape would emerge that resembled a living
creature—an odd combination of snake, stag, eagle, and panther, or
other strange hybrid Beast—but most of the designs were distinctly
stylized, although always rhythmically organic. The stream cut a
deep swath through the stone, the natural result of an ageless flow.

She stopped once to peer into the water but stepped away with a start when she could see no bottom through the clear depths.

As she neared the end of the tunnel, Tarsa heard a soft, low rustling in the distance, a gentle pulse on the air that sent sudden tremors through her sensory stalks from wave after wave of pure, unbound *wyr*. She stopped and clutched at the damp wall, gasping from the intensity as the sensual charge throbbed through her body, trailing down through every hair and length of flesh. Her entire body trembled with awareness, and she let the feeling wash over her for a long time, until her body grew accustomed to the rhythmic sensation. Tarsa had never known such a wholly energizing power, not even in the depths of her bloodsong frenzy. It cleansed the body and unraveled the tension that coiled around her consciousness.

The light beckoned her on, and she stepped into the blinding blue. All she could see and feel lay beyond that blazing brilliance, now azure, now cobalt, flowing into hues as bright as the daytime sky, as deep as midnight's mantle. She moved forward, eyes streaming, and felt a voice in her mind, low and rich, untouched by the heat of life.

"None may look upon the Tree without a true face."

The light dimmed. Tarsa blinked and squinted. Her eyes slowly adjusted to see two worn and moss-thick standing stones, each looming tall above her and carved with the rough representation of a scowling Kyn face, flanking a brown path that disappeared into shadows. The stones glowed with a soft light of their own, but all else was darkness. Between the stones stood a short, bowlegged creature less than half the warrior's height. Its limbs were thin and lanky, shining red-brown like polished cherry wood. Tarsa couldn't tell anything about the creature's face, for it wore a thick wooden mask that somewhat resembled the wide-mouthed images on the standing stones. The mask was painted brightly in red, black, blue, and white, with strips of animal fur glued onto the surface to resemble facial hair and eyebrows. The creature's bright eyes gleamed in the light of the stones. Its green hair was unkempt and flowed wildly down its back and over the edges of the mask. In its right hand, it held a thin stick topped with a rattling gourd and various small bird skulls, feathers, talons, and pierced fragments of polished turtle shell strung together with rough twine.

The creature pointed its stick at the she-Kyn and rattled it. Tarsa felt the voice again. *"None may look upon the Tree without a true face."*

"I don't understand," she said. "This is the only face I have." Her voice sounded muted and hollow in this shadowed place.

"You must have a true face. You must be honest in your choice."

Tarsa looked around. The tunnel gaped dark and empty behind her, but she gave no thought to going back.

"How do I choose my face?"

The figure shook the stick in a wide arc. The rhythm of the rattling gourds matched Tarsa's bounding heartbeat. *Shukka-shukka. Shukka-shuk. Shukka-shukka. Shukka-shuk.* The creature turned around and around, lifting its feet high and bringing them down hard to the ground again, spinning slowly, moving faster and faster still, until it jammed the end of the stick hard into the ground. Tarsa cried out as thousands of glowing faces burst from the darkness like a horde of hungry ghosts. She stumbled back toward the tunnel, but she stopped as her outstretched hands moved toward the dark opening. The tunnel was still there; she still had the choice to leave. She looked back to the standing stones and saw that the shapes weren't ghostly faces at all but masks of all kinds. Some were made of thin sheets of gold and silver, others of heavy clay, still others of rough wood, hornets' nests, beaten copper, thick cloth, leaves, or feathers. Everywhere she looked the masks stared at her, an arching curtain of empty faces watching from the darkness.

"To see the true Tree you must wear your true face."

The young Wielder's head swam. There were so many. How was she supposed to choose the right one among them all? How would she know which one was hers? She turned to the creature, but it offered nothing else as it stood looking at her with dark, shining eyes.

Tarsa looked back at the curtain of masks floating in the shadows. She would never be able to decide—not this way. She thought for a moment. "The eyes deceive when the will overwhelms thought," she whispered, remembering Oda'hea's advice during her early days of Redthorn training. The older warrior had said these words after Tarsa's fifth failed attempt to hit a water-filled sack target that swung from a tree branch. The younger she–Kyn's impatience had lost her both the lesson and Oda'hea's praise . . . but only until she'd returned the next day with firmer resolve and determination to defeat the other hopeful initiates and even Oda'hea herself, much to the older she-Kyn's pleasure.

Tarsa closed her eyes. One of her hands rose into the darkness; the fingers of the other traced along the knotted pattern of her chanting-sash. She felt her spirit grow lighter in the space between that touch and the guided bloodsong, and she drew her thoughts away from herself and into the medicine songs that were wrapped in the fabric. The stories within those songs came free, and the young Wielder felt a sudden rush of mingled fear and peace flow across her body. She felt herself fading for a moment into something greater, and the thought both thrilled and frightened her. The only barriers to the *wyr* in this place were stubborn flesh and spirit. She pulled those walls aside and let the *wyr* course unchecked through her consciousness, again feeling that wondrous tingling flow through her flesh, hearing the spirit-voices whisper beyond sound to the very core of her being. The voices throbbed with her blood, riding deep in crimson currents, drifting with unbidden ease from heart to hands and beyond.

The sound of a soft gourd rattle threaded its way into her awareness, and she felt herself returning from the *wyr*-flow to her tender flesh. Her skin tingled still. She held something in her outstretched hand.

"You hold your true face. Wear it now, and you will see the Tree as it is, as it was meant to be."

Without opening her eyes, Tarsa lifted the mask to her face. It was light and made of wood, with a soil-deep spice to it, but it felt unadorned and unmarked, little more than a rough strip of wood with holes for eyes and mouth. She didn't hesitate. As the mask touched her skin, a tremor went through her body. Something opened up and flowed free inside her.

The rattling stopped. Tarsa opened her eyes and touched her face. The mask was gone. Her skin was different; her forehead and cheeks felt strange, almost numb.

A sudden shift in the light drew the Wielder's attention away from the sensation, and she turned again to the standing stones. They were as before, but the little creature with the gourd rattle was gone. The path was clear, bathed now in a soft green light, like sunshine through a leafy curtain.

The path back to the waterfall was open as well, but she gave it no thought. She wouldn't leave now, not until she had done what she came to do. She walked between the great mossy stones.

Although she'd entered the hollow cliff face and stood now in a tunnel, she could see no sign of being underground. Above, beneath, and all around her was night sky unlike any she'd ever seen. There were thousands of brilliant stars in a firmament as deep as midnight. Dozens of blue, purple, red, golden, and silver moons and planets hung like shining jewels in the darkness. Comets blazed both far above and below the Wielder, their streaming tails shimmering into stardust as they passed. There was no end to the heavens on any side of her. Tarsa looked into endlessness, yet felt no fear or hesitation. The trail beneath her feet was soft moss and wildflowers floating in the night, the air rich with the light, earthy fragrance of spring rain.

Standing tall and ageless before her, growing green from the center of a gleaming blue lake, stood the Eternity Tree.

Ever after, when her thoughts would return to her first visit to the Tree, Tarsa would never be able to fully describe the sight. But then, no mortals ever were. The Tree didn't fully belong to the ways of the Melded world; it was a remnant and reminder of the Elder Days, a living symbol of the bonds between the Folk and the land from ages past, when all the Eld Green grew wild and whole, when life stretched past forever. What she saw was the Eternity Tree at its closest point to the Folk between the present and the past. It was larger than it seemed at first, or else it changed its size according to whim or purpose, with wide-spreading silver branches that disappeared into the heavens, boughs reaching past sight above and beyond her. She didn't know whether she'd walked to the Tree or whether the Tree had found her. All she'd later remember was that one moment she stood at the stones and the next she stood by the shining waters floating in eternal night.

Tarsa felt again as she had when she reached for the mask. There was no room for what she knew as Tarsa'deshae or even Namshéké here; everything she was, everything she took such pride in, faded to nothingness in the Tree's presence—she was small, insignificant, fleeting. Her fire was doomed to fade, but the Tree would continue. Her mind pulled back, but her body no longer responded to her will, and, before she realized what she was doing, she stepped forward into the water and felt it caress her body. Her clothing dissolved; there was no barrier between her flesh and the rippling touch of the water. The pool was deep and warm, and she was a good swimmer, so she dove down and let the waters embrace her worn and battered body, bruised in flesh and spirit, the pain now eased beyond any expectation or even hope. She opened her eyes and saw undulating flashes of silver light shimmer through the waves. Rushing upward, she surfaced with a joyful shout. The air was afire with energy, like a new-birthed storm, but she felt no more fear or shame. She swam easily toward the Tree, cutting through the water like an otter, and there looked upon it with awe.

The Wielder couldn't identify the color of the Tree's bark—there didn't seem to be a word to describe it. It was neither silver-blue, nor grey, nor green, but a shifting marriage of the three, sometimes distinct, sometimes blending together as one. The bark itself didn't remain constant either but changed from the craggy roughness of spruce, with streaks of blue light shining through, to the smooth and silver silk of aspen or wyrwood red-gold. Every time her eyes seemed to fix the Tree, to define it in some way, the image changed, swirled, and twisted out of known description to become something else entirely, to tempt her away from expectation. It rose far above her, its branches stretching out wide over the horizon; only the brightest stars shone through the canopy.

The leaves, too, defied Tarsa's mind, but she turned her thoughts from grasping the Tree and instead sought only to observe, to allow the Eternity Tree to exist beyond the limits that her mind would impose. The leaves were of all seasons and none. The burning red, brown, and orange of autumn flared amidst the young green of spring-born morning, and these mingled with ageless silver, copper, brass, and gold. The Tree was of all species, all forms, all genders and none, but each image was unique in its way, and each leaf grew large and lush, wild beyond living memory, as tendrils of endless generations of ivy wrapped themselves around the great trunk and branches, dipping deeply into the waters that lapped against the wide and reaching roots.

Tarsa's head spun from the heavy scent of earth and wild undergrowth, the deep embrace of rooted life. The stars could just as easily have dangled from the branches as from the sky, for the leafy canopy glimmered with the light of thousands. Sapphire and emerald fire danced on the leaves, across the branches, down the trunk, but no smoke rose into the sky, no char remained after its passing. The flames slid across the water and Tarsa's skin and hair, and, though it gave no heat, her flesh thrilled at the touch. This was *wyr* as it was meant to be. It burned with the rushing brightness of life.

A soft wind rustled through the leaves, sending its whispers in unknown tongues through the world, to bring precious pain to those whose hearts could still know longing. The whisper wound its way around the Wielder, lifting her soaking hair around her trembling shoulders, and she wept to hear the sound, for in that gentle rustle sang the voices of the Ancestrals, all the Folk who'd gone before her, heroes and traitors, friends and family, the loved and the forgotten. Tarsa floated in the warm water's embrace and heard, at last, her mother's honor song among the chorus. These voices were the heartwood of the Eternity Tree, and of all the Everland: their memoried story was life incarnate, the abiding currents of green beneath skin and soil.

This flame burned within all that was of the Everland, within the Folk and all that they honored and guarded. The Kyn were more than just the children of Zhaia, the seedlings of the Eternity Tree: they were the living embodiment of the Tree itself. Only through them did the Tree blossom fresh and fertile; only through them could it give life to the Everland and to the memory of elder days. Tarsa realized that she wasn't insignificant—she was part of something far greater than she'd ever imagined. The sacred word-fire—the *wyr*—burned brightest here. And in that endless night, in the healing waters of the Eternity Tree, far from the memory of Men and the shadows that crouched on the borders of the Everland, Tarsa sang and laughed and wept anew, mourning the pain of the past and singing into life the dawning world, adrift within the endless ebb and flow of the *wyr*.

When, far into the deepening night, Tarsa emerged naked from the tunnel and walked slowly past the waterfall, Unahi and the other members of the Wielders' Circle stood waiting for her, soft torches sending flickering light across their smiling faces. With Unahi were eight other Kyn Wielders, including the venerable Braek the Older, the eldest of the gathering, and the militantly traditional Sinovian, little older than Tarsa, who even now barely contained his contempt for the shining grandeur of Sheynadwiin. Biggiabba was the eldest representative of the Gvaergs within the Circle, and she held the trust of her people. She and a trio of shorter deep-rock Gvaergs, two male and one female, stood wrapped from head to foot in their wyrweave cloaks. Tarsa's eyes widened when she was introduced to Athkashnuk, the serpentine and antlered Wyrm whose multicolored bulk spread out like a molten rainbow of fire far beyond the confines of the waterfall. More figures stepped forward to meet her: four Tetawi Wielders, the mushroom-shaped Oakman Grugg and his shy daughter Mim, and assorted Ferals—including the famed Uru Three-Claw, one of the bear-faced folk who inhabited the rocky narrows of the Kraagens; the standing-fox Ryggin; and Ixis, the aerie-mystic of the reclusive eagle-bodied Harpies.

The Tetawa healer Jynni Thistledown stepped forward to congratulate the new Wielder, and beside her was Tobhi, his shapeless brown hat in his hands, his round face beaming with pride. Unahi held a long, trailing cloak of white swan feathers and red wyrwood leaves sewn cunningly together, and this she draped over her niece's wet and shivering form. It would be Tarsa's cloak of passage; she'd seen the Tree's true form, felt the sacred fire, and knew at last the Heartwood of the People. Her voice would be for understanding, whether in war or in peace, and the good of the Folk would stay utmost in her thoughts.

Tarsa's body still glowed with the light of the Tree, and, while this would fade with the dawn, the new azure sigils on the young she-Kyn's flesh would remain a sign of her true face and matured Awakening: two rows of small dark circles on each temple and down both arms and legs, three blue claw marks that stretched across each cheek, and an angled slash beside a bright ring between her brows, the same symbol that now shone on the foreheads of all the Wielders, and which Tobhi and Tarsa had once seen on the Governor's seal one night a lifetime ago in Nine Oaks Town.

Unahi straightened the cloak and stepped away, and old Biggiabba gently placed a garland of juniper berries and green aspen leaves in Tarsa's hair. They turned with the reborn she-Kyn between them and offered her to the People. A shout of applause rang out from Tobhi and the gathered *wyr*-workers, who rushed forward to embrace Tarsa and welcome her to the Council. They presented her with new wyrweave clothing, bracers, and other gifts, then led her to the great longhouse, where a rich feast awaited them.

It was a joyous night, for the Redthorn Wielder had come to Sheynadwiin.

12

Gatherings

MARKET DAY WAS GENERALLY THE HIGH POINT of every sevenday for Quill, but lately little lifted the pall from Spindletop. The Dolltender pulled her thick shawl tighter around her shoulders to drive out the cold of the morning mist. The deep-bone chill of autumn often clutched at the woods these days—it hardly seemed like the start of high summer at all. She shifted her river-cane basket on her hip to balance the weight of the small honey crocks inside. On the path ahead stood a couple of other *firra* who waited patiently for her.

"*Shoya*," Quill mumbled in greeting. Her cousins smiled. Gishki, whose short black hair glistened even in the dull and misty morning, carried a long sheaf of high-marsh tobacco, dried and wrapped in thick paper. Medalla, a quiet *firra* who stood a head taller than the others, held a long, curved stick in one hand, from which hung three dozen small ears of red-kerneled corn, tied together in thick bunches with brightly colored ribbons. Both were bundled up for the cold, but neither fussed as much as the Dolltender.

"What a wretched morning." Quill held out her hand to show a couple of swollen red bumps on her palm. "Even the bees are unnerved by this weather. Summer, indeed."

Gishki chuckled. "You can't very well squeeze the honey out of 'em, Quill."

The Dolltender swatted Gishki's arm playfully, but her mood went sour again, and she sighed. "Do you think we'll hear anything today?"

Medalla shrugged. "Maybe. Things are changing awfully fast these days. I'm just hoping for good news this time."

They continued walking in silence. The news from beyond had been troubling for much too long. Settlements burned to the south, travelers ambushed, boneyards looted, trade disrupted. *Fahr*, both elder males and striplings, had gathered together to patrol the roads in the four-settlement district, and, although they had thus far encountered nothing more dangerous than an orphaned bear cub, they continued their walks day and night. Everyone felt the tension, especially after Bryn's gruesome murder. Something unwelcome still lingered on Spindletop's borders. Sometimes the hair on Quill's arms would stand up in alarm, like the tingle in the air preceding a storm, or she would wake in her root-framed bed, gasping and quivering with fear, and watch the shadows scatter in the darkness outside her window.

The moundhouse cabins of Spindletop were thinly spread throughout the windswept Terrapin Hills and, in some places, even among the sparser reaches of the Edgewood itself. Quill's family home was on the eastern edge of the settlement, beside a gnarled and massive oak that stretched its heavy bulk around her squat little cabin, but even there she was only a brief, brisk walk to the nearest neighbor. Gishki and Medalla lived with their husbands, brothers, sisters-by-marriage, and father—Quill's maternal uncle—in some of the adjoining cabins; they were the core of Spider Clan in the region. This was the common way of Tetawi settlements: families lived with one another or close by. It was a bit unusual that Quill didn't share her home with anyone, but it wasn't unprecedented, especially for a *wyr*-worker; if she would have even wanted to live completely apart from her Clan, she would have been considered eccentric, or worse, for witches were known to be particularly antisocial.

The well-worn path to the trade center and ceremonial mound of Spindletop meandered through the tall, tree-scattered hills that dotted the southwestern reaches of the Everland. The trail wended its way across the marshy bottoms beneath the hills, and it wasn't uncommon to see deer and the occasional sage-hungry hill antelope grazing on the thick grasses that grew in the rich red earth of the bottom lands. Grouse, turkeys, rabbits, and well-fed grizzled foxes made their homes among the trees, but the *firra* were the only creatures on the path this morning.

At least, that was their assumption before a massive shape darkened the fog in front of them.

Medalla saw it first and held out her hands to either side, abruptly stopping her companions. Quill opened her mouth to protest until she, too, saw the shadow move through the thickness, and she swallowed her retort. The morning light was in their favor; they hadn't been seen. Gishki glanced nervously to her left and led them toward a tight thicket of willows off the trail, taking care to walk as swiftly and silently as possible. The grass was wet and the air heavy, so their movements were veiled, but all nervously watched the mist for any sign of pursuit. Quill's heart throbbed painfully—she wondered how the shadow could possibly fail to hear the raging beat, as the noise was nearly deafening to her own ears.

She'd seen that silhouette before, and it was unforgettably etched upon her memory. It was the shape that crouched outside her moundhouse in the darkness, watching and waiting. It was young Bryn's killer, the creature in her vision that had torn out the cub's heart.

The three *firra* crouched in the thicket, hands clasped together, their fearful breath held as much as they dared, as they watched the murderer's bulk move closer. It was huge and Man-shaped, at least three times Medalla's height, but thin and gangly. Its movements were awkward, jerky, with a strange, choppy hop, like a buzzard stranded aground. And the noise it made was hideous. Quill nearly cried out as a bubbling, deep-throated gurgle echoed eerily in the mist.

Medalla squeezed Quill's hand tightly, almost painfully. The Dolltender looked up. The haze was lifting in the warming sunlight, and it was lifting too quickly for them to escape to safety unseen. The shadow still stood on the road, its head bobbing carefully, a sniffing sound muffled in the murk. It was searching for them.

The *firra* glanced fearfully at one another. *I should have brought the dolls*, Quill thought desperately. Then she remembered—old Pinchface, one of her granny's dolls, had tried to talk to her shortly before she left, but the Dolltender had been in too much of a hurry to meet up with Medalla and Gishki to pay much attention. She gritted her teeth. *It's a little late to be worrying about what I should've done. I've just got to figure out a way to . . .*

A beam of sunlight cut through the grey veil, followed by others. *The fog's breaking up!* Quill could barely hold down the scream. She couldn't see the creature's features yet, but it wouldn't be too long.

There was a crackle of frost-rimed grass by the trail: the monster had seen the willow thicket. It was heading toward them.

Then, muffled in the haze but still distinct, came the low sound of Tetawi voices in the distance. Panic clawed at Quill's throat. She wanted to scream, to call out to the *fahr*, but all she could see was the dark figure moving closer, its gibbering growl shifting toward intelligible, almost familiar speech. Her mind raced to make sense of the burbling noise as a flash of sunlight shot into her eyes, dazzling her before it disappeared again into the mist. The Dolltender bit her tongue until the salty tang of blood bubbled up in her mouth. Her head spun.

A hand stretched out from the fog. The fingers were long and moist, almost translucent, each as long as Quill's forearm. The blue-black veins under the flesh pulsed with an irregular rhythm. It was nothing like a heartbeat, but its movement captivated the young *firra* in spite of the terror that drove through her belly like an icy spike. Dirt-caked fingernails twitched as they moved ever closer toward the thicket. The world went silent. Even Quill's heart seemed to stop beating. All she could see were those grasping fingers stretching out.

The voices grew louder. The shadow hesitated, uncertain. It splashed through the boggy growth near the thicket, then stopped and listened. Quill thought she had the briefest glimpse of pale white flesh through the fog, but then strong Tetawi hands wrapped around her arm and dragged the Dolltender to her feet.

"Run!" Medalla hissed, as she pulled Quill behind her down the road. There was no attempt at silence now as the shape erupted into pursuit. Medalla slipped onto one knee, the fall jarring the stick from her hand, but she was up again in a moment, dragging Quill with her. Gishki ran ahead of them, her voice calling for aid. A heavy, slavering grunt filled the air. Quill wanted to look back, to fully see this creature that rushed through mud and reedy pools, but she could only run until her sides burned like fire and each agonized breath tore through her lungs. The fiend wasn't just hunting at random: it sought something that had evaded it before.

The Dolltender had little doubt what it was after. It wanted *her*.

Gishki led the way, calling out to the voices. A half-dozen well-armed *fahr* emerged from the vapor, wide-eyed but at the ready, spears and strung bows in hand. "Behind us," Gishki gasped, grabbing a farming sickle from one of the younger *fahr*. Medalla peered through the dwindling mist, her sharp eyes taking in every strange shape and shadow. Quill looked around in terror, clutching her basket tightly to her chest.

They stood together, tense and unmoving, until the fog vanished in the sunlight. The stalker was gone. Quill told them of her vision, and the others muttered amongst themselves.

"We should tell the Clan mothers," Medalla said at last. "We'll all have to arm ourselves now."

Perwit, one of the elder *fahr* in the group, handed her a short bow and fringed quiver. "No one should walk alone. Keep friends and family close, 'specially you," he pointed to Quill, who nodded hesitantly. "We'll come back and look for its tracks; it won't get away for long."

"Come along, cousin," Gishki said. "You can stay in the big lodge with us for a while."

Quill was quiet all the way back to Spindletop as the warning spread throughout the settlement. Medalla and a couple of their older cousins stood waiting outside the Dolltender's moundhouse while Gishki helped her pack, even though they weren't going more than a few hundred steps. As they wrapped the dolls in cloth and placed them gently into a stout lidded basket, Gishki asked, "What aren't you telling us?"

"What do you mean?"

"Please, Quill—I'm no fool, you know. You've never been one for silence."

The Dolltender wiped the back of her hand across her eyes. "It's just . . . I don't often get lonely, even with Granny and my folks gone, but I've been feeling it more lately. I wish . . . well . . ."

"You wish Tobhi was here, don't you?"

Quill swallowed against the lump in her throat, but it remained lodged firmly in place. "He'd know just what to do. Nothing scares him. He grew up in the deep woods, and he's faced pretty much every kind of danger there is. He makes me feel like nothing could possibly go wrong in the world when he's near me."

The older *firra* shook her head, bemused. "Spidersilk save us, Quill—sometimes I'm amazed at you. Not long ago you followed your dolls into the Spirit World and drove that creature away before it killed the rest of those cubs, and you didn't so much as shiver. But now you're behaving like a kitten mewling at shadows. You can't expect your love-addled *fahr* to make you strong, Quill. You've got to do that yourself." Seeing the stricken look on the young Dolltender's face, Gishki sighed. "Do you know when Tobhi's supposed to return from the Council?" She frowned at Puckerlips, a sweet, down-haired doll whose dried apple lips were tightly squeezed into a perpetual kiss, as she handed it to Quill.

"No," the Dolltender shrugged. "Whenever it's over, I guess. But I do wish he'd hurry. I'm tired of being so scared all the time, and he's not afraid of anything. I don't care what you say, Gishki: he'd make everything better."

"To be honest, I en't never been so nervous in m' life," Tobhi whispered to Tarsa as the delegates to the Sevenfold Council filed together into the soaring Gallery of Song, its great walls melded seamlessly into the massive trunks of the ancient wyrwood trees that made the seven cardinal points of the structure. The Wielder nodded, her face pale. The leaf-and-feather cloak lay light upon her shoulders, but, as the significance of the gathering became clearer, it took on a greater weight. They were witnesses to a momentous event; in a very real way their future—and that of the Everland—depended on what happened here.

Tarsa had never seen such a grand structure before; its spacious expanse was crafted of the finest Wielded materials and was thus pleasing to the senses in ways that gouged and wounded wood and stone could never be. Hundreds of cushioned benches stretched from the floor of the amphitheatre to the rainbow-paned windows near the top, with fine, bold-patterned wyrweave carpets lining the walkways between them. The seashell half-dome remained folded back to allow free passage to starlight and fresh air, but brawny young he-Gvaergs sat ready at the winches to pull it closed when necessary. Everlights were scattered along the walls in sculpted sconces to drive away the shadows, sending out no heat or smoke to bring discomfort to the gathering.

The only open flame in the Gallery came from a large stone-lined pit in front of the Wielders' seats. Seven kinds of wood burned in the fire, their cleansing smoke curling over the twenty-eight *wyr*-workers and their closest allies. Many more Wielders should have been among them, but death and misfortune had followed the messengers from Sheynadwiin, and relatively few had survived to share their news with the remaining Wielders. This knowledge cast a heavy pall over the Circle. All those who'd celebrated Tarsa's remaking ceremony were present, along with a few others who were newly arrived. Some of the Wielders were not of the Eld Folk—including the Oak-folk, the Wyrm Athkashnuk, and Kidarri, a Jaaga root-worker—and had no official representation within the Sevenfold Council, but their voices joined those of the other followers of the Old Ways, and they watched the proceedings with as much concern as their Eld kindred.

The Shields sat directly opposite the Wielders. In contrast to the green vines and bright blossoms that adorned the seats of the Wielders' Circle, a gauzy, silver-colored curtain fell across this wing of the Gallery, veiling those behind it from the prying eyes of others but enabling them to observe the events without obstruction. Tarsa had watched many of the Shields before they disappeared behind their curtain, which was held aloft by tall silver poles that lined the wing. Whereas Wielders dressed for comfort, wearing few unnecessary adornments, the Shields left little flesh untouched by silver or silk, although it was unclear to Tarsa whether pride or humility dictated such coverings. Most wore long white robes with tight, lacy cuffs that shimmered in the warm glow of the everlights, fabric that caught the light and sent it dancing in prismatic brilliance, and they draped their arms and throats with silver bangles, bracers, rings, and collars. Few Shields allowed their hair or sensory stalks to fall free in the way of the Wielders; instead, they pulled both into ornate caps, often molded to resemble the rough outline of a crescent moon, or they bound them tightly into star-shaped arrangements with their stalks wrapped deeply into the hair. The Shield of Red Cedar Town had followed some of these practices, but his style seemed quite simple in comparison with his brethren in Sheynadwiin.

The central seats of the Gallery belonged to the scores of lower-level delegates of the First Folk. Most of the Seven Sisters were represented here, all but the Ubbetuk, who were expected at any moment. Even the rare and beautiful Wyrnach Spider-Folk had come to the Sevenfold Council. They stood taller than the massive Gvaergs but were slender and graceful, with six long-limbed arms beneath their ornate blue, gold, and black robes. Others, such as the Strangeling Jaaga-Folk of the open prairie-lands—descended long ago from inter-married Kyn and Men, and now a distinctive people in their own right—and a few trusted Human friends, had no official spokespeople but were welcomed along with the others. Scattered throughout the various wings of the Gallery were scribes and translators, including Tobhi, who had received his auntie Jynni's permission to assist Tarsa during the Council. Jynni, though a healer and *wyr*-worker, sat among the delegates in the central section. Here she was acting as the elder speaker of Bristlecone Hollow, one of four small Tetawi communities in the Terrapin Hills.

At the northern end of the Gallery stood the empty Speaker's seat, a striking synthesis of sweeping stone and wood formed into the shape of a butterfly in flight, flanked by two giant doors that led into the chambers of the Governor of the Kyn Nation. A massive table, smoothed and shaped from the trunk of a fallen wyrwood tree, sat in the wide space between the Speaker's chair and the assembly seats: this would be the council table of the leaders of the Folk, and this would be where most of the debate would take place. No one sat there now. The Council members were finishing their last discussions with their assorted parties before entering the Gallery.

"I've never seen so many Folk in one place before, Tobhi," Tarsa whispered in awe. "I suddenly feel very small."

He nodded. "I know what ye mean. But don't forget that this en't exactly common for anyone here. After all, this is only the fourth such Council since the Meldin', so we're in good company." He looked around. The dark, timeworn wood of the Gallery gleamed in the everlight glow, and all along the rafters he saw birds of every size and variety crowding and preening in the light, their bright eyes fixed on the proceedings below. More flew in through the narrow windows with each passing moment. In the more shadowy places were gathered bats, flying squirrels, and other night-flyers. Between the delegates in the chamber, all along the benches and aisles, gathered all manner of Beasts—from bumblebees and wasps, whispering moths and buzzing mosquitoes, to the tiniest shrews and mice, squirrels and toads, up to the largest of creatures, including proud moose and grumbling bears. None expressed any fear or scorn for the others here; even traditional enemies in the animal world honored the sacred law of peace that held sway in the Gallery and the city beyond. And it wasn't only the four-footed and winged creatures that gave their attention to the proceedings—the tall trees and small plants that grew untrimmed within the Gallery's walls also seemed to tremble in anticipation, as did the mountains and river beyond.

Tobhi's eyes misted over. All the peoples of the Everland stood assembled this night.

The Tetawa started to speak again, but he stopped when the doors flanking the Speaker's seat swung open to herald the beginning of the Sevenfold Council. A group of Redthorn warriors sitting together beside the seats of the Wielders' Circle struck a large upright drum, accompanied by two Tetawi shell-shakers and a chorus of Gvaerg chanters. The union of sounds and voices rolled together through the Gallery. It was a song of sadness, a song of defiance, a reminder of the ageless strength and endurance that had traveled with the Eld Folk through devastation and back again. Now was the time to sing again, to remind all gathered here just what their survival meant. The music grew louder as voices throughout the Gallery took up the chant; rattles materialized from traveling packs, joined by flutes, string-drums, fiddles, and all manner of improvised instruments. Even the great Wyrm Athkashnuk entered the song, hir undulating red-gold scales scratching in rhythmic time with the shake of the turtle-shell rattles.

First to enter were the eldest of the Folk, the Wyrnach of old, four blue-cloaked, six-armed siblings who had watched so many of their kindred fall to the ravages of the Melding. They stood beside their chairs, tall and gaunt, with glossy black hair that fell in silken waves to pool on the floor, while the rest of the delegates entered. As with the Kyn, Wyrnach eyes had no pupils or whites, but whereas those of the Kyn shone in many hues, the four eyes that shone out of the Wyrnachs' delicate, round features were deep red, like old rubies or cooling embers. The Spider-Folk wore their old grief like threadbare garments, but their faces still held a spark of love for the world and its peoples.

Four giant animals followed the Wyrnach elders, and their leader sent a ripple of admiration through the Gallery. He was Myrkash the Unbroken, a bearded bull elk of extraordinary size. While his great height and proud demeanor commanded attention, most eyes lingered on the two wide-branching racks of antlers that stretched out from the great bull's temples, each rack polished until it gleamed; the end of each tine was capped in delicately carved bronze from which hung long crimson tassels. Unlike most of his kind, whose antlers fell in the spring, Myrkash held his proud spread throughout the year, a symbol of his authority. All the Beast-people with him—an aged and scarred grizzly bear, an enormous, black-scaled rattlesnake, and a grinning mountain lion—were strong with wild musk, and Myrkash pawed at the floor and let out a long, shrill bugle upon his arrival into the chamber. The Beast-people in the crowd raised their voices proudly to welcome the great Beast-Chief and his companions.

The third group of Council members waited until the shell-like roof was raised to blot out the starlight to make their appearance. Three she-Gvaergs emerged from the shadows, their protective wyrweave body wrappings now cast aside to reveal helmets with golden spikes rising from their temples, craggy features, and wide, solid bodies in gleaming armor that flowed with the unsmithed grace of Wielded ore. The brutal smith's hammer and anvil were abominations to the Gvaergs; only the soft caress of a sanctified Wielder—a Hand of Kunkattar—was permitted to draw the shape of armor and axe from the Everland's precious metals, which the Gvaergs knew to be the sacred blood of their fallen ancestors.

But it was the figure who followed the she-Gvaergs that was truly a surprise to most of those gathered in the Gallery. Tobhi's astonished gasp joined those of others as Guaandak, the Emperor Triumphant of the Marble House of Kunkattar, entered the chamber, his beard of living flame burning bright against the smoky grey of his flesh. The only items of clothing he wore were a cap and scale kilt made of flowing stone and streaked with precious ores— the blood of Kunkattar, first father of the Gvaergs. He held a golden spear in his ring-encrusted hand, and this he stood beside his seat as he waited for the other Council members. Biggiabba bowed low at his entrance, and he bent his head in respectful response.

Tobhi leaned over to Tarsa. "He almost didn't come. Gvaergs don't generally care much for us *rijjik* unbelievers." A low grumble from Biggiabba, who sat behind Unahi, caused the old Kyn to turn a disapproving eye at the Leafspeaker. "Sorry," he whispered, blushing. Tarsa nudged Tobhi in the ribs and turned her attention back to the floor.

Four Tetawi followed the Gvaergs, among them Molli Rose, the brown-haired Spirit-talker of Victory Peak, who would be the primary voice of the Tetawi in the Sevenfold Council, and Tobhi beamed with unabashed pride as she stepped into the Gallery. Though barely over three feet tall and far more humbly dressed than the others, the famed seer, in her simple green homespun dress and brown shawl, was known and loved by many Folk across the Everland for her unbreakable devotion to her people and her unrelenting opposition to the rare but always destructive corruption among some self-serving Folk. She spoke plainly and without concern for diplomatic niceties; her concern was for truth and good sense, two things sadly rare in the world these days. Her presence brought deep joy to the Wielders; if anyone truly had the best interests of the Everland at heart and understood the links of spirit, law, and land, it was Molli Rose.

The Brood Mother of the North Wind Aerie, Kishkaxi, flapped gracefully to her perch at the table. Three massive golden eagles, each as large as Molli Rose, preened themselves beside the bare-breasted Harpy, whose wrinkled Woman's face scanned the crowd and nodded, ever so briefly, to Ixis, her brood-sister among the Wielders. Kishkaxi wore a circlet of shells, pearls, and beads on her stringy-haired crown and a tinkling abalone shell necklace around her thin neck.

"I've never seen such an unhappy face on any living creature in my life," Tarsa whispered to Tobhi. She almost wept when the Harpy's gaze passed over her. Such a depth of sorrow in those dark eyes. A cold chill crept over Tarsa's skin. It was said that the Harpies could sometimes see the future. If this was true, what did those sad old eyes see for this gathering?

The young Wielder's thoughts shifted back to the door as the harsh clang of a gong broke through the drumming. From the darkness emerged the Ubbetuk contingent, dozens of small, pale figures marching with practiced precision into the central aisles of the Gallery. Utterly hairless, with sharp-toothed grins and luminous eyes that seemed much too big for their round skulls, each wore a long-tasseled cap that marked his or her social rank according to color and fashion—Goldcap merchants, Redcap soldiers, Greencap mechanists, and the like. The Ubbetuk were the most removed from the Eld Green of all the Folk. They'd long ago surrendered their attachment to the *wyr* in favor of their hidden airborne cities and the earthbound lands of Humanity. Iron held no fear for them; indeed, over the past thousand years the Ubbetuk had become the most accomplished inventors and industrialists in either the Everland or the Reach of Men beyond. Steam engines, cloud-galleons, mechanical lifts and automatons, and all manner of exotic weaponry had emerged from the smoking Ubbetuk factories, and these creations had enhanced their reputation across the two lands. They'd also increased suspicions among Folk and Humans alike that the Ubbetuk Swarm posed a powerful and growing threat. The name given to them by Men—Goblins, for a race of mythical creatures who'd supposedly inhabited the Human lands before the Melding—seemed fitting to many, as it held a heavy note of disgust in its brevity.

It didn't matter that there were none who could rival the Ubbetuk in stately grace, social etiquette, and genteel manners, or that Ubbetuk had held little tolerance for greed, selfishness, or undue violence. The Swarm had no equal in the world of diplomacy or military strategy; many were the wars that had been lost because an Ubbetuk councilor's suggestions went unheeded, or the desperate battles won through Ubbetuk design. Yet common knowledge held that there was one unbreakable rule among the Ubbetuk, one that cast a shadow over their otherwise unblemished reputation: "The Swarm Above All." No one knew if or when that precept would be called into service, but many looked at the indispensable Ubbetuk councilors, strategists, advisors, and scholars in every corner of power throughout the Reach and the Everland, only to shake their heads in foreboding. Dark glances followed the brightly capped representatives as they threaded their way through the Gallery to take seats, blushing and apologizing for the disruption with their softly musical voices.

The last of the Ubbetuk to enter was the undisputed head of the Swarm, the Goblin Chancellor, Blackwick, one of the most feared and respected political leaders in the known world. He wore robes of the purest white that outshone even the luminous glow of the Celestial Shields. Around his neck stretched a broad white collar, like a ridged sunburst, and on his bald head sat a white cap inlaid with golden thread. He wore a fist-sized blue pearl on a long silver chain around his neck. His only other accessory was a long, wasp-headed walking stick carved from a single length of unknown black wood. His eyes, though surrounded by innumerable wrinkles, were clear and unclouded by age or infirmity. The Chancellor smiled serenely, revealing a mouth full of dagger-sharp teeth, and stepped to his own chair at the table with three Whitecaps of the Swarm's Ruling Council at his side.

The last to enter the Gallery were the Kyn representatives, and Tarsa's eyes widened when a familiar figure stepped up to the Speaker's chair. Three other Kyn, including a copper-haired she-Kyn Shield, joined the others at the massive table, while a fourth, the Speaker's zhe-Kyn consort, sat on a cushion beside hir lover's great butterfly seat. The young Wielder stared at the silver-haired Speaker as the realization sunk in fully. *The Pine Branch elder at the waterfall—the one who pointed me to the Tree—is the Governor of the Kyn Nation and the Speaker of the Sevenfold Council. Oh, Mother, if only you could be here with me now! The Old Ways are still strong in our people.* "There's nothing to fear now," she whispered softly, a thrill of pride rushing through her.

Yet the slightest tingle of discomfort clutched at her sensory stalks, for the Wielders belonged at that table rather than relegated to the audience, where they were separate from the doings of the Council. That the Shields had a representative at the main table was more troubling than she wanted to admit.

Garyn Mendiir lifted his hands into the air, and the drumming slowed to a halt. Everyone in the hall stood and faced the Speaker. For a moment all was silent, and then Garyn lifted up his voice, a deep, ageless timbre that echoed through the Gallery of Song.

"*Hanahé*, my kith—the deepest welcome and wishes for good health to you all from myself and all the Kyn Nation. May our gathering this night, and over the six nights to come, be filled with the spirit of peace and good judgment, and may the decisions we make bring benefit and peace to the generations that follow. *Hanahé!*"

The Gallery erupted in applause and shouts of *"Hanahé"* in response. Garyn waited a few moments for the noise to subside before motioning for everyone to take their seats.

That night was devoted to introductions and the first giving of gifts from the Kyn to the other members of the Council, to be followed by a similar ceremony each night of the assembly from the representatives of one of the other Folk. Tarsa noticed that each gifting brought a glower of disapproval from the Shield at the Council table, who had been introduced as Neranda Ak'shaar, one of the leading Lawmakers of the Kyn Nation. It didn't make much sense to the young Wielder that Neranda would be present, but Tarsa wanted to trust in Garyn's wisdom, and she knew too well that the complexities of this world of politics were still outside her experience. *He must have a good reason for including her among the Kyn delegates,* she told herself, and she tried to push the whisper of doubt from her thoughts.

When the first gifting had finished, Garyn turned to the Council members. "It is time to begin the Sevenfold Council. Remember, even in these changing times, that the old rules of council still stand strong: harmony above all, consensus at the end. Those who do not agree with the collective voice may do so without rebuke and without obligation, but they must stand outside the circle of rights, protections, and responsibilities at that time. Once consensus has been reached, after deliberation and discussion with those gathered here, the decision is made. If there is no consensus, the Council fails."

His shoulders sagged slightly, and a shadow of pain flitted across his face. "My kith, my friends, my people—this is our dilemma. We are faced with a decision unlike any other since the Melding, and this choice, like that ancient catastrophe, has been forced upon us by the greed of Men. We have been commanded to abandon the Everland."

A great uproar shook the Gallery as those gathered cried out their rage and anguish in response to Garyn's words; even the aching groan of leafy trees joined the throng. Tarsa's voice rose with the others, and Tobhi called out a battle trill. At the table, only pale Neranda and the Ubbetuk Chancellor remained composed.

Garyn raised his hands again, and the noise dimmed. "These are dangerous times in the Everland. The recognition of our autonomy, which once kept our lands safe, is no longer honored by the nations of Men, particularly the Iron Fist of Eromar, Lojar Vald, to whom we sent food and medicinals during the plague years. He has forgotten that kindness, or has chosen to repay it by threatening to steal our homes. Whatever his reasons, we have been given a choice: to surrender our ancient homeland in exchange for a territory to the far west, toward the setting suns, and some measure of gold and trade goods to reestablish ourselves in the new land, or to face the wrath of Eromar and its Dreydmaster. Vald's foundries are belching out black smoke in preparation for an invasion. Our scouts tell us that even the farmers of Vald's land have surrendered their plows for iron swords and armor." His maroon skin paled slightly, but his eyes burned like grey fire.

The cloak on Tarsa's shoulders seemed heavier as she considered Garyn's words. There was no outcry in the Gallery now. All sat in silence as the full significance of the Speaker's message descended.

"If any doubt the sincerity of Dreydmaster Vald's demand, look upon this." He nodded to a Redthorn warrior who stood beside the antechamber door. She exited and returned with a large covered basket that she placed on the table. Garyn reached down and pulled the cloth away to reveal three bloody Kyn heads, each branded with a jagged, three-tined mark on the forehead—the symbol of the House of Vald. A wave of shock shot through the Gallery. The Kyn gasped as their sensory stalks recoiled in agony; a few fainted from the swift and unexpected pain.

The Speaker breathed heavily, his jaw clenched, but continued. "These were three of our wisest elders, all of whom were part of the diplomatic delegation to Eromar City. Of the fourteen ambassadors who left for Gorthac Hall not quite a year past, only five remained three sevendays ago, and I greatly fear that none of them will return. This is a reminder, delivered to us on the eve of the Council by unknown hands, to make clear what Vald believes to be our choice: removal or death.

"You have been called to this place during these seven nights to decide, as the gathered Nations of the Everland, on our response to Dreydmaster Vald and his people. Will we surrender our homeland, or will we resist? Pain and darkness rule either path, but it is a choice we must make. This is the matter before the Sevenfold Council. This is the matter we decide."

13

The Folk Consider

DEBATE RAGED IN THE COMMON trade tongue through that night and would, after a few hours' respite, continue through the nights to follow. Though she often had to rely on Tobhi to translate some of the more esoteric terms, Tarsa was generally able to follow most of the discussion. That first night was largely devoted to a lengthy discussion of the increased conflict on the borders of the Everland; Myrkash, the Beast chieftain, told of small bands of Humans who had even reached the inner Kraagens on slaving raids. A pack of wolves and bears had devastated those bands and freed their hostages, but some of the slavers had escaped, and rumors crept into the forests and valleys of larger groups armed with weapons far more deadly than mere iron. Tobhi, Tarsa, and Unahi exchanged knowing glances at this news.

Blackwick, the Ubbetuk Chancellor, told of increased intolerance in towns and cities throughout the Reach, hostility that increasingly ended in the death or mutilation of Ubbetuk diplomats and merchants. It had become something of a favorite hobby for young Human thugs to kidnap an Ubbetuk and pierce one of his bulging eyes with a thin iron skewer. Blackwick recounted these horrors with stoic calm, but the air crackled when he spoke, and none doubted his outrage.

Debate of Vald's demand, which the Dreydmaster had euphe-
mistically titled "The Oath of Western Sanctuary," followed the
gruesome list of towns and settlements razed, Folk butchered and
violated, kidnappings, land theft, and torments almost beyond
telling. The Shields, and a small but vocal group of Celestial Kyn
delegates, stood firm on the side of accepting Dreydmaster Vald's
conditions and migrating to the western lands as the most sensible
choice for survival. Even the Wyrnach, the firstborn of the Folk,
leaned toward that choice. They were few, with no new younglings
in many years, and their hearts were heavy with loss. They wanted
no part in war or bloodshed; they wanted merely to withdraw and
remember times when they walked freely through leaf and shadow.
The most eloquent speaker for the Shields and their allies, Tarsa
soon learned, was the lovely blue-skinned Lawmaker who rivaled
even Garyn in her speaking skills and who, like the Governor, was
fluent in many languages, including the shared trade-tongue used at
the Council.

"We cannot pretend that rejection of this treaty will aid our survival in any way; if anything, it will merely strengthen Vald's resolve
to remove us by force. This is, to him, a purely domestic issue: our
resistance is an uprising of subject peoples, not the independent asser-
tion of liberty by self-governing nations. My Celestial kindred and
I understand the ways of Men, and we know the internal politics of
both Eromar and the larger Reach better than anyone here. As we
have already heard with heartbreaking clarity, the Humans are growing bolder with each passing day, and more of our people are falling
prey to the violence. How many more must we sacrifice before we
face the grim certainty of our present situation?"

Molli Rose stood up, her dark eyes narrow. "Maybe ye understand
Men a bit *too* much t' keep your judgment unclouded. What makes
ye think that this Man will honor his promises? Seems to me we'd be
givin' up an awful lot on the word of a thief and a murderer."

Neranda nodded. "Yes, it is a risk, but what is the alternative?"

Myrkash, the elk chieftain, snorted in his deep, hollow voice.
"We can fight. That's a good alternative, eh? Would you have us
give up our homelands without spilling the blood of the kith-killers?" A few wolverines, bears, and eagles in the main chamber cried
out in agreement.

Neranda turned a cold eye on the great bull elk. "Are we then creatures without any thought of the consequences of our actions?" A number of Beasts growled, but she continued. "We can fight, certainly, but there are far more Men than you can possibly realize. I have traveled beyond the Everland and seen the menace that the Humans pose. They breed like plague-year rodents, overwhelming the land, consuming all until the rivers go dry and the skies are choked with ash. They have four children to each youngling born among the Folk, and all are raised to hunger beyond need. There is no end to their growing numbers, no end to their greed, no end to their desire. Beasts who once roamed free in Human lands have learned to flee or die, and sometimes even flight is not enough to ensure survival."

The elk snorted in anger, but it was the Harpy Kishkaxi who responded, in a voice like claws scratching stone. "Thou art not the only one well traveled, blood-hair. We have seen much cruelty in the hearts of Men, and much treachery. Surrender promises naught but prolonged death and destruction." She settled back on her perch, her feathers puffed up in agitation, and cocked her head at Neranda. "T'would be best to strike while yet the fire burns in our hearts and leave no doubt of our resolve."

"Perhaps." The Ubbetuk Chancellor leaned forward. "And perhaps not. We should not dismiss the suggestion without considering its merits. What are the features of this land to which Dreydmaster Vald would have us move? Is it a territory that would be more defensible than the one we hold now?"

"*We?*" roared Guaandak, the Emperor of the Gvaergs. "Your people are hardly a consideration. You've surrendered your right to any voice in this matter. You hide in your hidden cities and deign to join us only when it suits your advantage. Only those who've not abandoned the first teachings to embrace the unclean ways of Men should have a place at this table. *Rijjik* do not belong here." His eyes shot to both Blackwick and Neranda, who returned his gaze without flinching. Guaandak's beard burned white hot, scorching the table. The Whitecaps with Blackwick shifted uneasily in their seats, but the Chancellor waved away their concern and the sulfurous smoke.

"My Gvaerg kinsman, we are not enemies. I am not advocating removal, nor am I advocating resistance. I merely believe that we should be fully aware of our options before making a decision that will affect everything we hold dear. And though it is true that the Ubbetuk have long traveled to other lands outside the Everland, this will always be our first home, and we hold nothing but love and respect for it. Please forgive me if my words offend; such was not my intention."

Guaandak glared at the Chancellor but, seemingly pacified, leaned back in his stone seat. Molli Rose turned back to Neranda. "There's a lot to think 'bout here," she said softly. "One thing we haven't talked 'bout is heavy on m' mind. Have ye never thought 'bout what the move will do to our old customs and traditions? They come from our kinship with the land, after all. What happens if we break faith with the spirits that abide in our most ancient home?"

The she-Kyn shrugged slightly. "That is hardly a matter of importance to this Council."

Molli Rose laughed. "'Course it is! What could possibly be more important?"

The tension in the Gallery thickened instantly. The old Kyn conflicts between Greenwalkers and Shields had often bled into the affairs of the other Folk. All eyes were upon Neranda. For only the shadow of an instant, a flash of unease crossed her powdered face, but it disappeared just as quickly, leaving those who saw the expression unsure of their eyes in the soft glow of the everlights.

"Luran will guide us, no matter where we go," Neranda responded with a smile.

"Really?" Tarsa called out from her seat, unable to restrain herself any longer. She'd listened to the Shield with growing impatience and chafed at the cold she-Kyn's condescending tone toward the plain-speaking Tetawa. The Council members turned to the Wielders. Most seemed unconcerned by the breach of protocol, but Neranda's face flushed with anger. "And what of those who aren't Celestials? Luran speaks only to the Shields, not to those Kyn of the Deep Green, nor to the other Folk. What do you say to us?" The young Wielder stood tall, her dark hair cascading down her back, eyes burning like winter lightning.

Tobhi grinned. He was always up for a fight, and nothing would please him more than to see Tarsa batting the strutting Shield around the table. It didn't look likely to happen, but it was a pleasant thought.

Neranda turned to Garyn. "With respect, Governor, please bring order to this situation. It is not the place of observers to interrupt these proceedings."

Garyn waved away her objection. "As the Shields are proudly represented at Council, it would be irresponsible to deny the Wielders the same right to represent the Kyn. She may speak . . . once."

Neranda nodded in acquiescence, but her lips tightened.

"Again I ask, what of those who do not follow Luran's way?" Tarsa asked.

All was silent in the Gallery. Neranda looked hard at the young Wielder. She hesitated for a moment longer, then said, "The differing paths of the Celestials and the Greenwalkers have too long divided the Kyn; in truth, each party must choose the path it wishes to walk. Yet it would certainly be both unfair and unwise to allow the unfortunate divisions among the Kyn to determine the fate of *all* Folk. Vald does not draw such fine distinctions; the danger of Eromar is hardly discriminating. The survival of *everyone* must hold precedence over the particular beliefs of any given Kyn. Such questions will do nothing but distract us from the true importance of the issue before us."

A number of Folk in the crowd nodded in agreement, but Tarsa shook her head. "If you honestly believe that, you don't know anything about the Everland, or about what's at stake. There's nothing more important than this question." She addressed the entire Gallery. "We belong to this land; its heartblood pulses through us, giving us strength and life." For the first time, she understood how deeply her encounter with the Eternity Tree had changed her. There was no longer any room for doubt or fear. She spoke with the strength of a Redthorn warrior, and with the understanding of a Tree-touched Wielder. "The bones of our ancestors are buried here; the Eternity Tree blooms in its soil. Our words and stories flow in its winds and waters. Our strength abides in the Everland."

Her voice rose through the Gallery. "Our lives are bound to this world, and its survival is bound to us. We belong to one another— life to life. If we abandon our responsibilities to our homeland, it will weaken, as will we. And we know what happens when Humans perceive weakness. You Shields may be deaf to the bloodsong, but you're still connected to the *wyr*. This is our home. This is our inheritance, our legacy. What could possibly matter more?"

The Gallery erupted in applause, from all but the silver-curtained wing where icy silence reigned. Unahi nodded approvingly to her niece. Even some of the Council members joined their voices in support of Tarsa's words. Garyn motioned to the drummers, and they pounded loudly on the drum to quiet the raucous crowd. Neranda sat back in her seat, face pale as the Greatmoon, her burning eyes fixed firmly on the Redthorn Wielder.

As the applause rolled through the Gallery, one of the golden eagles perched beside Kishkaxi erupted into flight and shot like a burning spear into the rafters, its keen eyes fixed on a black shadow that fluttered toward the partially open roof. Before anyone could stop her, the eagle extended her talons and slashed out in bloody fury. A collective gasp echoed through the Gallery of Song at this violation of one of the peace-city's most ancient laws, but the shock became anger as the shadow fell to the ground, changing from a twisting mass of raven feathers to a jumble of tattered black shreds of cloth covering a spindly, pale body no larger than a Tetawi cub.

"Witchery!" Tobhi whispered as the creature stood and turned, with hunched back, to glare upon the silent crowd. It looked like a wizened Human infant, utterly hairless, with seeping black holes gaping wide where once had been soft eyes. Dozens of tiny sharp teeth jutted out of a mouth too large for the head, and long, black-nailed claws glimmered in the light. The horrified Folk looked upon a Not-Raven, malevolent ghost summoned to the Human world by fell sorceries, brought to this strange shadow life for the sole purpose of unraveling secrets to share with its unknown master.

For a moment it seemed that the Not-Raven would speak, but the eagle dropped from above, talons extended, and smashed into the ghost-creature again. A burst of raven feathers scattered in the air. The eagle flapped upward, joined now by her two aerie sisters, and they circled around the wounded, fluttering ball of feathers and twitching flesh as the Not-Raven tried in vain to reestablish its shape. Again and again the eagles tore into the ghost, driving it farther back with each attack, until, with a furious simultaneous assault, they forced it into the Wielders' fire pit. The flames flashed a noxious yellow. A long wail of anguish erupted from the sickly blaze and pierced the shocked silence of the Gallery, but it lasted for only a moment, fading with the stink of burning flesh in the cleansing scent of the seven woods.

Garyn nodded at Kishkaxi and her eagle companions. "Our words have not remained unheard this night, but that is of little true concern, for there are no secrets in the Sevenfold Council. What we say is given to all; the honest do not fear our words." A rush of murmuring rippled through the crowd.

The Governor held his hands out to the Gallery. "Dawn approaches," he called out when the chamber grew quiet again. "We will continue this debate later, when our minds are firmly focused on the matter before us, and when the taint of witchery is no longer upon this hall. All delegates are released until dusk, when we will convene again." Garyn turned to his consort and whispered to the zhe-Kyn before following the Council members back through the doors to his inner chambers.

Most of the Wielders departed together. Tarsa joined them while Tobhi gathered up his charcoal and bark-paper. A shadow drifted over him as he stuffed his writing tools into his big satchel. Looking up, the Leafspeaker recognized the dark-haired zhe-Kyn who'd sat at Garyn's side that night. Tobhi hadn't seen many zhe-Folk; the only such Tetawa he'd heard about was a much-loved healer who lived not far from his home settlement. Neither male nor female, nor truly separate from either, the zhe-Folk walked between the worlds; they had strength unmatched by other Folk and were honored for it, at least among those who followed the Old Ways. Celestials tended to see the zhe-Kyn and other zhe-Folk as disturbing abnormalities, but their whisperings hadn't yet erased the place of the zhe in the Everland, though they'd done much to make the zhe-Folk less welcome in Sheynadwiin. This young stranger wore dark, finely woven wyrweave breeches and a knee-length jacket of midnight blue tied with a green sash. Hir dark knee-length hair was draped over one arm as zhe bowed low.

"*Hanahé*," the zhe-Kyn said. Hir voice was deep and gentle, like spring water over smooth stones. "I am Averyn of Ash Branch, a healer of Sheynadwiin and consort to Garyn Mendiir. You are Tobhi, the nephew of Jynni of Bristlecone Hollow?"

The Tetawa nodded and extended his hand, palm forward, in greeting. "Ye've helped m' auntie a few times with her medicinals. Glad we finally got to meet. Can I help ye?"

The zhe-Kyn held out a small cloth bundle tied tightly with a blue cord. "You are the one who has been teaching the ways of Sheynadwiin to the Redthorn Wielder?"

Tobhi nodded again, his eyes narrowing slightly. "That's me, too."

The zhe-Kyn smiled. "Molli Rose was right—you are most certainly the one we seek. I will look forward to speaking with you again soon. *Hanahé*." Zhe held hir fist to hir chest and left the Gallery.

Tobhi opened the bundle and pulled out a piece of birchbark paper. Holding it up to the light, he read the message, and his face went pale. He didn't move until the throbbing of his heart eased slightly, then he slid the paper into a belt-pouch, swept up his satchel, shoved his hat down on his head, and rushed up the stairs and out of the Gallery, his black braid blowing behind him. He gasped in alarm as a hand landed on his shoulder. He swung around to face Tarsa, who regarded him with concern.

"Sorry," he said, as he gathered his fallen satchel. "I guess I'm just a bit skittish after all them doin's in there."

"I understand." The young Wielder pointed toward a small crowd that was walking up toward the waterfall and the Eternity Tree. "We're gathering for breakfast soon; will you join us?"

The Tetawa shook his head. "Don't think I can." He showed her the package Averyn had given him.

She pulled out the folded paper but handed it to Tobhi after a glance. "What does it say?" As fluent as she was becoming in new languages, she still hadn't learned to read.

Tobhi swallowed thickly. "I'm goin' away, Tarsa. Garyn is sendin' a group to Eromar, to protect the last of the ambassadors before the Council's vote. I been asked to help bring 'em home."

14

Choices

"WHY WOULD YE WANT *ME?*"

Tarsa and Tobhi sat on plush raised platforms on the floor of Garyn's rooms at the Gallery House, clay mugs of honey-sweetened sassafras tea in their hands. The curtains were drawn. A few stone bowls smoldered with burning cedar branches, and the soft smoke curled through the large, wood-paneled room. Although Redthorn warriors stood watch outside, Garyn didn't want to risk another uninvited guest like the Not-Raven, and the cleansing scent of cedar was a sensible precaution.

Garyn and his consort, Averyn, sat next to the she-Kyn and the young Tetawa, but they weren't alone. Unahi, the Greenwalker Sinovian and his sister Jitani, Tobhi's aunt Jynni, and Molli Rose completed the circle. All were grimly quiet, but none more so than Tarsa, who'd been under a deep pall since Tobhi's announcement.

Garyn turned to the Leafspeaker. "Our people in Eromar are in danger, Tobhi. While officially the guests of Dreydmaster Vald, they are little more than prisoners, playthings that he destroys at whim. As yet, he still maintains the veneer of diplomatic courtesy—he claims that the dead ambassadors were assassinated by brigands on the road back to the Everland, branded with his sigil only to ensure their 'safe' return home. 'Collectors' would think twice before laying claim to the head of a Kyn thus marked. This is apparently his idea of diplomatic charity."

Sinovian barely managed to stifle a snarl. Tarsa looked at him. His hair was shaved in the old fashion, with only a long braided top-knot remaining between his twitching stalks; intricate honor markings emblazoned his face, arms, and bare chest. Great copper hoops hung from his stretched ear lobes; copper armbands, similar to Tarsa's own, wrapped around his upper arms. Sinovian wore an etched-shell gorget around his neck, another sign of his bravery and leadership skills. He was handsome, but a rage that bordered on hatred coarsened his features, making him more sullen than sensual.

His sister was entirely different. She was a striking beauty, with dark bronze skin, pine-green hair, and golden eyes that caught the dancing firelight. She wore well-traveled leathers and high brown boots, and a loose-fitting blouse that left little to the imagination. A stout scabbard hung low on her wide-buckled belt. But while her body was memorable, her uncovered head was even more so: where four sensory stalks should have been there were only two, wrapped tightly in copper bands. Jagged scars were all that remained of the others. Few Kyn survived a stalk slashing; few would want to. The sensory world was rendered intelligible by their stalks, and the thought of such a loss was sometimes enough to kill a captive Kyn. But this she-Kyn didn't seem tortured by her loss, for she smiled at the young Wielder and lowered her eyes shyly, almost playfully.

Tarsa caught her breath. Jitani's nearness was intoxicating. The sweet scent of the she-Kyn mingling with the cedar smoke made Tarsa's head spin, almost as much as did Jitani's lingering golden gaze.

Garyn's words brought Tarsa's blushing attention back to the discussion. "Yes—it is all pretense. Vald is toying with us while at the same time abiding by the letter of the laws of the Reach, which hold him accountable for the fair treatment of all ambassadors who visit his home. But that pretense will not last much longer. If the Council stands against Eromar, nothing will hold back Vald's fury, and those Kyn who remain at Gorthac Hall will die. I cannot allow that to happen."

He reached out and touched Tobhi's shoulder. "Vald is watching, waiting, preparing. The Not-Raven is surely not the only spy sent to observe the proceedings of the Sevenfold Council, and such Darkening-brood are only one threat. The hearts of some in Council, and in the Gallery at large, have turned in Eromar's favor. Though I do not believe that they will sway the entire Council, I fear a deep schism. Without a near-unanimous vote, we will find consensus nearly impossible, and the Sevenfold Council will have gathered for nothing.

"We have six days remaining before the Council votes on Vald's demand—six days for a small group of trusted delegates to travel the vast distance to Eromar, meet with our people there, and return to the Everland with them and all of the information that they have gathered from months of close observation. They have done their job admirably; now, it is time to bring them home."

Tobhi nodded. "They're spies, then?"

Garyn shook his head. "Not entirely. We have other allies, other ways of observing our enemies without putting our diplomatic envoys fully in harm's way. The ambassadors' first duty was to serve as the diplomatic voice of Sheynadwiin, but yes, they were also charged with learning as much about Gorthac Hall and the inner ways of Eromar as possible, in the hope that such knowledge could protect us when the Iron Fist closed. I had not thought that Vald would move so soon. But such is the way of Man's world."

"But I still en't sure why ye want *me* t' go," Tobhi said. "I en't a diplomat."

"No, you are not. But you are wise in the ways of the Folk, you speak the Reach-language of Men, and you are calm and brave in a crisis. We need someone there who will not draw suspicion; Sinovian is sending a follower of the Deep Green to keep attention focused away from the others in the party, someone who will be an overt symbol of our resistance." He pointed his chin toward Jitani, who nodded her head in assent. Tarsa's chest tightened.

"The time for trained politicians is past, Tobhi. We have already sent wise ambassadors—mostly Kyn, but some Tetawi and Ubbetuk as well—to the various ruling houses throughout the Reach: Eromar, Harudin Holt, even great Chalimor itself, and all that they have found is rejection, if not worse. The hearts of Men have turned against us, even among many whom we believed to be our friends. What we need now is someone who is devoted to the Everland, not to the promises made by Men, whose words have no more strength than dust. You have clearly demonstrated those qualities in your work with the brash young Wielder here." Garyn smiled at Tarsa, who weakly returned the gesture. "Yet it must be someone subtle, someone who might be overlooked as he goes about his business. There are none better suited to this task. And you come with the highest recommendation."

Unahi and Molli Rose both nodded, their faces grim. All knew too well the dangers Tobhi would face, but they also knew the risks for the Folk if the last ambassadors died without sharing what they'd learned in their many months at Eromar. There was no certainty that anything of value would be found, but the possibility was worth the risk. It was a thin hope, but it was something.

"I cannot command you to go," Garyn said. "Nor would I wish to do so. As all the Eld Folk are born into life with freedom, so, too, must we exercise our freedom throughout the days and seasons that follow. The power given to the Firstkyn is not the power of coercion; only courage and some measure of wisdom. I do not command this, but I ask you: will you go to Eromar?"

Tobhi looked at Tarsa, then to the others in the circle. Unahi's eyes were downcast. Molli Rose and Jynni smiled sadly at the young Tetawa. Sinovian and Jitani stepped away to a shadowed corner of the room to allow them some privacy.

"I'd talk with m' Clan mothers," Tobhi said. Garyn nodded, and the three Tetawi withdrew to another corner.

The Governor and his consort stood. "We will leave you to discuss this together," Averyn said, and they joined Sinovian and his golden-eyed sister. Tarsa moved to sit beside her aunt, who reached for the younger she-Kyn's hand.

"Do you think he's really going to go?" Tarsa asked.

Unahi nodded. "I do."

"He can't leave," Tarsa whispered. "He's the only one who has any time for me here."

Unahi's expression grew hard. "The world will have its way whether it suits our personal whims or not. Your time will come, but it's not now. Tobhi will do what's best, and so will you. Sometimes we've simply got to let life take its course. The Governor is right: Tobhi has the strength and the training to succeed where others can't. The knowledge these ambassadors hold could be Eromar's undoing, so we need them back home."

A sudden thought struck Tarsa. "I want to go with him. I want to help."

"No, I don't think so. It's much too dangerous." The firmness in Unahi's voice indicated that the discussion was over.

"I'm a Wielder, as much as you. Why shouldn't I go?" Tarsa asked, not trying to mask her anger.

"Enough!" the elder Wielder snapped. The others glanced over, and Unahi leaned in toward her niece. "This isn't a sprout's game, Tarsa. This is a matter of enormous importance to the survival of the Everland, and frankly, you are *not* ready. Leave it be."

"But . . . "

"I said, *leave it be.*"

Tarsa pulled away from Unahi, her face flushed with fury and humiliation. Bitter words pushed at her lips, but she knew better than to set them free here—she didn't want to add public disrespect of an honored elder to her embarrassment. Swallowing her anger, she turned to see how Tobhi was faring. Molli Rose and Jynni had gathered Tobhi into their arms, and all three wept.

He might not survive, the Redthorn Wielder thought suddenly, a hard knot of fear clawing at her stomach. *Even if he returns with the diplomats, there's no guarantee that they'll be able to do anything to stop the invasion. This might be the last time that he'll ever see any of us. They all know it, and they're afraid for him.* Her eyes darted to Jitani, who stood calmly beside her brother. *They could die in Eromar, far from the Everland.* Her own words at the Council echoed again in her mind. *"Our strength abides in the Everland." What will happen if they don't go? The remaining ambassadors will die, away from home, their spirits lost in the world of Men, their knowledge—perhaps our only real hope—lost to us.*

Tobhi wiped his eyes with the sleeve of his shirt and walked over to Garyn. "I'll go. When do I leave?"

Tarsa went numb at the words; she couldn't speak. She didn't understand why she was so attached to the Tetawa—she'd only known him for a few weeks. But he was one of the few dependable features in her life. He was the only one who listened to her with any real interest. He shared his stories with her; his family embraced her with a warmth she'd rarely known among her own kith. He was, she suddenly realized, the only real friend she now had. Unahi was family and generally kind, but she treated Tarsa as a sprout, not as a full-grown she-Kyn who'd proven her mettle both in battle and in her transforming encounter with the Eternity Tree.

No, Tarsa couldn't let him go to Eromar without her. She still had such need of a friend.

A second arrow whistled through the air, followed by many others; the surrounding trees popped and cracked like sap-rich logs in a fire. Vergis Thane hugged the ground as another missile smashed into the branches above. He trusted his weathered cloak and hat to make him nearly invisible in the undergrowth, and they seemed to be working well so far, but it was only a temporary measure—the damned Deermen knew he was there. But Thane had survived much more dangerous situations than this. Besides, they weren't likely to strike too carelessly for fear of injuring their spirit-weaver.

The Unhuman struggled against the Seeker's grasp. Thane drove his knee sharply into his prisoner's belly in response, and the trussed creature went limp. It knew well enough to refrain from crying out. Thane didn't believe in waste, but he wouldn't hesitate to kill the creature if it made itself a nuisance or threatened his own escape.

Thane listened carefully. There were at least a dozen armed Deermen in the trees, probably more, and certainly others on the way. Though little over four feet tall from hoof to antler, with the furred torsos of savage Men, mixed by some strange Unhuman witchcraft with the heads and lower parts of black-tailed deer, the creatures were fiercely defensive of their home grounds and of their kind. If Thane hoped to get away, this would be the time to do it, before the odds were more difficult to manage.

He reached down and pulled the little Deerman's face toward him, yanking hard on one of the creature's long ears. <<I don't know if you understand my words, but you'd better understand my tone,>> he whispered, his voice no louder than a sigh. <<If you cause me the slightest bit of trouble, I'll slice you from seed-sack to eyeballs and leave your guts for the buzzards. If you behave, I might consider taking that collar off you.>> He squeezed the iron band around the

Deerman's hairy neck. The creature gritted its teeth and whimpered as the increased pressure dug the metal deeper into the blistered flesh, but it didn't cry out. Satisfied that his intent was unmistakable, Thane turned his attention to their escape.

The Seeker and his prisoner lay crouched in a leafy hollow on the slope of a thick valley in the heart of the Everland. He'd followed the trails of at least five Fey-witches, but most of these hunts had faded to nothingness. It was as if the creatures had simply vanished. At one location, the ruins of a town within a massive stone bowl, he'd come across dozens of shrouded Kyn bodies on scaffolds and the remnants of a recent campsite. The stink of twisted power—Fey witchcraft— was heavy in this place, especially around a ravaged stand of disfig- ured pines. Whatever had happened here was still fresh, but the thin trail of the powerful Unhumans he followed had been swallowed up by the massive energies of death and destruction in the town.

He'd lost that trail but found others, a few of which had van- ished like the one within the stone ring, but some remained fresh. It was one of these that had brought Thane to the small band of Deermen and their wide-antlered Fey-witch. The creature had been injured before Thane arrived, and this made the capture that much easier: one leg was bound in a willow splint, and one tine of its noble antlers had been snapped in half. But these creatures were wily, and he'd barely managed to get his quarry out of the village before he and his prisoner were attacked by a large group of cloven- hoofed archers.

The Seeker slid slowly upright, like a patient rattler preparing to strike, until his ice-blue eye was clear enough of the undergrowth to scrutinize the terrain around him. Most of the stone-headed arrows had come from upslope, toward the creatures' village. Escape down- hill was the most direct route, but it was also the most dangerous, as Thane would be at a disadvantage and a clear target. He scanned the ridge again, and a thin smile creased his features. He might be a target, but he wouldn't be alone.

The sharp blat of a horn echoed upslope through the trees, fol- lowed by others on the left and right, quickening downward to cut off escape. This was the moment he'd been waiting for. Thane rolled over and spun his captive onto his back, then jumped up and raced down- hill, the terrified witch acting as a living shield from behind. The

Seeker held the creature over his left shoulder by its bound legs, while in his right hand he held his long knife. A few arrows smashed into the ground around his feet, but most of the archers restrained themselves, hesitant to strike at the Man for fear of hurting their kinsman.

A hairy shape rose out of the undergrowth before Thane with a heavy oak cudgel in its hands, but the Seeker drove onward, his blade shining like silver fire in the midmorning light. The club swept down, and Thane twirled around, shifting his weight slightly for balance as the cudgel smashed into his bellowing captive. He completed the spin to drive his knife into his stunned attacker's throat, slicing viciously to the side until it stopped short against bone. Kicking the blood-spurting body to the forest floor, Thane flew down the slope. The Fey-witch cried out in pain and horror, and they were surrounded again by armed Deermen, spears and clubs swinging. Thane never missed a step. As each weapon flew toward him, he turned his captive toward the threat, while sending blood splattering across the trees with his own knife. The creatures quickly fell away from the Seeker, and he was moving again, this time without pursuit. The battered Fey-beast over his shoulder shook with deep sobs.

Thane ran until he was certain that the hunt had ended, if only briefly, and dropped his prisoner to the ground. The Fey-witch groaned. Its face was battered and bloody; there were fresh wounds on its chest and a nasty gash on its upper thigh. Pulling some leaves and a flask of water from his pack, Thane chewed the leaves and washed the wounds, layered them with the leaves, and wrapped the most serious of them with coarse linen strips. He gave some of the water to the Deerman, finishing the flask himself.

<<I don't have either the time or interest to carry you. Remember what I said before: if you disobey me, you die. Now,>> he cut the bindings on the Fey-witch's hoofed legs, <<you're going to walk, or limp, or crawl—whatever it is, you'll be doing it on your own. I'll give you a little time to prepare yourself, and then we're moving on. Understand?>> The spirit-weaver nodded, breathing heavily, and struggled to its hooves.

<<Good.>> The hillside rang with loud wails and cries. For a moment, the little witch-creature looked as though it might answer, but a glance from Thane sent the prisoner into pained silence.

<<Let's go. It's better for you and your friends if we leave quickly.>> The Deerman nodded and stumbled desperately into the trees, following the heartless Man with the brutal blades.

Jitani looked at the young Wielder in astonishment. "You want to *what?*" She'd been pleased and surprised when Tarsa followed her out of the Governor's chambers, but this was far from what she expected to hear.

"I want to take your place among the diplomats to Eromar."

The golden-eyed she-Kyn shook her head. "That's impossible. It's not my decision—Sinovian is the war-leader, and it's his responsibility to decide these matters. He needed someone he knows, someone he trusts. And I've already given my word. I . . ."

Tarsa's lips trembled. "Please," she whispered, taking Jitani's rough hands in her own. "This is something I need to do."

The touch of Tarsa's flesh was like fire, but Jitani couldn't bring herself to pull away. "Why?" she asked softly. "Why does this matter so much to you?"

"He's my . . ." She struggled for a word. This wasn't anything like a romantic attachment, but it was more than simple friendship. He was kith and family to her now, generous beyond acquaintanceship.

She smiled. "He's my brother." Such a simple word, but it was thick with feeling. Jitani suddenly understood some of the deep, aching loneliness that radiated from the young Wielder. She'd heard stories about Tarsa from Biggiabba and Unahi, but it wasn't until now that she understood just how isolated the Redthorn Wielder had been in her life. Jitani had always had family and friends; some had given their lives in her defense. Standing here, holding Tarsa's hands in her own and looking into her wounded, hopeful eyes, Jitani knew that what she took for granted was, in large part, alien to the Wielder. True family was rare for Tarsa, and thus precious.

It was crazy, foolish, and dangerous. It put Jitani firmly against her brother's wishes, and, although he couldn't challenge her choice, as all Kyn were acknowledged to have the right to decide their actions for themselves, he could certainly be unpleasant about it, and he was well trained in surliness and long-harbored grudges.

Still, she couldn't do otherwise. She might not have the same sensitivity she'd had when all four of her sensory stalks were whole, but she didn't need them to understand Tarsa's desperation.

She pulled one hand away and held her fist against her chest. Reaching down, she handed Tarsa a long wyrwood knife, straight and leaf-bladed, from a scabbard around her calf. "Your heart is strong, Redthorn Wielder, though I'm not entirely sure about your mind," she said with a hesitant smile. "We'll fight boldly here, never fear. Fly quickly, and care for your Tetawa brother. And when you finish, return safely to us."

Tarsa slipped the knife into her belt and brought her fist to her chest, her eyes brimming. "Wait," she said as Jitani turned away. "Tell Unahi that I didn't mean to . . . No. Just tell her that I had to do this. I'm sure she'll understand."

Jitani nodded, but she wasn't as optimistic. If what she'd seen of Unahi was any indication, the grumpy she-Kyn would likely take the news worse than Sinovian, if that was possible. As the young Wielder rushed back to her rooms to gather her traveling gear, Jitani walked back to speak with her brother and Unahi, dreading each step along the way.

15

To Ride the Storm

ALTHOUGH HE'D SEEN MANY wondrous things in his travels across the Everland and through areas of the Reach, Tobhi had never imagined anything quite as fabulous as this Stormbringer, the Ubbetuk cloud-galleon that descended from the sky above Sheynadwiin to take them to the border of Eromar. He'd wondered how they would travel the many miles to Eromar City in such a short time, especially as they only had six days remaining until the Council's final response to Vald's demands.

The Tetawa stood with four Kyn and all of their traveling trunks on a wide wooden platform that hung over a rocky outcropping on the western edge of the Sheynadwiin grotto. The only member of their party still missing was Jitani, and she'd be arriving soon. He was surprised and a bit disappointed that Tarsa hadn't remained to say goodbye to him, but her unhappiness was clear when she left the Governor's rooms, so he tried to not be too hurt by her absence. All people dealt with their grief in different ways; perhaps this was easiest for the young warrior-Wielder.

Tobhi turned his attention to a last check of his own gear. He never left anywhere without his well-worn hat, but his beaded belt and wyrweave vest were new, as were his fringed leather boots, all gifts from his aunt Jynni. Aside from a few changes of clothing, some rope, minor medicinals, and a week's worth of dried fruit and yam cakes, he was traveling light this trip. He had his lore-leaf pouch hidden under his oiled overcoat, and his satchel—containing quills, ink, charcoal pencils, bark-paper, a long-stemmed pipe, and a pouch of smoking tobacco—was slung comfortably over one shoulder. His stone-headed hatchet lay tied by its travel thong across his back.

The Kyn councilors were an unremarkable bunch. They stood a bit apart from Tobhi and talked quietly among themselves. Two were elders; the others were a little younger than Tarsa. All wore satin jackets, and the two she-Kyn were regal in their flowing dresses. Tobhi frowned. They didn't look at all like the battle-hardened veterans he'd been expecting; indeed, the younger two looked to be little more than bored cubs. Tobhi returned his attention to the far more interesting spectacle of the black clouds and cracking blue lightning lowering toward the platform.

Blackwick spoke quietly with Garyn and Molli Rose nearby as flashes of the Stormbringer came into view. The Ubbetuk airships were said to be all gears and steam and bulging gas-balloons, translucent sacks that deflated and inflated in rhythm with the grinding of machinery deep inside their bulbous frames. On occasion, Tobhi thought he could see the sails of this one among the clouds, along with glimpses of what looked like a strange, insect-like hull, with metallic oars that hung like segmented legs over the side. But glimpses were the most he could have, for the airships were mysterious, and their appearance changed depending upon the viewer. Humans saw great misshapen monsters in the air, and they drew from their most fearful legends to name them "Dragons"; many Folk perceived the Ubbetuk wonders as nameless mechanical abominations that resembled nothing of either the green or primal worlds. All agreed on one reality about the airships: the fierce black storm clouds that surrounded the galleons and gave them their honored name among the Ubbetuk: "Stormbringers."

The clouds twisted and boiled around the airship, obscuring most of the structure from view and adding to its strangeness. More unnerving was the crackling blue fire that skittered across its length and breadth, occasionally streaking to earth, and giving an otherworldly aura to the already imposing vessel. It was said that a flight of Stormbringers could upset the natural weather and cause catastrophic changes in the lands around them; Tobhi had overheard a

group of Human hunters in a Béashaad border tavern speculate that
if a full flight of Dragons ever took to the clouds, they would likely
blast a hole in the sky to rival the Melding.

The first spatters of rain struck Tobhi's upturned face, and with
them came a sudden fierce wind. Above those sounds, the air was
alive with a buzzing hum and the sharp smell of a spring storm.
He had to turn his face away from the sight, for between the rain,
wind, and lightning, he couldn't keep his eyes open long enough to
make out the dim shapes on the deck of the ship. He was glad that
Smudge was back with the roaming deer herd in Sheynadwiin, for
the Stormbringer would have driven the little stag into a panic. It
was no surprise to the Leafspeaker that the Ubbetuk were treated
with some measure of suspicion; the cloud-shrouded shape did nothing to welcome closer observation. Was it a cloud-skimming galleon
that moved closer, or some gigantic creature out of nightmare?

As the Stormbringer descended and the rains increased, the rolling taint of iron crushed down upon Tobhi and the others, and he felt
himself wilting as it approached. The Tetawa's skin burned. "How
we s'posed to travel up there surrounded by all that iron?" he called
out to Molli Rose. "We'll never make it to Eromar like this."

Head bowed in the rain, Molli walked over to him. "Ye don't
think I'd let ye go without a bit of help, do ye?" she shouted through
the rising winds. "Well, here ye go, one for you, and one for Jitani
when she arrives. The others already have theirs." She reached into
her jacket pocket and pulled out a bracelet and a matching choker of
alternating rows of white and black shell beads—the choker, set with
a crimson stone, for Jitani and the thick bracelet with a glimmering
lilac pearl for Tobhi. "They're iron-wards, and powerful ones at that.
They'll keep the worst of the poison from bringin' ye low. Ye may
find that they'll be a far sight more useful in Man-lands than even on
that Ubbetuk contraption."

Tobhi slipped the band over his wrist and felt the burning tug
under his skin fade. His stomach still rolled awkwardly, but it at least
now it didn't threaten to overwhelm him. He smiled with gratitude
at the Tetawa matron, for iron-wards this powerful were precious.

"Now," Molli Rose took his hand and smiled, "I've got to be
gettin' back down the hill; there's lots to do, as it's the Tetawi who'll
be hostin' the giveaway tonight." Her eyes grew soft. "Take care,

cub, and know that our prayers are with ye all. Ye've already proven y'self more than able to handle some difficult times, so just do what ye can and then get back to us." He nodded and embraced her, and she headed through the rain down the path toward the grotto.

The Chancellor and Garyn walked toward the group. Two blue-capped attendants held a large parasol to shield the Chancellor, but Garyn contented himself with an oiled longcoat and a wide-brimmed hat. "Where is Sinovian's emissary?" Blackwick asked. "There is little time remaining."

"I'm here!" Tarsa called out as she ran up the hill toward the dock, her arms heavy with a hurriedly gathered pack of supplies. Tobhi stared at her in surprised delight.

Garyn frowned. "Where is Jitani?"

Tarsa stuck out her chin defiantly in spite of the rain and the nearly overwhelming force of iron. "I'm taking her place. She's going to stay and continue to help the Sevenfold Council. I'm here to help my brother."

Tobhi grinned. *Brother.* The word had a nice sound, as much for its truth as its purpose. He nodded his acceptance, and she met his smile with one every bit as wide.

"The airship is nearly ready to depart," the Governor said, his voice sharp. "Sinovian chose Jitani as his representative, not you. This is no time for such nonsense, Tarsa'deshae."

"It en't nonsense," said Tobhi decisively as he handed the other iron-ward to Tarsa. "She's a Redthorn warrior, and a Wielder of no mean skill. That could come in pretty handy."

"That is not what concerns me . . ." Garyn began, but he stopped as another group of figures came over the hill to walk toward the dock: Unahi, Jitani, and a visibly furious Sinovian, all thoroughly drenched by the sudden rains.

"Wielder," Garyn called to Unahi. "Please, we are running short of time."

Unahi looked hard at Tarsa. "Is it true what she told me?"

Tarsa glanced at Jitani and nodded. "Yes."

"I see." Unahi's lips tightened into a thin line. Tarsa would have almost preferred to see fury and burning rage in Unahi's eyes instead of this cold disappointment. "Very well. She's made the choice, as have you. There's nothing more to be said." Sinovian glared at the young Wielder with almost murderous fury, but Jitani's golden eyes were warm. Tarsa looked away.

Blackwick cleared his throat. "So be it. The cloud-galleon will take you as far as Lake Ithiak, which is a little over a day's journey to the east of Eromar City. I have provided a coach and four rather special ponies, along with an Ubbetuk groom, to take you the rest of the way. May your feet find you swiftly on the road home." Without another word, he and his attendants followed the path taken by Molli Rose.

Lightning crackled around the platform, and the ground shook as thunder rumbled through the grotto. Garyn's face was worn with worry and indecision. His piercing eyes assessed the young Wielder for a long time. At last he sighed and handed a fist-sized copper ball to Tobhi while addressing all of the travelers. "When you are ready to return, break this in starshine or moonglow, and the nightwasp will summon the Stormbringer again to bring you home. We will look for you within the week. Be wary, my kindred. Lojar Vald is a cunning Man, and a cruel one. He has no love of justice or the Eld Folk, but he will not likely challenge you openly—not for a while, at least. 'Accidents' abound for Folk who enter Gorthac Hall. The sooner you are free of Eromar City, the safer you will be."

He looked at the other Kyn diplomats and slid in close to Tobhi, his voice low, nearly drowned out in the noise from the Stormbringer. "The travelers I had originally chosen for this journey have fallen ill and are unable to accompany you. Apparently, Tarsa is not the only unexpected change in our plans. I have my suspicions of the reasons for their 'illness,' but, until they have recovered, I cannot say for certain. These four are not trained as warriors—they are traders and minor dignitaries, but all are dependable, if uninspiring. If we had more time . . ."

His eyes followed the other Kyn as they moved toward the loading platform. *Dependable, but also expendable,* the Governor thought darkly. *These truly are unhappy, desperate days.*

"All that they know is that they are to finish trade negotiations and help to escort the remaining diplomats home again. They will do their job efficiently and effectively; you need not worry about them endangering your true purpose. I would send you alone, but that would arouse Vald's suspicions too much, and we cannot risk it. It is a heavier burden that I am placing on you, Tobhi, and I am sorry for it. But it cannot be helped."

The Leafspeaker held his fist against his chest. "We'll be strong, I promise ye that. And I en't alone, so don't ye worry 'bout us."

Garyn's eyes flickered toward Tarsa, but he nodded. Turning back to the larger group, he said, "Hurry back to us, all of you. We will have much need of your wisdom upon your return." They all bowed low, gathered their travel packs, and walked to the edge of the platform, where a single rope ladder descended from the dark clouds. Tobhi walked ahead of Tarsa, his eyes wide and neck straining to discern the shape of their strange transport.

As Tarsa stepped beside the Tetawa, Unahi called to her. "Niece, wait!" The younger she-Kyn turned, preparing for a firm lecture or Garyn's refusal. Instead, the elder Wielder held up her wyrwood staff, its golden surface still etched with the marks of thorns from Tarsa's battle against the Human grave-robbers.

Unahi wiped a strand of silver hair away from her drenched face. "Take the staff with you; it has a spirit of its own, and a name—Dibadjiibé. It served you well before; perhaps it'll continue to do so on your present travels." Tarsa tried to protest, but Unahi bristled. "Don't argue. You'll have more need of this help than I will, and if you won't heed my warnings, you should at least be prepared for the dangers to come." Her voice softened, but her lips were still drawn and disapproving. "Show it respect, for it's both powerful and helpful. And don't make too much of this—it's only a small thing."

A wave of love rushed through the Redthorn Wielder, and Tarsa swept the bent old she-Kyn into her tattooed arms. "It's not such a small thing to me, Auntie. *Tsodoka*."

Unahi stiffened and pulled herself free. "You've got a long, darkening road ahead of you—it's a road you've chosen freely, though I tried to spare you. Take care of yourself, and of Tobhi. He's kith to you now, and that brings responsibility. Don't fail him. Come home as quickly as you can. May Zhaia bless and keep you safe in her leafy bower." She lightly touched the azure Wielder's mark on her niece's forehead, and then the old she-Kyn was gone, lost in the screaming wind and rain.

Tobhi glanced around and waited for Tarsa to slip over the railing before following to his seat. As their transport rose upward, he turned back to peer over the edge. For a moment something caught his eye beside the receding platform, but it was just a flash of color in the storm-shadowed trees below, not enough to really tell if something was truly there.

"That bit o' witchery last night is spookin' me," Tobhi mumbled to himself as he craned his head back toward the site, trying fruitlessly to catch another glimpse before black clouds and blue fire obscured his vision completely. Something nagged at his memory, a troubling thought just out of reach.

Tarsa's hand on his arm broke his reverie, and he promptly forgot about the movement on the ground below as the she-Kyn pointed in awe at the bubbling liquids, strange whirring gears, and smoke-belching machinery. He was too lost in excitement to remember where he'd seen before that brief glimmer of burnished copper tresses, that momentary gleam of violet eyes that now gazed coldly upward through the rain as the Stormbringer disappeared from sight.

Cycle Three
In Remembrance of Trees

This is a story of the Eld Days, long before the Melding, long before these troubled times.

It is a teaching.

The Wielders were not the first among the Kyn to comprehend the voices of the wyr. *If not for the Makers, those voices would have remained unintelligible, for it was the Makers who first revealed the spirit-ways of the* wyr, *and who first harnessed its transformative powers for the benefit of the Folk. The Makers stood tall and proud among the Kyn, and they were honored above all others, save for Zhaia, the True Tree and mother of the Kyn, and her mossy-haired husband, Drohodu. The seven nations of the Folk knew and gave respect to other powerful spirit-beings—Avialle, the gentle river mother; Shobbok, the ice-hearted Winter Witch; Jenna, Granny Turtle of the Tetawi, and her adopted nephew, the mischievous squirrel-spirit, Kitichi; Skyfire and Thunder, the powerful Storm-Born Twins; among others—but for many of the Kyn, it was the Makers who were first in mind when needs arose, when danger threatened, when desire crested.*

The Makers were powerful medicine-people and conjurors, at once beautiful and terrifying to behold. Flesh and fear held no mysteries to the Makers, for they were the strongest of their kind. They could change their form at will and whim, and none knew if they had a true shape or were simply meant to be ever-changing, untouched by the ravages of the elements, unburdened by fragile flesh. When they did take embodied form, they were the fairest of the Kyn, with dozens of tendril-like braids that fell to their knees, with feathers, stones, bird bones, twigs, and other detritus woven into their thick hair. Their multicolored skin was covered with bright sigils and signs of unknown origin, as though the very words of Creation were etched onto their bodies for the wonderment of the world. They were armed with wyr-shaped staves and cudgels, and wore tunics of crafted bark, leaves, grasses, and flowers as armor. None could best the Makers in combat, nor endurance, nor passion. Never many, the Makers would sometimes gather in remote place to share their knowledge with one another, then bring it to the towns of People, their generosity untouched by pride or avarice.

It was they who learned the healing powers of the wyrwood trees, they who rode the winds and waters, who first comprehended the nature of stone, flame, and whirlwind. They embodied the voices of the wyr and showed the People how to open their spirits to the hidden depths of the Eld Green. In so doing, the Makers unveiled the very heart of the Eld Green and its many peoples, and gave the Kyn knowledge of their primal connection to the verdant world that flourished, untamed and bountiful, around them. Born of wyrwood and skyfire, moss and rain, the Kyn came to know themselves as true inheritors of the Eld Green's lifeblood, and this understanding made them stronger than they had ever been.

And as the Kyn grew stronger, their need of the Makers grew less, though their gratitude remained strong. Yet the Makers, once humble teachers and wisdom-bearers, came to fear the growing strength of the People, and remembered the days when they walked alone in the high places of the Eld Green. Now, after generations of sharing the Makers' powers, others came to know and wield the delights of the deeper wyr-ways, and the greater medicine-makers grew jealous of the time when others trembled in fear, awe, and hunger in their presence. They saw only through the veil of memory, seeing loss for themselves instead of gain for their people, unwilling or, perhaps, unable to see what wonders had been achieved through the wise use of their once-unselfish gifts. That other Kyn might aspire to speak in the language of Creation was unimaginable to the Makers, and they began to hoard their knowledge, parsing it out in small fragments, and only to those who lowered themselves before the Makers in submission and, later, debasement.

Watching in growing despair, the ever-patient Zhaia and Drohodu warned their proud children that this path would bring nothing but pain to all. Once housed in the spirit, pride and resentment could never be sated; the firstborn were turning against their own, and no family could flourish when its members fed upon each other. A common fire burned in the hearts of all the

Kyn: when one spark faltered, it diminished the strength of all. It was wisdom that the Makers themselves had taught to their kith, yet in their resentment they had forgotten, and they grew prouder, crueler, and more selfish.

The Makers soon called themselves masters of their younger kindred; fear and pain reigned where once blossomed honor and pleasure. They turned away from their own teachings and the deeper ways of the wyr. They would be the first and greatest, or nothing. They even began to quarrel and fight among themselves, for their parents' warnings had come to pass: envy had burrowed into the heart of every Maker, and they all ceased to see themselves as part of the Eld Green and its elemental ways. They could no longer see the tender ties that bound them to the green, growing world and its peoples.

No one remembers how the War began; that story is lost to the ages before the Melding. All we know is that, once begun, the ravages of War consumed the great Makers, and their wisdom withered like the drought-shrunken vine. Hot blood flooded the land; the mountains and oceans writhed in pain; the People fled, yet died anyway. Each Maker saw the world as enemy or posses-sion. There was no love, no joy, no balance. The green lands turned brown; great rivers shrunk to ash-choked trickles; the parched trees cried out first in thirst and then agony as greedy flames consumed them. All was desperation, terror, and pain.

Yet the teachings endured, and it was the very wisdom that the Makers had discarded that, in the end, saved their younger kindred. The lesser medi-cine-keepers of the Kyn called to Zhaia and Drohodu, and they opened their minds and hearts to the Deep Green. The wyr of the world responded, and, on a blistering summer night when the air sat still and heavy, the Wielders gave themselves fully to the wyr, surrendered themselves to whatever balance was necessary.

And the land rose up against the Makers. Too late the great ones realized how far from wisdom they had fallen—too late, because they had long ago forgotten the songs that had calmed the spirits of earth, skyfire, whirlwind, and rain. The Eld Green rose against the Makers, who fell screaming into jagged, dark places of cold stone, or were tossed, torn and wailing, into the burning heart of the raging storm. They tried to remember the songs, but their voices were broken and cracked, and their once-lovely forms had become corrupted by the harvest of selfishness that they had sown so carefully, so heedlessly.

By the morning, when the amber glow of the sister suns filtered through the first soft rains of the new era, the Makers were no more. They had returned to the land that had given them birth, and only their memory remained. It was *the first dawn of the days of the Wielders, who, even now, keep the teachings of their predecessors and learn with each Awakening of the terrible lesson of the Makers' rise and fall. The memory makes them mindful of their duty to serve the People, not rule them. It was a lesson well learned.*

Yet they know well that their people have remembered this story, too, for it was the memory of the Makers that the proud Shields used to herald the Purging, when so many of the Kyn turned against the Wielders and their wyr-rooted ways. And thus continues the legacy of the Makers, and thus endures the threat of blind, prideful power.

This is a teaching, and a remembrance.

Interlude

Awakening

EVEN WITH HER EYES PINCHED tightly closed, Denarra couldn't avoid the dawn, as the single sun's first light cut through her consciousness like forge-heated needles. She groaned with overdramatic emphasis and pulled her pillow over her head, but there was no escape—she'd forgotten to lower the curtains before falling into bed, and now the morning's brightness was omnipresent. She couldn't quite bring herself to face the dawn today, or any day, for that matter; she normally slept until midmorning, or early afternoon if she had spirited company the night before. Once awake, she generally found it impossible to go back to sleep, at least until later in the afternoon, when the lush interior of her brightly colored wagon would be a welcome respite from the prairie's afternoon heat.

Though the cool shadows of twilight were long gone, and though she was well aware that sleep was equally elusive, the curvaceous Strangeling lingered in bed for a little while longer. When she mustered the courage to finally open a bleary, sleep-crusted eye, she let out another groan and slid back under the silken coverlet. The wagon was a mess: overturned crockery, half-drained jugs of various local and regional wines, a partially eaten loaf of bread and a rather pungent piece of white-skinned cheese, and miscellaneous articles of bright, perfumed clothing scattered on the floor, chairs, and tables, with the most intimate articles hanging from her cabinet doors and draped over a small statue of a strutting peacock.

As her thoughts came together through the haze of wine-addled sleep, the last items brought a flash of recognition to her face. She sat up, slowly, and stared at the three shapes slumbering in the bed beside her, their well-muscled chests rising and falling softly, sun-bronzed limbs wrapped together, damp locks curled and pasted to their foreheads. As the pleasing memories of the previous night's events slowly returned, Denarra shook her head, then winced as a pounding headache announced itself with the force of war-horns.

Farmhands, she berated herself. *Suns save you, Denarra Syrene, what's the appeal?*

She lifted a corner of the blanket and gave the young Men a more thorough appraisal. She couldn't help but grin; it all made perfect sense now. Gorgeous farmhands *and* triplets.

Of course.

It took her a while to disengage herself from the firm, sweat-moistened knot of arms and legs—a struggle that, admittedly, she didn't particularly mind—but she eventually managed to stumble to her wardrobe and into a snug emerald dressing gown that she'd chosen specifically because the striking hue matched her eyes and complemented her auburn hair. While her guests remained soundly asleep, Denarra stepped outside into the already warm air and walked barefoot to the oaken water barrel at the back of the wagon. The water was ice-cold and clear. She squeezed her eyes shut and took a quick breath before dunking her head into the barrel. She rose up again, sputtering and gasping, and finally felt the morning's mind-fog clear away.

As she'd forgotten to bring a towel with her, the water streamed down her face and neck and pasted the clinging gown to her skin. She was fully awake now, and she idly considered waking up her young guests to show them how transparent and form-fitting the wet cloth was. Given their performance the night before, she had no doubt that they'd be more than eager for a frolic before breakfast. She was half inclined for a pinch and giggle herself. But with full awareness came a sudden unease that had nothing to do with the glistening tangle of luscious Man-flesh in her wagon.

Denarra turned to the east, toward the Everland. The caravan was miles away from the southern edge of that territory of dark forests and reaching peaks, but she could always feel the green lands calling her back. It had been years since she'd been home; she shared her parents' mutual restlessness, and she'd long ago given herself to the road and all its unpredictable ways. Hers was a sometimes wearying life, with too few opportunities to sit and enjoy the quieter side of sociability. Besides, her temperament wasn't much suited to domesticity, nor to tradition, and her father's people had no great love for a Human-born Strangeling who had little facility with those ways.

Over the years Denarra had found many places to call home, at least temporarily, and Mother Baraboo's theatrical company was among the better of them; she didn't stick out as particularly freakish among this motley company of actors, acrobats, musicians, and minor miscreants, and her various mundane and magical skills were quite useful for a group of wanderers who skirted propriety and legality at the best of times. This life would do for a while, at least until she could get back to the marble-lined streets and gilded domes of Chalimor, the greatest city of Men in the Reach. It was the one place besides the Everland that always called to her, and it was the only call she happily answered. The ways of the road could be lonely, but it was better than being a foreigner in your own homeland.

Still, as her clenching stomach reminded her, Denarra would always be tied to her birth home through blood and history. She could keep running for the rest of her life, but she'd never be free of the Everland; it would always inhabit her, no matter how far the road might take her. And the closer she came to the often-unseen barrier between the Reach of Men and the lands of the Folk, the clearer that link became.

Yet as she looked off to the eastern horizon, squinting her eyes against the hot sun, the knot in her stomach became a sudden, searing pain, and she bit her lip to keep from crying out. The boundary between the haven of the Folk and the world of Men wasn't unseen any longer. She could see it just fine now.

It was smoke. The border of the Everland burned.

16

Flight and Fury

ANOTHER BURST OF JAGGED WHITE skyfire exploded in the air, followed within the space of a breath by a blast of thunder so loud that it rocked the Stormbringer and its battered passengers. The freezing rain smashed against them with blistering force, and nothing seemed to keep its chill from clawing into their muscles and bones. The galleon spun around in the air again as another spear of lightning flashed across the deck to fill the air with a bitter, metallic tang.

Tarsa was bent nearly double, holding her head between her knees, trying to find a *wyr*-fed place of calm from the terror and gut-twisting sickness that upended her senses. She and Tobhi were firmly tethered to a stout oaken mast; they wouldn't be lost overboard in the upheaval of the storm, but the constant swirling and slamming of the ship had bruised them badly, and the constant drenching of cold rain did nothing to help their discomfort.

She'd long since given up any attempt at maintaining her poise; she simply sat curled in a tight ball in the failing hope that this nightmare would finally come to an end. The iron-ward had kept the poisoning at bay but not the sickness, and the Wielder had vomited more than she could imagine had been in her stomach in an entire lifetime. Her sensory stalks were firmly wrapped; had they not been, the sickness would have been even more incapacitating. She, Tobhi, and the diplomats had earlier tried to enter the Stormbringer's inner hold, but the intensity of being surrounded by so much of the toxic metal was too much, even for their protective talismans, so all the non-Ubbetuk aboard found makeshift seats on the upper deck, where the chill open air gave some small bit of relief—for a short while.

Tarsa almost regretted that decision now, for her thoughts were jumbled and tangled with dizziness and fear. Her senses had gone wild when the galleon entered the perpetual black storm that lay on the northwestern edge of the Everland. It was past these brutal clouds, where lightning and thunder ruled supreme, that the lands of the Folk ended and the world of Men began. This was an elemental borderland unlike any other in the Melded world, and Tarsa's growing awareness of the *wyr* seemed to make her more vulnerable to the flood of sensations and atmospheric phenomena than the others.

For his part, though drenched by icy rain, bruised by the chaotic movement of the airship, and more than a little sick himself, Tobhi found the journey fascinating. While not much of an inventor himself, Tobhi had always liked strange and unusual things—he was a lore-keeper, after all, with a particular love of weird and heroic tales—and this was by far one of the most unusual experiences of his life. The rumors of Ubbetuk airships were creative, but they fell far short of the brutal, visceral reality of skyfire, ice, and wind. He spent most of his time watching the bulging gas-sacks and clanging machinery on deck, or catching occasional glimpses through the lightning-shattered darkness of the silver storm drakes who flashed through the clouds past the ship, their massive fanged mouths open in roars of defiance against the puny land-walkers who dared take to the skies in their iron-wrapped abomination. This world was so unlike the heavy earthiness of the great forests below, and though his heart lurched from time to time as the galleon jolted away from another arc of drake-summoned lightning, Tobhi felt as much exhilaration as fear.

They'd left Sheynadwiin in the early afternoon and traveled through the night before reaching the storm. Now, hours later, the wind grew louder, more intense, becoming a desperate wail of anguish and grief. This time Tobhi and Tarsa both bowed their heads and clung tightly to each other as the merciless burn of rain on flesh tore into them. They couldn't breathe, could barely think, as the air itself seemed to crush down, forcing their bodies against the deck, smashing the breath from their lungs, the very heat from their bodies, with unrelenting fury. Their hands squeezed tighter, and this connection was soon the only reality either could focus on. The wind and rain and ice and thunder and suffocating pressure grew fiercer, more brutal, and still they held tightly to one another, groaning in pain and defiance.

And then, without warning, it was over. As though a door slammed shut behind them, the Stormbringer slipped from the rain-choked darkness of the storm and into bright sunlight. The air at this frigid height was little warmer now than it had been before, but the thin light of a single sun and blue sky were welcome to those who had been buffeted around for hours in the stinging rain. Some of the Ubbetuk whispered amongst themselves about the surprising violence of the storm on this journey; it was almost as if the dark clouds had been targeting the galleon with their full force of rage. Yet now, as the wall of roiling gloom receded in the distance, it became a shadowed memory in the brilliant light of a new day. All on the deck lifted their squinting eyes to the sky, and some shed grateful tears.

But Tarsa was not among them. Her face was hollow with something more than pain.

"What is it?" Tobhi asked, wiping his eyes with the back of his hand, as the she-Kyn unwrapped her sensory stalks and pulled her dark hair away to let them move, unhindered, in the sunlight.

Her voice was ragged. "I didn't know this would happen. It's worse than I could have imagined."

"What are ye talkin' 'bout?" He asked the question, but he had a guess; his eyes were fixed on Tarsa's sensory stalks. They nearly always danced and curled with a rhythm all their own, as though each had a quickening heartbeat pulsing within. But now they all hung limply down the sides of Tarsa's head.

"The *wyr*, Tobhi. It's almost unreachable here . . . I can barely feel it. What are we going to do? I can't be a Wielder without the *wyr*."

The cloud-galleon landed on the banks of Lake Ithiak and unloaded the diplomats and baggage, as well as a large, four-wheeled coach and four strange brown ponies, each identical with a trimmed mane and bobbed tail, along with a green-capped Ubbetuk groom named Gweggi. Blackwick had explained that landing a ship of this size in Eromar City itself would be a threatened sign of invasion, so the wiser course was to land in a location with a sparse population and move swiftly across the ground using the carriage in the hold. The Humans might still be suspicious upon their arrival, but at least this option had the trappings of diplomatic normalcy.

In less than an hour the Dragon was airborne again, and its passengers were left to travel the rest of the journey alone.

Tarsa stood apart from the others and looked out over the lake. She held Unahi's inspirited staff firmly in her hand; the gift gave her some small measure of comfort. It wasn't enough that she felt so exposed and vulnerable outside of the deeper channels of the *wyr* that she'd so recently come to know; she was a Wielder, true, but she was also a Redthorn warrior, and she observed the world around her with a warrior's unflinching eye. Uncertainty and fear were no enemies here, but only if she maintained control of herself. Clear-minded response to this strange land and its ways, more than emotional reaction, was needed now.

Stark, rocky hills stretched out far into the distance. There were no trees, although the Wielder could see the remains of an ancient forest in the charred tree trunks scattered like broken teeth throughout the hills. Those jagged fragments poked out through scrubby thorn bushes growing wild and unchecked in the shallows of the hills, which were themselves broken only by the grey expanse of Lake Ithiak. Linked to Eromar City by the river Orm, Ithiak was a lengthy stretch of silt and ash-choked water that stank of dead fish and sulfur. Orange foam clung greasily where the waters lapped sickly against the shore. Though she stood in the bright, alien light of a single sun, the water was impenetrable.

This wasn't just a dead place—it was a murdered world, poisoned and left to rot. The Wielder, though a stranger to this land, could still feel the deep, burning ache that radiated off the waves, the soil, the bloated bodies of fish so poisoned that not even insects sought sustenance. And everywhere lingered the stench of iron-wrought blood and death.

As Tarsa took her first view of the Human world, she slowly began to realize how much she would need both her warrior's wits and whatever Wielder's strength she could muster in this strange and devastated world—a world that she didn't understand in any way. And in spite of her earlier bravado, the fear returned, stronger now, weighing her down like a snow-crusted blanket. *My coming here was a mistake*, she thought to herself as she rewrapped her sensory stalks against the pervasive corruption. *I'm a danger to Tobhi and the others. I should never have come.*

She heard the Tetawa call to her. Blinking away sudden tears, Tarsa turned and saw him waving to her from beside the coach, slapping his floppy brown hat gleefully against his knee. "They's machines, too, just like the Dragon!" he called out to her. "They en't real ponies at all! No wonder we didn't hear no commotion durin' the storm. I was wonderin' 'bout that." He returned his attention to Gweggi and began plying him with questions.

She couldn't share in Tobhi's excitement. *Lifeless ponies in a dying land—what kind of nightmare have we entered?* Tarsa took a deep breath, held it for a few moments as her thoughts cleared, and returned with a heavy spirit to the coach. The younger two diplomats stood talking softly to one another beside the coach door but stopped and nodded when Tarsa drew near. The dark-haired he-Kyn bore an undisguised sneer on his face, but the she-Kyn beside him merely looked bored.

"There isn't any more room remaining in the coach, so you'll have to ride in the front with the Goblin and the Brownie," the he-Kyn said blandly as Tarsa approached, ignoring the Wielder's bristling response to the slurs.

Just as the Wielder began to retort, the coach door opened and another he-Kyn diplomat waved Tarsa forward. "Nonsense, Hak'aad, there's plenty of room for all here. The Wielder is, after all, a distinguished member of our company as well. Please, forgive him—he is quite young." Hak'aad glowered at his elder's comments, but he lowered his eyes and stepped aside.

Tarsa motioned to Tobhi, who shook his head. "Thankee, but I'd rather sit up here with Gweggi and find out more 'bout them ponies." The Wielder nodded and entered the coach, followed closely by Hak'aad and the young she-Kyn. The door closed. A strange, metallic ping clicked across the length of the vehicle, and the coach slid forward with the smooth, measured movement of a flat-bottomed canoe on ice.

The interior of the coach was spare, yet comfortable, with cushioned benches along each wall and curtained windows that could be opened for fresh air. It was well lit by two green everlights on either end, but these could be veiled by hinged shutters. There was little decoration, as gaudy excess was shunned by the Ubbetuk, but such modesty was suited to the vehicle.

The he-Kyn who had intervened on her behalf introduced himself to Tarsa as Reiil Cethwir of Ash Branch. He was fluent in the Upper Rinj dialect of Mannish, the most common tongue of Eromar, and had frequently traveled through the lands of Men on trade runs. One other trader joined Reiil on this journey, the young she-Kyn Athweid, as well as two career diplomats: Imweshi, an unpleasant, thin-lipped she-Kyn who pointedly ignored the young Wielder, and her son Hak'aad, whose attention had again returned to the young and blushing Athweid.

The smooth rhythm of the coach lulled everyone out of conversation and into a steady, drowsy silence, their thoughts their own as they moved ever closer to Eromar City. Tarsa fell asleep for a short time, awaking with a start to find everyone but Reiil leaning against the cushions, slipping in and out of sleep. In the distance she could hear Tobhi's voice in enthusiastic conversation with the Ubbetuk driver.

The old trader looked at her and smiled. "You should try to get a little more sleep, Wielder. It was a rough journey."

Tarsa wearily returned his smile. "Don't remind me—my stomach has only just started to settle down. But I can't sleep right now. Everything is so strange here, and I need to stay awake to learn something of this place and its spirits."

"I understand," Reiil nodded. "It's always difficult when you first leave the Everland. I imagine it's even worse for someone like you, who's still connected so much to the land and its hidden ways." He shrugged. "That was never a driving concern for me or my family. We turned from the Tree to the Pillar of the Stars a long, long time ago. It has not often troubled me to leave the Everland."

"All the more reason to give it up," a hard voice responded. Old Imweshi was awake now, and her cold eyes were fixed hard on Reiil. She glanced sidelong at Tarsa before shifting to the trade tongue, unaware that Tarsa was able to understand nearly everything she said. "The only way to be a part of the world is to look to the future, not to the past. And the future belongs to Men."

Tarsa wanted to respond, but she held back as Reiil interjected, "I hope not, old friend, because Men have little use for us, Celestial and Greenwalker alike." He looked at the Wielder. "Don't you ever wonder what we could have become, Imweshi, if we'd have been raised like she surely was, strong in the Old Ways, certain of our place in the world rather than being tossed around on the ever-changing wind, never sure if we're worthy enough even to be an afterthought in the world of Men?"

Imweshi's lip curled scornfully. "You speak blasphemy, Reiil, and you speak of foolishness. Where you see strength I see stubbornness, and a dying past that should be hastened to its grave. Look at her. Look at those witch-marks on her skin. This isn't something to praise, Reiil: she's a barbarian and a conjuror—at best misguided, at worst perverse. She clearly put some witchery on Garyn to convince him to send her on this delicate mission. She wasn't meant to be here." She shook her head. "No, you'll not find any longing in me to be of her kind. She sickens and fails when beyond her trees; her kind could never appreciate all the greatness and grandeur given to us. Ours is the way of redemption, not hers. No, never hers." Her root-brown eyes narrowed at the Wielder. "Far better to die among enlightened Men than to live in faded disgrace among the lost."

Reiil turned his face to the window and pulled the curtain aside to stare silently at the passing landscape. A thousand different arguments flew to Tarsa's lips, but she said nothing, sinking instead into her own thoughts. She looked again at Reiil and saw now the heavy longing in his eyes, a deep hunger for something just beyond his reach.

After a few moments in silence, Tarsa gently touched the old he-Kyn's shoulder and spoke in the trade tongue. "It's never too late to return home, Reiil. I was raised in a Celestial home, but the Eld Green endured. You don't have to be poisoned and made bruised and bitter by shame. You don't have to listen to those who hate themselves and want to become like our persecutors. You can choose despair, or you can choose an honorable life with your People."

Imweshi's face went white with rage, and she rose slightly toward the Wielder, but Tarsa turned calmly toward the old she-Kyn and slid her hand to Jitani's gift knife on her belt. Not a word was spoken between them, just brown eyes locked on blue, and then Imweshi slid back against the cushions, her hatred of the Wielder palpable in the intimate space. Hak'aad and Athweid remained asleep and curled against one another in the cushioned corner. Reiil nodded before returning his gaze to the window.

Tarsa slid to the opposite curtain and pulled it aside to see a bit of what lay beyond. They'd long since left Lake Ithiak behind, but the main road to Eromar City followed the Orm River, and its blasted banks gave mute testimony to the nation's history. The waters of the Orm, like those of the lake into which it sluggishly flowed, were choked with sediment and bright with strange liquids that drained from the jumbled stone and brick buildings squatting at its sides. These massive buildings stretched high into the air like tortured stone hands reaching for the sky, with few windows but many dark chimneys that belched out clouds of dripping black smoke. Even sophisticated Ubbetuk coach-craft couldn't keep the acrid stench from creeping into the carriage and nearly choking its passengers. Hak'aad and Athweid coughed themselves awake.

A wrongness pervaded these harsh stone structures; they were festering wounds, infected to the very core with a seeping miasma that stretched into the soil and air. Yet Tarsa's shock at seeing these caustic towers and fumes was nothing compared to the sight of the creatures who lived in and among them. This was the true horror. Worn brittle with hunger and want, poisoned for years by the massive foundries and mills, the Humans lived now as they had since the first wars of conquest that the Dreyd and their followers used to solidify their hold on the province and extend it to the lands beyond. The children were ragged and covered with open sores, their bruised and pinched features sullen, nothing like the playful Kyn sprouts who ran with abandon through their mountain homes. Old before their time, Women gathered in groups of four or five, heads covered by dull brown or black caps, and crouched with long, rough skirts trailing in the frigid river waters to slap shreds of cloth against oil-slick rocks. The upper banks of the river were covered with bearded Men of various ages, but each bore the heavy weight of poverty on his wasted features. They sat together and stared after the carriage with hungry eyes.

"Why do they look at us that way?" Tarsa whispered, her voice tight at the unfamiliar sight. A bubble of bile rose up in her throat.

Reiil sighed and let his curtain drop. "Why shouldn't they? This is the only life they know. They live and die by the will of their masters in the mills and the mines, thrown away when they aren't of any more use. And ever in the shadows is the will of Eromar, demanding more iron, more weapons, more labor, always driving the people further and further. But they do it, all with the hope that their Dreyd-blessed next life will be better than this one."

"That is not the only reason," Imweshi growled, but her sharp features had softened to something resembling pity. "They blame us for their misery."

"Us? But we've done nothing to them?"

Imweshi stared out the window. "No? Look at them, conjuror, and remember them well. The masters of Eromar have told them for decades that their poverty, their suffering, their pain and degradation are all a result of those greedy, selfish, and brutish creatures lurking in the green and fertile Everland. They are told that we worship evil spirits, that we engage in debauchery and bloodshed, that we kidnap, violate, and butcher Humans of all ages, that life means nothing to us beyond the gratification of our animal pleasures. As evidence of our witchery, we have tainted their lands, sent evil winds to curse the crops, poison their cattle, kill children still in the womb, and bring down the strong. It has to be our fault—after all, hasn't all this happened since the Melding? And while their lands suffer, we have used those dark arts to make our own land rich beyond measure, with gold and other precious metals deep in our mountains, just waiting to be found by those with unbending strength and will."

"But those are lies!"

Imweshi turned with a frigid smile. "Of course they are! But who cares? Does it matter to *them*?" She gestured toward the window. "Who are they going to believe? Us? We well-fed, clean, healthy, wealthy, coach-riding Kyn? Perhaps you with all your savage finery can convince them that the mechanical beasts that draw this carriage are something other than dark sorcery. What will you say to them, my truth-telling Wielder? Will your truth feed them, clothe them, give them warm homes? What would they rather hear: that Lojar Vald and his kind have driven them halfway into their graves out of greed and selfish ambition, that the promises of another life are mere manipulations to ensure their subservience, or that a small group of backward barbarians are the only thing between them and their salvation? If you stood in their place, who would *you* believe?"

The carriage crested a hill and left the foundries and the empty-eyed Humans behind. Tarsa slid a hand to the window and let the curtain fall.

17

Unleashed

EROMAR CITY WAS BUILT ON A HIGH, wind-smoothed butte that stretched in a wide arc over a steep canyon, through which flowed the wildest stretch of the Orm River. "The City on the Water" had once been the seat of learning in the North, the northernmost outpost of the Reach, a city of stark beauty and people who were dignified and free. Yet it changed when the old gods of Men were overthrown and the rule of the ambitious Dreyd took their place. One massive building dominated the city from the apex of the butte. The structure—Gorthac Hall—was a mass of gables and shadowed nooks, named by Vald to honor an obscure but influential legal sage who advocated the rule of Dreydlaw over the secular philosophies dominant in the rest of the Reach. The city itself was built between six descending stone and timber walls that led to the foot of the butte, each wall marking the social stratification within the city, with the boxy, narrow buildings growing progressively shabbier, the streets narrower and more dangerous, as they moved closer to the city's edge. The smelting foundries and mills squatted at the lower levels of the city, as did the most impoverished of the people, who found shelter anywhere they could among the ash-choked factories. Mountains of crushed tailings and burnt-out cinders stretched from the city's walls for miles in the distance, and great gushing sprays of acidic liquid bubbled from the mills through lead pipes into the river below.

The carriage sped along at an easy pace through the ruined structures that flanked the road toward the city. In spite of the surrounding dilapidated buildings, old trestles, and stone columns, the road itself was remarkably smooth and clear. The mechanical ponies needed little care, as they had been ingeniously crafted to wind themselves by their forward movement. Angular and sleek, the automata were lesser marvels of Ubbetuk design: hundreds of individual sheets of darkened metal joined cunningly to one another so as to resemble the wrinkling of flesh; the wheels, springs, weights, and toothed gears within were fully protected from the elements by the careful Ubbetuk artistry. Gweggi's primary duty was to lead them in the right direction and to watch for any irregularities on the path ahead; the ponies took care of the rest. It was an easy task.

Tobhi had stopped talking, choosing instead to wrap himself in a blanket and settle into the steady movement of the carriage for some much-needed sleep. The driver's bench wasn't very comfortable, but the Tetawa had slept in much more awkward locations than this one, so it took little time for him to be snoring softly, his well-worn hat pulled down over his eyes to keep out the dimming sunshine.

Though he was much too polite to say it aloud, Gweggi was thankful that the chatty Tetawa was asleep. Ubbetuk were generally reserved amongst strangers, and the constant questions from the long-braided scribe had nearly driven the Ubbetuk to agitation. He hadn't been pleased with this assignment—he was, after all, the private driver of Lady Shudwagga, a member of the white-capped Consulting Council of the Swarm. Yet the request had been made by the Chancellor himself, so Gweggi accepted the duty without complaint. It was a short enough drive, and in a land that he was quite familiar with. He had, after all, driven Lady Shudwagga and even the Chancellor down this very road not so long before on trade-related meetings, and he anticipated few surprises that would distract him from continuing work on the short book of lyric poetry he'd been writing over the past few years.

So it was that Gweggi was mumbling over a complicated rhyme scheme about the moral virtues and difficult delights of faithful service when the crowd of Men stepped from behind the crumbling walls of an old smelting mill to block the road ahead. The Ubbetuk looked up and pulled steadily on a lever beside his seat. Slowly, gently, the clockwork ponies came to a halt. The fiery smokestacks of the foundries in the city beyond burned bright in the deepening gloom, casting a reddish pall across the sky.

Gweggi could make out at least twenty Men slipping out of the darkness, and the scuffling sound of boots on rocks behind the carriage made his heart beat faster. He reached over and touched Tobhi's arm. "We're not alone, friend Tetawa," the Ubbetuk whispered evenly.

Tobhi's ears twitched at the warning in Gweggi's voice. He slowly lifted his hat brim and scanned the approaching Men. His hand slipped to the thong that held the hatchet to his back, but he remained curled in the blanket like a watchful badger. "I was beginnin' to think we wasn't gonna have much excitement on this trip."

Although the golden-haired Seeker was young, he wasn't stupid; he and his hunting hounds had trapped Merrimyn in the ravine rather easily, relying on the exhausted Binder's terror to do most of the work. Like coyotes driving a stray sheep to exhaustion, the dogs loped on each side and kept him moving in the desired direction, forcing him down the creek bed, staying just far enough away to further undermine his already strained reason. Now that he saw the high cliffs of the gully above him, Merrimyn cursed his panic and lack of good sense, but it didn't change anything—he was still in worse danger than he'd been since fleeing Eromar City. The snaring-tome pulsed painfully in his arm, as if emphasizing his precarious situation. If he didn't think of something quickly, he'd be on his way back to Vald's prison; unless, of course, this hotheaded Seeker had orders otherwise. As a fugitive, he could be killed with impunity here; as far as Merrimyn knew, he was still in Eromar and still under the authority of the Dreydmaster. The merchant train he'd seen earlier in the morning was too far away to help him now.

The narrow ravine opened up, and the creek emptied into a wide, cold pond that stretched across the base of the cliffs. He was trapped; the only exit stood at the other end of the pond, and he couldn't swim. He might try wading, but the pond looked deep and murky, and he didn't relish his chances in strange waters. Harsh howls from back up the creek ended all hesitation, and he plunged forward. Whatever his chances might be here, they were better than he'd have with the Seeker's kill-trained hounds.

The escape from Eromar City had been easier than Merrimyn expected, and that, he now realized, had eased him into a dangerous overconfidence. After leaving his Unhuman rescuer, he'd slipped through the stables and out one of the granary chutes, grabbing a saddle blanket and a sack of biscuits and bruised apples on his way. He'd wound his way down to the gates, where he joined the late-morning rush of laborers for the smelting mills beyond the city walls. From there he simply slipped off the road and followed the foul-smelling Orm River south. He was occasionally harassed by thugs and children on the road, but each time he simply revealed his snaring-tome and chains, and his assailants backed away, too frightened even to mutter against him.

Such moments of self-preservation were, unfortunately, a glaring trail that doubtless took the Seeker no real effort to follow. Merrimyn didn't know he was being followed until just a few days past, when the hounds rushed out of the darkness and woke him from a deep sleep in the small, mossy hollow where he'd camped. It was a simple strategy but effective. The dogs kept him from sleeping or resting; each time he tried to slow down, they moved in closer with teeth bared and menacing snarls. These Dreyd-raised creatures had no fear of the snaring-tome, so he'd stumbled ever onward, increasingly more exhausted, until at last their master was ready to move in.

And that time was now. Merrimyn gasped and coughed in the pond, the water up to his chin. His eyes were wide with fear, but he still struggled on in the brown water, unwilling to turn back.

<<Enough running, coward—it's time to go.>> The Seeker knelt by the edge of the water with his sword unsheathed. He wasn't much older than the Binder, although his travel leathers testified to a much more worldly existence. His pale hair and sparse mustache stood out starkly against sun-bronzed skin. He smiled, clearly quite pleased with himself and his successful catch.

<<I . . . can't . . .>> Merrimyn gasped. <<I can't swim back!>> He struggled against the muddy water, sinking under the waves for a moment, then his head surfaced again. <<Help me . . . please!>>

The Seeker shook his head in disgust and whistled to his dogs, but they stopped at the edge of the water and whined, unwilling to move forward. He sighed. <<I don't know why you're worth all this trouble, long-neck. You'd better not get my hair wet.>>

He slid into the pond and recoiled slightly as the frigid water flowed over the tops of his boots. Seeing Merrimyn's terrified eyes focused firmly on him, the Seeker shrugged off the discomfort with a laugh and swaggered his way through the water. But when he reached the flailing Binder, his arrogant features clouded with confusion. The water was only up to his waist. Why was the Binder drowning?

Merrimyn exploded out of the pond with a guttural howl and threw his snaring-tome chain around the Seeker's neck. Before the stunned Man had a chance to react, Merrimyn whipped open the pages of the strange, flesh-bound book and pushed them hard against the Seeker's face. The hunter shrieked and splashed backward as acrid smoke billowed from the eldritch tome, but the Binder pulled the chain tighter, his eyes wild, trapping the Man in the book's deathless hunger. There was a sizzling, popping hiss. The Seeker's hands fluttered desperately against the binding, like the wings of a wounded bird, but the struggle was brief, and his body quickly went limp and dropped heavily into the water. Merrimyn didn't need to look to know that the Seeker's face had been completely eaten away.

A raw, vital rush of strength pulsed from the cursed book into the Binder's veins, and he groaned with fear-filled pleasure. He wasn't a cruel Man at heart; this life had been chosen for him by a tyranni-cal, Dreyd-fearing father, and his soul recoiled every time he opened those pages to force eternal imprisonment on another living creature. This self-loathing was why he'd failed Vald, and why he now fled Eromar City. But he couldn't deny that there was a tantalizing ecstasy in Binding; it gave him pleasure and vigor like nothing else. Binders were forbidden from physical gratification with other living flesh, as their links with the snaring-tomes required unyielding chastity to keep them from the madness that came with the excess of sensation, but he thought that these moments of light-headed delight must be some-thing akin to the sensual joys experienced by the rest of Humanity.

The sudden cold realization of the dead Man floating in the water beside him brought Merrimyn's thoughts back to the present.

Whatever other Humans experienced, at least their pleasures didn't require the snuffing out of another living spirit. Their connective ecstasy was something he would never know; he would always be untouched, alone. He stumbled out of the water, and the dogs fled, whining and yelping as they ran back up the creek bed. The Binder wanted to cry, to rage against the unending horrors of this life, but he was too soul-sick and weary. It was his fate to bring death to the world around him; only in self-imposed exile could he hope to struggle against it.

He thought back to the traders' wagons on the road a few miles back from the upper end of the gully. They were heading south. Perhaps he could find a respite among strangers, at least until he was far from Eromar. Then he'd find his own way in the world—unloved, but a danger to none. Tears stinging his eyes, Merrimyn staggered back up the ravine and away from the faceless body that sank slowly into the cold, dark water.

"We've stopped," young Athweid said.

Reiil pulled himself up and rubbed his eyes. He smiled at Tarsa. "I didn't know if I'd be able to fall asleep. I'm glad the journey is over; it'll be nice to get out and stretch for a while." He reached for the door handle.

Tarsa's sensory stalks twitched slightly in their wrappings, and she bolted upright. "I don't think we should—"

The door opened. Torchlight flashed in the darkness beyond, and Reiil jerked backward, eyes wide, his bright blood spraying like a hot red rain from the iron-tipped crossbow bolt that tore through his throat.

"*Bandits!*" Tobhi's shout echoed shrilly in the twilight.

Athweid screamed out and grabbed Hak'aad, who squirmed away from Reiil's thrashing form. Tarsa pulled the gurgling trader toward her, desperately trying to stop the flow of blood, but she dove to the carriage floor herself as the roar of a musket blasted through the air and shattered the windows. Imweshi and the others dropped beside her.

"We've got to help him!" Imweshi screamed, wrapping her hands around the steaming wound in Reiil's throat. Tarsa nodded, but her mind was on what was happening outside the carriage. She'd already felt Reiil's spirit escape in the brief moment she held him; there could be no help for this sad, lost elder—not from here, anyway. Now she had to make sure the rest of them stayed alive. She crouched low and tried to listen beyond the weeping cries of the three Kyn beside her. Though a Wielder, her first training was in the arts of war and defense. She was a Redthorn still.

The carriage suddenly lurched forward, throwing everyone askew, and then it was moving again, flailing wildly back and forth, plunging down the road. Stripping off her cloak, Tarsa kicked the door open. She slid to the side to see what was beyond before swinging onto the outer side of the carriage.

So much was happening that it was difficult to see what was going on. The Ubbetuk was dead or wounded; she could see his thin, green-capped shape slumped down and lodged tightly between the seat and baggage rack behind it. Tobhi was bent double and viciously fighting off two Men who were balanced precariously on the seat over him. Another Man clung to one of the mechanical ponies with one arm while readying a large crossbow with the other. She turned to see several more Men on horseback galloping toward them from behind. And in the distance ahead rose the fiery shadow of Eromar City.

"Grab something secure!" Tarsa shouted to the Kyn in the carriage and pulled herself up to the roof, where she saw another Man kneeling precariously with a long knife in his hand. He lunged toward her, but the knife slashed empty air as the Redthorn warrior ducked back to the side of the carriage, tensed, and flew upward again, her momentum carrying her fully to the roof. Her fist shot out and snapped hard into the Man's throat, propelling him backward, up and over the back of the carriage, and down screaming into the road.

A sudden jolt shook the coach again, and Tarsa stumbled down, cracking her knee on one of the luggage chests lashed to the roof. Gritting her teeth, the Redthorn warrior pulled herself forward. One of the Men fighting Tobhi had stumbled backward to the roof's edge. He was too busy trying to maintain his footing to notice the she-Kyn who slid behind him, or the wyrwood knife that flashed over his back for the briefest moment to slice cleanly across his throat.

Saying a silent prayer of thanks to Jitani for the blade, and ignoring the Man's death agonies that pulsed through the wrappings of her stalks, Tarsa kicked his twitching body off the coach as Tobhi smashed his head into the other attacker's chin, opening enough room between them to drive his hatchet into the Man's belly. The Man screamed, and then Tarsa's booted foot struck into his mouth, knocking him into the air. His screams were lost in the heavy crunch of his body smashing into a jagged rock wall.

The carriage rolled on.

Tobhi nodded in gratitude but had little time to relax, as a crossbow bolt splintered the wood beside his hand. The Man on one of the front gear-work ponies had secured his position and readied another bolt. Tarsa reached down, jerked the bolt out of the seat, and threw it at the archer. It sped past the Man and skittered harmlessly into the dirt. He turned his crossbow on the she-Kyn with a leer. The smile vanished, though, as Tarsa launched herself through the air with knife in hand and landed, too heavily, on the pony beside the Man's. Something snapped in her side, and a red haze of pain swept across her vision. Gasping for air through broken ribs, Tarsa pulled herself up on the unyielding pony, and jerked the knife at the Man beside her. He dodged and readied his crossbow again but slipped a bit on the mechanical creature as Tobhi yanked on the braking lever.

"No!" Tarsa gasped, barely able to speak, pointing her knife behind them. Tobhi turned to see the horsemen gaining ground. He spun back, released the braking lever, and pushed hard with all his strength on the propulsion lever. The ponies shot forward again, sending the carriage snapping back and forth from the sudden shift in momentum. The Tetawa fell to the floorboard with a curse.

Tarsa lost her grip and slipped between the ponies; the Man clung helplessly to his rushing mechanical mount, his crossbow now lost on the road behind them. The she-Kyn kicked her legs out, and she hung there, suspended with her feet on one machine and her back tensed against the other. Sliding her knife into its scabbard, she crept upward until she was free of the gap and could push herself backward toward the pony she had landed on. She nearly fainted from the searing agony in her side, but she made it to the top, where she sat breathing heavily and trying to focus her thoughts. The Man ignored her; he just clutched the pony with white knuckles and shaking hands.

Tobhi picked himself up and looked backward. The riders were lost in the thick dust; he wasn't sure if they were still following. He heard a metallic crack from one of the rear gear-work ponies and saw a billowing cloud of black smoke rise from its underbelly.

Tarsa could barely breathe; her broken ribs burned with every jolting movement. Looking up, she saw the log palisade of the city gate yawning open toward them. She turned back to see the Man watching her, and a cold chill crept across her skin as her gaze drifted toward his chest, where the crest of the House of Vald was emblazoned on his vest. He was waiting for the gate, too, waiting to call down the guards upon them.

Their attackers all wore these jerkins. She understood now.

The diplomats were never meant to reach Gorthac Hall.

Heedless of the pain in her side and stalks, Tarsa flung herself at the Man with a shrill battle trill, her unsheathed knife slashing through the air like cougars' claws as she landed on him and clamped her legs tightly around the pony's belly to trap him face-down beneath her. The Man thrashed and screamed, struggling to free himself while maintaining his grip, but it was useless—he couldn't stop the ferocious storm of blade and fist. Blood sprayed into the air, and the screams rose to a thin, screeching wail of torment that went suddenly silent as the coach bore down on the gate.

Guardsmen rushed out of the shadows of the gatehouse to see a handsome Ubbetuk carriage, pulled by four brown ponies shrouded in smoke, rushing toward the massive wooden gates with the sound of clanging thunder. The Men barely had time to duck out of the way when the ponies and carriage smashed with a deafening roar into the gates, scattering springs, shards of metal, and fragments of wood everywhere. Black smoke rose up in thick clouds from the wreckage.

The Men stepped from cover to examine the strange ruins, stopping in fear and amazement as a blue-green radiance suddenly shone through the smoke. A small shape stepped out of the light, followed closely by three bent, coughing figures. The strangers moved away from the debris and stood together, faces grim, staring at the glowing haze as if in expectation.

A great rolling plume of radiant smoke billowed forward and parted to reveal another shape stumble from the wreckage, her head held proudly, honey-brown braids flowing behind her on an unseen wind. Her bright eyes burned in the torchlight, and her tattooed face was grim. She carried something under her right arm; the other cupped her side protectively.

Tarsa walked up to the wide-eyed militia guards and held the head of the crossbowman in the air. Her voice icy, she growled with obvious distaste in the Mannish tongue, <<Tell Dreydmaster Vald that his guests have arrived.>> She tossed the brigand's head to the ground at the guardsmen's feet. <<And thus far, his hospitality is rather lacking.>>

18

Gorthac Hall

TARSA HISSED AS TOBHI PULLED the linen strip tighter beneath her breasts to keep her broken ribs from moving. He waited with lips tight and brows furrowed while the Wielder took a few shallow breaths and tried to push her thoughts past the pain. At length she nodded, and Tobhi carefully continued wrapping until the bandage was tight and secure. Tarsa sighed heavily and nodded in thanks, sliding the thick wyrweave blouse back over her chest, securing it again with her wide chanting-sash. This was followed by her leaf and feather cloak, which was singed and blackened in places. Her eyes were heavy with pain and exhaustion, but rage burned there, too, and it was that fire which gave her strength now.

Their present accommodations were hardly welcoming. The militiamen at the outer walls had led the group to a squat stone building, where they would wait until summoned by the Dreydmaster. So Tobhi and Tarsa sat, together with Imweshi, Hak'aad, and Athweid and most of their recovered gear, on rough wooden benches in a smoky, low-ceilinged meeting room that stank of stale Man-sweat and fresh blood. Four long tables, each pitted and gouged with the wear of time and rough use, stretched down the length of the room. The muted crackle from the fireplace at the northern end of the narrow chamber gave no comfort; if anything, its furtive light gave a decidedly ominous mood to the shifting shadows. The shrouded bodies of Gweggi and Reiil lying on a table at the other end of the room chased away the few remaining flickers of warmth.

Tobhi walked to the table nearest the fireplace, drew out his badger-etched leaf pouch, and sat down. He withdrew the leaves from the pouch and unwrapped them from their protective red cloth, checking each individual leaf for signs of damage or wear. Though all eighty-six were unharmed, they felt different now, heavier and less responsive. The Tetawa focused his thoughts and lifted a couple into the air, but they dropped to the table and snapped apart.

"What does it mean?" Tarsa asked, slipping carefully onto the bench beside him.

The Leafspeaker folded the broken leaves together and sighed. "Just what yer own dampened Wieldin' means. We en't much in touch with the *wyr* no more, so we gotta be careful. We en't got these gifts to rely on now."

"Can you read them at all?"

"Sure," Tobhi nodded. "But I can't be certain what I read is truthful, 'cause m' thoughts and their voices is all muddled up with this smoke and foulness around. I en't as sharp here as I was in the clear air back home. But I can still do it. Do ye want me to try?"

Tarsa considered but finally shook her head. "No, not yet. I don't even know what I'd ask you, anyway. Let's think about this for a while. We've got enough to try to understand right now." She looked at the three Kyn diplomats who huddled together at the far end of the room. Lowering her voice, she said, "Those Men who attacked us weren't just roving thugs. They wore the badge of Eromar."

"Yeah, I saw 'em. Ye think he sent 'em after us?" Tobhi returned the leaves to their pouch.

"Why not?"

"It just don't make no sense. Why would Vald risk goin' after us on the open road, where we might be able to get away? Wouldn't it be more sensible to just wait 'til we was up at Gorthac Hall, where nobody would see what was goin' on, and throttle us in our sleep or somethin'? We was probably a whole lot safer on the road than we'll be in his house."

The Wielder smiled grimly. "Yes, but don't forget one important thing, Tobhi: *he'll* be much less safe once we arrive at Gorthac Hall, and he knows it."

The night was deep upon them when the door to the meeting house swung open and a group of armed Men entered. The three Celestial Kyn had remained at a distance from Tarsa and Tobhi since first arriving in the room, but now they skittered to the Folk warriors with faces pale and eyes wide. Tobhi puffed calmly on a thin-stemmed pipe and remained on the bench. Tarsa stood to face the newcomers, her hands crossed over the wyrwood staff in front of her.

These Men wore long black coats that reached to their knees, matching in grim tone their wide-brimmed grey hats. Most of the Men had thick beards or muttonchops, and all wore heavy leather boots and brass-buttoned leather vests that rose nearly to their chins. Most bore long daggers, thin clubs, or crossbows in their hands, although Tarsa noticed short flintlocks strapped over the shoulders of two of the Men. The three-tined star of the House of Vald was emblazoned on each Man's vest.

For a moment the two groups regarded each other warily, until the Men's ranks opened to reveal another figure, a green-eyed he-Kyn with black hair and golden skin, who stepped forward and held his open hand to his chest in greeting. With a sidelong glance to the Men around him, the he-Kyn said in Mannish, <<Welcome, my kindred. Dreydmaster Vald sends his greetings, tempered by heartfelt condolences for your loss. The Dreydmaster has asked me to escort you safely to your chambers at Gorthac Hall, with the request that we break fast with him in the morning. There is much for us all to discuss.>>

Imweshi's sour features softened into a well rehearsed smile. <<Please tell the illustrious Prime of Eromar that we would be honored to join him at his leisure, and that we send our most sincere thanks for his hospitality.>>

Tarsa turned toward the elder she-Kyn and opened her mouth to speak, her eyes narrowing dangerously, but Tobhi turned toward her and, while knocking the ashes from his pipe, gave his head the slightest shake. The room bristled with tension. The Men shifted uneasily at the sight of the angry, tattooed she-Kyn, but Tarsa took a quivering breath and stepped back beside the Tetawa.

Imweshi turned to give Tarsa a cold smirk, and walked across the room to join the dark-haired he-Kyn, whose own eyes lingered for just a moment on the Wielder before he took the elder she-Kyn's arm and led her out of the room. Athweid and Hak'aad followed Imweshi.

<<What about our other companions?>> Tarsa pointed to the covered bodies on the table beside the door. The language of Men was cold ash in her mouth.

A Man who was clearly of some authority said, <<We're here to take you to the Dreydmaster. Nobody said anything about carrying corpses. Leave them here and come with us.>>

Tarsa laughed bitterly. <<No, I don't think we'll leave them. I've seen too well how your kind treat the dead.>> She slipped the staff into the back of her waist-sash before bending down to lift Reiil's body over her shoulder. Tobhi did the same with Gweggi, who was lighter than the Tetawa had anticipated. He could see Tarsa's pain as Reiil's body pushed down on her broken ribs and made each breath like a fresh wound in her chest. But the Wielder stood proudly, her muscles and jaw tight, and glared at the Men, who looked uncertainly at one another.

Finally, the leader pointed toward the door. <<Just go—and don't expect any help from us.>> He frowned at the defiant Folk and stepped out of the meeting house. Taking a deep, measured breath, Tarsa followed, Reiil's body held gently in her arms.

The group moved from the guardhouse toward the brick-cobbled street that stretched up the butte toward Gorthac Hall. The streets were crowded with dull, soot-smeared Humans, but they gave Vald's militiamen a wide berth, thus providing the Folk free passage through the filthy streets. Tobhi gagged at the heavy stench in the air; it clutched at the back of his throat, the thick, sour weight drifting in part from roughly chiseled sewage ditches on each side of the street that snaked down the side of the butte toward the river. Rats and worse slid across their feet and between their legs as they walked. Athweid was soon sobbing in terror, but Hak'aad was no comfort, for he was beside his mother fighting down his own fear. Acidic smoke rolled through the alleys and buildings from the foundry stacks above to join the stink of sewage and the bitter, ever-present tang of iron. The thick air held an eerie, greenish yellow hue, sometimes so heavy that it choked off the sputtering light from the coal oil street lamps lining the streets. The newcomers soon found themselves fighting for breath from the foul air, and even those who had lived here for some time found the stench almost overwhelming. But they continued on.

The journey was worst for Tarsa, whose proud endurance was crumbling with every step. The toxic air burned her lungs; each cough drove burning agony through her ribs, and Reiil's body weighed heavier on her shoulders. By the time they reached the third palisade, Tarsa could barely move. Although most of the smoke and fetid air crouched behind them over the lower levels of Eromar City, every new breath tore through her like a knife. She was ill again, and her stalks, although bound and eased somewhat by the iron-ward, were almost overwhelmed by the pain of this place.

Step, step, step. Breath. Step, step, step. Breath. Breath. Step, step. Breath. She had a pattern now, yet it was breaking down. She would never make it to Gorthac Hall. But how could she leave Reiil behind in this place of poison and misery?

She stumbled, and as she fell she knew that she wouldn't be able to stand again. But then a hand was under her arm, pulling her back to her feet. The binding on her chest tore slightly, and Tarsa groaned from the searing pain.

It was a strange voice in a familiar language. "Be strong, Wielder. We don't have much farther to go. Let me help you."

Tarsa's mind cleared a bit, and she turned to see the green-eyed he-Kyn beside her, his polished black leathers shining in the Men's dull torchlight ahead of them.

"I don't need . . . your help," she growled. Though she tried to pull her arm away from him, he held her firmly.

"Then let me help Reiil, for he was long known to me, and I always thought him a friend." Tarsa noticed for the first time that the he-Kyn's golden face was haggard with exhaustion and sorrow.

Her strength wavered, and she nodded. The he-Kyn slid Reiil's body from her and staggered under the weight as he shifted the body to his own shoulder. He looked at the Wielder with surprised admiration but said nothing. Tarsa slid Dibadjiibé from her sash and leaned heavily on the staff as they walked together up the dark street.

Gorthac Hall was far more imposing from afar than from closer observation. Built of heavy granite and stout timbers torn from the now vanished 'Hold forests of northern Eromar, the Hall stood on the top of the butte, where the Dreydmaster could survey his world without obstruction. Known throughout the province as the "Hall of a Thousand Gables," the edifice was a rambling mass of sharp angles, jutting gables, hooded eaves, stout doors hidden in shadowed recesses, narrow balconies, and wide, darkened walls. Its clay-shingled central tower stretched eighty feet into the air, reaching like a piercing spike into the night sky; a broad wooden balcony, lit by iron braziers on bars that stretched outward from the roof above, was Vald's favorite observation point. None found comfort when the Dreydmaster strode the tower.

Secrets were comfortable in Gorthac Hall, and things crawled among the shadows without fear of daylight. The will of its makers had penetrated the Fey wood with every iron nail, the stone with every mason's chisel mark. Many rooms in the rambling estate had never been seen by living eyes, and others were known to the Dreydmaster alone. Indeed, strange corners and chambers appeared on occasion, although the ring of builder's hammers had been unheard for nearly a hundred years. A steady stream of servants came and went, or arrived and were never seen again, lost in the wandering, oak-paneled walls. With every passing year, the Hall rooted itself deeper, clutching the wind-blistered butte with a determination beyond reckoning.

Tarsa was nearly delirious with pain and sensory exhaustion when the group arrived at Gorthac Hall; their duty done, the militiamen returned to their quarters in the city. The green-eyed he-Kyn asked the Hall Steward to find a suitable place for the dead Kyn and Ubbetuk to be kept until proper funeral services could be arranged, then led the survivors to their quarters in the western wing. The Steward joined them shortly after.

All the Kyn were housed in the same hallway, a cold, drafty series of rooms with narrow windows that looked to the jagged northern highlands. Hak'aad had a room to himself, while his mother and Athweid shared a small chamber with a single bed. All of the bed linens were rough and musty, but they were clean.

When they reached the room where Tarsa would stay, Tobhi said, <<If ye don't mind, I think I'll just bed down here with her. There's plenty of room.>>

The Steward blanched. <<That's impossible.>>
<<Why?>>
<<I'm afraid I cannot allow it. It's improper.>>

Tarsa, clutching at the door frame, whispered hoarsely, <<I would very much like . . . for him to be here. He's trained in medicinals, and he . . . >>

The Steward waved his hand dismissively. <<We have a fine alchaemical doctor here. You will be well cared for, I assure you. I will send for him.>> He turned to lead them down the hallway but stopped when Tarsa lunged forward and caught him by the throat, her eyes wild.

<<I'll have nothing to do with your Mannish witchery!>>

Gasping, the Steward clutched at the she-Kyn's hand, and though she was weakened by her injuries and stood a head shorter than him, he couldn't break free of her grasp. The green-eyed he-Kyn stepped forward and pulled her hand away, gently but firmly.

<<She is ill, Steward, and is in need of particular skills found only in the Everland. This Brownie is here to care for her. There can hardly be anything 'improper' in that, can there?>>

His eyes bulging, the Steward frantically shook his wispy-haired head. Tarsa pushed the Man against the wall and staggered into the room. Tobhi smiled and bowed to both the Man and the he-Kyn. He followed Tarsa and shut the door behind them.

<<I will speak to the Dreydmaster about this outrage, you can be assured, Ambassador,>> the Steward coughed, smoothing the wrinkles from his silken jacket.

The he-Kyn spun around. He drove the Steward to the wall again and held something cold and sharp against the Man's bristly neck. His green eyes burned with barely contained frenzy. <<Are you threatening me, you gibbering imbecile?>> he hissed into the Man's ear. <<If you are, I'll cut out your tongue and feed it to you in slivers. Don't forget: alone of my people *I* have survived. Don't imagine that you'll be able to succeed where better Men have failed.>>

The Man's mouth gaped and quivered, and the sharp tang of hot urine filled the hallway. The he-Kyn looked down at the floor beneath the Steward and smiled with grim satisfaction. <<Get out of here, stink-skin, and don't return unless it's to clean up this mess. I won't be so gentle with you again.>>

He stepped back, and the Steward stumbled away. The he-Kyn stood watching the darkened hallway long after the Man had fled. At last, a voice in the Everland trade-tongue broke his reverie. "I heard some commotion out here. Seems ye en't the drag-tailed dog I took ye for."

The Tetawa stepped into the hallway and pulled the door closed behind him. His hat and satchels were in the room, but he held his lit pipe out to the he-Kyn, who took it and drew deeply. "It's been so long since I've heard a familiar word, or shared a pipe. I am Daladir Tre'shein, Ash Branch brother of Sheynadwiin. *Tsodoka.*"

"Name's Tobhi—Badger Clan of my people. It's a pleasure." They leaned against the hallway wall for a while, passing the pipe between them. The cleansing scent of fresh tobacco lifted the gloom somewhat. When the bowl was finished, Tobhi tapped it against his boot, knocking the ashes to the ground. "Where's the other diplomats? We en't heard nothin' about 'em since we got here."

The he-Kyn gave Tobhi a haunted look. "There are no others here. Of the fourteen who came here last spring, and of the five who survived the winter, I'm the only one who remains."

"*Nashaabi!*" the Tetawa cursed. "The only one?"

"Until now, yes."

"Well, it'll be easier than we was guessin', although it's grim news, to be sure."

The he-Kyn looked at Tobhi quizzically. "What do you mean?"

"C'mon in. We better talk out of the hall." Tobhi led the he-Kyn into the room and slid the door bolt firmly behind them.

The he-Kyn looked around. A smoking oil lamp glimmered softly on the windowsill, casting its gentle light across the small room. His eyes were drawn immediately to the bed, where Tarsa lay asleep, her dark, tangled hair floating across the thick coverlet, one tattooed arm resting on top of the blankets.

"How is she?" he asked, his voice barely above a whisper.

"She'll be better after a bit of sleep, I think; fortunately, Wielders heal fast. It's been a long trip for us all, but 'specially her."

The he-Kyn smiled. "I think you could use some rest, too, Tobhi."

"Yeah." The Leafspeaker yawned. "Ye won't hear no complaint from me there. But that'll have to wait a bit, I think." He smiled warmly. "Daladir, we're here to take ye home."

Relief and fear flooded the he-Kyn's face. "It's over, then?"

"Not yet." Tobhi refilled his pipe bowl and lit it with a flaming sliver of wood from the oil lamp. "But the Sevenfold Council en't takin' too kindly to Vald's terms. When they do make their decision, it en't likely that ye'd want to be anywhere near here. So we're here to make sure you en't."

They sat in smoky silence as the Ambassador reflected on the news.

"It won't be easy," he said at last, his eyes returning to Tarsa's sleeping form. "The Dreydmaster is no fool, and your sudden arrival, especially with a Wielder, puts us in terrible danger. You won't know it for some time, however—Vald is nothing if not the measure of rigid courtesy. He'll toy with us, like a sated cat, until he tires of the game. And then he'll strike with as much mercy, as he's done so many times before."

Exhaustion pulled at the he-Kyn's words, and though he looked hale and strong, there was a furtive quality about him, a dread that lurked behind his green eyes, the certainty of oblivion crawling slowly toward them. Tobhi suppressed a shudder. *What happened in this place to fill him with so much worry?*

"I must go—I've been here too long. She made an unnecessary enemy in the Steward this evening, and I didn't help matters afterward." Daladir stood suddenly and walked to the door. "Be wary, Tobhi, friend of the reckless Wielder. You're in the hound-pit now, and they hunger." The darkness returned to his eyes as he looked to Tarsa's sleeping form, and then he was gone.

Tobhi finished his pipe, lost in thought, before returning it to his satchel. He chewed for a bit on a piece of cleansing birch wood, then lowered the lamp wick, took off his overgarments, and slid under the covers beside Tarsa, curling close to keep her warm in the deepening chill. He slipped easily to sleep, but those haunted green eyes lingered long in his thoughts, and his dreams brought no comfort.

19

The Dreydmaster's Welcome

<<WELCOME TO MY TABLE, honored guests.>> Dreydmaster Vald stood at his seat and bowed to the visitors as they entered the dining hall. The wide room was bare of decoration, except for a long table of burnished cherry wood and a series of benches that stretched nearly from the door to Vald's massive seat. A large fire blazed in the Man-high hearth behind the Dreydmaster. The dull light of morning crept into the room through uneven panes of thick glass set every few feet in the paneled walls. Though weak, the sunlight was welcome, as it brought more warmth to their flesh than did the leering fireplace that belched out smoke and hissing embers.

Daladir led the group to the seats nearest the Dreydmaster, who, except for a few faithful retainers, was otherwise alone in the room. Tarsa's observed the Man who'd orchestrated such fear in the Everland. He was nothing like she'd expected. He had no striking features other than the thick brows that bristled over his hawk-like nose, no dark aura of malice. A tallish Man, neither fat nor skinny, handsome or ugly, Vald was indistinguishable from the hundred other Men she had seen in the past few days, except for his fine dark garments, neatly trimmed peppered muttonchops, and broad, ink-stained fingers that were free of callus and wear. She had expected a monster, but instead she'd met a surprisingly ordinary Man.

Daladir bowed low. <<Dreydmaster Vald, Sanctified Voice of Authority in the Province of Eromar within the Reach of Men, I wish to introduce you to my recently arrived companions, who have traveled at great urgency from the Everland to speak with you at your leisure and grace. I believe you have met one of them before, when she was last assigned to this post.>>

Tarsa and Tobhi exchanged quick glances.

<<Yes, I recognize the Lady Imweshi,>> Vald said, his deep voice a resonant purr. <<It is a pleasure to welcome a Celestial matron of such wisdom to my home once again. Please introduce me to your companions; I am quite curious about them.>>

The elder she-Kyn flushed as she turned to the others. <<This is my youngest son, Hak'aad, and with him is Athweid, daughter of my cousin's wife. They have accompanied me to learn better the wisdom of Men, so that they might one day bring that wisdom to the service of our people.>>

Vald smiled slightly, and he nodded to the younger Kyn. Then his eyes turned to the tattooed Wielder who wore her singed leaf and feather cloak of office over her travel-worn leathers. <<And who else have you brought on this visit?>>

Imweshi began to speak, but Tarsa's hand slashed through the air, silencing the matron. <<I am Tarsa'deshae, the Spearbreaker.>> Even in Mannish her voice was clear and strong. <<I was born into the Cedar Branch of Red Cedar Town, daughter of Lan'delar Last Born, niece of the Wielder Unahi Sam'sheyda, granddaughter of Ayeddi'olaan. My people know me as a Redthorn warrior and Wielder of the Deep Green. Imweshi's words are her own; she does not speak for me.>>

All held their breaths as the Dreydmaster and the Wielder coolly regarded one another in the tense silence. Tobhi's sharp ears caught the sound of boot nails on stone in the hallway, and though he knew the gesture was futile, he slid his hand toward the tiny sheath on his belt. Vald was indeed no fool; while his hall spoke of welcome, he left nothing to chance. Tobhi hadn't wanted to leave his hatchet in the room as protocol demanded, and now he wished that he had more than a little wyrwood dagger between his flesh and Vald's militiamen.

Vald bowed, breaking the tension. <<Welcome then, Tarsa'deshae of Cedar Branch, to the world of Men. It has been many years since a

bearer of the ancient traditions of your people has come willingly to Eromar. Perhaps this is a sign of a new spirit of cooperation between our nations.>>

Tarsa nodded but remained silent.

Daladir introduced Tobhi, whom Vald ignored as he motioned to the main door of the hall. The air crackled like the air before a spring storm, and the door swung open to reveal a small, pale Woman in a dull saffron dress and white head cap, followed by two thin, dark-eyed girls in green.

<<My goodly wife, Betthia, and daughters, Sheda and Methieul.>> Vald clapped his hands. <<My son, Sadish, will be unable to join us today, as he is touring the foundry district. We will eat, now.>> Betthia and her daughters bowed their heads and slipped like shadows through the door behind the Dreydmaster, to emerge moments later with thick platters of greasy meats and gravies, long loaves of thick-grained breads, and bowls of thin oat porridge. Vald didn't share their food; he had his own plate of meat and bread, delicately spiced. The Women kept their eyes averted from their guests. When young Methieul brought the porridge to Tarsa, the young Woman trembled visibly.

Vald watched as the plates were piled high, all but that of the Wielder. <<Does our food displease you, Wielder?>> he asked gently.

She shook her head. <<The breads and vegetables are more than adequate for me, Dreydmaster.>>

<<But my wife prepared the suckling roast in your honor.>>

<<I thank you, Dreydmaster, but I cannot eat animal flesh. It is not the way of my people, even though some may have forgotten this.>> She looked at Hak'aad and Daladir, who both held meat forks in hand.

The master of Gorthac Hall leaned forward, and his voice took on a hard edge. <<It is discourteous to refuse food given by your host.>>

Tarsa smiled in response, but it didn't reach her shining eyes. <<A courteous host wouldn't prepare food that his guests couldn't eat.>>

Imweshi dropped her knife, her face pale, and Daladir coughed on a bite of food. Tobhi listened to the conversation without much interest and continued to eat his roast, as this Kyn tradition was not shared by the Tetawi. The meat was overcooked and had a slightly bitter aftertaste, but it was a welcome change from the nuts and dried fruit in his satchel. The bread tasted fine, especially when dipped in the greasy gravy that sloshed at the edge of his plate.

The Dreydmaster suddenly broke into a smooth laugh. <<Too true, Wielder, too true. Very well—you will be served those foods that best suit your delicate constitution. I trust you do not object too strenuously to your companions' eating habits?>>

<<What they eat is none of my concern.>>

Vald clapped his hands. <<Good. All is settled, then.>> He turned back to Imweshi. <<I understand that you lost companions yesterday during the attack by ruffians. My condolences to you all.>>

Tarsa glared at the Man, but Imweshi pointedly ignored her. <<Yes. A Goblin, and one of our own, Reiil Cethwir, whose uncle Damodhed once served beside you in the Battle of Downed Timber on the borderland of the Everland and Eromar.>>

<<Kyn and Men fought together?>> Athweid asked, incredulous.

<<Yes,>> the Dreydmaster replied. <<We need not always be enemies. When I was much younger, brigands swept down from The Lawless to the north, threatening both the lands of Men and of the Folk. It took us many months and a great many lives, but we managed to stop them before they reached Lake Ithiak. In fact, it was Damodhed who saved my life during that battle. I had been struck from behind and knocked to the ground. Just as an enemy was preparing to run me through with his spear, Damodhed crushed his skull with a well-placed blow from his war-club. I am sorry to hear that his kinsman has died in such unfortunate circumstances.>>

<<It was more than unfortunate,>> Tarsa growled. <<We were ambushed.>>

<<Yes, so much hatred, so much unnecessary pain.>> Vald shook his head sadly. He smiled at Athweid. <<And yet there is always hope. Misunderstandings arise, and people suffer because of them. But there are always opportunities for brave individuals to take control of their own destinies and take a new path, a wiser path that can break down these age-old prejudices and bring us all closer together, to give all people the hope of a good future, not just the remnants of a fading past.>> The young she-Kyn smiled at his words and turned to Hak'aad, who returned her smile and clasped her hand under the table.

Tarsa looked toward the windows that overlooked the city. <<If I may ask, what is the future you're offering us, Dreydmaster?>>

Vald turned to her and smiled, as though indulging a petulant child. <<Why, progress, my dear Spearbreaker. What could be
more important?>>

<<Progress? By whose measure? I'm not sure I understand what
that word means here. Iron machines belching yellow smoke, hungry people and poisoned waters. It seems to be a gift my people could
do quite well without.>>

Hak'aad let out a strangled gasp, and Athweid held her hand to
her mouth. For the briefest moment Tarsa saw the Dreydmaster's
face contort into something else, something ill-concealed and ravenous beneath the Man's skin. Then it vanished. Vald sighed heavily
and turned to Athweid with wounded eyes. <<This is what I speak
of. The Wielder, not understanding the power of industry, its ability
to strip away shiftlessness and weakness, instead chooses to attack
it, to surrender to her lower urges, to give way to fear. But gentle
lady, do not be angry with her. Pity her. Her time is at an end, and
she knows it. You and your solid friend there are the future, for you
understand that the ways of Men are only dangerous for the weak
and the corrupt. These goodly ways can help you live virtuous lives
beyond the feral wilderness. Why slink around like whipped dogs
when you can fly with eagles?>>

Vald stood and wiped his mouth with a napkin. <<The world is
changing, my friends, and you must change with it or be washed away
by the flood. None of us can stop this storm—it is inevitable. Now
you must decide, will you build a boat that will carry you to safety,
or will you stand and let the waters wash over you?>> He held his
hand out to Athweid and motioned for the others. <<Come. Let me
show you what this future can bring. We have created a world unlike
anything imagined by your ancestors, or ours, for that matter. Let me
show you what Men can offer to the Folk.>> Hak'aad and Imweshi
followed, leaving Tobhi, Tarsa, and Daladir alone in the dining hall.

"*What are you doing?!*" Daladir hissed when the door creaked
shut. "Are you trying to get us killed? Do you have any idea what
Vald can do?"

Tarsa walked over to the window and looked out. "Of course I
do. Look for yourself. He's killing his own people, poisoning their
bodies as well as their minds. When was the last time a tree grew in
this land? The hills ache from deep roots left to rot. The Everland

sent medicinals to help plague victims in Eromar years ago. Did you notice that he never mentioned this gesture of kindness? He cares nothing for healing. His stories are all of metal, war, and bloodshed. What would you have us do, just sit around and wait for him to kill us and our people, like you've done since you've been here?" Her eyes flashed with building rage.

"You don't know anything about me, about what I've had to do to survive here! And you don't know a Dreyd-damned thing about Lojar Vald. I do. I know what he's capable of, and I've seen him do things that you can't imagine. You think you can just walk into this monster's lair, spit in his face, and walk away? This isn't your back-country village, Wielder, and things aren't so easy here. I've had to watch as my friends, as much my family as my Branch kith, died one by one at Vald's whim. They died, Wielder, in order for Vald to break me down, bit by bit, to tear me into pieces, all for the simple joy of watching me crumble. Why he chose me, I don't know. I could just as easily have died in the darkness with a knotted bedsheet around my neck, just one more of many 'accidents.' But I survived. And then you ride in, the great brave Redthorn Wielder, and you're going to stand up to the Dreydmaster of Eromar? You're arrogant, you're a fool, and you're a danger to all of us. You don't know anything about this," he spat and stormed out of the room.

Tobhi stood up and walked to Tarsa's side. "Don't ye worry 'bout him," he said. "He's just scared, that's all."

"Yes, he's scared. But he's right about one thing." Tarsa looked out the window. "I don't know anything about this world or these people. This place is built on lies and pain and cruelty, all twisted up and tangled like a briar thicket. I don't understand this place, Tobhi." The cloak was heavier than ever with the weight of sudden doubt. "Maybe I *should* have stayed back in Sheynadwiin. Why should I think I know any better than Imweshi, or Hak'aad, or even Vald?"

"Because, Tarsa, ye know what's goin' on *beneath* them lies and pain and cruelty. I watched ye as his wife and daughters came slinkin' through with our food, and you saw what the others didn't want to see. These Women is sufferin' terribly, that they fear this Man like nothin' else in the world. That their great fear should come from the one Man who should love 'em the most is a sad, sad thing. Imweshi and her kind don't see none of that, and Daladir is too caught up in his own hurt. There's a lot more to the world than what's on the surface, and in this place it's what's under the skin that's most important. He can't deceive ye, not unless ye let him break ye down."

Tarsa placed a hand on the Tetawa's shoulder and squeezed gratefully. "Besides," Tobhi whispered as they moved toward the door and their room beyond, "I don't trust nobody who serves a meal with more grease than gravy. There's a sure sign that somethin's wrong. If nothin' else, Tarsa, trust yer stomach."

When the big people were all finally out of the room, the rats sped out, rushing around to capture stray bits of food. As no one came out to take the dishes, the brown creatures clambered up the chairs and onto the table, where they fell upon the chunks of roast and the few crumbs of bread that remained. The sound of the kitchen door swinging open sent the rats scurrying back to their hiding places, back into the safe shadows in the walls.

And it was there, a few hours later, that they died, their claws scrabbling at the fouled floor, their bodies contorted into grotesque shapes, squealing through foam-flecked mouths as the poison burned like liquid fire through their blistered bellies into their blood. The poison didn't work so quickly in larger bodies, but in small forms it was swift. The end result, however, was always the same.

None survived.

20

The Council Decides

"OUR OPTIONS ARE FADING quickly, Captain," Neranda whispered to the he-Kyn beside her. It was the seventh and final night of the Sevenfold Council; six days had passed since the Redthorn Wielder's outburst. Pradu Styke, whose minion Myyrd had not long ago been thoroughly rebuffed by the Lawmaker, now sat beside her at the table, having arrived in the afternoon at her request to watch with growing alarm as debate slowly gave way to consensus. The Beast-tribes, Tetawi, Gvaergs, and Ferals were unanimous in their opposition to the Dreydmaster's Oath of Western Sanctuary, and their counsel seemed to be swaying the Wyrnach. The Kyn were still divided, but, even with Styke's recent arrival, the Celestials were losing support.

Neranda looked over at the Ubbetuk Chancellor, who sat with this hands folded beneath his chin, his eyes narrowed in concentration. He would be the key. The bonds between Ubbetuk and Humans—through trade, politics, and culture—were stronger in many ways than those between Ubbetuk and the rest of the Folk. Blackwick wasn't likely to alienate one of the growing powers in the Reach, certainly not for a group of wayward forest-dwellers who refused to face the inevitable.

The Ubbetuk were Neranda's greatest hope. They were everyone else's greatest fear.

Blackwick suddenly looked up and caught her gaze with his own. His face was inscrutably distant. Then, almost imperceptibly, he nodded at her. His eyes closed again in thought. The Lawmaker leaned back in her own seat, heart throbbing wildly. For the first time in days, she had a spark of hope.

Though the debate might have raged for weeks more until a consensus emerged, with those few opposed eventually withdrawing from the issue, all who were now gathered in the Gallery of Song felt the heavy press of time upon them—a new and unwelcome pressure largely unknown before the arrival of Men. By dawn they would have to reach a decision, and it would determine the future of the Everland—perhaps even the very future of the Folk.

When a brief silence descended, Neranda stood and addressed the Council. "My kith, older sisters and younger brothers, I have heard many good words, many brave words about standing against Eromar and its demands. I do not doubt your hearts, nor your courage, but you speak from the safety of your mountain valleys and deep forests, your caves and aeries. Listen to one who understands the ways of Men, one who has traveled among them, learned their speech, given himself to the study of their minds and passions. Before we close this Council, before the coming of the dawn, listen to Captain Pradu Styke, guardian of the western border."

Garyn nodded, his face haggard with exhaustion and the creeping shadow of the future. Some of the Council members shuffled uncomfortably in their seats, and Molli Rose exchanged a knowing, suspicious glance with the Gvaerg Emperor Guaandak, but all were silent as Styke stood to address everyone in the Gallery. Even now Neranda didn't fully trust him, and his earlier attempt to coerce her vote still burned in her righteous heart, but her allies and friends were increasingly few, and she needed the Captain more than she cared to admit.

Styke brought his fist to his chest in salute and turned to the Gallery. He was a proud Celestial warrior, dressed in a long, split-backed black jacket of the Human fashion so common in the borderlands. His stalks were bound and wrapped in tight blue cloth around his head, his thick hair was cut at the shoulder, and his green leather boots were buckled and brightly polished. Yet he was still Kyn, still marked with honor tattoos and scarred from many battles over the past thirty years of protecting the western edge of the Everland. Captain Styke was arrogant and opportunistic, but he'd long since proven his qualities as a warrior of courage and skill.

"Men are hungry creatures," he began. His was the voice of a born orator: deep, smooth, and sincere. The Folk listened, and even those who knew his intent found themselves drawn to his words. "Men feed wherever they can find sustenance, and when that's gone, they feed on one another. They don't know balance. They poison themselves with everything they consume, and even then they can't stop themselves. Hunger and life—these are the same things to Men. I've seen what they can do. I've seen more than one town fall to this unending hunger, and I've seen Folk torn to pieces by the ravenous will of Men. Don't try to fool yourselves into thinking that this will end, because it won't. They'll keep coming, slowly now, but eventually more and more, wave after wave to crush us while they feed on what little remains."

He walked slowly around the great table, pulling all eyes toward him. "Sunflower Hill was a small Tetawi settlement not far from my well-guarded Kyn town of Defiance. We used to trade with the Tetawi—they brought us river reeds and honeycomb, and we gave them wild rice and meadow deer, having long ago given up the prohibition against eating animal flesh." The Beast-lord Myrkash snorted. "We even celebrated a few marriages between the towns, and raised our voices in joy when seedlings were born to our people, Kyn or Tetawa by the blood of their mothers. I danced and sang with the small Folk of Sunflower Hill. I was proud to call them my kith.

"One morning, when I stepped from my cabin and looked out over the western ridge, I saw thick smoke climbing into the sky above Sunflower Hill. We gathered about twenty warriors and rode as fast as we could to help our friends. But we were too late. The settlement was gone, destroyed in the night by Men hungry for blood, for slaves, for whatever they could plunder. What they couldn't carry with them, they destroyed, simply because they could."

The Captain stopped. His eyes were locked on the etched stone floor, and he was quiet for a long time. When he spoke again, his voice was pierced by remembered hurt.

"We walked through the settlement, hoping against reason that some had survived. A few still lived, but the Men had done terrible things to them, especially the she-cubs; few were ever able to walk again, let alone look on the world without haunted eyes. Seedlings, elders, those between the rich bounties of youth and adulthood—all were dead, or worse. I've never seen such horror, and I've been a warrior since I could hold a hatchet. The Humans didn't stop with driving people from their homes, or with raiding the storehouses. No, their hunger went deeper. They wanted pain. They fed on it, needed it like parched tongues need water. And the blood . . . it flowed in steaming streams that morning.

"Two warriors ran for reinforcements to come to Sunflower Hill, and the rest of us went after the Men. We found them soon enough—there were only nine of them, and they were laughing and celebrating their easy raid. They still stank of death.

"I don't remember much of the battle that followed, but it was short. We butchered them, crushed their bones to dust, ground them into the dirt and burned even their ashes until nothing remained, not even their memory. They didn't even have time to scream." He looked up, and tears streamed unchecked down the sides of his face. There was no deception in his face—only deep, scarring pain. "I remember only one thing clearly. A Man was tying something to the saddle of his horse when we attacked, and, after he was dead, I looked at the saddle. Hanging from the saddle horn, tied delicately together with long ropes of bloody black hair, were the tender, secret parts of nineteen Tetawi—male, female, and the between-worlders, young and old alike—carried away as a memento of the attack."

The Gallery of Song was silent except for the scattered sounds of weeping. "Do not doubt, my kith, that the Men will come again, because their hunger grows every day, and they have no love of the Folk. We can leave our homeland now, while we still live, or we can stay and wait to share the fate of Sunflower Hill. We can't withstand this tide forever. We can bend like the storm-tossed willow, or break like the rigid oak. We must withdraw. We have no other choice."

"Before your courage fails you, listen to what *I* have to say." Sinovian, the young Greenwalker, stepped down from the Gallery. The consensus of the Council threatened to unravel after Styke's passionate speech. It had been easy to dismiss the Celestials as selfish or cowardly before, but the testimony of one who had fought for years against Men was difficult to ignore.

Cutting off Neranda's objections, Garyn waved Sinovian forward. It was past midnight. Dawn would bring either consensus or collapse, and time and hope for all sides were diminishing. Tobhi and his companions hadn't returned yet, as the Governor had desperately hoped; there would be no sudden reprieve, no timely information from the surviving ambassadors. All would depend on the eloquence of those present.

The young warrior turned to the Wielders' Circle and brought his fist to his chest in greeting as he stepped to the Council table. The grey eyes that gazed on the Council were filled with deep anger, but love and anguish lay there, too, and it was these qualities that now drove his words.

"The words of my he-Kyn elder have some wisdom. He speaks the truth about these Men that he's encountered, for I've seen the same cruelty to the north, where my home once lay. I don't disagree with anything Pradu Styke says about the ways of Men. But it's for this reason that we *must* fight Lojar Vald and his demands."

Styke stood up. "Did you hear nothing I said? We can't fight Vald—it's hopeless pride to claim otherwise."

Sinovian turned a harsh eye on the Captain, but Garyn intervened. "You have had your opportunity to speak, Captain Styke."

"What more has to be said?" Styke persisted. He glared around the table. "We can continue debating this issue until the next Melding, but it's not going to change a thing. We'll never have another opportunity like this one. We can take these terms and move someplace safe, someplace where we'll be free of Humans once and for all."

"And where would this be, Captain?" Sinovian said, his voice suddenly soft, the shift in tone breaking the spell of Styke's words. "If, as you seem to believe, we're all destined to die anyway, what does it matter if we die now or later? If we can't possibly fight these Men, and if they're never going to stop trying to take what's ours, why should we leave?"

Styke glared at the young warrior, but Sinovian persisted. "Have you ever thought that running might be the very worst thing that we could do? If we give up our homelands now, the most precious bond we have to the Deep Green and the Ancestrals, if we deny the trust that we've shared with the land for all these ages, how can we possibly imagine that we'll be able to cling to anything we have in the future? Maybe by surrendering we'll actually be abandoning ourselves to a false fate. If we make a stand here, and lose, we'll at least know that we've done the very best we could to hold fast to those things that are most important to us. What's more, these land-hungry Men and their kind will know it, too. But if we give up now, if we abandon our homes, the bones of those who came before, and the covenant of the Tree, with the expectation that Men will treat us fairly in the future when there's less at stake, we're setting ourselves on a path to certain destruction."

No sound came from the Gallery. A weight of exhaustion and creeping fear now settled over the gathered assembly. Neranda stood angrily and turned to Garyn. "I implore you, Speaker, to put an end to this charade. Think of the dignity of this Council. This . . . Greenwalker has made his point quite clear."

Garyn nodded. "You are right, Neranda, and thank you for reminding me—it *is* time to finish this." He looked at the delegates of the Sevenfold Council. "We have deliberated for seven nights, and heard voices in support of Eromar and others in opposition. What say you, my kith? Do we stay in our homeland, or do we surrender?"

Neranda's face went pale, and her mouth hung open in shock. It was too soon. "Uncle, wait. There's still more time. We must not rush—" she cried, but Garyn slashed his hand down angrily, cutting her off. She wanted to remind the wavering Council members about the wisdom of accepting Vald's terms, to end the discussion with the understanding that survival depended on surrendering this land that tied them to the savagery and ignorance of the past. But the situation was now beyond her control.

The Speakers of each of the Folk Nations gathered with their councilors for long, tense moments. Neranda remained at the table as the other Kyn representatives gathered beside Garyn's seat of office. She had little hope that her voice would make much difference in their negotiations, but Pradu Styke met with them in a last effort to sway their thoughts. His words this night carried a great deal of weight; he might open ears that were now deaf to her. The only other leaders at the table were the Ubbetuk Chancellor and the Emperor of the Gvaergs, as their sole decisions would guide their people.

Do not fail me, Chancellor. Do not fail the Seven Sisters of the Folk. Neranda's nails dug into the arm of her chair. Blackwick looked up again, as if reading her thoughts, and nodded to her again. Exhilaration raced through the Lawmaker's body. She was dizzy with fear and anticipation.

Molli Rose and the Tetawi representatives returned to the great table. "For the Tetawi people, and for the Everland, we reject the Oath of Western Sanctuary. We won't surrender our home." Her hands trembled, but her voice was firm. Neranda barely heard the Tetawa's words; there had been little doubt that the small Folk would refuse to sign the treaty—they were a stubborn, ignorant people anyway, and certainly not worthy of the admiration Garyn seemed to have for them.

Kishkaxi, the Brood Mother of the Harpies, ruffled her feathers and hissed in her dry voice, "The Feral-Folk will remain in our aeries and villages. There will be no alliance with Men. We will continue as of old." The golden eagles called out in agreement, answered by a chorus of birds and other winged creatures from the windows and rafters of the Gallery.

"No Human will desecrate the caverns of the Gvaerg Empire," growled Guaandak, the Emperor Triumphant, as he struck his golden spear on the ground. "The Gvaergs are now and have always been a free people; that will not change. Let Men do their worst—we will drive them from the mountains with forge-fire and stone. We join with all true Folk in the defense of our 'Hold. I reject Eromar and its *rijjik* Dreydmaster. They will find nothing but death in the Everland." A low, proud chant rose up from the Gvaergs in the Gallery in praise of their leader and his decision. Guaandak sat back, his flaming beard sparking with righteousness.

Myrkash the Unbroken, the chieftain of the Beasts, smashed his hoof on the floor in agreement. "Our blood may fall, but we'll take many Men with us. We're not leaving our mountains." The Gallery was filled with the sound of animal people praising Myrkash's decision.

The four Wyrnach representatives returned to the table. Neranda shifted slightly. They might shift the balance; if the Wyrnach and the Ubbetuk expressed reservations at this point, consensus would be impossible and the work of the Sevenfold Council would collapse.

Sethis Du'lorr, the serene speaker of the graceful Spider-Folk, bowed low to the Gallery. In a hollow voice that seemed to come from the deepest shadows of the Eld Green, the ancient creature whispered, "Though my heart is filled with fear, and though darkness crouches on the horizon, we shall stand beside our younger siblings in defense of the Everland. If we fade, we will fall with the fury of all our lost kindred in our hearts. The Wyrnach reject the Oath."

Styke stomped back to his seat beside the copper-haired Lawmaker. Garyn's voice was stronger than it had ever been. Now, at last, he spoke the words that had long been on his heart. "I have long consulted with my people, and I have heard their voices. Though some may disagree with this decision, there is no doubt that the vast majority of the Kyn do not wish to leave the Everland. As Governor of the Kyn Nation, bound by duty to serve my people and their interests, and with the blessing of the Assembly, I reject Eromar's demands."

All eyes turned to the Ubbetuk Chancellor, who sat unmoving, his hands curled over the handle of his wasp-headed walking stick. All depended on the Ubbetuk. Would they add their voice to the consensus, or would they step away? If they exercised their right of dissent, would the rest of the Sevenfold Council be able to withstand the inevitable assault?

Neranda could barely breathe. All her work, for all these years, came to this moment.

Blackwick looked at the Council and out at the Gallery beyond. His smooth voice was heavy but calm. "It is a dangerous road we travel, dear friends. We have been given two terrible choices, and, although there are doubtless other options, they have thus far eluded all our collected wisdom." He turned his penetrating gaze to Neranda, who sat trembling in her seat. "The Ubbetuk do not eagerly wage war, and we do not seek conflict with anyone, either Men or Folk."

Neranda's violet eyes brimmed with grateful tears. Her legacy was assured.

"And yet," Blackwick continued, his eyes still focused on the copper-haired she-Kyn, "we do not turn away when injustice falls upon us—or upon our kith, no matter how distant. The Sevenfold Council will have consensus: the Swarm stands with the Folk."

There was a moment's pause before the Gallery erupted in thunderous applause. Guaandak burst out laughing and grinned at the

Chancellor, who merely nodded in return. The golden eagles who guarded Kishkaxi lifted themselves into the air and cried out as they raced through the Gallery of Song, the joy of those assembled lifting their wings higher.

Molli Rose walked to Garyn and took his hand in her own small brown fingers. He watched, his heart heavy, as Neranda strode swiftly from the Gallery, her face ablaze with anger and shame, Pradu Styke and the gathered Celestials following behind her. He shook his head. "I fear, Molli, that we have made more enemies than Eromar this night. And with the Kyn divided, our future is still uncertain."

The Tetawa didn't respond. Garyn was right—the real struggle was just beginning. She gave Garyn what she hoped was a comforting smile, but she stopped abruptly. "Where is he?" she asked, looking around the crowded Gallery.

"Who?" the Governor asked, exhaustion heavy on his shoulders.

"Blackwick. The Chancellor is gone."

It was cold in the shadows near the platform. Neranda's ceremonial robes would not have generally kept her warm in the darkness before dawn, but this night her body burned with fury, and she felt only the slightest chill. Her business wouldn't take long; she would have time enough to gather more suitable clothing for the journey to come.

Everything had started well, but the unraveling had started with Garyn's pet Wielder and her speech from the audience that first night. It was a flagrant breach of protocol, but Garyn's decision had already been made; by allowing the young she-Kyn's outburst, the Governor had surrendered the integrity he'd once had as a leader. His failure went beyond poor judgment; he'd actively worked to undermine a fair debate, and could no longer claim the mantle of responsible leadership.

Neranda had thought that the unexpected departure of this so-called Redthorn Wielder would minimize the damage of those inappropriate words; the Shield had stood in the shadows and watched with no small satisfaction as the Ubbetuk Stormbringer departed with the tattooed warrior and her Brownie lapdog. Yet Tarsa'deshae had had a strange effect over the Council, and though gone for the subsequent six nights of discussion, her spirit remained powerful in the Gallery of Song.

The Shield's lips curled in bitter scorn. This young Wielder represented all that was blind and unnatural about the wild ways of the Deep Green. Those who walked the Celestial Path these days were still a sizable group, but there should have been far more, especially given the recent chaos. Their ranks should be swelling with Kyn and other Folk looking to benevolent Luran for guidance; there were sadly too few who were willing to give themselves to the pain and sacrifice necessary for true seekers of wisdom. It didn't help that the barbaric rituals of old were no longer hidden in furtive darkness. Even Garyn Mendiir, the leader of the Nation and Speaker of the newly announced Sevenfold Council, had given himself back to their embrace. Irresponsible and foolish, he would lead them all to misery; of that Neranda had little doubt.

These are dangerous times, Uncle, she thought darkly, *and though you are unwilling to make the necessary choices to ensure our survival, there are others who are most certainly prepared to do so.*

Neranda closed her eyes, forcing a calming reason through her rage. She had to conserve her strength. The struggle was great, but the goal was greater. The People would survive. She wasn't defeated; the true battle was only now beginning. Tarsa'deshae would find that she was not the only she-Kyn warrior to be reckoned with. And there were many ways to be a warrior.

A chorus of harsh croaks called down to the Shield from the shadowed tree canopy. Neranda looked up. She couldn't see the creatures, but their mocking voices had become all too familiar to her over the past few weeks.

The Lawmaker nodded. She'd tarried long enough; a storm was gathering, and the Not-Ravens were awaiting her answer. Now, at last, she knew what that answer would be.

21

The Dark Before Dawn

"I'M SORRY TO HAVE BROUGHT YE such unhappy news, Wielder."

Unahi sat in silence at the table of the small, two-story round-house she shared with Biggiabba. The kind, hulking Wielder was gone this night; the only time she could meet with her people was in moonlit darkness, when the sister suns' deadly rays offered no danger to the he-Gvaergs who'd traveled down from the far north mountains to join the discussions of the Sevenfold Council. Sunlight harmed only he-Gvaergs, turning their living flesh to frozen stone, and only great wrappings of wyrweave prevented that terrible fate for those who had no choice but to travel under the suns' watchful gaze. As wyrweave was an increasingly precious commodity due to the recent disruptions of the trading network, the most practical option for the stone-born Folk was to gather beneath the softer light of the midnight stars.

On the nights when Biggiabba was away, Unahi generally retired to her pallet early for much-needed rest, as her days were becoming busier with the swelling numbers of refugees from around the Everland. More invading Humans meant more displacement, danger, and death for the Folk, and the great peace-city of Sheynadwiin was still one of the last safe places for them to flee. Kyn, Tetawi, Gvaerg, Beast, even an occasional Ubbetuk and allied Human, along with all manner of unusual and rare Folk-creature, now called Sheynadwiin their temporary home. There was food and water enough, for now, but space was dwindling, and tempers were fraying with each passing day. There had already been a few outbreaks of violence and illness, which the Wielders and some of the Shields had managed to keep from growing out of control. All the medicine workers who remained in the city, Greenwalker and Celestial alike, were overwhelmed with the needs of their respective peoples. They were already exhausted, and everyone knew that it was only going to get worse as the days went on. Much, much worse.

An early rest would have been very welcome, but it wasn't going to happen tonight. Her guest had brought unexpected news that had deeply shaken the bent old she-Kyn, and she sat in stricken silence for a long time. At last, she licked her lips and said, "Tell me again, please. What happened?"

Molli Rose, the principal speaker of the Tetawi delegation at the Council, sighed deeply. "We don't know too much, but some of the survivors arrived earlier tonight. I was already in the refugee grounds and heard 'em talkin' to one of the Shields who's helpin' organize things down there. It was raiders, that's for certain. The attack was well planned. They had caging wagons ready for those they could catch."

"And for those they couldn't?"

Molli Rose hesitated for a moment. The Tetawa was well known in the Council for her frank speech and forthright manner, but she knew well that such a style wasn't ideal for all occasions. This conversation required special care, even if it was difficult to know how to possibly share such horrible news in a gentle way. Molli Rose admired honesty and courage, and for this reason was quite fond of the old Wielder, who considered issues deeply and spoke her own mind with conviction. It was this warm regard that had made the Tetawa decide to bring the news to Unahi directly rather than entrust it to someone else.

She pulled her brown shawl tighter around her shoulders. The room was cold, but Molli Rose couldn't tell if it was from the strange weather that had recently affected the Everland or Unahi's grief. "Most of the grown he-Kyn were killed on the spot. A few zhe-Kyn may have escaped, we en't sure, but at least one was mauled to death by the Men's war-dogs. As for the survivin' she-Kyn and cubs, they were rounded up and put into the cages. They're likely on the way to Eromar, like those from other burnt-out towns and settlements."

It wasn't a new story. Slavers and bandits were growing bolder and crueler with every passing day. Hundreds of Folk had been kidnapped and taken to slave markets throughout Eromar, and thousands of animals had been killed already. It wasn't an exceptional story, but this attack was on Red Cedar Town, the sapling home of both Unahi and her niece, the Redthorn Wielder, Tarsa'deshae. And there was no word of the fate of Tarsa's aunts, Unahi's four surviving sisters.

"I'll keep askin' around down there, to see if anybody knows anythin' else. I'll let ye know as soon as I learn more." She patted Unahi's wrinkled grey-green hand softly and stood to leave.

The Wielder didn't look up. "*Tsodoka*, Molli Rose. I appreciate you coming here yourself to let me know."

"My prayers are with ye and yer family, Unahi. I'll be back tomorrow to tell ye what I hear."

Unahi sat at the table for a long time after the Tetawa had gone. She couldn't quite absorb the news. It was almost impossible to imagine that the town was destroyed. Even though she'd been exiled for years from Red Cedar Town, even though its inhabitants— her family—had rejected the Deep Green for so long, it had never occurred to her that the town wouldn't always be there. That place was immovably rooted in her mind and memory. Though the town had changed in significant ways from her earliest days, it was still her home more than any other place in the world. To hear that Red Cedar Town was now gone was too much to fathom.

And her sisters. Two of the six had died years before, including Tarsa's mother, Lan'delar, and were buried in the red soil of their ancestors amidst the now-smoldering ruins of the town. Unahi's relationship with most of the others was strained beyond repair, but they were still kith, still her flesh and blood, and she still loved them. Sweet, fragile Geth. Dignified Vansaaya, haughty Sathi'in, petulant Ivida. What had happened to them on that terrible day? Did they still live? If not, did they die quickly? If they weren't yet dead, what were their lives like now? Though few spoke openly of it, everyone knew what horrors awaited she-Folk at the mercy of Men, and the very thought brought a choking sob from the Wielder's trembling

lips. To think that the she-Kyn she'd grown up with, played along-
side, loved and fought and wept with would know brutalized lives
in Eromar . . .

Eromar. She dropped her face into her hands, her heart too
heavy for tears. It wasn't just her sisters who faced the threat of that
dangerous land. Tarsa was there now, too, and likely in as much danger as the others, if not more, as she was in the bleak beating heart
of Eromar itself: Gorthac Hall, the home of Lojar Vald. The elder
Wielder had tried to keep Tarsa from going, but the young warrior
was every bit as stubborn as her aunt, and more resourceful than
Unahi had anticipated. In the end, the old she-Kyn had watched,
fearful for her niece and furious with herself, as the Ubbetuk airship
disappeared into the storm-choked skies.

Yet, unlike the situation with her sisters, Unahi wasn't entirely
helpless with Tarsa. She reached into a pocket of her skirt and pulled
out a jagged chunk of red-veined amber, the match to the Wielder-
marked piece at the tip of Dibadjiibé, the wyrwood staff she'd gifted
to the headstrong warrior. The two resinous shards were linked across
the vast distance between the Everland and Eromar, both by origin
and by special Wielded art, and it was this link that would help Unahi
track Tarsa's journey through her niece's dreams. A partial picture,
admittedly, and a treacherous one—the dream-world was inevitably
erratic and difficult to decipher, even in ideal conditions—but it was
the old Wielder's only way of being of help. She was powerless in so
many other ways; she needed to know that she could be of service
to the one she-Kyn in her family whom she'd promised to protect.
With the news about Red Cedar Town, it still gave her hope, no
matter how thin.

Unahi quickly gathered the materials she needed from doublewoven cane baskets and brightly painted clay vessels scattered
throughout the room. She took a few cinders from the fireplace,
placed them in a blackened abalone shell, and covered them with a
handful of tobacco leaves, some cedar sprigs, and a few blue-green
berries. Cupping her hand over the shell, she blew on the dried plants
until they began to smoke, then whispered a prayer as she wafted the
smoke across her sensory stalks, forehead, face, and body, taking care
to leave no flesh or clothing untouched by the sweet-smelling vapor.
When satisfied, she rummaged through another basket for a small

black root that she immediately popped into her mouth and swallowed, ignoring the bitter taste and sudden light-headedness.

Returning to her seat, she brought the piece of amber to her forehead and closed her eyes. Her eyes grew heavy, and her head began to spin. The chill in the room faded, replaced by a dry, heavy heat. The fingers of Unahi's free hand ran across the medicine songs beaded onto her chanting-sash, and as the words formed on her lips and her sensory stalks began to pulse in unison, she let her spirit drift free into the dream-world, where a blue-green light in the misty darkness drew her forward.

Tarsa stood in the cavern again, but it was an empty darkness. She was naked, and alone. No water flowed from the cavern's depths, no rich blue light sent her skin tingling. Even the waterfall was gone now. The deep pool was dry and cracked, and she could see down almost to its sandy center. The wind whipped mournfully across the old pool's weather-worn walls.

Dust swirled listlessly around her. She could almost taste iron in the air, just the slightest bitter tang that clutched with dry claws at the back of her throat. She looked around—it couldn't possibly be the same place. But the same slender vines and leaves were etched into the walls, and though the water was gone, the trough in the floor that led into the darkness was achingly familiar.

"Why am I here?" the young Wielder asked, but silence was the only response. She looked back, just once, at the empty pool, then turned and walked back into the cavern toward the Eternity Tree.

Her bare feet scraped painfully on jagged pieces of rock torn out of the wall. The only light was the dim, blue-green glow of her tattoos, but it was enough to guide her way. It was a short journey. The brown-legged creature in the mask was gone, but the standing stones remained, the sole reminders of her first journey through this place, a shroud of deep, impenetrable gloom crouching around her.

Tarsa felt something in her hand. It was a small bundle of red cloth, wrapped delicately with a white thread. She knelt on the ground and unfolded the cloth to reveal dozens of leaves, each marked with a different image. Yet as she reached out a trembling finger, they crumbled into ashes that were carried into the darkness by a sudden gust of icy wind. Tarsa cried out and tried to grab them, but they flew out of reach, and then she lost her balance and plunged headfirst into that unending darkness, flailing wildly, and all she could hear over her screams was the mocking, gasping wind as she fell downward, downward, down . . .

She shot awake, her heart throbbing painfully in her chest. The bedroom was stiflingly hot. Her skin dripped with perspiration. She put her head in her hands and tried to calm her racing thoughts. "Just a dream," she whispered, but the words gave her no comfort. Her stomach burned. For five nights she'd slept beneath the roof of Gorthac Hall, and each evening brought nightmares and a growing fear. Vald had been the model of cold courtesy, joining them for dinner each evening, spending time in vigorous conversation with Imweshi and the others, paying little attention to Tarsa and Tobhi. Even Daladir avoided her, his eyes growing more remote with each passing day. This evening the Dreydmaster had seemed almost giddy, and this disturbed the Wielder far more than his earlier condescension.

Her stomach clenched violently. Something was wrong. She remembered Vald's pleasant smile as she ate her bland dinner of boiled carrots and potatoes and drank a bit of the salty wine. Another jagged pain tore at her belly. The wine had been strange, but she was unused to alcohol, and the dizziness seemed normal.

A thin, muffled gasp caught her attention, and she turned to see, in the lamplight, Tobhi's small, sweat-drenched form twisting beside her, a pinkish white froth on his bloody lips, his eyes rolled back and hands clutching at the air.

"Tobhi!" Tarsa whispered in horror, but he couldn't hear her: his body was contorted nearly beyond recognition. A deep, gurgling noise slid from his throat. The Wielder pulled herself on top of the Tetawa to keep him still, but the convulsions were too strong, and her own pain was too great to hold him down. His legs flew out, catching Tarsa in the chest and her earlier injuries. She fell onto the plank floor, and blinding pain exploded in her side.

It took a long time before she could crawl back to the bed and pull herself up. Her breath came now in shallow gasps, but she reached down and grabbed a blanket from the floor that Tobhi had thrown off in his unconscious flailings. She threw it over him as his spasms became more desperate. There was a streak of blood on the headboard where his head had smashed against the wood.

Tarsa pulled the blanket tight around him, desperately hoping that this measure of restraint would keep him still. She didn't know what to do. For an instant she almost called for the Steward and his alchaemical doctor, but Tobhi would be dead before they arrived.

She touched his bloody forehead, but pulled back as the iron-ward around her neck went ice-cold. Tarsa snarled in fear and frustration— the iron-ward protected her from that poisonous metal, but it did so by dampening her own link to whatever thin thread of the *wyr* remained in this cursed place. The amulet turned cold again in warning as she reached out. Tobhi's body twisted violently beneath her, nearly lifting her off the bed again. He surrendered a bubbling shriek.

There was no other choice. Choking back tears, the Wielder pulled the iron-ward from around her neck.

The world collapsed. Tarsa fell across her friend, gasping in renewed pain and shock, as the presence of every piece of iron in the room burned into her flesh and mind like liquid fire. Wood-nails, hinges, knobs, bedposts—all flared to caustic life when the amulet left her flesh. Her sensory stalks twisted in pain, like earthworms held to a flame. She turned her head and retched until tears streamed down her face and her body trembled from pain and exhaustion.

But she couldn't succumb, not while their lives ebbed with each heartbeat. She was getting weaker, too. Driving the pain to a hidden corner of her mind, Tarsa took a deep, quivering breath and pulled the convulsing Tetawa against her, chest on chest, heart to heart, their pain-filled bodies linked by the touch of tender flesh.

The *wyr* was weak in this toxic land, but it still endured, and it flowed between them. Tarsa took Tobhi's pain, and her conscious-ness flowed into his blood, following those burning currents to find the deadly imbalance raging there.

It didn't take long. Her heart chilled as she suddenly touched the poison of weltspore in his blood, a bitter yellow fungus that lost its distinctive taste when mixed with something stronger, like the juices of cooked meat . . . or heady wine. As a young sprout, she'd seen a playmate in the early stages of weltspore poisoning; he'd mistaken one of the enticing yellow buds for an edible mushroom. It had been a swift and terrible death, as he'd eaten an entire cap at once.

For an instant Tarsa saw Vald's piercing eyes at every gathering over the past five days, the sudden veil that dropped over his eyes as he ate his own meals, and she knew. Vald's vengeance was subtle, and patient; he'd played with them the whole time, dropping only enough poison to weaken them, day by day, watching them die a bit more with each passing dawn. It was brutally fitting that he'd chosen a poison from the Everland to do the deed.

No, Tobhi, her mind spoke to his, and she shared her fading strength. *I won't let you die. I can't survive in this place by myself.*

She opened her spirit wide and surrendered to the bloodsong that she'd so long held in check. Now, at last, it was free, and the flood drew her down into its swirling depths. The *wyr* grew stronger, unhindered by the iron that surrounded them, gaining speed and strength, racing through them to cleanse the weltspore from their blood, from every tissue and fiber of their calming bodies.

She trembled now with renewed strength. The poison hadn't affected her as much as it had Tobhi, but even the one goblet of wine would have been deadly in the night if the dream hadn't wakened her. Tarsa held Tobhi tightly as the *wyr* drew the poison away from the bodily depths, coming closer and closer to the surface. She retched again, felt the poison rush away from her own flesh in a gout of orange ooze, then placed her mouth over Tobhi's and pulled the weltspore out, spitting it on the ground. She repeated the process over and over again, sucking out the poison until her mouth was numb and she was certain that they were both past danger.

The Wielder's body pulsed with the growing rush of *wyr*-fed power, as if all the *wyr* remaining in Eromar was flowing through her, summoned by her need to strengthen her fragile flesh. Tobhi lay unconscious but alive. She sighed in relief, but it was short lived, as she suddenly remembered that Tobhi was not the only one who ate from Vald's poisoned table.

She was strong again—stronger than she'd been in a long time. Grabbing her knife-belt and vest, Tarsa jumped to the floor, staggering a bit as the blood rushed to her head. The feeling passed; the bloodsong still flowed strong, and her senses were intensely alive. It was a strange moment, to be in control of her senses and yet feel them pulsing at the edge of her strength and conscious thoughts, but the delicate balance endured. Unahi's patient training and calming chants had worked. Tarsa was no longer a slave to the bloodsong. She waited for her thoughts to clear a bit before leaving the room.

The hall was empty, and there were no noises in the chambers beyond. She pushed on Hak'aad's door, but something blocked her way. She shoved again, hard, and the door slid open to reveal the he-Kyn's stiffening body on the floor. In the bed, twisted into filth-stained sheets, lay poor, gentle Athweid, who had slipped into Hak'aad's room and arms deep in the night. Their bodies were mercilessly convulsed, mangled and broken until they were both almost unrecognizable.

The Wielder pulled the door shut. They were far beyond any help she could give.

Tarsa moved silently down the hallway and pushed Imweshi's door open, but the room was empty. The mystery of the elder she-Kyn's disappearance was solved, however, when Tarsa stumbled down the hall to find Daladir. There, crumpled at Daladir's doorstep, lay Imweshi, her hands twisted into claws of pain. Her delicate fingers were bloody and torn from trying to drag herself to the he-Kyn's door. Tarsa choked back a sob and reached out, but she stumbled back as Imweshi let out a wheezing hiss.

Falling to her knees, Tarsa pulled Imweshi to her own chest. As before, the *wyr* rushed to draw them together, but something stopped it, and Tarsa felt the Celestial's proud spirit push against her.

Imweshi! Let me help you!

—*No. Leave me be. You and all your kind have brought this fate upon us.*—

You stubborn fool—you'll die if you don't let me help you!

—*Then I will die. Better to die sanctified than to abandon the Pillar for the Tree. Curse you, Wielder, and your witchery.*—

Imweshi . . . please. I'm here to help!

Imweshi?

Imweshi . . .

The *wyr* drew back, and Tarsa was alone in the hallway again, Imweshi's body a limp weight in her arms.

Tarsa lowered the elder to the stone floor and stood, shaking and weak. She'd never felt such anger, such hate, not when she battled the Stoneskin, not even when she'd fought the grave-robbing Men. So much death and shame, and so much poison. It was worse than the weltspore; at least the weltspore had its place in the way of things. Its origins were far from the seeping lies that crept across the Melded world.

She thought back to Reiil's words in the coach as they rode toward Eromar City. He'd looked so sad. There was a longing in his eyes, a wish for a past that could have been, choices that might have been unmade.

But Reiil was dead now, as was Imweshi. Hak'aad. Athweid. Garyn had compromised on the latter three when he sent them on the mission, but he'd put his hope and faith in Reiil, Tobhi, and—though reluctantly at first—Tarsa. He'd given them his trust that they'd bring hope back to the Nation. Trust that they'd bring Daladir . . .

Daladir! Tarsa pulled away from her reverie and threw the door open. The he-Kyn lay moaning in his narrow bed, a thin, flickering candle the only light in the cold room. He pulled himself up as Tarsa stepped into the room. Sweat streamed down his pale face; the poison was swiftly spreading through his body.

"Wielder," he whispered hoarsely, but his words were lost in a fit of coughing. He slipped back to his feather pillow as Tarsa pulled his shivering body toward her. "I don't want to die here, not like this."

"Don't struggle, Daladir. Let me help you, as you once helped me." Their flesh touched, her mouth closed over his, and she felt him surrender.

You won't die, Daladir, she promised as the *wyr* pulsed between them.

We're going home. Tonight.

The boiling black clouds spread across the sky like an army marching to the beat of thundering drums. The air crackled dangerously. Storms were not uncommon in the skies above Spindletop, but there was a dark spirit to this thunderhead, and everyone felt its presence. Wind and rain and hail stretched out ahead of the lightning, smashing into the fragile land below, tearing at flower and flesh alike.

Medalla joined Gishki in pulling the shutters and doors closed while their pepa, Lubik, finished bringing in an extra store of firewood before the storm prevented him from reaching the woodpile. The rest of the family was at Medalla's house, preparing that building for the storm. Quill stoked the fire again. Though it was nearing midsummer, a bone-burning chill had crept into the world as the storm crept closer, and without the fire they would have nearly been frozen. As it was, they all wore various winter robes and mittens, and these were inadequate to the task.

Gishki rubbed her hands together. "Did you ever hear of anything like this before? What a wretched night. Pepa, are you sure we have enough wood?"

Old Lubik scratched his tattooed chin and nodded. He was a quiet elder, a *par fahr*, more inclined to listen than speak, like most of the older generation. Quill respected that. Indeed, she often wished that the Tetawi her age were like the elder *fahr*, especially the young he-Tetawi. She sighed and drove the greenwood stick back into the embers and pushed them around. It hardly mattered. There was only one *fahr* that Quill spent much time thinking about, and he was far away. There was no telling when, or if, she'd see him again. She didn't like to think about that possibility, but it always returned, unbidden.

Quill glanced up to see Gishki and Medalla looking at her, their eyes warm with concern. The Dolltender smiled weakly.

"If you don't need me anymore, I think I'll just go check on the dolls." Old Lubik nodded, and Quill slid down to the room that she'd share this night with Gishki's young daughters. The room had one window looking out over the Edgewood with a view not so very different from that of her own little cabin, which now stood empty since the recent sightings of the cannibal Skeeger. The creature had been far too interested in the Dolltender lately, and though her home was a short walk away, she felt better with her cousins in the next room rather than across the meadow.

The dolls stood side by side on makeshift shelves around the room. Their dark, shining eyes followed her in irritated resignation. Quill shrugged her shoulders.

"It's the best choice, you know. It isn't safe to be at home by ourselves tonight. We either stay here with family, or we take our chances out there. I prefer to stay here, at least until things get a little calmer."

It was time to feed the dolls. The Dolltender pulled a small leather bag of tobacco and dried cedar from her apron pocket and walked to every small spirit-figure, talking in a low, quiet voice to each in turn and leaving a small pile of the fragrant shavings at their feet. Though they weren't pleased about being taken from their shadowed cedar boxes in the old house, where they could dream undisturbed through the night, they seemed to be willing to accept the change without much fuss. The Dolltender had to spend a little more time talking with Green Kishka, the most stubborn of the bunch, but eventually even that old apple-headed spirit gave the *firra* a smile.

Quill turned to the window as the hail grew more ferocious. The hailstones were large—each at least as big as her thumbnail. She crawled on the bed to look outside. Suddenly a flare of lightning illuminated the night, followed closely by a roar of thunder so loud that the entire moundhouse trembled. The Dolltender threw herself flat on the bed with a gasp.

In the moment between the lightning and the thunder, something pale and massive flashed into view. She'd seen it before.

The Skeeger had come for her.

Another lightning blast burned through the darkness, and then the thunder tore the night apart. The roof beams quivered and groaned. Quill heard the splintering of wood and screams from the other room, and Medalla, Gishki, and Lubik rushed down the hallway to her room. The front door gave way, and a rush of cold wind found them. Lubik held a stone hatchet in his hand with the easy grace of an old warrior who'd never forgotten the ways of war. Gishki had grabbed a stick from the woodpile, and Medalla held a stout clay jar. Quill shivered behind them and watched the door.

They stood together for a long time. The cold wind whipped through the room, burning past their winter wear. Then, outside, they heard the pigs screaming, a high-pitched, desperate sound that grew more and more hysterical. Quill covered her ears and burst into tears.

"They're being butchered alive," Medalla whispered. Lubik started down the hall, but Gishki stopped him. They said nothing, merely looked in each other's eyes, but he nodded and held his daughter's hand.

As suddenly as the squealing started, it stopped. One long, groaning cry, and then it was over. But the silence was almost worse than the screams.

"We can't just stay here all night," Gishki whispered at last. The thunder continued to shake the moundhouse, but the silences between grew longer and longer. "Maybe the door opened on its own. After all, we were in a hurry to—"

A large shadow filled the doorway, and the Tetawi fell back in alarm. Old Lubik lunged forward, but a foot flew out and sent him spinning into a corner. The three *firra* grabbed one another in terror.

Lightning flashed through the window to illuminate a bearded Man standing in the room. Water dripped from his wide-brimmed hat and his wrinkled cloak. A patch covered one eye, but the other gazed at them with a frigid blue calm.

"Don't be stupid," he growled to Lubik in the trade tongue as the *par fahr* slowly regained his feet. "I want food, a fire, and shelter. Do as you're told, and I won't hurt your family. Cross me, and none of you will live to see dawn." He turned to the window. "Besides, without me and my friend here, that creature out in the pen wouldn't have stopped with the pigs."

Quill's eyes strayed to the common room, where another, shorter figure crouched. In the dull firelight she could barely make out the shape of a Feral deer-kith, his arms bound behind his back. She shuddered and quailed away as the Man caught her gaze. He regarded her in silence for a moment, then turned and stalked down the hall. Gishki and Medalla helped old Lubik to his feet. The Man said something, and they followed carefully.

Quill slid over to the dolls. They were more agitated than she'd ever seen them before. "So you felt it, too?" she whispered.

"Quill," Medalla called out, her voice trembling. "He wants us *all* in here."

The Dolltender turned to the little figures on the shelves around her. "Don't worry. He'll be gone by dawn." Ignoring the fear in their wrinkled faces, Quill smoothed out her apron and headed down the hall, feeling for all the world that times were getting very bad very quickly . . . and they were only going to get worse.

Biggiabba finally lumbered back from the Gvaerg gathering in the early hours before dawn, where she found Unahi sprawled unconscious on the floor, a small shard of amber glowing softly in her outstretched hand. The she-Gvaerg bent swiftly and carried her friend to a sleeping pallet, then watched over her with growing concern as Unahi thrashed in delirium for hours. River willow tea and cold compresses seemed to help, and to Biggiabba's great relief the worst of the fever finally passed by midmorning.

At last the old she-Kyn slowly opened her eyes. "It's begun, Biggiabba," she whispered hoarsely. "May Mother Tree save us all, it's finally begun."

22

Revelations

IT TOOK VERY LITTLE TIME FOR TARSA to gather their gear together in Daladir's room, but it was nearly dawn by the time Tobhi was well enough to travel. She returned her iron-ward to its place around her neck. Tobhi had kept the golden globe with the nightwasp in his satchel. Tarsa transferred it to her belt-pouch; when they were in the open air of the night, she would break it open and summon the great Ubbetuk Dragon to return them to the Everland. She would need to carry Tobhi's belongings, as he was still very weak.

Her first instinct was to hunt down the Dreydmaster and kill him. After healing herself and her two remaining companions as best she could, she'd called upon the medicine of her chanting-sash and muted the bloodsong again. In its place rose a rage so bitter that she could almost taste it. She wanted Vald to know pain, and she wanted to be the one to inflict it. Twice she stepped to the door, the wyr-wood staff in her hand, only to stop, trembling, with the knowledge that Daladir and Tobhi would never be able to escape the Eromar City without her. She would help them, but it was almost all she could do to restrain the call of blood revenge.

"I hate this. I en't much use to ye now, am I?" Tobhi whispered as she helped him dress. The Tetawa leaned heavily on his hatchet, careful to avoid the sharp blade.

She gently pinched his nose. "Not much, little brother, but you'll be better soon enough. All you have to do is move silently and as quickly as you can; we'll be fine."

He smiled weakly. "Sure am glad ye came, Tarsa."

"Me, too," she said, her voice thick with sudden emotion.

Daladir sat on the edge of the bed, still regaining his strength. "Do you really think we can get free, Wielder? Vald has more than mere Men at his service."

Tarsa's face hardened. "He'll *need* more than Men if he hopes to stop us. Yes, Daladir, we'll get away from this place, and we'll be home soon. Trust me."

"I do." He smiled. "I'm sorry for my earlier words."

She began to respond, but a noise in the hallway reminded them of their continuing danger. "Wait here," she hissed. Taking her staff firmly in hand, she snuffed out the candle and moved to the side of the door, waiting.

A few tense moments passed in the darkness. No one moved, though they all watched the doorway and listened, senses straining, for the slightest sound.

At last, the door creaked open. The Wielder felt the biting chill of iron radiate through the doorway as the shining point of an iron-tipped crossbow bolt shimmered in the dull lantern light from the hall. The door opened wider, and the weapon inched forward.

And then the Redthorn Wielder was upon the intended assassins, her thirst for vengeance finally unleashed, the wyrwood staff whirling in the narrow corridor with fierce accuracy. Her first blow shattered the crossbow and sent the Man sprawling backward. The second caught another Man in the throat, and he fell with a strange, high-pitched squeal. The sudden ferocity of her attack caught the other three Men by surprise, and they stumbled away in alarm.

A blast of *wyr*-drawn wind tore through the corridor, snuffing out their lanterns: the darkness now belonged to the Redthorn Wielder. Her boot caught the crossbowman in the face, ending his threat for the moment. Tarsa crouched low and listened, her *wyr*-heightened senses drawing in every sound, scent, and shift in the air around her. She was still for a heartbeat. Then, like a whirlwind, she flew forward and spun Dibadjiibé in a diagonal arc, snapping another soldier's arm and sending his long knife flying.

"Now, Daladir! Take Tobhi and go—I'll finish them!"

He didn't hesitate. Pulling Tobhi onto his back, Daladir slipped out the door, stumbling down the hall and away from the chaos of the battle. He didn't let himself think about what Tarsa was facing on her own; he simply had to trust her, and hope that he and his companion didn't encounter any of Vald's troops on the way.

It was almost too dark to see in the hallway, but with Tobhi's guidance Daladir was able to make his way toward the eastern stairs, which would lead them to the stable yards. They slid quietly along the darkened corridor for a long time—Daladir couldn't tell the distance, and Tobhi was concentrating on listening for approaching enemies.

Once they reached the stairs, the quickening dawn through the windows aided their movement, and they made good time. Daladir was once again amazed at the size of Gorthac Hall—the place seemed so much bigger on the inside than it looked from without. It wasn't a comforting thought, especially at this moment, when sanctuary already seemed so very far away.

Tobhi was still very weak, and the rough bouncing on the he-Kyn's back sent his head spinning, but the Leafspeaker was aware enough to trust his instincts. The darkness ahead was dangerous.

"Wait," he hissed as they neared the top of the stairs. "Someone's comin'."

"Is it Tarsa?"

The Tetawa listened. "I can't tell yet. No, I don't think it is. Mebbe it's comin' from beneath us."

"Let's hope not," Daladir whispered, continuing forward.

The sound grew louder. It *was* coming from down the stairs, and approaching quickly. Daladir slid Tobhi to the floor and pulled out his knife. The shuffling of boots on the rough planks of the stairs grew louder, and suddenly the Steward appeared, a short-stocked musket in his quivering hand.

The Man and the he-Kyn stood staring at one another in surprise. A leering grin twisted the Steward's pockmarked features into an expression that was far from friendly. He pointed the musket's barrel at Daladir's head and pulled back the hammer.

<<What was it you said, Ambassador? That you'd cut my tongue out? Do you remember? Well, I'll splatter that and the rest of your Unhuman face all over the walls, then let the hounds lick up the

pieces. I'll show you what happens when you don't show respect to your betters.>> His finger tensed on the rod's firing lever.

<<Ye talk too much,>> Tobhi growled from the floor as he drove the sharpened end of his hatchet up into the Man's paunchy belly. The Steward let out a piercing shriek as Daladir shoved the barrel of the gun under the Man's chin and jerked on the trigger. The air exploded in blood, bone, flesh, and fire. The Steward's half-faceless body teetered for a moment, then fell backward with wet, crunching sounds, smashing limply against the stone stairs on its descent.

Wiping the gore from his face, Daladir swept Tobhi into his arms and slipped down the smoky stairs, barely missing the Man's twisted body in his haste.

He stopped and peered around a corner. Satisfied that they were alone for the moment, he slid into the shadows of a long, westward-leading hallway. The only stairs downward met in the center of the wood-paneled corridor. He and Tobhi said nothing, for at that moment they reached one of the few large windows on the second floor and looked outside. Dawning twilight lit the hallway.

"The Ubbetuk galleon!" Tobhi sighed. "They've arrived already! Tarsa must've already called 'em." The giant ship was anchored to the upper parapet of Vald's tower. It was a rather bold move, but perhaps the best option. It was a different Dragon from the one they'd arrived in—grander and much larger, shaped like a massive silver wasp—but this one looked quite a bit more protective than the last.

"We've got to find Tarsa." Daladir looked around. He now recognized where they were. This hall led to a central stairwell that opened to the first floor and various back passages. If they could avoid detection, they'd soon be at the stable yards.

Grief caught in Daladir's throat. He remembered all too well the murder of his friend Fear-Takes-the-Fire in those very yards not so long before. It was an unwelcome memory right now, and it filled him with growing dread.

"We'd better go, Tobhi. Maybe she's already at the galleon." Shifting the Tetawa to a more comfortable position on his back, Daladir looked back to the shadows one more time before dashing down the hallway toward the waiting Dragon.

The battle was fiercer than Tarsa had anticipated, especially after she encountered another group of Men on their way to ensure that the diplomats were dead. By the time she'd chased, battled, and disarmed the last of eight militiamen, she was in an unfamiliar part of the house. Her ribs were sending sharp spasms through her chest, and the shallow cuts and darkening bruises she received during the skirmish were slowing her down, but the pain was manageable, for now. What mattered most was reaching Tobhi and Daladir and getting out of Gorthac Hall. She would break the globe with the night-wasp, summon the Dragon, and then they would be on their way. Daylight wouldn't be their ally, but the galleon would be swift, and once aboard they would have little to fear.

She rushed down the hallway, which ended in a narrow door. Listening intently for a few brief moments for any suspicious sounds, Tarsa pulled on the latch, hopeful that this was the direction her companions had traveled.

The door opened easily. The Wielder slipped into the dark room beyond and pulled the door shut behind her.

A thin window in the wall was the only source of light, but it was enough to show Tarsa that dawn had nearly arrived—time was precious. Looking around, she noticed that this small chamber was merely a linked room to another that lay beyond a stout wooden door in the corner. The biting stench of iron was heavy here, and it made her weak in spite of the iron-ward. She closed her eyes, breathing deeply as she rewrapped her stalks against the sensory inundation. Something strange was strengthening the iron here.

Still, she had to go forward. Each moment brought them closer to discovery.

The she-Kyn tried to use the staff to softly lift the iron latch on the door, but it didn't move. She hissed angrily and looked around for something to help her. There was nothing. She would have to grab the latch by hand.

Cutting a strip from her leathers, Tarsa wrapped it around her hand and pulled on the latch, ignoring the sharp pain that streaked through her flesh. The door was heavy, and stubborn, but it was unlocked, and after straining a bit, Tarsa was able to pull it open enough to look out.

The door led to a narrow balcony overlooking a large, grim chamber with stark, unvarnished plank walls. The three-tined iron star of Eromar dominated the wall opposite Tarsa's hiding place. A series of benches stretched across the lower floor, all facing a tall raised dais where Lojar Vald stood with a large group of Men, as if in anticipation. A narrow door in one corner was closed, and all eyes lingered there. Vald wore a fur-lined mantle over his thick jacket and well-tooled breeches, and a wide black hat with silver buckles covered his head. The Men with him were similarly dressed, although none wore a hat in the Dreydmaster's presence.

They're waiting for something, she thought to herself. *I should go.* Her thirst for vengeance was largely sated; now she just wanted to find her friends and escape. She was tired, and the pain was getting worse.

She started back when the far door opened below. The Wielder's eyes opened wide. Blood filled her mouth as she bit down on her tongue to keep from screaming. She couldn't breathe.

It was a trick—it couldn't be the truth.

No.

Not now.

Not here.

Neranda Ak'shaar, the leader of the Kyn Shields in Sheynadwiin, stood in the doorway, her silver cloak flowing like liquid moonlight down her shoulders, her pale blue features cold and proud. Behind the regal Lawmaker walked an unfamiliar Kyn wearing a blue headcloth and black jacket, along with a handful of Celestial Shields that the young Wielder recognized from the Sevenfold Council.

Vald stepped forward and took Neranda's hand in his own. <<Welcome, Lady Neranda. I was confident that your people would at last accept the inevitable. I assume that you have come to announce the happy news yourself.>> His voice was almost too loud as it echoed through the chamber.

<<Dreydmaster,>> Neranda's demeanor was icy; she was in no mood for Vald's sarcasm. <<the Sevenfold Council voted against your terms. They rejected the treaty . . . unanimously.>>

The Man dropped her hand. <<Is that so?>>

<<It is.>>

Vald looked at the group of Kyn and smiled softly. His features became almost gentle. <<I see. If the Sevenfold Council has rejected this most generous offer, my Lady, why are you here?>>

For a moment Neranda seemed to shrink slightly, but she took a deep breath and stood tall again. <<Most of the Folk are superstitious and ignorant of the wider world. They are easily influenced, especially by the long-discredited conjurors of the Old Ways who use the fear of ghosts and spirits to separate the People from their good sense. They are not capable of making a wise decision in this matter. It is thus a heavy burden that my compatriots and I must assume. We have come to make the difficult choice for all the People, even if it against their baser wishes. We have come to sign the Oath.>>

Tarsa shook with rage and terror and grief. *I can stop them*, she thought desperately. *I can bring this hall crashing down on them, crush their treacherous bones into dust, drive them to the shadows for all time.* Her skin began to burn as the *wyr* bubbled up, fighting past the iron-ward around her throat. The songs woven through the chanting-sash no longer restrained her fury; reason and self-protection could no longer hold back her vengeance. The wyrwood staff responded to her need, and the spirits of the living world flowed toward the quivering she-Kyn. It might mean her death, but she could destroy all the enemies of the Everland in one swift, certain strike.

Slowly, the power swirled around her, building in strength and fury, as Tarsa watched, horrified, while Neranda and the other Kyn in the chamber below each took a black quill in hand and signed their names to the Oath of Western Sanctuary. When they finished, Neranda turned away and walked slowly out of the room, her head bowed. Vald rolled up the parchment and smiled.

In that moment, at long last, the wave crested. With a roar, Tarsa flew from the balcony and landed, hard, just yards away from Vald and his retainers. A guard rushed to block her, but Dibadjiibé flashed with green fire, and the Man fell screaming, his body consumed by unquenchable flame. She drew Jitani's knife as other soldiers stepped in. Smiling broadly from a safe distance, Vald tipped his hat at the howling Wielder and followed Neranda through the door.

One of the soldiers leapt toward Tarsa, bringing his sword down with practiced ease. She easily blocked the blade, twisting the knife around to catch the Man's tunic, cutting down to the flesh. He cried out and stumbled away as another soldier threw himself at Tarsa's back, catching her around the waist and pulling her to the ground.

Dibadjiibé flew across the chamber. Three more Men ran in with weapons drawn, and the wounded swordsman followed closely behind. They slid to a horrified stop, however, as their companion on the ground shrieked in writhing desperation. Tarsa slowly stood, and the Men saw that her flesh had *changed*—dozens of long, wicked spikes covered her moss-green flesh, and the soldier who'd grabbed her was pierced through in a dozen or more places. He was delirious with agony, and his blood-slick hands tried to push against the jagged barbs, but it was hopeless, and he soon quivered in his death agonies. The Wielder's gaze was cold fire.

Tarsa arched her back. The spikes that held the Man's body impaled against her withdrew, and he fell to the ground. She then lifted her hand, and a stout vine flew from her outstretched palm to the staff, drawing it back to her grasp. The remaining Men turned toward the door, but a wall of spiny tendrils spread across their path with terrifying speed. There would be no escape.

"The reckoning has begun," Tarsa whispered, her eyes glazed over, her gaze distant. There were voices on the wind, voices that had too long been silenced by cold iron and willful forgetfulness. She was the spark, and they were tinder. They inhabited the Wielder; she couldn't understand their words, but she understood their rising grief, and she became their embodied fury.

They would be heard now.

The Men cried out and begged for mercy, but the Wielder ignored them. Holding Dibadjiibé high, she began to chant in a hollow voice, and the chamber crackled. A warm wind rose up, followed by blistering rains and a crash of thunder that shook the building's foundations. The floor split apart, and great green stalks as thick as tree trunks whipped upward, breaking through the ceiling and sending a shower of tile, plaster, and shattered wood plummeting on the screaming Men below. The she-Kyn's eyes glowed azure as she pointed the amber-topped staff at the doorway. A rush of green flame roared outward, and the chamber exploded in blood and fury.

The room was slick with sap and mud, and smoke hung heavy in the air. A great hole gaped wide where once the door had stood strong. Vald's militiamen lay dead around the room, their bodies ravaged by the elemental forces Tarsa's grief and rage had unleashed. But it didn't matter: Neranda and the Dreydmaster were gone, and with them the treacherous treaty. Tarsa fell screaming to her knees, driving her bloodied fists against the shattered floor tiles.

Something jabbed the she-Kyn in her side, breaking through the haze of fury. Her pouch had been knocked open in the chaos, and small, golden shards of thin metal lay crushed where she knelt. Her heart stopped as awareness flooded back. Hands shaking, Tarsa reached into the pouch and pulled out the fragments of the nightwasp's orb, along with the summoning insect's broken silver body.

"No," she groaned. "No . . . "

The nightwasp was dead. There would be no cloud-galleon, no rescue for her and her friends. The Expulsion had begun, and they were trapped in Gorthac Hall.

23

Betrayal

"THAT EN'T THE RIGHT SHIP," Tobhi whispered hoarsely. He and Daladir looked up at the docked Dragon with growing despair. They had followed the stairwell to the lower levels of Gorthac Hall, rushed through the servant galley to the stable yards, and slipped from shadow to shadow until they found an unused stall to catch their breath and prepare for the next desperate rush. Now they crouched in moldy, dung-strewn hay that made Tobhi's nose wrinkle and slowly comprehended the bitter certainty of the danger they now faced.

Daladir watched the great cloud-galleon with burning green eyes. Even though he wore his own iron-ward—a necessity of all Kyn diplomats to Human lands—he shrank from the great iron machine and the clank and whirr of the gears and great gas bellows. But he couldn't look away. Tethered to the great tower of the Hall, the Dragon hovered at just the right angle above them to obscure the ship's passengers from view. Another smaller airship—one of the numerous Ubbetuk trading skiffs that carried goods to and from the city—lay docked at the far end of the stable yard.

A memory fluttered at Tobhi's thoughts. There was something familiar about the larger ship, something about the great wasp's alien visage carved onto the bow. He'd seen it before. His eyes widened suddenly. "That wasp. It belongs to—" he began, but the sharp blat of horns silenced him as they tore through the early morning stillness.

Darooomah. Darooomah. Darooomah.

Horns of warning. Horns of war.

A flurry of activity caught their attention. The great gas-bladders of the cloud-galleon began to swell, jets of steam and smoke shot out from the ship's underside, and the gangplank sagged from the march of feet hurrying across it. The Dragon would be leaving very soon.

Darooomah. Darooomah. Darooomah.

Then, something else came into view, a flash of green flesh with braided brown hair flying behind. Tarsa was running toward the ship, and boiling storm clouds followed, the staccato flare of lighting shimmering through the darkness in her wake.

Darooomah. Darooomah. Darooomah.

Tobhi and Daladir watched in fascinated horror as the wooden gangplank began to *wither*, like a creeper left too long in the hot sun. It buckled and twisted, groaning with the pressure until it exploded against the galleon in a shower of piercing fragments. A red-capped Ubbetuk cried out and plunged from the deck, followed by a figure wrapped in fluttering white robes, its body impaled by a massive spike from the shattered gangplank.

Casting caution aside, Tobhi and Daladir rushed out to find the broken bodies lying tangled together in the ice-rimmed mud of the yard. Tobhi called upward, uselessly trying to catch Tarsa's attention, but Daladir was focused on the dead. The Redcap lay with wet eyes staring sightlessly into the sky, his body twisted backward, arms akimbo. It was the other shape, however, that now commanded the he-Kyn's attention. The shimmering white silks, like moonlight dancing on snow, revealed as much as did the figure's oak-leaf ears, bronze skin, and two tightly bound sensory stalks.

"What is a Shield doing here?" Daladir asked softly, but he knew the answer. He knew even as Tarsa stood on the tower parapet and pulled the iron-ward from her throat, her anguished voice empowered by such primal rage that the wooden timbers throughout Gorthac Hall buckled.

"*SHAKAR!*" A sudden surge of *wyr* crackled around the he-Kyn and the Tetawa, sucking the air from their lungs. Thunder and lightning exploded above them, and the early dawn was replaced by icy sleet and blistering hail. Daladir stumbled back to the stable, dragging Tobhi with him, and they watched the bodies of the Shield and the Redcap disappear under a sudden blanket of gleaming white ice. The small cloud-skiff slid in slow helplessness to the earth, overwhelmed by the storm.

"*SHAKAR!*" Tarsa shouted again, and again, through the raging tempest, as the great Dragon rose up and away from the tower. A jagged fork of lightning skittered across the hull of the galleon. The air was alight in fiery response, but when the glow faded the Dragon sailed on, disappearing at last into the roiling clouds.

The Wielder remained standing on the tower, unfazed by the maelstrom around her. She had given a name to her quarry.

Shakar.

Traitor.

And the horns of Eromar blared on.

Neranda stood on the deck of the cloud-galleon and watched the tower of Gorthac Hall disappear in the distance, and with it the young Wielder whose grief-ravaged voice still burned in her ears.

Shakar.

The fury of the storm abated, the clouds thinned, and the cold daylight of early morning ruled the sky as the Dragon moved eastward toward the Everland. Neranda still watched the uncontrollable storm in the west, unwarmed by the morning sun at this frigid height.

"Do you think we're safe?" Pradu Styke emerged from below deck to stand beside the Lawmaker, who pulled her cloak closer to her chilled flesh. Though they were allies now, it was an alliance of necessity, not choice, and she still hadn't forgiven him for his earlier insult to her honor. She'd called him a traitor, yet the word was ashes in her thoughts now. Styke's voice still dripped with his characteristic arrogance, but he now visibly trembled from more than the cold.

The Shield shook her head. "We will never be safe again, Captain Styke. As you said before we arrived last night: 'We go to sign away our lives.' They will not forgive this treachery."

"This was not betrayal, Lawmaker. We simply did what no one else had the courage to do."

Shakar.

"Yes, of course we did." Neranda turned abruptly away from the he-Kyn and walked into the hold, pulling the dirty hem of her sky-blue robe away from her feet as she descended the stairs. The oak-paneled hallway was softly lit by small oil lamps placed in recesses along the wall. Unlike the steady Kyn everlights, the glow from these lamps flickered and danced with the movement of air on the galleon, casting shifting green shadows along the walls. The Lawmaker thought for a moment about returning to wind and fresh air on deck but instead opened the door to her own quarters. Styke's presence sickened her. The whole affair had gone too far beyond her control. She felt much like the cloud-galleon, tossed and battered by a storm not of her own making.

"Perhaps a restful sleep will ease your mind." The lamplight in the hallway grew dim, almost dark, and then flashed to life again. Blackwick, the Ubbetuk Chancellor, stood in the open doorway. "May I join you for a moment before you retire?"

Neranda smiled gratefully, and the Chancellor limped forward, leaning heavily on his wasp-headed staff. His robes were less ornate than those he'd worn at the Sevenfold Council, but the lack of adornment seemed merely to enhance his presence; the white fabric shimmered with the iridescence of woven diamonds. The she-Kyn and the Ubbetuk regarded each other for a few heartbeats before slipping into the plush chairs bolted securely to the floor.

"The return journey will be a bit more leisurely than the first." The Chancellor scratched at his chin with a well-manicured claw. "The Dragons are marvels of engineering, but I would not risk such strain again, especially with the . . . unusual weather thus far. We should arrive in Sheynadwiin by tomorrow's dusk."

"Thank you, Chancellor. Your kindness eases my mind, although I must admit that I am not entirely eager to return." She leaned back stiffly in her chair.

They sat in silence for a while, easing into the slow rhythm of the ship. At last Neranda cleared her throat. "I had hoped that my legacy would be an enduring one, that future generations would see my leadership in the Sevenfold Council as the turning point in the creation of a promising future for all the Folk. Now everything is so muddled and confused." She hesitated, her voice thick with emotion.

"Please forgive my impertinence, Chancellor, but I must ask you a question. Why did you bring me here to sign the Oath after you voted with the rest of the Council? Do you not fear discovery?"

Blackwick turned to her, his eyelids heavy. All trace of the smile was gone, and in its place settled a deep sorrow. For the first time Neranda saw the weight of age bleed through the near-mythic reputation of preternaturally shrewd diplomacy, political maneuvering, and strategic machinations that had built up around the Chancellor over many long years. No figure was so respected, or so feared, in the lands of Humans or the Folk; he saw details and possibilities that evaded others, and his uncanny ability to choose the best moment to take action or delay had kept him well ahead of even his most determined opponents for decades. There was a cost, surely, though Neranda didn't dare imagine what Blackwick had surrendered to achieve this reputation. One thing was certain, however: his was a powerful mind, but he was mortal, too, and bound by the same laws of mortality as the rest of his kith.

"Life is too often the unhappy path between painful choices, and this is the reality that besets us now. War would come to the Everland whether we signed the Oath or not; signing the document merely gives the appearance of tacit acceptance, an appearance that all involved know to be an illusion. Yet had the Ubbetuk turned away from our kindred and split the Council, the Folk would be torn apart from within, thus stripping us of any hope for withstanding the coming onslaught."

He shrugged and crossed his hands over the top of the staff. "Vald no longer has any need to use terror to compel us to sign; there may still be battles, but by signing the Oath you have given his crusade legal standing in the Reach, and no Human state will challenge its validity—not, at least, with force of arms. Without that hope to cling to, the spirit of resistance among the various Folk will be lessened, and emigration will be far more peaceful than it would have been if Vald had thrown his full fury upon us. Had that happened, we could have perhaps expected aid from the Humans of the Allied Wilderlands, Béashaad, or perhaps even Sarvannadad, and both the Everland and the lands of Men would have been torn apart by civil war and bloodshed. Vald will be cruel, certainly, and many of your people will die under the terms of the Oath, but more would have died if Vald had been defied entirely."

"You do not believe that the Dreydmaster will honor his word at all?"

Now a frigid smile passed over the Chancellor's thin lips, and his eyes narrowed to slits. "I am neither a fool nor an idealistic dreamer. Your colleague Captain Styke is wise in his assessment: Vald cannot be trusted—the Man is hunger incarnate. He seeks blood and power, and each taste leaves him greedy for more."

"But what would it benefit him to violate the Oath?"

"Have you heard nothing, Lawmaker?" he hissed, his soft voice almost too low to hear. "These treaties and agreements are fragile, written on paper that is easily burned. The Folk may regard words and promises as sacred, but Men have forgotten those truths. To them, treaties are merely convenient and efficient means to achieve what they want while appearing to be eminently reasonable and conciliatory. There will be more agreements, which they will violate again and again, and then they will insist that we negotiate again and again based on the unjust terms of those same documents. They are some measure of protection, but only as far as Men are willing to honor them, too. Vald is a liar, a thief, and a murderer. Eromar is drenched in the blood of his own people, and the blood of the Folk will flow there before this storm passes. There is no hope for fidelity from such people. Our only hope rests in his belief that we are no obstacle to his ambitions. You have given him reason for that belief."

Neranda leaned forward, her face stricken. "Is death, then, the future you see for your people?"

"The Ubbetuk live in every Human nation throughout the Reach. No general goes to war without first consulting his 'Goblin' tactician. No wealthy maiden attends a party without asking her 'Goblin' retainer for advice on etiquette and the latest fine fashions. There is no house of power in all the Reach of Men that is untouched by the hand or thought of the Swarm. Even Eromar itself depends on our machinery and iron-craft for their great foundries and factories. Do you think this is mere coincidence? We survive by making ourselves so necessary to the functioning of this Melded world that we *cannot* be removed. If a new Purging begins, everything Men have built will collapse. They cannot kill us without killing themselves. Their survival depends upon our own. The Ubbetuk have no need of the Everland to endure."

Blackwick held up his walking staff and examined the carved head intently. "Do you know why the wasp is the symbol of the Swarm, Lawmaker? Above all else, the Ubbetuk are a people dedicated to survival—there is nothing more important than that. We will always survive. Your people, too, are swift and beautiful, with duties and passions of your own, but you are more akin to bees. Your hives are lovely, your honey sweet, and you are fearless when enemies attack. But a bee can sting only once, and then it dies.

"The wasp, however, is different. It may not have the golden comb and flow of honey, but it can sting again and again and again. It is merciless in its defense of home and nest. And there is no place that a wasp cannot make its home. No place at all."

His words hung in the air. Neranda grew pale as she studied the alien visage on the staff. "If such is the case, why not simply vote with your conscience and against consensus?"

Blackwick laughed, a thin, dry sound, like ripped birch-paper. "I *did* vote with my conscience, Lawmaker. The Folk will be driven to the shadowy West, but they will do so with a feeling of righteousness, and this will give them strength to survive in the dark days to come. Had I voted in favor of the Oath, the other Folk would see the Ubbetuk as the architects of their suffering, with unnecessary death as a result on each side. I did not lie at the Council. We are kith yet, and though your peoples' dependence on the Everland is a grievous weakness that we do not share, we still acknowledge our bonds of kinship. If the Folk saw us as enemies, the enduring hatred and deaths that would result could never be made right. Such division could bring nothing but suffering. I would not have that burden on my shoulders, Lawmaker."

"But *I* signed the Oath. Will not that create division? Will not—" She suddenly stopped, her eyes widening with dawning horror. It was all becoming terribly clear.

"No, it will not." The Chancellor shook his head, his expression impassive, emotionless. "That division already exists among the Kyn. Once the dying starts, once the elders and young ones fall, your betrayal will bring your people together as one again. They will look past the silly squabbles between the Old Ways of the forest and the New Ways of the sky, for a while at least, and turn their attention to survival. Their rage and sorrow will fall upon you and all the Oathsworn, and as your blood falls, the Kyn Nation will be reborn."

"But you . . ." she whispered. "You helped me. That Wielder saw you. They'll know . . ."

"What will they know? I never stepped into the Hall; indeed, I never once left the galleon. I came to Eromar City simply to ensure the safe transport of two high-ranking Goldcap trade merchants back to Sarvannadad, both of whom are now aboard and resting comfortably; I was both shocked and saddened to discover that a Lawmaker of your reputation used my generous offer of transportation to engage in such unlawful and unethical activities. Such betrayal particularly grieves me because of my very public opposition to the odious terms of the Oath of Western Sanctuary."

Blackwick stood and gently smoothed the wrinkles from his robes as he stepped to the door. Without turning, in a voice little louder than a whisper, he said, "It seems that you have left your sting behind, Lawmaker. But do not fear: your betrayal may yet ensure the survival of your people. In years to come, they will speak your name, and those of your compatriots. The Oathsworn will be known for generations, and the Kyn will curse your names. Rest assured—your legacy will most certainly endure . . . *Shakar.*" The lamps in the hall dimmed, and when they flickered back to life, the Chancellor was gone.

Neranda buried her face in her shaking hands, her nails scoring long, jagged lines down her cheeks. She rocked silently back and forth as the lamplight danced around her. The only sounds to be heard in her chamber were the mechanical groans of the great Dragon as it cut eastward through clouds and air currents, and the Lawmaker's soft weeping.

The horns continued to bleat, even as the massive cloud-galleon vanished into the clouds and the storm raged around the tower. The hail had ended, but the rain that drove down continued pummeling the earth. Tobhi and Daladir could still see Tarsa on the parapet, her hands tightly clutching the wyrwood staff.

"Why isn't she coming down?" Daladir yelled, trying to be heard over the roll of thunder and the maddening horns.

Tobhi peered through the rain. "She can't. There en't no way down but the tower stairs, and I'll bet m' knock-kneed deer that

Vald's butchers is blockin' that route." He looked around. "I guess we'll just have to figure out some way up there our ownselves."

"We can't go back into the Hall." Daladir shook his head. "There isn't any way."

The Leafspeaker turned to the he-Kyn, his face beaming, and pointed to the stable yard. "Oh, I en't so sure 'bout that." Daladir followed the gesture to a handful of golden-capped Ubbetuk rushing around a large shape that lay indistinct in the raging storm.

Before the he-Kyn could say anything, Tobhi unslung his hatchet and rushed out into the rain. With an exasperated sigh, Daladir followed after.

Fight on, spirits of the raging sky. Share your fury with me for a while longer, I beg you. Let your cleansing wrath fall upon this poisoned place.

Tarsa again felt the *wyr* surge through her body in response to her desperate appeal. The air pulsed with blue-green fire that danced across her skin to burst across her attackers' swords in a blistering arc. The first Man fell, followed by a second, and then a third, but Tarsa knew that she wouldn't be able to stop them all. The tower doorway was too wide, and she was weak from despair and the storm summoning. As her thoughts wandered, the burning gleam of an iron crossbow bolt flashed past her head.

She heard the click of another bolt being readied. The Men were preparing for the final assault; she no longer had the strength to stop them before they brought her down.

Very well. If she were to die this night, she'd make sure that the event would haunt Men's darkest dreams for years to come. The Wielder took a deep breath and flung herself at them again. The Men were ready. A club clipped her in the shoulder, and she stumbled backward with a grunt. Her staff shot out, parried, smashed into an arm, a jaw, caught the edge of a sword and crushed a kneecap. A blade slashed across her hand, a bolt pierced her upper thigh. The storm grew in intensity as her bright blood now glistened in the flashes of skyfire.

She smiled grimly. If nothing else, it would be a memorable death.

Tarsa could feel the *wyr* drain from her as a wreath of lightning suddenly crackled around the tower and struck the parapet, sending stone shards flying and Men screaming. The wood on the east side of the tower caught fire from the intense heat, even in the heavy rain.

Another explosion of thunder shook the tower. Buffered by the ebbing *wyr,* Tarsa felt nothing more than a sudden shift beneath her feet, but the Men around her covered their burst ears and crouched screaming on the trembling planks. The horns stopped. A low groan crawled from the structure's stones and timbers, growing louder from below, like a creature of the deep earth clawing its way to the surface. Slowly the tower began to sway back and forth, each return movement longer than the one before. Those militiamen unbroken by the storm jammed the stairwell, trying desperately to escape the shifting edifice, the she-Kyn Wielder now long forgotten.

Tarsa leaned wearily on Dibadjiibé as another burning blast illuminated the tower like sudden daylight. It was over, or soon would be. She slipped to one knee, her flesh tearing on the jagged plank, as the tower shifted again. She couldn't do any more. The *wyr*-call had been answered; her focus was slipping, and though the storm remained, the sated spirits of this strange land were drifting back into slumber—she didn't have the strength to call on them again.

Then, as though stepping from midair, Tobhi appeared out of the storm-shrouded darkness.

"Tarsa! Grab m' hand!" And he was gone again, lost amidst black smoke and clouds.

But only for a moment. He swung wildly in the air, tied securely to the end of a thick rope that hung off an Ubbetuk cloud-skiff. Tarsa could see the small ship through the flashes of lightning and rising flame. It bounced and fluttered like a giant moth, buffeted by the ferocious winds and driving rain she'd unleashed.

Tobhi swung back into view. His hat was missing, and his long black braid whipped viciously around his face and neck.

He thrust out his hands again, and this time Tarsa tried to grab him, but the tower moaned and the planks moved under her feet, and she fell sprawling. Breathing heavily, she pulled herself up on trembling legs, weakly holding her free hand to the sky, reaching out to his flailing hands.

"Down!" Tobhi screamed up to Daladir and a young Goldcap Ubbetuk at the he-Kyn's side. The winds were dangerously erratic. The Tetawa gasped in pain and sudden disorientation as the little Dragon dipped down and shot up again, sending him spinning in a wide, uncontrollable arc. "Tarsa, hurry!" he cried out to the wind,

not at all sure where she was, where he was, or whether she could even hear him. His stomach twisted into a knot of nausea as he reached out one more time.

The tower's groan shifted again, now rising to a calamitous roar. The screams of the Men in the stairwell were lost in the cacophony, and at last the structure crumbled into flames, fragments of shattered stone and wood, broken flesh, and crushed iron. The shattered mass plummeted to earth, and a choking cloud of fire and hot ash burst up from the ruins.

In the air above the broken tower of Gorthac Hall, a cloud-skiff bobbed awkwardly. Below it, hanging from a thick rope, were an airsick Tetawa and a worn and weary she-Kyn. Half conscious, Tarsa clutched at Tobhi with one hand; in the white-knuckled grip of the other, she held Unahi's wyrwood staff, its amber head aglow in the dawn's light. Daladir tugged at the rope, slowly drawing them upward.

Wounded by the storm but not broken, the small ship limped its way through the sky to the east, toward the Everland.

Cycle Four
The Hill of Broken Pines

The Dreyd were not the first gods of Men. They were usurpers, unsatisfied with the knowledge given to the dying world, unwilling to accept the Chain of Fate as it was forged, link by link, within the great soul-foundries of the Immortals of Old. Chaos was the bastard child of the Old Ones, and Men despised and feared Him, for He gave honor to none, and He loved many, capriciously cruel and kind in turn. None stood high in the eyes of Chaos, so Men created Law, and She brought Chaos to heel and sought to bind Him in walls of stone, shackles of iron, and words of unyielding certainty. Law, too, was cruel, but She was predictable, and Men loved Her even as they feared Her. But Chaos could not be contained, and He slipped free of Law's embrace and laughed at Her fury. And He returned to the world of Men, unchanged, bringing joy and pain with every step, caring no more for one than for the other.

The Old Immortals were drinkers of blood and wine, slaves to sacrifice and adoration. They indulged their wild son and scorned the hard-eyed daughter of Men. And they laughed when the Dreyd sought the hidden mysteries of the Veil Between Worlds. But their laughter was short-lived, for Kaantor, the Great King of the rich valley of Karkûr, had penetrated into the mysteries and returned again with their secrets. The Veil tore apart, the Old Immortals fell screaming to earth, and the Dreyd rose up to take their place. These priests and alchaemists thought to bring Law with them into eternity, but they were deceived, for when the Blind Lady removed Her mask, the Dreyd wept in despair: it was Chaos who looked laughing upon them.

And yet the Dreyd still seek to trap the bastard son of the Immortals of Old, but they know now that Law is a lie crafted for Men's comfort. So they try to give Her flesh, to place life in those nerveless fingers, and the more desperate their efforts, the greater the mirth of Chaos. So it has been for a thousand years, and so it will always be, as long as the Dreyd reign and the memory of the world remains lost.

24

Thresholds

THE DREAM ALWAYS BEGINS *the same way. It's a soft purple evening, the spice of pine sap heavy on the drowsy air. Quill sits in her bent-root chair beside the fireplace. The apple-head dolls crowd around her, singing a low, soft melody, their distinct voices melting together, digging as deeply as taproots, in words as old as stone. The Tetawa doesn't sing, but she listens and taps her foot in time to the song. The dolls nod approvingly, and their voices grow stronger, the words fading beneath the rhythm. Soon the entire cabin is alive with the sound—every tile, every swatch of cloth, every kiln-fired plate. It's an ancient song, with words unknown to any but the dwellers of the Spirit World. It ties the Dolltender to her memas and grannies, all those* firra *before her who spoke to the dolls and knew of those ancient days in the Eld Green, when the world belonged to the Folk alone, when there were no barriers between the Folk and their Spirit cousins. Those days are lost to all but memory now, and to the dolls, who remind her.*

Quill sits in her chair, listening to the song, and finishes sewing a tight edge on the long red sash in her lap. The sash is the color of old blood. She has double-stitched black trim to the edge, from which emerges the silhouettes of flat-bodied badgers dancing across the long red field. It's a gift.

She feels the knock more than she hears it; it's too soft to be heard over the song. The dolls move aside, singing still, as the young firra *drapes the sash across her arm and steps to the door to welcome her visitor. The door swings open, but it's not a welcome guest who stands in the doorway.*

A claw flashes in the firelight and catches the sash, tearing a jagged hole through it with a single motion. Quill sees yellow, watery eyes, and hears the gurgling giggle, and the figure stands tall, looming above her, its jagged teeth dripping with slime and blood.

She sees the clawed hand rise again, and she tries to scream, but her voice is lost in the song, which goes on and on and on . . .

Quill jerked awake. She gasped and clutched at her hand, where the bone embroidery needle dug into her palm. Pulling the needle free, she lifted her hand to her mouth and looked down at the sash. A thick droplet of dark red blood glistened for a moment on the surface before vanishing into the thirsty cloth.

Someone was at the door. She looked around, her heart suddenly beating wildly. The dolls were on their shelves, where they'd been since Medalla and Gishki helped her put her own house back in order. Her cousins now lay in Quill's bed, sleeping soundly after the stress of recent days; the Dolltender hadn't been able to sleep and chose to sit beside the fireplace and continue working on the sash. She'd slept in her chair for the past three nights, unable to find comfort in her own bed. A few logs crackled softly in the hearth; a kettle steamed from its hook above the flames. Otherwise, all was silent.

The knock sounded again, more insistently now. Her heart was a deafening drumbeat in her ears, but she stood anyway, bare feet dragging slightly on the stone floor. There was desperation in the sound, a need calling out to her. Quill glanced up at the dolls, but their eyes were dull and vacant, nothing like the brilliant black stars they'd been in the terrible dream.

One brown hand closed firmly over her smoothed-pine walking stick beside the door, while the other slid hesitantly over the door latch. Her breath rose and fell in quick, short gasps. There was silence beyond the door now, waiting for her to open the threshold wide. She clutched the stick until her knuckles went white, and then the door was open, and she was standing with weapon raised against a trio of figures barely illuminated by the light streaming out from the cabin. Quill froze as she stared at one figure in particular, the mundane world suddenly lost in impossibility, and the staff was on the ground and she was in his arms, crying with joy and relief, as the words she'd dreamed of saying for so long at last found voice.

"Etobhi, my love, where have you been?"

<<Only one this time?>> the Woman asked impatiently, her thin voice already grating. <<You seem to be losing your touch, Vergis.>>

The Seeker shrugged as he watched the guards drag the Deerman toward the holding pens, where the creature would be kept until the wagons to Eromar were full and ready to transport. Thane and his prisoner had arrived at the assembly hall in the early afternoon, and now Thane was finishing the obligatory interrogation. <<The Fey-Touched are getting harder to find these days, Carinne, especially in the outer reaches. I caught the trace of a few others, but I wanted to deliver this one before following after them.>> He leaned back in his chair, his mud-stained boots propped up on the Binder's desk, and drew deeply on his pipe.

After casting a cold eye at Thane's breach of etiquette, the old Binder nodded and returned to scribbling in the voluminous tome shackled to her bony wrist. <<It's a good thing that you arrived when you did. The Dreydmaster of Eromar has called for all the faithful to prepare for the Expulsion. This should make your Seeking easier.>>

<<No, it won't.>> Thane spat out a loose piece of tobacco. <<The last thing I need is for a bunch of flat-footed farmboys and murderous glory-seekers to be pushing my quarry deeper into those damned hills. It's hard enough to find them in their villages without having to ferret out their hiding holes.>>

<<It can't be as bad as all that.>>

<<I don't tell you how to Bind, Carinne, so don't try turning Seeker on me now. I've been over more of that land than any Man I've ever met, and I *know* these creatures—they're far more resilient and far more tied to this place than you can guess. I'm telling you that this latest plan of Vald's is going to cause us all a lot of trouble.>>

Carinne's bird-like features jutted forward. <<That's *Dreydmaster Vald* to you, 'Seeker' Thane. You've been a little too independent for too long, I think. Your impertinence is going to get you into trouble one day. The Purifiers are always eager to bring the proud and haughty to the High Hall in Bashonak. Talented you certainly are, Vergis, but don't count yourself too precious. Perhaps you could use a reminder about the proper respect for the inspired dictates of our honored leaders . . . >>

Thane's lip curled slightly, but he knew that this was a battle he couldn't win—not now, anyway. Carinne may have looked like a half-drowned buzzard, but she was the undisputed voice of the Dreydcaste in the Half Moon Hills and the southern edge of Eromar, and her fidelity to the upstart Dreydmaster of Gorthac Hall was unwavering. This was an argument for another time. For now, Thane merely nodded and continued smoking his pipe; Carinne smiled victoriously and continued writing in the book.

When she finished, the Binder motioned to Thane, who read over the transcription account of his latest journey and signed at the end with her ink-stained quill. The Woman sprinkled a handful of sand liberally over the wet ink, blew the excess back into the bowl, and shut the great scarred tome, her Binding chains rattling loudly in the largely empty room.

<<We may not have many more opportunities to find them in their wild places, Vergis, while they're still pure in their powers, so I'm sending you out again as soon as you're ready. We haven't much more time. Do you, perchance, have any objection to that proposal?>>

Even if he had, it wouldn't have made much difference; though she pretended to offer gracious options, it was all a counterfeit, as the Binder permitted no defiance—her word here was Law. It hardly mattered. Thane had little interest in remaining in Chimiak for any longer than a bath, new travel gear and hardtack, a little fun with a wide-hipped whore, and a good night's sleep.

He finished his meeting with Carinne and headed to the barracks behind the main hall, where he could begin with the bath while a novice filled his supply order. The whore and sleep would come later.

The barracks included both a communal bathing room and, for Seekers, a series of smaller bath chambers for the use of the more unsociable of their kind. It was the latter that Thane sought, and he found an unoccupied cell without difficulty. The white stone walls of Chimiak were built on the site of natural hot springs, so most of the public buildings and all of the Dreydcaste structures had a plentiful supply of hot water. Thane undressed and eased himself into the small stone pool, feeling the tensions of his latest journey slowly work themselves out of his muscles as he descended.

He pulled the patch away from his eye and slid under the nearly scalding water, delighting in its burning tingle. It wasn't so hot that it blistered the flesh, but it was enough to drive the flesh to its sensory limits, and that's what he wanted now. He didn't mind the sulfurous smell, nor the gritty residue that remained after even a short bath in the springs. These were far better than the mud, sweat, and other accumulated grime of life in the wild. He surfaced and floated to the side of the pool, the safety of this healing moment guiding his mind toward calm reflection.

Though the lowest of the Dreydcaste, the Seekers were also the most vital to its survival, for it was through their clarity of purpose and diligence that the Fey-Touched were found and claimed. Without the Seekers, the Binders would have to draw upon their own life-blood in their alchaemical incantations, and they would burn away much too soon. As it was, the soul-tomes that were shackled to their wrists were the only true defense they had from being consumed by their spirit-manipulating powers.

Seekers had no such weaknesses. The greatest risk a Seeker faced was sympathy; the many faces of their prisoners rarely faded with time, and many nights were haunted by the fear-filled eyes of those who had fallen prey to the Seeker's patient pursuit.

Thane had little worry about this risk. If he'd ever needed a reminder of how dangerous the Fey-Touched could be, the eye-patch and a grotesque series of scars that spread across his belly were enough. No matter how many tears his quarry shed, no matter how great the ransom promised or brutal the vengeance sworn, they rarely found an escape from Vergis Thane.

Only a small handful had successfully evaded him, a Fey-witch and her other Unhuman friends who'd long ago wounded and cast him down into the personal darkness from which it took him years to emerge. Already one had fallen to swift, certain death at the merciless edge of his blades; another he'd mutilated and left nearly dead; if she'd survived, hers was no doubt a greatly diminished existence. As for the last one—the witch who'd taken the most from him, the creature whose treachery had led him directly into the life of a Seeker—he knew they'd meet again. And he would never cease hunting her, even into the next life, if necessary.

But it wasn't the mocking face of his long-sought quarry that floated before him now. Instead, the sandy-haired image of a young Brownie maiden returned to his thoughts. Though so inconsequential on the surface, Thane had always considered Brownies amongst the most nettlesome of the Unhumans. He didn't understand why, but those little people had a strange ability to shroud their Fey-Touched radiance, and he'd had few successful hunts in Brownie country. Still, the little maid with the dolls had lingered in his thoughts long after he left her house, and Thane was sure that this feeling was more than simply the disquiet left by the strange, hunchbacked hound with yellow eyes that scampered away from the household's slaughtered pigs.

That little Brownie was Touched—of that he was certain. But she was different from anything he'd encountered before. This alone was reason enough to return.

But there was something else. Whatever that hog-shaped creature was, it was there for more than fresh meat. It was on the prowl for something, too. Thane knew the sweet, tangled scent of a hunter and its prey.

He reached into a copper urn resting on the side of the pool and pulled out a handful of coarse soap flakes. The mystery would resolve itself soon enough. For now, he turned his attention to the bath. In his long experience, no whore liked a dirty Man.

Quill's happy cries had woken Medalla and Gishki, and they now sat with the visitors—young Tobhi, whom they had known for many years, and the two grim, silent Kyn with him—eating a makeshift dinner of rice stew, deer-milk cheese, thick bread, and winter willow tea. Quill glowed as she sat beside her travel-weary lover, her fingers twined in his long hair, her head leaning softly on his shoulder. Tobhi pulled her close to his side as he ate, content in spite of the deep circles under his eyes and the ache in his muscles. After hearing about Tobhi's recent adventures, the Dolltender told the visitors about the recent events around Spindletop, the Skeeger's murderous cruelties, and of the strange Man who'd driven the Skeeger away and left before dawn.

Tobhi nodded. "I en't surprised, givin' what's been happenin' throughout the Everland lately. Men are gettin' bolder than ever, and all sorts of creatures is comin' out of the dark pockets of old

stories. We'll see more of these shadows afore the end, I reckon."
He glanced at Tarsa and Daladir, but they'd long ago lapsed into a
thoughtful silence.

The Leafspeaker shook his head. Had it really been only five days
since they'd fled Eromar? The damaged cloud-skiff had borne only
enough fuel to reach the far western edge of the Everland, on the
southern edge of Meshiwiik Forest. It was far from the best site for landing, as the territory was still dangerously close to the grasp of Eromar,
but the Ubbetuk refused to push the small Dragon beyond its strength.
When they'd landed, the youngest and most sympathetic of the merchants gave Tobhi some travel rations, but he couldn't convince his five
companions to assist the travelers any further. Tobhi could hardly blame
them, as he and Daladir had forced the Ubbetuk into this sudden and
dangerous journey when they'd commandeered the ship. While he
would have preferred to take the skiff all the way to Sheynadwiin, he
knew they were lucky to have gotten as far as they had already.

Still, good fortune had been with them, for although they
were farther from the heart of the Kyn Branch-hold, they'd landed
quite close to the wild, tree-thick country that Tobhi called home:
Spindletop, the Edgewood, the Hollow Hills. They would find help
here, and then they could hurry to Sheynadwiin.

Besides, he had a long-overdue visit to make.

It had been nearly two years since he'd set out from the forested
hill country Spindletop to meet with his aunt Jynni Thistledown at the
Gathering of Clans in Mossydell. That was where everything began
for him. But before he'd left on that snowy morning, he held a sandy-
haired *firra* close and kissed her full lips with the promise that he'd
return. He'd sent letters and gifts with the occasional traveler heading
that direction, but it wasn't as much as either of them had wanted.

So tonight, he kept the full measure of his promise.

But what now? Tobhi turned to look at Quill. Her dark eyes were
warm, and they drew him deeply. Yet he knew that he couldn't stay.
And he also knew that, if things went as badly as Tarsa and Daladir
now feared, he might never be able to come back.

He might not even have anything to come back to.

Medalla stood and clapped a hand on his shoulder, interrupting
the Leafspeaker's troubled thoughts. "Welcome home, Tobhi. We'll
leave you now; I'm sure you've got plenty to talk about." She glanced

sadly at Quill. *She knows,* Tobhi realized, but before he could speak, Medalla was moving toward the door and motioning to Gishki. "It's nearly dawn. We'll check back on you around midday."

Quill smiled and held her cousins' hands tightly as she walked them to the door. "I told you he'd be home again, though I almost didn't believe it myself. It's better than I could have hoped for!" She could barely keep her eyes off him as she spoke. "We'll have a welcoming feast tomorrow night to celebrate!"

"I'm so happy for you, Quill," Medalla said, her voice hoarse. With a doubtful glance at Tobhi and his companions, she slipped into the darkness beyond, followed silently by Gishki.

After bolting the door, the Dolltender turned to her visitors. "My room is on the left, and my spare room is on the right. You're welcome to either one."

Tarsa looked at the Tetawa and nodded, smiling in spite of her exhaustion. "Thank you, Quill. It's been a long time since we've slept without fear or cold as our companions. I'm only sorry that we can't be better guests."

The *firra* shook her head. "You're welcome regardless, Tarsa. If you're Tobhi's friends, then you're mine as well. Please, make yourselves at home. I'll have hot water ready for a bath when you wake up."

Tarsa began walking down the short hallway but stopped and turned to Daladir. "You'll need your sleep, too, Ambassador. We can share the room and give them some time alone."

He looked up, his green eyes heavy. "Should I take the floor?"

The Wielder laughed, the shadows momentarily slipping from her face. "No need, so long as you're less selfish with the blankets than you've been with the bedroll these past few nights! Given these past days together, modesty doesn't hold much between us, Daladir. I think you've been too long in the world of Men. You're back on home ground now, or near enough to it. Things are different here."

Daladir smiled thinly and followed her into the guest room.

The Tetawi were alone now in the main room of the cabin. It was still dark outside. Tobhi stood and scratched his chin nervously. "Well, I s'pose I can lay m' bedroll here aside the fireplace. Ye reckon I might have a bit of that hot water later, too?" He cleared his throat.

The Dolltender didn't respond. She stood and walked around the room, blowing out the oil lamps, leaving only the dancing flames of the hearth to light the room. Then she returned and took his hand as she led him to the fire, where she slowly unlaced his sweat-soiled jerkin. Tobhi trembled at her touch.

Quill left him again, but only for a moment. The Leafspeaker heard splashing, and then she was beside him once more, a washcloth draped over her forearm, a large wooden bowl in her hands that was half-filled with cold water and a handful of dried flower petals. She filled the bowl now with hot water from the steaming kettle. Pulling the *fahr* closer, the Dolltender slipped his jerkin off, then dipped the rag into the fragrant warm water and ran it over his skin. Tobhi moaned.

"Quill, ye don't have to . . ." Her finger pressed against his lips, and then her own lips were there, soft and full and warm. She brought the moist rag against his chest and felt his nipples harden beneath her fingers.

They sank together onto the tiles before the hearth. Quill's own garments joined Tobhi's on the wooden floor, and soon their unbound bodies shimmered and moved with a gentle rhythm, brown skin glistening like liquid bronze in the firelight.

Vald examined the ruins of the tower impassively and with little interest. The center of Gorthac Hall had been crushed by the falling stones and timber, and with it, remarkably, only eighteen members of the household, not counting the score of soldiers killed in the attempt to dispatch the witch and her friends. It hadn't taken long for Vorgha, the Dreydmaster's personal attendant, to organize both laborers and militia together to repair the breach in the Hall, and even now, in the darkest hours of early morning, there were hundreds of Men and Women swarming over the broken structure like so many dusty ants, desperate to appear busy under the Dreydmaster's unyielding gaze.

The Man turned back to the stable yard, where the bodies of the Kyn Shield and the Redcap Goblin lay swollen and crumpled, now five days dead. The terrible storm invoked by the Fey-witch had continued long after her departure, turning the yard into a pasty mass of mud and slimy dung, but Vald cared little for such trivialities. He looked up again to the site of the tower, which was brightly illuminated by hundreds of torches jammed here and there in the ruins.

<<Your Authority?>> Vorgha slipped across the muddy yard toward Vald, limp hair sticking to the thick sweat on his pallid brow. The attendant was unused to such labor, but he didn't dare to complain in word or deed. The Dreydmaster had no patience with laziness.

<<What is it?>>

<<We've completed our search of the rubble, and it's certain that both airships escaped intact. However, by all reports the smaller vessel was heavily damaged in the storm, so it's quite likely that they crashed somewhere between here and the Everland. I've ordered seized some of the city's remaining airships and loaded our soldiers into them; they've begun a broader search for the witch and her associates.>>

Vald looked to the darkened east. <<Don't waste your time—we have more important matters at hand. Let the Fey-witch go, for now. We will see her again soon enough. At dawn, use those ships to deliver leaflets announcing the details of the Oath to all cities within three days' march to the Everland. Make it clear that the spoils of Sheynadwiin are mine alone, but everything else is free for the taking; I won't punish anyone protecting what they claim by right of settlement.>>

<<Yes, Authority.>> Vorgha moved slowly backward, careful to avoid plunging into the muck. <<Will there be anything else?>>

The Dreydmaster's attention was focused on the ravaged tower. His thoughts drifted back to the sight of the Wielder in the storm, her dark hair wreathed by blue lightning. *Spearbreaker,* she called herself. Such power—and such potential.

He turned to his attendant. <<No—go on. I will take care of the witch myself.>>

As Vorgha crept back to the Hall, Vald strode to the western walls. The mud was no obstacle to the Dreydmaster—it hardened beneath his stride before each boot struck earth. Under the sun, one could see that the sky was black with storm clouds in the eastern sky, a perpetual wall of gloom that now rose up on the border of the Everland. Night's fading darkness now held sway over Eromar City. The damage to the Hall looked terrible now, but it, like the sky, was revealed to be so much worse in daylight. A massive pile of rubble as tall as a Man lay in the center of the Hall; those stones and broken timbers that had been scattered in the collapse were gone, swept away by Vorgha's efficient organization. Half of the eastern wing roof collapsed two days after the tower's fall, but the only casualties were some maidservants and a cowherd who had snuck into the house for a brief liaison—an insignificant loss, and a fitting end for such lechery. The western wing, where Vald's family chambers were located, had never been in any danger—the Dreydmaster had long ago ensured its stability with powerful, bloodletting Craftings. The world itself would crumble to dust before that part of Gorthac Hall fell.

Vald ignored the Men who saluted him as he passed through the western doors and through the north-leading hallway toward his private gardens. Three more soldiers—all picked years before by Vald himself—guarded this doorway. The Dreydmaster held up his right hand, bending the middle two fingers into his palm, and whispered a few words under his breath as his other hand released a handful of ash into the air. The Men nodded, their eyes glazed, faces pale and drawn tight like the skin on a drum, and stepped to the side of the door, their muskets still held high in defense of their eternal post. Vald walked through the doorway.

The garden was as dead in summer as it had been in the spring. None of the trees bore a sign of leaf or greenery. The tangled weeds that choked the dried fountain and broken garden pathways were brittle and desiccated. The acrid stench of sulfur—and something worse—hung in the air, a yellow haze that singed the Dreydmaster's throat and eyes and left an unpleasant film on the flesh. The place burned, not with the blistering heat that often accompanied his visits, but now with a preternatural cold. This chill oozed with slow deliberateness from the pulsing hole of shadow that the Dreydmaster had opened months before. It was from this rift that he'd sent the first shadow-stalkers—all dark feathers and claws—in pursuit of the Sevenfold Council's messengers and some of the more troublesome witches. Seekers took care of the minor Fey-Touched. Other shadow-servants he'd pulled from this dark nether-region, each bound to Vald's will through freshly shed blood and words of great power.

He generally showed restraint in bringing these creatures forth, as he never knew what would answer his bidding, but his visions had become progressively clearer over the past few months, and he knew now that he was on the cusp of achieving the ambition that had so long evaded his grasp. Hesitation now might well undermine his resolve: he was, after all, a Dreydmaster, and it was both his right and his duty to bind these creatures to the will of Men.

The words of the Dreyd were so much clearer now that the gate was left open, and it was their purpose that pulled him forward. It was their words that haunted his nights and left him gasping in exquisite fear and pain. It was their thoughts that bled the living world of joy, promising so much more in the shadows beyond than mortality could ever offer.

They promised him ascension. They promised him everlasting life.

The first message came to him years ago, when he'd first joined the Ruling Council of Eromar, a sullen lawyer from a merchant family with more money than influence. The other Councilors had ignored him, dismissed this young, kinless upstart without connections or a lineal heritage of significance. It was one night during that humiliating time, while he'd been fiercely mounting his unwilling young wife and ignoring her tearful pleas as he took what was his by marital right, that Vald had first heard the voices. He screamed and clutched at his head, falling backward from the bed, and the voices vanished in the commotion. But they returned, over and over again, year after year. He grew used to them and longed for their presence, for their words were like golden honey, an all-too-brief sweetness that lingered longer in memory than on the tongue.

And they *always* came back.

Do not fear, they assured him. *You will be among the Foremost, the Dreyd. We were once Humans like you—frail and easily broken. We knew the frustration of mortality, of giving fealty to the Immortals who cared little for our people, except to use us for amusing playthings and then to discard us in petulant boredom. We knew hunger, and pain, and loss, and we watched as the Immortals of Old played their games and hid their glories in other worlds.*

It had been the Dreydcaste who'd offered young Vald the quickest route to power. With disease and famine spreading like fire through the land, the purifying rites of the Dreydcaste brought comfort, and the people had rallied to the cause. Vald had reminded them that witches and conjurors were everywhere among Men; only a ruthless cleansing could bring back hope. Fear had given strength to the rising power of Dreyd-law, and Vald had been well suited for bringing order to a lawless land.

The lawyer became a judge, and the judge became the name of law in the province.

So we watched, and we waited, and when our strength was at its peak, we sent Kaantor into the Fey World, and on the night when he drove cold iron into the Veil Between Worlds, we drew upon the Power he unleashed, threw down the Immortals of Old, and rose high in their place at last.

He'd orchestrated the First Cleansing that had swept away the old Ruling Council. Soon after, the High Hall of Bashonak, the center of Dreyd power in the Reach, had sent word that Eromar would know its first Dreydmaster, the great Purifying Authority and defender of the Dreydcaste and its principles: Lojar Vald. The Man who had once known only frustration and dismissal was now the most feared and respected figure in the northern Reach. The people had loved him then, and they overwhelmingly chose him to be governing Prefect of Eromar.

We are the Dreyd. We are more than the new Immortals—we are the unyielding certainty of Power.

The Reachwarden of the time, Kell Brennard, had protested from the safety of faraway Chalimor, claiming that no Man should hold the power of both the Dreydcaste and the Prefectorate, but he'd been powerless to intervene. Chalimor was the great gaudy jewel of the Reach, but its gilded grandeur masked both its distant decadence and its impotence in these hard lands. The people of Eromar had chosen: the Dreydcaste would oversee their lives, in this world and those to follow.

Vald had immersed himself in both the political life of his harsh province and the deeper studies of Dreyd-Crafting. And he became an efficient master of both.

You are meant to be one of us. You must sacrifice. You must give for what you receive. Do not fear that the cost will be too great.

And in the years that followed, the voices pushed him further. When his temporal ambitions became so great that the Reachwarden's army finally threatened invasion, Vald conceded the authority of Chalimor, then turned his attention to Crafting, where fearful, small-minded Men could never interfere. Though he had no doubt of the strength and martial skill of his militia, he had too much work to finish, too many plans to put into place to risk being distracted by a yet unnecessary war.

Finally, after over thirty years of unyielding discipline, the voices revealed the path to him. He knew at long last what the Dreyd required of him, and he was more than willing to surrender to his destiny. The Melding of a thousand years past hadn't finished its work. Remnants of the first great power remained scattered across the Reach, that power the Dreyd had unleashed to fuel their own ascension.

Be the master of your fear. Strike hard, strike fast, and be merciless. There is no room for the weak among the ranks of the Dreyd. Only power will be remembered.

The Everland.

Remember your legacy.

Vald called into the rift, and from it flew a great flock of creatures, each as large as a small Human child, with ragged garments that seemed at times feathered wings and at other times the shredded black remnants of grave-clothes. Their bald and wizened Men's heads were too large for their fluttering bodies, and they had wide mouths ringed with scores of sharp teeth. Slimy holes gaped wide where once eyes might have glimmered with life.

The Not-Ravens hopped around the Dreydmaster's feet and cooed affectionately while they rubbed greasily against his legs and each other. They gladly served him; the blood he provided was intoxicating, and although they didn't belong in this world, there was still joy to be found in its unpredictable shadows. Vald waited for a few moments, until no more of the creatures emerged from the gate, and then he lifted his voice in a series of low cackling whistles and grunts, which the Not-Ravens echoed enthusiastically.

Within moments they were aloft in the early morning darkness, hundreds of the creatures flying with grace and purpose toward the storm-ringed Everland. They would find the Fey-witch who'd destroyed his tower, and they would watch her until he was ready to claim her and her power. And that would be a day this long-cursed world would never forgot.

Yes, Vald would see her again. Soon.

They lay together in the indigo twilight before dawn. Half-covered by a supple white deerskin, Quill nestled tightly in the crook of Tobhi's arm, the clean smells of sweat and passion filling her senses as she listened to his strong heartbeat. Tobhi softly stroked the damp hair on her forehead, marveling as he did so that she was now so much more beautiful than before, when she'd already seemed the loveliest *firra* in all the Everland.

Sunrise was coming, and the thought chilled them both. When Tobhi shivered, Quill held him tighter and ran her fingers along the line of sparse black hair that traveled from his chest to his most delicate parts. She wanted to talk to him, to share all her dreams and fears, to remind him of their vow and beg him to stay with her to protect her from the gathering storm. But even as they made love that night, their promises at last more than mere words, she'd known that he wouldn't stay with her. He couldn't, not now.

As Quill thought about the tender truth of this moment, anger blinded her, and she stiffened at his side. Tobhi looked down at her face. There were tears in his eyes, pain that she didn't expect to see. He swallowed thickly and opened his mouth to speak, but Quill leaned over and kissed him, taking his words into her, knowing now how much he wanted to stay. She didn't need to hear the words spoken.

As the sky brightened through the windows, the room grew warmer and the shadows receded. The Tetawi lay under the deerskin in a tender embrace, unwilling to let go, but knowing, too soon, that they must.

Dawn came and went in Spindletop. Daladir still slept in the guest room, lost in long-needed sleep and adrift in the thick feather bedding. Tarsa sat, freshly bathed, on a large rock near the door of Quill's moundhouse cabin, drinking a steaming mug of mint tea and relishing the sunshine of an early afternoon. She'd unwoven her braids, and her long hair was drying in the warming air. It had been far too long since she'd enjoyed the daylight for its own sake, and it was almost enough to drive the fear and anger of the events in Eromar from her heart.

"May I join ye?" Tobhi asked softly. Tarsa looked up. The Tetawa's hair was disheveled and tangled, and his eyes were dark with grief. He plopped down on the mossy ground beside her. They sat together listening to the sounds of the early day.

The Leafspeaker broke the silence. "First time I ever seen her, we was at a turtle dance." He smiled at the memory. "M' pepa, Jekobi, took me with him to Spindletop, where we was gonna sell some of our tobacco and pick up some fresh supplies. I'd never gone with him afore, as our settlement was so deep in the woods, so it was a real treat. We worked real hard all day, and that night, when the work was done, we heard that there was gonna be a dance. Well, Pepa wasn't about to dance 'round the fire without m' mema, but he didn't have no worry about me joinin' in. Prob'ly thought it was about time I enjoyed m'self with others m' own age. So, I slid into the stompin' line and started to dance, a fresh-faced cub from the hill country. M' old-fashioned britches prob'ly made me stick out in that place like a third ear, but nobody said nothin'. Quill's pepa, Mungo, was leadin' the dance and shakin' his turtle rattle. I followed along with the other *fahr* as they sang back to Mungo's song, him startin' the songs and us continuin' the tune. The *firra* slipped in between each of us, alternatin' one after the other. It took me a long while, but I eventually caught on that the same light-haired *firra* kept movin' into the line right ahead of me with each dance. Once I finally figured that out, I started noticin' little things, like the way her hair smelled like fresh strawberries, the way her silver earrings shined so pretty in the firelight, the shape of her hips, and the sweet, slow way she danced. Finally, when that last dance was over, she turned and smiled at me afore runnin' off to catch up with her cousins. I tell ye, Tarsa, I en't never seen nothin' prettier than that smile. I fell in love with her that night, and I made it back to Spindletop every chance I got. Though I've held a fair share of soft flesh in m' time, in m' heart there en't never been nobody else; never will be, I reckon."

He sighed. "I never forgot 'bout her, ye know, even though I been gone such a long time. Every dream of every night has been 'bout her. I just never knew how deep and empty m' heart's been since I left. It en't too hard to put that aside when ye keep ye'r thoughts busy elsewhere. Now I'm back . . . " He pointed at the roof. "Them tiles could use a bit of care. That chimney smokes a bit too much for m' likin', too. She sure could use a bit of fresh venison hangin' in the cold room. That stuff ye buy at the Spindletop market is too often just the fatty leavin's the hunters don't want 'emselves."

Tobhi's face darkened. "She shouldn't have been alone with all them Men and monsters about. She shouldn't ever have to be alone." His voice fell to a near-whisper. "I en't told her I'm goin' yet."

Tarsa nodded and looked sidelong at the Tetawa. Tears shimmered in his dark eyes as he stared, unseeing, into the distance. The Wielder reached down and squeezed his hand, and they lapsed again into silence. After a while, she said, "We'll understand if you stay, Tobhi. You've done so much already. You don't have to go on."

"Yes, he does, Tarsa." Quill stepped out of the cabin, her eyes sad but clear. Tobhi looked down, unable to meet her gaze, even when the *firra* stroked his cheek with her hand. "He can't stay here. Tobhi's given himself to this path, even if it wasn't of his own making—I've seen it in his eyes, a shadow behind his love for me. He'd stay if I asked him, but that would be asking him to turn his back on everything he's fighting to save. Besides, if things are getting as bad as we've been hearing, Spindletop won't be any better off than Sheynadwiin pretty soon. And if what we all fear *can* be stopped, that's where it's going to happen, not here. I understand that."

He looked at her now, and she pulled him close, draping the newly finished badger sash around his neck. "I'll be well, I promise, but you've got to come back, sweetness," she whispered. "I'm letting you go now so I can keep you later. Promise that you'll come back to me."

Tears trickled down her round cheeks as he buried his face in her shoulder. "Keep your friends safe, and keep yourself safe, too, my sweet, strong *fahr*. Don't forget your black-eyed *firra*, Tobhi, because she won't forget you."

Medalla and Gishki returned to Quill's home after walking Tobhi and his friends to the edge of the forest. Quill sat beside the cold hearth. Her face was swollen, but there were no new tears in her eyes. She'd tried to be cheery and strong as the travelers gathered supplies for their departure, and although everyone could see her grief, they'd played along. It all seemed easier to bear that way.

"Do you want us to stay?" Gishki asked.

"No, *mishko*. I think I'd rather be alone right now, if you don't mind."

Medalla squeezed the Dolltender's arm. "We'll be back in the morning. It's market day tomorrow. It'll be good to get out of the house again." They slipped out the door.

Quill remained beside the hearth until late in the night. Her thoughts spun wildly, and they kept coming back to Tobhi's tale the night before, when he'd recounted his adventure. She felt so helpless. She couldn't go with Tobhi; his path was dark to her. But there was another option, a path that grew clearer even as her heart grew heavier from the thought of it.

She turned to look at the dolls on their shelves, their puckered faces pinched into looks of disapproval. Her own lips tightened defiantly. She was tired of sitting and waiting for things to happen. Tobhi was willing to sacrifice so much to save their people. He needed her, now more than ever. Maybe she could do something to help, even if she wasn't by his side in Sheynadwiin.

"Yes," she whispered. "Somebody's got to tell the Reachwarden about Vald's treachery. He's the leader of all the Humans in the Reach, more powerful than Vald, even. I know that good people won't let this happen. They've got to be told the truth." She stood up. "And I guess I'll just have to go to Chalimor to do it."

25

Hunter and Hunted

THE FIRST THING THAT VERGIS THANE noticed was the smoke. It rose in long columns throughout the Everland, creeping skyward like hundreds of oily eels, thick and black against the afternoon suns. His brows narrowed. Such waste. This bountiful land was more than adequate for all the settlers; there was hardly any sense in burning the crops and houses to useless ash. Such was the foolishness of land hunger. Silly, weak-minded Men without any purpose beyond greed and the cowardice of mob force, gathering together to take what they could and destroy what they couldn't. The Seeker cared little about the Unhumans themselves, but he saw no reason for unnecessary devastation—it would merely strengthen the creatures' resolve to remain in the Everland and stiffen their resistance to the inevitable. They would die, Men and Women would die, the land would be torn and broken in the conflict, and everyone would suffer—all but the politicians, those Men who'd set this conflict into motion to begin with.

He didn't need to make his way to the forest to know that Spindletop, too, was aflame; it wasn't likely that the little Brownie he sought would still be in her cabin. This would make his job much more difficult.

<<Dreyd-damned fools,>> he growled under his breath, sliding his battered hat back on his head and spurring his sure-footed horse

forward. If the Brownie still survived, she'd probably be seeking refuge in the forest, or else be among the prisoners in the slaving wagons. Either way, she was now bringing him a great deal of trouble. It
would take time and talent to find her. If she was Fey-Touched, as he
thought, she'd be well worth the effort; if not, well, hunting practice
was never wasted.

He was at the ruins of the cabin by nightfall, and it was as he had
expected: she was gone. A quick search through the rubble revealed
little. Looters had taken everything of value and destroyed the rest.
None of the cabins in this part of the settlement remained standing;
even the stables and barns had been destroyed. He found nothing of
interest in the ruins he'd come to that first night, so he walked down
the hill to what remained of a small house at the base of an old, fire-
scarred pine. In the broken wood and embers of what had once been
the main room of the cabin, Thane found the smashed remnants of
one of those strange dolls he'd glimpsed for just a moment during his
first visit, half of one apple head now glaring reproachfully at him
with a glittering, polished-stone eye. He removed a glove and slid his
hand over the piece.

The prickling burn on his fingertips confirmed his suspicions: the
doll-maker *was* Fey-Touched! Whatever the purpose of these dolls,
they were a powerful part of her witchery. So much stronger than
the Deerman he'd captured, yet she'd been able to veil her powers
from the Seeker with little apparent effort. The corners of Thane's
mouth creased slightly. He had to admit a growing admiration of
the little Brownie; whatever else she was, she clearly wasn't stupid.
Naive, maybe, but not stupid. Whether she'd known that he was a
Seeker or not, she'd certainly understood upon their meeting that he
was a threat, and she'd kept him from sensing her secret.

But the secret was his now. He slipped the broken apple-doll into
a pocket and looked around again. No body or bones, no blood-
stains. No more dolls. She hadn't died here, that was certain. The
place was empty of her presence, other than the lingering memory
clinging to the blasted and torn roots of the trees that reached into
the base of the cabin from the east. His bare hand rested softly on the
roots. They still remembered the Brownie, even through their dying
ache. His palm twitched slightly in response. He slipped on the glove
and headed toward his horse.

Thane looked toward the direction of the still-smoldering village of Spindletop, some distance from the Brownie-witch's house. That would be the start of the true hunt. He rode quickly away from the ruins of the house, closing his ears to the trees, their whispering voices calling endlessly for the she-Brownie, wondering where she'd gone, why she'd left her cozy little cabin behind.

Come home, Spider-child, they wept. *Come home.*

The most difficult decision about leaving home was deciding which dolls to take and which to leave behind. Quill had gathered them together near the hearth, all seventy-three, their dried apple faces pinched with worry and corn-husk garments rustling nervously, and told them of her plan. There was no changing her mind, so the debate would center on which dolls would go with her. That was a decision that only the dolls could make, so Quill had left them in council and busied herself with the final preparations for the journey.

She'd returned to the common room to find only three dolls together beside the hearth. The others were back on their shelves, their eyes cloudy with grief. Holding back her own tears, Quill sat on the tile floor and pulled the three dolls to her. They were all from her granny Pearl's days as Dolltender: Cornsilk, the quiet, sleepy-faced doll whose contemplative spirit helped ease the tension from thoughts and flesh; Green Kishka, a dour doll with a feather skirt and multicolored corncob body; and Mulchworm, the oldest of the dolls, whose white-capped head was so deeply etched with age that his features were almost lost in the wrinkles. Old friends all; brave friends, too. Their willingness to join her was more of a relief than she'd expected. This wouldn't be a midsummer trip to market.

For the first time, she was beginning to understand just what her decision to leave truly meant, and a wave of grief and longing hit her. It was more likely than not that she'd die out there, far from home, and the other dolls would never know what happened to her. Cornsilk, Kishka, and Mulchworm weren't just going along on an afternoon stroll—they were risking themselves and likely giving up their lifelong fellows to accompany her on this mad quest into the heart of the Men's Reach. The pain in Tobhi's eyes returned to her then, and she now understood the fear he'd tried to keep from her.

Oh, Granny Jenna, Mother Turtle, help us.

Quill had left in the early hours of the morning, when the fragrant dew still lingered on the pine boughs of Edgewood. A note tacked to the front door explained everything; Medalla and Gishki would find it when they stopped by to walk to market in the early afternoon. She'd struggled with the note, wondering if it was cowardice that kept her from telling them goodbye in person, but she also knew that they'd try to convince her to stay home. Her resolve was already shaky; if she were ever going to leave, she'd have to do it now, before her new fears overwhelmed her. At the end of the note, she left instructions to her cousins for the dolls who remained behind. They'd be well cared for in her absence.

The first two days had been more fun than she'd expected. Although her knowledge of the lands around Spindletop was limited to the main dirt roads and favorite harvesting paths she used for gathering doll-making materials, she'd been surprised at how little discomfort she experienced. Some of this was certainly due to her foresight in choosing traveling clothes. Thick-soled leather boots and a high-collared, oiled-leather coat protected her from the worst of the elements. Her hair was bound into a tight topknot and away from her eyes, and the neck and chest of her blouse were covered by a long scarf studded from end to end with small white shells that clicked softly together as she moved. Gloves, rope, a small knife, fire-stone and tinder, two more blouses and another pair of cotton breeches, soap and menstrual rags, tooth-cleaning sticks, purifying herbs and bandages, a sachet of dried tobacco leaves, and a thick blanket joined a full week's worth of thick cornbread, dried fruit, tea leaves, and a waterskin in the travel satchel on her back. Across her waist hung the leather purse that carried the dolls and a gourd hand rattle, each wrapped firmly with red cloth. She carried a farewell gift from Tarsa in her hand—a stout cedar walking stick, its shape etched by the *wyr* with trailing vines and blossoms. Quill marveled at the delicacy of the wielded wood; it looked as though the flowers had grown along the wooden shaft of their own will.

Two days had taken her beyond the southern limit of the Edgewood. She'd guessed it would be not much more than seven days to the southernmost edge of the Everland, although she couldn't know for certain, as there were no maps in her cabin, and she had to rely on the dim memory of traders' conversations and the growing beyonder rumors that had so haunted the region in recent months. Still, she knew that the Old Windle Road stretched across the entire expanse of the Men's Reach south of the Everland, and the east-ernmost point of that ancient roadway was Chalimor, the political and cultural heart of the lands of Humanity. All she had to do was continue south, and she'd eventually find it. It would be quite sim-ple, really—little more than a lengthy hike. She might even be back home again before the first winter snows.

Quill awoke on her third morning from Spindletop to find a giant, sharp-toothed raccoon with pale fur ravaging her pack. She screamed in surprise, then fury, as the creature crouched backward with Green Kishka in its mouth.

"Put her down," Quill hissed, but the raccoon simply stared, its yellow eyes regarding her with something like amusement as it crunched down on the doll's corncob body.

The Dolltender's eyes widened in horror. A red stream trickled from the pierced kernels.

She stepped back, trembling. Blood. The doll was bleeding. The raccoon remained still, its jaws clenched tightly around Kishka's body. A noise from behind caught Quill's attention, and she turned to see the other two dolls standing beside her, their eyes fixed on the raccoon and poor Green Kishka, whose face was now twisted into a grimace of pain. The air thickened, and Quill's mouth went dry.

The Dolltender reached down slowly, hoping to wrap her hand around a log from the burnt-out fire or a sharp rock, but she stopped when the raccoon lowered its head, its gaze fixed on those of the dolls, and gently dropped Kishka to the ground. With agonizing slowness, the creature crept backward into the undergrowth, its yellow eyes never turning from the dolls, and disappeared into the undergrowth.

The weight on Quill's chest relaxed, and her vision cleared. It was over.

Looking down, she saw Cornsilk and Mulchworm lying side by side on the ground, no longer standing in bold defiance. The Tetawa took a deep breath and picked them up, then lifted Green Kishka and wrapped a cleansing cloth around the doll's wounds.

"I don't know if this will be enough," she whispered, her voice labored. She'd never doubted the reality of the dolls' spirits—they'd spoken to her too many times to deny that—but this was the first time she'd ever known one of them to bleed. She wasn't entirely certain that the knowledge was welcome. It was one thing for the dolls to be filled with a life spirit; it was another thing entirely for that life to include such mundane mortal realities. If Kishka could bleed, then she could die, too.

The thought stripped the journey of any fleeting romance.

The rest of the day wasn't much better. Quill returned to her satchel to find that the raccoon had eaten most of her travel food. One of the gloves was missing, and the cake of soap had been chewed into a half-dozen small pieces. After kicking out the remains of the fire pit in a tantrum, she gathered everything together and stomped southward in the late morning, now fully submerged in her foul mood.

The rain started as a light, easy drizzle, but it soon swelled into an icy downpour that soaked through both her coat and her boots. Her topknot drooped down her back, and her blouse clung to her skin with a frigid embrace. Lightning regularly split the dark rain, and the thunder was so loud and so close that Quill cried out in terror more than once.

She was now in the Downlands, a series of rough, rocky hills that took up where the Edgewood left off. The thick pine and cedar forest gave way to broken country, covered with low, bushy pines, alders, and scrub oaks, knee-high thorn bushes with dagger-sharp thorns, wild roses in late bloom, and prickly raspberry plants still far from ripeness. Occasionally Quill's ears twitched at the strange sound of tinkling bells that echoed across the open hills, its source unknown but welcome. Even through the driving rain Quill could see that the land had a harsh beauty, and she could hardly help but be impressed by the sight, especially the towering stones that stood as far as she could see through the downpour, which wasn't far. The stones were rough and worn, nearly featureless, painted by the elements and layers of grey-green lichen. Some were only as tall as the Tetawa, while others stood six or seven times her height. Many were carved with shapes that had long since lost their meaning to the wind and ages. She'd never seen the Downlands before, but as she crouched beneath an overhanging stone to avoid the worst of the storm, she recalled that she'd heard stories of the place when she just was a youngling cub.

She froze. Yes, she *had* heard stories about the Downlands, and now she was beginning to remember what they were. The Downlands had another name, one best known by grannies and cubs during dark-night stories: the Barrow Hills. Quill looked at the stone that leaned over to protect her from the rain, and she knew.

It was a barrow stone of the ancient days. She was sheltering in a boneyard.

Lightning pierced the storm again, and the Dolltender crouched quivering in the rain. Had she seen something out there in the storm, in that momentary flash of skyfire? Was it tall and thin, with fierce eyes, glistening white flesh, and the bloody heart of a Tetawa cub still burning in its hand? Had it followed her here, to this land of ghosts and death? Her fingers tightened on the walking stick, but she lowered herself down to the muddy earth and pushed as far against the side of the stone as she could.

The dolls shifted in her pack, but she ignored their discomfort. She couldn't risk unwrapping them and revealing her presence to whatever waited, not while something might be out in the rain looking for her.

Thunder shook the ground, and Quill slid her hands over her ears, but not before she heard another noise, a squelching sound, like broad feet moving slowly through mud. Her hands dropped back to the walking stick. Whatever was making the noise, it was close.

A shape moved out of the plummeting rain, followed by others, but Quill didn't relax. If anything, her heart beat even faster as figure after figure moved past her hiding place. Six, then ten, twenty or more, some on horses, others on foot, all heading north through the Downlands.

They were Men. Men were marching through the Everland.

The dolls twisted violently in the purse. Quill bit her lower lip. She could feel it, too. The Men carried iron. Swords, flintlocks, even the iron buttons on their jackets, the nails in their thick boots and the shoes of their horses radiated and burned all they touched. But there was more, far more; it made her stomach cramp and eyes water. A ponderous wagon moved into view, the creaking whine of its axles shredding the dull rhythm of the rain. It moved closer. The bulk of the vehicle was a squat cage, perched at an unwieldy angle on the back of a wheeled wooden pallet. Iron bars glinted dangerously in the flashing lightning, and Quill saw shapes huddled miserably inside, shapes of captive Folk.

"A slaving wagon," she whispered, more to herself than to the dolls.

Terror swept through her. Here she crouched, not even thirty paces from the Men; all it would take to join the poor Folk in that wagon would be for one Man to turn and look her way. *Please, keep going. You don't see me. Keep going. Please . . .*

But one Man did turn, and he saw her. He lifted his hand to his eyes and peered into the shadows of the rock, stopping his horse as he did so, and called out in a harsh language the Tetawa didn't understand. Quill didn't stop to think. Like a panicked mouse, she burst from her hiding place and skittered around the side of the rock, boots slipping in the muddy earth, her thoughts on one thing only: escape.

The rumble of hooves shook the earth. She spun around to see the Man riding hard, a long knife in his hand. Quill lurched back again, but she slipped in the rain-softened soil and landed hard, mud filling her eyes and mouth. She was too terrified to even scream.

And again she heard the bells, the same sound that had echoed throughout the hills in the early afternoon. It was closer now. The Man's voice roared out again, almost on top of her now, but it lifted into a howl when a blast of heat swept like a curtain in front of the trembling Tetawa, choking the air with the stink of burning hair and flesh. The horse shrieked in terror, the land trembled, and another burning burst split the air. All was chaos. Quill tried to lift herself up and wipe the mud from her eyes, but something hard smashed into her, and she rolled to the ground again. She couldn't breathe. From the other side of the barrow-stone she could hear the roar of the muskets, and then more screams and shouts. The tinkling bells rang again, nearly on top of the flailing Tetawa now. In between the explosions and cries, Quill thought she heard laughter. The gentle sound didn't belong in this place of sudden fear and death.

The Dolltender wiped furiously at her eyes, enough to clear the gritty mud away, and sat back on her knees in wide-eyed astonishment. The Men had been routed. Those who remained were dead or wounded, their horses racing off in various directions. But it wasn't the Men who captured her attention now.

A small train of brightly colored wagons stood in a semicircle around the Tetawa. Wandering through the ruins of the slaving train and looking after the imprisoned Folk was a motley group of figures, all dressed in strange and garish clothing. Some were impossibly thin and tall, others as short and squat as toadstools, and still others seemed of average build. Most were Humans, but they looked and sounded nothing like the slavers: the tinkling sound Quill had heard came from the rows of bells and tambourines hanging from bright cloth belts around their waists or bracers on their wrists and ankles. Men and Women alike moved to the slave wagon and pulled the prisoners free, tending to their wounds and gently administering medicinals and fresh water.

"By Bidbag's hairless goat, darling, you're a remarkable mess." Quill had heard the voice before; it was the source of that laugh, the merry sound that had split the storm during the battle. She turned around, and her mouth flew open as a buxom, bronze-skinned figure knelt down and wiped the mud from her face with a soft silk cloth. The stranger wore a billowing lavender dress, its bodice cut daringly low. Her thick auburn hair was held back by a wide-brimmed white hat fringed boldly with iridescent, blue-green feathers. Bright emerald eyes sparkled as they examined the Tetawa for injury.

"What happened?" the Dolltender coughed, spitting mud and grass out of her mouth.

The stranger laughed. "Why, we rescued you, of course," she said in the Folk trade-tongue. Her accent was fast and oddly lilting but not unpleasant. "To be unashamedly honest, my dear, it was a truly magnificent sight, one of the most dramatic rescues I've ever attempted. I've rarely impressed myself so much, and that's hard to do, believe me."

"I'm a bit confused."

"Well, of course you are—it was admittedly a rather bold and sudden entrance, one designed specifically to induce both chaos and confusion." The figure slipped her hat off to reveal four knobby protrusions that swayed gently from within the thick hair at her temples. Pulling the curls away from her oak-leaf ears, she grinned. "But you needn't worry, my mud-stained wanderer—you're among friends!"

"A Strangeling," Quill whispered breathlessly, then blushed at the spoken word.

The stranger brought the back of her hand to her forehead and staggered back in a melodramatic swoon. "Born of two worlds, welcome in none—ah, the tragic life of the tortured Strangeling!" She laughed again, and the sound was so carefree and infectious that the Tetawa couldn't help but smile. "How quaint—I'd almost forgotten what weight that silly word carries around here!" Smiling, she bowed slightly and held her fist to her chest in greeting. "Yes, darling, my father was Kyn, my mother Human. Love worked its sweet, sweaty magic, and not long thereafter I was born. You are now in the presence of the radiant, emerald-eyed beneficiary of their inspired exuberance: Denarra Syrene, daughter of Walks-with-the-Winds and Zoola-Dawn Bandabee. It's a pleasure to meet you."

Nearly overwhelmed by her rescuer's enthusiasm, Quill hesitantly lifted her own hand. "Quill Meadowgood, Spider Clan of Spindletop at Edgewood. Many thanks—I'm so lucky you arrived when you did!"

Denarra stood and wiped the mud from her dress. "Please don't mention it, darling. Always glad to help out, especially with these uncouth and depressingly unhygienic raiders lurking about. Can't have a sweet and tender maid like you wandering around alone in such a dangerous place. Besides, I'm not much of a believer in mere luck, unless we make it ourselves; you and I were meant to cross paths, if only so that my compatriots and I could offer a rescue of exquisite and rather memorable spectacle. Come along, then—it's best to not thwart the fates. You'd better stick with us for a while."

Looking around with some trepidation, Quill asked, "Who are all these Humans?"

Denarra grinned. "You're in for a magnificent treat, my disheveled little friend. You've been personally delivered from a fate worse than death by the illustrious, Reach-renowned traveling fellowship known to all and sundry as Bremen and Crowe's Medicine Show and Repertory of Thespian Delights."

"Repertory?" She'd never heard the word before. The Tetawa's eyes lingered on the wagons. She could see large letters, brightly painted, with strange symbols weaving their way around the characters. Their meanings were unknown, but the pictures were quite charming. "Is that what you call your army?"

The Strangeling giggled and pulled Quill along behind her as she moved toward the gaudiest wagon of all, a pink-and-yellow structure with golden, fan-tailed birds etched on the side. "Our 'army'? Oh, my dear, you *are* a peach! We're no army, Quill—we're actors, dancers, singers, performers of rare and distinguished quality! I'm rather versatile myself—a little of this, a little of that, you know." She winked conspiratorially. "And let me assure you, with all due modesty, that although we are a small company there are none better anywhere—not in the Everland, and certainly not in the length and breadth of the Reach of Men."

Quill looked back to the shattered slaving train, where the cooling bodies of the slower slavers lay scattered in the mud and rain. "I've never heard of actors being able to do something like this."

Denarra nodded sympathetically. "No? Ah, but then you've never performed in Harudin Holt, either, where they hang bad actors and off-tune troubadours naked in the city square and let angry critics skewer their backsides with heated pins—a lenient sentence for such aesthetic heresy, in my ever-humble opinion. If you can survive the audiences there, then scattering a little gang of high-smelling thugs is no difficult matter. Besides, I have a few tricks that come in quite handy from time to time." The she-Kyn held up her hand, and Quill saw a sheet of shimmering lavender, pink, and silver flame burst to life and dance across Denarra's fingers.

An actor *and* a Wielder, Quill mused—an unusual combination.

Smiling broadly, Denarra led Quill to the wagon door. "Now, let's get you cleaned up and get some dry clothes on you. This rain is starting to soak into my boots. I'll wager my best brassiere that underneath all that grime you're actually rather charming to look at. Maybe we'll do something with your hair while we're at it, if you don't mind. No reason to look like a waterlogged prairie dog, even if you feel like one, don't you think? I've got an extra cot; you can sleep there for now, at least until we can figure out more appropriate and certainly more comfortable sleeping quarters."

Too tired and bewildered to protest, the Dolltender followed Denarra into the wagon, where she found a hot bath, a clean robe, and the endless but pleasing chatter of her flamboyant host, until the day's fears drained away and sleep found her a few hours later. Denarra smiled and snuffed out the lantern before snuggling deeply into her own bed, drifting asleep to the sound of the rain falling on the wagon's cedar shingles.

In the darkness and the rain, far beyond the reach of the caravan's night lanterns, yellow eyes peered hungrily at the wagon holding his prey. The creature had been interrupted in its hunt three times this day—first by the Brownie herself, then by the Men, and finally by the newcomers and their skyfire. He'd hungered for the little sand-haired female for a very long time, since she and her dolls interrupted his feast those many months past. But he didn't mind further delay; the wait made the kill that much sweeter. He held her lost glove up to his nose and breathed in, savoring the smell of her salty skin and imagining its taste on his serpentine tongue.

There were other ways to get to her; he could make a game of it. It would be fun. After all, her new friends couldn't watch her forever.

26

Ghostlands

THE NEWS OF THE OATHSWORN'S BETRAYAL swept through Sheynadwiin like a brushfire. Few knew how the news reached the city before the airship arrived, but there were rumors that strange Ubbetuk machinery helped to relay the message. It didn't take long for two large crowds to gather at the landing dock in anticipation of her arrival. The first was an armed group of Shields and their supporters, thirty strong, with a fitted carriage and four swift horses waiting to bear the Oathsworn to safety. They stood nervously against a much larger group of at least two hundred angry Kyn and Tetawi from across Sheynadwiin, who milled around in agitation. The Shields were closest to the landing, but they weren't the only ones with weapons. The air was hot with rising rage; one stray spark, and an inferno would erupt.

It was early evening when the great wasp-faced Dragon emerged slowly from the storm-torn sky, gears whirring and bellows groaning from the exertion of the long journey. It hovered for a while over the ground, its four great metallic wings moving with slow, rhythmic precision, finally descending on the dock's far edge, where a dozen Ubbetuk swung on ropes from the upper deck to finish mooring the ship. When all was secure, the gangplank slid to earth, and Neranda Ak'shaar emerged alone, her head held high, her face pale but proud.

Three long red scars burned on each cheek. No one else exited the ship with her, but the plank remained lowered.

"*Shakar!*" someone hissed, and others took up the chorus. "Traitor!"

The Shields closed the circle tighter around the Lawmaker, holding their ornate bladed staves and pole-arms against the crowd. No one tried to break the circle, but the chant grew in intensity even as the numbers of the opposition swelled. "*Shakar!*"

Neranda stared straight ahead at the carriage as she walked. They would not break her poise. *I did only what others were too cowardly or foolish to do. We had no choice. One day they will see this, and they will honor me. They will understand.* It was why she returned to Sheynadwiin, even knowing that her life was likely forfeit—she would help them to understand why she had to make this difficult choice. She wouldn't hide in the shadows like the others who remained cringing in the ship but would instead face her people proudly, defiantly, and they would see that she had no alternative.

She moved forward with renewed determination. The voices of her enemies faded beneath this certainty. She'd been preparing for this moment ever since leaving for Eromar City, speaking the words to herself over and over until they became a sort of armor, pushing away the nagging fear that clutched at her vitals, the memory of the Dreydmaster's chilly smile as the she-Kyn Lawmaker took the quill in hand and signed her name to the Oath of Western Sanctuary. There was poison in that smile, and it burned deeper with every remembrance.

We had no choice. They will understand.

We had no choice. My people will listen.

The copper-haired Lawmaker was vaguely aware of a shift in the bodies around her, the swelling numbers pushing against the knot of frightened Shields, but she paid them little attention. The carriage door was open, and she drew her shimmering white robes away from her legs as she moved to enter. The first rock hit Neranda in the small of her back. Pain brought her thoughts back to the moment. A second stone smashed into the carriage door beside her, while another struck her shoulder. She cried out and turned. Something wet and foul spattered in her face. Gagging, she wiped it away to see the Shields lashing out at the crowd pressing against them. Bleeding shapes fell to the cobbled street. Shouts and screams rose up as the dam of bodies broke, and the Shields were overwhelmed by the mob. The carriage shot forward. Neranda had just enough time to fling herself into it before the angry Folk swarmed over the carriage, rocks, clubs, hatchets, and hands striking its sides. The driver shouted and lashed the fear-maddened horses through the furious throng, crushing a dozen bodies beneath hooves and wheels before shooting free.

Neranda shook with terror and humiliated rage. The windows of the carriage were broken. She looked at her dress, soiled with spittle, dirt, and mud, along with unidentifiable filth that filled the carriage with its acrid stench. The carriage careened through the streets but not without difficulty, for the people of Sheynadwiin now knew who rode in the coach, and they were rushing to share their displeasure. Rocks, sticks, clay pots, root vegetables, arrows, spears, and other weapons struck the vehicle and flew through the open window, but Neranda remained largely uninjured.

The voices—they were what tore into her, each screaming a single word that burned like pitch-fire in her mind.

Shakar. Shakar.

Traitor.

Tobhi always preferred dawn over any other time of day. It wasn't simply that the arrival of the ever-reborn suns over the eastern horizon was a sacred time to all the Tetawi, although that certainly had something to do with the joy he felt in the morning. Rather, it was a moment of renewal, a reminder that each day brought with it unknown possibility and promise. Tobhi's heart was lifted by daybreak, and he generally tried to greet the sister suns with a prayer of welcome and a bit of cedar-sweetened tobacco.

This morning brought with it no dawn, only storm clouds, and the Tetawa's spirits were as soggy as the day's promise. But he nevertheless whispered his prayer and scattered the tobacco to the grey sky and red earth before returning to camp, where Daladir sat rubbing his hands over the small cooking fire, a small gutted trout skewered on the end of a cut green willow branch hanging over the flames.

The he-Kyn looked up. "Another long day ahead of us, I think."

Tobhi nodded and joined him beside the fire. "We got us 'bout a tenday 'til we're there, if we move fast and don't run into any more trouble on the way, which en't likely." He pointed to a dark blur on the northeast horizon. "That's the Eldarvian Woods. If we can find ourselves a good road, we might cut it down to an eightday or so. There's better roads up north than down in the south forest. Either way, we still got us a bit of a haul yet."

Daladir handed the trout to the Tetawa, who peeled away the blackened skin and began munching on the steaming pink meat inside. They sat quietly, looking off into the distance, until Tarsa appeared over the embankment. Her hair still dripped from the cold lake bath. Daladir held up another skewer, this one piercing a thick sweet potato that they'd brought from Quill's home.

"It's not cooked yet," he said, his eyes bright, "but it shouldn't take too long; the fire is quite hot."

The Wielder smiled and accepted the stick. "*Tsodoka.*" Tarsa's turquoise gaze lingered on the he-Kyn for a moment, but she looked away when he shifted toward her. Looking skyward, she asked Tobhi, "Do you think we'll be able to make it to the forest before the storm hits?"

"Nah. We'll be lucky to even break camp afore it gets here."

As if in response, a low rumble of thunder echoed through the hills. The storm was moving fast. Tobhi sighed. It was going to be a long, dreary day.

The storm struck hard and lingered all morning and afternoon, but they pushed on, even when blisters burned through the drenched and bunching leather of their boots. Time wasn't their ally these days. It had been seven days since their flight from Gorthac Hall, and they would have at least as many to go through dense forests and the western heights of the Kraagen Mountains. Word of the Oathsworn betrayal had surely reached Sheynadwiin by now, but no one knew how long it would take Vald to send an organized force into the Everland, and the trio wanted to be in the city before that happened.

Tarsa felt a particularly heavy pull on her spirit. All Wielders were needed at this time—now more than ever, as the darkest days were approaching with the clouds of invasion. The sooner they reached Sheynadwiin, the safer their people would be. In their more optimistic moods, this was their thought. In their less sanguine moments, they wanted merely to stand beside their people at the end.

The Wielder was lost in the latter thoughts when they reached the edge of the Eldarvian Woods, the vast forest on the western side of the Kraagens. She'd tried to not chastise herself for leaving, for abandoning the city and her people, but those thoughts returned again and again. *Unahi was right*, Tarsa thought to herself. *I'm still a sapling, too caught up with my own wants to pay attention to what's really important.* Then her eyes flickered to Tobhi and Daladir. *But they would have died if I hadn't have been there. Oh, Green Mother, will we always be forced to choose only between death and devastation?*

The rain continued to fall steadily through the late afternoon, turning the world the dreary color of slate. In spite of their aching feet, they trotted the last few miles into the trees, where the thick canopy gave them some measure of protection from the storm. The tree cover at the forest's edge was sparse, mostly thick firs, cedars, and some scattered birch and aspen stands, but the woods would become much denser as they moved to the northeast, where the land was shrouded by massive, green-bearded wyrwood trees, ferns, blankets of thick moss and mushrooms, and shadow-tangled undergrowth. This part of the forest provided little protection from the elements, but they could at least spot anything approaching them; that wouldn't be the case in the deeper trees.

Tarsa lowered her travel pack and stretched, wincing slightly at the catch in her back. "Should we try to go farther tonight, or should we find a dry place to camp?"

"I doubt there's any such place in all the Everland today," Daladir muttered. He was limping badly now. The other two were far more experienced with the rigors of such travel, and the he-Kyn had been weakened by his months as Vald's reluctant guest. He was wounded now, in both spirit and body.

Tobhi took off his new hat, given to him by Quill as a farewell gift to replace the one he'd lost in Eromar, and looked around, his dark eyes squinting through the trees. "I en't sure we'd be able to keep goin' if we stop now; m' feet is hurtin' somethin' fierce. Let's keep on for a while, least 'til we find ourselves someplace to wait out the storm." He pulled his long hair over his shoulder and tried to wring the excess water out of it, but he quickly gave up and tugged the lumpy hat back over his pointed ear-tips.

Tarsa slowly slid her pack back onto her aching shoulders. "Will we make it in time?"

The Tetawa shrugged, his face troubled. "I really don't rightly know. Vald don't seem like the kind of Man who takes well to waiting. Then again, he en't the kind of Man who rushes into trouble, neither. I don't think he'll do much yet, but it won't be long 'til he does. I'm pretty sure we'll get back to Sheynadwiin in time to find out just what he's got in mind."

The cawing of ravens in the trees echoed through the rain. "That's what worries me," the Wielder muttered.

The sister suns cut a bloody swath across the darkening horizon, their red glow giving little light or warmth to the Everland as they surrendered day to the curtain of twilight. No one would sleep in Sheynadwiin this night. Already wails of grief echoed through Dardath Vale from every house, den, nest, and burrow.

Garyn watched the setting suns disappear past the great Eldarvian Woods to the west. He was alone in his bedchamber, sitting in the darkness with his narrow-backed seat beside the window. He had very few opportunities for quiet reflection these days, and he cherished each one with more than a little selfishness. Even now, with his people in mourning, all he wanted to do was sit by his window and watch the day pass by before his eyes.

He was tired beyond reckoning. It was over. They'd fought tirelessly for so very long, and now all their work had come to nothing. The Sevenfold Council stood firm against the raging greed of Eromar. The Folk had been unified as never before, and this might once have been enough to gain support from Chalimor and its enlightened Human leaders. Yet everything they sought to defend, all the lives and legacies of the Everland—it had all been unraveled in an instant by the treachery of his own niece and her Celestial associates.

Among Men, fathers gave guidance to their children; among the Kyn, it was the uncles who guided their sisters' children into the ways of the People. And with Neranda he'd failed terribly. She'd always been headstrong and willful, more interested in her father's Human-leaning ways than those of her own people, traveling to Chalimor to live among Humans and learn their customs, even against the wishes of her family. And she'd returned changed, her heart distant. Perhaps her betrayal was inevitable; perhaps all the guidance he'd tried to give had been useless. He wanted to believe otherwise, but she was Oathsworn now, and that spoke more about her than any teachings he'd once tried to share.

He could hear the weeping rise up from the city. This would be only the beginning of the grief. Soon the brigands, robbers, thieves, cutthroats, and border trash would descend, emboldened by the threat of Eromar. When they had taken away what treasures they could carry, the militiamen would come for the Folk. The Kyn and their kith would stand strong in defense of their homeland—of that Garyn had little doubt—but they were so few, and the teeming hordes of Men were driven by a voracious hunger that would never be sated.

Such different ways. Were all Men like those who swarmed over the Everland? Was his father? Garyn had only a few memories of that long-dead Human, more sensations than actual memories, but they held no taint of fear or hatred. If anything, the Governor felt the lingering touch of love and laughter from those brief seedling days, before the raging fever took his father and before his Pine Branch mother fell into the long grieving silences from which she rarely emerged.

What was it that made some Men so grasping, while others found contentment in the gentle joys of life? What had his father found in Thornholt to convince him to surrender his former life and choose that of Kei'shaad Mendiir and her people? He didn't know. All he knew now was that Humans like Reiss Thalsson were rare beyond measure in the Everland these days, but he hoped that other Human leaders would respond to Vald's aggression with the righteous fury it deserved. He'd written so many letters and appeals, making the Kyn case to Human politicians and lawmakers, intellectuals, moral leaders, social crusaders—anyone who could shift public opinion in their favor, anyone who could convince the people of the Reach that the Folk's cause was a just one. It was the last, best hope they had, and Garyn hated this fact. He'd learned all too often how dangerous it was to trust in the kindness of Men.

A soft knock sounded at the pine-slat door. Garyn turned to see his consort, Averyn, enter with a mug of tea on a tray, which zhe placed on a small table beside the window.

The black-haired zhe-Kyn rested hir hand on the Governor's knee. "You'll catch a chill if you stay here too long, my love."

Garyn returned his gaze to the window. The suns had passed below the horizon. It was twilight. "Do you hear them?"

"Yes," Averyn whispered. "The night aches with sorrow."

"You know what is to come?"

"Everyone knows. It is why they weep. It is why they need your strength now, more than ever before."

Garyn's face darkened. "I cannot be the strength of the entire Everland. I am weak. I have failed."

Averyn knelt between the Governor's knees and took the silver-haired he-Kyn's face gently in hir hands. "Our people live still, Garyn Mendiir, and as long as that truth endures, so will your strength. You have not failed us, not yet. If you cannot find strength in yourself, find it in us . . . in me. Give us a reflection of our own strength, and that will be enough to sustain us in the times to come." Zhe kissed Garyn tenderly. "You are needed now, beloved. Pradu Styke is dead, as are most of the other Celestials who signed the Oath—all executed by fear-maddened Folk." Seeing the grief rise up in Garyn's stricken face, Averyn added, "Neranda still lives—she alone of the Oathsworn was able to escape the vengeance of the People, but I have had no word of where she fled. There are rumors that she is rallying her supporters, and the killings have added both fuel and fear to her cause."

The zhe-Kyn brushed a lock of hair from Garyn's face. "Our Nation threatens to split apart from within. The People are in pain, and you must help them. It is the duty that they entrusted in you."

Garyn nodded and pulled the young zhe-Kyn into his strong arms. They held each other for a while, sharing grief and fear in their embrace, until a noise in the distant forest pulled Garyn away from his lover's touch. It was a strange, mocking sound heard often these dark days, cruel birds calling to one another in the darkness.

The Governor's eyes narrowed. "Not all creatures mourn this night." He stood and stepped to the bed, where his coat of office lay tossed across the thick blankets, its much-frayed edging trim a mark of honor and endurance. Averyn wiped the tears from hir face, stood up, and stepped forward to help Garyn make himself presentable. They could hear the gathering rumble of Folk in the room beyond who waited for the reassuring presence of the stalwart Governor of the Kyn Nation.

Averyn slid a polished silver gorget over Garyn's head and let it rest on his chest, where it gleamed in the soft moonlight through the window. The silver-haired he-Kyn softly stroked his lover's cheek. Straightening his shoulders, he pulled the door open and stepped out to confront a growing throng of terrified Kyn.

"Be strong," Averyn whispered softly from the shadows of the bedchamber as the Governor spoke to the crowd. Already he was easing their fears with his powerful words and solid presence.

The strange noise echoed again from the shadowed forest beyond the city. Averyn moved to the window and closed the shutters against the night. But before zhe headed to the common room to join Garyn and the others, hir thoughts lingered on that troubling sound, and the many enemies that crept ever closer toward Sheynadwiin.

"Be strong, beloved," zhe whispered under hir soft breath. "We have never needed your strength so much, and we will need so much more before these dark days are gone."

27

New Worlds and Old

LIFE AMONG ARTISTS in a performing caravan was very different from anything Quill had imagined. She'd seen few performers in her life, other than the occasional ceremonial mask-dancers who visited Spindletop and Harvesthome during the high-season festivals. Those dancers would appear from the night's shadows, their faces hidden by hideous carved masks, their bodies covered by long, shaggy reed cloaks that made them look even more monstrous. They'd rush around and frighten the cubs and young *firra*, wheeling around the dance grounds and howling to the stars, before fleeing back to the darkness with relieved laughs following them into the night. The mask-dancers took the People's fears and uncertainties with them, and when the young *fahr* stepped back into the settlement, the masks and cloaks hidden, they returned to a community that had faced its shadows and surrendered them to the mask dance.

Those Tetawi dancers were nothing like these peculiar Humans and the fascinating Strangeling who accompanied them. Quill couldn't understand anything the Humans said, but their acting skill was such that she had little need to know their words, for they made their stories known through the delicacy of their movements, the passion in their voices, the pain and power in their expressions.

Theirs was an exotic and mysterious world but one that was, for all that, surprisingly comfortable.

At first Quill was surprised that there were few Women among the main performers, but Denarra explained that in many Human lands it was still considered indecent for Women to perform in public plays, so Men often assumed the feminine roles. "They don't give a dirty damn if a whore or she-Kyn steps onstage, just as long as a good Woman of stature doesn't soil her tender virtue," Denarra said, spitting on the floor of the wagon. Thinking better of it, she pulled a handkerchief from her sleeve and bent to wipe up the mess. Then she giggled and stuck her chest out, and her frown vanished. "Still, I must admit that these silly prejudices have worked out pretty well to my advantage. I get all the best and most provocative roles, and our customers all know that when they see these great bulging mams onstage that they're getting nothing but the best!" Quill blushed, and Denarra laughed even harder.

The Medicine Show and Repertory, about thirty strong, moved south, then eastward at a leisurely pace. They rarely remained in any one place for very long, preferring to share their stories with new audiences every few weeks. Their last few performances, however, had ended a bit abruptly, as the Strangeling had an uncanny ability to attract unwelcome attention with both her exuberant *wyr*-fed pyrotechnic displays and her equally enthusiastic effect on leading male citizens of the towns. The troupe usually had a few days before a mob came looking for the Wielder who'd seduced one or more of their handsome young he-Kyn or *fahr*, and then the folk of Bremen and Crowe pulled up and headed to the next town. It surprised the Tetawa that Folk could be so inhospitable, but these lands were very close to the danger-riddled border of the Everland, and those who lived here were far more suspicious than the Folk of the interior—these people had learned long ago that strangers more often than not meant trouble.

Yet even with all the quirks and upheavals, Quill understood why the troupe never got rid of Denarra. As maddening as she could be, the Wielder was also a dauntless protector of her friends. The mobs always came looking for trouble, but they scattered like corn-crib mice when the purple fire started dancing on the Strangeling's fingertips.

The main entertainers generally kept to themselves, as they spent most of their time writing and rehearsing the extended performances that were their specialty. Denarra spent some time with them, especially with a lanky, acrobatic young Man with pale hair and a charming smile named Kinnit, but most of her time was with the eccentric specialty performers who appeared during intermissions. The she-Kyn introduced Quill to some of them: Lartorsha, a painfully thin Woman with wide, sorrowful eyes and lifeless hair, who danced with such frenetic abandon that Quill thought her feet might burst into flame every night; Colonel Bedzo, a scarred but distinguished Man with sweeping mustaches who swallowed wicked-looking blades and performed long, emotional monologues that brought tears to the Tetawa's eyes, even though she had no idea what he was saying; Mother Baraboo, the leader of the company, an immensely fat Woman who sang beautiful songs and smelled like winter-mint tea; and the harpist Adelaide of the Veil, whose beauty was hidden beneath a series of gauzy, mist-like scarves that seemed to dance of their own power. Though not an actor, the most imposing of the group was grim, silent Klaus, a huge bearded Man with dark eyes who was the troupe's hunter, groom, and wagon-mender.

There were few grand performances, as the lands they traveled through were sparsely populated by Folk, and the Humans weren't interested in performing for the animal tribes in the region. Quill figured that was for the best, as she didn't think the plays were quite suited to the tastes of sage deer, coyotes, badgers, or burrowing owls. Still, whenever they met travelers, hunters, traders, farmers, or herders on the way they generally stopped the wagons and gave a brief show, asking in payment only what the viewers believed to be fair. As a result, the troupe was always well stocked with fresh meat, nuts, fruit, an acorn-fattened piglet, and even a freshly woven fishing basket from an old Tetawa *fahr* and his grandson. It was a thrilling time.

Denarra woke Quill in the early morning of her third day with the troupe. The Strangeling was dressed in an uncharacteristically drab grey gown and forest-green cloak. Her unadorned hair was pulled back in a simple braid, and her face was solemn. There was a moist heaviness in the air, a strange weight that caused Quill's pulse to quicken.

"What is it?" Quill asked, instantly awake. She reached for her leather purse in the bed beside her. The dolls were still there, but she could feel them twisting in unexpected discomfort.

"We're about to leave the Everland." She handed Quill a small beaded bracelet. "We're coming to the Human lands now, and you'll need this handy little accessory that I picked up some time back. Keep it on you at all times, and it'll guard you from the worst of the iron sickness. I'm afraid it can't help with what's coming up right now, however. It's a rather unpleasant experience, so I thought it best to give you a bit of warning. Don't worry, though; I've left and returned many times, and the feeling won't last for too long, I promise."

"What feeling?" Quill whispered, just as it struck. The wagon seemed to spin, moving from its slow, uneasy movement to a wild rush of vertigo in the span of a heartbeat. A bitter spasm of bile filled the Dolltender's mouth, and she vaguely heard Denarra fall moaning to the floor beside her cot as the entire world descended into thunderous madness. Horses screamed, people shouted, Quill sobbed, and above everything roared the piercing shriek of the spirits on the Threshold of the Everland, torn and twisted in the Melding-made barrier between the worlds. She couldn't breathe—the very air itself bore down on her lungs like a crushing weight of stone.

The torment seemed endless, but just when Quill was certain that death was the only way free, the chaos passed, as thoroughly as if she'd simply opened her eyes and wished everything back to normal. An easy calm descended over the wagon, and the air grew cool and light again. Quill fought to sit up, weak and trembling from the sudden shift, and turned to the Strangeling, who remained lying on the floor.

"How . . . how many times have you gone through that?" the Dolltender whispered. Her mouth had a bitter, earthy taste, as though she'd been chewing on one of her leather boots.

Denarra shrugged wearily and pushed herself into a seated position. "No idea. I've crossed the boundary more times than I can count, but I've never felt *anything* like that. Something terrible is happening. It was worse than the time I drank a whole tray of Ramavarian flame-brandies, and let me tell you, darling, I thought I was sick *then;* my housekeeper told me that I apparently ran through the city wearing a soup tureen on my head and a gravy boat on my . . . oh, well," she stammered, blushing slightly. "Those trivial little details aren't all that important right now. At least that time the vomit was mine alone."

Quill looked at the wagon's floor in sudden shame. "Oh, Denarra, I'm so sorry. I didn't know. I mean—"

The Strangeling waved away her concern and smiled weakly. "Nothing to be concerned about. Sister suns know I've cleaned up worse messes in my life, and I've certainly made more than my share, too. Besides, why do you think I wore this uninspiring old gown? It's not as if I have any intention of giving up my wardrobe and joining the ranks of Dreyd-addled penitents on pilgrimage, you know. Say what you want to about the overthrown Immortals, those ancient spirits had far more appreciation for fine fashion and beautiful things than the pinch-faced Dreyd and their pleasure-hating followers. Come now, let's get you cleaned up, then we'll see to the rest of the wagon." She pulled a covered jar of water from a bin against the wall and poured some of its contents into a large clay bowl. "And while we're at it, maybe you could share your little secret with me."

"What are you talking about?" Quill's face hardened in suspicion.

The Wielder laughed as she dipped a cloth into the water. "Darling, if there's one thing I've learned in my many travels, it's this: *everyone* has a secret. Myself, I've got more fabulous secrets than I know what to do with, though admittedly most of them belong to other people, and fortunately my discretion has been rather richly rewarded. So when I see a wide-eyed Tetawa traveling alone and prepared for a long journey in Man-infested hills far from any settlement that could be considered even remotely civilized, I know there's got to be something more going on in her thoughts than an afternoon stroll."

Denarra shrugged at Quill's reticence. "But of course you know that I wouldn't *dream* of imposing on you. You're more than welcome to keep your secret to yourself if you'd like, but I'm a pretty good judge of these sorts of things, and I think this might be something you could use a little bit of help with. There's no shame in asking for help; I do it all the time. It's why I'm here right now, in fact; a little financial miscommunication with a fellow secret-keeper back in Chalimor, Illirius Pym, which he'll no doubt have reconsidered by the time we return. It's not at all unlike the time I got into a bit of trouble in this unpleasant little town in the Allied Wilderlands called Swampy Creek. It was an unfortunate misunderstanding involving a rather handsome and remarkably endowed spice merchant, his utterly unsympathetic wife—who was, I might add, both surprisingly agile and utterly impervious to reason—as well as a three-legged mule with an aversion to freshwater pearls. You see, I'd been inadvertently stranded there after taking the wrong turn at Edge-of-the-Woods—"

"I'm going to Chalimor to ask the Reachwarden to stop the Expulsion."

The Strangeling stopped, one eyebrow raised in disbelief. "You're going to do *what*?"

Quill took the rag from Denarra and rinsed it in the bowl of clean water before handing it back. "I'm going to talk to the Reachwarden in Chalimor and tell him how Vald cheated to get the Oath signed. Tobhi told me all about it. I've heard good things of the Reachwarden, and I know he'll help if he could only hear the truth from one of us. So I'm going to talk to him."

Denarra shook her head. "You sweet, adorable, ridiculously silly little thing! You clearly don't have *any* idea what you're doing. You don't know where you're going, and you don't even know how to speak the Reach-tongue of Men. I'd be willing to wager my snakeskin corset that you've never been half this far away from home in your life. How do you expect to get an audience with the most powerful Man in the Reach, let alone get him to risk a war for a bunch of Folk whom most Humans would be enthusiastic to be rid of?"

"Simple," the Tetawa said. "You'll help me."

"Me?"

Quill nodded, studying the bracelet thoughtfully. "You're right: I don't know what I'm doing. All I know is that I've got to do something. I couldn't just sit at home and wait while our world fell apart. But I didn't think it through too much, and if you hadn't saved me, I'd be in some slave pen or worse right now." She held up her wrist. "Without this, I wouldn't have lasted long in these lands. It didn't even enter my mind to worry about iron. You're right about me. I'm silly, and naive, and small, and I don't know the first thing about Men or their world. What I do know terrifies me. But there aren't many Folk who could travel the Reach for as long as you have and still live to tell the tale. You've got more wisdom, experience, and courage than almost anyone I know, Denarra, and I need your help." She smiled. "Besides, you did tell me to ask for help. So I'm asking: will you help me save our people?"

The Strangeling gazed at the Tetawa in open-mouthed surprise, the dripping rag held limply in her hand. Suddenly she burst out laughing. "And here I thought that *I* was the crafty one! Well, I'm heading to Chalimor anyway to clear up that little matter with Pym, so it's not as though it's out of my way. All right—I'll help you, but only on one condition."

"What's that?"

"We've just *got* to do something about your hair. You can't very well meet the Reachwarden looking like an ill-tempered porcupine—I won't have my reputation sullied by such an unfashionable distraction. Well, not with that complexion, anyway." Denarra planted her hands firmly on her hips and surveyed Quill with a critical eye. She sighed. "It's a good thing we've got a few weeks left before we get to Chalimor."

"The weeping reaches even here," Unahi said. Biggiabba moved down the grotto steps to sit beside her friend. The waterfall still roared, and the air still flashed heavy with dawn-brightened mist, but all of Sheynadwiin was in mourning, and even the gateway to the Eternity Tree was no sanctuary.

Biggiabba said nothing. They were an odd pair—the hulking Gvaerg-matron with the weathered face and eyes as dark as deep-mountain pools and the bent she-Kyn with the faded tattoos whose black hair had long ago turned to braided silver—but they understood one another well.

The world had changed much in the years since the bloodsong called them to be Wielders, and not for the better. The Awakening was a joyous occasion among both Kyn and Gvaergs in the old days, before the Shields came to power among the Kyn, before Men haunted the shadows. Biggiabba's Awakening happened late, much like Tarsa's, but in those days she'd had a community to embrace her and ease the unguided bloodsong toward calmer channels. After her own Awakening and long before her exile from Red Cedar Town, Unahi learned at the feet of a trio of great elders, including Mashamatti, her grandfather, who lived in his own Branch-hold near Thistlewood and took in his strange, frightened granddaughter, sharing the stories of the ancient days of the People and the Eld Green.

And then there were the Gatherings, when Wielders from all the Folk came together to share their wisdom, to dance moonwise around the fire and sing, to mourn the dead and celebrate the newly Awakened, and to share news of their world and the lands of Men beyond. It was at Biggiabba's first Gathering, at the edge of a feast-fire, that the awkward she-Gvaerg and the shy she-Kyn first met. They'd been fast friends ever since.

Biggiabba had wept with Unahi when the Shield of Red Cedar Town exiled the she-Kyn Wielder from her home, separating her from the sisters and the young niece who would one day have her own Awakening; Unahi in turn nursed her friend through the scourge that mottled her grey skin and killed her only child, a fat-faced he-Gvaerg named Ore-Runner. They'd gathered medicinals in the mountains together, planted trees and healed wounded animals, driven poachers and other invaders from their homelands, and often just sat beside the other's hearth-fire in silence, content simply to smoke a fragrant pipe and gaze into the fire with a friend close at hand. And often lately, they shared the visions of Unahi's dream-world travels, where she caught glimpses of Tarsa's difficult journey and the dangers that threatened them all.

Because they had shared so many times like these, Biggiabba could tell what was going through Unahi's mind without need of words, but she wanted to hear something besides the sobs that echoed through the redrock walls of Sheynadwiin.

"She'll be here, you old worrier. Nothing will keep her away. Blackwick told us that his merchants dropped them close to Tobhi's old home ground. You've seen for yourself, and she's still strong. It's not far past a sevenday yet. They'll be fine. She'll be here soon."

Unahi looked up and smiled. "I know. We're connected more than she understands; it's one reason I gave her the staff, to keep track of her through our dreams, to share something of the journey with her. She's strong and stubborn, just like her mother—those roots run deeply in this family. But I still can't help but worry. She's had to understand so much, with so little time." Her voice weakened. "I wish I might have spared her some of it. I wish I would have had more time to give her everything she's going to need in the days ahead. With so much lost and threatened . . .. Maybe I should have stopped her. So much depends on her, and on the rest of these young ones."

Biggiabba nodded sympathetically. "It's awful lonesome, some-times, thinking that we might be the only ones left."

"Do you think they're ready?" The she-Kyn stared off into the water.

"They'll have to be. You've done all you could, grey-eyes, so all you can do is hope for the best and trust them. There's no stopping this storm now. We just have to pray that the seeds we planted will have roots deep enough to endure."

It was a small fire, just large enough to give off much-needed heat but not so large that it would attract unwanted attention. They'd already had a few close calls with Humans this day and didn't relish another, especially when they were all so weary and worried. In just a matter of days, Men were now everywhere in the Everland, even this far into the interior. Things had accelerated far beyond anything they'd expected.

This stretch of the woods was littered with piles of mossy gran-ite boulders that jutted through the leafy canopy like green icebergs. Tobhi had found a defensible spot for them to camp for the night beside a small creek at the fern-covered base of one of the outcrop-pings, and he took first watch at the top of the rocks while the others tended to the fire and themselves.

Tarsa removed her travel-worn boots, hissing as her blistered toes stretched free in the cool evening air, and leaned back with a groan. She was more tired than she'd ever been in her life. It would have been almost beyond endurance if so much didn't depend on their haste. They'd come so far in such a short time, and they were still so far from Sheynadwiin—so far from the Tree that called to her day and night, pulling her forward with increasing insistence. Tarsa didn't know what was coming in the days ahead, but the ice-cold knot in her stomach gave her more hesitation than hope.

A hiss of pain caught her attention, and she saw Daladir trying to pull his own boots off, without success. His face was thin and drawn, but he stubbornly kept at the lacings.

"Your feet are swollen, Ambassador," Tarsa said, pulling herself to his side. "If you get those boots off, you'll never get them on again."

He shook his head. "It doesn't matter. I've got to bathe them. They burn like fire."

"Then let me help." Tarsa took her wyrwood dagger and cut through the side of the first boot, almost to the sole, and helped the he-Kyn squeeze his foot out of it. Tarsa winced at the sight and smell; it was no wonder he was in so much pain, as some of the blistered flesh had gone bad, and infection had set in. She leaned with him to the bank and helped him remove the second boot, then gave him support as he draped his misshapen feet into the creek. With a smile, Tarsa joined him, nearly laughing as the cold water rushed over her flesh and eased the ache of the journey.

They sat there for a long time. When they could no longer feel their feet from the cold, Tarsa helped Daladir limp to the fire and began to softly massage the feeling back into the flesh, drawing on the *wyr* as she did so, trying to knit the damaged skin and drive out the festering sickness. Daladir never said a word. He didn't even flinch as her fingers probed his tender feet, but he watched her intently, his gaze bright in the firelight.

At last Tarsa nodded and released his feet, her face drawn but victorious. "I haven't tried much healing before, certainly not like this, but I think it worked. It's different from drawing out poison; you have knit the flesh back together, not just remove something that doesn't belong. You'll still hurt, but if we cleanse your feet every day, you should be able to walk without much difficulty."

She leaned back, but Daladir caught her hand tenderly. "Thank you, Wielder . . . Tarsa."

The she-Kyn looked at him now, blue eyes locked on green. His touch was inviting, and her body responded with an almost forgotten hunger. Her breath caught in her chest. There was something familiar in his gaze, something that she'd seen not long before.

But Jitani's deep eyes were like golden flame in her memory, and they'd burned there since she'd left Sheynadwiin. Pulling away from the he-Kyn, Tarsa retreated, suddenly shaken, to the far side of the campfire. When she finally slept, deep in the night, her dreams were of eyes, green and gold, in the darkness.

28

Hide and Seek

THANE'S SEARCH TURNED UP NOTHING for the first few days, even though he thoroughly scoured the woods and the remaining slaving trains in the area. It was as if the little Brownie witch had been swallowed into the very earth itself. When at last luck came to his aid, it was unbidden but welcome.

He sat on a rough wooden bench in the ruins of the Brownie village, waiting for the blacksmith to finish looking after his horse, which had lost a shoe during the previous day's explorations. Being a practical Man, Thane thought it best to take care of the creature rather than push it farther into the forest and risk injury, so they'd returned to the village, and the smith now attended the mare, though not with the care Thane would have preferred. He looked around. Now named Chestnut Grove in honor of the massive old trees that darkened the landscape for miles around, it hadn't taken long for Men to turn this ruined Brownie settlement into the bustling beginning of a Human outpost, complete with makeshift smithy, trading tents, and rum merchants. The trees were now being felled at a tremendous rate for lumber and to make space for cropland. Soon there wouldn't be any more chestnuts anywhere near the place, and the name would be just an empty symbol. A few ragged homesteaders and their families were preparing to move farther into the Unhuman territories, ready to claim lands by any force necessary.

Thane grew increasingly irritated as he watched more and more Men enter the town from the west. The stink of smoke, horse dung, and Human waste increased with every new traveler, and the road had been churned into slimy mud by the recent storms and hundreds of strange feet passing through Chestnut Grove toward anticipated riches to the east. The numbers would only increase.

He remembered the last time he traveled through the town, shortly before he'd first discovered the dark-eyed dollmaker, when the town belonged fully to the Brownie-folk. So different from now. Their little round cabins, though rough and unobtrusive, had been cared for with pride; the path to the river had been well-maintained; privies were deep and kept clean and the outbuildings free of rubbish. The hundreds of small, almost tame animals that lived amongst the Brownies were now long gone, having fled with their Fey friends or died under blade, bolt, and musket shot.

His single eye scanned the remaining buildings. The wooden statues that had once adorned the town were gone now, either sold as curiosities and mementos or destroyed for kindling. Although the Dreydcaste generally condemned statuary as objects of witch-inspired superstition, Thane regretted the destruction of the Brownies' animal idols. The Man-high blocks of wood were carved to resemble various beasts and stood proudly in front of the larger structures. Some had been strikingly lifelike, while others were given a mere hint of resemblance to recognizable creatures. Either way, the artistry of those idols had been exquisite. Thane had an eye for fine craftsmanship, but there was no longer anything to admire here; now those statues, too, were gone.

He sighed and stood. It was likely going to be a while before the smith was done, as there was only one forge in the town and many people were clamoring for his help, so Thane decided to examine the rest of the town to familiarize himself with the other changes in the new Chestnut Grove.

He was sipping from an unwashed mug in the rum trader's tent when the first Men arrived with news of an attack in the rocky country to the south. Thane listened as one Man stepped up to the trader and began telling the story of a powerful witch and her monstrous warriors who'd called down lightning from the sky on his friends. Thane could smell Fey-sorcery on the Man, even through the stink of sweat and sour-mash. It was a familiar scent, one he knew as well as the scars on his own flesh, though he hadn't smelled it in years.

Things were finally looking far more promising.

Thane turned back to his drink and waited. A group of Men and Women gathered around to hear the details of the story, and the Seeker was among them, listening past the Man's self-serving lies and the mists of drunkenness for details that might be useful. Eventually the crowd shifted toward the other survivors of the attack. Thane kept his attention focused on the first Man, as he carried the strongest taint of Fey-sorcery.

When the drunkard lurched off behind the trading tent to find a bush for release, Thane followed noiselessly.

He slid behind the Man and waited for him to squat with his stained breeches bunched around his ankles. Knife in his left hand, Thane swept his right arm around the Man's throat, cutting off his air and jerking him into the underbrush and away from any unintended observation. His prisoner flailed wildly for a moment, but stopped instantly when Thane nicked a bit of flesh off the end of the Man's nose.

<<Keep struggling, I'll peel that little wrinkly nub you prize so much,>> the Seeker whispered into the Man's ear, wiggling the knife downward. <<Cooperate with me, and this might be the only blood I draw.>> The threat worked. The Man's knees quivered, but he didn't cry out when Thane dropped him to the rocky ground.

The Seeker knelt close. <<No more lies. Tell me everything about your encounter with the witch. I want every drunken detail.>>

The Man's voice cracked, but he shared his information without hesitation. <<It's like I said before. Me and my mates was bringin' a load of them Brownies to the market when we was attacked by this witch—one of them snake-heads from up north. She was terrible—gold skin, purple robes, and them eyes—like green fire. It was supposed to be an easy job, quick—just in and out. There wasn't supposed to be any of them down here. And now I see them eyes and hear that laugh all the time. And the smell of the lightnin', and burnin' skin . . . I never would'a come along if I'd have known she

was goin' to be there. That's what I told Cobbert before we left. I said, 'If any of them snake-headed'—>>

<<I don't care,>> Thane growled. <<You said there were others. Describe them.>>

<<They wasn't too easy to see. It was rainin' hard, and there was fire everywhere, and screamin'. Their wagons appeared out of nowhere. Lightning started flashing around us, and then the arrows came. Cobbert went down first. He'd chased that Brownie up the hill on his horse, and it was about then that—>>

Thane leaned in swiftly. <<Stop. What Brownie?>>

The Man's eyes bulged. <<I don't know! I never seen her before! All of a sudden this Brownie runs out from under this rock, like a rabbit from hounds. Cobbert sees her first and yells at us to stop, and then he kicks his horse toward her. He's almost got her when this big bolt of lightning comes down and . . . >> His voice trailed off. <<I ran after that. We all did. The witch suddenly showed up, laughing and calling down fire all over us. We lost a lot of good Men that day, I'll tell you.>>

<<And what of the Brownie? Can you describe her? How do you know it was a female?>>

<<I saw enough of her to know that, if you know what I mean. Her hair was all pulled back on her head, light-colored, I think. That's all I remember. I don't know if she was still alive or not. I got out of there as soon as I could.>>

Thane leaned back on his heels. It could be the little dollmaker; her hair was the color of sun-dried sand, so that feature fit. Then again, it could be any one of a thousand Brownies in the world. The Fey-stink on the Man was distinctive and unmistakable, so he had a good idea of who the Unhuman witch was, but the description of the Brownie was too vague to be certain. Still, it was better than anything else he had to go on, and it was consistent with everything else he knew about the Fey: witches were drawn to one another, like flies to filth.

<<Where was this, and how many days past?>>

<<Two days ago, in the hill-country south of here. We followed the main pass.>>

Thane lifted the Man into the air again and shook him like a drowned kitten. <<I'll feed you your own liver if I find out that

you've lied to me. Now, clean yourself up—you're fouling this place with your stink.>> He tossed his prisoner into the thorny underbrush and returned to the smith's yard, where he found his freshly shod horse waiting.

After examining the work and paying a brass penny less because of the poor quality, Thane spurred his horse southward, leaving Chestnut Grove behind in the distant dust.

<<The first . . . messengers have arrived, Authority,>> Vorgha whispered from the outer edge of the door.

Vald looked up from his desk, his brows knitted in annoyance. The Dreydmaster rarely tolerated interruptions during his studies, as this time was increasingly sacrosanct. Although he'd ordered his attendant to notify him as soon as these particular visitors returned, the timing was rather poor. He was in the middle of a vexing translation from an ancient Rinj prophecy scroll to the Reach script of his workbook, and the older Eromar text was veiled in a deceptively simple Crafting that required intense concentration to maintain the intelligibility of the symbols. There were far too few opportunities for research lately: the voices of the Dreyd were growing ever more insistent as the days passed, and even solitude brought little freedom to fully unravel their enigmatic messages; the unexpected repairs on Gorthac Hall were an unwelcome distraction, as was the sudden disappearance of the Fey-witch and her associates. And earlier today the emissaries from the Reachwarden in Chalimor arrived demanding explanations for the unorthodox and possibly illegal circumstances surrounding the signing of the Oath.

Meddlers and incompetents. At least the visitors of this night were wanted.

<<Dreydmaster?>> Vorgha said, louder this time. With a deep sigh, Vald shut the dusty book with a snap of his hand and stood to sweep his silver-buttoned coat from the back of the chair. This evening's guests were certainly welcome, but they weren't patient, so the deeper nuances of the Dreyd mysteries would have to wait. Vorgha led the way from the room, and Vald carried his own oil lamp. There were things in this subterranean chamber that loved

neither light nor heat, and in his absence an unguarded flame might well cause great mischief.

They traveled together through the roughly hewn tunnel that wound like a serpent through the underbelly of Gorthac Hall, moving sharply downward for only part of its length, then rising gradually upward again toward the highest elevation of the steppe upon which the Hall squatted, where Vald's cursed garden lay inaccessible from above. Few Human feet had willingly wandered through this dark passage since its creation in the time of the first Prefect of Eromar. Of course, in those days the rooms were saved more for illicit liaisons that often ended in the bubbling screams of Women and the occasional Man, but times had changed. Vald had ceased to enjoy such mundane carnal pursuits; the dictates of the Dreyd offered so much more satisfaction than mere flesh could provide.

Yellow bones stained red and brown with the wet mineral moisture of the tunnel still sat amidst crumbling rags in most of the rooms along the corridor, but Vald needed few chambers for his studies, so he generally left the rest undisturbed. On occasion, when especially displeased, Vald would order a bound and blindfolded transgressor brought to one of these long-abandoned alcoves and then go about his business while the perpetrator awoke in the company of the decaying dead. Those who managed to survive the shock and numbing cold were occasionally released and nearly always shattered by the experience. And those fools never caused him further difficulty.

Those who escaped were the ones who nettled him. But they were few, and rarer still were those who managed to evade his grasp for good. Years might pass away, the world might change, bodies might age and familiarity fade, but vengeance was enduring, and the Dreydmaster's reach was long. Some, like the incompetent Binder, Merrimyn, weren't worth much pursuit at all; one Seeker was enough to take care of the problem.

Others, like the Fey-witch who called herself Spearbreaker, were a different matter entirely.

The entrance to the under-tunnel stood behind the great wall tapestry in Vald's bedchamber; Vorgha, Vald, a handful of trusted mercenaries, and the fugitive Merrimyn were the only Men now living who knew of its existence. The nosy Unhuman spy Daladir was another, but he'd be dealt with in good time, too.

They stepped from the darkness. Vorgha set their oil lamps on the bed table and quickly wiped dust and debris from the tunnel off the Dreydmaster's jacket. Stepping toward a plain wooden box on the table, he returned with a small brush that he used to fluff out Vald's muttonchops and bristling eyebrows. Such ministrations enhanced the Dreydmaster's leonine appearance, as did the high collar on the jacket. The effort was likely wasted tonight, but Vald insisted upon being fully presentable, especially with guests such as these. One could never be too careful during these delicate times.

His toilet complete, Vald sent his attendant on an errand and walked alone to the garden corridor, where he released the sanctified ash and hissed the necessary words to pass the Craft-bound guardians unhindered. The doors opened, and Vald grimaced slightly at the raucous, cackling laughter and rancid stench of sulfur and rotting flesh that hovered among the ragged brown plants in the enclosure.

The Crafted gate hovered over the dry fountain, its iridescent surface shimmering like dark oil in weak sunlight. Vald's eyes lingered on the dozens of knee-high, sniggering Not-Ravens that crouched with gleaming talons on the withered branches of the garden's long-dead fruit trees. Like stillborn infants brought back to life against their will, they bobbed back and forth, warily watching him approach with preternatural awareness oozing from glistening black holes.

<<What news do you bring me?>> he asked, and then caught himself, realizing that these Not-Ravens likely did not speak the languages of Men. He repeated the question, this time in the trade-tongue of the Fey. His mouth struggled over the words with obvious distaste.

As one voice, the creatures hissed in chorus, "We have found the ones you seek, oh Man, yes, we have found them all, short and tall, and She with the shining eyes and skin green as swamp-moss, yes— *she* walks proudly, yes. Unbroken still." Trails of black slime dripped from their mouths as they cawed and giggled.

The Dreydmaster nodded. "Where are they?"

Again the creatures chanted in unison. "Among the trees, in the deep, dark trees, where the beasts and the shadows reign, where their shining eyes seek dark wings and feathers, oh Man. They wander toward the weeping city, still many days away, but moving ever closer, oh yes. Soon, too soon, they will find the city where tears flow warm like rabbit's blood. Still they walk untouched, oh Man, and still we watch them, never failing in our duty, as promised to you, oh Man. Watch them still we shall, yes, as we promised. We are faithful to our duty."

"You have done only part of what I asked. There are others I told you to watch."

The Not-Ravens nodded and clucked at one another. "Yes, yes, yes. None escape us, none walk unnoticed. All is well, oh Man. All is well. Their feet carry them quickly, but our wings, yes, yes, they carry us faster, and the night hides us well. None walk unnoticed. Faithful we are, now and always." Their movements ceased, and their heads leaned forward menacingly. "Now, faithful you must be, yes. We hunger. Your promise you must keep."

The Not-Ravens giggled harshly to themselves. Sickly green points of light flared to life in their eye holes, and they grew more agitated on the crackling branches, flapping their ragged black wings and sending rolling waves of foulness through the garden. Vald nodded curtly and snapped his fingers. A chime echoed deep in the inner hall. Vorgha appeared at the open doorway after a few moments, his pale features set in an expression of bland docility.

<<Vorgha, I must discharge a debt to these visitors. Is all in order?>>

<<It is, Authority. I will call the guards.>>

The attendant returned quickly, and with him were two grim-faced Men, their black jackets soiled with mud and the blood of the chained figure who knelt limply on the ground between them. Vald looked on without emotion.

The Wielder-witch had left too soon, paid too little attention when she'd examined her poisoned comrades. Not all were dead when she left.

Young Athweid glared up with her one remaining eye, fear and hatred burning like a guttering flame across her mangled face. The iron chains sizzled into her wrists, blistering the flesh, but it was hard to tell where the freshly burned scars ended and those of the previous days began. Her oak-leaf ears were gone, along with her dark azure hair—nothing but blackened stumps remained of either—but Vald had kept her silky sensory stalks intact and tightly bound. She might have cursed him then, but her tongue and teeth had long since been torn away under the skillful ministrations of the Dreydcaste Purifiers. She hadn't known much more about Spearbreaker and the others, but by the end of the interrogation had surrendered that sparse information as well as minor but useful details about Sheynadwiin and the Sevenfold Council. Even she had been surprised at how much she knew, when provided with the proper incentive.

And now, once again, she was going to prove useful.

Vald turned to the other Men and nodded. Vorgha led them away, and the Dreydmaster was alone with the pain-ravaged she-Kyn and the eager Not-Ravens who crowded around his legs. Vald stared at her for a long while, unperturbed by her hatred.

<<What a sad, wasted creature,>> he whispered in Mannish as he stroked her trembling cheek. <<To think that the salvation of this broken world depends on such as you.>> His hands moved quickly, and the bindings on Athweid's stalks fell free. Her bloody mouth gaped impossibly wide with the sudden, hissing rush of agony. He turned away, and the Not-Ravens surged forward, a giggling flood of bright teeth and dark feathers.

Vald reentered the hallway only after the guttural shrieks abruptly ceased; he wanted to ensure payment in full. The door shut on its own, and he returned alone to the long, dark tunnel that led to his library.

There would be no further interruptions this night.

Mother Baraboo's tea wasn't very good; it was thick and a bit gritty, with only a little honey to please the tongue. Quill didn't mind too much, though, as she'd grown quite fond of the gentle old Woman and her strange associates. The Dolltender was willing to suffer the tea to sit around the wagons. She enjoyed watching the troupe's interactions with one another, and listening to the heavy rhythm of their alien speech.

Since Denarra spent most of her nights with doe-eyed Kinnit, Quill's visits with Mother Baraboo had become a nightly custom, but her days generally involved chatting with the Strangeling and learning more about the Human lands around them. They were in the arid southern reaches of Eromar now, nearing the great Windy

River that separated the Dreydmaster's domain from Béashaad, the province of the Reachwarden and the city of Chalimor. This world was so very different from the fragrant hills and verdant forests of the Everland. The scrubby brush and trees were short and hugged the dun-colored earth, as wild winds howled unchallenged in the rocky hills. It all felt less tangible, somehow, as though this world of Men had been drained of some of the vitality of the Folk Threshold.

The caravan now traveled on the Old Windle Road, an ancient track that had cut across the Reach before the Melding. That catastrophe had placed a great sea in the middle of the highway, so it had long ago ceased to be useful for westward travel, replaced by the more serviceable Great Way Road to the south. The Old Windle Road was still used by those on the eastern side of the Riven Sea, heading toward Chalimor, and although highwaymen and other bandits were known to menace travelers on this grassy track, the Repertory was large enough to make all but the most ambitious robbers reconsider an attack. And with the Strangeling Wielder in tow, even those rogues didn't stay long.

All these things Quill had learned from Denarra, who embraced her role as teacher with great enthusiasm, though with no particular structure or order, sharing mixed bits of geographical history, cultural lore, botanical curiosa, and social customs of the Human provinces with her young friend during the daylight hours. Then, at night, after Denarra left for Kinnit's athletic embrace, Quill would hide her dolls beneath the quilts and pillows on her cot and wander over to the bonfire in front of Mother Baraboo's massive wagon, where she'd sip her bitter tea while the members of the Repertory laughed, sang, and danced together into the early-morning hours. Occasionally Denarra and Kinnit would join the revelry, but they rarely stayed for long, preferring instead their private celebrations in his wagon on the edge of the camp.

Quill sat on a cushion beside Mother Baraboo's massive bench every night. She still didn't understand much of their language, but from this unobtrusive seat she'd quickly learned something about their personalities from the way they interacted with one another. These Humans were louder and more abrupt than was customary among the Folk, and they tended to be rather physical and familiar with one another in ways that the Tetawa found a bit unnerving, especially since they were so much larger and more imposing than she. Still, these Humans smiled and laughed when they were happy, just like the Tetawi, and they were always kind to her.

Of all the Human members of the Repertory, Mother Baraboo and Klaus were Quill's favorites. The old Woman cooed and fussed over the Tetawa like a mother pigeon. She kept a wooden box of small mint candies in her wagon, and every night she handed a few to Quill to enjoy. Mother Baraboo often chattered away in the Reach-tongue, which Quill still didn't understand, but the Woman didn't expect a reply; she just seemed to be happy to have someone new to talk to.

Klaus, on the other hand, never said a word, to Quill or to anyone else, but he never objected when she helped to clean the wild game he brought to the fire each night, and he always put aside cuts of the choicest meat for the Tetawa before returning to his unpainted wagon. His silence comforted her. Denarra was lovely, and Quill adored her, but the Strangeling's exuberance was sometimes overwhelming, so the hours alone in the wagon were something of a relief. Similarly, a loving hour of Mother Baraboo's endless giggles, sweeping hugs, and incessant cheek-pinches often left the Tetawa feeling much like a cub's play toy, and she came to relish her quiet moments with Klaus. The thick-browed and long-limbed Human never intruded on her thoughts. After Quill made clear her willingness to help, he would return from each hunting trip with a small deer or a handful of prairie quail and rabbits and hand her a stone-bladed knife. She'd sit beside him near the fire and dress the meat for cooking. Once finished, she might grab her walking stick and follow him as he checked the horses one last time for the night, or wander back to help at the cooking pots while the others danced or played lively songs on their fiddles and horns. Klaus spent little time among the crowd, but he always nodded appreciatively to Quill as he retired for the evening.

The other Humans were friendly enough, but they generally kept to themselves, so the Tetawa had little real contact with them. Lartorsha danced wildly to the music, her narrow arms thrashing back and forth, until just before dawn, when the gallant Colonel Bedzo would wearily lead her back to her wagon. Adelaide of the Veil never joined the evening gatherings, although she would occasionally slip through the shadows to the campfire to fill a wooden bowl with ember-cooked meat and bread and slip just as carefully back into the darkness. Other performers came to the fire to join the fun, but their revelries rarely brought them close to Mother Baraboo or the young Dolltender beside her.

Quill had been with the caravan for ten days when the newest visitors arrived at the evening fire. For two nights Klaus hadn't returned from the hunt until after the Dolltender went to bed, so there'd been little for her to do but sit around until drowsiness claimed her. Denarra had come back to the fire more often now, generally without Kinnit, but on this night she'd been gone, too, and her young Human plaything sat dejectedly on a log at the opposite end of the fire.

A sudden commotion caught Quill's attention. Klaus stepped from the darkness with two strangers tucked gently under in his arms. One was a skinny young Human with unkempt brown hair, pale skin, and green eyes. His blue cotton shirt was torn in places, and dried blood darkened the fabric, but he seemed otherwise healthy enough. He held a large cloth bundle in his left arm and clutched it tightly to his chest as he unsteadily found his footing. The second figure, however, filled Quill with joy, for it was a Tetawa, a *fahr* with roughly chopped bangs and a long, dirty jacket with frilled cuffs. He was one of her own people, and after Klaus set him down he brightened at the sight of Quill at the fire's edge.

"Praise to the Old Ones, I'm among friends," he laughed in the trade-tongue, tucking his pointed cap under his armpit with one hand and offering a vigorous handshake with the other.

She pulled back, a bit overwhelmed by the enthusiasm of his greeting, but responded with a smile of her own. "Welcome, cousin! I was beginning to feel awfully short around all these Humans! What happened to you?"

He frowned. "A brutal attack . . . couldn't tell what it was. If not for the help of your long-legged friend there, we might have been torn apart like the others." He bowed and swept his travel-bent hat in greeting. "You're a welcome sight in this wild land. The name's Jago Chaak."

"I'm Quill Meadowgood, of Spider Clan in Spindletop Hollow."

The Dolltender started to speak again, but the young Human

suddenly collapsed, and Mother Baraboo pulled her massive frame forward to stanch his wounds. Then, as though called from the darkness, Denarra appeared, her recently tinted hair and emerald-green dress disheveled, her face troubled. After a brief consultation with Mother Baraboo, who handed the Strangeling a small clay jar and clean linen strips, Klaus swept the youth into his arms and followed Denarra back to her wagon. She undressed the stranger and began binding his wounds. Quill and Jago followed along, but at the door Klaus stopped the *fahr* and pointed to another nearby wagon that was to be the Tetawa's resting-place for the night. He then motioned to Quill to join Denarra.

Before leaving, Jago moved in and whispered to the *firra*, "There's something wrong in all of this. Something terrible attacked us tonight—it seemed to change, becoming something different each time we fought back. If your friend hadn't arrived when he did . . ." He shuddered. "The boy's been strange ever since; he's not himself. He's changed, too." Casting a fearful glance back at the wagon, Jago skittered back to the campfire.

Quill looked up at Klaus, who'd remained beside the door, a grim, silent sentry, and trudged hesitantly up the stairs and into the wagon. All the windows were shuttered against the outside darkness, and a flickering oil lamp glowed over the pale face of the young Man in the bed, who moaned softly in pain. Denarra motioned to the Tetawa. "Hurry, Quill, and shut the door!"

"What's wrong?" She dropped the bar across the door before walking over to Denarra's bed.

"Something dreadful, I'm afraid." The Strangeling finished wrapping the last of the bandages across the young Man's head. "I didn't want to worry you before, but Klaus saw a prowler on the edge of the camp a couple of nights past when you were with him near the horses. He only caught a quick glimpse, but he saw enough to know that you were being watched."

The Dolltender's mouth went dry. "What . . . what did it look like?"

Denarra's eyes were warm with sympathy. "Well, I've never seen it, but it certainly sounds familiar. You know the description, darling, because it was you who shared it with me. Tall, pale, yellow eyes—a rather unfriendly acquaintance of yours. It knows you're here."

Quill's legs buckled, and she sagged to her knees on the wagon floor. Denarra sighed. "As soon as he shared the information with me, Klaus and I decided to look after you, day and night. We followed the creature's trail for the past two nights, but every time we got close its track just seemed to vanish, which of course hardly makes sense. Klaus is a splendid tracker, yet he lost all sign of the creature; the tracks got all mixed up with others, a raccoon, a pig, a youngling child. And, to be perfectly honest, I have more than a little experience hunting down unsavory types, and even my own skills didn't help us out much. For such a large creature, it's surprisingly cunning."

"What happened tonight?" The Dolltender's voice was thin and strained.

"Well, we hadn't been gone for too terribly long when we heard some screams away to the north. It was a small merchant train, though not a particularly reputable one, from what little remained to see. One of those shady vagabond trains that picks up every troubled, desperate wanderer with a sad story, no questions asked." She stopped and considered Quill for a moment, then went on. "We got there as soon as we could, but we were too late to stop the worst of it. Whatever this creature is, it didn't worry about leaving a mess. Just ghastly." The Wielder shuddered. "There were only two survivors when we got there—this boy and the Tetawa you met near the fire. The creature was nowhere to be found."

Quill looked up in alarm. "So it's still out there?"

"I'm afraid so. We didn't have time to keep looking, especially since this poor boy seemed badly hurt. We figured it was best to get these two back to the caravan before going out again. But we'll keep an eye on you, I promise. Whatever this creature is, it won't slip past us again. You're safe here with us."

"*Mishko*," the Tetawa whispered.

"There's a bit more," Denarra said, casting a worried glance at the bed. The flushed young Man shuddered, feverish and unconscious.

"I'm not sure I'm ready to hear anything else." Quill was dizzy. The safety and comfort of the past days had vanished with the grim news, and she suddenly felt as alone and vulnerable as when she'd crouched in the rain under the standing stone in the Downlands, hoping to escape the eyes of the slavers.

The Strangeling held up the Human's left forearm to reveal a three-tined black star tattooed on the flesh. A thin chain stretched from a cuff on his wrists to the locked binding on a small purple book on the floor, which had been hidden in the bundle he bore so carefully. The tome was ribbed with a dull grey metal that seemed to absorb the light, and its pulsing toxicity made Quill thankful yet again for the iron-ward Denarra had given her. "This isn't just some trader's brat out to make some money with a band of mercantile vagrants. I don't know what he was doing with them, but he can't be here by accident. If I've learned anything in my travels over the years, it's this one little bit of timeless wisdom: there's no such thing as coincidence."

"Why not? Who is he?" Quill's eyes were riveted on the book shackled to the young Man's arm. Whatever strange mottled skin or fabric had been used to Craft the tome shimmered in the soft glow of the lamp with an unpleasant rhythm of its own.

"He's a Binder from Gorthac Hall, Quill. He bears the mark of Dreydmaster Vald."

29

The Spirit World

THE EVERLAND NIGHT POSSESSED a beauty unmatched in the lands of Men. In daylight, the sister suns warmed the world: Goldmantle, the elder sister, was the largest and most beautiful, her hue that of gilded bronze; Bright-Eye, the younger, was smaller, and she burned white-hot. They traveled across the sky-vault together, Bright-Eye's heat tempered behind Goldmantle's ample sphere, both looking down upon the Thresholds of the long-shattered Eld Green, ever-faithful sentinels over their fragmented kindred.

It was the night, however, that truly revealed the Eld Green's beauty. The Greatmoon, Pearl-in-Darkness, loomed large in the heavens. Even in the daytime the Greatmoon was an impressive sight, although only a milky shadow of his luminous radiance in the night. He was more mercurial than his sisters, more mysterious and remote; his wounded face changed shape and temper throughout the month and year. But Pearl-in-Darkness brought comfort, too, of a sort, for he'd survived the Melding intact, even while his two brothers were shattered to become the silver, sparkling rings that circled the Greatmoon and spread far across the sky-vault.

Men feared their own sky. Tobhi couldn't really blame them, as their own moon was a small, feeble guardian in comparison to the magnificence of Pearl-in-Darkness. The evening stars in the Reach were distant and aloof, not the shining, beckoning spirits of the Everland night. The single sun of the world of Men, too, seemed strangely lonely, although its white heat was similar to that of Bright-Eye. The Tetawa hadn't realized the unhappiness of that sky until he'd spent so many nights under its vault. Now that he was in the Everland again, he could hardly remember the strangeness of that time, and he was glad of it.

Tobhi looked over at his sleeping companions. They'd been so strange lately, all fire and frost, sometimes laughing together, at other times falling into grim and awkward silences. Tarsa lay curled within the moss-covered roots of a great wyrwood tree, her moon-touched face partially hidden by her tangled brown hair. Daladir lay closer to the fire pit, his face turned away from the dull flames. The Leafspeaker didn't have to see their faces to know the pain and fatigue etched there. Tarsa never complained, but Tobhi knew that her cracked ribs had been slow in healing without time to focus her healing arts on herself, and it was a matter of sheer stubborn will that kept her moving so quickly and so far each day. Daladir, too, was wounded. Most of the Ambassador's life had been spent in Sheynadwiin, where he'd learned the arts of writing, music, and diplomacy, but his knowledge of the wilds was limited to day-trips into the woods around the city—hardly sufficient preparation for this grueling march.

Yet the trip was wearing on Tobhi, too. He missed Smudge quite a bit these days. The ill-tempered little riding deer was a nasty biter, but he'd also saved the Tetawa a lot of traveling aches over the past few years and had become a cranky but dependable friend, so on the whole it seemed a reasonable balance. He wondered where the little stag was, as he hadn't seen him for weeks, not since trusting him to the care of one of his cousins after arriving in Sheynadwiin. Smudge was probably ensconced in some well-stocked stable in Sheynadwiin or wandering free among the city's resident deer population. Either way, he was likely getting fat and lazy and annoying the other animals.

Tobhi sighed. Such reminiscences didn't do much to ease his own aching muscles. Although the Kyn were only a couple of feet taller than the brown-skinned scribe, they had a wider stride, and he occasionally found it difficult to keep up with Tarsa's unyielding pace. Still, though his feet were swollen and blistered each night, he was probably the least exhausted of them all, as his solid frame and journeying life had given him strength, patience, and calluses enough to travel without too much difficulty. Being back in the Everland helped, too.

He was strong enough, in fact, to let their turns at watch pass, and to allow them to catch up on a bit of sleep. The days ahead weren't going to be any easier than those of the past, but he was certain that Tarsa would need to be stronger than any of them; that wouldn't happen if she kept pushing herself so mercilessly. They were all desperate to get to Sheynadwiin, but the Wielder was especially agitated, becoming more so with every passing day. Something drove her forward, and Tobhi wasn't entirely sure that it was a good thing. They had to stand beside their People during this terrible time, and warn them of Vald's murderous hospitality and the full measure of Neranda's betrayal. Daladir knew about Vald's arsenal and military capacity; his months as a careful observer in Gorthac Hall had resulted in some success in this subversive regard, if not so much in overt diplomacy. But they were still three days, maybe four, from the grotto city. Sudden, savage storms and the increasing presence of Humans had delayed their arrival by at least a day already, and there was no telling what difficulties still stood between them and Sheynadwiin.

The Tetawa looked at the Kyn again, this time more closely. Neither Tarsa nor Daladir stirred; their exhaustion would keep them from waking too soon. Tobhi had another reason to let them sleep. Something unpleasant had been lingering in his mind since their arrival in the Eldarvian Woods, and it was getting stronger as they neared Dardath Vale. Something awful was waiting for them. He had to know what it was.

Tobhi reached into his badger-faced satchel and drew out the red cloth bundle, which he untied and opened to reveal the lore-leaves to the moonlight. He'd chosen their campsite deliberately, for it was one of the few places in this dense forest that had a clear view of the night sky. The radiance of Pearl-in-Darkness would be helpful for what he wanted to do.

As he'd done so many times in his young life, since his pepa had first showed him how to read the stories woven into the movements of the leaves, Tobhi settled his mind into the right thoughts, pushing away the hot ache in his feet, the awkward bite of a sharp tree root in his thigh, the exhaustion that weighed down on his eyes. It took a little while, but when the shift took place, he settled easily into the familiar change in his senses. His hearing and sight went distant and dull, but he could now smell the deep and earthy spice of lush vegetation and rich soil around him, and his tingling fingers almost burned with that renewed awareness. The strains of the journey vanished as his full attention focused on the ridges and smooth webbing of the leaves. He followed their spreading veins, stark against the nearly transparent membrane in the moonlight, and traveled across their varied textures, sometimes rough, sometimes soft and cool as glass.

Ordinarily, this would be where he drew on the stories embedded in the leaves and their dancing patterns to understand the wisdom of the past and present. This time, however, he was moving toward divination, which was something he generally disliked. Too many things could go wrong; the future was always mixed up with emotions, fears, passions, and expectations. In spite of his discomfort, he didn't have much choice. The world had grown so much more dangerous, and he needed something to hold on to, something to prepare him for the darkness at the end of this road. It was hard to clear the mind of all that muddled mess to get to the single question that most concerned him: *What's gonna happen to us when we get to Sheynadwiin?*

He fanned the leaves gently through his fingers to mix them up, but his brows knitted in sudden worry, and he stopped. Two of the leaves were broken. He thought back, remembering the brief attempt at reading he'd tried with Tarsa in Eromar, the night of their arrival at Gorthac Hall. Frowning, he pulled the leaves out of the pile and felt them more closely: *Ehk-shewi* and *Ghwai-shewi*—the fawn and the doe. Both leaves broken, both now useless, their part in the story missing. Whatever wisdom they could bring to his speaking was lost for the moment. He'd have to prepare two replacement leaves, and he had neither the time nor the strength to do so now, as those forming prayers required fasting and days of concentrated attention.

He'd just have to make do without them.

Suddenly, his father's voice echoed in his thoughts. *They's seventy-seven leaves here, cub—no more, no less. They's ages of wisdom tied up in 'em, too. All the stories of the Folk are tied up somehow into them lore-leaves, so you got to give 'em honor and respect. Don't be thinkin' ye can change the stories just 'cause ye don't like what ye'r hearin'. And don't be puttin' some aside thinkin' ye can fool y'self in learnin' the story. They's all necessary, even if ye en't sure of how they go together. Ye'r just part of the story; ye can't always see the whole story until it's passed, if even then.*

Tears sprang to Tobhi's eyes. It had been a while since he'd seen his pepa, Jekobi, or Nenyi, his mema. With all the chaos, he hadn't given much thought to them. He'd always just assumed that they were like the mountains, the Moon—they would always be there.

A sudden chill crept over him. Even the Greatmoon vanished in the world of Men.

His hands trembled over the leaves in his leathery hands. Should he continue? *It en't like I'm tryin' to hide the story,* he thought. *If anythin', I'm tryin' to find out the truth of it. Mebbe them leaves don't matter none to this particular tellin'. It en't like we got much choice, anyhow. It's best to walk into the shadows with a dim lantern than with none at all.*

His pepa's words were wise, certainly, but this situation was different. There wasn't time to follow every detail of the tradition. Besides, it was only two leaves, and he hardly saw what significance they had for the current question. Too much was at stake to give in to fear. He had the gift of Leafspeaking—it would be irresponsible to avoid using it in such a time of need.

Although uncertainty still troubled him, Tobhi slid his fingers through the stack of leaves, feeling each for the warm edge that called to its place in the story. When he'd pulled twenty-five free, his fingers reached out again for more, but he hesitated and nearly jolted out of the deep calm he'd entered—there was an unexpected space in the story, a gap he hadn't expected. He waited a moment longer to see if the gap would close or widen. When nothing further happened, he continued, lifting the twenty-five leaves to the air, following a pattern that opened up before his extended fingers as his mind returned to stillness. One leaf here; the next above it; the next to the far left of the first; the next beneath that one, and so on, until each leaf was in place. Again he pushed his thoughts toward his question, and this time he didn't hesitate.

The pattern glimmered for a moment in the moonlight, and then the leaves began to spin their story, moving back and forth, above and below, spinning faster and faster. Tobhi watched carefully. His eyes grew wide in horror.

Clash of kindred. The Wielder in war. Blood in the water. The Tree falls. Death rides soft wings.

Trembling, Tobhi closed his thoughts to the question. He'd seen enough. The leaves stopped and slowly drifted to the ground, and the Tetawa joined them, his body trembling as the reading became clear.

Tarsa was marching to her death.

"What are we going to do?" Quill asked the next morning, disheartened. They'd spent a restless and uncharacteristically silent night caring for the young Binder, and dread had gradually settled over the Tetawa's heart. She wondered if she'd ever feel safe again.

Denarra sighed and looked down at her hands. "We're just going to have to prepare for the worst. At least we have each other in dreadful times like these." She held up her fingers and examined her painted nails from different angles in the light. "The periwinkle is going to be last month's color in Chalimor, but there's simply no getting around it. We're just going to have to grieve and go on bravely, chin up, a song on our lips and in our hearts, and hope that not too many people notice our regrettable lack of fashion foresight."

"I meant, what are we going to do about *him*?" Quill motioned irritably toward the Binder.

"Oh, of course, darling, of course." Denarra stood and shrugged. "Well, I'm not exactly sure what the end result is going to be, but I don't think he's much of a danger to us right now. He's lost a lot of blood, so he's not too likely to wake up strong enough to cause much mischief, for a little while, anyway. He slept pretty soundly last night. Besides, I've added a few 'special' features to this wagon to protect us from any unfriendly guests, and they didn't make a fuss when we brought him in, so I'd wager that he's not too much of a threat."

"But you said he's a Binder from Eromar. They're the witch-Men, aren't they, the ones who trap spirits with those chained books?" The Tetawa shuddered as her gaze drifted to the strange purple tome laying atop the quilt, but she averted her eyes quickly, as it seemed to respond to her attention, and its awakened interest sent a sickening ripple through the wagon.

Looking back at the bed, Denarra nodded, her eyes dark. "Yes. That book is part of him, wrapped by dark powers into the very weave of his Human soul. It grows with him as he becomes older and ever more powerful. The oldest Binders have massive tomes often carried by groups of unfortunate slaves, as they're much too heavy for the Binder to bear by himself. But they're not the worst of the Dreyd-pledged. The Binders are the middle rank of the order. The Seekers hunt us down and bring us to the Binders, who use their sorcery to force our spirits into their ancient snaring-books. But it's the Reavers who are the worst, Quill. They're the ones who take the powers collected by the Binders and Craft them into terrible conjurations. Vald is said to be a Reaver of incredible power. And I doubt that he'd let a Binder wander free, especially during this awful time. Something's not right here."

A strained voice whispered, "You're right. I'm not what you think."

The she-Kyn and Tetawa turned to see the young Human struggling to sit up. His face was a sickly grey, and a nasty green-and-blue bruise discolored his right cheek, but his eyes were bright.

Stepping in front of Quill, Denarra planted her hands on her hips and glared in irritation. "An eavesdropper as well as a Binder—you're a rather discourteous little vagabond, aren't you? You're *supposed* to be unconscious." She folded her arms. "It's only fair to warn you that I've taken on a few Binders *and* Seekers in my time, so you'd better not try any tricks. I know a thing or two about your kind."

He smiled slightly and slid back into the blankets. "Nothing to fear—I just wanted to let you know that I'm not going to hurt you."

Denarra snorted. "You'd better be more worried about your own hide, boy; we can take care of ourselves."

Quill stepped out and peeked at the Binder, curiosity and suspicion mingled in her eyes. "Denarra—he's not using the Reach-speech." She moved forward slightly. "Who are you? What are you doing here?"

The young Human's smile disappeared. "I'm just a pilgrim heading eastward."

"I've never seen a true pilgrim with such a lovely snaring-book shackled to his wrist, or one wearing such fine silks—they may be tattered and dirty from travel, but they're undeniably of more than modest origin. You'll have to do better than that." Denarra laughed, but there was a hard edge to the sound. "Besides, I saved your scrawny skin, so the least you can do is tell me on whose behalf I ruined my favorite green riding dress."

For a moment the Binder looked as if he might resist, but his wounds and exhaustion were too much. He crumpled back into the blankets. "Merrimyn Hurlbuck."

"Very well—what are you doing all the way here, Merrimyn? Did you see what attacked you? What are you doing here all the way from Eromar City?"

His face flushed and grew petulant, like that of a stubborn child. "My reasons for being here are my own. I told you that I'm not going to hurt you, and I meant it." He turned away, his face toward the wagon's walls.

Denarra swept haughtily toward the door. "I'm bored now, Quill—it's time for supper, anyway. We'll let him sit here and pout in grim solitude. Maybe later he'll be a bit more talkative. I just pray that whatever it is that attacked him isn't still creeping around the camp. After all, my wagon is outside the main circle of the caravan. We probably wouldn't even know if he was being massacred until it was too late. Fortunately, however, we now know his name for the lonely gravestone; I hear it's the way Humans prefer to be memorialized after death . . . for those who are actually missed, that is."

She looked over her shoulder, but Merrimyn remained with his back to the she-Folk, unresponsive except for a slight defensive shrug of his shoulders. As she followed Quill out of the wagon, Denarra called back, "Let us know if you change your mind, Merrimyn Hurlbuck. A good hot meal among friends is a rare thing these days, but we can't have you in the circle if we can't trust you." She shut the door softly behind her.

Jago Chaak was waiting for Quill at the morning campfire. Mother Baraboo embraced Denarra and began regaling her with a breathless story in the Reach-tongue, so Quill was somewhat relieved to have someone to talk with. Ordinarily she'd have been forced to simply look around, a docile and smiling mute.

Jago patted the log beside him. "Where have you been? I was up with the dawn waiting to talk with you."

The Dolltender picked up a small clay bowl and ladled stew into it, then grabbed a chunk of thick grain bread. "We were talking with the Human you came in with."

"Really?" The *fahr*'s eyes grew fearful. "What did he say?"

Sitting down, Quill began to eat. "Not much, although he does speak the Folk-tongue," she said between bites. "He's not very talkative. I don't think he trusts us much."

"Doesn't trust *you*?" Jago laughed. "It seems like it's the wrong way around, doesn't it?"

"Maybe." She went back to her meal. She didn't want to talk about the Binder anymore. She just wanted to eat.

Sensing a shift in her mood, Jago blushed. "I'm sorry—I shouldn't be so direct. We've only just met. Please, forgive me. It's been so long since I've been around another Tetawa so it's easy to forget myself."

Quill smiled gratefully and returned to her meal. They sat together in silence for a long time. Finally, bored and a little bit ashamed, the Dolltender said, "We didn't get much of a chance to talk last night. Who's your family? Why are you all the way out here?"

Jago grinned, grateful for the return to conversation. "I'm glad you asked. I'm a toymaker. My father, Jervik, also made toys, so I learned the craft from him. We lived in a small village near the Tuskwood to the west. I set out on the road after he died, and I've been traveling ever since. The brigands destroyed my wagon, or I'd show you my dolls."

Her eyes shining with interest, Quill put down her bowl. "Your what?"

"Dolls. They're my specialty."

The *firra* clapped her hands together joyfully. "I make dolls, too! Apple-head husk dolls." It was the first time she'd ever met another doll-maker. She wondered if he could speak to his dolls, too, although she rather doubted it, as he referred to them as toys.

"Now this is a rare and wondrous pleasure! My own dolls are painted wood—nothing quite so soft and expressive as apples. I'd be most interested in seeing how you make yours." Jago's enthusiasm nearly matched her own. His bright gaze was so intense that Quill turned away, flushing scarlet. Only one other *fahr* had ever been able to make her blush like this, and he was far away on his own dangerous path.

Something caught her eye beyond the fire. Merrimyn stood in one of Denarra's dressing robes at the edge of the firelight, his shackled arm and snaring-book wrapped tightly in a magenta quilt from the Strangeling's bed. He smiled wanly at the Dolltender and approached.

359

"I hope you don't care if I've changed my mind," the Human said. "You'd better talk to Denarra. She wants to know a little more about you before you get too comfortable."

The Human looked a bit hurt at Quill's curt tone, but he moved in the Strangeling's direction. Her eyes followed him. He was young, perhaps no more than twenty summers, if her limited experience with Humans could be a reliable measure. It was clear, though, that his youth hadn't spared him a hard life. His eyes darted nervously back and forth, watching every movement. His shoulders were hunched slightly, as though anticipating danger from any of the people around him. Last night's attack wasn't the first or only time he'd been hurt; the fading bruises around his neck and shoulders gave testament to a much longer familiarity with pain.

They were too far away to hear, but whatever Merrimyn said to Denarra seemed effective, because she flashed her most charming smile and led the young Binder back to the fire, where Mother Baraboo gave him a hug and a bowl of stew. He sat beside the massive Woman and was soon lost in conversation with her.

"There's no such thing as coincidence," Quill whispered, recalling Denarra's observation as she studied the Binder. "I'm not sure I like what that means." She turned to Jago, but Merrimyn's arrival had ended the conversation. The toymaker was gone.

PROCLAMATION
Declared by His Esteemed Martial Authority,
The Governing Prefect,
LOJAR VALD
Dreydmaster and Pledged Defender of the Sovereign State of Eromar,
Independent Affiliate of the Reach Confederacy.
Dated the Third day of Sun-mark,
one thousand and eight years since the Ascension of the Revered Dreyd

Be it here Declared to all Lawful Citizens of the Sovereign State of Eromar, and to all Lawful Citizens of the Reach Confederacy, that the Insolent, Self-Styled leaders of the Unhumans of the Territory formerly known as THE EVERLAND have been Cast Aside by their Right-Thinking Kindred who seek a lasting Peace with Men.

Be it here Declared to all Lawful Citizens of the Sovereign State of Eromar, and to all Lawful Citizens of the Reach Confederacy, that the Prefect and his Governing Council have long Asserted the Sovereign Rights of Eromar to the Territory formerly known as THE EVERLAND, a Land that Rightfully Belongs under the Authority and Domination of Eromar. The Sovereign Rights of Eromar, and indeed of the Reach Confederacy, can no longer Countenance the Flouting of Law and Order in the Reach by Self-Proclaimed non-Human nations. The Grotesques of the Territory formerly known as THE EVERLAND have too long Threatened the Common Safety, Challenged the established Authority, and Defied the People's Will of Eromar and the Reach Confederacy by Proclaiming an Independence that is not recognized by Law, by Civilized Tradition, or by Sound Judgment.

Be it here Declared to all Lawful Citizens of the Sovereign State of Eromar, and to all Lawful Citizens of the Reach Confederacy, that the Wiser, Braver Leaders of the Territory formerly known as THE EVERLAND have Now been Convinced of the Folly of Resisting the Magnanimity of the Prefect and Council of Eromar, and They have Affixed their Signatures to the Right Lawful Oath of Westward Sanctuary, which Exchanges the Wilderness of the for-mer EVERLAND for Cultivable Lands in the Eastern Expanse of Dûrûk, Procured for the Benefit of the Unhumans of the Territory formerly known as THE EVERLAND by the Sovereign State of Eromar.

Be it here Declared to all Lawful Citizens of the Sovereign State of Eromar, and to all Lawful Citizens of the Reach Confederacy, that the Unhumans of the former EVERLAND are now Legally Bound to Surrender their Claims to their Former Territory, which is Now under the Sovereign Dominion of Eromar, and to Repair in Reasonable Haste to their New Homes in Dûrûk. Those Creatures who Refuse to Acknowledge the Legitimacy of the Oath of Western Sanctuary are henceforth Declared to be Outlaw Lawbreakers and Trespassers, and thus Beyond the Protection of Eromar and the Reach Confederacy. Those Unhumans who Obey the Lawful Authority of Eromar are Hereby granted Safe Passage to those Territories reserved for their Use in Dûrûk.

Be it here Declared to all Lawful Citizens of the Sovereign State of Eromar, and to all Lawful Citizens of the Reach Confederacy, that the Territory formerly known as THE EVERLAND is now under the Sovereign Dominion of Eromar, and thus Under the Authority of the Articles of the Reach-Pact. All Lawful Citizens of Eromar and the Reach Confederacy are Hereby Given Notice that the Territory formerly known as THE EVERLAND is open for Settlement and Lawful Cultivation to those who acknowledge the Authority of the Sovereign State of Eromar and its Prefect and Governing Council through Actions and Oath. The Laws, Customs, and Demands of Eromar are Henceforth the Supreme Authority of the Territory formerly known as THE EVERLAND.

Be it here Declared to all Lawful Citizens of the Sovereign State of Eromar, and to all Lawful Citizens of the Reach Confederacy, that Settlement and Cultivation under the Above Terms is open in Measured Parcels under the Following Guidelines: Unmarried Men may Claim no more than Five Hundred parceled Acres without a Writ of Property from a Designated Land Claims Minister; Married Men without Children may Claim no more than 1,000 Parcels without same Writ; Married Men with Children may Claim no more than 2,500 Parcels without same Writ. Parcels will be Forfeit if less than Half of the Claimed Parcelage is Left in its Present Uncultivated State, but will be Verified by the Land Claims Minister if said Cultivation is Undertaken with Due Diligence.

Be it here Declared to all Lawful Citizens of the Sovereign State of Eromar, and to all Lawful Citizens of the Reach Confederacy, that Settlement is to Begin Immediately, and Will Continue until all Parcels have Been Allotted. All Laws, Customs, and Demands of Eromar will Prevail in Deliberations and Conflicts resulting from Settlement. Any Unhumans of the Territory formerly known as THE EVERLAND who Resist Settlement are henceforth declared Outlaws beyond the Protection of Law. All Lawful Citizens of the Sovereign State of Eromar are hereby Absolved of Penalty in Defending their Persons and their Claimed Property against such Insurgents. All Unhumans who Refuse to Repair to their New Lawful Territories will be Removed by the Martial Representatives of

Eromar and Transported to those Territories, with all Due Care taken for their Swift, Merciful, and Permanent Re-establishment.

This Proclamation is Hereby Authorized by Lojar Vald, Dreydmaster and Governing Prefect, and Witnessed by the Governing Council of the Sovereign State of Eromar. Their Seals are thus Affixed Hereto on the Third day of Sun-mark, Year of Ascension 1,008.

30

Darkenings

AT FIRST JITANI THOUGHT that Sinovian had been injured, or worse; she hadn't seen him resting so quietly in months. He sat on the upper wall of the first great gates to Sheynadwiin, his chin in his hands, as the sister suns rose upward toward the sky. Jitani stood on the far end of the wall. The gates themselves were older than living memory. Some believed that the magnificent gates, drawn together by wyrcraft from the red granite and the living heartwood of two colossal wyrwood trees on either side of the roadway, carefully and cunningly carved with intricate leaf and vine lacework, had been formed by the ancient Makers themselves. The gates once stood wide open, welcoming all to the great city of peace. But that was before the betrayal of the Oathsworn and the subsequent assassination of most of those who'd signed Vald's treaty. Now the gates were shut against both the world beyond and the growing shadow within. It was an unhappy reminder of grim times.

Shaking her head, green hair heavy in the moist morning air, Jitani pulled herself along the narrow ledge to her brother's perch. His stalks twitched, but he ignored her as he stared off to the east. She sat down beside him and followed his gaze.

"Not much smoke this morning," she said. "The Redthorns are keeping the fires in check."

The warrior nodded. "So far. But it's more difficult every day."

"Can we hold the city?"

Sinovian didn't respond for a while. When he did speak, his voice was soft. "Our people are brave and strong, but the days of war and blooding are long past for most of them. I don't know. Perhaps. If we can keep the gates from being breached, we should be able to resist. We have enough food for a few months. Beyond that, I can't tell. This is a place of peace; it was not built with war in mind."

They sat together in silence. After a long time, Sinovian placed his hand on her knee. All was forgiven. It had always been their way, ever since they were hot-tempered saplings sparring with homemade spears and hatchets, neither one giving ground or expecting mercy. They might rage against each other, they might battle and fuss and quarrel and sulk, but they always sat down at the end and let comfortable silence speak their forgiveness for them.

Even so, Jitani had wanted to explain to Sinovian why she'd given her seat on the diplomatic mission to the young Wielder. It wasn't just passion, although the mercenary couldn't deny that motivation—she'd wanted to touch the tattooed she-Kyn from their very first meeting, and the feeling had merely intensified with the realization that Tarsa shared the attraction. Just being in the Wielder's presence made Jitani's remaining sensory stalks throb.

It had been a very long time since she had known such desire. Since the brutal wounding of her younger days, when two of the stalks had been cut off in an ambush, the ability to feel the world and its sensations had diminished, sometimes so much that she wondered if she'd lost the ability to feel anything at all beyond hot anger and cold rage. Tarsa's sudden arrival in Sheynadwiin was a welcome reminder that she could still have such hunger, though the Wielder's subsequent departure to Eromar had considerably complicated matters.

Jitani had wanted to share these reasons with her brother, along with the more relevant one: Tarsa was better suited to the task of helping the diplomats in Eromar. Although Jitani had traveled throughout the lands of Men and understood their words and ways, the Redthorn Wielder walked with a kind of protective innocence that had long been foreign to the golden-eyed adventurer. Jitani had seen far too much of the Reach and its customs; the poisons she would have encountered in Eromar City might well have driven her past the point of endurance. Tarsa was so very strong.

To survive the coming days, Jitani knew that she'd need to hold on to whatever hope still remained in her heart, and she knew too well that Eromar would have extinguished that flickering spark. It was the only thing that kept her sane. It gave strength to her sword arm and fear to her enemies. It enabled her to sit on the great gates of Sheynadwiin and contemplate the peace-city's precarious future without hurling herself headfirst off the walls and into blessed oblivion.

There was so much that she wanted to say to Sinovian, but silence was familiar, and it carried far less risk of misunderstanding. She didn't want to open up another argument, or worry her brother, who was charged with planning the city's defense. They would talk another day, when there was less to burden them both.

Jitani scanned the horizon, knowing that Tarsa wouldn't be there but hoping to see her anyway. Hope. Such a small, fragile thing, but so very powerful. It was what made these dark days bearable.

The dolls were agitated again.

Quill had tried to give them their daily ration of tobacco and cedar, with a bit of corn-mush added as a treat, but they remained clustered together on the bed, their dark eyes boring into her as she tidied the wagon on her scheduled day of chores. For two days now the dolls had refused their meals, preferring instead to sulk. Green Kishka was the most unpleasant about it, with Cornsilk and Mulchworm mostly feigning disinterest.

Quill's tending wasn't going too well these days. She'd tried a couple of different times to sit down, clear her mind, and engage the dolls in conversation, but even before she fully relaxed into the chant, a nagging disquiet would rise up and scatter her thoughts. There was little time for such concentrated ceremonies these days, with all the necessary duties that kept the caravan functioning smoothly, and the addition of Merrimyn to Denarra's wagon cut sharply into the private time she might otherwise have had to speak with the dolls.

But there was something else that made communication that much more difficult. The dolls were afraid. The Skeeger had followed them from Spindletop. They kept trying to speak with her, but the shadow in Quill's mind held them back, so now they stared at her in frustration and fear, pushing hard against that barrier. Sometimes Quill would bolt awake and glance out the window to catch the flash of yellow eyes shining in the night. Even in daytime she could feel the hot track of those eyes on her neck.

Others, too, felt the strain, and stories were spreading. With the exception of Mother Baraboo, Klaus, and Merrimyn, all the Humans now avoided looking at the Dolltender, and some shunned her presence entirely. A few fights had broken out among the performers in the troupe, causing even the gregarious Mother Baraboo to get angry. She waded into each fight, her massive bulk listing precariously, and boxed every ear she could reach, sending all aggrieved parties to opposite sides of the camp until their tempers cooled. Klaus rarely came around anymore, preferring instead to scout around the camp both day and night and keep their elusive stalker at bay. His grim face went gaunt from exhaustion, but he maintained his unyielding vigil in spite of its clear toll on his health. Merrimyn helped around the camp, but he said little to anyone but Denarra and Mother Baraboo, preferring instead to take afternoon rides with the Strangeling or, when Denarra was otherwise occupied, to sit and brood on the steps of the wagon. On occasion, Quill would look up to see the young Man's brown eyes regarding her with a strange, distanced gaze. This didn't ease her discomfort.

Jago had become increasingly clingy and followed Quill everywhere; the Dolltender had never met a more skittish Tetawa in her life. He refused to go anywhere near Merrimyn and had even taken a clear dislike to Denarra and the others. The only person he seemed to regard with any goodwill was Quill, and that growing bond held little appeal for the Dolltender.

Of everyone in the caravan, only Denarra seemed relatively unfazed by the tangible tension. She'd broken off her dalliance with Kinnit, preferring instead to remain with Quill and Merrimyn at night, regaling them with various tales from her many travels throughout the Reach. Quill half suspected that the Strangeling was making up most of the outlandish stories, but as she was in need of distraction, and as Denarra was impossible to dislike, the Tetawa had come to look forward to the evening storytelling session. Even

Merrimyn seemed less burdened by whatever memories and grief had followed him here. He might not have been any less of an enigma to them than before, but he was quickly becoming something of a friendly acquaintance—and perhaps even more than that with Denarra. They'd been spending a great deal of time together lately, especially in the afternoons, when they'd disappear together for hours at a time while Quill sat under Klaus's watchful eye.

The hilly country was becoming more domesticated, with small towns and homesteads scattered throughout the gentling land. Their early evening shows had more of an audience, and twice now they'd been able to stop beside one of the villages and entertain a larger crowd. Although the hills were generally rocky and often rugged, the lower country seemed to grow more fertile as they moved eastward, and massive fields of wheat, corn, and other grains spread out around the road. Quill had never seen anything like these before, as Tetawi crops tended to be small and tightly nestled among their orchards, with all sorts of plants growing in the same soil. These Human farmers seemed to prefer segregated crops that couldn't nourish one another. It hardly seemed a sensible way to cultivate food, but she wasn't a farmer, and this land was so very different from her own, so she just left it as yet another strange mystery of Human behavior.

Chalimor was still well over a week away, and then the truly difficult part of the journey would begin. Quill shuddered. What then? She'd planned to go right up to the Reachwarden and argue her case, but that was before she'd realized just how enormous her task was. The Reachwarden was the single most powerful Man in the Reach, the elected representative of what was clearly a massive and expanding population. Why would he listen to a single little Tetawa? Would he even be able to understand her? Denarra was here now, but would she follow to the end of this journey? What if the Reachwarden refused Quill's plea? Would she ever be able to get back home?

Would she even have a home to go back to?

A loud rapping on the wagon's door broke through Quill's reverie. It was Jago's characteristic knock: five rapid taps, followed by two more. She breathed a deep sigh and swept a scarf over the dolls to hide them from prying eyes.

As Jago consistently refused to enter the wagon, Quill opened the top half and let it swing outward. The *fahr* stood on the stairs and smiled.

"What is it, Jago?" Quill asked, not even trying to keep the irritation from her voice.

He smile wavered. "Well . . . I was just wondering if you might enjoy an afternoon walk. It's a lovely day."

Indeed, the weather was quite fine. They'd been in this site for a couple of days, a small, spring-fed hollow, just off the main track of the Old Windle Road. It was a good place to refill their supplies, as it was nestled in the hills just north of the small town of Widley's Pike. Their first day in the hollow had been marked by unyielding rain, but dawn had brought sunshine and a dry crispness to the air. The perfume of midsummer flowers wafted through the wagons along with the sounds of music rising up from among the wagons. It was a day to treasure.

Jago shifted uncomfortably. Quill blushed, suddenly realizing that she'd ignored his request as she stood lost in her thoughts. For a moment she considered returning to the wagon and finishing her chores, but the sudden urge to run through wildflowers and get away from all the stress and strain of the caravan took hold of her. Besides, Denarra and Merrimyn had been gone most of the day themselves, probably enjoying a ride to the market at Widley's Pike. There was still plenty of daylight remaining; she could get back in time to finish cleaning up.

"Of course I'll go, Jago," she smiled as she untied her apron and threw it on her cot. "It's far too lovely an afternoon to waste it inside." She followed the *fahr* outside, taking special care to shut the door firmly behind her. Jago's mood brightened considerably as they walked away, and his own infectious eagerness took hold of her. They raced each other through the wagons, laughingly dodging various tall people as they rushed toward the wooded hills.

In the shadows of the trees, a large figure watched as the two giggling Tetawi slipped out of the safety of the caravan and moved closer to the forest. There was no need for pursuit . . . not yet. They would arrive in the trees soon enough. He didn't want to surprise his quarry too soon.

The hunt was almost over.

Tarsa crashed through the underbrush, her heart in her throat, as the next blast of the musket exploded behind her. The Men were everywhere. Tobhi and Daladir rolled together into the ravine at her side. The Tetawa's breath was slow; the wide cut on his forehead bothered him more than Tarsa had first thought. Daladir's glance met hers as he pulled Tobhi to his feet.

They could hear voices behind them—the Men weren't going to give up quickly on this pursuit. Taking a deep breath, Tarsa pulled her sensory stalks free of their soiled linen wrappings and slipped both hands into the rich black soil at her feet. As her fingers wove through the roots and around worms and beetles, the *wyr* flowed through her, and she chanted out to the spirits in the trees around them, to those of the deep earth beneath them, to those of the thin stream that soaked through her travel leathers. Even the air responded to her need. A thick cloud of mist rolled down the ravine and swallowed the Folk in its chill embrace. They could hear the Men shouting out in sudden fear, their voices muffled and faint.

A crashing burst echoed through the trees, followed by a sound like branches thrashing in a mighty storm. A deep, rolling groan moved through the earth, and Daladir threw his hands over his ears. The ground trembled again, and again the noise repeated, but closer this time. Sweat streamed down Daladir's face. The fog obscured his vision, but he could hear enough to know that the Men had forgotten all about their quarry—they were fighting for their own lives now. Screams and shouts of pain bounced strangely off the mist-shrouded trees for a long, agonizing time, and then all the he-Kyn could hear was the soft, easy whisper of leaves as they settled back to rest.

Tarsa looked at the he-Kyn, her eyes heavy with exhaustion. "The mist will move ahead of us for a little while, at least until we get near the city. I don't think we'll have any more trouble today—we're almost there, and Sheynadwiin is well defended from outside attacks." She sighed deeply and rewrapped her stalks. "At least these Men will think twice before coming any closer to the city."

Daladir nodded. "These ones, yes, but you can't stop them all."

The Wielder turned away and moved down the ravine.

Tobhi's wound had rattled him a bit and left him with a raging head-ache, but he was soon able to walk on his own, and they started off again. They moved more slowly now. Even with the mist to guard their movements from unfriendly eyes, all three were weak, wounded, and hungry, and although Sheynadwiin was relatively close, they were more in danger now than they'd been since coming back.

Men had never penetrated so far into the Everland, not even dur-ing the Battle of Five Axes, when a small battalion of Mannish troops foolishly entered The Wild to the north to protect Human prospec-tors from Gvaerg and Tetawi attacks. That short, definitive battle left no doubt that the Folk were the sole inheritors of the Everland, and the memory remained strong, even three hundred years later. But now Men roamed freely through the forests and mountains, growing bolder and more brutal as they drove birds, animals, and the other peoples from their ancient homes and deeper into the hidden heart of the Everland.

Daladir watched Tarsa closely. Tobhi had confided the results of his Leafspeaking to the he-Kyn, with the hope that together they could protect the young, willful Wielder from harm, so now they both moved carefully, hoping to challenge whatever evil waited in her future. Tarsa didn't seem to notice, or even to care; her need to reach Sheynadwiin filled her waking thoughts and tormented dreams.

As the Redthorn Wielder came closer, she finally understood what had been driving her for so long: the Tree called to her. She had no choice but to answer.

As they moved out of the ravine and back toward the city, Daladir noticed that although the ground was torn up in places and there were scattered weapons and fragments of clothing, no blood or bod-ies remained behind to mark the devastation.

"Did the earth take them?" he asked, his voice low in the thick murk.

Tarsa turned. "They aren't dead."

"But all those noises, those screams. It sounded like a slaughter."

The Wielder smiled grimly. "That's what I hoped they'd believe. Some fog, a few moving trees and shifting stones, and they scattered like sparrows in a storm."

Daladir looked puzzled. "Why didn't you kill them?"

"I considered it," Tarsa said, moving forward again. "I really wanted them to die. But their bones don't belong on our land. This soil holds and nourishes *our* people, not theirs."

She stopped and looked at Tobhi, whose face was thoughtful. "I've thought about this many times since the last time I fought Men in the Everland. Back then I responded with hate—I hated those Men for digging up our graves and defiling our lands. And I unleashed a terrible abomination upon them." She shook her head. "I wanted them to suffer as I did, to know the suffering all our people are experiencing. But I don't hate them anymore, not after seeing so much pain and hunger when we were in Eromar. Those empty-eyed children . . . all the hope in their lives has been destroyed by the Dreydmaster's unending hunger. He's used his people's fear and need against them. And I don't want to become like him. Even the Men lost in the *wyr*-storm at Gorthac Hall weren't wholly to blame for what they did."

Tarsa's voice wavered for a moment. "That's what Unahi has been trying to teach me. I'm finally coming to understand what she said. It's not enough to be a warrior if your heart is burdened by hate. I can still fight those who mean us harm, and I can still be filled with pain and rage; I'll still kill if I have to. But I'm not going to corrupt everything I love with the poison that has so tormented Eromar. Hate isn't our way. It won't be my way any longer."

They stood together in silence. Suddenly, the fog closed in around them again, thick and clammy. The sound of muffled voices echoed for a moment through the trees, only to be swallowed once more by the thick vapor. Fear again settled down on their spirits. It was impossible to know if these voices belonged to Men or to one of the occasional Kyn patrols in the area, but they weren't interested in finding out. Hearts pounding, they waited for a while longer until the voices faded, and moved again toward Sheynadwiin.

31

Shadow and Smoke

ONE OF QUILL'S FAVORITE SONGS as a cub had been a sweet tune about an adventurous young wildflower who sought freedom and adventure in the wide world beyond sheltered garden walls. As she and Jago picked a thick bouquet of sunflowers, daisies, and strange, cup-shaped purple bulbs with brilliant golden streaks through the petals, her thoughts drifted back to the song, and to the longing she'd once felt to be free from the predictable life of Spindletop.

She'd long ago forgotten that dream, yet now she was here, part of a traveling performance company, living with a flamboyant Strangeling Wielder and a Dreyd spirit-Binder, wandering up a flower-strewn hillside with a strange Tetawa toymaker. Never in her most ambitious dreams would she have imagined such a life, but it wasn't such a bad one, even considering the creature that stalked the night searching for her. In the golden sunshine of the late afternoon, all danger seemed so distant. The only reality was here and now, among the fragrant flowers and whispering grasses. Indeed, she couldn't remember when she'd felt so fully alive.

No, that wasn't exactly true. There was one other time, one that returned to her every night, one that brought both pain and pleasure with its memory. *Etobhi.* Her heart ached with sudden longing. *Where are you, beloved? Have you reached your destination safely? Will you be waiting for me in our little cabin in Spindletop when I return? Will either of us . . .*

She sniffled softly, and Jago looked up from the grass where he was sprawled fanning himself with his hat. "Everything okay?"

"Yes." Quill returned to picking flowers, but the pleasure was gone, and an aching loneliness took its place. Now all she wanted was to be back in the wagon, where she could cry with the dolls, away from the open, eager eyes of this young *fahr.* "I'm just not feeling too good anymore. I probably shouldn't have come."

Jago's face fell. "Well, we probably ought to head back, anyway; it's getting late," he said, his voice soft, and Quill looked up at the hill with a start. She hadn't realized how far away from the caravan they'd wandered. The sun was still above the horizon, but it was descending swiftly.

Wrapping the flowers together with a small ribbon from her pocket, Quill followed the toymaker down the hillside. Jago's shoulders were hunched, and he walked ahead of her with a wounded air. He fancied her; his every movement made that abundantly clear. For a moment the Dolltender thought about explaining everything to him, to let him know that he had nothing to do with her mood, but it was just too much effort. Besides, it wasn't as though she'd ever given him any reason to believe that she had intentions toward him; if anything, she'd become increasingly impatient with his presence over the past few days.

Jago stopped and looked off into the distance. Quill followed his gaze to the top of the hill. Her stomach clenched. In the blinding light of the failing sun, a large shadow moved down the hillside toward them. She couldn't make out any features, but it was enough to send terror surging through her.

"Whatever it is," the toymaker said, "it's awfully tall, and it's coming here." He pointed to the line of thick trees to their right. "We'll never make it to the caravan, but maybe we can lose it in the trees." He grabbed Quill's hand, and they rushed together toward the woods. She could hear something cry out in the distance behind her, but the noise was swallowed by the pounding drum of her heart as she followed Jago down the hill and into the trees.

The smell of dry pine washed over them. They wove back and forth through the trees, feet slipping on the thick bed of brown needles that blanketed the forest floor. She could barely think through the fear. Jago led the way, moving up the hill and down again, back and forth, until all sign of their pursuers and all direction were lost. The light of the approaching sunset streamed through the forest canopy, but the golden shafts of light did little to brighten the trees; if anything, the gathering gloom seemed deeper, more malevolent.

Quill collapsed to the ground, her legs weak. Jago's pale face was flushed now. He looked like a pale bullfrog, his cheeks bulging with each deep breath. They lay on the ground and tried to catch their breath.

"What . . . do we do . . . now?" Quill gasped. Her lungs ached. She wasn't sure if she'd be able to stand, but her mind screamed for her to move. Their pursuers weren't gone yet.

"I don't know," Jago began, and then he screamed. A shadow loomed up from behind Quill. She turned to see a massive figure rise from the enveloping twilight.

Jago's cry became a piercing scream. The shadow dove forward. It grabbed Quill by the arm and flung her to the side, where she rolled headfirst into the bristly trunk of an ancient pine. A strangled howl tore through the trees, but the Dolltender didn't hear it. Her body bruised and battered, her mind stunned by the fall, Quill fell into merciful darkness.

Behind her, after a brief struggle on a thick bed of crushed pine-cones and broken needles, the feast began.

Garyn stood on a rocky outcropping overlooking the city and valley beyond, his cloak wrapped tightly around him in spite of the heat of the night. The forest burned throughout Dardath Vale, the flames lifting high and bright even through the thick smoke that surrounded the city. Men torched the wyrwood trees as a warning, and a promise of more to come. The influence of the Eternity Tree kept the smoke from choking Sheynadwiin, but the rest of the Vale lay cloaked in the ashy fume. Right now a wide assembly of Kyn, Tetawi, and Gvaergs fought to control a few of the blazes that had started in the city; others had taken up arms and prepared for the first wave of invaders.

Guerrilla warfare had kept the first groups of Men from coming too close to the city and other Everland settlements, but as the numbers of invaders grew, harassment and delaying tactics became less successful, and many towns and settlements now lay abandoned as the Folk and Beasts fled into the more inhospitable reaches of the mountains, forests, and deep swamps.

Small groups of warriors still struck at the edge of the advancing horde, but there was little hope that they could fight off an entire army of Men, especially Men armed with the murderous mechanical weaponry of Eromar. These killers knew no honor in war, no restraint or balance. They came to kill, to destroy, and to steal— nothing less. Garyn had hoped that the emissaries he'd dispatched to Chalimor after Tarsa and Tobhi went to Eromar would arrive with a timely reprieve, but there was little hope of that now; any Kyn traveler returning to Sheynadwiin would be dead or captured long before reaching the gates of the city. Besides, the Reachwarden in Chalimor had little support from the Assembly of States to interfere with what Eromar claimed was an entirely domestic matter. No Man had the courage to risk civil war for the Folk, no matter how just the cause.

Now it was a simple choice: fight or surrender. And surrender wasn't a choice at all. They'd prepared for any eventuality, and though they'd fight to keep the invaders from the city, the elders, she-Folk who weren't warriors, and younglings were preparing to flee into the vast cavern system of the Gvaergs, who would hide and protect them. Garyn had also ordered that all the important artifacts of the city be taken to the caves, so wagons full of medicine sashes, codices chronicling the histories and ceremonies of the Folk, rare stone carvings and wyrwood statuary, flutes, baskets, rugs, and other precious articles joined the refugees beneath the earth. If the city fell, Redthorns and other warriors would fade into the forest and strike from the shadows. Yet if the city fell, so would everything, including . . .

Garyn shuddered. No. He had to believe that it wouldn't come to that.

He turned and moved down the trail, back toward the Gallery of Song, to speak to the Wielders. Of all his many counselors, Garyn trusted their guidance the most. It took a little while to get down the cliff face, as the path was narrow and steep, and his bad leg made such movement treacherous. Although his beloved Averyn had protested against the vigil on the cliff, zhe didn't intervene; instead, zhe waited patiently for the Governor at the base of the trail. They walked together in silence, hand in hand, and tried to drive from their thoughts the screams and shouts that filled the air around them.

Only a few Wielders remained at the Gallery of Song, most having gone throughout the city to assist the warriors and wounded as best they could. The Oakfolk elder Grugg and the elder she-Kyn Unahi sat on one of the many benches carved into the lower exterior of the Gallery, sharing a small pipe between them. Garyn's own weariness increased as he looked at them. Those two had spent the better part of the day extinguishing fires; the exhausting toll of their Wielding etched their faces like weathered bark. Yet here they were, at the Governor's request, ready to advise him in this desperate time.

Unahi nodded as Garyn and Averyn approached. "Any sign?"

"None of the raptor scouts have seen sign of aid." Garyn shook his head in resignation. "We can expect no help from Chalimor. I fear that we are now truly alone."

"What of the northern Gvaergs? Are they not concerned with Sheynadwiin's fate?" Grugg's deep, woody voice rose up from the ground, where he had lowered himself to dig his roots into the moist earth. "Do they not know of our need?"

"They know," Averyn acknowledged, "but they're under siege themselves. This was no random movement; it was a carefully planned invasion. Eagle and sparrowhawk messengers have arrived throughout the day to tell us of battles going on to the south, in the Tangletop Forest, between Men and the allied Tetawi and Kyn towns. To the north, in the Wyrmwall Mountains, the Gvaergs are being driven back by Men with massive thunderburst cannons. Even the swamp-dwarfs of Blackfly Fen are under attack and the swamp is aflame. We were prepared for the troops of Eromar but not for the waves of squatters and land-robbers that surged ahead of them. They've had a great deal of help from within, and much of the terrain that we'd expected to slow their advance has been mapped and bypassed by the earlier invaders . . . and by some of the Human merchants we'd once trusted as kith, friends, and allies. Vald's fist is closing over the entire Everland, not just Sheynadwiin."

Unahi frowned and drew deeply on her pipe. "True, but the Tree is *here*. Vald is going to strike us the hardest, because we offer the most powerful resistance, both in fact and in symbol. As long as the Eternity Tree stands, the Folk will be able to withstand the rise of Men."

A thunderous roar split the air, and the earth at their feet exploded, sending them all sprawling. As the noise and smoke subsided, Garyn found himself on the ground trying to catch his breath. Averyn moaned softly behind the Governor; Unahi wheezed loudly on the other side of the bench and struggled to rise. Garyn couldn't sense Grugg's presence.

Through the dust and smoke a stately figure emerged. Her shimmering white robes fluttered on the rising wind in sinuous rhythm with her copper tresses and unbound sensory stalks. In one shapely hand she held a long, silver-hafted axe; in the other, she held the shredded flag of Sheynadwiin—a golden tree on a green field, surrounded by seven leaves representing the seven branches of the Kyn Nation.

"If it is the Tree that holds back our fated future, then perhaps we should remove that unnecessary obstacle," the newcomer said as she casually dropped the flag before Garyn's horrified eyes. A group of armed Shields followed her, bearing between them a still-smoking cannon.

He stared at the ravaged remnants of the city's standard. "Neranda," he whispered, "what have you done?"

"No, dear Uncle—I no longer answer to that name. Have you not heard? My loving people have given me a new name to treasure, a new name that honors the lifetime of sacrifices I have made for them, a new name to reflect the unending toil, the pain, and the misery I have experienced at the hands of those so blinded by shadows that they cannot see the light they so desperately require." She looked toward the waterfall and lifted the axe to her shoulder, red scars bright on her pale blue face. "Remember my new name, dearest uncle, for it will echo throughout history when I finish what the Purging has too long delayed.

"I am Shakar."

32

Playing Games

THE PAIN WAS EXCRUCIATING, but Quill fought to open her eyes. If she was going to die, at least it would be with a fight. She'd come too far and seen too much to surrender to her fate with her eyes shut.

She groaned softly and rolled over. It was still light; she couldn't have been unconscious for too long. A sudden wave of nausea struck her, testing her newfound resolve as she tried to keep the bile from rising. The raging ache in her head remained, but the sickness wasn't as crippling as she'd feared, so she took a deep breath, pulled herself up on trembling knees, and looked around.

Just up the hill from her, beneath the trees, lay a long form, its face obscured by Jago, who sat kneeling with his back to the Dolltender. His shoulders shook.

Her knees still weak, Quill leaned against a tree and slowly stood, using the tree for support. She didn't try to walk; she wasn't sure she'd even be able to stay on her feet. At least the threat was over.

"Are you hurt?" she whispered hoarsely.

Jago, still shaking, didn't respond.

Taking another deep breath, Quill pushed herself forward and was surprised to find that her legs, though shaky, held her weight. With infinite care, she moved up the slope, until she was close enough to see past Jago to the body on the ground.

Her heart froze.

Klaus.

"He's been watching all this time. I should have expected that he'd be here today, too," Jago said, his speech slurred. Quill's legs began to quiver again. The toymaker wasn't crying. He was *laughing*.

"What's happening here, Jago?"

"All these days, all these nights, they've been watching me—all of them, the nasty spies." Jago turned, and Quill let out a strangled shriek. The skin on his face was tight and translucent across a skull that seemed to grow longer and more grotesque as she watched. His watery eyes shimmered yellow in the deepening dusk. But it was the jagged teeth and long, serpentine tongue that riveted the Dolltender's horrified gaze, for they were coated thick and crimson with the blood that steamed from Klaus's savaged chest.

And as she watched, Jago's body *changed*. His arms and legs grew long and mottled, splitting through the Tetawa-sized clothes with ease. Thick, ropy muscles rippled under the writhing skin, and glistening ooze bubbled up on the grey flesh. His hair seemed to be drawn back into the massive head, and long, craggy claws erupted on pale hands where once five small brown digits had held Quill's own. It happened so quickly, and the Dolltender's mouth went dry as the nightmarish figure stood tall before her.

The creature smiled, his bloody teeth shining with a light of their own. "Now, don't you worry about old Klaus, here. He was brave to the end. He even put up a bit of a fight, until I chewed his heart out."

The Dolltender stumbled backward into the old pine. "All this time—it's always been you."

Jago slid toward her with eel-like grace. "Such a smart little dolly." Talons slashed across Quill's face, sending her tumbling and screaming down the slope.

"You're smart, like the rest of them. But not smart enough. I belonged to Magpie Clan, one of the few changelings in the flock. I used to fly for days, unrestrained, unhindered." He loped down the hill and landed beside her again, an eager leer on his face. She held a hand against her cheek to stanch the heavy flow of blood. Her head spun. He was toying with her, drawing out the moment, and the fear, as long as possible.

"They didn't like my games, couldn't understand them, and so they punished me. They threw me from the Clan, and they took away my wings forever." His face twisted, and he snapped his teeth in fury. "They never understood how delicious fear could be—not until they felt it themselves. They took away my Clan-shape, but they couldn't take my power to change, to take new, stronger, hungrier shapes. So I made them play lots of games, and I won every time, until they bored me."

Quill struggled to her feet again. His taunts were meant to scare her, to make his feast that much sweeter. But he'd misjudged the Dolltender. A steady stream of blood dripped down her face, but the fear in her eyes was now mingled with fury.

"That's why you killed poor Bryn, and all the other cubs—they were just *toys* to you?"

"Just toys." He stood tall, and his face went slack. "They thought they were stopping me by stealing my wings, but I didn't need them." He skittered forward on all fours, his body suddenly that of a familiar pale raccoon with yellow eyes, then a slavering, hog-killing hound, and Quill stumbled back, a scream lodged in her throat.

He giggled and moved forward slowly, returning to his monstrous Man-shaped form. "I didn't need them at all. I just went inside and changed *myself*. And it's so much more fun now. They used to be afraid when I'd sneak into their rooms and wrap a rope around their necks before having my fun." Grinning, Jago twisted his hands across an invisible rope and made a cracking noise deep in his throat. "But then—ah! When I became *this*, their terror lasted even longer, even after death. And it was . . . beautiful."

Jago lowered his head, and his eyes flickered orange in the darkness. "But one night, as I was about to have some real fun with a handful of little playthings I lured all alone to a forest, a mean and selfish maggot and her nasty little dollies spoiled all my fun. They took all my soft little toys away from me." He looked up at her. The smile was gone. "They never asked if they could play; they never even said thank you. They just took my toys and left me all alone."

He moved forward, slowly, menacingly. "But I don't like that sort of game. I play by the rules, and I'm going to teach you how to play, too."

Jago's hand slashed out again, but this time Quill was ready, and she dropped to the ground as his claws ripped into the thick bark of the old pine. Jago howled and pulled his hand away. A bloody nail remained embedded in the tree.

"Cheater! You're a cheater! That's *not* the way you play the game!"

The creature lunged again. Quill rolled down the slope, hands scrambling at the ground as she fell, and stumbled to her feet as Jago launched himself into the air and landed on all fours beside her. He caught her this time, and she cried out as his claws tore at her upper shoulder.

Leaning down, his breath hot and rank in the Dolltender's ear, Jago hissed, "I'll show you what happens to cheaters. It's a long, slow lesson that you won't like *one bit!*" The blistered purple length of his squirming tongue slid wetly between his glimmering teeth.

Quill went limp. Jago leaned in, giggling triumphantly, but it was a mistake. On her fall down the wooded hillside, the *firra* had pulled a small, sharp branch from the ground and held it close to her body. Now the creature was close, and she was ready. Quill's hand snapped forward and drove the sharpened point of the stick deep into his left eye, sending yellow slime spurting across her hands and face. Jago threw himself backward with a piercing howl and rolled his face into the dirt, trying desperately to escape the agony.

Leaping to her feet, the Dolltender looked around. The area was thick with dead wood, so she pulled a stout, lichen-rimmed branch from the mulch and swung it with all her strength at Jago's head as he looked up again. The branch caught him full in the mouth, and he rolled shrieking to the ground, leaving teeth, blood, and a chunk of his ravaged tongue behind on the forest floor.

Quill bellowed inarticulately as she swung the branch again. Jago sprang out of the way, and the momentum of the aborted blow set the Dolltender off-balance to tumble hard to the ground. The creature, now insane with rage and pain, threw himself at her.

But he never landed, because the night erupted in a flash of mauve fire that sent the Skeeger crashing into a stand of young pines. Fragments of sap-coated wood rained down on the shapeshifter's writhing body, but it wasn't the pain of the tree branch that pierced his lower belly or the pulsing torment in his shattered face that drew his wails now.

"Let's play a different game, shall we, darling?" A familiar voice echoed eerily through the woods. "I like this one much better than that nasty fun you seem to enjoy so much. I call this new game, 'let's-send-this-vicious-little-degenerate-back-to-the-Darkening-pit-where-he-belongs.' But I should warn you—I play to win." Denarra stepped out of the trees, her emerald eyes blazing, and lifted her right hand in the air, where a ball of blinding purple fire flared to life. She flung the fireball with a deft twist of her wrist, and it caught Jago full in the chest.

"Now, Merrimyn!" she cried out, and the flushed-faced Binder emerged from the darkness to stand beside her with his snaring-book held high. Jago flailed and shrieked, twisting maniacally to free himself from the crackling flames that raged across his body, but he was helpless to resist their combined efforts.

Denarra raised both hands into the air and drew Jago through the air toward her. Filaments of blue lightning now streaked from all directions among the dark trees to wrap around the struggling creature. Merrimyn chanted, his voice strange and resonant, the words unlike anything spoken by mortal Men. The air itself sizzled and hummed. His voice seemed to suck the very life from the green wood around them. Denarra shuddered. The lightning dimmed slightly, and it seemed for a moment that she might collapse, not from the strain of her own Wielding but the nearness of Merrimyn's hungry Crafting. She gritted her teeth. Sweat beaded on her brow, and her auburn hair slipped free of its braided coil, but the Strangeling ignored the distractions and maintained her poise, her hands still holding the Skeeger high from afar. At last, Denarra straightened and grinned widely. The moment of danger had passed, and more lightning streamed out of the forest to wrap ever tighter around Jago's flailing body, lifting him high above the duo.

The Binder held his snaring-book open and thrust it forward toward the thrashing figure. There was a sudden flare of white light, accompanied by a scream of unearthly torment that ripped through the night. Then all went dark. There was a heavy thump, and the Skeeger's Tetawa body fell lifeless to the earth, its spirit lodged firmly within the depths of the snaring-tome. Silence shrouded the darkness, settling heavily on the hillside.

"Denarra?" Quill called out in a trembling voice.

"I'm here, Quill. We both are." The Strangeling suddenly appeared at the Dolltender's side, her body wreathed by a soft blue glow to light her way. She was followed closely by Merrimyn, who held his shackled book tightly to his chest and trembled with the mingled ecstasy and revulsion he always experienced when Crafting.

"Jago . . . is he . . . ?"

"Yes, darling, he's gone. He's not going to hurt you again." She dabbed a kerchief at Quill's bloody cheek and held the shaking Dolltender tightly.

"How did you know where we were?"

Denarra's eyes were soft. "We saw you two in the meadow. Didn't you see us? We were riding as fast as we could. I even called out to you."

"That was you? The sun was in my eyes. I . . . I couldn't see."

"Well, we were just fortunate that Klaus was keeping watch over you both from the forest."

Quill began to cry, her voice lost in her sobs. "Jago . . . k-killed him. I didn't know."

"Shhhh. Of course you didn't. Klaus was a good and loyal friend; he wouldn't have thought twice about protecting you, even with his life. He died honorably. We'll give him a good burial."

<<No, you won't. We have a long journey ahead of us, and we'll be starting . . . now.>> Denarra looked up to see a cloaked Man standing in the clearing, his face obscured by a beaten, broad-brimmed hat. The stranger stepped over Jago's twisted body and looked up, his single blue eye shining in the eerie light.

<<Disappointing. I'd expected you to be a bit more difficult to track down this time. Your penchant for melodramatic pyrotechnics isn't the only thing that hasn't changed, Denarra; you and your friends seem to make a habit of blinding your enemies.>> He kicked Jago's cooling remains. <<Fortunately, some of us have ended up a bit better off than this wretched creature.>>

"Vergis Thane," Denarra whispered, her face suddenly pale. "Wouldn't you know that he'd *insist* on having the better entrance." She sighed and stood up, wiping the dust from her hands.

"Well, darlings, I hate to be the bearer of unhappy news, but we're in *real* trouble now."

33

The Doe and the Fawn

SHEYNADWIIN WAS IN CHAOS. The gates of the city still held against the invading Men, but the battle within was between the Folk themselves. The Shields were locked in battle with the Wielders at the great waterfall. Fire, ice, crackling storm, living stone, walking tree, club, cudgel, axe, and dagger met one another, and blood fell hot and steaming into the pool.

Biggiabba drew rocks down from the cliff above and sent them spinning into the Shields and their followers, but one of the Shields drew a small iron globe from his robes and threw it at the Gvaerg, where it exploded into hundreds of small, piercing splinters that buried themselves in her flesh. Her concentration broken, the rain of stones ceased, and the Shields rushed forward, their axes raised to hew down the ancient Gvaerg.

But then Jitani was at the Wielder's side. A he-Kyn Shield swung his axe at her head, but he was a scholar, not a fighter, and his aim was careless and far too slow. Jitani caught the blade with the edge of her wyrwood sword, using the momentum to twist her body inward and send the weapon flying. In the reverse movement, she brought her sword back down in a wide arc and cut through the stunned Shield, dropping him dead to the ground before he even knew that he'd lost his weapon.

Jitani wasn't alone in coming to Biggiabba's defense. She was joined by her brother, whose own hatchet dripped scarlet. There was no more powerful Redthorn warrior in Sheynadwiin than Sinovian Al'daar, and his raging war-cry reminded everyone of the reason. He moved with a cougar's deadly grace, his scarred body marked with fresh battle-paint and blood, and those few Shields who tried to rush him lay sightless on the reddening earth.

Still, there were many Celestials, and even together Sinovian and Jitani knew that they couldn't hold them all back. The roar of cannon-fire echoed loudly through the city, followed by a chorus of screams near the gates. Civil war within, and invasion without. The great peace-city of the Kyn Nation was falling.

The Redthorn lifted his hatchet and began his death song.

"You might want to wait on that," Tarsa called out as she rushed past him into the crowd of Celestials. She was a green-skinned whirl-wind, Dibadjiibé funneling her fury, the staff piercing armor and flesh with *wyr*-shaped spikes. The Redthorn Wielder was followed by her Tetawa friend and his darting hatchet and a dark-haired he-Kyn who bore the spear of a fallen Redthorn and wielded it against the Celestials with desperate rage. A wild wind erupted around them, wrapping the Shields' own long robes around their legs like winding sheets, dragging them to the ground, where Tobhi struck at their weapon hands. Sinovian, Jitani, and the newcomers fell upon the Celestials like a thunderstorm, pushing them backward and away from the sacred pool. The sudden ferocity of the defense broke the invaders' spirit, and they scattered in panic.

Catching their breath for a moment, Tarsa and Jitani turned to each other and shared a small, secret smile of recognition. It was fleeting but long enough for Daladir to catch the exchange. Its meaning was unmistakable.

"Hurry," Biggiabba called out weakly. "There are many more inside—they're trying to hew the Tree!"

Tarsa nodded and rushed to the cave behind the falls. Tobhi, Jitani, and Sinovian followed closely behind. Daladir trailed them, his face dark with sudden grief.

They had thought it would be difficult to get into the city, but Tarsa had called upon the *wyr* of the earth to guide them swiftly and safely inside. The soil had parted and roots unraveled themselves, opening a newly formed tunnel beneath their feet. When the ground closed over their heads again, Tobhi and Daladir had watched in amazement as a passage spun open through the earth ahead.

That strange cavern oozing with mud, roots, and worms was nothing like the tunnel they were in now that led to the Eternity Tree. This passage radiated the weight of hallowed age, yet there was no time for either of the he-Folk to admire the lichen-covered markings on the wall, or the glowing water that rushed down the center of the tunnel. Already they could hear the clash of arms in the chamber ahead, and Tarsa was running desperately toward the radiance.

The young Wielder reached the standing stones at the bridge and stopped in dismay. The small masked guardian was dead, his head cut apart by a single brutal blow. The shattered remnants of dozens of masks lay scattered across the ground, and hundreds of comets streaked in bloody trails across the shimmering sky above. Tarsa looked ahead to see a pitched battle raging at the edge of the gleaming lake. A handful of Wielders held the shore against twenty or more Shields, but their defenses were weakening, and the invaders gained more ground with each clash of arms. Wielding was impossible in the presence of the Tree, as its power overwhelmed any attempt to call upon the *wyr*, so the guardians depended on their ancient skills with arms and war-craft. In the front ranks stood Unahi, her silver hair flowing free behind her, a bloody club in her hands. It had been many years since she'd last used a weapon to fight an enemy, but she'd never forgotten how to do it. What age had slowed, wisdom had honed to deadly precision.

Tarsa rushed across the bridge, heedless of the danger, and threw herself into the rear ranks of the attackers, Dibadjiibé smashing skulls and slashing bodies with abandon. Unlike the Shields at the waterfall, these Celestials didn't move away. They were steadfast in their purpose and had trained well for such an eventuality. They closed in against her, meeting each blow with their own. Soon Tarsa's warm blood mingled on the dark earth with that of her enemies.

Tobhi reached the bridge and watched Tarsa and the others cut a swath through the Celestials. His eyes moved upward, and he froze. One Shield stood slightly apart from the others, her copper hair falling in long curls, an axe with a glimmering haft in her hands. She

moved forward with grim certainty, toward a bent, silver-haired figure who'd been pushed backward into the water but still fought on,
fiercely undeterred.

No! his mind screamed. *Not her!*

But he knew now that he'd been terribly wrong. *Clash of kindred.*
He'd been so sure that he knew whose death the lore-leaves predicted.
The Wielder in war. The two broken leaves, the gap in the story; there
should have been twenty-seven leaves in the reading, not twenty-five.
Blood in the water. It wasn't Tarsa at all.

The Tree falls.

It was the doe who would die, not the fawn.

Death rides soft wings.

It was Unahi.

Daladir and Jitani rushed into the melee to aid Tarsa, but Tobhi
ran around the swarming mass of Shields and Wielders in raging combat and threw himself into the lake. He lunged forward, splashing
frantically, but fell back as a great tremor tore through the waves.

There was too much death and destruction in this sacred place.
It was breaking the balance, sending catastrophic ripples through the
fabric of the Everland. The Tree was in pain. Tobhi would never
reach the old she-Kyn in time.

Unahi fought on, her stout club holding its own against the
iron blade of a Shield's sword. She never saw the copper-haired
Lawmaker at her back.

Tobhi called out to Tarsa, who turned to see Neranda raise the
axe high.

The Redthorn Wielder struck out furiously, screaming to Unahi,
who'd been pushed nearly to the trunk of the Tree, still unaware of
the danger behind her.

Neranda looked up, her violet eyes shining. With a choking
sob, she brought the silver axe down, splitting Unahi's skull, driving
the elder she-Kyn's body forward, where it was impaled on the iron
blade of the Celestial who faced her. Their bloody task finished, the
Shields pushed Unahi's broken form into the water and stepped back
to the shore.

There was a crack, and a thunderous groan rose up from the
very heart of the Eld Green, as though all of Creation was being
torn apart from within. The stars rained down above the horrified

spectators, the moons and planets faded into endless shadow, and the pool became a raging cauldron of blood. The light of the lake faded, and darkness took its place.

The Eternity Tree fell. From the lightless depths flew thousands of white-faced owls, as quiet as despair.

And in their silent wake came Death.

Cycle Five
The Revenant Oak

The dead bring no comfort when they return, no matter how much you long to see them again in life. The journey to the Spirit World changes them. They still perceive love and pain, fear and joy, but those emotions are like smoke, easy to see but impossible to grasp. The dead forget many things—how else could they endure their halfway existence? But sometimes they remember us, and those are the times when we're in the most danger. If they make the journey back from the Spirit World, they bring a poisonous longing with them; no matter how much love they had for us in life, that poison eats away at our own love of living, moving us from this world to the next before our time, turning us against ourselves. Life is meant to flourish; death is meant to end all things . . . for a short while, at least.

When I was just entering my adulthood, in the cold month of deep-wood slumber when the snows are high in the forest hollows and the dark nights so often ache with loneliness, my favorite uncle died of the wasting sickness. I prayed fervently at his rock-strewn grave that he'd return, for he was one of few in my family who showed me unhesitant love and regard. Later, the following summer, when a friend and sometime lover, Kajia, was killed in a hunting accident, I made the prayer again at the base of her scaffold. One night, some months later, while my spirit wandered in the Dreaming World, they both returned, and they warned me. These prayers are powerful, *they* said, and dangerous. It's a long, difficult journey through the ghostlands to the Waking World, and if I called them across in my prayers, it would change them, and I wouldn't like what they'd become.

In the given way of things, the dead belong for a short while to the Spirit World, but in time they come back to the Middle Place in the fussy, forgetful flesh of wide-eyed seedlings, here to learn again of the terrible beauty of this world. But when our grief drags them back across the ghostlands before their time, the torment of the journey makes them forget what it was to belong to a people. They forget about the balance, and the necessary divide between life and death. All that these tortured souls remember is the hunger and need that called them forth, and they seek it out, thoughtlessly destroying the living as they try to ease a thirst that can never be quenched.

So these loved ones came to me in the Dreaming World to tell me to let them go, to unbind them from my love and loss, to love them enough to let them continue on their given path. And I did, reluctantly. Life and love must always continue. It is the way of the Middle Place. Pain is here, true, but so is passion, and we're not meant to stand between worlds in mourning. We're meant to remember; we're most dangerous when we forget ourselves and our histories.

But for the dead it's much different. The dead are dangerous when they remember.

34

Unforgotten

"DO YOU REMEMBER ME?" the Seeker asked in the trade-tongue, idly scratching his ragged beard, his gravelly voice strangely soft in the heavy silence of the pines. He faced the buxom witch and her two friends—a disheveled she-Brownie with fear-filled eyes and a bloody cheek and a quaking young Man with a Binder's snaring-tome shackled to his wrist—but it was the Strangeling that drew his fixed attention.

"I remember you, Vergis Thane," Denarra replied. She stood straight and proud, her fingers extended, arms tensed and ready.

She didn't wait long.

When Vergis Thane's thoughts wandered through memory, three images rose up to displace all others.

The first was his younger brother Darveth, a golden-haired youth of exceptional courage who'd long looked to Vergis for guidance, his heart full of awe and adoration for his elder sibling. Darveth had been an awkward youth in body, but no one could doubt the courageous determination in his eyes when he reached maturity, or the stubborn jut of his jaw. He had the promising future of a Man of strength and honor.

The second image was of a low wooded valley at the base of a flat-topped butte, the grassy slopes dotted throughout with fat cattle. That herd, branded with the Thane family arms of two fighting goshawks in silhouette, was the brothers' living inheritance, their investment in a promising new life for their mother and sisters, and for the wives and children surely to come. The family had labored and sacrificed much, and within just a few short years Vergis and Darveth Thane were on their way to becoming Men of substance. Their cattle were strong, their house and outbuildings solid, their family well fed and increasingly esteemed among the Human settlements in the Certainty Hills.

The third image that haunted his thoughts was the least welcome but most bewitching, a Fey-Woman with golden skin and bright green eyes who'd come to stay briefly in the bustling trading post of Verdant Grange, not far from the Thane homestead. She and two Unhuman companions were destined westward, to the coastal city of Harudin Holt. A fierce winter storm had blocked the higher mountain passes on the Great Way Road, so they'd decided to wait a few weeks until the weather cleared and Goblin steam-wagons in the employ of the Holt's trading guilds could clear a traveling path for the profitable westward traffic.

From the instant he'd seen her, Darveth was in love with the beguiling Denarra Syrene, and although it was obvious to anyone with clear eyes that the Fey-Woman had no enduring interest in the youth, he'd pursued her with dogged determination. Vergis had warned his brother about her, knowing that no good could come of such a union, even if there had been any interest on her part, but his words were useless, and Darveth continued on, undeterred.

It was then that Thane first began to understand the fickle, unfeeling nature of these Fey-Touched Unhumans, these Fey-Women who fittingly called themselves the "Sisters of Wandering Virtue." Darveth had the desires of a Man, but he was still a boy in experience, and in Denarra he'd found a captivating object of unrequited love. Her early flirtations faded under his persistence. He gave her armfuls of rare hill-country flowers; she returned them to the earth with a shudder and a glare of reproach. He killed a magnificent, six-tined buck and dropped it at her door; she turned away in horror. When a local farmer asked Denarra for a dance at the Spring Planting festival, Darveth challenged him, only to be dismissed with a laugh by the arrogant creature that both Men desired. She'd danced instead with her Unhuman friends and ignored the hungry glances that followed the curve of her shapely hips and the revealing dress, so different from the humble fashions of decent Women. Such was the unthinking cruelty of these she-Fey, unconcerned as they were with the passions they provoked among lonely and love-hungry Men.

And poor Darveth. Each attempt to win Denarra's heart brought nothing but teasing scorn, yet he refused to surrender. He was determined to have her for his wife. He even started naming their future children when he and Vergis checked the cattle in the early evenings, much to his older brother's growing irritation.

Then one night, after they'd finished their rounds, the brothers returned to the house to learn that the upper passes were clear: Denarra and her friends would be leaving the next morning for Harudin Holt. Darveth went wild. <<She can't leave!>> he'd shouted at their mother, who advised caution. <<She just doesn't know how much I need her.>> His voice grew soft. <<If I can just make her understand, she'll stay here with me.>> Shrugging off his brother's comforting hand, Darveth rushed from the homestead, driving his horse mercilessly toward Verdant Grange. Vergis stayed behind, but dread clutched at his heart, and he followed soon after.

When the older Man arrived at the Grange, the place was in an uproar. Darveth had burst into the Unhumans' rooms, sword in hand, demanding to see Denarra. When her friends tried to intervene, he attacked them and forced his way into her bedchamber, where he found her preparing for the next day's journey. He'd locked the door behind him and tried to talk with her, but she wouldn't listen. They argued, and when she turned away from him again, he swung her around and slapped her, hard, knocking her to the floor. He crawled on top of her, weeping and screaming, and held her down, trying to kiss her. All he'd wanted to do was show her how much he loved her, how much he needed her to return that love. But it had all gone wrong, and he was plunged into cold, aching despair as she spat in his face and clawed at him.

The boy couldn't have known that she was a Fey-Touched witch. All he knew was that his dreams were gone, that she'd never loved him or even thought of him as anything more than an amusing nuisance. His desperation, pride, and strength made him dangerous. But she was Fey, treacherous and heartless, and she had no sympathy for what her beauty had done to him. He meant to show her that he wouldn't be any Woman's fool, whether Human or Unhuman. He was a Man, and she'd learn to respect that.

When Vergis arrived at the inn, Denarra's desperate friends had ripped the thick oaken door from its hinges. He rushed in to find Darveth lying in a spreading pool of blood, a long hunting knife broken on the floor beside him, smoke rising from his clothes and charred flesh. Denarra stood over the boy, the glow of purple fire fading in her hands, her eyes glazed and face pale with pain from the deep cuts that Darveth had inflicted across her hands and upper arms.

Vergis knocked her friends aside with a terrible cry and attacked the Fey-witch with his own drawn blade, but Denarra wouldn't be caught off-guard a second time. The dullness in her eyes cleared, and she stood firm, a sinuous wooden staff suddenly flowing into existence in her hands. He lunged low, but he was a simple rancher, unprepared for the twisting coil of crackling violet flame that leaped from her staff, burning into his sword and up his arm, sending him spinning to the ground. He threw himself forward again, but this time she stepped aside and caught the edge of his sword with the impossibly hard end of her own staff. The impact threw off the momentum of his attack, and when she drove against their clashed weapons, he lost his footing and again went sprawling. His sword landed at her feet. He grabbed for it, and she stomped on his fingers, sending the ringing blade under the bed with a decisive kick.

Giving only a backward glance to the broken, sobbing Man who clutched the motionless body of her much-jilted suitor, Denarra gathered her belongings and left the ravaged room, followed closely by her friends.

Vergis carried Darveth home, where the boy was buried the next morning. That evening, Vergis took his weapons and traveling gear and left his ashen-faced mother and weeping sisters with the promise that he'd avenge his brother, no matter how long it might take.

It wasn't that he'd fully approved of his brother's actions. If Darveth had lived, Vergis would have beaten him for trying to take a Woman against her will, even if she was a Fey-creature without morals of her own. There was no honor in rape. But neither was there honor in making a Man into a laughingstock, or denying him the love he rightly deserved. Darveth had wooed her, given her gifts, promised her a fruitful life. Any one of a hundred Women throughout the Certainty Hills would have been more than willing to marry the youth for less than that. Darveth would have been a good, faithful husband to her, but she'd dismissed him, threw him away, and then killed him when her scorn drove him mad.

It was this dismissal as much as the murder that Vergis couldn't forgive. It was one thing to kill him; it was another thing entirely to geld him in the eyes of his family and people before spilling his blood. Darveth had done what he needed to keep his pride, and Denarra had denied him even that. When he was buried, he was a boy, not the Man he should have been.

Vergis knew that he was no match for his brother's killer and her accomplices—not then, anyway. He was just a cattle rancher, more familiar with herding cows through the Blue Sage Valley than tracking three Fey-Women to an unknown city far from home. But he was clever, and he was patient, and he relied on these skills to guide him to Harudin Holt, where he robbed, bullied, and butchered his way through the underbelly of that lawless city, slowly strengthening his skills and learning to push the limits of his abilities, until he found what he was looking for.

They'd lingered in the city for months, enjoying the wild culture of a settlement renowned for its excesses, even hiring themselves as adventurous mercenaries to one of the many trading guilds that ruled the city through guile and force. When Thane picked up their trail, the Unhumans had just left on a raid against some of the many pirate clans that attacked merchant ships off the Reaving Coast Cliffs. By the time they returned, Thane knew where they lived, the names of their employers and friends, and their arrival date, and he'd even been inside their small suite of apartments overlooking the roiling waves that crashed against the city's jagged coastline.

Thane was waiting in their suite when they finally arrived home, drunk and singing a sea-chant, and his attack was swift. The first Fey-Woman stopped and screamed when she saw him silently emerge from the darkness, just before he cut the blue-haired creature down beneath a rain of swift, savage blows. He'd brought his sword down on another one, a green-haired female who dressed more like a Man than a Woman, and cut off two of her head-stalks before she could raise her sword to defend herself, but Denarra had stopped him before he could finish the task. That hated brown staff—which he knew now to be made of ensorcelled wyrwood—exploded again in flames and pushed him away from his wounded prey.

Thane was stronger now, faster and more skilled with sword and Darveth's reforged hunting knife, but Denarra was stronger still, more merciless now that she'd lost one of her friends. She and the stalk-wounded warrior fought back against him, and the blood of all three combatants stained the ornate carpets as the Unhumans drove him out onto the roof where, in a frenzied joint attack, the Fey-warrior's wide-bladed sword tore through his cheek and left eye as the Fey-witch unleashed a bolt of crackling fire that threw him from the roof and into the surging waves below.

He remembered the pain of that night, the smoking flesh of his belly, the hot desire for vengeance that drove against the freezing coastal water, the stubborn Thane pride that kept him from drowning. He remembered the pale-faced Human healer who found him on the rocky shore and introduced him to the philosophies and goals of the Dreydcaste, who were then still a widely dismissed but growing sect whose commitment to the purity of mind, body, and nation had few friends among the sensual masses. And he remembered his *subsequent initiation into the Dreydcaste and his training as a Seeker, which he pursued to aid in his fulfillment of another vow he'd long ago taken over the grave of his beloved younger brother.*

Thane was too much of a pragmatist to pretend that he fully believed in the promises of the Dreyd; the only thing he now believed in was himself. But the Dreydcaste could give him what he wanted, including the freedom to live as he saw fit, with minimal obligations to others. Such an arrangement worked well for both the Man and the institution. Each new bit of training honed his skills, strengthened his flesh, will, and spirit, and made him ever deadlier and more determined. He learned to hunt Unhumans and how to turn aside their foul witchery, all the while knowing that these early lessons would one day serve him well when he once again faced his brother's killer. The weakness of his former life soon faded away, and the name of Vergis Thane came to be known and feared by both Men and Unhumans throughout the Reach. There were more skillful warriors, flashier and more romantic fighters, but there were few blades as certain, and none of their bearers had Thane's patience. What he didn't have in physical strength he more than made up for in unrelenting diligence and cunning.

All these memories haunted his nights and shadowed his days. Two images—brother and home—were lost to him. He'd never been home or even sent word again after they'd buried Darveth; it was likely that one of his sisters had married and now ran the ranch, for his mother was probably long dead. The wounded Fey-warrior who nearly blinded him had largely vanished after that night in Harudin Holt, and although he caught her trail a few times in the years that followed, it had been nearly ten years since he'd seen the last signs of her existence. She'd simply disappeared from the world like mist in the morning sun.

But the other one, the third vision that came to his thoughts in the darkest hours of night—she was a different story altogether. She couldn't seem to keep out of trouble, and she was known in small towns and large cities throughout the Reach, a notorious, unpredictable creature who took an uncanny delight in chaos and devastation. He'd been too busy with his Dreydcaste duties to hunt her down, but he knew that time and patience would one day bring their paths together. If anything was the will of the Dreyd, it was this simple truth: he would one day have justice, for himself, for Darveth, and for the dreams of a peaceful future that the Fey-witch had so cruelly denied.

And he was right. Here she was, after nearly twenty-five years, the treacherous creature who'd murdered his brother and aided in his own disfigurement.

While green-haired Jitani was in Thane's mind when he gazed at his shattered face in a looking-glass, it was the shapely witch's face he saw when a whore recoiled at the sight of the fire-forged scars on his belly; it was the witch's eyes that burned into this thoughts when the pains would come, the scar-tissue deep inside that constantly ate away at his innards, a wound that would never fully heal; it was the witch he recalled when a hunted Unhuman begged for mercy to find only cold scorn in response.

Yes, Vergis Thane had given much thought to Denarra Syrene.

Merrimyn stepped in front of Denarra and Quill, his body trembling with fear but lips tight with determination as he faced one of the deadliest Seekers in all the Reach.

Denarra shook her head and gently pushed him to the side. "While I appreciate the chivalrous concern, darling, I'm no weepy princess in need of a hero with a big codpiece to rescue me. There's not a lot you can do here."

<<Listen to her, boy,>> Thane growled, switching to Reach-speech for emphasis. <<I'm not here for you, although I'm sure the Purifiers in Bashonak will be interested to know that they've got a rogue Binder wandering in the wild. Anyway, that's not my concern. My business is with them.>> He pointed to the Strangeling and the Tetawa. <<Don't interfere, and you're likely to stay healthy for a while longer.>>

Quill looked around in growing despair. She remembered the Man quite clearly from his brief visit to her home that terrible night, and now she understood why his presence had filled her with such dread. He was a Seeker, dedicated to hunting down Wielders and all Folk with *wyr*-rooted talents. But worse still was the icy disdain in his expression; she and Denarra were just *things* to him, and barely that. Even the thin, mocking smile on his face was devoid of humor. He wasn't evil so much as casually unconcerned, and for some reason that was so very much worse.

And the expression on Denarra's face filled Quill with horror, for it was clear that the Strangeling wasn't going to have an easy victory against this enemy, who now stood amidst the litter of shattered pine trees and branches that surrounded Jago's ravaged corpse. If appearances were any measure, Thane wasn't much to look at. Rather plain, even homely by Mannish standards. But even twenty yards away Quill felt his deadly menace and saw thick muscles working beneath the worn leathers. The distance and growing darkness were meaningless to this Man.

Escape was futile. Quill could see that certainty both in Thane's shining eye and in Denarra's resigned gaze.

The Strangeling had no intention of fleeing. She'd dealt with this Man before, more than once, and she was as familiar with his reputation as he was with hers. Of the many enemies she'd encountered in her long adventuring life, he was the only one who still gave her nightmares. That long-ago night in Harudin Holt still burned in her memory, when he rose out of the darkness and butchered Essiana, a gentle she-Kyn fiddler and dear friend. So much pain and death, and all because Denarra had killed Thane's fawning, pimple-faced brother when the boy tried to rape her after months of unrelenting harassment.

The Strangeling had always expected that she'd face the Seeker again, some day. She wasn't certain which of them would walk away this night, but she didn't much like the balance—three to one odds weren't nearly good enough when facing Vergis Thane. For the first time in many years, Denarra Syrene was afraid.

Still, there wasn't any use embracing that unhappy possibility of fate. If she *was* going to die this night, Thane would be taking a few new scars away with him, or at least invest in another eye patch. She clenched her fists. The air crackled and hummed as Denarra called the *wyr*-spirits to her aid.

Thane nodded. It was no less than he'd expected. Her powers had increased significantly over the years.

But so had his.

Almost at the same instant, Thane and Denarra burst into movement. The Wielder's eyes glazed over as she ran forward with arms extended in a wide arc. The air warped and buckled in front of Thane to become a wall of howling wind that snatched his hat into the air and wrapped his long cloak around his body, pinning his arms to his sides. Without stopping to admire the results of her first Wielding, Denarra began the second. She cupped her hands and twisted them back and forth rapidly, as though smoothing a clay ball. There was a sudden flash, and a small globe of writhing blue fire came to life between her carefully manicured fingernails. As her hands moved faster, the globe grew larger, until it was nearly the size of her own head. With a triumphant grin, Denarra dropped the wall of wind and released the crackling ball.

The fireball exploded where Thane had been standing, but Denarra's smile vanished as she saw the Seeker roll to the side with blinding speed. His cloak bulged, and the silver gleam of a knife blade sliced cleanly through the thick cloth. He was free now, and moving forward.

Merrimyn's face contorted in rage, and he moved to intercept Thane, but the Seeker had fought Binders before and knew their limitations—the unusually high number of Binders in parasitic administrative duties among the Dreydcaste was testament to their general uselessness beyond great Crafting rituals. Merrimyn's one victory against the young Seeker he'd killed in southern Eromar made him overconfident; against an enemy like Thane, that was a consequential mistake. Thane met the Binder head-on, using his bulk to drive the spindly youth backward a few steps. Merrimyn cried out in fear, then pain, as one of Thane's callused hands jerked the youth's snaring arm up and away from its protective stance over the closed book. The tome fell open. Thane's knife flashed again, and he plunged it fully into the pages. Merrimyn shrieked in wordless anguish as scarlet-bright blood exploded from the book and showered the two Men. It wasn't a fatal wound—the entire hand would have to be removed for that—but it was more than enough to incapacitate the Binder for the rest of this fight, and perhaps days to follow.

Thane swung toward Denarra, expecting her to be distracted with worry for her fallen friend, but a blistering purple conflagration met him instead. She'd learned many years ago, on that dark night in Harudin Holt, that a battle with Vergis Thane required total attention. Whatever part of her heart ached to help her fallen young friend was shadowed by the immediacy of the battle; sympathy would be their undoing. So she held out her arms, and a slender wooden staff shimmered into existence out of the air. She held it tightly and waited, watching the Seeker's movements with the fixed intensity of a she-wolf.

Thane stumbled back from the wall of fire that singed his beard and eyebrows. He was impressed. In their last battle she'd hesitated, and the cost then was nearly her life. In spite of all the laughable stories about her addled adventures, Thane could see the steely resolve of a hardened *wyr*-warrior beneath those gaudy silks and jewels.

An itching tingle at his back warned Thane that the flame had surrounded him. His eye narrowed. The flames were trouble enough, but he could feel the breathable air swiftly disappearing within the shrinking circle. Of the two, the fire was the better chance. Taking a deep breath, and trusting to the Craftings that offered some protection from Fey-witchery, Thane pulled what remained of his cloak over his face and whispered the protective words as he threw himself through the blazing circle.

It was the moment Denarra was waiting for. She snarled and swung the flowery head of her staff hard against the Man's skull. The staff erupted in golden light, and Thane bellowed as he hurtled through the air and back toward the tree where his horse was loosely tethered. He smashed into the muscled flanks of the screaming animal, and they fell together in a dusty, smoking tangle of bodies and tree limbs. Denarra leaned heavily on her staff, the weight of her Wielding heavy on her spirit, and turned toward Merrimyn, who lay sobbing in a pain-wracked ball.

The Strangeling suddenly staggered. She looked down to see the charred, feathered shaft of a small dart sticking out of her thigh, tossed at the moment Thane emerged from the fire. The warm tremor that pulsed across her skin gave Denarra a good idea of what coated the end of the dart. Not likely a lethal poison, but it would be enough to end this battle, and not in her favor. She shook her head weakly and looked up. The flames had diminished, and just beyond them stood Thane, his face crisscrossed with cuts and small scratches, his cloak in tatters, one boot nearly gone. But he was smiling, and as she sagged to her knees, Denarra knew that she'd lost.

Watching in horrified fascination as the battle began, Quill felt suddenly distanced from the events taking place in front of her. She wanted to help Denarra and Merrimyn, to drive Thane away, but as much as she tried to be mindful of the struggle at hand, something else pulled at her attention.

Time slowed down. The dolls were coming.
Shakka-shakka-shakka. Shakka-shakka-shakka.
She turned to see the trio walking out of the dark forest, their

dried-apple faces bobbing in rhythm with their corn-husk garments. Her eyes bulged. Although she'd long known they were alive, they'd never moved like this before—she'd only ever seen the results of their secretive travels. But now Green Kishka, Mulchworm, and Cornsilk shuffled forward in a line, each step part of a rhythmic dance, moving in a growing circle that edged closer to the Dolltender with each rotation.

Shakka-shakka-shakka. Shakka-shakka-shakka. Shakka-shakka-shakka.

Her eyes grew wider as the air shimmered inside the circle to reveal another night sky, one much different from that of the land of Men. A familiar world opened up to her within the dancing circle, and tears streamed down her face as she saw the Greatmoon of the Everland come into view, its ringed, pearly expanse shining brightly in this strange, faraway land. A wave of homesickness washed over her.

When the dolls reached her, Cornsilk smiled broadly, her polished stone eyes gleaming. *We've got to go, Spider-child. It en't safe here for ye no more,* she said, her rustling voice inside Quill's thoughts.

"I can't go yet. My friends need me."

Green Kishka shook her head. *There en't nothin' we can do for them, cub. But we promised to look after ye, and that's what we're here to do.*

Quill squinted at them in puzzlement. "Vergis Thane is too fast. He'll come after us."

Not where we're goin', he won't, Mulchworm laughed, his wrinkled face pinched tight.

"I don't understand," the Dolltender whispered. "Where *are* we going?"

There en't time to talk now, Spider-child. Cornsilk looked at the skirmish in strangely slowed movement beyond them. *Just know this: we walk the hidden ways of the world, as we did in the Old Times. That's how we served the People, by comin' back in the dried-out bodies of these spirit-dolls, cared for by generations of firra and bringin' guidance from the Spirit World when needed.*

Quill knelt beside the dolls. "Why didn't you ever speak to me before?"

We did, they all insisted, *but only in the Dreamin' World. Ye weren't ready to hear us in the Wakin' Time.*

"And what's different now?"

Yer need is different. If we don't leave here now, the line of Dolltenders will be broken, and we'll fail to serve the People as we was meant to do. Come with us, Spider-child. We must go, now.

Tears welled up in Quill's eyes. She'd heard so many stories from her mema and granny about the dolls, about the joyful friendships they'd shared with the little beings during their own days as Dolltender. Those stories had filled her with such longing as a youngling cub. In the years that followed, when she became the keeper of the dolls, the longing often turned to dejection, for although she never doubted their power, she always wondered what was wrong with her, for they were mute in her presence. She'd despaired of ever really knowing the dolls as the *firra* in her family had done for generations.

Now she'd come into her own, and she could leave with them. But the price was much too high.

"I can't leave my friends," she said, her voice quavering. "Either you take them, too, or the line of Dolltenders ends with me, right here."

A wail broke out from the dolls. *We don't have the strength, Spider-child. There en't enough of us to do the ceremony. We're too few, and they're much too big—they'd draw too much strength from us. We'd need more of our kind to do it.*

A wild look suddenly flared in Quill's eyes. "Then teach me the ceremony."

The dolls stared at her in surprise. *Ye don't know what you're askin'. The teachin's take much more than ye know. If ye failed, ye could kill your friends, all of us, and then there wouldn't be any help. Even if ye do succeed, it will take more from ye than ye know. It demands too much of the livin'. Be sensible!*

"I don't care," the Tetawa said stubbornly. "Those are my friends, and they've saved my life more than once. Let me help you, and let my strength be part of the whole." They looked at each other, and then to her again. "Please do this," she whispered. "I can't leave them behind to die."

Mulchworm sighed heavily. *Just like her granny,* he groaned. *These Spider-Clan firra are goin' to give me an early rot.*

He nodded. *Let's go, then. We're runnin' short of time.*

Even with the sleep poison coursing through her body, the Fey-witch could be dangerous, so Thane moved quickly. She'd already proven more resourceful than he'd expected, and the damage was significant. His head spun; he could barely think through the red haze of pain from a dozen or more injuries. One hand was swollen and useless, at least two fingers broken; blood dripped from his nose and mouth. His left shoulder had been dislocated from the force of being thrown against his now-crippled mare, who lay screaming on the ground, her back hip shattered. At any other time Thane would have killed the creature and put her swiftly out of pain, but not tonight. The Seeker had far more immediate concerns.

As he'd expected, the poison slowed the witch down, but it didn't make her helpless. The ground broke open beneath his feet, and great tree roots shot up through the soil, a swift, woven tangle of dirt-crusted spikes rising to block his way. Even he could feel the suffering of the trees as the desperate Fey-witch twisted them against their will into a dying defensive wall.

But he was close enough to put his next plan into action. Reaching into his belt-pouch with his good hand, Thane removed a thick handful of dull grey granules and tossed them over the barrier. The witch cried out as thousands of minuscule iron shavings rained down on her exposed flesh, searing her skin like a sudden swarm of stinging wasps; even her iron-ward couldn't protect her from this Craft-strengthened weapon. The simplest tools were often the most effective. There would be no more witchery this night, not while the iron blistered her skin and the poison slowed her blood.

He smiled through his battered lips. The Fey-witch was down, and the traitorous Binder with her. It might take him a while, but he'd make it over the tree-root wall and collect his prizes.

Suddenly he stopped and cursed his stupidity. In the heat of battle, he'd forgotten the Brownie.

Thane's good eye peered through the cracks in the barrier, which writhed with slow suffering like hook-skewered worms. He'd half expected her to run away in terror, but what he saw instead filled him with amazement. The Brownie and three small, wizened creatures no taller than her knees were walking in a slow circle, shuffling their feet as they moved. Rivulets of sweat pasted her sandy hair to her brown forehead, but her face was radiant. The Man imagined that he could almost hear her singing, but the screams of the crippled horse were too loud to tell for certain.

<<What is she doing?>> he whispered, then choked on the words as he watched another world open up in the center of the dancers' path. A tunnel shuddered into being, swirling larger and larger with each expanding circle of the dance as the Brownie and her dolls moved toward her wounded friends. The Strangeling wobbled unsteadily to her feet and tugged at the Binder's coat, trying to drag him toward the gate.

Thane cursed with wordless frustration. Taking a deep breath, the Seeker grabbed his left shoulder and heaved himself into the wall with the right, heedless of the blinding pain. He pulled back again and drove onward. Fragments of wood and dirt-crusted roots flew high, and again he lunged at the wall, feeling it give way a bit more with each attack. The pain sent his head spinning, and a wave of sudden nausea nearly forced him to his knees, but his desperation and persistence were rewarded, for at last the barrier crumbled beneath his frantic assault, and he stumbled into the circle.

The gate was closing. The Brownie, her dolls, and the Binder were gone, but the witch was still in sight. Gritting his teeth, Thane jumped out and grabbed the trailing edge of her dress. Denarra screamed and fell forward, her back legs sliding out of the shrinking passage. She spat and kicked and cursed, and his grasp held true until one of her sharp-heeled boots connected with his inflamed left shoulder. He howled in agony, and his fingers released spasmodically. The fabric disappeared from his grasp, and with a soft sigh, the gate slid closed.

Thane lay shaking on the ground. For a moment all he could do was clutch at the broken pine needles and shattered earth as his shoulder pulsed and he vomited his last meager meal. His vision gradually cleared. When he was finally able to breathe without wincing, he slowly rose to his knees, and at last to his shaky feet.

He was alone. He kicked furiously at the crumbling wall, cursing under his breath with each blow, until the movement sent his shoulder spasming again, and he had to stand still to let the rage and dizziness pass. The Fey-witch was gone; her witchery no longer had power, so the ravaged roots slowly returned to the earth. The Seeker pushed his anger down and buried it, but his body still trembled.

Vergis Thane was a patient man, much accustomed to the unexpected and to delays of many kinds. It was one reason he'd survived for so long in an occupation that had killed more Men than he could count. And he knew the Fey-Touched witch and her habits. She wouldn't return to her wagon among the traveling actors—she was too badly injured for that. But she was too vain to go for long without her pretty clothes and fancy playthings. He knew where she'd be soon enough; the brief glimpse he caught of tall spires and bright lights at the tunnel's far end confirmed it. They'd meet again.

And the next meeting would be the last.

35

Hauntings

A LETTER FROM THANAEL TIBB-WOOSTER, Dreydcaste Proselytor
and delegate to the Everland affiliate of the Friends of the Folk, to
the honorable Mardisha Kathek, Friends general secretary (no record
of a response sent):

1,008 Year of Ascension
14th Day of Markmeasure
Dear Madam Secretary,
It is with deep sadness and no small frustration that I inform you of the
temporary suspension of our outreach efforts to the Unhumans of the Ever-
land. The continuing controversy and discord surrounding the passage of the
Oath of Western Sanctuary has made our heretofore-tireless work untenable,
as there is much resentment among the unsanctified, and increasing fear among
the edified. Even these difficulties we might be able to overcome if not for the
influx of the basest sort of Men into these surrendered lands, callous brutes who
seem to delight in proving true all the worst prejudices and expectations of our
opponents among the Unhumans. Our teachings of undying hope and humility
among the enlightened sons and daughters of Men are every day undone by
the thieves and brigands who now claim this soil, and nothing we do will avail
against the daily humiliations our ignorant charges endure.
*   While I have no doubt that the Dreydmaster's purpose and policies are*
noble, the practical reality of those policies is difficult, especially for the Friends,

who have so long labored to teach by our own lived example. We are now overwhelmed with requests for our assistance, and for each Unhuman we assist, ten others stand waiting. There are now few safe havens in these lands, and the Proselytor settlements are islands of relative security, at least for the moment. As much as it pains me to admit it, we have even suspended our Creed instruction for the services provided, as the need is too immediate and our numbers too few.

At present we have five score Kiin and half again that number of Brownies housed in a temple built for no more than forty, with thirty unredeemable half-Beasts in the stable yards. I realize that the latter are quite explicitly outside the purview of my purpose here, but Madam, the Creeds instruct us to be merciful, even to those who have no hope of elevation, and these once-proud creatures have been driven to such an undignified station that even the most rigid adherent to the Supremacy Creed would be moved to tears of pity. And every day more come to us for protection that we simply cannot provide, for not only are our numbers utterly inadequate to the task, we have had our own properties threatened with seizure for our continued service to the unsanctified. How much longer we will be permitted to remain is known only to the blessed Dreyd.

Should we be forced to leave these lands, I have instructed the other Friends in the affiliate to return to Chalimor to share the story of our struggles. I will remain with my charges to further demonstrate the importance of Creed teachings to their own sanctification. We have worked too hard for far too long to surrender in these times of trial. The Unhumans are growing more frightened with each passing day; their faith in their foolish ways of old is greatly weakening. I will walk with them and give them guidance so that they will understand the true purpose of these difficulties. It may well be that these unhappy days will lead us to the victory that has so long evaded our efforts.

In service to the Sanctified,
Your servant,
Friend Thanael

After the Tree fell, the dying began.

Even though less than a month had passed since the destruction of Sheynadwiin, Tobhi's mind could barely contain all the misery of that short time. All he knew was that sleep was always long in coming, and it was unwelcome when it arrived; the nightmares were often just as bad as the horrors he saw in his waking hours. Indeed, he sometimes preferred not to sleep; there was no escape from the consuming darkness that now stalked his dreams. At least in the daytime he could bow his head and turn away from the sights that sent his spirit quailing back in numbed despair.

He was tired beyond imagining, and he was afraid in ways he'd never been before. Past fears were brief moments, temporary frights followed by a defiant, rallied heart. The fear of the Darkening Road was something else entirely. It was the unyielding fear of uncertainty, of watching the world die around you and wondering when you'd be next. It seeped its way into his very bones, dogging his weary steps, settling down with him at night. It was a hated constant companion, and it sapped his spirit until the living world took on the grim grey haze of the ghostlands.

It was no comfort that their path took them westward, toward the land of the dead.

Tobhi had never known the particular fear of dying. He'd always expected that life would endure, that he would see the next dawn and sing its praises. Even the toxic madness of the world of Men wasn't enough to destroy his certainty of purpose; that was one reason why he'd traveled to Eromar City without hesitation. He'd faced death a hundred times before, and in all those times it had never once touched his heart. But it was all different now.

Something inside the little Leafspeaker had vanished in these days of endless death and marching. At one time he might have called this lost thing hope, or anger, even hatred: these were all things that gave a measure of strength. But he knew now that it was something else, more basic and essential to the deepest part of his understanding of the world and his place within it. Without this lost bit of himself there was nothing left.

He'd lost the fire within.

The spark had dimmed with the hundreds who died in those horrible days following the fall of the Eternity Tree, and it faded with each death along the Darkening Road. It had dwindled so much that he didn't even try to find hope in the storied patterns of the lore-leaves; they'd remained wrapped in their red cloth since the fall of Sheynadwiin. All the Folk felt the Tree's destruction. The severing of the link between the People and the land was a cold iron blade in their spirits. They'd fought on, valiantly, desperately, but their hearts were broken, and there was too much hatred against them, too much greed and cruelty and unrelenting madness as Men poured into the sacred valley and set upon its *wyr*-born people like blood-maddened hounds.

The Folk died by sword, club, knife, axe, musket-ball, bolt, and arrow. They died defending themselves, fleeing, or hiding. The weakest were the choicest targets—few younglings and elders survived—and too many she-Folk and zhe-Folk met horrors worse than death at the grasping hands of the Men who found them. Iron was everywhere: in the black smoke that boiled into the sky, in the muddied water that brought no relief to parched tongues, in the blood as lives slipped away and keening wails rose in waves of wordless grief.

After the first bloodbath, the city's survivors were herded together in the ruins of the great Gallery of Song, now a blackened, ash-coated skeleton so utterly decimated that not even the ghost of its glory remained. Tobhi tried to find Tarsa, to learn if she'd survived, but no one had seen her since the destruction of the Tree. Daladir was also missing. The Gvaerg Wielder, Biggiabba, still lived, as did the he-Kyn leader of the Sevenfold Council, Garyn, and good old Molli Rose, the Tetawa Speaker, although she'd nearly lost a foot in the chaos.

Black-nosed Smudge had spotted Tobhi in the first attack and rushed to be by his side, heedless of the horrors taking place around them. Tobhi's initial relief at seeing his four-footed companion turned to sudden panic when he spotted a grinning Man raise his flintlock and take careful aim. The Tetawa screamed and waved his arms, trying to drive Smudge away, but the stag was too far in panic and ran on, nearly reaching his frantic friend when the musket thundered and a crimson blossom burst on the deer's flank. Smudge flipped over, crumpling to the ground, his legs kicking in confusion and remembered desperation as the life-fire drained from his brown eyes.

Tobhi's sudden grief turned to blind rage as the killer approached. Lifting his hatchet, Tobhi let loose a howl and attacked, driving the surprised Man backward with blow after powerful blow in spite of the difference in their size, until another invader, unseen by the furious Leafspeaker, came behind the snarling Tetawa and smashed him in the temple with a hand club. Tobhi didn't know how he ended up with the other exiles after that, but he vaguely remembered the zhe-Kyn healer Averyn patching him up as well as zhe could, hir own face ravaged by grief and filthy with ash and dried blood. There was an ugly red scar on Tobhi's forehead now to match his earlier injury, but he barely remembered it was there any longer; there were other, more important memories crowding his thoughts these days.

Others had lost more than blood or a friend or two. Sethis Du'lorr, the eldest of the Wyrnach Spider-Folk, was the only known survivor of her family—the other three were butchered in the first sweep of Men through Sheynadwiin. She walked alone, head held high, crimson eyes unseeing, speaking to no one, refusing all sustenance, until the day she collapsed at the side of the road and never stood again. The history of her brave, melancholy people—always few—was now lost to the Spirit World, for she was the last of them to stride beneath the suns.

Myrkash, the Beast-Chief, fell at the very gates of the city, although over twenty Men were broken under the great elk's hooves and piercing antlers. His skinned skull and rack now hung on the food wagon, an obscene, bloodstained trophy that brought no glory to its leering possessors. Although the Harpy brood-mother Kishkaxi survived the invasion and was able to escape to her faraway aerie, all her great eagle companions fell to iron-tipped arrows, and their feathers now decorated the belts and hatbands of many a Man who drove the Folk down the Darkening Road.

And what of Guaandak, the Gvaerg Emperor? Sinovian Al'daar, the great Kyn warrior, and his golden-eyed sister, Jitani? Ixis, the Harpy Wielder? Jynni, Tobhi's own wise and loving auntie? So many of the People were lost now. Were they dead? Wounded? How many orphans had fled into the mountains, only to die lost and alone? Did they escape, or were their bones smoldering in the ashen ruins of Sheynadwiin? So many others were fading away. Each morning was filled with weeping, and every night the sky was filled with white, moon-faced owls. No cry escaped the uncanny birds, no flutter of wings announced their arrival. They covered the forest trees, although the branches didn't bend or break from the weight. When the trees thinned and became wind-swept prairie, the carth was a blanket of feathered whiteness, and endless dark eyes watched the camp relentlessly.

The Men seemed oblivious to the owls' presence. Occasionally one of the Folk would grow frantic and rush at the owls to drive them into the air, but the birds would always return to their patient vigil, the only movement their bobbing white heads in the shadows. No one ever spoke about the creatures, or of the fact that with each day's march, more owls appeared in the night. But all the Folk watched and waited with dread for the day when the denizens of the darkness would outweigh those of day.

Too many were dying these days—there was no time for burial or proper condolence ceremonies; nothing more than a brief blessing was allowed each day before they were on the Road westward again. The sufferings of the young ones were the hardest to watch. Some died quickly, in their sleep or while resting against a weak but comforting shoulder. Others were taken by fever and died in wracking pain and endless crying, some orphaned or abandoned and alone. Those families that remained whole watched helplessly, or raged against the sky and the Men in thick black coats who rode spur-bloodied horses beside the walking exiles. Each day the Sheynadwiin Folk became fewer, but even now other Folk from throughout the Everland were joining the exodus, driven forward by Men wearing the three-tined star of Eromar. And with them came other stories of pain and torment. Tobhi had no way of knowing whether his family and friends from the southern Everland were in these new groups, or if they'd managed to join the resistance and avoid capture. He wanted to see his parents and the others, to know they were alive and as healthy as life on the Darkening Road would allow, but another part of him wanted them to be far, far away from this misery-filled world, even if it meant that they'd never touch again. There was no hope of anything here but fear and anguish.

There was one face, though, that often filled his thoughts during these burning stretches of daylight and gave whatever strength came to his step when the inner fire faded and finally vanished under the despair that crushed him down. The presence was brief and fleeting at night, but those glimpses brought the only calm his life had known since the destruction of the great peace-city. Yet he didn't dare hope to see that face again, because he knew now that such hope was doomed to die with so many other precious things on this nightmarish march. He could survive anything but that. He could survive the terrible screams that ripped through the rough camps each night and stole away the slightest shred of much-needed rest. He could survive the rancid meat that twisted his stomach in pain all day long, the gritty, beetle-infested bread that stuck like dirt in his thirsty throat. He could survive the bloody blisters that burst anew each night as he pulled his boots off his swollen feet. He could even survive watching and experiencing the abuse from the Men who drove the Folk westward—the whip across the face, the fist against the bleeding mouth, the boot in the side, the nighttime visitations that too often left their victims crippled or cold with the dawn. All these things Tobhi could endure, but not the thought of Quill sharing in these torments.

Let her be safe, he whispered each morning, gently stroking the red badger sash she'd gifted to him, its surface now stained with sweat, blood, and grime, his empty eyes raised in solemn acknowledgment of the single sun that blazed down upon the Human lands in this too-hot early autumn. *If I never see her again, please, Granny Turtle, let my beloved be safe.*

They passed Eromar City. Tobhi imagined Vald smirking triumphantly as the long procession of the Folk marched slowly across the bridges that flanked the poisoned Orm River on their way to their new "homeland." The Tetawa was too tired and heartbroken to call up hatred for the Dreydmaster. He didn't look at the city or even try to remember when he had felt so defiant and unbreakable by Tarsa's side as they faced down the Prefect of Eromar in naive certainty of their righteous resistance. It was just a memory now. All he could do was put one foot in front of the next, step after step, neither knowing nor caring what would come with the next day. The Darkening Road was the only thing in his thoughts now. It was his past and future. The present was nothing but pain.

There was little conversation on the Road. Most of the Folk had long since fallen into their own mute unhappiness, except those for whom madness was a constant companion. Many exiles had been separated from friends and family, and solitude tended to encourage silence. Some waited until the brief evening encampment to whisper words of hope, comfort, or simple acknowledgment to others, while just as many returned to their solitary sanctuaries and curled into their threadbare blankets. On occasion the strain of a mournful song could be heard faintly wandering through the dark shadows of the camp, but it was always lost to the sounds of ever-present misery that chilled the darkness.

The suffering of the Road was so extreme for the Kyn that their earlier stalk-wrappings were no longer enough to keep the pain from overwhelming them. Now they wrapped long swatches of salvaged cloth around their heads to protect their sensory stalks from both emotional and physical agony. It seemed to help a little. It certainly helped to guard against the blazing sun. Without his hat, lost in the scuffle over Smudge, Tobhi's exposed skin burned and peeled until he followed the example of the Kyn around him. His head-wrapping came from the thin striped blanket of a Tetawa elder who'd died earlier in the journey, given to Tobhi during the one brief visit he'd had with Molli Rose. It wounded Tobhi to cut the love-worn cloth, but it was better to use the cloth for the living than leave such precious things behind for the brigands who prowled the edges of the camp each night and looted the bodies of the dead after the mass of exiles moved on.

The Men who led the Folk down the Road were little better than the outlaws who followed. If anything, they were worse, as they found sadistic pleasure in tormenting the increasingly fragile Folk with foul water and pest-ridden food, inadequate clothing and firewood, late camps and early risings. Each new indignity seemed designed less to destroy the Folk outright than to make them wish for a death long denied. Tobhi couldn't understand why the Men didn't just kill them, instead of dragging them hundreds of miles across the Reach. It didn't much matter. The results seemed calculated to end the same, whether accompanied by humiliation or direct brutality.

There were rebellions, to be sure, and the Folk themselves had curbed some of the worst excesses of their captors. The militiamen now gave the Gvaergs a wide berth after Biggiabba and some of her she-kith went on a rampage and crushed three soldiers into the dust before being subdued and chained to supply wagons. The old Gvaerg Matron may have been devoid of her *wyr*-fed talents since the fall of the Tree, but her massive muscles and thick, nearly impenetrable hide commanded respect. The Men now generally ceased attacking the she-Kyn, zhe-Folk, and *firra* during the night but more out of haste and efficiency than any benevolent change in attitude.

New threats now took the place of these attacks. The Everland had been a place of menace as well as bounty; the Wielders of all the Folk had kept many evils bound in words and rituals, to protect their various peoples and the land from dangers like the malevolent Skeeger shape-shifters and the predatory Stoneskins. Now that the Tree was destroyed, *wyr*-weavings of all kinds were unraveling throughout the Old Everland, and these hungry creatures were freeing themselves and taking advantage of the chaos. Some remained to ravage their fading homeland; others followed the exodus, haunting the shadows, waiting for a lonely traveler to wander too far from the firelight, or feasting on the recently dead and dying as they lay far behind in the lonely darkness.

A more mundane but even more corrosive threat came from both soldiers and lawless Men in settlements along the road. They'd grown bolder as the Folk had grown weaker, and were now giving fermented sour-mash to some of the exiles. In another time this would have offered little trouble. Few Folk had any use for sour-mash madness in times of contentment and security. But the appeal of escape—in mind, if not body—was overwhelming for many. Now the she-Folk found entirely new and unexpected dangers, for it wasn't only Men or monsters who stalked them in the night.

Early one morning, the Leafspeaker awoke to discover that someone had snuck beside him in the night and stolen his boots. Although so worn and tattered that they were hardly sufficient for the journey, they were better than nothing, for to fall behind was surely to die. Tobhi limped through the camp, furious that someone would endanger his life in such a petty way, until he finally spotted the culprit with the boots bound tightly to his thin legs with strips of dirty cloth.

His teeth gritted tightly in barely suppressed rage, Tobhi tackled the thief and raised his clenched fist, ready to strike. "Give me m' boots, ye thievin' sneak!" he hissed, swinging his quarry around to reveal a young he-Tetawa, face pale with terror, an oozing wound on his jaw. The stink of illness and neglect wafted off the gaunt cub, who looked as though he hadn't eaten or slept in days.

Tobhi stared at the youngling with wide-eyed pity. Then he saw the cub's fear. Self-loathing flooded over the Leafspeaker, choking off his words. Tobhi lowered his fist, fell to his knees, and began to weep. *"What are we becomin'?"* he screamed, smashing his hands against the ground until blood streamed down his arms.

When he looked up again, his boots lay in the dirt beside him. The cub was gone.

The days and nights flowed together. Dawn was still a long time away, but Tobhi couldn't sleep. It was a cooler morning than most had been lately, yet he could barely feel the change, for his attention was focused on the increasing pain in his right knee. It had started off as a simple twinge that he could ignore in favor of the innumerable other aches that gripped his body; he had no idea that such a small frame could hold so much pain. But the knee grew worse as the days went on, until each step was like a broken stone blade under the flesh. Without adequate time to rest, evening encampments brought him only slight relief, and the rigors of the following day stripped away any hope of healing.

But no matter how bad the pain was, he couldn't stop walking. Those left behind were easy prey for the scavenger Men who lurked beyond the soldiers. There were a few healers left among the Folk in this group, but they were generally overburdened with those far more injured than the little Leafspeaker. He would have to keep going. Death was the only other option, and even after all the horrors he'd witnessed and experienced, it was no real option at all. Not yet.

"When do you think they'll let us go?" a voice whispered. Tobhi turned to the old he-Kyn who sat up from beneath a thin blanket beside him. The Tetawa had seen the elder many times during the long death march, but they'd never spoken. He hadn't really spoken to anyone in days, maybe longer. He couldn't actually remember the last time he'd had a conversation with another person. For a moment he thought about ignoring the question, but he was lonely, and there was a sudden surge of need, a longing to speak and to be heard, to feel someone respond to his living presence. He needed to know that he was really still alive.

Tobhi's voice was thin and raspy. "I don't know. It don't . . . it don't seem like they're ever gonna do it."

The he-Kyn nodded sadly. His head was wrapped in a filthy fringed blue cloth from what looked like the remnants of a coat sewn loosely together. The thick wrinkles on his face left his features pinched and tired. "What will we do when it's over? It seems like the Road is all I can remember now. It's all I know; it's everything."

"Me, too," Tobhi whispered, grief rising up, threatening to choke off any other words. They sat together in silence for a while. Finally, the Tetawa turned and said, "M' name's Tobhi. M' people are Badgers, from Birchbark Hollow."

"Braachan, of Apple Branch." The he-Kyn smiled weakly. "I remember you from the Sevenfold Council. You were with the fiery young Wielder during her speech."

The Leafspeaker nodded. "I was. I don't remember seein' ye, though. Where was you sittin'?"

"You probably didn't see me. I was with my brethren behind the screen."

Tobhi's face darkened. "Behind the screen?" he spat with sudden vehemence. "Then ye're one of them twice-cursed Shields, and a bad death would be too good for yer treacherous skin. What're ye doin' here with us? E'nt ye s'posed to be collectin' yer blood money from Eromar? Why don't ye be on yer way and leave the rest of us to die in peace."

The old he-Kyn turned away, but his voice held more hurt than anger. "Not all Shields are traitors, Tobhi. You haven't the right to blame us all for the offenses of a misguided few. We're Folk, too, just like everyone here. We have no love of the Dreydmaster or his minions, and we didn't all desire to leave our homeland behind."

"Mebbe so, but it don't change the fact that none of this would'a happened if not for yer hate for the Old Ways and the Tree. It was yer whole way of lookin' at the world that brought us here, as much as Vald and his earth-killin' poisons. Ye'r as much to blame as he is."

"My dedication to the Celestial Path doesn't imply a hatred of Greenwalkers, Tobhi. Love of one needn't depend upon destruction of the other." His voice grew softer. "The Celestial Path was never intended to destroy the Deep Green, not by those who really understood it. It was simply another path to understanding. It gives me something that the Green couldn't, just as the Green gives to its followers something unique for them. The Purging of the Wielders should never have happened; it was an abomination, as much to the *true* teachings of the Celestials as to those of the Wielders. It was more about power and fear and shortsightedness than about our Great Mother-Tree Zhaia and Her wisdom. The destruction of the Eternity Tree shouldn't have happened, either. The stars don't shine any brighter when the earth is broken and barren. Too many have forgotten these teachings."

Tobhi looked at the he-Kyn with puzzlement. He'd known very few Shields in his lifetime—they were generally unwelcome among

Tetawi, who much preferred to be left alone and to be helped by their various Wielders and Wielder-kin: Beastwalkers, Dolltenders, Cropminders, Leafspeakers, and others. Those Shields he'd known were far closer to the treasonous Shakar than to Braachan, who seemed entirely different from those proud, aloof Kyn. Shakar and her kind made no room for other ways of living and believing; it was the One Moon Path of mind purity and body scorn for all, or nothing, and Braachan's words would surely have been nothing short of heresy to their thinking. This he-Kyn troubled the Tetawa, but there was a peace about him that was missing from those other Shields.

Still, Braachan might be a Celestial of peaceful principle, but his was not the guiding voice of their kind, nor from what Tobhi could see did it carry much influence. The Leafspeaker could not drive away the memory of the mass of murderous Celestials as they rushed toward the Tree, their white robes stained with the blood of their kith, nor could he easily dismiss the burning violet eyes of one copper-haired Shield as her shining axe came swinging down toward brave old Unahi.

He closed his eyes against the image. It was too much. He'd grown quite fond of the elder Wielder during their brief time together, and it had been a point of brotherly pride to know that he could help care for her niece when Unahi wasn't around. Now they were both gone, and he had failed.

A single tear trickled down his grimy face. He hurriedly wiped it away and curled into his blanket with his back to the he-Kyn. The stink of the journey washed over him again, as it always did when he let the pain bubble to the surface. *Great Badger, what I wouldn't give for a bath!*

Braachan didn't say anything else, and soon Tobhi heard the he-Kyn's breath rising and falling in a soft, regular rhythm, interrupted only by the occasional soft cough or groan. But it was a long time before the Leafspeaker was able to fall asleep, and the pain that kept him awake had nothing to do with his knee.

Braachan looked worried. "Here, use my walking stick."

"I don't want yer help," Tobhi snapped. After a moment he shook his head. "Sorry. I en't tryin' to be ungrateful; I know ye'r only tryin' to help. But ye'r gonna need that stick more than me. No reason to waste it."

After their initial introduction, Braachan made a point of seeking out the Tetawa, even though Tobhi tried to avoid his presence. But the he-Kyn seemed harmless, and it was nice to have someone to talk with regularly, even if the conversation consisted mostly of insignificant comments on the weather, the length of the day's march, or the changing landscape.

There was little indeed to say about their surroundings. Western Eromar seemed to be little more than brown grasslands stunted and worn by the merciless winds that tore through the prairie with maddening regularity. They encountered few Men other than the militiamen around them and the thugs behind, though the Road seemed well traveled. It was a stark and desolate land for those who had spent their lives in deep green forests and high mountain valleys. They felt exposed in the day beneath the wide sky, utterly vulnerable to the one-sun world. The star-choked heavens, far from the belching smokestacks of the Eromar City factories, might have given comfort if not for the owls. Instead, night simply heightened their sense of passing through a strange and hostile land. Being watched and dominated by Men was bad enough; now the earth itself seemed ready to strike at the Folk.

For two days Tobhi had struggled to keep up with the rest, and for two days the pain in his knee had grown worse. The daily heat made things even more difficult, as he felt himself wilting with each step under the blazing sun. The only time the soldiers let the Folk rest was when the Men couldn't stand the heat anymore themselves. They were pushing hard ahead, at any cost, for a purpose that was yet unknown. The dead and exhausted were left where they fell; there was no time for mourning or aid. Tobhi wouldn't be able to keep up the pace, and he knew it. So did Braachan, and for whatever reason, the old he-Kyn seemed almost desperate to help the Leafspeaker endure.

"Please, Tobhi, I insist. Use my walking stick. We can take turns, if you prefer." He held out the well-worn staff of twisted walnut. Sighing deeply, Tobhi took the stick and managed a thin smile of gratitude.

"I lost m' hatchet in the battle; it made for a pretty handy stick when I needed it." He peered off into the distance. "I imagine it'll be a while 'til I can get m'self another bit of wood like that, 'specially if we stay much longer in this damned treeless country. Don't know who'd want to live here. It en't fit for nobody but wind-addled flatlanders."

Braachan leaned forward and slid his hand under Tobhi's right arm to steady the Tetawa as they walked. "I do hope they don't leave us here. Where would we live? What would we eat? It would almost be kinder to just slaughter us now than to leave us to linger in this place."

Tobhi sucked at his teeth. He felt it, too. It wasn't just that this land was so different from the Old Everland in spirit; it was fundamentally different in form, too. They could find edible foods in most any place. He'd seen enough antelope and rabbits to know that there was enough for bodily sustenance in the grasslands. It was the other things that worried him, especially medicinals. Each people of the seven Folk had ancient knowledge about the healing plants and herbs that grew in their various lands. But this knowledge was rooted in their relationship with that very soil, and it was specialized in ways that took years to understand. It would normally take generations to learn about the spirits of a place, but the *wyr*-draining influence of the Man-lands made the normal process so much harder. What new sicknesses would they find in this new world? Would they be able to find medicinals similar to those of their old homelands, or would they be helpless? Would they ever be able to speak to the spirits of this strange place? If not, their vulnerability would increase dramatically. Worse still, the strange autumn heat, the rigors of the journey, and the inedible food was weakening even the strongest of the exiles. Winter wasn't that far away. What would happen if the snows came too soon? They were utterly unprepared for winter and its certain cruelty on these wind-blasted lands. Things seemed about as bad as they could get now, but winter's devastation would be beyond imagining.

Tobhi's knee suddenly buckled, and he cried out as he smashed to the ground, the walking stick snapping beneath him. Agony and despair overwhelmed him. It was over. There was no use continuing; it would be best to just finish it instead of lingering on to become a desperate wraith in some faraway country, torn from kith and ceremony. At least here he still had his memories of home. If he went on, even those would be swept away in the ever desperate search for hope. He didn't want it anymore. He just wanted to be left alone.

Callused hands clutched at Tobhi's shoulder, but he remained on the ground, unmoving. He could hear Braachan's voice calling to him, then the growl of a Man telling the old he-Kyn to keep walking. A boot smashed into the Leafspeaker's side, and excruciating pain filled his senses, but then he felt the pain slip away, and no kick followed the first. He opened his eyes slightly. Bloody, bandaged feet marched past, tattered boots, thick-soled bare feet, dusty hooves, claws, talons, and pads, hundreds in all shapes and sizes moving forward in a slow, erratic rhythm. He watched them, detached but slightly pleased to be free of the need to continue. His eyes closed, and he drifted away into darkness.

When Tobhi opened his grit-rimmed eyes, it was still daylight, although the solitary sun moved swiftly toward an orange dusk. Waves of heat still radiated off the rolling grasslands. His only companions were a couple of mean-eyed buzzards who glared at him, as if annoyed at his rudeness for not being dead. He shared their confusion, if not their motivation. For a moment he wondered if he actually might have passed beyond the mortal world, but the burning thirst in his cracked and dusty mouth was evidence enough of life— if the old Tetawi stories were true, as they so often were, the dead certainly wouldn't be thirsty. His hair was tangled and matted with dried blood; he couldn't remember the last time he'd washed it.

Tobhi waited for a long time to move, but when there was no doubt that he wasn't dead, and that the buzzards weren't likely to go away on their own, he painstakingly pulled himself up, and promptly collapsed again. After a few more false starts, he finally made it to his knees and remained there, unsteady but determined. The buzzards hissed and flapped away in disgust. Looking toward the west, he saw the wide stretch of dusty road and beaten grass that moved far into the horizon, but he didn't see any of the uprooted Folk or the Men who drove them forward. Except for a couple of buzzard-mobbed bodies lying motionless on the rough path in the distance, he was the only Folk in sight.

A sudden chill went up his spine. He might be alone at present, but the Human and monstrous scavengers who followed behind the exiles would be along shortly—the pickings were good these days, and the Men were well armed with iron and other poisons. If not for Vald's soldiers and their unknown reasons for protecting their wards from further attack, these various two-legged parasites would have decimated the Folk long ago. A single crippled Tetawa would pose no problem to them, especially one weakened by thirst, hunger, and heartbreak.

Still, death by oblivion was one thing. Allowing himself to be murdered was another entirely. Tobhi looked to the east and groaned. He could see them now, a line of figures in the far distance, moving fast. They would reach him by sunset.

He tried to stand, hoping to hobble into the tall grass and find a hiding place, but the pain in his injured leg was too much, and he collapsed again with a groan. His knee wouldn't possibly hold his weight.

He scanned the ground for options. The grass beside the road was matted down for a long distance, but a couple of wide depressions beneath the broken vegetation caught his attention. An idea suddenly took hold of his thoughts. He might not be able to hide above the ground, but escape might be possible *below* it. He didn't know much about this land, but there was one thing he could recognize, even in this alien place: he knew the look of badger territory. He was, after all, born to the Badger Clan, and the spirit of Buborru the Keeper, wisdom-bearer of the Tetawi Clans, was in the Burrows blood.

Taking a deep breath, Tobhi pulled himself forward on his elbows, ignoring the pain as sharp stones tore into his tender flesh. It took longer than he expected to get to the dip in the grass. By the time he reached it the daylight had turned crimson, stretching like a bloody stain across the prairie. The Men would see him soon, and then there would be no opportunity for escape.

He dug into the grass and pulled thick wads free of the hole, spreading dry brown soil across his fingers. It was as he'd hoped—an old badger burrow, not long abandoned, if the musty odor was any indication. The residue of the badger's presence and scent marking was still strong; a young and vigorous male, off to find a mate or a slow-witted ground squirrel. For a moment Tobhi felt woefully alone, until he realized that, had a badger been in the hole, he might have had to send it fleeing into the very danger he himself was trying to avoid.

Still, he realized with growing desperation, it would be good to have a badger's help, as the hole was too small—he couldn't fit. His wide brown hands dug frantically at the dirt, which crumbled in his fingers and collapsed into the tunnel, filling it further with each movement he made. The heat and drought had damaged the soil and weakened the den walls. Even if it had been large enough, the burrow might well have fallen in as he tried to dig into it.

This knowledge didn't stop his digging. It was still his best choice, his only real hope. He was much too big for the hole, but if he could just open enough to drag part of his body into it and then pull the broken grass back over his exposed body, the fading light might be enough to hide him. He had to try. Frustration burned his eyes as the dirt flew. His hands moved faster and faster, digging deeper and deeper as soil fell again.

The soft crunch of boots on dry grass nearby brought an end to the Leafspeaker's efforts. He stopped digging and remained head first in the hole, breathing heavily, tensing for the attack. If he was going to die, he'd do it with some measure of dignity. Badger Clan was proud and defiant—he was too weak to put up much of a fight, but he'd at least draw blood before dying.

His teeth bared, Tobhi spun around with a snarl. At first he couldn't tell what he was looking at, as the blazing light of the prairie sunset burned so brightly on the figure. It wasn't until something dropped beside him that he began to comprehend.

The familiar shape was battered, worn, and slightly more crumpled than it had been the last time he'd seen it, but there was no doubt about it.

It was his hat.

"I think you dropped this a little ways back, little brother," Tarsa said as she knelt down and pulled the Leafspeaker to her. Tobhi trembled in disbelief for a moment, then collapsed in her arms, his body shaking with sobs of joy and relief. She gently rocked him, her fingers stroking his hair, and soothed him like a frightened cub awakening from a nightmare that had lasted much too long.

He pulled away and looked at her, as though unable to make himself believe that she was really there. "But Tarsa, where've ye been? I thought ye died."

She smiled. Her face was lined with sadness, but there was something new in her turquoise eyes that Tobhi couldn't quite understand, a strength in her arms that went beyond the tight muscles of a trained Redthorn warrior. "We were separated in the great chamber of the Tree—I couldn't find you. Jitani and Sinovian saved us. We've been following you for weeks."

Tobhi was dizzy—Tarsa was alive. If she still lived, then others lived, too. The heart-spark was rekindled, flickering uncertainly. He looked over her shoulder to see Daladir, Jitani, a small group of hard-eyed Folk, and even a few Humans dressed in Kyn travel garb. The Tetawa turned back to the she-Kyn.

"It happened so fast. I tried to find ye too, but them Men and Shields was everywhere, and then I was bein' pushed out of the city. Last thing I really remember clearly is the Tree fallin'." His voice went hoarse. "Tarsa, I saw Unahi die, in the lore-leaves, before we got to the city. I didn't know it'd be her. I didn't know that her death would destroy the Tree. I would've said somethin'—."

The Wielder's eyes glowed strangely in the fading light of the setting sun. "The Tree wasn't destroyed, Tobhi."

"What d'ye mean?" he whispered. "It was—we all felt it. It was like the heart was torn right out of me. I en't never hurt like that. The Wielders can't touch the *wyr* no more. It's all gone."

"No, Tobhi. It's not gone. It's just changed, that's all." A cool emerald flame flowed across Tarsa's skin and over the Tetawa's body, and he felt the spirit-deep exhaustion vanish in the healing fire that suddenly surged through his veins. There was no more pain, no more fear. He gasped with surprise and delight and watched the flame rise into the air to become a blazing shower of radiant green sparks. The grass danced around the pair, and the wind tousled their shining hair. The sparks scattered on the wind to fall on the parched earth, where lush vegetation erupted through the dry soil and spread out in wild, joyful abundance. Tobhi could smell the sweet perfume of rain and flowers. The Wielder's unbraided hair rose up like liquid bronze, and her sensory stalks moved in an easy, gentle rhythm, like willow branches adrift on a cooling summer breeze.

"The Tree is fallen, but it still endures." The green glow faded, but Tarsa's eyes still shone with blue fire. "I am the Eternity Tree, Tobhi. And now, so are you."

36

Truth

THICK BLUE SMOKE HUNG like a gossamer curtain in the parlor, so dense that Padwacket could barely see the other side of the room. He smiled, well satisfied with the purchase. Lower Rinj smoke-leaf was hard to find in these days of increasingly erratic trade through Eromar, but it was undeniably worth both the expense and the trouble. Eight months of savings, two months of waiting, and a few not-quite-legal favors went into this small purchase. Now, at long last, he had the time and solitude to enjoy one of his preferred vices. He was determined to savor the experience.

The Ubbetuk loosened his cravat and nestled deeper into the red plush sofa. His eyelids grew heavy, and he felt the sweet bite of the smoke on his tongue as he took another deep draw on the brass pipe. It made his head spin a bit, but unlike most Ubbetuk in his position, Padwacket had no deep-seated desire to maintain constant control over his mind and behavior. Even if such a silly principle had intruded into his character, it would hardly have been an advantage in this household, where a smoke-addled mind gave things a more calming perspective.

The world seemed to sink into a haze of drifting tingles, and a low moan of pleasure slipped from his grey lips. He reached out with exquisite lethargy for the wine decanter on the sideboard but stopped as a jingling noise in the hallway caught his attention. Someone with a key was coming to the parlor, someone with a firm purpose.

Sudden panic set in. Padwacket leapt up and rushed to a window to clear out some of the smoke, cursing himself for his inattention. Meggie Mar had no love of smoking, and the slightest hint of smoke in the parlor rugs or draperies would unleash her freckled fury. She had an uncanny nose for the stuff, although, sadly, she didn't discriminate between common ditch-weed leaf and premium stock like Lower Rinj. It hardly mattered that Padwacket was the head valet and ostensibly beyond the authority of the house-matron—all were trembling vassals in Meggie Mar's domestic domain.

He threw open the window and cursed. The unnatural heat of the evening provided no cross-breeze to pull the smoke outside; if anything, it simply added the heavy stink of rotting fish and other pungent sea life to the mix. The door shuddered slightly, and the rattle of keys in the corridor beyond echoed eerily in the claustrophobic room. In desperation, Padwacket grabbed the edge of a heavy red curtain and tried to wave it back and forth to encourage the smoke to move outward. But the curtain was too big, his movements too abrupt, and the Ubbetuk squeaked in terror as the velvet tore away from the hanging rod and the entire mass of cloth tumbled down, swallowing his flailing body in its thick folds. He fought for escape until he heard the door open and someone enter the room. He was caught. Resigning himself to his fate, which would no doubt include an hours-long lecture and painful ear pulling, Padwacket poked his head out of the red fabric, only to see an unexpected figure shaking her head.

"Really, darling, I hardly think that a change of drapes is necessary at this time of night, especially with everything else that's been taking place lately. Have you discussed this with Meggie Mar? I'm not entirely sure she'd approve." Denarra walked over to the open window and looked out. "No, I'm quite sure she's not going to be happy about this at all. Well, we'll worry about that in the morning. You'll be sure to tell her, won't you? In the meantime, let's close this window. This ghastly heat is making all of Chalimor smell like a cod-fisher's privy. This is hardly the cultivated atmosphere I promised my guests."

The Strangeling turned and sat in the chair opposite Padwacket's sofa. "I've never known such an autumn. These past few weeks have been absolutely exhausting. Do you have any idea how difficult it is to get a free moment with the Reachwarden? The Man is like a ghost, flitting here and there, always at a different party from the one I'm attending. It's almost as if he's intentionally trying to avoid me."

Finally free of the clinging curtain, Padwacket stood, smoothed his vest, and wiped a layer of fine red lint from his pendulous nose. He poured two glasses of amber-colored wine from the sideboard and handed one to Denarra, who nodded appreciatively.

"Perhaps a direct meeting would be more profitable than the casual encounter. It seems rather unlikely that he would make himself available for an issue of such significance during a mere dinner party." The Ubbetuk drained his glass.

"I've tried that already," Denarra pouted. "He won't return my letters or answer my queries. His private secretary refused to sign my name to the audience register for the next three months." She glowered as she sipped the wine. "That hateful little bureaucrat has far too much nose hair to be entirely trustworthy."

Padwacket refilled his glass. "Yes, one's true moral character is generally reflected in one's nasal hygiene," he said dryly, his eyes wandering over to the still-smoking pipe on the end table beside his sofa.

"I couldn't agree more," Denarra said, nodding absently. She held the glass up and swirled the golden liquid around, watching as bubbles drifted through the wine like pearls. "Chalimor has changed since I've been gone, hasn't it, Padwacket?"

Yes, he thought to himself as he cast a quick glance at the dozens of small, pitted scars on her upheld arm, a reminder of her recent encounter with Vergis Thane. *And it's not the only thing that is different.* "Changed in what way?"

She turned to him. Makeup concealed most of the iron-wrought wounds to her face, but nothing could hide the hurt in her eyes. "I haven't even been away a year, but the whole place has been transformed. My old friends don't invite me to their dinners and dances anymore; most of them carefully ignore my invitations to visit here. Illirius Pym didn't even care that I was back; after all that bluster and drama, he barely acknowledged me when I went to reimburse him—I didn't even merit an acknowledging snarl. Last week's dinner party was a disaster—only two people came, and they both left before dessert. I've only been to six parties in the month I've been home, and most of the guests had little to say to me, even people I've known for years! Last week, when I went to Ashanna dol'Graever's wedding reception, I was actually relegated to a table half-hidden behind a potted fern, along with a watery-eyed Woman who couldn't speak without her chin-wattle flapping around like a live trout in her throat. I didn't even get an invitation to the wedding, just the reception. I'm rather glad now that I didn't take Ashanna a gift. What's going on here?"

Her hurt bewilderment was transparent, but so was her anger. She knew what was happening, but she didn't want to be the first to mention it. It had always been that way between them, from the first day the Ubbetuk came to work for his eccentric employer nearly fifteen years past, rescued by her from an ill-planned and extralegal business venture that nearly went fatally wrong due to his inebriation and an ill-timed bit of sarcasm. Denarra had saved Padwacket's life and his family's reputation, both of which created a debt that he could never fully repay. Soon, however, friendship replaced duty, and the Ubbetuk became both a trusted member of the household and a confidant. Denarra expected him to tell her both what she wanted to hear and what she *needed* to hear, and she trusted him to know the appropriate time for each, even if she didn't always like what he had to say. That was the least he owed her.

But it wouldn't be easy. This wasn't something that her special charms could fix. Their world, indeed, had changed.

Padwacket coughed once and refilled their glasses. "Men are less trusting of the Folk these days, more willing than ever before to see difference as deficiency. At one time such poison found safe harbor only among the ill educated or Dreyd-tainted, but it is the houses of learning now that nurture these ideas. Alchaemists and philosophers of Men claim to find evidence of intellectual and moral degeneracy in everything about us, from the hue of our flesh to the sizes of our skulls, from the timbre of our voices to the cut of our clothes and devotion to our own customs. The hatreds nestled in Dreyd prophecies have made their way into the Academies, and they feed upon each other."

Her face was composed, but Padwacket could see that each word wounded the Strangeling's spirit. She was used to rejection and resentment in the wild lands of Men, but Chalimor had been, for some time, a cultivated haven from such ignorance. It was her escape and sanctuary, a place of healing. It was more of a home to her than anywhere else in the Melded world. Now, it seemed, there was no place free of the cruelty of Men.

"Worse still to their minds," Padwacket continued, his heart heavy, "is the idea of any Human bedding an Unhuman. Such unions are seen as tainting virtuous Men, weakening them, stripping away the dignity of their rightful place at the apex of creation. And the products of such unions are to be especially scorned, for they are corruption incarnate."

He stopped. Denarra's green eyes flashed, but she remained seated and drank slowly, purposefully, until her glass was empty. She held it out for a refill and drained that glass, too.

After a long silence, Denarra cleared her throat. "So, the exotic Strangeling lusted after by Men and Women of high station isn't welcome at their parties anymore? The Kyn-blood that used to warm them with desire is now a bit too hot, I suppose? I wonder what so many of these petty society tyrants would say if they knew that their husbands and wives had spent time in my bed, joyously 'tainted' by this Unhuman temptress? And not one of those simpering society sops had the courage to say anything to me. They just thought I'd slink away, tail tucked between my legs like some hide-whipped bitch." She threw her glass across the room, where it smashed against the cold fireplace. "Well, they'll see a bitch soon enough, but this one has sharp teeth!"

A smile crossed her red lips, and she turned back to her valet. "In the meantime, let's have a bit of that pipe. I haven't smoked Lower Rinj in ages, and I have a lot to think about right now; we'll just have to deal with Meggie's wrath in the morning." Her eyes darkened. "And then I think it's time to tell Quill what's going on."

They'd arrived in Chalimor during an unseasonably fierce thunderstorm, although whether the storm came with them or was waiting in the harbor was beyond Quill's knowledge, as this was her first gate-walking experience. It was terrifying. She had no clear sense of time or geography. Howling winds tore at them, and rippling currents of white lightning burned through the darkness between worlds, a fiery tunnel through a raging black sea of otherworldly chaos. Worst of all, though, were the milky white faces that faded in and out of sight from the swirling shadow, their eyes deep, dead hollows that ached with endless misery. The trio was wounded in flesh as well as spirit: her own body ached from the battle with the Skeeger and from the gate-walking itself, which had drained her every bit as much as the dolls said it would. Her belly cramped worse than in her moon-time, so much so that the spasms nearly bent her double from the pain. She knew then precisely what the ceremony was demanding of her body, though she didn't want to dwell on the thought. It was a blood sacrifice in every sense of the term, and thus far too frightening in its implications.

She'd been scared for more than herself, too, as poor Merrimyn was still barely conscious, and Denarra was bleeding and nearly unable to stand after the battle with Thane. Between the two she-Folk, though, they half-carried, half-dragged the young Man through the otherworldly storm, more certain of their survival even in this alien place than back in the world of Men with Vergis Thane. Quill wasn't even sure if they were going the right way, but when the gate opened all she could think was Chalimor, the home of the Reachwarden and their long-sought destination.

The Dolltender wasn't sure how Denarra had managed it, but a carriage with a well-dressed Ubbetuk attendant stood waiting for them when the gate opened into the stormy streets of the great city. The valet seemed unsurprised to see them as he helped to drag Merrimyn into the carriage, although his eyes widened a bit when he saw the snaring-tome shackled to the young Human's arm.

A long ride later, and then a brusque Woman with tightly bound brown hair and a freckle-covered face opened the door of a two-story, red-tiled house somewhere in the city. It took her little time to bustle the two she-Folk into the house and into steaming baths on the ground floor while she attended to Merrimyn's injuries upstairs. Quill couldn't remember falling asleep, but she awoke the next morning nestled in a soft bed beneath bright quilts in a sunny, oak-paneled room. Her cramping had nearly stopped, though there was still an occasional twinge of discomfort to remind her of the strange journey. Her old, travel-worn clothes had disappeared in the night, but fresh replacements lay folded on a small table beside the bed, each garment sized and fitted to her exact dimensions. The Woman, Meggie Mar, arrived a few moments later with the announcement of breakfast. The smell of fresh bread and spiced meat wafted through the door, and the Tetawa was dressed and in the kitchen, almost on Meggie's heels.

Denarra and Merrimyn were still sleeping, but the Woman—of whom Quill had heard a great deal during her evening wagon-chats with the Strangeling before the chaos of the previous day and night—was clearly someone of authority in the house. Meggie Mar wasn't old, but she carried herself with the certainty of a Woman many years her senior. Her crisp blue dress and ironed apron were clean; the smooth calluses on her hands were worn deep and strong like wind-polished wood. She grumbled and snarled at length, in both Mannish and impeccable Folk trade-speech, but her touch was gentle, and Quill noticed kindness and concern in the fuss the Woman made over the maidservant and the Ubbetuk valet. No one went hungry in Meggie's household, nor did they stand idle. When Quill was finished eating, Meggie put her to work right away helping the maidservant, Ellefina, on her daily shopping expedition into the mid-city market.

It wasn't until later that Quill understood Meggie's reason for sending her so soon into the city: if this was to be her home for a while, it was important that she familiarize herself with it as quickly as possible. And the giggling young Ellefina was a charming guide, if somewhat addled and rather too flighty for the Tetawa's comfort. They wandered through stalls and into shops, the girl occasionally gossiping with other domestics and flirting with handsome young Men idling on the cobbled street corners, and all the while Quill walked in mingled fascination and terror through the masses of Humans, Folk, and other odd and wondrous creatures who inhabited this strange city. By the time she and Ellefina returned with their arms full of fresh vegetables, a suckling piglet, flowers, and various cooking herbs and pastries, the young *firra* was only just beginning to understand the remarkable character of Chalimor, the Jewel of the Reach.

In her most ambitious daydreams she'd never imagined anything so huge and overwhelming. The sheer scale of the city staggered her. It stretched for miles, from the hewn-granite base of majestic Mount Imor all the way into the calm center of Chal Bay, where the city was built up on massive limestone reefs that jutted out of the clear blue depths. The greater buildings were in the shadow of the mountain, all white marble, whitewashed stone, and colored tile. It was here, too, that Denarra's stuccoed brick house stood on a flowery hill that provided a stunning view of the city, which spread out in the shape of a great crescent moon, with the more fashionable districts lining the coast and those on the lower end of the social scale extending outward into the fish-rich bay. Ships of every conceivable design and style passed through the harbor, from the great scarlet-sailed merchant sloops of the Sarvannadad trade guilds that cut proudly through the sapphire waters, to the swift white Chalimite sculls that slipped past the high-hulled city scows bringing goods from ship to market, to the frail and weather-worn scalloping punts that kept close to the docks and often ended up swamped by the white-capped waves made by the larger vessels—such a common event that dock laborers were disappointed when a day went by without the opportunity of a water rescue.

Humans of all sizes, shapes, and colors swarmed the streets like so many ants, and the noise they made was deafening—all shouting and laughing and calling out to one another. Spices of both exotic and mundane origin were favorite trading goods in the city, but anything that could be procured by coin, deed, or bargain could be found somewhere in the city: bold and vibrant dyes drawn from crushed beetles and unpronounceable plants from faraway ports; soft silks, hardy linens, lustrous leathers, and other fabrics drawn from worm, sheep, rabbit, goat, bear, and more unusual creatures; wood and stone in great supply for both building and fine artistry; rare oils, cheeses, honeys, teas, spirits, and Folk-grown tobacco found their way to the city's finest homes. Soothsayers and fortune-tellers had a brisk business in talismans, amulets, Craft-touched bones, sanctified chalices, and other strange magics, much to the vocal dismay of both Rationalist philosophers from the Learnèd Academy and Dreydcaste Proselytors who lectured against such superstitions—and each other—in every market square. It was said that in the more dangerous areas of the city even Human or Folk slaves could be purchased; though slavery was ostensibly against the laws of the Reach, indentured servitude was a flourishing legal business, and the line between the two was often quite thin.

Beasts of every temperament and kind were sold as food, pet, or plaything, with little regard to the creatures' own preferences. Fresh beef, mutton, poultry, pork, seafood, and less identifiable meats were readily available, and Ellefina confirmed that many Beasts offered as pets one day often ended up in the butcher's stall the next. The smells resulting from so many goods and animals and bodies in such close proximity were also new to the Tetawa. The stench of decaying fish and refuse from the alleyways and docks was bad enough, but when added to the sickeningly sweet perfumes that the wealthier Chalimites used to mask the other smells—it was sometimes all Quill could manage to get through a trip to market without spending the remainder of the day with a pounding headache and rolling stomach.

She had no idea how all these people managed to survive in such a place. The shadow side of the city was as terrible as its beauty was magnificent. Orphans, urchins, and the other desperately poor lived in squalor in the alleys and abandoned buildings of Mariner's Quay, the wharf district, but Quill rarely saw them, for they were driven out of the finer neighborhoods every night by the city guard to prevent them from offending the sensibilities of the moneyed and powerful. She saw few Folk, either; those who inhabited the city were either celebrated outsiders, like Denarra, house servants, like Padwacket, or struggled to live among the other unfortunates in the more dangerous parts of the city.

It was all quite amazing to Quill, yet troubling, too, like an endless dream with more possibilities than a lifetime of slumber could uncover. Her first few weeks in Chalimor passed in a whirl. She traveled with Ellefina and Meggie through the city, observing most of its respectable areas during the daylight as she was put to work carrying parcels, packages, baskets, and armfuls of vegetables and other goods. She strolled Denarra's private garden, where a pair of bold and beautiful peacocks strutted regally among the dusty grey peahens; aside from the carving on Denarra's faraway traveling wagon, Quill had never seen the unusual birds before, but she was unsurprised that the boldly preening males were the Strangeling's particular favorites.

With her exuberant hostess, Quill witnessed something of the glittering nightlife of Chalimor, and bedecked in soft-hued silk dresses and some of Denarra's more demure jewelry, she was introduced to many of the people whom the Wielder hoped would get them an introduction to the Reachwarden to plead their case. They'd spent a few nights on starlit terraces, or in shimmering gilded ballrooms filled with the music of soft flutes and harps. One night they saw a play with an elaborate stage designed to resemble the inside of a golden conch shell, far more extravagant than any of the motley shows put on by Denarra's scruffy old performance troupe. The following week they attended a late-night literary salon at the Luminescent Observatory in the People's Academy, where Quill was brought to tears by the Strangeling's lovely friend Pixi, a warrior-poet of Jaaga heritage whose word-weavings lingered in the heart and spirit long after the evening's entertainments were finished. The lightly seasoned food at these parties was, without exception, exquisite, although Quill often preferred the loving weight of Meggie's meals of corn, sweet potatoes, beans, and fresh meat to the florid but impersonal pudding-based cuisine of the High Houses of Chalimor.

At one time she might have felt awkward and rustic among these bewigged Men in velvet coats and high white collars and their tight-faced Women dripping in pearls, gems, and endless folds of bright cloth, but she was pleasantly surprised to find that Denarra's kind supervision helped her to navigate this strange world with little discomfort. If anything, she enjoyed the new experiences and grew eager for each night's new revelry. Even the dolls seemed more relaxed in this place, especially after their worlds-crossing efforts. They spent most of their time in sleep, barely noting her presence when she came to feed them their daily ration of tobacco and cedar shavings. It was a period of peace for them all.

But the invitations soon dried up, and Denarra became increasingly despondent. Even Quill could see that things weren't going very well.

The Strangeling's tensions grew with her concern over Merrimyn. He lingered for a long time in fever after their arrival, and when he emerged from it, he could remember little of the past few months. The binding of his snaring-tome was cracked and pitted as a result of the battle with Thane; a biting black smoke occasionally trickled out of the book's seam. Merrimyn recalled Denarra and seemed to remember Quill, but of the rest, there were mere glimpses and hints. This discovery threw the Wielder into a deep depression. It was only later, after Denarra came to the moonlit garden from a talk with her valet in the parlor, that Quill discovered the depth of the Strangeling's concern.

"He was our key to Vald's plans, Quill," Denarra said, dropping down onto a vine-wrapped bench on the terrace. "He knew something of Vald's preparations for the Expulsion, and after; he was going

to give the information to the Reachwarden, to make him understand just how terrible this is for *everyone*, Folk and Human alike." She
grimaced. "Merrimyn told me what's happening, at least as far as he
knew, but a Man's word is far more valuable these days than that of a
half-breed Strangeling."

Quill's throat went dry. She'd come outside to enjoy the peace
of the evening, but it was gone now. Now all she felt was a smothering darkness reaching out over them. "What do you mean, Denarra?
What's happening?"

The Strangeling smiled sadly. "I didn't want to tell you yet, Quill.
I promised to look after you, and I've taken that vow quite seriously.
You've been enjoying yourself so much, and after everything you've
been through I wanted you to have as much fun as possible before . . ."

"Before what?"

"The Expulsion isn't just about land, Quill—it never really was.
Certainly, that's what's been getting everyone's attention. That's
what's driving the endless streams of land-hungry Men rushing from
all over the Reach for some choice farmland or mining stakes. That's
what the politicians are arguing about; it's what the condescending philanthropists who call themselves 'the Friends of the Folk' are
yammering about, too. But it goes much, much deeper than that.
Vald seems to be seeking nothing less than the utter destruction of
the Folk in this Melded world."

A chill breeze embraced them, but Quill took no comfort in
the cooling change from the salty humid heat of the earlier evening.
Mind awhirl, she looked off into the distance, to the shining lights
throughout the city around them. Denarra's terrace looked out over
the bay and some of Chalimor's most famous structures: the great
Jurist Temple; the House of States, where the legislators of the Reach
Republic endlessly debated government policy; the Hall of Kings,
where the Reachwarden worked to unite the contentious territorial and political factions; the grand library and lecture halls of the
Learnèd Academy. It was a lovely sight at all times, but none so much
as this cloudless night, as the light of the nearly full Man's moon
bathed the marble structures in a radiant silver glow.

But the beauty gave no warmth. It was as cold as the fickle sea
air, stripping her heart's heat and leaving only emptiness behind.

"There's more, isn't there?"

"I'm afraid so, Quill. I'm sorry."

The Tetawa nodded once. "Tell me what's happened. Please, Denarra, don't try to protect me. I'm tired of everyone thinking I'm so fragile that I always need to be coddled and cared for. I'm not a youngling cub anymore. I've shed the blood of my enemies, and I have the scars to show it, so that should have more than earned your respect. We can't be friends if you won't trust me with the truth."

Denarra's eyes filled with tears. "It's not that I don't trust you, Quill. It's just that I know how hard . . ."

"Tell me."

The Strangeling sighed and reached out for Quill's hand. It was freezing. "Sheynadwiin was destroyed on the day we arrived in Chalimor. I only found out a couple of weeks ago. Some of the Folk escaped—perhaps your Tobhi was among them."

Quill's face grew pale, but her voice didn't shake. "You said 'some' escaped. What about the others?"

"Some . . . many died. But most survived. They're being driven westward by the Eromar militia with iron swords and muskets, to the broken land promised in the Oath of Western Sanctuary, a land once known as the Pit Fields of Karkûr."

"I see." Quill jerked her hand away from Denarra's grasp. "Then we've failed. We've danced and sipped fine wines and lived in grand style while my people—*our* people—have been dying on a lonely road far from home." The Dolltender stood abruptly and turned an accusing glare on her friend. "You promised to help me, and I trusted you. You lied to me."

"Quill, truly, I thought this would work," the Strangeling cried, stricken. "I've always been respected among the right circles in the city; I've always had the ear of the most powerful Men in the Assembly. But things have changed! They don't want anything to do with me anymore. Their hearts have hardened against the Folk, and I don't know why."

"I have an idea," Quill snarled. "Maybe they're tired of shallow, jaw-jabbering actresses with more love of fine food and fashion than concern for their own dying kith."

Denarra's anguished sob followed Quill as the *firra* spun angrily on her heel toward the house. She'd said she wanted to know more, but now she was sorry to have heard it. There was a certain false comfort in these shadows, in the pretense that the world would go on as it always had and that nothing was changing. She could keep dreaming of parties and dances, of perfumed candles and soft music, and nothing would intrude into that hopeful, dreamy peace.

But then she saw Tobhi's broad smile. She could almost smell the spice of cedar and pine on his vest, feel the silky softness of his long black hair in her fingers. He'd given up hope of a false dream, and in doing so fought to make a reality of peace. She could do no less, even if he was gone. Even if . . .

Wiping her hand across her eyes, she straightened her shoulders, pulled her hair away from her face, and turned back to the door. A sudden commotion inside caught her attention, and she ducked out of the way as Padwacket rushed outside and threw himself over the edge of the terrace into the garden below, Meggie Mar close behind him, her voice raised in an unintelligible stream of curses about smoke and curtains.

Quill shook her head angrily. Her world was crumbling, and they were worried about the household draperies. Everything she'd known was gone now: her cousins, Medalla and Gishki, her home of Spindletop, all her other dolls . . . Tobhi. The Everland itself. Who was she, if not part of this web of history, friendship, family, and love? She could never return home again, not unless the Reachwarden came to their defense. But for all these weeks her people had been dying, and the Reachwarden had done nothing—indeed, it mattered so little to the Humans of this city that she hadn't heard even the slightest whiff of rumor or gossip. The icy silence of social sanction reigned supreme in Chalimor, and against that she had no defense. Not without Denarra, anyway.

The peacocks cried out in the garden, their shrill voices so different from the beauty of their proud tail fans, and Quill's knees buckled beneath her. She fell to the cold tiles and watched the birds slip in and out of the garden shadows, their iridescent plumage shimmering, ghostlike, in the moonlight.

Betthia Vald could barely remember when they'd first met. Her few friends could all reminisce in fine detail about when they'd met their husbands—first glances exchanged, first furtive kisses, first declarations of love—but Betthia's memories held few tender moments. It had been a mournful loss when she was younger, but after many years of marriage, the missing memories worked well on balance; she'd also forgotten the first tirade, the first bloodied nose, the first broken arm.

She sat at the dressing table in her private room, a small fire burning in the grate, and carefully ran a brush through her greying hair. The rooms on this side of Gorthac Hall were cold, even in a strange hot autumn like this one. Many things were strange these days.

The tortoise-shell brush had been a childhood gift from her mother, one of the few things that the emotionally distant Woman had ever given freely. Betthia had been only fifteen when she married Lojar Vald and moved from her beloved seaside home in Chalimor to the weathered butte that crouched over Eromar City. Even now, almost forty years later, she sometimes awoke to the smell of salt water on the breeze and the shrill call of gulls ringing in the air. Even now, she wept at the loss.

Her pale green eyes took a survey of the image in the mirror. It had been a long time since she'd been young. Though she doubted she'd ever been truly beautiful, whatever beauty she'd once possessed had long since been worn away by life in Gorthac Hall. Other Women many years her senior were radiant in comparison.

Betthia's face was thin and drawn, her long nose bent at the bridge from being broken numerous times over the years. Her hair was brittle and growing thinner with every year, even drawing away from her forehead a bit. It was one of many gradual changes she'd noticed and accepted with stoic disinterest, including the slightly yellow pallor creeping into and hardening her flesh. Betthia suspected that the constant pains in her back and the irregular bleeding from below had something to do with these changes in her skin, but the alchaemists and surgeons insisted that it was a natural consequence of age among the aristocracy. They suggested less sun and more face powder. And she obeyed them, growing ever weaker, becoming a living ghost that even her own children could hardly bear to visit. <<The doctors and your father insist,>> she'd say to them, and the matter would be dropped, for a while, anyway. She'd long ago given up arguing with Men, even though they were killing her.

Betthia had no doubt that she was dying. The possibility secretly thrilled her. She wasn't strong enough to die on her own; if she'd ever had that strength, she would have killed herself the night her father dragged her screaming from her bedroom and into the wedding coach. She knew then that she'd never see the ocean again, and her long, slow soul-death started that night. No, she couldn't kill herself, not that day, nor on any one of a thousand days and nights of humiliation, pain, and fear. It was her lot in life. She was a Woman, and there was little hope in the world of Men for such as her.

She pulled the brush through her hair again, repeating the movement with practiced ease. There had been a time when this evening ritual would bring a certain luster to her hair, a slight, soft beauty of which she'd been uncharacteristically proud. Now, though, her brush came away with more hair tangled in its bristles than ever before, and those once-thick tresses were growing sparser. It didn't matter. The brushing hour was one of the few unchanging routines in her life these days, a time when she was left to her own thoughts and image in the mirror. It was *her* room, *her* time, and she hoarded it with miserly insistence.

She didn't know when she'd started talking to that image in the mirror, but she was glad to have the company. Strangely, though, she'd never thought to name her mirror-self. It wasn't so much that the figure was a distinctive personality as it was just nice to have someone to talk to again. It was the only company that never demanded anything from Betthia; the mirror-self only gave, never took, and she was always a welcome guest.

<<He visited me tonight, like I told you he would.>>

<<I know,>> her mirror-self answered, as she brushed her own fragile hair on the other side of the glass. <<I saw him come in. He looked . . . different tonight.>>

<<Yes, I suppose he did.>> She pulled a few loose strands away from her face. They fluttered to the shabby rug.

<<What did he want?>>

Betthia sighed. <<He came to say goodbye.>>

Her mirror-self stopped brushing and looked at her. <<So he's really going through with this? Did you try to stop him?>>

She laughed then, a harsh, awkward sound from a mouth unused to such expressions. <<I long ago gave up any hope of changing

Lojar's mind on anything. Once he's set his thoughts toward a goal, he follows the swiftest path to its end. He's leaving tonight. There's nothing I can do.>>

<<I see,>> her mirror-self said, then shrugged. <<If all goes as planned, he won't be returning, will he?>>

<<No. Nor will he return if things go poorly.>>

<<Do you have any idea what will happen?>>

Betthia turned her head sideways and stroked the brush downward; the image in the glass did the same. <<It's difficult to tell. If the Dreyd prophecies are correct, he should ascend after the power is released. If they're wrong, well, he's prepared for that, too.>>

<<I see.>> The mirror-Betthia lifted her head and turned it the other way.

<<He thinks it should happen quickly, if the Seekers have gathered enough fuel for the transformation, and if there are enough Binders for the transfer. He's lost a few of both, but he insists there will be enough in time for his passage through the Veil.>>

<<It seems like there's a good chance of problems, don't you think?>>

Betthia's expression was more a grimace than a smile. <<Oh, yes—this won't be easy. It's quite likely that he'll unleash something that he can't control. It happened before, you know.>>

<<The Melding. But that worked, didn't it?>>

<<It did, but it was a close thing at the end. There were many Dreyd in those days; they were committed to the task, and they helped each other.>>

Her mirror-self smiled, too. <<Lojar is at a disadvantage there. He doesn't have many friends.>>

<<No.>> Betthia's strange smile faded. <<But if anyone can succeed in solitude, it's him. He's put all this in motion already, and no single Man has ever accomplished that much before. The High Hall at Bashonak has sent all its Binders to help; they don't realize they'll all be consumed, of course, but I suppose it's all for the good of the Dreyd.>>

<<If he has the Binders, what's left?>>

<<Fuel. He thought that the witch-raids would provide enough, but they were weaker than he'd expected, and the iron shackles cut off some of their strength. So his soldiers are bringing a horde of them

in a few different groups to the site. He says there are some strong ones in the last nasty bunch. They should give him more than enough fuel now.>>

They sat together for a while, brushing their hair in silence. Finally, her mirror-self said, <<Will you miss him?>>

Betthia stared intently at the mirror. <<What?>>

<<Will you miss him? He's your husband, after all.>>

The Woman shrugged. <<I don't know. I've never thought that far ahead. I might, I suppose.>>

<<Do you think he'll miss you?>>

A soft sigh slid from Betthia's lips. <<Yes, I think he will.>>

Her mirror-self looked at her dubiously, but Betthia continued. <<He visited me tonight, just after dinner. I didn't expect him to say goodbye, but there he was, tall and dark and grim, as always. Then, before I knew what he was doing, he reached out and touched my cheek, but kindly. He had an odd look on his face, like he'd only just seen me for the first time and . . . and he was pleased with what he saw. He was gentle. It . . . it was the first time I'd ever seen anything like love in his eyes.>>

The face in the mirror seemed to grow soft and misty. <<What did he say?>>

Betthia placed the brush on the dressing table and stared off into the looking-glass, past her twin, into memory. <<Nothing. He didn't say anything. He just touched my face and looked at me, then turned around and left, closing the door behind him.>>

She looked up, but her mirror-self had grown silent. The fire in the grate had burned itself out, and a deep chill had crept into the room. She stood, stoked the fire, and rang for an attendant to build it up again. Her body trembled violently from the cold, so she reached to the back of her chair for her shawl. Pulling it away, she noticed something wet on the end nearest the seat of the chair. Lifting it into the light, she saw that it was her own blood.

Betthia looked down at the pool of crimson spreading beneath the seat. Her legs sagged slightly, but she shook her head in annoyance. The attendant would come, then the doctors, then the leeches, then her devoted but incessantly mewling children. And she'd survive this yet again, most likely to witness the results of her husband's success.

But then, if she lived that long, she likely wouldn't live much beyond it—very few would, especially this close to the site of the ceremony. Lojar Vald was a Man of no small ambition. He would show himself worthy to rise to the ranks of the Dreyd, and in doing so would unleash a power like nothing the world had known for a thousand years of Men.

And in the second Melding, Lojar Vald would be among the supreme.

Betthia sighed and returned to her dressing table. Her hair was askew again. Picking up the brush, she began the long, delicate process again, hoping to finish by the time the attendant arrived.

After that . . . well, after that, it wouldn't much matter.

"All right, Denarra, I want to know what's going on. Who in this Melded world *are* you? How do you have a house like this, with all this finery and caretakers?"

Quill stood defiantly before the Strangeling with her arms crossed and lips tightly pursed. She'd had enough of hints and secrets. She teetered on the edge of a vast abyss, and she was on the edge of losing her very world. She had to stand firm, and it would happen now.

"I've been a good friend to you, Denarra, and you've been like a sister to me, but I can't stand by your side if you're going to keep things from me. I've got to know that I can trust you."

"Now, wait a moment," sputtered Padwacket, his big ears quivering angrily. He sat beside the Wielder, holding a cold steak to the swelling knot on his head from Meggie's wooden-heeled shoe. "She's only saved your life a half-dozen times. She's only put herself in mortal danger every time, and given her home and hard-earned—"

Quill held up a hand, silencing him. "I wasn't talking with you, Padwacket—I'm talking to Denarra. It's as simple as this: either you tell me who you are and give me a reason to trust you again, or I'm leaving and doing whatever I can on my own. I need your help but not at the cost of everything and everyone I love." Thoughts of Tobhi strengthened her resolve. "I want to know. Now."

Padwacket opened his mouth again, but Denarra shook her head wearily. "No, darling, she's right. Thank you for your valiant defense, but she's right. She deserves to know what's going on. Please, leave us alone for a while." The Ubbetuk reluctantly departed, and the Strangeling turned to Quill, who still stood glaring. "I know you're angry, and I don't blame you. But you really must know that I never lied to you, not fully, anyway. There are just some things that I didn't think you needed to know."

"That kind of secret is still a lie. It hides your heart from the people who deserve to know it."

"Very well," Denarra nodded in surrender. "If you must know, I'm not really a legitimate participant in the world of theater, although my heart certainly tugs in that distinguished direction."

Quill raised an eyebrow. "I pretty well guessed that by myself."

The Strangeling sighed. "In fact, I'm really not associated with *any* legitimate organizations. In fact, you might say that my true associations are likely as *illegitimate* as they come."

"And those would be . . . ?"

Meggie poked her head into the room, her brow furrowed in annoyance. "Oh, for goodness sake, Denarra, enough of this child-ish dance. Just tell her that you're the most notorious smuggler and pleasure-broker in Chalimor and get it over with. And *you*," she turned and hissed with a quick, withering glance back down the hall, "don't think I don't see you sneaking away. As soon as that swelling's gone down, you're to get yourself down to the scrub-tub and *clean those drapes!*"

As Meggie stomped away after Padwacket, Denarra shrugged. "It's true, Quill. My true calling rests in the procurement of pleasurable entertainments and rare items of fine quality, which I provide to an interested clientele at a significant profit to myself and my employees."

"You mean, you're a . . . you're . . . ?" Quill didn't know quite how to phrase the question. She'd heard of such things before, but only rumors and hints. *Firra* weren't prudish about their bodies, but they reserved such pleasures for those with whom they shared an abiding emotional connection, or at least a degree of trust and friend-ship. Joinings for money were alien to Tetawi ways.

"If you like, you can call me a 'bringer of happiness.' I give pleasure, and I receive pleasure. Whether it involves a visit to the home of one of Chalimor's First Families on Rosewood Hill, where I might have a perfectly lovely evening with a lonely merchant, or simply bringing a rare, blood-heating, and legally inaccessible spice to a customer in the Brownbrick District, I give joy to those denied it by convention or circumstance. I don't harm anyone, and I don't allow anyone to harm me. It's that simple."

The Dolltender sat down. "Have you always been a . . . 'bringer of happiness'?"

"No," Denarra replied with a shrug. "Actually, I was once a rather unremarkable student at the Learnèd Academy just up Assembly Height. There was a movement among Humans at the time to rescue poor, downtrodden Folk from our 'barbaric' lives, and I was by that time living on my own and rather ambitious to see what excitement could be found in the rest of the world, so I ended up here in Chalimor. Thanks to a *very* earnest group of bored society wives and their browbeaten husbands—they call themselves the 'Friends of the Folk,' though in truth they're anything but—a small group of us, all Kyn-born or Kyn-sired, were brought to the city and paraded around like well-dressed lap dogs, poised and polished to demonstrate how virtuous and self-sacrificing our sponsors were." The bitter edge of resentment slid into her voice. "And I loved every moment of it. As long as I was an obedient pet—adored by the sages, attending lectures at the Academy every day, memorizing the inane Dreyd creeds and mind-numbing lyric poetry that were so fashionable at the time, and avoiding the slightest whiff of scandal, which wasn't always easy—they patted me on the head and made sure that I had all the pretty dresses and perfumes I wanted."

"What happened?"

The Strangeling chuckled. "I didn't take too well to domestication. Actually, it really wasn't my fault, not entirely. Some of my friends and I were studying in one of the gardens of the Academy when a group of Human students started harassing us, Men of the most unpleasant sort. Jealousy, bigotry, and fear are a bad combination. I'd Awakened a couple of years before but had kept those powers well hidden until that day, when the teasing escalated into something much more threatening. As a result, my friends and I walked away from the garden. Two of those brutes didn't."

She stared out the window. "It didn't matter that we didn't start the fight, or that we were only fighting to defend our lives. All that mattered was the fact that we were Kyn, and that we'd attacked Men.

We were expelled from the Academy that day, and we found our few belongings in the street when we returned to our sponsors' home. We heard later that some of the Kyn who hadn't been involved in the fracas still remained in the good graces of the Friends of the Folk, but the three of us had been erased as fully as if we'd never existed. So, being of a theatrical bent and hoping to hide the pain and shame of our situation in frivolity, we took the name 'the Sisters of Wandering Virtue,' and we learned quite quickly what it took to survive in the shadows beneath the marble grandeur of Chalimor. I found that I had unexpected and not entirely unpleasant talents that were very much in demand among the more discerning sons and daughters of the city; my training in social etiquette turned out to be a quite marketable addition to those other talents. In a relatively short time my friends and I gathered enough money to leave the city and head west, toward Harudin Holt." Her expression was unreadable. "After a few years and numerous adventures I returned alone to Chalimor, one friend dead and the other vanished, and aside from the occasional foray into the larger world, I've been here ever since, honing my skills, learning a thing or two about the nature of Humanity, and ensuring that I will never again need fear the leash and collar. I'm no Man's pet, not anymore. I'm free to choose or refuse, and I take pleasure where I find it."

"But why were you with the Medicine Show?"

Denarra smiled. She was pale after the story but calm. "Darling, a vocation like mine doesn't limit me to one place. I'd been visiting some business associates in Iradîl, to the south of the Allied Wilderlands, where I hoped to pick up some new . . . pleasure-giving accessories that one of my clients was eager to experience. Because of a brief but rather unpleasant misunderstanding with the High Jurist of the city, I was unable to make it to my ship before it was scheduled to leave, so I was forced to find another way home. As there'd been a somewhat similar misunderstanding in Chalimor before I left, I decided that discretion was wiser than haste, so I continued on with the troupe for quite a few months, and that was when we encountered you. Complicated, as I said, but completely true." She gazed earnestly into Quill's face. "I promise—no more secrets, ever again."

They sat in tense silence for a long while. At last, Denarra reached out. "Quill? Are we . . . ?"

The Dolltender stood again. "I don't know. I'm still trying to understand what's happening, and there's still a lot to decide." She walked to the door but stopped before leaving the room. "Thank you for finally telling me. I'll see you in the morning."

Denarra was still sitting in her chair when Padwacket returned a while later. He pulled a footstool beside her seat, and together they gazed through the window at the city shining in the darkness beyond.

37

Lamentation

THE EVERLAND IS GONE. *Forests burn to grey ash, and the People bleed and die under crumbling branches and smoke-choked skies. Birds can't flee this devastation; not even the burrowing creatures find safety in the damp, dark earth. There is no escape. The Everland is gone.*

I rush into the raging waters as the Tree cracks apart, the sound like screaming thunder in my ears. I'm blind to the chaos, to the screams of the dying and the wounded. I'm deaf to the fear that surrounds me, to Tobhi's cry as he's swept away into the mass of fleeing Shields who rush in panic from the cavernous great chamber of the Tree. Even the falling stars and trembling earth fail to give me pause. I plunge under the boiling waves and flail for a moment, and then I see the bent shape bobbing in the water and swim desperately forward. I'm sobbing now, barely able to breathe from the aching emptiness in my chest, but I wrap an arm around Unahi's limp body and cling to it. I can't look at her face; her eyes are wide open and empty, staring at the falling sky.

Why am I so devastated? In truth, I barely knew her. But she was kind to me, and the closest thing to a mother than I've ever known. I want more time—to know her, to know who my own mother was, and to know myself. What will happen to me now that she's gone? There's so much I still have to learn. I try to shout, but my voice is lost in the howling wind, and when I pull Unahi's head back, away from the water, my hand jerks away from the grievous wound in the back of her skull. But I keep chanting the words; I can't do anything else. I can't let her go, not yet.

I turn to swim to the bank, but the waves are too high, and I can't see anything but the blood-red water under an endless black sky. The water seems to thrash in its own death throes. I gasp and choke as I'm drawn under the waves. Unahi begins to slip out of my grasp until rage fills my flailing limbs and I push myself upward to clutch her body. We surface again, together now, and I weep in frustration. There's nothing to see but boiling waves, and I'm growing weaker. The exhaustion hits me hard, and I sink again. Now my own wounds begin to burn in the smoking water. The shore, like the rest of the world, is gone. I am alone.

"Look to your roots." It's Unahi's voice, but only in memory. There's no chance visitation, no last-moment-before-death resolution. Unahi died before striking the water, and it's only her body now that I hold—the spirit has fled on soft wings in shadow. But even remembered words give strength, and I feel a light tug at my thoughts, the swiftly fading tingle of familiarity in my blood. The wyr *is calling to me.*

The waves roll over me again, and I know now that I have to make a choice. Death and destruction rage everywhere. I scream beneath the surge, lungs burning, but my strength is seeping away with every passing moment, and the water smashes me with growing fury. I'll only have this one chance. If I wait, I'll die, and with me all my auntie's dreams.

I make the choice, and Unahi's body vanishes into the flood.

The Wielder awoke crying. A cold wind blew across the prairie, and it chilled her. The others slept in twos and threes throughout the camp, except for Tobhi, who lay curled soundly in a thick blanket beside the fire, and Daladir, who stood watch at the flames. The he-Kyn caught her gaze and nodded. He'd heard her. It wasn't unusual; her nights were filled with this dream and others, many far worse, and she often called out in her sleep. Most of the others seemed used to the late-night disturbances by now. Few of them were silent in the darkness, as they'd all witnessed too much horror to find peace in the Dreaming World, but Daladir was always awake to greet her. He never asked about the dreams, and she never offered any explanation for her cries, but she was glad that she didn't have to spend these times between the dreaming and waking worlds alone. She pulled her blanket around her shoulders, trying to regain some of her lost warmth, and sat beside him on the grass.

"Don't you ever sleep?" she whispered, trying to avoid waking Tobhi, who snored softly on the ground beside the he-Kyn.

Ignoring her question, Daladir looked down and smiled. "You don't have to whisper—I tripped over him a while ago and he didn't even move. I think this is the first real sleep he's had since . . ." His words trailed off, and he turned his gaze to the western horizon.

Dawn was still a long time away, but the nearly full moon gave the prairies a soft blue glow. It was difficult to imagine that these gentle grasslands were the site of so much suffering. But the evidence cut through the land like a silver scar this night, and the Darkening Road would continue for many days to come. Both Kyn turned away from the sight. They would see enough of it come morning.

"You're going to need some rest," Tarsa persisted. "Everyone is more than willing to take watch for a while; you don't need to do it every night."

He shrugged. "I don't mind. It's hard to sleep these days, anyway."

She looked at him. The struggles of the past few months had changed the he-Kyn. There was still a gentleness in his eyes when he looked at her, but his face was harder now, made haggard by more than exhaustion. It was more than the burning sun and wind. They'd all seen so much misery, and the experiences had made them all different, but Daladir had seen more than the others. After months of Vald's manipulations at Gorthac Hall, the he-Kyn had grown painfully used to the cruelty of Men, so none of this was a surprise. Now there was something brittle about him. His unyielding strength would shatter under its own force. He might walk to the Road's end and fight the enemies of the Folk every step of the journey, but he was wounded in a way that Tarsa didn't understand.

The thought alarmed her. She was comfortable with him; he didn't look at her with the same awe and fear that everyone but Tobhi and Jitani shared. She wasn't some strange creature out of old stories to these three kind friends. She was just Tarsa, not the unpredictable salvation of the Folk.

She reached out and touched his hand. He was cold. "You don't have to carry this burden alone, Daladir. I can bring you a healing, if you'll let me." The familiar green flames flickered down her arm toward her fingers.

He pulled his hand away. "No." Seeing the sudden flash of pain on her face, he smiled and slid closer to her. "Don't misunderstand. It's not that I don't trust you, because I do. And it's not that I don't want to know what all these others have felt, Tarsa, because I do, desperately. But we don't know how much of this strength you have left, and we don't know how much we're going to need in the days ahead. There are so many others who are going to need your help; I'll be fine. I promise."

Tarsa let the lie pass, and the green glow faded. The main thing keeping Daladir going these days was pride; she had no intention of denying him that. She took a small stick and absently stirred the coals for a while, then wrapped her blanket around her shoulders and moved back toward the soft, grassy hollow where she'd rested before. Daladir watched the Wielder nestle into a ball for warmth and slowly fall asleep again. He watched over her until dawn.

"What's a body to eat around here?" Tobhi chirped to Jitani as he drew his fingers through his sleep-tangled hair.

"Nothing different from yesterday," growled the golden-eyed she-Kyn, her eyes darting over to Tarsa, who sat with Daladir a short distance from the remains of the campfire. "And nothing different from what you'll eat tomorrow." She handed the Tetawa a crumbling biscuit and a couple of strips of dried meat of unknown origin. Tobhi studiously avoided looking at the withered stumps of her wounded sensory stalks.

"Really, Jitani," a tall, dark-skinned Man named Oryn said in the trade-tongue behind her, "you should try to be a bit more pleasant in the morning. Your sour face is giving me a stomachache." He laughed and reached over to grab another chunk of meat, but the she-Kyn dodged his hand and grinned.

"I doubt your burbling belly has anything to do with me, fat one. Maybe you've forgotten again that you're not supposed to eat the hide with the meat." The others laughed as the Man roared in mock anger and chased her around the camp. Tobhi joined the revelry, even while sneaking a glance at Tarsa, who was regarding the western horizon with concern. He briefly considered going to her, but the freedom of the moment was too irresistible. He'd have to face the grim journey soon enough as it was.

Oryn stopped, wiping the sweat from his face. "Would you deny a starving Man a bit of sustenance?" he intoned with dramatic flair. Tobhi laughed again. Although not exactly fat, Oryn of Deldmaar was gifted with a seemingly equal share of firm muscle and ample stomach. He also possessed an endless good humor that served him well in the strains of these times.

At first the Leafspeaker had been shocked to see Men and Women among the warriors, but Daladir assured the Tetawa that these Humans were firm allies. Some had lived peacefully among Folk for years and had joined the others to help rescue their Folk friends and families; others had watched the horrors of the Expulsion and fought in righteous indignation. It was sometimes still hard for Tobhi to be near the Humans and not be filled with bitterness, but at those times he'd think of Tarsa and all that she'd lost since leaving Red Cedar Town. If she could see past her anger, he could do no less.

There were about thirty others in the group, mostly Kyn, with two Tetawi brothers, a she-Feral with cloven hooves and two horns that curled impressively behind her pointed ears, six Men and two Women, three Ubbetuk, and a handful of the Strangeling Jaaga-Folk, who traveled these grasslands in long caravans of canvas-covered wagons and followed great herds of antelope, bison, and prairie deer in the summer months. The travelers had a few horses and ponies to carry supplies but not enough for everyone to ride, so they remained on foot and pushed themselves to cover as much ground as possible each day without being spotted by the main company they followed. They'd escaped detection thus far; it would be disastrous to reveal themselves too soon and to risk more deaths among the exiles.

The thought of detection brought another, more disturbing fear to his mind. Tobhi looked up at Jitani. "What about them bandits? En't ye worried that they'll come up after us?"

Jitani's smile sent a chill through him. "Not unless they can do it without their heads." The others around them shared a harsh laugh. "We took care of them a couple of days back, the day before we found you."

"There were no survivors, Tobhi," Tarsa said as she walked back to the group. "We couldn't risk them raising up an alarm in the settlements behind us. We've got enough to worry about already." The conversation faded at the Wielder's presence, but she didn't seem to notice. If she did, she didn't betray any discomfort. Among the exiles, only Jitani and Daladir seemed unfazed by her arrival. Indeed, Tobhi noticed with awkward surprise, they both shared a similar soft warmth in their eyes when they looked at her.

This was certainly unexpected.

His thoughts returned to the perils of their situation as Tarsa went on. "We've been talking with our Jaaga friends and looking at the maps we were able to salvage from Sheynadwiin. It's another two days to the Shard Ford. They'll be stopped for a few days there, because it'll take a while to get so many of our people into the barges and across the gap into Dûrûk and the Pit Fields. We should be able to strike the boats first; the militia won't be expecting trouble now, not after avoiding it for so long. If we can stop them before they get anyone on the barges, we'll avoid being separated, and they'll be without transportation across the Riven Sea. We won't have another opportunity like this."

"How do you suggest we handle things when we get there?" one of the Women asked. Her hair was shorn down to the scalp, and she wore a heavy wool cloak over her body; the clatter of metal beneath the fabric hinted at dangers unseen from outside. Tobhi noticed that the earlier sense of frivolity among the company had vanished, and deadly purpose now took its place.

"Men are creatures of habit. The Jaaga scouts have confirmed this," Daladir said. "Vald's soldiers have followed the same procedure each night: three guards for every twenty prisoners, with replacements coming at midnight. That makes about one hundred twenty guards on duty at any one time, with just as many in reserve."

One of the Tetawi brothers snorted. "You don't expect the thirty of us to take on eight times our number, do you? You forget, they've got muskets and cold iron. Our bows and spears won't do much against those weapons."

"Those weapons are nothing against the arsenal we've got," Jitani said, and she drew a wooden weapon from the sheath at her side. Tobhi's eyes widened. The sword's *wyr*-shaped edge was as sharp and strong as any piece of metal. Jitani spun the sword in a dangerous arc, and the Tetawa understood immediately that the she-Kyn and her weapon had a long, deadly history together.

Tarsa looked at the top of her own wyrwood staff and the piece of amber glowing there, gold in the light of the early dawn. "Yes, our weapons will match anything the Men of Eromar have, but if we're smart and lucky, we won't have to use them. We can't yet risk a direct assault; our people are too weak to fight, and the threat to them is too great. Chaos will follow the destruction of the boats, and it's that chaos that will be our greatest ally—that, and the Jaaga-Folk, who are tired of Men crossing their lands, disrupting their hunts, and stealing their herds. They'll help us afterward, but the barges will be our responsibility."

"I don't understand," the cloaked Woman said. "What happens after we've destroyed the boats? The Folk are sick and exhausted; they won't be able to help us much."

"Don't you bet on it," said Tobhi, crossing his arms proudly. "There's plenty of fire left in the Folk. Ye just give 'em some good reason for hope, and ye'll see how much help they'll give ye."

Oryn eyed the Leafspeaker critically. "I share Eladrys's concerns. No matter how defiant they are, they're still weak and underfed. The soldiers will be relatively well rested and fit, not to mention fully armed, with many on horseback. Without good weapons, the Folk would be in a bad way, even in their best health. As they are, they're not going to be much help to us. We can't just wait for them to get stronger."

"You're right," Daladir interjected. "We can't wait. But we don't have to." He looked at Tarsa. "It's time for the Wielder to share her power with the People."

The wyr *pulls me through the thrashing waves. The world isn't falling down around me anymore. I'm joined with the thunder, a daughter of the storm. It rages in my blood like a war-chant lifted high. My voice is the wind, my tears the sea, my flesh the stars and stones. Spirits of this world and those beyond join the song. The words are unfamiliar, but I know them and I know the rhythm, if not the meaning. I've sung them before, when I first Awakened to the* wyr, *when I lost my sapling name and came into the name that has shaped my life: Tarsa'deshae—She-Breaks-the-Spear. Now the fear is gone. I still don't understand this dangerous gift, but it's no longer a stranger. I belong to the* wyr. *The Deep Green courses through my veins, and with it the memories, dreams, and voices of a thousand generations.*

My grief for Unahi mingles with that of all those who are dying, who have died before. There is life here, but pain, too, and it's almost more than I can bear. But they belong together in the Deep Green, both life and death, joy and pain, the earth and the underworld and the sky. Balance in all things. It's a hard lesson, sometimes. Sometimes, it's the only lesson that endures.

Waves crash over my head, and still I fight forward. My body is dying, but the knowledge brings no grief. All I want to do is reach the shattered Tree before my body fades and my spirit joins the exodus of dark-eyed owls. If I can have that moment of connection, at least, I'll be content.

A shape rises up out of the water, and grief rises up with it as the shattered silver skeleton of the Eternity Tree appears through the crimson flood. The branches are bare; the leaves have all been stripped away by the ferocity of the storm. It is split through the middle, as though hands of lightning have torn it wide from crown to roots. But this wound comes from within. The Tree withstood ages of fire, storm, and drought. It weathered the catastrophe of the Melding, and the years of chaos that followed. Even the Purging of the earthborn Wielders by the sky-blinded Shields didn't dim the Tree's brilliance. But blood in the water, the blood of the Folk, shed in the sacred waters of the Eternity Tree by one of Zhaia's own children—the Tree couldn't survive this violation of the ancient covenant between the People and the land. It is this blood of treachery that threatens to drown me.

The wyr *pulls at me still, but its strength is fading. The surge of the bloodsong has diminished, and I can hear the screaming storm lift above the spirit-voices in the brutal rush of wind and water. My own weakness is nothing compared to this slow, mournful bleeding away. I can't bear the knowledge of such loss. It's more than death. It is erasure from the very memory of the world.*

"Unahi, help me," I whisper through the salty red liquid on my lips. "Mother. Tobhi. Daladir. Jitani. Biggiabba. Garyn. Averyn. Sinovian. Geth. Spirits of skyfire and earth, of all the worlds we call home. Zhaia, Green Mother, help me. Mothers of old, give me strength. I can't do it on my own."

I sink beneath the waves again, and this time I don't surface, but still I keep whispering, even as red water fills my mouth and the Tree fades into darkness. I'm on the edge of oblivion. It is silent.

No, not quite silent. I look down; a shape is swimming up through the red water toward me, his voice raised in familiar song. I remember him well. Wyrwood spikes still pierce his body, and his yellow eyes narrow in exultation as he approaches. The monster Wears-Stones-for-Skin swims with a speed and grace he never possessed in life. As if to prove it, he spins in an upward arc and laughs through the song, teasing me, his voice bubbling up and surrounding me.

He reaches out with a gnarled hand, and I pull away, but he keeps singing, and the fire rises in my blood. In life he was one of the Eaters of Old, and he's still dangerous in the Spirit World, but not to me, not now. His blood is my own. The song endures from the ancient days through the lives and deaths of those who hear it, and I'm just one more thread in a woven cord that travels through the Deep Green to the first days of the People. It will endure long after my own flesh has joined the rich soil and stars, but only if I survive now. If I'm lost in this place, I'll be lost forever. That's why he's returned. He's come to keep me a part of the wyr-*woven pattern. I'm no more special than all those who came before and those who'll come again after me, but each is needed in its time and place for the pattern to endure. And my time is now.*

The bloodsong burns in my ears, and I reach out. His touch is surprisingly gentle; the pebbled flesh of his palm is worn smooth and soft. He grins again and sweeps me upward, moving like a heron toward the surface. The water parts, and I'm alone and gasping for breath amidst the great roots of the Tree. I look up at the devastation. The silver glow is fading. Scales of shimmering bark rain down into the water, and the branches quiver in the shrieking winds. Lightning dances through the sky, but I can see without it, for a deep blue-green glow shines from the shattered trunk, and it calls to me.

I slip back into the water; the wood is too slick. Then I remember the knife Jitani gave me. It's still in its sheath at my side. As I start to slide toward the beckoning waves, I draw the knife and drive it into the wood. It slides easily, locking in, giving me something to hold. I slowly pull myself up, exhaustion finally catching me, and look down through the broken wood of the trunk into endlessness. Vertigo—my head spins, and I begin to drift away. My hands flail out for balance and take hold of something unexpected, and then I feel a sudden surge of strength as the Heartwood of the Eternity Tree bursts into living flame and envelops my body, binding me to the pulsing heart of the Everland. My chanting-sash unravels and falls away; it's kept my mind and spirit whole, safe from being overwhelmed by the wyr, *but I don't need it anymore.*

The Tree lives again.

Dark clouds finally moved in to ease the afternoon heat, but Tarsa felt little comfort. The fickle sky was a constant reminder of the strange and sudden shifts in weather that plagued these lands and made their journey increasingly difficult. Two full days of hard travel through biting cold nights and brutally hot days had brought them to this place, and yet, for all their cautious speed, they were too late: the Folk were already starting across the ford in barges. The Wielder stood in shadow on a small wooded rise overlooking the ramshackle settlement of Kateline Crossing, where hundreds of bent figures stood at the water's edge. More a rough collection of haphazard shacks and unkempt stables, the Crossing served a single purpose: to provide basic trade goods at excessive prices to travelers preparing to cross Shard Ford into the broken lands of Dûrûk beyond. The Jaaga-Folk had long chafed under the traders' ruthlessness, watching as the Men of the Crossing grew increasingly fat from the hard-earned pelts that the Jaagas brought in trade. The place was even less hospitable to the Everland exiles.

Two barges, each loaded with Human militiamen and far too many Folk, moved with ponderous slowness across the unsteady water. Unlike rope-drawn ferries on some of the smaller rivers they'd traveled, these barges were propelled by coal-fired Ubbetuk steam-engines and paddle-wheels that vomited out great clouds of sparks and black smoke. Even from this distance Tarsa could feel the sweep of iron sickness move off the water. It was little wonder that the Folk below huddled on the shore in quiet, unresisting misery; the barges would no doubt be the final journey for the weaker wayfarers.

"Something terrible is driving them on," Jitani hissed, rage and growing fear mingled in her voice.

Tarsa didn't need to respond. They could all feel the desperation that pushed the Men forward through the days and nights, with little more than survival sleep for the past few days, and now compelled them mercilessly forward into storm-savaged waters. More of the Folk were dying each day on the Road now than had died in a full week before. Where Tarsa and her allies once had time to honor the dead as they walked past in pursuit of the other exiles, they could now only move on and try to ignore the hunger-ravished bodies with their sightless eyes and puckering skin scattered everywhere along the Road. A few members of the group had, like Tobhi, been rescued after being abandoned by the Eromar soldiers in previous weeks, but there were no more survivors these days.

Tobhi lifted the brim of his hat and wiped the sweat from his forehead. "What d'ye suggest we do now? There en't much use in stoppin' those boats, since they already got half the Folk on the water. If we move in now, we'll only be trappin' them on the other side."

A snap of thunder rolled across the sky to signal the arrival of a sudden cold rain. It drove the warmth from the body, but at least it hid them from view, and for that Tarsa was thankful; surprise was their only real advantage now. Even so, it wasn't much.

The winds grew wilder with the rain. Most of the others moved back into the trees for cover, but the Wielder remained just on the edge of the thicket and watched as one of the barges moved ponderously away from the dock and into the rolling waters. It wasn't as big a boat as she'd expected; indeed, it looked far too small for the number of Folk crammed onto it. Where once the barge had carried hundreds of cows, pigs, sheep, and other livestock across the Riven Sea, it strained now under a different burden.

Tarsa's cloak slipped away in the wind, but her attention was fixed too closely on the sea below to notice. Something was wrong. She couldn't see very well through the heavy rain and blinding lightning, but the boat was moving strangely sideways, the waves dragging one side downward, into the water. Another burst of jagged skyfire tore through the growing darkness, and she saw it clearly: the barge was sinking.

One side of the boat tipped dangerously, and although the Folk rushed frantically toward the other edge, their panic simply caused the ship to shift more precariously into the water. Screams of desperate horror rose up from the Folk gathered at the water's edge in response to the cries from the boat. Bodies fell into the raging surge, and for a moment it looked like the barge would right itself. It hung on the edge, quivering, as dozens of Folk clung to ropes, wood, and each other to keep from being lost in the ravenous waves, their voices a unified wail. But then a piercing crack split the stormy air, and the barge split apart under the rushing weight of the water. It was gone in mere heartbeats, a few last clouds of black smoke and steam snaking upward through the rain, and with it went the Folk, many still holding tight to one another as they slipped beneath the swell and died.

The Wielder raised Dibadjiibé to the sky and called out to the *wyr*, to stop the storm and calm the waters, but the sudden deaths of so many Folk rushed over her, and she stumbled back with a primal scream that shook the hill. She could feel them dying even as she reached out, and now that the gate was open, she couldn't shut it. Each death was like a physical blow, and she thrashed wildly under the overwhelming assault. The staff fell from her hands.

Through the searing torment she now understood her terrible danger. True, the Heartwood had made her strong. The elements brought little pain, and she could withstand hunger and thirst like no other mortal. She could change the course of rivers, call down storms, and heal the hurt and dying, all without fear of harming the spirits who rushed to her call. But she was terribly vulnerable, now more than ever before.

Except for the few healing sparks of the Heartwood she'd shared with her companions, the essence of the Tree was now woven into her own. She and the Tree were one. And as the Tree connected the spirits of the living and the dead to the remnant shards of the Eld Green from which all the Folk had emerged, so now did she, and her fragile flesh couldn't bear the burden.

She fell back again, clutching at her head. Voices filled her mind. She saw their faces, but they were shifting, changing, and then the world became blood and white feathers as the owls dove toward her through a red-black sky, their dark eyes glowing. Screams of the dying became rasping shrieks in the night. Her blood boiled. The spirits were talking to her, desperate to tell her something, but she couldn't make out the words.

A burning pain spread across her forehead, and the red fog began to lift as she saw her own blood trickle to the waterlogged soil. She was on the ground, her head against a large rock, as the faces of her companions faded in and out of view. They were with her, but they were muddled and indistinct among the owls that still hissed and screamed out to her. She tried to understand, but it was too much, and she shook her head, trying to push them away. "Not yet," she groaned to the voices. "Not yet."

The red curtain dropped again, and soon another face moved into view, different from the others. He was clear and distinct, and the owls flapped silently away from the small darting shapes that surrounded him. Tarsa held out her hand and watched with delight as a large blue dragonfly landed on the edge of her finger, its translucent wings shining like diamonds in the strange light. Soon the air was filled with streaks of gold and ruby and emerald and sapphire, and the Wielder laughed.

"*Ev'rybody wants to tell their story, Tarsa. Remember ol' Akjaadit, the first Dragonfly, and her meetin' with Strivix the Owl? Sometimes we don't know the story afore we tell it, but it gives us strength anyhow. And sometimes we can't hear nobody's story 'cause we're so wrapped up in our own. Ye got to give their stories some room afore you'll understand 'em. 'Til then, ye got a lot of work to do."* The mist-formed image of Tobhi smiled again, and then faded into darkness. But the dragonflies remained to keep the owls away until the world became rain and earth again and the vision disappeared. Tarsa lay huddled in Jitani's strong arms as Daladir wiped mud and dead grass away from her face. A very real Tobhi knelt on the ground beside them, his face dark with worry.

Tarsa breathed in deeply and turned to her friends, her bruised face firm with resolve. "Hurry," she gasped as she reached out for her wyrwood staff and her travel pack. "This is our chance. We won't have another."

I don't know how long I've been unconscious, but when I open my eyes I see Daladir beside me. His face is covered with ash and dried blood, but it doesn't seem to be his own. The deep shadows under his eyes seem to lift, and he lifts my head to a clay jar and gives me a drink of cold water. The liquid has a bitter bite to it, but it's clean, and it eases my terrible thirst.

I want to talk, to know what's happened, to find out if the destruction of the Tree is real, but it's safe here by his side, and I don't want to hear what my heart tells me is undeniable. Unahi is dead. Sheynadwiin has fallen. Men have taken the Everland.

My eyes wander upward. We're in a cave, but it's not the massive gallery of the Eternity Tree. It's a rough, soot-stained chamber that smells of sweat and unwashed bodies. The air is thick with smoke; it doesn't seem to be coming from this tunnel. The cave is full of Folk huddled together with faces turned toward the entrance.

Daladir's green eyes never leave mine, and I'm more grateful than I care to admit. There's comfort in his presence. It's more than just familiarity. The concern on his face speaks to something deeper than simple friendship, and this time it doesn't frighten me. It's all that I want right now.

I finish drinking the water and nestle deeper into his arms. He stiffens for a moment, uncertain, but finally pulls me close and gently strokes the hair away from my face as we lie together and drift to sleep. And although the world we knew is shattered beyond recognition, and although death and pain and terror fill the air as much as the smoke of the burning forests, we sleep peacefully for a while.

High in the air above the Riven Sea, buffeted by vengeful winds and drenched by fierce rains, flew a score of Goblin airships commandeered by Vorgha for the Dreydmaster's final journey. They and their captured crews belonged to Eromar now. Vald was pleased. It was fitting that he arrive at the ritual site in the style and dignity befitting an ascending Dreyd, and even he had to admit that the artistry of the Unhuman Goblins surpassed all others in this regard. His present transport was cunningly shaped like a large scarab, a diplomatic vessel belonging to an enormously fat Goblin matron whose protest against its seizure resulted in chains, imprisonment, and toil in the iron mines of Eromar. When her sons protested, they joined her. There were no further complaints.

The Dreydmaster sat in a deep chair of crushed black velvet in the old matron's observation room and watched the world through a large, cunningly wrought window that was shaped like an insect's multifaceted eye. He almost regretted not having had such a ship before, but it was too late for such thoughts. He'd have much more remarkable experiences soon enough. For now he was content to listen to the whirring hum of gears and pulsing air bladders rumble through the ship and watch the savage storm from the carpeted splendor of this wood-paneled chamber.

Storms never bothered Vald. Even when he was a child, he had spent hours on his uncle's covered porch and watched as his dull town became a more fascinating world through the haze of falling rain, snow, and hail. He'd always enjoyed the massive spring storms the best, especially those with much lightning, and thunder so loud that the house and smithy rattled from the blast. It always seemed a shame that his uncle never stopped at the forge long enough to enjoy the town's transformation from a grimy little hamlet, with mangy dogs and scabby-kneed children skulking along the streets, into a silver-grey wonderland filled with wondrous strange shapes and unexpected mysteries. But his uncle had no appreciation for a world beyond his nose, and he'd stomp to the porch, box the boy's ears, and drag young Vald back to work among the biting fumes and sparks of the smithy. But even from the forge the boy could see what he wanted his world to be, and it helped him through the nastiness of the world he inhabited.

He'd watched hundreds of storms from the tower of Gorthac Hall. After joining the Dreydcaste and advancing up the ranks of the Reavers, he was the source of many of the storms, as he'd found that the Fey-demons of the air responded most powerfully to his commands. He'd order a Binder to draw unseen victims to him, and when the air-demons were firmly trapped within the Binder's chant, Vald would focus his will and begin the slow, delicious process of stripping sparks of life from them, forcing them through his Crafting into eruptions of frenzied pain. They couldn't harm him or escape, but in their desperation to free themselves they created the most fantastic tempests in Eromar's history—at least until the stormy night that Spearbreaker toppled the tower.

The witch's face was burned into his memory. He didn't care about the tower, barely cared about the damage to the rest of the house, but he greatly resented her strength, and the clear knowledge that those air-demons didn't destroy half of Gorthac Hall out of fear or pain but out of rage. The green-skinned creature didn't force them to do anything; she had awakened them, and they responded out of desire, not hers, but their own. And the power that resulted was unlike anything the Dreydmaster had ever experienced in all his years of endless study and toil as a Reaver. The demons never responded like that to his pleas, entreaties, or bribes, and although they followed his commands when torture was applied, it was always a ruthless struggle of wills.

Here he was, undeniably the most powerful Man in the Reach, a political leader whom even the great Reachwarden hesitated to openly challenge, a Dreydmaster who had reached the highest ranks of learning and daring among Men, and yet even he was forced to watch as a snake-headed Unhuman witch commanded powers that were, until now, still far beyond his reach.

In another time it would have been galling beyond tolerance, and he would have sent Seekers and other minions to bring her to him, bound and humiliated, so he could slowly unlock her secrets and show her just how futile it was to defy the iron will of Men. But however appealing such leisurely pursuits might be, they were also a distraction of both time and energy. Why hunt her down when she would be walking right to him? The Not-Ravens had followed her throughout her journey and kept Vald informed of her movements, and although he'd been surprised that she survived the razing of

Sheynadwiin, he knew that her eventual fate was just as certain. If anything, her approaching death would be more useful to him than if she'd died before the preparations for the great ritual were finished. Her commitment to her broken and ragged kind was an admirable but predictable weakness. It was a shame that someone so strong would be so unimaginative.

Vald turned to the figure who sat on the long sofa across from him. There were others among the witch's people who were far more interesting, others who knew well the pains and joys of sacrifice. He held up his empty crystal cup, and a trembling Goblin crept out of a corner of the room with a steaming silver decanter.

<<Would you care for more moché, Lady Shakar?>>

The copper-haired she-Kyn held up her hand and smiled wanly. <<No, thank you. I haven't the taste for it, I'm afraid.>>

Vald waved the Goblin away and returned his gaze to the window. <<An acquired taste, perhaps. It is one of the few vices in which I freely indulge—far less disruptive and far more invigorating than the fermented filth so popular among the Unpurified. My wife prefers hers with cream and honeyed chacatl, but I enjoy the honest bitterness of the undiluted seed. It is too easy to get lost in the weaknesses of the senses, and such a bite keeps one's mind clear and undistracted.>>

He took a sip of the black liquid. <<You have changed much since last we met; I nearly did not recognize you. I trust, however, that you are still committed to the cause?>>

Shakar nodded. Her flowing copper tresses were gone now, cut short to just a few fingers' width past her scalp. Her sensory stalks were covered by delicate white lace netting that draped down to her shoulders. Each cheek was lined with three bright scars, and her face was harder and slightly gaunt, making her violet eyes seem larger and that much more striking. But it was her robes that had changed the most. Shakar no longer wore the white robes of a Shield; she now wore silken robes of azure and midnight blue. The Kyn colors of mourning.

<<If I have changed much, it is because I have lost much, but not because of you, Dreydmaster. Visionaries are often called upon to challenge the world's blindness, even at the cost of comfort and rightful recognition.>>

<<Yes.>> Vald put the cup to his lips again and inhaled the acrid steam. <<And your new name?>>

<<A term of shame among my people.>> Her eyes narrowed. <<I wear it now as a badge of honor.>>

<<The nations of Men will look kindly on you, Lady Shakar, even if your own people do not, for it is in the histories of Men that your future is ensured.>> Vald set his cup on the table but never took his eyes from the window, through which he scrutinized her using the reflection of the glass. He knew that she was fully aware of his actions, but she seemed resigned to let him continue with the masquerade, so he turned his back to her and continued his double gaze: first looking to the storm, then to the she-Kyn's reflection.

At length the Dreydmaster grew tired of the game and motioned for the Goblin to clear the dishes. After the creature left, he turned his attention to Shakar.

<<You truly *are* a visionary among your people, my dear Lady, and that is why I am so pleased to have you join me on this journey. You above all others understand what it is to sacrifice all that is precious to you for a cause that is even greater still. There are few, Man or Kyn, who can say the same.>>

Shakar gave him the hint of a smile, but Vald could see the shadow of doubt in her eyes. *Sad creature*, he thought to himself. *She still stings from their rejection. They are only common animals, and she is so much more than they are now, but she cannot free herself from her roots. No matter how far she travels, no matter how much her people despise her, no matter how honored she is among Men, she will always share their weak natures . . . and she fears this unyielding truth.*

Vald walked over to Shakar and sat beside her on the couch. He leaned in, his leonine face taut and suddenly hungry. His voice was low, little more than a growl. <<The world will soon change, Lawmaker, more than you can imagine. And you have been a part of that. You alone of all your kind have understood the inevitability of the changes that are to come. Although your help was scorned, you alone freed them from blind superstition. But it is not over yet, not quite. There is still much that must be done.>>

Shakar's eyes glowed in the bursts of lightning that illuminated the room. <<What would you have me do, Authority?>> she whispered.

The Man smiled. <<Among the exiles there is one who still holds great power over the backward and superstitious of your kind.

She is much loved by the people, and they will no doubt turn to her in their doubt and fear.>>

<<She is dangerous, then?>>

<<Dangerous? Yes, she is certainly that. But she is also . . . useful. The old Tree was a powerful symbol, but it was but a tree, and its fall was seen by few. But this witch—she carries an uncommon strength with her, and that can be helpful in showing your people the futility of defiance. Until they come to fully accept that truth, they will be unable to free themselves from the shackles of the past toward a more certain future. Symbols are more powerful weapons than any blade, and they can be used for any purpose, vile or virtuous. It is up to you, my brave, wounded friend, to finish the task to which you committed yourself not so long ago. It is not too late to find favor among your people and to give them an honest future unclouded by superstition. It is not too late to find your redemption.>>

The she-Kyn's wounded face was radiant. <<What must I do?>>

"Wielder, you mustn't leave!" Sinovian says, his face torn between rage and despair. "You are needed here!"

I shake my head and look at the crowd, three hundred strong and growing: Kyn, Tetawi, Gvaergs, Ferals, and others, even a few allied Humans who chose to be fugitives rather than surrender their friends and freedom to the grasping hand of invasion. They are all survivors of the siege of Sheynadwiin; all somehow managed to avoid capture or death by the mercenaries and militiamen, the ravenous land-seekers who even now crawl close to this remote valley. There is little food here now, and precious little hope of more to come, especially with winter on its way and all the storehouses burned by the Mannish horde. Survival will be very, very difficult.

The Heartwood has healed them of physical injury, but there is nothing I can do to ease the nearly overwhelming grief on their hearts, or the painful memories of loved ones lost and butchered. There is no room for hope here. There is room only for survival. And so many of our people are defenseless on the Darkening Road. It is they who need me most.

Daladir stands beside me, his stalks bound in green wrappings. I can't cover my own stalks, though, for the Heartwood within refuses to be dampened. So my stalks move with a life of their own, charged with strength beyond under-standing. I'm fully alive as never before. All of my body sings to the world. It's all I can do to keep my thoughts together, to keep from fading away into the Tree, but for now my will is stronger than the power flowing through me, and I know I can't stay here. In one hand I hold Dibadjiibé, Unahi's last gift to me. In the other, I hold Tobhi's hat, found beyond the chamber of the Tree, next to the cold carcass of his fierce little deer-friend, Smudge. These things keep me rooted. They remind me of how much we stand to lose by waiting. The battle for the future of the Folk won't take place in fugitive caves and furtive shadows. The Tree can no longer be hidden from the world, not here, not anywhere. I must go to where the Tree can grow free and tall again, as it was meant to be.

Sinovian sees the answer on my face, and he turns away. He has lost most of his family—his wife, his eldest son and only daughter, his uncle. But he refuses to surrender. He's still a Redthorn warrior, and if anyone can keep these scattered people together, it will be him. His rage will be the fire that warms them.

I desperately want to say something, but words seem inadequate, and the rising tide of anguish that rolls through the crowd is almost enough to make me turn back. I grieve for Unahi, and dear Tobhi, and all the others who disap-peared in the chaos. But Daladir is beside me, as are others who understand my task and wish to join me. I'm not alone.

We're moving away from the crowd toward the tree line when Sinovian calls out. He walks to me, and by his side is his lovely sister, Jitani, who let me take her place on the airship to Eromar, almost a lifetime ago, and who fought beside us in that last terrible battle for the Tree. The pain of her many losses must still be immense. But when she looks at me, it's not hurt I see, but kindness, and something else, something I also see in Daladir's eyes. They've both given me my life back. I think of her knife; it has saved me more than once. More than love of the People brings her to me.

Sinovian turns to me. "You bear a precious burden, Wielder. I wish I could talk you out of this madness, to make you stay here with us where you'll be safe, but I can't force you to listen to reason. I can only pray to whatever spirits still watch over us in this blighted land that you know what you're doing, and that you won't forget us if you succeed."

My throat tightens. "I won't forget you, Sinovian. You have my word on that."

He frowns and continues. "I can't make you stay, but I don't have to let you go without good protection, either." He turns to the she-Kyn at his side. "You know my sister. She's a respected Thorn Branch warrior and tracker who has traveled widely in the lands of Men. She knows their ways very well." His glance flickered for a moment toward his sister's two savaged sensory stalks. "There's no one braver, or more dedicated. Take her with you. Do this for me, at least."

Jitani draws a wyrwood blade from the beaded scabbard at her side and holds it to her chest. "You asked me once to protect Unahi, and I failed to do so. But I give my blood vow to you now, Wielder, that I will defend you with my life, and with my death, if it comes to that. Will you accept me?"

I'm speechless. Blood vows are rare and inviolate; they demand much of both the giver and the receiver. But the Darkening Road will be long and perilous, and I'll need every bit of strength I can get. It's not just the mortal dangers I fear; I also dread the loss of myself within the Heartwood. To know that others are depending on me may be enough to keep me sane and safe. Besides, I'm drawn to her smile, to the curve of her hip and the easy, unhesitant way she balances the blade in her hands. She intrigues me.

"I accept your oath, Jitani of Thorn Branch. Be welcome at my fire."

Sinovian embraces his sister, turns, and walks stiffly away. Jitani watches him for a moment. When she looks at me, there are no tears in her golden eyes. Just acceptance. They have both lost so much, and yet they're willing to take this chance, too, with the hope of something better on the other side of the journey. Finally, I take her strong hand and lead her to the small group.

"It is time," I say, and we begin the long walk west.

"Garyn."

"Beloved, get up."

"*Garyn!*"

Averyn shook hir lover's arm, but the old Governor ignored hir. Garyn was tired. No, he was broken and blasted to the root. The loss of the barge and all the Folk on it was the last horror he could face. Over all these terrible weeks he'd tried to be so strong, and for a while he really *had* been. He'd comforted mothers when their saplings passed into the Spirit World; he'd calmed striplings when their parents were racked with delirious fever; he'd challenged the mercenary policies of the Kateline Crossing merchants, and personally emptied one trader's sour-mash barrels out of fear that the Man would try to cheat some of the more easily tempted Folk of what little they still had; he'd held young she-Folk who'd been brutalized by Men in the night, and helped plan vengeance attacks with such subtlety that they seemed nothing more than strange and bloody accidents. If Garyn Mendiir had been a loved and honored leader before the Darkening Road, he was doubly so now, for none of his people, nor any of the other Folk, had ever seen his strength and grace falter. They didn't see him, deep in the night, in the darkness of his wagon, when he silently wept in Averyn's strong arms. They didn't see him when he awoke, or the raging grief that choked him with such violence that Averyn often thought the old he-Kyn would die from the power of his fury. No, the Folk saw in Garyn Mendiir, and in many of their leaders, the strength they needed to continue each day's dark journey.

But Garyn wouldn't get up again, not after what he'd seen, not after the sea consumed all those gentle spirits. *Let the others go on if they can. My walk is over.*

"Beloved, you *must* awaken. Someone is here to see you."

There was a strange quality in Averyn's voice that caught the Governor's attention. It wasn't the ever-present heartache of these dark days. He couldn't quite remember the sound, but it seemed reminiscent of something like hope.

The old he-Kyn lifted his head from the thin blanket on the floor of the wagon. Averyn was smiling—actually *smiling!*—beside another figure. Garyn tried to make out the other, vaguely Kyn-like shape, but its features were blurred by a burning blue-green radiance that filled the wagon. The thought occurred to him that he ought to feel fear at this strangeness, but it was a soothing light, and familiar, as though he'd seen it a lifetime ago.

A lifetime ago. And then he knew.

"It can't be," he gasped, pulling himself up to his knees, his eyes shining with wonder. "It was dead . . . I saw it myself. The Tree is gone."

Tarsa held out her hand and led him from the wagon into the open air. "It's come back, Garyn, to all of us." Their fingers touched, and life returned to the he-Kyn. He was reborn.

"Now come," the Wielder whispered. "We must hurry. There's still so very much to be done." She looked to the sky, where distant shadows disappeared into the clouds.

The attack comes suddenly, but it's not unexpected—we knew there would be no easy way to leave the Everland. This small ridge is dense with scrub oak and shaggy pine, their fallen leaves and brown needles blanketing the rock-strewn ground; these Men are loud and ungainly, even in attempted stealth. They're arrogant, too, filled with bloodlust and greed and warm with the flush of their earlier victory against Sheynadwiin. They think that slaughtering the aged and infirm makes them courageous. They think that they're made strong by heedlessly destroying a place of ancient beauty and unbroken history unique to this Melded world. They expect us to flee, to run screaming from them and their murderous weapons.

They are wrong.

As planned, the Tetawi brothers, Jorji and Jothan, turn and kneel, aiming carefully as they unleash a rain of deadly arrows on the Men to cover our counterattack, while Eladrys darts in among her former kind with long knives flashing, drawing hot blood with every swift movement. Daladir and Oryn rush to join the battle, guarding one another's flank as they strike hard with spear and miner's pick. Others take their positions, and the Men are soon pushed to a desperate knot, striking back with more fear than ability.

I'm standing away, at the bracken-filled hollow below the ridge, with Jitani by my side, waiting for the right moment to strike. We can't leave any survivors to warn others of our presence, as we must travel swiftly and without unnecessary delay, but so much killing sickens me now, and I wish we had another choice. Jitani's attention is split between the fight in front of us and watching our surroundings for unexpected dangers. She doesn't seem concerned about the fate of these creatures, and I wonder why I should care so much myself. After all, they've destroyed so much that I love, so much that is woven into my being. How can I forgive that?

But I remind myself that forgiveness isn't our concern right now—life is what matters, and every new death, whether Man or Folk, diminishes what we're fighting to maintain. I'm tired of death and bloody deeds, but at the moment it's a balance: they die, or we do. Too many people rely on us to permit failure. We must finish this.

Three Men, large and well armed, break through the knot and rush our way. They want to escape, but we stand in their path, and they're terrified and desperate—thus doubly dangerous. Jitani's sword is ready, and her eyes have gone hard, as they did when we faced the Shields at the chamber of the Tree. She closes something of herself when in the heat of battle, and although I know that it makes her stronger and smarter, less likely to be swept away by her rage, it frightens me, because I don't know what's behind that inner barrier. I wonder if there will ever be a time when she won't be able to return through it. A Kyn distanced from the pains and pleasures of the sensory world isn't fully Kyn; most who've suffered such a mutilation of their sensory stalks go mad from the loss of that deeper tie to the world and its harsh beauty. How has she maintained her spirit for so long? Has she?

I watch as she plants her feet firmly in the red earth and swings her broad-bladed sword in a wide arc around her, catching one of the Men in its path. He screams and falls as another drives forward, his own sword raised high. She steps slightly to the side and meets his blow, staggering slightly from the force of it. He's much larger, and he's in a frenzy—he wants nothing more than to escape, or to bring Jitani down with him.

The third Man runs around them; he's no longer interested in killing . . . he just wants to escape. He's fast, but I'm faster. I extend my hands, a glowing green mist flows across my vision, and the wyr *goes hot in my blood. I call out to the earth and sky, and a blinding whirlwind of dust and choking debris responds. It bears down on the Man just as he reaches the top of the ridge, and he's dragged shrieking into the air, rising higher and higher until he's far from sight and sound. There's a thunderous crack above us, and all is silent except for the groans of the wounded and dying, and a sudden thump on the ground behind me.*

My eyes clear, and I turn to see Jitani stagger slightly, her face pale, golden eyes wide in shock. Her attacker is dead just a few steps away, but she's clutching her throat, and blood streams through her fingers. I rush forward, and she sags into my arms. The wound is ghastly; her hand slips away, and the blood spurts like a fountain with each rhythmic heartbeat. She took the wound intended for me—she's already honored her blood vow, and we're not even out of our ravaged homeland yet. I barely know her, but I have no intention of letting her go. She's a warrior of uncommon skill and strength. We need her. I need her.

Her pulse is weak, and fading; her breathing is getting deeper, more desperate. I cover her wound with one hand and draw her close to me with the other. My thoughts extend into the world, and the wyr *answers my call. A link is forged between my flesh and hers; our hearts are on different beats for a few uncertain moments, but they soon find a shared strength and rhythm, drumming with renewed power as the slashed skin on her throat begins to knit under my warm palm. Her labored gasps ease as my lips close over hers, and my* wyr-*touched breath fills her lungs and pulls her farther from death's grasp. We breathe in unison, and as she gets stronger, she finally begins to breathe by herself. But I don't pull away.*

This was not how I'd imagined our first kiss. Her blood soaks my hands, the earth, and her wyrweave tunic; dead Men and injured friends are all around us; our homeland is broken, our people are in exile on a darkening road west. But as her warrior spirit heals and becomes strong again, and as her bright eyes open and grow clear with a welcome understanding, I don't pull away.

And neither does she.

38

Homecomings

<<SOCIETY IS A FICKLE MISTRESS, *but she is the only thing that survives the decrepitude of age. The bloom of youth may fade, but good station endures.*>> It was a philosophy that Mardisha Kathek followed with single-minded devotion. The Woman had gone from being the envious younger daughter of a mid-level wine merchant to becoming one of the most sought-after socialites in the First Families, the upper ranks of Chalimor's elite High Houses. The journey had been a hard one, but her studied charm, unyielding ambition, and statuesque beauty certainly helped to ease the pains of the journey, as did her marriage to Yelseth Kathek, heir to the much-envied Kathek mining fortune. The Man might be unrelentingly boorish and unimaginative—in bed as well as conversation—but he had money and family connections, and as long as he was well stocked with fine liqueurs and a good number of dull-witted but enthusiastic mistresses, he gave Mardisha plenty of freedom to follow her own pursuits. Such a situation was far from uncommon in their social circle, but Mardisha and Yelseth had none of the jealousy or bitterness that seemed to poison similar arrangements among their friends and acquaintances: Yelseth was honest about his affairs, and Mardisha was honestly relieved to be freed of the burden of sharing his bed. As a result, theirs had been a truly harmonious home for nearly thirty years.

There had been a time when Mardisha Kathek had an open invitation to every house on Rosewood Hill, the most respectable neighborhood in Chalimor and the ancestral territory of most of the First Families. All the Woman had to do was ride in her black-lacquered carriage down the cobblestone lanes of the Hill, past luxuriant gardens and marble-columned stone mansions, and she would have a dozen or more invitations to breakfasts, teas, dinners, salons, and other amusements waiting for her when she returned to her own home at the upper end of the Hill. She'd only accept a few of the invitations each week, thus whetting the appetite of those who sought her company and ensuring a steady stream of admirers for months to come.

Yes, Mardisha Kathek had once been the pampered dove in the gilded cage of Chalimor's finest neighborhood. But those times were sadly past. She'd fallen from grace so quickly, so thoroughly, that she didn't realize she was outside the cage until the door had closed behind her. Such was the way of the First Families. Confrontation was unthinkable; anything other than pleasant decorum and unruffled refinement was surreptitiously and mercilessly purged from the delicacy of the Hill. But while the surface remained smooth, a glance beneath would find a boiling world of intrigue, cruelty, and deception. It was here that Mardisha now saw her life being ripped apart by those with sharp tongues and tenacious memories, whose festering jealousies, long nursed and well nourished, were now released to spread their venom throughout the only world she knew. Gentle smiles often hid sharp teeth.

It would be a little while yet before she was fully exiled from the life on the Hill, but that day was approaching. In the meantime, the pace of invitations would steadily slow to a trickle; the conversations would get shorter, and eyes once locked in rapt attention would begin to wander with instructive boredom; her staff would drift away to houses of more respectable reputation. Then the long-feared day would come when the callers disappeared altogether, and her rejection would be complete. She would be like the dead, snuffed out of Chalimor's favored circles, denied even the courtesy of a wake in her memory.

And all because of the Dreyd-cursed Folk! Their stubborn, selfish refusal to embrace the gifts freely given by the Dreydmaster of Eromar had tainted public sentiment, even though the Reachwarden was still an unapologetic Unhuman supporter; the creatures' outright violation of the terms of Vald's generous treaty was worse than stupidity—it was arrogance, if not betrayal, and there was no room among civilized Men for such faithless creatures.

They hadn't always been this way. Indeed, she'd once held great hope for the eventual domestication of all the Folk; it had become her life's work. Her charitable service with the Friends of the Folk had brought enormous prestige to the organization. With her contacts, the Friends had become more than just a group of high-minded socialites; they became a political force with growing influence among the Assembly members and even the Reachwarden himself. The Friends were now the undisputed authorities on Reach policy toward the Folk. No law passed the Reach Assembly without their consultation and endorsement. Bringing the Folk into the Nations of Men was a gargantuan task, but it was one that Mardisha and her associates relished. It eased their boredom and gave them myriad little projects of character improvement to pursue.

And they could actually see their work making a difference. She had set an example by bringing a number of the benighted creatures from the howling wilderness into her home, with the hope of teaching them the ways of Men. She'd given them schooling and taught them to read, to speak, to behave appropriately, to do everything necessary for unburdening themselves of the toxic taint of wild beasts and dark forests. And, on occasion, she'd been successful, so much so that the funds kept flowing, and all the First Families added their participation among the Friends of the Folk as one more measure of prestige on Rosewood Hill. The too-frequent failures were quickly cut away before they could cause a scandal and corrupt their ever weak companions, and they vanished as thoroughly as if they'd never existed. All she had to do was dress a little Brownie-child in a blue velvet suit with ruffles on the sleeves and collar and black buckled shoes on his tiny feet, stand him in front of a crowd of bewigged and lace-dripping Men and Woman, and have him sing a plaintive chorus of "To the Argent Moon Sang the Pensive Whippoorwill," and Mardisha's virtue would be the talk of the Hill for weeks on end. The money would always flow.

All these thoughts burned in the Woman's mind as her carriage bounced and shuddered through the rough, shell-strewn streets of the Merchant's Ward, returning far later than she desired to her fading house on the Hill. She could no longer shop in her favored Rosewood marts and boutiques. She'd placed orders with a different merchant every day for the past week, and each returned a brief, unsealed note with the same message: *We regret to inform you that the items you have requested are no longer available from this establishment.* The ink fairly dripped with sneering sympathy. If Mardisha had doubted her swiftly accelerating fall before, this was all the evidence she would have needed. She was being pushed out of the Hill, and all with poisoned pens and smiles.

She might have sent one of her trusted maids to do the shopping, but most of these Women had disappeared over the past few weeks, and the few who remained were those she desired to see least: backcountry Kyn and Brownies, all trained by the Friends to be dutiful domestics. They were no longer welcome among the other First Families, and, indeed, weren't very welcome in her home, but she couldn't get hardworking Women to remain in her employ, so she had to make do with the very creatures that had brought about her downfall. And now she was finally seeing them with eyes unclouded by romantic charity. Where she'd once seen noble Unhumans in need of enlightenment, she now saw surly creatures who turned their backs on all the precious opportunities she'd provided to them; where once they'd been sweet, faithful children with unlimited possibility, they were now selfish, unkempt, and unmotivated brutes no better than the forest beasts from which they'd descended. Mardisha could barely contain her disgust every time she walked into her home and saw one of the creatures pawing over her lovely furniture with a filthy dust-rag. Something would have to be done, and soon, or her fall would be irreversible.

Still, all was not lost, not yet. A week earlier she'd received her invitation to tonight's festivities—the Reachwarden's Jubilee, *the* social event of the year, held in the atrium of the Hall of Kings. It was the celebration of the overthrow of the old royalty and the installation of a more egalitarian republic, that of the freely elected Assembly and Reachwarden. It would be a time of unsurpassed goodwill and, she hoped, forgiveness. Although most of the First Families had abandoned her, there were still some who held her in esteem, and these would be her greatest hope for returning to the warm bosom of Chalimor society. Today's quick shopping expedition brought the necessary accessories that would make her fully prepared for tonight's festivities; if she made it home soon, she'd be able to put the finishing touches on a penitent but still elegant jade-green dress and pearl-beaded turban and still have time for a light dinner before the Jubilee. If she could prove that her former sympathy for these Unhuman animals was firmly behind her, she might be able to salvage her position, perhaps even return to something greater.

The wagon jolted again, and Mardisha slapped the carriage door with her parasol. <<Mind where you're going, you black-eyed brat, or you'll be paying for the repairs. You've been careless enough with my property as it is.>> She waited for a sullen response from the Brownie driver. Hearing none, she smirked and nestled back into the cushions. Perhaps her husband was right. All these creatures truly understood was a sharp tongue and the occasional thrashing. She'd tried to change them, but most had proven incapable of abandoning their wild ways. Even red-haired Neranda, her most promising and accomplished pupil, had returned to the wilderness of her ancestors, and by all reports it seemed that the girl had paid a heavy price for such foolishness. Admittedly, she'd wanted to share her education and new ways with her people, but such training was best left to the firmer minds and hearts of Men. If only she'd stayed in Chalimor . . .

But it was past time for regrets. Neranda made the choice to go back to that lawless world. She could hardly be surprised that the wild animals would one day bite her outstretched hand.

Mardisha cursed as one of the wagon wheels smashed into something hard, sending the Woman sprawling across the seat. Where had she gone wrong? She'd once been loved among Folk and Men, but now she received resentful glares from the former and cold dismissal from the latter. It was all terribly unfair. Her perfumed world was crumbling, and now her Unhuman driver was trying to destroy the only good carriage she had left. She had already suffered enough—surely there was hope for redemption?

To her surprise, the carriage came to a stop just as she was about to start screaming again. She pulled up the shade and looked outside. Her face turned red as she watched the Brownie jump down, throw his coat and hat on the ground, and disappear around a corner.

<<Petyr!>> she screamed from the window. <<Petyr! Where are you going? This isn't the house! Come back here immediately,

you little brute!>> The smell of seaweed and fish was almost overwhelming. She was in an alley at the dock ward. What was he thinking, abandoning her in this low-district cesspool just before dark?

Mardisha opened her door and stepped outside, only to recoil in disgust as her boot and the hem of her dress dipped into a stinking pool of fish grease floating on brown water. She tried to back up into the carriage, but the heel of her boot was now too slick, and it slipped off the step. Her arms flew out wildly. There was nothing to grab for balance, so with a high-pitched shriek she plummeted, face-first, into the stinking street. "*Petyr!!!*" Mardisha screamed, her face purple now with rage and filth.

<<He's gone, Mardisha,>> a soft voice responded, and the Woman pulled the dripping hair away from her eyes to see a curvaceous figure in gaudy silks leaning against the rear wheel of the carriage. <<Besides, his name is Pishkewah, or it was until you insisted that he change it to something you thought more appropriately civilized. He's gone to find his family, as have the rest of your rather underappreciated staff.>>

<<What are you talking about? What have you done with my servants?>> Mardisha hissed.

The newcomer's green eyes twinkled. <<I just helped them along a little, that's all. I didn't think you'd mind.>> She jingled a small belt purse in front of the Woman's face. <<After all, this money was donated for the noble goal of helping the Folk. I guess one could say that it really belonged to them all along. It wasn't doing them much good in that little locked chest in your study.>>

The Woman stood up and tried to wipe her face free of fishy ooze. <<I knew you were a whore, Denarra, but I didn't know you were a thief, too. The marshals of Chalimor have no love of either, and they'll be quite interested to hear about this latest venture of yours.>>

The Strangeling laughed. <<My dear Mardisha, you've become such an unpleasant old catfish! You used to be so sweet and condescending; I wonder what happened. Why, I remember when you were so desperate to be seen in the presence of Folk that even a tainted specimen like me was welcome to hold your clammy little hand to demonstrate your patronizing generosity.>> Ignoring the Woman's speechless fury, Denarra shrugged. <<But I'm not here to argue with you, darling. I've come to have a little talk, just like in

the old days, when you were more pleasant and I was naive enough to believe that you really cared more about the Folk than your own bootlicking reputation.>>

Mardisha turned back to the carriage. <<I'm not going to trade false pleasantries with a strumpet. Good evening. Expect to hear from the marshals about my stolen property.>> She lifted her boot to the coach-step, but she slipped again and nearly tumbled back to the street.

As the Woman caught her balance, Denarra laughed. <<Same old Mardisha. I'd almost forgotten what a terrible temper you have! It's almost as distracting as that enormous mole on your forehead. Don't worry, darling—I won't let either of those things get in the way of our little reunion. I'm a forgiving person. You see, I understand that you still have a bit of influence in high places, and I'm ever so eager to go to the Jubilee tonight. In fact, it's most urgent that I attend. If anyone can help me, I just know it would be you . . . especially these days.>>

It was now Mardisha's turn to laugh. <<Help you? You've lost the little mind you once had. If I wouldn't be seen in public with one of my own maids, what makes you think I'd be seen with a creature like you? You're positively pestilential, and you've lost whatever worthy reputation you could claim before. I have no interest in wasting my time or what little standing I still have among the good *Human* people of this city by being seen in your demented company.>> She looked at the coach. <<Damn Petyr, and damn you, too, Denarra Syrene. Find a more receptive audience. I wash my hands of all your cursed kind.>>

Turning with a sniff of disdain, she shut the door and moved toward the street, stopping short as a group of figures stepped out of the shadows. One was a dark-eyed she-Brownie who held a long silver dagger in her gloved hand, light gleaming along its sharp edge. Beside her stood a grim young Man in purple silks and leathers with a book chained to his right arm; in his left hand he held a long-hafted hammer that he swung with slow menace. The last of the figures was a well-dressed Goblin valet with two small hand-crossbows, each pointed at the Woman's vitals.

Mardisha looked back to Denarra, who still leaned against the carriage. The Strangeling smiled coldly.

<<Mardisha, darling, I think you've misunderstood me. Let me clarify this in terms that even a half-wit like you can understand: this *isn't* a request.>>

Neidam read the letter again and shook his head in disbelief. The Reachwarden, Qualla'am Kaer, had summoned the guardsman to his private office in the Hall of Kings. Neidam had already served his shift hours, but he'd dutifully crawled out of bed, pulled on his boots and longcoat, strapped on his sword, and hurried to the waiting coach, ruefully scratching his three-day stubble. The Reachwarden placed the letter in his hand the moment he arrived at the White Chamber. Neidam wanted to pretend that it said something else, that the words would rearrange themselves into something that made sense and didn't send his stomach into knots. But no matter how hard he tried to wish the words away, they always returned to the same firm message in a tight black script, so precise and forceful that the pen had nearly ripped through the bleached paper:

To My Honored Colleague, the Estimable Reachwarden, Qualla'am Kaer:

You have made your point well known to me, Kaer—your curious concern for the criminal Unhumans in the "Ever-land" is unfortunate but not surprising. The weak-kneed statesmen in the garish halls of Chalimor have little under-standing of the savagery that is the true nature of these creatures in the western lands. Ignorance, however, is no justification for cowardice, or stupidity.

It is well that you remember one thing: you are Reachwarden, but I am Eromar, and Eromar bows to none, especially when we are well within our sovereign rights. This "Ever-land" belongs to Eromar, not to Chalimor, and certainly not to a handful of unredeemed nomads unable to put the land to the uses for which it was intended. We will have what is ours, with or without your blessing.

Proceed on this course, and you will find fire at your feet. The Law protects Men; it recognizes neither tree nor stone nor beast, except as they belong to the service of Men. Have you the mettle to enforce this decision? Shall we test it?

V.

Neidam refolded the letter and handed it back to Kaer. <<So, he's come out and said it directly: he's declared full treason.>>

The Reachwarden nodded. His face was drawn and ashen; it seemed that silver had streaked the thick black hairs of his goatee almost overnight. He looked older than Neidam had ever seen him before. A former military campaigner himself, with a sterling reputation for bravery and integrity, Qualla'am Kaer was a Man of indomitable spirit and unyielding moral courage, one whom the guardsman served not only willingly, but with pride. Neidam was honored by his work as the Captain of the Reachwarden's Guard, and each day brought more opportunities to make the Guard an effective defensive force like no other. Although he'd seen too much death, deception, and cruelty in his life to think anyone worthy of idolatry, the soldier had enormous respect for the Reachwarden.

It wasn't Kaer's clear fear that filled the guardsman with foreboding but rather the sudden realization that peace in the Reach now stood balanced on the narrow edge of a knife . . . and the blade sat in Lojar Vald's hand. Worse still, public sentiment was clearly on Vald's side, no matter how wrong-headed or dishonorable his behavior. Hordes of eager young Men—and not a few Women—had already left the city for the Old Everland with the hope of finding land, riches, and glory.

Neidam cleared his throat. <<Sir, has anyone else read this note?>>

<<Not yet. You're the first.>> He drained a long-stemmed glass of sweet mead and reached again for the decanter. <<Of all the nights to do this, he had to choose the Jubilee. I've got to be at the Crystal Court in an hour to begin 'the celebrations of the unification of the Reach under the republican will of the people,' and this is when that viper-tongued bastard makes his move.>>

Holding the folded letter up to the oil lamp at the desk, Neidam examined a series of sharp gouges in the paper. <<Who delivered the note?>> he asked.

Kaer grimaced. <<You wouldn't believe me if I told you.>>

<<I've seen some strange things in my time. Try me.>>

<<Never saw anything like this in my life. Nasty creature; I first took it to be a ragged raven, but its face—all oozing eyes and sharp teeth. I only saw it for a moment as it flew in and dropped off the letter, and that was more than enough. It took me a long time to even pick up the letter, let alone open it.>>

Neidam's brows wrinkled. <<Was there anything else? Did it say anything or do anything unusual?>>

<<Well,>> Kaer snorted, <<I'm not exactly sure what is 'usual' for such a thing, so I'm not in much of a position to speak to that, but no, that was it. It flew in, dropped the letter, and flew back out. That's it.>>

The Reachwarden and his captain stared at the note. Finally, Neidam said, <<I took the liberty of planning for a quick deployment after your last declaration to the Assembly. Come morning, they can be ready to advance into Eromar.>>

<<No.>>

Neidam stared at Kaer. <<But the Reach has recognized the rights of the Folk to those lands for almost two hundred years, and it has taken sacred oaths to protect those claims. You promised to uphold the covenants of defense. Vald's note has made his treachery clear. What more do you need?>>

Kaer turned a sad but firm gaze on the other Man, who wasn't that much younger in years or worldly experience. In political life, however, Kaer was a reluctant master, and his mind saw webs of action and response spreading out endlessly, whereas his friend saw a few clear paths, some easier than others. Neidam was an unyielding idealist, but the wearying world had long ago worn away Qualla'am Kaer's idealism. <<There's much more to think about now, Neidam . . . much more. If only it were that simple. There's little support in the Assembly for such interference; there's even less among those on the street. It's not a simple world, not anymore, not ever again.>>

<<But sir, how can you turn away?>>

<<I haven't turned away,>> he snapped. <<I have much to consider now, and very little time in which to do it. Wait for me outside. I'd like you to accompany me to the Jubilee.>>

The guardsman stood and bowed stiffly. He wanted to argue, to shout, to do anything that would lift the despairing pall from the room, but he'd been given a direct order that ended further discussion.

Neidam left the room, and Kaer stood. In the White Chamber, by the fading light of a single flickering oil lamp and the crackling ashes in the fireplace, the Reachwarden opened the letter and read it again. Unlike Neidam, Qualla'am Kaer didn't hope to find something new among the black lines on the page. All he wanted to find was courage, and there was little room for that in the words of Lojar Vald. No matter what his choice would be, it would mean devastation.

A sudden chorus of trumpets rang through the corridors of the Hall of Kings to announce the beginning of the Jubilee. Kaer looked up, his brown face haggard. Walking to the fireplace, he let the letter fall among the glowing coals and watched as the paper burst into orange flame. He waited until nothing existed of Vald's missive but a slender sheet of ash, then took up his jacket and strode purposefully from the room toward the Crystal Court. His decision was made; it was the only one he could possibly live with. He hoped such conviction would be enough.

Right or wrong, it would have to be.

The Hall of Kings was a fitting testament to the ambitions of the founders of the Reach. In the days before the overthrow of the monarchy and the establishment of the Reach Republic, the Hall stood as a reminder of the military might of the great kings of old. It had been designed to inspire awe and no small amount of fear in those who viewed it, and the six generations of kings who once ruled over the Reach had each made the Hall their own, drawing slaves and resources from throughout the provinces and other lands to enhance their own grand dreams. It was a half-mile-wide rectangle flanked by two massive octagons built of white marble and granite, with a columned central tower—the Crystal Court—capped by a massive dome of cut glass and joined to the rest of the structure by lacy stone arches radiating from the middle like the tines of a sunburst. The dome blazed so brightly on cloudless days that it nearly blinded those imperious enough to look skyward. Marble-topped towers rose high and proud at the apex of every side of the building, but none stood taller than the wondrous vault of the Crystal Court.

The deep and well-patrolled waters of Chal Bay kept most unwanted visitors from the city's center, while the cliffs of Mount Imor and the outer city walls amply defended the inner wonders of Chalimor, so the Hall of Kings was unmarred by protective partitions. Rather, its open corridors, wide halls, and carved white columns gave a sense of imposing, spacious welcome, even under those kings better known for cruelty than wisdom. It was a hub of culture and law, where poor and wealthy alike were free to enter, though on different floors of the structure. Lush, fragrant gardens and wide green lawns spread out on every side of the Hall as well as in various open chambers throughout the estate.

The Hall of Kings was the greatest treasure of the people of Chalimor, and when the kings were overthrown there was no thought of replacing such a magnificent structure with anything else. It belonged to the people now, and though it kept its former name—in spite of occasional attempts to replace the antiquated term with something more befitting a republic—the Hall became even more beloved in the new age of the Reach of Men. It was said that the Crystal Court would never fall, not as long as the glory of Men stood strong.

Quill had heard of the Hall of Kings even before she came to Chalimor, but nothing had prepared her for the sight of the great crystal dome at night, shining from the moonlight without and the thousands of candles and torch sconces within. Light danced through the massive central chamber with such a bewildering array of colors and patterns that it was all she could do to keep her thoughts focused on their reason for being at the Jubilee in the first place. Her eyes strayed upward at the terraces that ringed the great atrium, and her senses swam with the smell of flowers in bloom and the sweet spices that wafted from enormous incense braziers scattered through the growing throng. The delicate sound of soft harps and flutes wove through the crowd and gave a calming note to the slow hostility that built around them.

The Dolltender tried to ignore the dark glances and whispered remarks, but it was impossible to pretend that their small group was welcome. If not for Mardisha's admittedly reluctant presence, they would have been stopped at the Hall's great doors. But the Woman's invitation had said *Guests Generously Received*, and all the guests were dressed in the expected finery: the Strangeling wore a sky-blue dress with a white silk wrap across her shoulders, bright pearls draping her throat and earlobes, and a wide-brimmed white hat trimmed with her signature peacock feathers; a simple but elegant gown of shimmering, copper-colored cloth adorned the Tetawa; Merrimyn cut a dashing figure in a black suit and polished riding boots, his snaring-tome hidden beneath the folds of a long, red-lined cape that gave him an air of mystery and slight menace. As the invitation was quite explicit and made no comment about Folk being excluded from the ceremony, the guards were unwilling to cause a disruption, so they admitted Mardisha and her three strange companions.

The group walked down a long staircase from the front hall to the atrium as the low, incessant buzz of scornful voices filled the air. Mardisha's shoulders fell. When they at last reached the center of the great chamber, Merrimyn moved to a high spot from which he could see a long distance, and Denarra released the Woman's arm. Fixing the Strangeling with a glare so venomous that Quill stepped back, Mardisha rushed into the crowd and disappeared from sight.

"Aren't you afraid she'll tell someone that we forced her to bring us here?" Quill whispered.

Denarra grinned mischievously. "Mardisha and I know each other quite well, too well, perhaps; if she says anything about us, the world will learn about how Yelseth Kathek discovered young Mardisha don Haever in a two-shack brothel in the small fishing town of Waterborne. If not for a popular talent she exercised quite freely with her regular clientele, he probably wouldn't have brought her back with him at all. Her association with Folk has cast a shadow over her reputation, but it's redeemable; this little bit of news would destroy her place in society forever. It would be worse than death for someone like her."

"And what about you, Denarra?" asked Quill. "What about your place in society? Do you miss what you gave up for us . . . for me?"

Denarra looked down with surprise. She seemed to hesitate for a moment before reaching out to brush a loose strand of hair away from her friend's eyes. "It hurts sometimes, I won't deny it. But I knew this day would come eventually—there's no permanent place of affection among Humans when you're Kyn-sired. Admittedly, I always thought that the cause of my exile would be some terrible scandal involving me and the virile son of a local politician or other such outrage, not this particular type of smooth-faced nastiness. Still, in this matter I'd rather be on the unfashionable side and welcomed with love by people of good heart than be the pet of fools drooling over the dregs of their attention and regard. That kind of life has never much appealed to me."

Quill's eyes misted over, and she reached out to squeeze Denarra's hand. In spite of everything they'd said to each other in the past few days, all the suspicious recriminations and biting words, there was no doubt now about the Strangeling's allegiance.

"By the way, Denarra," the Tetawa mused as they threaded their way through the crowd in search of the Reachwarden, "how did you know about Mardisha's past?"

The Strangeling cleared her throat and pulled Quill quickly behind her. "Lucky guess. Hurry now; let's get this over with before the wine starts wearing off."

Merrimyn wandered through the crowd for a while but eventually returned to the top of the great staircase leading down into the lower atrium. He was restless. Ever since arriving in the city, the young Man had seen far more of Humanity than he'd ever expected or desired. As a Binder, he was cursed to always be separated from his own kind, and so many beautiful people and so much grandeur filled his heart with a longing that was easier to deny than acknowledge. Binders had to devote all their energies—physical, emotional, and erotic—to maintaining the alchaemical locks on their snaring-tomes. Surrender to passion could be more than just awkward—it could be catastrophic, for the release of the captured Fey-spirits would bring a vengeful death to the Binder and anyone near him. If not for his obligation to Denarra and Quill, and their growing friendship, Merrimyn would have fled the city just after regaining his strength, for there was too much temptation all around him. As it was, he was planning to leave when they were finished talking with the Reachwarden about the Expulsion.

He tried to reach one of the upper terraces to get a better view. All the other stairs were blocked by soldiers armed with muskets and short swords, so he resigned himself to a place at the top of the sweeping stairway. It was the best height he could find, and enough to see most of the atrium floor. He watched the movements of the Strangeling and the Tetawa below.

At present he couldn't see the Reachwarden, but there was no doubt where Denarra and Quill were located, because the crowd always seemed to split apart when the Folk were present. A dull knot of rage burned in the Man's throat at the sight. He was young, but he was far from being naive. He understood all too well the petty hatred that pervaded the Hall of Kings this night, and he despised it. He despised everything that reminded him of the knowing cruelty he'd seen in Eromar City and throughout most of the lands of Men. He despised everything that threatened his strange, brave friends, and he especially hated the stupidity that led to so much bloodshed in the world.

It was a large world with many people and possibilities, but in the many lands he'd traveled during his twenty-one short summers, he'd found very little that gave him much hope for a future free of death and destruction. Yet below him, winding their way through an increasingly hostile crowd, walked vibrant vessels of that slim hope. It wasn't just that Denarra and Quill had saved his life and brought him along on their quest to save their people; it was also that they considered him a friend—family, even—and trusted him with their lives, just as they trusted each other. Trust was a rare thing these days. Even if he didn't survive this grand adventure, it was enough that he knew such a precious thing existed.

Trumpets blasted above the young Man, and he looked back to see what was happening in the atrium. His eyes scanned the crowd below and moved upward. Suddenly, he froze. The Reachwarden had entered the Crystal Court with his entourage and guards, but it wasn't this group that caught Merrimyn's attention. His gaze was fixed instead on a short, solid Man in travel-stained leathers and a wide-brimmed black hat on one of the upper terraces, a Man who prowled past the columns lining the chamber's edge and watched the milling crowd with burning intensity.

Vergis Thane had found them.

"He's here!" Denarra shouted over the roar of the crowd. Quill could barely hear anything, but the sudden noise seemed to be a good indication of the Reachwarden's arrival. The Dolltender was too short to see anything other than the well-padded posteriors of Men and Women, but Denarra shoved through the crowd with abandon. The press of bodies seemed to shift slightly; there was less hostility now, as most attention was focused on something happening ahead of them.

Denarra held tightly to Quill's hand as she pushed, prodded, and sometimes kicked her way through. She didn't know how long the Reachwarden would remain, and she wasn't much in the mood for trying to come up with another clever scheme to get into his presence. It would be this chance or none.

The trumpets rang again, and a voice echoed through the chamber. They couldn't hear much of his speech, and they doubted that anyone else could either, but the energy of the crowd grew, and the Humans seemed to be enraptured by whatever the Reachwarden was saying. The excitement was contagious. They could feel themselves caught up in the thrill that raced through the throng.

"Hurry, Quill," Denarra called out, pushing through a tight knot of bodies, and then they stood at the front of the crowd, looking upon Qualla'am Kaer, the fifth Warden of the Reach of Men, who stood upon a stone dais speaking to the assembly before him. He was a tall, dignified man, with silver streaks in his tight black hair and well-trimmed goatee and broad shoulders that spoke to his military past. Kaer glanced over at them, and his dark face flushed slightly, but he continued his speech for a few moments, occasionally interrupted by exuberant shouts of assent. Finally, his address finished, Kaer bowed low and turned to walk swiftly out of the Crystal Court.

"He's leaving!" Quill wailed. "We're going to lose him!"

Denarra cocked an eyebrow. "No caterwauling yet, please!" The Strangeling rushed shouting toward the Reachwarden's guards, followed closely by Quill, who pulled off her belt and jumped free of the binding weight of the lower dress. Although taken by surprise, the guards were well trained, and they met Denarra's desperate lunge with swords drawn.

<<No!!!>> a voice roared through the chamber, and the blasting smoke of a musket erupted from the edge of the stairs. A few small chunks of marble rained down on the crowd from a columned terrace above. Denarra looked back to see Merrimyn wrestling with a soldier on the stairs, each trying to keep a smoking flintlock from the hands of the other. More troops rushed in to restrain the Binder, and the mood of the gathering shifted instantly. A scream echoed in the atrium, followed by hundreds of babbling voices. As though of one mind, the crowd surged toward the exit, and guards hustled the Reachwarden from the Crystal Court. Others leaped on Denarra and Quill, who surrendered without resistance.

"I hope you know what you're doing," the Dolltender gasped before being led away into the dark recesses of the Hall of Kings.

"Don't worry!" Denarra called back with a grin. "I'm making it up as I go!"

Tarsa slept at last, though fitfully. She lay beside a small, flickering fire that gave more smoke than heat. Like all the wounds she'd suffered since becoming the guardian of the Heartwood, the cut on her head had healed completely, but Jitani still stared at the spot, unable to look away, and unwilling to try. It gave her comfort to know that the Wielder was still mortal enough to be injured and to bleed.

She stretched a knot from her back and looked around. Tobhi sat at another campfire talking with an old he-Kyn Shield that he'd befriended earlier, during the hardest part of the Darkening Road. Oryn and some of the other Humans had gone to help search for bodies from the wreckage of the barge. Most of the other fighters who'd traveled with Tarsa from the Everland had gone off to find their families, hoping that they were among this group of exiles, but Jitani stayed beside the Wielder, true to her blood vow and a deeper need that grew stronger with each passing day.

She wasn't the only one. Daladir sat there, too, his careworn face turned away toward the darkness, his hands clearly aching to reach out and stroke the Wielder's tangled hair. He and Jitani rarely spoke to one another. There was little need, for each knew what the other desired.

They had no reason to put those feelings into words.

So it came as a surprise when Daladir walked over to sit beside her. They regarded each other warily. "She's slipping from us," he said at last, his voice low.

Jitani nodded. Tarsa was fading into the Tree, drifting away from everyone, even—*especially*—those who loved her the most.

He frowned. "It's going to be bad very soon. We'll need to be ready . . . for whatever happens."

"Yes."

His green eyes shone brightly in the dull firelight. "You fashioned your brother's warrior lock, didn't you?"

Her eyebrow rose. "I did. And he fashioned the one I wear."

"Will you help me with mine?"

It was a simple request but one that shocked the she-Kyn. A warrior lock was an ancient symbol of a Kyn's dedication to the defense of the people. It was painful, especially for he-Kyn and zhe-Kyn, for it required a plucking or shaving of most of the hair from the head, all save for a long topknot of hair at the crown, which was bound, greased, and braided. She-Kyn had a longer stripe of hair that stretched down the center, from the forehead to the back of the skull, like a horse's mane with a long braid at the end. For all Kyn, however, the fashioning of the lock involved a scarring of the temples by the warrior's most trusted friend or closest family member, generally a sibling. None were permitted to bind their sensory stalks during the ritual; it required full awareness, no matter how extreme the pain.

That Daladir would ask such a thing of her was unheard of. He either didn't know what he was asking, or . . .

Turning to him, she pulled out her hunting knife—not quite the quality of blade that she'd given to Tarsa but suitable enough for this task—and began scraping it across the side of Daladir's scalp. He flinched at the pain, but even when his head was slick with blood from the shaving and the three angular gashes cut above each eyebrow, he didn't move away from her. Jitani went about her task with swift efficiency. When she finished, she unwove her own dark green braid, cut a long strip of hair, and wrapped it around the base of the he-Kyn's topknot. She nodded approvingly as she replaited her braid.

Daladir wiped the blood from his head with a dirty cloth. "*Tsodoka.*"

"It will be dawn soon," Jitani said. "We'll need to wake her before the guards begin to move."

He sighed. "She'll be annoyed that we let her sleep for so long. She's still strong."

Jitani glanced at him. "She's remarkable in *many* ways."

"She's never given up, not once, not in all this time." Daladir tensed, then whispered, "And I can't surrender."

"Neither can I. My decision was made long ago."

They looked at each other again, warrior to warrior, eyes warm with tangled emotion. They were both scarred and weary, covered with grime, blood, and the heavy burden of loss, wounded by a thousand aches that filled both their waking lives and their dreams. They didn't know how it would end, but they were connected now in a way that neither had ever expected or wanted, and it would have to suffice. It was enough to know what mattered most to the other, and to know that it gave them both purpose in a world that was falling to jagged pieces around them.

It was enough. For now.

It had been a long, long time since Mardisha had been in such a place, and she resented that long-buried world's intrusion into her new life. She'd once thought that those days were far behind her, but history was hard to escape. This time, however, would be the last, one way or another. Either her new acquaintance would be able to help her regain her rightful place among the First Families on Rosewood Hill, or she'd reach the unhappy end of the shameful path that her more reputable friends were so skillfully setting before her. It was her last hope.

She'd been close enough to Denarra's pet Binder to see that the boy wasn't a political assassin; he'd grabbed the musket and fired *above* the Reachwarden at someone else. The figure vanished, but only briefly, reappearing in the middle of the fleeing crowd moments later as naturally as if his ragged clothing belonged among the jewels and fine fabrics of the First Families and their respectable guests. Twenty years of high living hadn't erased her ability to identify a skilled mercenary; she'd known many such Men in her old life, and this one moved with the predatory ease of the best of them. She'd watched carefully and followed him from the Hall of Kings, hoping that he wouldn't expect pursuit in such chaos. Whoever he was, his goals seemed to match hers this night. Her social salvation was close at hand.

Mariner's Quay was a nasty place, especially for a Woman bedecked in finery. But delaying to change was absurd; she couldn't risk losing him in the stinking streets and back alleys of the city, because there was no way to know where he'd disappear. She had to stay with him, no matter the risks. She was terrified, of course, as any sensible Woman would have to be, but she feared what would happen if she didn't take the chance far more than any thugs in the shadows.

Now she was in Mother's Dashed Dreams, what had to be the most disgusting tavern in all of Chalimor, lit by nothing more than a mass of stinking peat in the smoking fireplace. There weren't many people in the common room—not surprising, given the rancid stench that filled the air. The few who were there seemed far more interested in pawing at the pockmarked serving girl than in the well-dressed Woman at the door. Mardisha took a deep breath, choked back a bubble of bile that rose up in her throat, and moved toward a dark corner, where a plainly dressed Man sat staring at her, his single blue eye glinting in the dim light.

<<I have information for you,>> she whispered as she slid beside him on the bench. <<Are you interested?>>

<<Not in the least,>> he said, sliding a knife blade against her ribs. <<Go away.>>

Swallowing deeply, Mardisha pulled a small piece of paper from her handbag. <<We share a problem, and I think I can help you take care of it to my satisfaction as well as yours.>>

<<And what problem would that be?>>

The Woman smiled. <<Let's just say, her mouth is much bigger than her brain.>>

The corners of Thane's lips twitched. <<I'm listening.>>

<<Now then,>> Kaer said, turning his brown eyes on Merrimyn, who sat in the White Chamber with his hands and snaring-tome chained immovably. Denarra and Quill sat elsewhere in the room, each wrapped in leather restraints. <<You say this 'Thane' is a trained assassin? How do you know this? *You* were the one with the musket.>>

Merrimyn sighed. <<I told you. I'd seen him a few times when I was a Binder for Dreydmaster Vald. He visited on occasion, and always with someone in custody that Vald wanted to . . . speak with.>>

A blond Man of middling height turned to Quill. "And you, small one? Do you want to add anything to the tale?" he asked in Folk speech. The Dolltender looked at him with more suspicion than surprise.

"It's just what they said. Thane's a killer. We didn't know he'd be here, but it was a good guess." She turned away from the Man, hoping that he'd let the matter drop. It was clear that he didn't believe them. All she could hope was that Denarra's charm would work on the Reachwarden, and at present, that hope didn't look too realistic.

<<I see.>> Kaer looked at the trio and frowned. <<There's some truth here, of that I'm quite certain, but it's not what you're sharing with me.>> He leaned toward Merrimyn. <<I'm going to ask you this only once, and you'd better be honest with me, or you and your friends will spend the rest of your short lives in the Trollmaw—which

is a place I honestly *don't* recommend. I know something about Vergis Thane, and he's most definitely a dangerous Man. I also know that whatever else he is, he's not a paid assassin. He was here for a purpose, and it didn't have anything to do with me. What was he doing here?>>

Merrimyn narrowed his eyes and pursed his lips but stayed silent. Kaer's gaze was unwavering. Finally, his patience at an end, he turned to the younger Man. <<All right, Neidam, take them away. I don't have time for—>>

<<He was after me,>> Denarra called out from the sofa.

Kaer folded his arms and leaned against his massive oak table. <<Ah, I see. And why is that?>>

<<We have a bit of recently resurrected history together. Our last meeting didn't go too well, so I imagine he was here to finish what he'd started.>>

<<So, we have a loose Binder from Eromar City and a half-breed Kyn-witch who's being hunted by one of the Dreydcaste's most notorious Seekers. Your defense isn't looking too good.>> He turned his cold eyes on Quill. <<Now, what about you? What's your story?>>

The Tetawa looked at Merrimyn's chains and Denarra's tattered dress, and tears sprang to her eyes. Although her facility with Reachspeak was still somewhat rough, it was enough to be understood. <<I came to ask for your help. I came to ask you to stop Vald from killing my people.>>

The Reachwarden stared at her. "What did you say?" he asked, reverting to the Folk trade-tongue.

"Please, don't be angry with my friends. They're here because of me. I left home months ago to tell you how Eromar is taking our lands from us, to tell you how much we need your help. I never would have made it here if it hadn't been for Denarra and Merrimyn. They've saved my life more than once. They gave up everything, just so I could be here with you today. We've tried for weeks to see you, to talk to you, but you wouldn't see us. Coming here, tonight, was the only way to do it." She fell to her knees in front of the table, and the tears streamed down her face as she sobbed. "Please. You're the only one who can stop them. You're the only one who can save us."

Kaer looked at the small figure on the floor. He stood and walked around to the front, where he reached down and ran his big-knuckled fingers through her hair. She stiffened for a moment, but the pain and fear and sorrow were too much, and she collapsed in another wave of tears.

"Be strong, Tetawa—be strong. You have my deepest sympathies," he whispered. Then he pulled away and stood up. "But I can't help you."

Quill looked up through her tears, her face stricken. "What?"

Kaer walked swiftly to the door. "As much as I want to help you all, there's nothing I can do."

Denarra stared at him, her mouth agape. "But *why*? We came all this way to get your help. There's no one else who can help our people! Would you let Vald drive us to extinction?"

The Reachwarden spun around furiously. "*Your* people? Did you ever stop to think about *my* people? Vald is threatening civil war if I intervene, the destruction of the Reach as we know it. The result would be devastation, famine, and death unimaginable. And we all know that the Man is more than willing to honor his threats. I could send soldiers after him, but our forces would be stretched past endurance, even if they were able to reach him in time. It's useless, anyway, because no Human army is going to fight and die for Unhumans, no matter how righteous the cause."

Kaer opened the door to leave. "Neidam, release them. That, at least, I can give." He turned and shook his head wearily. "I didn't make this choice lightly. I'd help you if I could. But the world is against you now, and your enemies stretch beyond Eromar. You have few friends even in Chalimor. Saving you would bring devastation on us all, and I can't risk the destruction of the Reach. I *won't* do it."

The guardsman stepped forward and placed his hand on the Reachwarden's shoulder, shifting tongues to express the full depth of his dismay. <<Would you trade their people's lives so easily, Qualla'am? Would you turn your back on your oath, on the justice that you promised to the weak and powerless? I never thought you were that kind of Man. I'm sorry to see that I was wrong.>>

Without turning, the Reachwarden said, <<If it saves the Reach, it's a small price to pay. Let it go, Neidam—it's done. I have spoken.

Chalimor has spoken.>> Shrugging off the younger Man's hand, Kaer left the room and slammed the door behind him.

The small group sat in stunned silence—all but Quill, who wept anew.

39

Surrender

THE SOLDIERS COULDN'T UNDERSTAND IT, but *something* was clearly happening among the prisoners. It started slowly, and most of the Men didn't even notice that the comforting familiarity of the journey seeped away, to be replaced by a growing unease. It might have been the gradual revelation that the creatures were no longer walking with their heads bowed and shoulders stooped. Maybe it was when a female refused to follow one of the soldiers into his tent, or the fearlessness in the eyes of her family as they joined in her defiance. Maybe it was the long-forgotten sound of children's laughter, or the gentle songs that rippled through the tattered crowd at night. The weather was worsening, food and fresh water were in short supply, and the relentless pace was exhausting even the Men on horseback, but the Unhumans weren't dying anymore. In spite of whippings and more thorough beatings, the creatures were no longer weighed down with resignation. Their eyes were clear of death's shadow now, more every day. The troops were worried; the balance of power had somehow shifted, and they found their pain-enforced authority slipping away with each new dawn. Insurrection was inevitable.

<<What would you have me tell the Men, Authority?>> asked Vorgha, his thinning hair still disheveled after his recent Dragonborne trip to the largest of the exile groups. The Goblin skiff had

encountered unceasing turbulence among the storm-ravaged clouds on his return to the makeshift camp, but Vorgha was a faithful retainer and knew his duty well. In spite of an aching desire to sleep, and his dry-mouthed fear of Vald's response to the news, he'd staggered off the airship and hurried to the Dreydmaster's sprawling tent to give his report.

Vald remained in his seat, seemingly unsurprised by Vorgha's tale, and continued to read from a small, well-worn book in his hand. This troubled Vorgha more than any outburst, especially now that his master's goal was so close to manifestation. So much could go so wrong. How could the Dreydmaster be so calm at such a time?

His fears overwhelming his good sense, Vorgha cleared his throat. <<Authority, what would you have me do?>>

Vald flipped a page of the book and kept reading. <<Nothing.>>

<<Nothing, sir?>>

The Dreydmaster's bristling brows narrowed. <<Did you suffer a head injury on your journey, Vorgha? A deafening blow, perhaps?>>

<<No, I . . . forgive me, Authority,>> Vorgha sputtered and bowed low. <<I did not mean to question your wisdom.>>

Vald returned his attention to the book. <<All is as it should be, you can be certain. There will be no uprising. Return to your tent. The troops have their orders, as do you. I will send for you shortly, so rest while you may.>>

The attendant bowed again and backed out of the tent into the dry mountain air of their present campsite. He shaded his eyes and looked around. The camp was located on a wide shelf of stone high on a sandstone mesa overlooking a rocky valley. Thirty or more Men from the other Goblin airships—mostly paid mercenaries, but some members of the Eromar militia, too—were finishing the construction of a rough-hewn log palisade around the camp. It was a precaution more than a practical necessity, as the Pit Fields were generally devoid of anything that might pose a threat to such a large and growing population. But seeing the devastation around them, Vorgha was still comforted by the presence of the wall.

There was no place in the Reach more blasted and bleak than the doom-haunted Pit Fields of Karkûr, the far eastern expanse of the now thinly inhabited province of Dûrûk. It was in this land of shattered stone and storm that the ancient Dreyd had drawn down the power of the Eld Green into the world of Men. The Dreyd lost their bodies in their ascension during the Melding, and the once-lush land of Karkûr became a desolation of broken mountains and columns of blood-red sandstone now twisted and tormented into grotesque shapes like nothing before seen in the world of Men. Vorgha shuddered involuntarily at the sight. Their camp was on the periphery of the Pit Fields, looking over the crag-ridden valley pass that led into the broken peaks surrounding the region. It was as if all the fiends of the Netherworld had risen from their stinking holes for obscene frolic under the stars, only to be turned to monstrosities of rock with the sun's light. In towering, blasted stone shaped by catastrophe and the unceasing gnawing of a thousand years of fierce wind and foul weather, Vorgha could see mute testament to the unbound ambitions of Man.

A strange shadow hung over the western horizon. It was their destination. It seemed to draw all light into itself, but Vorgha couldn't tell exactly what crouched in the distance. Each time he tried to focus his gaze on the shape he felt a burning tug at his vision, as if his eyes were losing their ability to see anything other than that awful, uncertain vagueness. He turned away from the sight and scuttled back to his tent.

Vorgha knew, better than most, the dangers that now faced the world of Men. The Dreydmaster had taught him much over the years. There was only one way to truly bring an end to the menace, and that knowledge, more than anything else, was why he was here in this horrible place.

Lojar Vald's great crusade wasn't just for himself; it was for all Men and their posterity. The ancient Dreyd may have succeeded in throwing down the old order and establishing another, but they were blinded by their pride; their victory was incomplete, and impurities corrupted the full potential of their grand ideal. Their Melding had been only partial; unnatural remnants of the savage world remained behind to torment, tempt, and bedevil the lives and dreams of untold good Men. And although driven back into the wild places for a thousand years, the Unhumans and their ilk had stubbornly refused to fade away.

But their time had, at last, come to an end. Like any good alchaemical doctor, the Dreydmaster had patiently observed the nature of the illness and tested various treatments, to finally conclude that only the most drastic surgery could fully cure the patient of such a persistent poison. It had been a long, painful, and bloody ordeal, but it was swiftly nearing its inevitable end.

Such a noble, necessary task was well worth the turmoil and trauma of the many years Vorgha had served as Vald's most trusted attendant. It was worth the blood he'd drawn, the pain he'd experienced and inflicted, the family and friends he'd lost along the way. It was worth anything, and everything. Vald's ascension would mean the end of the Unhuman taint.

And then, at long last, Men could live and breathe freely in a world fully their own.

Molli Rose leaned back with a sigh. "I en't never felt nothin' like that before," she said as the green glow faded from the Wielder's skin. "It's like all of Creation is swimmin' inside me. Makes me want to cry, or laugh, or dance, all at the same time."

"That's how it was with me, too," said Tobhi. He adjusted the pillow behind his elder's head to make her more comfortable.

"*Mishko*, Etobhi."

"*Ju'uba.*"

Tarsa sighed deeply, pale but contented. "That's all I can do for now. Give me a little while, and I'll be ready for the next few."

Molli Rose looked at the she-Kyn intently and said, "What's it like, Wielder? What's it feel like to have the whole world inside ye?"

Tobhi had wondered the same thing many times, but it always seemed too big to ask, too presumptuous. A lifetime of reflection and contemplation would scarcely be enough to begin to answer the question.

It seemed that Tarsa was having the same trouble. Her brows knitted in thought, and her sensory stalks caressed her cheeks. "I'm not sure how to explain it—I can't even remember what it felt like before. The *wyr* is so much a part of me now; I *am* the *wyr*. It's in everything I see, everything I touch. I can feel its rhythms and songs even in this spirit-hungry land of Men." Her voice went soft, and she spoke as much to herself as to them. "I hear voices in my dreams, thousands of them, all singing the same song, but I don't understand the words. The drumbeat is familiar, as are the songs, but they're in a language I no longer understand, if I ever did. The song gets louder as we move westward, and I get closer to knowing it, to hearing what's truly being said. But the voices escape me now. And I'm getting so tired."

Her stalks slowed down, and her eyes grew heavy, but she jerked awake just as her head bobbed downward. Tobhi reached over in concern. "Don't worry," Tarsa said with a reassuring smile, "I'll be fine. I just need to walk around a bit and stretch my legs. You stay here with Molli and enjoy your talk. I'll come find you later." The Leafspeaker started to protest, but Tarsa waved away his concern. "Really, Tobhi, I'm fine. I just need a bit of air to clear my thoughts."

He watched her pull a worn wool shawl tightly around her shoulders before she disappeared into the crowd. "She's workin' herself too hard. She's gonna end up sick if she don't start gettin' some rest."

Molli laughed. "That one can certainly take care of herself, little worrier! I'm glad she went with ye to Eromar all that time ago—I can't think of nobody better. If she can carry the essence of the Eternity Tree halfway across the Reach, I doubt there's anythin' 'round here that can cause her much trouble." She shifted the weight on her wrapped leg.

Seeing Tobhi's eyes travel to the grimy bandages, she laughed again. "And don't ye go worryin' y'self about me. I en't a Wielder, but I en't goin' nowhere. Good brains will serve me just as good as the *wyr*, I reckon. Besides, ye've been lookin' more than a bit wore out y'self, so maybe ye should be thinkin' to yer own health and stop yer frettin' over the rest of us."

"I s'pose so. I en't been able to get much sleep at night."

Molli Rose's face darkened. "They en't nobody sleeps well these days, cub."

Tarsa walked slowly through the camp and breathed in the smoke from the few fires allowed the exiles. Wood was scarce in this broken land, mostly strange, stunted pine and brush oak that burned fitfully at best, but the smoke was pleasing to the senses and to the spirit. Groups of four, five, and six were scattered in all directions for a half-mile or more, up nearly to the edges of the jagged valley that surrounded them, but no farther, as the soldiers were increasingly vigilant in guarding the perimeter—from without and within. The Men might be more watchful, but they were also frightened, so the nights were less dangerous than before. There hadn't been a beating or a death in the past few days. Although food was scarce for all, there were no more threats of withholding the wormy flour and rancid meat. It wasn't an ideal situation, but it was approaching something close to tolerable.

At least it was for the rest of the Folk. For the young Wielder, the journey was becoming more frightening. She could feel herself disappearing. At first the power was invigorating, but then came the voices, and the gradual realization that her own memories and emotions were growing more distant. She knew they were there, could sometimes touch and recall them, but with every passing day she felt more space between herself and the life she knew. The Tree would survive, and with it the Folk, but what about *her*?

A hand on her shoulder brought Tarsa back to the present. It was Jitani. They exchanged weak smiles.

"I promised to look after you, Wielder. You haven't made it too easy for me," the warrior teased.

"No, I suppose I haven't. I'm sorry."

"Don't be. I'm glad you're not too easy to catch; I enjoy the challenge."

An awkward silence fell as they continued walking, now with a bit of distance between them.

Tarsa cleared her throat. "You gave up a lot to be with us."

"No more than anyone else here. Some have lost much more than I did." Her golden eyes were deep and warm. "Tell me more about Unahi."

"What do you want to know?"

Jitani turned her gaze eastward, to the Everland that now lay so very far away. "My brother admired your aunt very much. She gave him wise teachings from the Deep Green, and he shared it with me. I was on my travels before I could get to know her very well, and during the Council she was so busy with the other Wielders. By the time it was over, it was too late."

Tarsa felt a clenching pain in her chest, and it took a few tense moments to catch her breath and be sure that it wouldn't become a sudden sob. "I wish I could tell you everything you want to know about her teachings, but I can't. I didn't know her long enough. There's still so much I have to learn, so much I don't comprehend yet. But I can tell you that she was brave, and defiant, and loving, in her own way. I miss her, more than I ever would have expected. She might have been able to help me understand what's happening to me now."

They walked together in silence to one of the fires, where a few of their fellow travelers sat huddled together. Tarsa recognized Oryn and Eladrys, as well as some of the Ubbetuk. The two Tetawi brothers had found some of their kinfolk. Someone was missing.

"Where's Daladir?" she asked.

Oryn pointed to a large boulder at the far edge of the camp. "He went to meet with the Governor and a few others over there."

Tarsa thanked the Man and started toward the rock but stopped to look back at Jitani, who stood hesitantly beside the fire.

"Well, my green-haired guardian," she smiled teasingly, "let's go. We have enough troubles as it is without adding my disappearance to your burdens." She reached out and took Jitani by the hand, as she had the day they left the Everland.

"It's a good plan," Garyn said. "But much will depend on our Jaaga friends. They know the land; they know what plants grow here and what animals are best for food and clothing." He shook his head sadly. "Our days of bounty are far behind us."

Daladir shrugged. "For a while, perhaps. But don't forget that we have many friends in the Reach. They might not have been able to strike against Eromar with force, but they won't abandon us here. Our trade partners in the Allied Wilderlands have always valued our weaving skills and other arts, as have many in Dûrûk and Sarvannadad. It might take some time to open up the trade routes again, but we won't be without options forever."

"Much will depend, of course, on whether the other Folk will agree to the idea," said Averyn, as Tarsa and Jitani joined them.

"What idea is this?" the young Wielder asked.

"We've been thinking about the future, now that it seems likely we'll actually have one," Garyn said. "We know that life will be different and very difficult in our new home. It will be hard, for all of us. Even when our enemies are gone, our needs will be great, and there is a grave danger that we will fall upon each other in a starved fury for the meager resources that remain. We are not used to living beyond the reach of Zhaia's generosity."

"I've tried to avoid thinking about it," Tarsa said.

"Well, we must start thinking, because things will likely get bad very quickly," said Daladir. "Rage is building out there, and when the Men are gone, our only target will be one another. We have to channel that pain and anger and fear and frustration into something useful, something that will give us reason to live, not an excuse to die . . . or kill."

"What's your suggestion?"

"A confederation of the free Folk, not unlike the Sevenfold Council," Averyn said. "Only this time it would be permanent rather than brought together only in times of great crisis. Each nation of the Folk would still remain independent; we'd all choose our own leaders and decide our own community concerns, but we'd be part of a larger group, an interdependent league of peoples dedicated to the creation of another strong homeland, linking ourselves to one another in an alliance belt for both conflict and peace. Perhaps together, with a hopeful vision, we can create and share as kith gathered around the same fire; we'll be able to stop our people from disintegrating when the Darkening Road is over. Without that hope, it won't be Men who will destroy us; we'll do it to ourselves."

Tarsa nodded. They'd all felt the slow, silent slipping away of those deep connections that had kept the Folk strong since time immemorial, even during the catastrophic Melding. With so many of their people dead and dying, with so much brutality and suffering, the traditional ties of kinship were slowly but certainly unraveling. It started with the little courtesies, the small observances of honor and respect, and then escalated to beatings and even worse. Far worse.

With his consort's help, Garyn stood and bowed to the two she-Kyn and Daladir, who stood up to bid him goodbye. "I must go to think about this idea some more. Molli Rose will be most interested, as will others. There is still much to be done." He leaned heavily into Averyn. "Now, beloved, will you—"

The Governor stopped abruptly as Daladir slumped to the earth. Tarsa rushed forward. Daladir was still conscious, but his face was gaunt, his breathing shallow.

"What happened?" Jitani asked.

"He's tried to be so strong, to deny himself the help he needed." The Wielder held the he-Kyn's head up. "He didn't want me to waste my strength on him, so he pushed himself, harder than anyone, until he couldn't do it any longer. I've got to help him."

"Bring him to our wagon—night has fallen, and you risk revealing yourself too much in the darkness," Garyn said, ushering them into the crowd. Tarsa nodded in agreement, her throat tight, as Jitani lifted Daladir into her strong arms and followed the others.

"You shouldn't have done it, Tarsa. I was just a bit dizzy. It would have passed." He looked at the Wielder in mingled irritation and gratitude. "Why do you have to be so Dreyd-damned stubborn all the time?"

She stroked his cheek with her fingers. "Do you feel any difference?"

"How can you ask that?" He closed his eyes and sighed. "It's like nothing I've ever felt before. The pain is gone, the fear, all of it. My whole body is singing."

"Then enjoy the song," she whispered. "Sleep now, Daladir. I'll be here when you wake."

The he-Kyn smiled. "I couldn't sleep if I wanted to. It's been so long since I've felt anything but endless exhaustion. I just want to lie here and enjoy it, and think about the future." He became more serious. "Perhaps a future with you."

Tarsa hesitated for a moment. "Daladir, I . . . we . . ."

He took her hand. "I don't want to bind you to me, Tarsa. Different fires burn inside us, but I do love you. And I know you care for me, too, though I'm not the only one your heart desires. If you'll have me, I want to share in your future, in some small way."

"Even though it means that you won't be the only one at my side?" she asked, looking back at Jitani, who sat nearby, uncertain, with her arms wrapped around her knees.

"Even then. Your love for her is part of who you are—I wouldn't divide your heart between us."

The Wielder turned to Daladir with a look of surprise. He smiled again. There was no hesitation in his expression, only love and the rising flush of desire.

An unexpected weight on her spirit slipped away. For now, the burden of the Tree was forgotten. Her love wasn't a finite, limited thing; it expanded and grew with the giving. She could let go of her grief and fear; these two brave and passionate Kyn didn't demand that she hide her difference or push it aside—her strangeness was part of her, and they both loved it, too. They saw beauty, not monstrousness, when they looked at her; in their loving eyes, she was complete, not fragmented and broken, as she'd so long feared. The choice wasn't between these lovers and those of the past; it was a choice between sharing love today or letting it wither into something small and cold and fearful. She felt her passion flow through the world, and she made the choice.

She would be whole again.

Tarsa slid over to Jitani, who avoided the Wielder's gaze. Tarsa could feel a pain there that required a different kind of healing than the radiance of the Heartwood could provide.

She reached out a hand to Jitani's temple, hesitating before softly resting her fingertips on the copper bindings of the severed stalk-trunks that lay nestled in the warrior's mossy hair. Jitani stiffened, and a flash of panic swept through her golden eyes. To touch another's sensory stalks was an act of unequaled intimacy. To lose a stalk through intent or accident was tragedy, as the loss drained the world of sensual possibility and connection. The world was poorer now without two of her stalks; the air lost much of its perfume, fruit its sweet delight. In all the years since her loss, no one had ever touched her injured stalks before.

But Tarsa's touch was gentle. She gave more than she took as her fingers loosened the copper bands and let them fall to the earth, revealing the pale, wounded beauty of the remnant trunks. Jitani had longed to know that touch since she first saw the young Wielder speaking defiantly to the Sevenfold Council in defense of the Old Ways of the People, dreamed of it since the day Tarsa saved her life with a healing kiss.

This moment, too, was part of the Old Ways. It was right and good. In all of Jitani's dreams and visions, the warrior-Wielder's touch had never been so tender as it was now.

"It happened . . . a long time ago," Jitani whispered and pulled Tarsa's hand to her lips. "But I remember pleasure, and passion."

Tarsa's eyelids fluttered as Jitani's kisses trailed down her wrist and inner arm. She embraced the warrior and kissed her deeply, then moved back to Daladir and slid atop his trembling body. Her shawl fell to the floor. As their sensory stalks intertwined and wove together, their hunger rising beyond the thin and fragile limits of their flesh, a soft groan escaped the he-Kyn's lips, and he rose up to meet her, hard and warm, sliding his hands beneath her blouse and pushing the garment from her shoulders. Tarsa's hands pulled at Jitani's belt, drawing it away, letting the breeches fall to reveal flushed bronze skin gleaming with fragrant sweat. The golden-eyed warrior hesitated, but only for a moment, and then her remaining stalks slid outward, strong and bold, as she knelt, smiling, to join the moist and tender caress.

"Let there be a healing," Tarsa sighed, and she slid into their waiting arms.

Cycle Six
Thorn and Flower

This is a story of the Tetawi Folk, from a time long before the Expulsion, when they and all their Sevenfold kith still lived and loved in the sheltered shadows of the great wyrwood trees and white-capped peaks of the home grounds once known as the Everland.

It is a teaching.

In the old days, before the Melding separated the Everland from the Eld Green, the greater spirit-beings walked the world among their children. Granny Turtle—old Jenna—would often dance around the fire in the form of an age-worn she-Tetawa with turtle shell leggings wrapped around her calves, pounding out a rattling rhythm as she moved, teaching her grandchildren the songs of thankfulness and celebration that would strengthen them for the hard times to come. Kitichi, the mischievous Squirrel-spirit, lived and loved among the small Folk, his foolish self-indulgence and laziness becoming part of the lessons that young cubs learned as they navigated the world in their growth toward maturity. Tetawi delighted in the exploits of Jippita, the whistling Cricket, and her dreamy but slow-witted Moth friend, Theedeet the Whisperer, and wisely avoided crossing Mother Malluk, the strong but foul-tempered Peccary who so often ended up the object of Kitichi's poorly planned trickery. The Clan-heralds of all the Tetawi traveled among the brown-skinned Folk, sharing their lives and wisdom as best they could, always giving honor to the Eld Green.

There were other spirits, though, who were rarely encountered by the Tetawi, for their purpose was not to walk among the Folk. Formed by the combined efforts of the Mothers of the Folk, these spirits came into being for one single purpose: to guard and protect their world and its inhabitants. One was Guraadja, the winged and antlered Bear-Snake. He was unlike the other Clan-heralds in that he resembled no other creature that walked the living world; there was no Clan named for him, no mundane versions of his kind inhabiting the deep forests or high peaks. Later, Human scholars studying the Tetawi story-cycle would say that Guraadja and his kind were abominations, the result of confused memories and corrupted stories of the most ancient times.

But Tetawi know differently. True, Guraadja was the only one of his kind, but he wasn't alone, for he and the other Anomalous were kindred to all the Tetawi—indeed, to all the Folk. They belonged to all the worlds, not just one, and could travel freely between the skies and the greenlands and the dark underworld, serving the People with all their varied gifts and talents. Yet first among them was Guraadja. Thus it was that the powerful upper body of a great brown bear and the broad rack of a noble stag of the Middle Place were joined with the shimmering scales and lower form of a monstrous snake of the Lower Place; Guraadja's kinship to the Upper Place was represented by four majestic wings, bright with the iridescence of a celestial rainbow. His swift friend and ally, Saazja the Dreamer, the winged Stag-Rabbit, traveled through the Eld Green bringing news of the other spirit-beings, the Folk, the Beasts, and the leafy peoples, understanding the ways of their homeland and its relationship to the worlds beyond. The other Anomalous and their rare descendants were tied to the three realms—the Upper, the Middle, and the Lower—and journeyed between them to keep them balanced, and to keep them safe, but most powerful among them were the Bear-Snake and his small but keen-eyed companion.

Saazja had seen Kaantor, the proud and greedy Man who would usher in the catastrophe of the Melding, and warned Guraadja of the visitor's strange ways, but the great Bear-Snake dismissed his friend's concerns, seeing little danger in a weak and solitary creature without wyr *powers or family to strengthen him. Saazja was more insightful—he knew from experience that the seemingly small and weak could harbor hidden strengths, and he'd seen a frighteningly insatiable hunger in Kaantor's dark eyes. So he watched, and waited, and was ready when Kaantor revealed his ravenous self.*

Too late Guraadja realized his folly, and as the Eld Green began to dissolve beneath the power of Decay, and the worlds of Men and the Folk collapsed into one another, he rushed to undo what his negligence had permitted. Yet not even a being of Guraadja's might could stop the Melding, and he raged against the cataclysm with a fury never before seen in the three great worlds. His great roar was a crash that shook the cosmos, and his claws were lightning that tore the skies apart. All of Creation trembled from his struggles, and from his blood rose Skyfire and Thunder, the Storm-Born Twins, who bore on their Tetawi-shaped bodies the wings, antlers, and scaled flesh of their three-world father. Yet even their efforts added to those of great Guraadja could not stop the Melding.

All was not lost, however, for as the Eld Green broke apart and the Everland became fused to Peredir, the world of Men, Saazja returned from his travels with most of the Eld Green's great spirit-beings following closely behind, unified in their fear and uncertainty. They gathered together beneath Guraadja's protective wings—turtle and squirrel and tree and moss and eagle and serpent-kind and boulder and others all shielded from the worst of the devastation—and watched in horror as the world they'd known disappeared into the cosmic maelstrom of the Melding.

What happened to the rest of the Eld Green is unknown. Some spirit-beings vanished with the Melding, others were broken and weakened by the experience, while yet others struggled to recover and guide their now-mortal children and grandchildren in the ways of their scarred and wounded new world. Grand Jenna, Kitichi, and most of the Clan-heralds of the Tetawi survived, as did the forebears of the Kyn, the Gvaerg, and most of the other Folk. But brave Guraadja and his faithful friend Saazja were lost in the chaos, their sacrifice ensuring the continuity of their exiled kith.

Of all the Folk, it is the Tetawi who best remember the Bear-Snake and the Stag-Rabbit in their stories and round-dance songs. Some say that these and other Anomalous died in the Melding, torn apart by the strange energies released by Kaantor's betrayal. Others claim that they did not die but were lost in another place, a strange and lonely shadow pocket between the Eld Green and Peredir, still fighting to ensure that Decay is not fully victorious, that when they are triumphant in their battle they will return to live among their kith in the green lands of their creation. No one has seen or heard from them in the long thousand years since, but their story is remembered in song, in spirit, and in dream. Theirs is a lesson of vigilance, of sacrifice, of endurance, no matter how great the struggle, no matter how terrible the cost. Theirs is a living legacy, for as long as the Folk live on.

This is a teaching, and a remembrance.

40

Secrets

MEGGIE MAR WAS A MOMAN WHO cherished order. It was purpose; it was life. In her world, all things had their place and function, and it was the duty of all right-thinking people to challenge chaos in its many manifestations. Some people fought such battles with swords or speeches; Meggie's own fierce crusade was on a smaller field. Her household was the first line of defense against anarchy, and her weapons were broom, cloth, needle, and ladle. Even Denarra's eccentricities were muted in Meggie's domain. Those who threatened the peaceful routine of the tidy house found in the narrow-eyed Woman an implacable foe, one who wouldn't rest until the known reaches of her world were brought back into the eternal harmony she desired. Love, for Meggie Mar, was expressed by commitment to this cause, and her love and commitment were boundless.

Thus, it was the house matron who suffered the most under the despair that descended after the Reachwarden rejected Quill's plea for aid. The Tetawa was inconsolable and refused to leave her room, even to eat. Meggie's strict rule about shared meals crumbled, and the maid Ellefina carried food to Quill's chambers in spite of the older Woman's grumblings. Denarra remained in her dressing gown all day long and rarely left her bed, further disrupting household custom. She did come to the dinner table for her own meals, but Meggie almost preferred the Strangeling's absence to the grim, puffy-eyed specter that appeared. Denarra even stopped styling her hair and never asked once about her beloved peacocks, which heightened Meggie's already significant concern.

Even Merrimyn was wreaking havoc in the household. He'd taken to staying out all night, only to appear in the morning, drunken and bruised, stinking from all manner of filth encountered in his carousing. After a few short hours of fitful sleep and minimal sustenance, he'd leave again, followed closely by poor Padwacket, who spent each night keeping the young Man from mortal danger. The valet was wearing down as a result, and both his health and his work were suffering.

The insanity had gone on long enough. Although Meggie rarely involved herself with matters beyond her little domain, she'd worked with Denarra for many years and knew well the best available resources. Life was changing much too quickly for her liking, as swiftly in the household as in the world outside, and if she didn't do something she knew that chaos would rule the day. So she found paper in Denarra's study, wrote a short note and sealed it, and called for Padwacket, who'd been sleeping and was barely coherent when he arrived. Meggie assured him that their troubles would likely be over if he agreed to deliver the note. She couldn't trust the errand to Ellefina, as Padwacket alone had access to some parts of the city enjoyed by no one else in the house.

When the valet was gone, Meggie replaced her dusty apron with a clean one, and took a broom to the front hall. If the forces of chaos expected an easy victory in this house, they were greatly mistaken.

A piercing shriek shattered the household's morning calm. Merrimyn shot upright in his bed, but the pain in his temples sent him sliding back to the pillows with a whimper.

Padwacket entered the room and drew the drapes away from the window to fill the room with blinding daylight. Another scream echoed down the hallway. It was coming closer, but the Ubbetuk seemed unconcerned. "What's happening?" Merrimyn choked out through the bitter paste that coated his tongue and sent his stomach churning.

Before Padwacket could speak, Merrimyn saw for himself the source of the terrible sounds. Meggie Mar and Ellefina were dragging

Denarra backward down the hall toward the downstairs bathing chamber, the matron's face set in an expression of patient efficiency, the maid's in a silly grin. The Strangeling fought and howled like a wounded panther, but the Womens' grip on her legs was firm, so Denarra could do little more than flail and curse unintelligibly. Merrimyn was shocked to see how disheveled the ever-fashionable Wielder had become. He swallowed hard, trying to push down his sudden grief and nausea.

"What's been happening?" he groaned as Padwacket tidied the room. The Binder looked down and realized that he still wore his Jubilee clothes from days ago. The sudden, stinking tang of cheap alcohol and other less savory smells in the fabric overwhelmed his control. He threw himself out of the covers toward the bedpan and crouched with streaming eyes until his clenching stomach was empty. Without any sign of emotion, Padwacket carried the pan from the room and returned with a hot wet rag, which he used to wipe the young Man's face. Merrimyn leaned back against the foot of his bed, breathing heavily, waiting for the world to stop spinning.

The sounds of what seemed to be an epic battle in the bathing chamber filled the house, along with a torrent of profanity that would have been impressive even for a sailing barge or prison, and in spite of his raging headache and swollen throat, Merrimyn smiled.

Padwacket raised an eyebrow. "Don't be too smug," the valet said. "Meggie's coming for you next."

<<What you are proposing is, well, utterly unprecedented.>>

<<Yes, it is.>>

<<And you understand the consequences and complexities of such an act, I assume?>>

<<No. That's why I'm here to talk with you.>>

The old Man chuckled. He finished pouring a cup of tea for his distinguished visitor before returning to his plush chair that stood in a small semicircle of cleared space among dozens of precariously high stacks of books, tablets, scrolls, and sheaves of papers, like a strong tower in the ruins of a once-great civilization. Though it was already midmorning, the First Magistrate's chamber was dark, lit only by a single oil lamp; the velvet drapes on the great leaded-glass windows were rarely pulled away, as direct sunlight threatened the delicate pigments on the maps and tapestries that hung askew on the few areas of wall not obscured by bookshelves packed nearly to bursting. Even in this unnaturally hot late summer, the Jurist Temple of the Sovereign Republic Court was frigid, for its stone walls were thick and ancient, and the fickle warmth beyond never reached the squat structure's heart.

Kell Brennard didn't mind the cold. He was used to it by now, having served in the Jurist Temple for nearly twenty years. He'd long ago taken to wearing ornate, fur-lined dressing gowns and slippers in his private study, and though he was older and more susceptible to the humid chill beyond the building, the stale cold of these wood-paneled walls was familiar and almost comfortable. Leaving the Temple for any reason these days was always unpleasant for Brennard, as protocol and good taste forbade him from wearing the dressing gown in public, and the threadbare but familiar garment kept him far warmer than the thin fabrics of his ceremonial jacket, breeches, and hose. Here he could dress in whatever way he wanted, fashion and protocol be damned.

<<Well, if it's advice you want,>> he said, <<I'm happy to provide what guidance I can. But I tell you, Qualla'am, this is new ground for me. I'm not at all sure that I can be of any help.>>

The Reachwarden wrapped his brown hands around the teacup. He respected his host too much to wear his overcoat in the study, but he was grateful for the warmth of the drink. <<Don't be modest, old Man—it doesn't suit you.>>

Again the First Magistrate laughed. He was bent and aged, with a thick mane of silver hair and trembling, blue-veined hands, but there was fire still in his watery green eyes, and a firm set to the jaw that even his ill-set porcelain teeth couldn't diminish. <<True, too true. I've always struggled against pride, all my life. You'd think by now that I'd be old enough to not care what others think, but those habits are too hard to surrender, and even the false veneer of humility is preferable to the unrelenting arrogance of the young clerks and solicitors who strut down these halls. At least I always had the talent to justify my haughty self-regard.>>

He slid into his chair and took up his own teacup. <<Enough about my own endless and rather uninteresting inner struggles. You have a far more pressing struggle of your own. So what do we do about the Everland, Qualla'am? You've made a rather bold suggestion.>>

<<Yes.>>

<<You know that a declaration of war against an allied province without Parliament's approval is utterly illegal, of course.>>

The Reachwarden sighed, almost imperceptibly. <<Yes, I know that, too. But I was hoping that . . .>>

<<That there would be a way to circumvent the Code of Confederation? That you would be able to assert absolute authority on a matter as important as the unity of the Republic itself? No, Qualla'am, it's quite impossible. You made an oath when you were selected by the Reach Assembly to serve as Reachwarden, and that oath was quite specific: 'I will honor the obligations of my office to ensure the stability, integrity, and expansion of the Republic of the Reach of Men, with no higher duty than to the Reach and its peoples, and with acknowledgment that I share these responsibilities with the Assembly and Sovereign Court and will defer to their respective powers.' *With no higher duty.*" His eyes were bright. "The Reach is what matters, Qualla'am. It's what brought us peace and prosperity after centuries of petty royalist feuds that soaked the land with blood and left the people poisoned with the hunger for vengeance. It's what we've fought to keep secure for nearly forty years, since the old monarchy was thrown down and a new government dependent upon the will of the governed was installed. We cannot afford a civil war, and certainly not for such a cause, no matter how righteous. The Reach will endure, but only if you keep true to the oath you gave. As long as you are Reachwarden, you must honor that pledge.>>

Kaer slumped back in the chair, his tea forgotten and quickly growing cool. He wasn't surprised that Kell Brennard knew the words of that oath by heart, for the elder statesman had once said those words himself, having served two controversial terms as the third and thus far most expansionist-minded Reachwarden. Qualla'am Kaer was the fifth in the line of leaders of the Republic, and to date his term had been the most peaceful of all his predecessors. <<It's not right, Kell, and you know it as well as I do,>> Kaer said, his words echoing the sentiment of his guard captain's disappointment when the Reachwarden refused to help the little Brownie maid and her friends. He hadn't talked with Neidam since, and the younger Man's dismay over his hero's apparent moral failure still wounded him.

Right was right. It had to be, otherwise what was the point of all this glory and grandeur? He couldn't accept that all the sacrifices he and others had made for so many years were hollow, without purpose beyond expedience and the ambitions of powerful Men. <<We can't just sit back while Vald destroys them. The Republic is a virtuous ideal, not just cold reality. If anyone understands this, it's you.>>

The old Man nodded. <<I've been a Jurist for far longer than I was in your position, Qualla'am, but in my deepest dreams at night I remain the Reachwarden who single-handedly doubled the territories claimed by the Reach. I'm the one who used both politics and pressure to extend our influence over the western lands with funds seized from Andaaka when we brought the province to heel after the last near-rebellion—a campaign in which you served quite bravely and with true distinction, as I recall. I knew that we couldn't survive as a nation if we didn't have unfettered access to both the eastern and western waters, and Andaaka was the test. Had we failed then, the Reach and all its promise would have shriveled and died.>> He frowned at the memory, but his features softened, and he smiled. <<Yes, I know what an ideal can do for a people. I saw freedom in those new lands, a great people growing even greater with the wide expanse of our possibility. Even so, the yammering Assembly balked at my actions, saying that I'd overstepped my authority and risked our economic stability; the Sovereign Court hotly deliberated the legality of both the seizure and the purchase, but the people rallied to support me and my vision. Eventually, protests faded. My legacy and the future of the Reach were preserved.>>

He leaned back in his chair and sipped at his tea. <<Yes, I was bold, and it served us well. I was elevated into the Sovereign Court after the end of my second term, and I've been here ever since. It's been a good life, and I have no regrets. But this is a different cause altogether, my friend.>>

<<Not entirely,>> the current Reachwarden corrected. <<It was the expansion west that first put the lands of the Folk under scrutiny. Their lands stand between us and the western sea. It was

just a matter of time before the pressure to surrender the Everland became overwhelming.>>

Brennard shrugged. <<It was inevitable anyway, Qualla'am. The Reach must be the sole sovereignty on this continent; any other claims to autonomy must be eliminated—through peaceful integration if possible, by force if necessary. If the Everland were to remain free, it would embolden every other disaffected region to take up arms and declare their independence. Andaaka will always be a problem, for the Dreydcaste hold the alliance in contempt, and it is only their rather feeble military position that keeps them from rebelling; the people who inhabit the Allied Wilderlands are far too enamored of their freedom, and they chafe at their subservience to the greater Reach; Eromar is one step away from armed insurrection; the Lawless and Dûrûk are only nominally part of the full alliance. Whether by Eromar's doing now or Chalimor's doing later, the Everland was always fated to become part of the Reach. It cannot be a symbol of resistance, Qualla'am. For our own survival, the Everland as it exists has to die.>>

<<No,>> Kaer said, setting his cup on the table beside him. <<I don't accept that. I *won't* accept it. Is our nation so fragile then, our vision so frail, that allowing others to live freely as they have since time out of mind threatens us so much? Can we not live as allies with a shared purpose and destiny rather than always be perceived as inevitably selfish potential enemies, facing each other with false smiles and poisoned daggers behind our backs? The Folk themselves manage to respect their differences and work toward harmony and consensus; is it unthinkable that we might do the same? Is brutal selfishness really what you believe to be at the heart of the Republic?>>

<<You and I both know that you're not that naive, Qualla'am, so don't pretend to be shocked.>> The First Magistrate had no anger in his voice; this was an old and well-worn debate between the two, grown more urgent with the political events of recent months. <<Men are fundamentally different from their kind. I, too, mourn the loss of life, and if this was a world in which ideals could survive self-interest, I would advise you to gather an army and march on Eromar on your way to liberating the Everland for its ignorant and idolatrous inhabitants. But you will not find an army willing to kill other Men on behalf of Unhumans, nor will you find the Parliament in any mood to support this cause. And while the Sovereign Court

would likely find Vald's actions illegal and a gross presumption of authority belonging to no provincial prefect, we can't realistically enforce our ruling, and you don't have the political support to do so either. At any rate, the Folk have no legal standing in the Republic: they are neither citizens nor slaves, and thus outside the laws of civil society and property. They do not exist, as far as the laws of the Republic are concerned, except in that they are recognized as having been the first inhabitants of their territories. Their continued presence on those lands is at the Republic's pleasure, and as the political mood shifts, that pleasure can be withdrawn at any time. I understand and share your desire to help them, Qualla'am, but you would serve them better by encouraging them to become citizens of the Reach and to abandon their failed dreams of independence. Whatever their past and present, their future is with the Reach, or not at all. Beyond that, there's nothing else you can do within the laws of this country and the terms of the oath you took as Reachwarden.>>

<<I didn't accept this office to be party to the wholesale degradation and slaughter of an entire race of people, Kell. That's not why I fought for the Republic for all those years.>>

The First Magistrate shook his silvered head, and he looked at his world-weary successor with genuine sympathy. <<Of course it is, my noble-hearted friend, though you may not have known or believed it at the time. How else do you think great nations come into being? The Reach stands for many fine and beautiful things, and its light is bright among nations in this world, but the more light we see, the more shadow stretches behind it.>>

They talked for a while longer, on topics far removed from the one burdening the Reachwarden's heart, but it was a courtesy conversation only, and Kaer was soon ready to go. The room was too cold, his mind too confused. But before Kaer left, Brennard placed a firm hand on his shoulder. <<You look upon the long shadow of the Reach of Men, Qualla'am. To destroy the shadow, you would have to destroy the light. Every Reachwarden comes to know one unhappy, inevitable truth: there are many shades of grey in this world, but in the end, you don't have grey without black and white.>>

"Quill, are you there?"

The answer was long in coming. "Yes. Come in."

Denarra entered the room, freshly scrubbed, perfumed, and dressed in a pleated green skirt with a puff-shouldered white blouse embroidered with gold and maroon glass beads. There was no evidence of the strain of the past few days, other than the dark circles under the Strangeling's eyes. Meggie had even taken care to braid and wrap Denarra's undyed auburn hair in a respectable crown around her head, tied firmly with a stylish green ribbon.

Quill looked up from the side of the bed where she sat looking out the window. Her three dolls sat on the windowsill, their faces drawn, their heads bowed in mourning. The Dolltender gave Denarra a slight smile, but her face was still swollen from crying. She, too, was clothed, having been the first one subjected to Meggie's special brand of therapy. Her plain brown dress was unadorned, except for a yellow belt with black spiders woven into the fabric.

There was so much to talk about, but neither wanted to bring the grief back to the surface, as the present semblance of normalcy was still very new and fragile. Yet they'd been brought out of their solitude for a reason. "You look lovely," Denarra said as she sat beside the Tetawa. "Brown clashes terribly with my complexion, but it really suits you, especially with your hair."

"Thank you."

Silence. The night of the Jubilee was an unwelcome subject for conversation. It had become a cruel, unhappy joke, and a wound best left to heal on its own.

"Have you eaten? I'm absolutely famished. Should we go see what Meggie's made us for dinner—that is, if she had time to cook anything in between driving us all into a scalding tub with no warning and precious little tenderness. My neck is still raw."

Quill shrugged. "No, thank you. I'm not really all that hungry."

"Darling," Denarra said, pulling Quill to her, "you can't surrender to despair. It's just not like you. You've come too far to stop now."

The Dolltender bit her lip. "What's the point, Denarra? It's done; it's over. The Reachwarden has turned his back on us, on everything we came here for. You have a good life here, but my life was with my people. When Vald is done with them, the Folk will be gone, and there'll be no reason for me to be here anymore. He's won."

"*NO!*" Denarra shouted. Quill pulled back as the Strangeling jumped to her feet. "I will *not* allow you to surrender! We haven't fought shape-shifting cannibals, Seeker assassins, and hundreds of miles of bad food and worse fashion to surrender to a petty tyrant with more bile than brains! Vald hasn't won *anything* yet, and he's not going to. Our people might be fighting for their lives, but they're not dead yet, and we're not going to let them die." She grabbed Quill by the shoulders. "Between you, me, and Merrimyn, we can shake this Melded world to its twisted roots. All we have to do is be clever about it, and be courageous enough to fight on, no matter what the cost. You're braver than you think, Quill. It's time now to be brave for your Tobhi, if not for yourself."

The Tetawa sat in silence. Memories of her last night with Tobhi came flooding back. He became a part of her on that night, not so long ago, and she him. After that love-bonding, she was certain that she would feel if he was truly dead. She felt pain and loss but not emptiness. Tobhi still lived. Of that simple fact, and that fact alone, the Dolltender had no doubt.

Denarra sighed and moved toward the door but stopped as Quill hopped off the bed. "Wait," the Tetawa said, smoothing the wrinkles from her dress. "I think I'm starting to get my appetite back."

They walked together to the dining room, where Merrimyn, Meggie, and Padwacket sat together drinking tea with a new visitor. The she-Folk stopped short. The figure sat framed in the golden light of the doorway. For a moment a flash of fear raced through Quill, as the shape resembled the hunching silhouette of Jago Chaak. But it was something else entirely, an elderly Ubbetuk in white robes and cap, a frilled lace collar around his neck, with a wasp-headed walking staff in his withered hand.

Blackwick, the Ubbetuk Chancellor, looked up at Denarra and reached out a hand in greeting. The Strangeling had regained her composure, but her eyes were wide in amazement. "Denarra Syrene, you are a vision of loveliness, now as always. We have never had the pleasure of a formal introduction, but I have seen you at many social functions, and young Padwacket here has kept me informed of your many remarkable exploits." He smiled. "I was most pleased to receive Meggie's note through my kithsman this morning."

"And this, I assume, is the remarkable gate-walker you wrote me about?" he asked the house matron. Meggie nodded, refilling his mug with boiling water. The Chancellor's large eyes turned to Quill. The Dolltender had the feeling that his very presence was reaching into her, ferreting out the secret places and fears that she kept well hidden in the recesses of her mind. She felt indescribable relief when he turned away.

Blackwick pulled a small silver whistle from a hidden fold of his robes and blew on it. Within moments the front door of the house opened and a small group of Ubbetuk in tasseled blue caps and long greatcoats entered with a large wooden box that shook and shuddered. The box was wrapped tightly with iron cords; from within came a high-pitched scraping sound. A foul scent seeped out from between the boards. The Chancellor nodded to the Bluecaps, who returned outside, and drank from his steaming mug as if nothing had happened.

"The news, as you know, is grim," said Blackwick as he sipped his tea, ignoring the loud rattling from the box. "It gets worse each day. I will spare you news about the Darkening Road, as you are already well aware of that dreadful and ongoing event. Instead, my information goes beyond that, to what appear to be Vald's true reasons for claiming the Everland. The most recent news from the Ubbetuk borough in Eromar City is that Vald has seized all the airships in the city, as well as their crews, and is using them for the transportation of himself, many Binders, and a wide variety of alchaemical instruments to a remote site in the Pit Fields of Karkûr. We estimate that he has at least thirty ships at his disposal, including twelve trade galleons that are easily converted into warships."

The Chancellor's face grew grave. "I have woefully underestimated Vald's potential for treachery, and the price of that mistake has been terrible."

"What mistake?" asked Denarra, her voice tight with sudden fear.

"When Vald first made his intentions toward the Everland known, I, like others, believed that it was a greed for land that was at the heart of his crusade. It was a reasonable inference, given the history of land-theft among the nations of Men. Reasonable, but mistaken. Land was always part of the plan, but it was the surface purpose only. No, Lojar Vald's dream reaches far deeper. He wants nothing less than godhood."

A hissing giggle leaked out of the box, and Quill jumped. The Chancellor looked searchingly at Merrimyn, who nodded. "Yes," the

Binder said, "but it's the way of all the Dreydmasters. They all desire to ascend to the ranks of the Dreyd, to break the bonds of this world and move into realms beyond, just like the first Dreyd priests of long ago."

"True, such ambition is not limited to Vald," Blackwick conceded. "But only Vald has discovered the surest path to ascension beyond the Veil Between Worlds."

Not sure she wanted to hear the answer but unable to restrain herself, Denarra asked, "And what would that be?"

"The eradication of the Folk, and with it, a new Melding."

Stunned silence blanketed the room.

"It can't be true," whispered Quill at last. "Nobody could do something so awful, not even him."

Blackwick shook his head. "Sadly, young Tetawa, Vald not only *could* do such a thing, he is in the final preparations of doing so even as we gather here. He need not kill all the Folk to accomplish his goal, but most will suffer grievously at his hands. If he succeeds, the new Melding may well result in our total destruction, and perhaps that of Humanity itself. As long as we all still live, it is a hopeful sign that he has not yet finished his task."

"He's right," Merrimyn said, his voice so low that they had to strain to hear him. "Of course. This is why Vald wanted me, why he wanted all of us."

Denarra put a hand on his shaking arm. The chain to his snaring-tome rattled loudly. "You remember?"

Merrimyn gripped the Strangeling's hand. "This is what he was doing all along, though I didn't see it then. It's so simple, and so perfect. Collecting Binders from all over the Reach, praising us, giving us gifts, making us part of his inner circle. And when the Seekers started bringing in the Wielders, I knew something awful was happening, but I didn't know that he was planning something like *this*."

"What is it?" Meggie asked. "What is Vald planning to do?"

"The Binders store power within their snaring-tomes," Blackwick explained to the house matron. "It is similar in principle to a dam on a powerful river. The higher you build the dam, the stronger the material, and the more cunning the design, the more of that precious resource you can control. If you have enough, you can release the waters to flood the parched world, or refuse to surrender it and by doing so turn the lands below into a desert. Wielders, above all other

Folk, possess great strength; if they are killed, that strength—what Kyn call the language of creation, the *wyr*—is dispersed throughout the few remaining Thresholds, to go back to the ancient world from which it first came. Binders are trained to draw that strength not just from the spirits of their own world but also from the spirits of the Folk. And, like a dam, the snaring-tome becomes a dangerous tool with enormous potential for devastation."

Meggie looked at Merrimyn. "So you could release that power on us at any time?"

The Binder shook his head. "No. I can only absorb spirits—I can't control them. I can sometimes let out small bits if I'm very desperate, like steam escaping from an overheated kettle, but there's no way of knowing what would happen or . . . who would get hurt." His shoulders sagged slightly, and a shadow crossed his face. "The only members of the Dreydcaste with that sort of will and strength are the Reavers; only they can channel and focus the bound spirits with any hope of success. And of all the Reavers in the Reach, Vald is the greatest."

The implications of Merrimyn's words sank in slowly. Denarra put her head in her hands. "So Vald sent out his Seekers to kidnap Wielders and steal their strength. Simple, but brutally effective. Why didn't he just stop there?"

"Their captivity was never his primary purpose," Blackwick replied, laying a hand on the box at his side. A low, muffled whine sounded from within, and then silence. "He had a much greater ambition. Yet he could not hope to win against the Everland if the Wielders were still strong, so he slowly stripped away their power through random attacks dispersed widely across the Everland. Wielders were rarely the only victims, so they were never identified as the primary targets of those early raids. The Purging of the Kyn Wielders by the Celestial Shields, though not of his doing, was remarkably advantageous, as it weakened some of the most powerful Folk who offered the greatest threat to his plans. So, slowly, inexorably, the Wielders vanished from the Everland, until all but a few of the most powerful of their kind remained."

He tapped the side of his empty mug, which Meggie promptly refilled. "The Wielders gave him great power, but there was much more to be had, and it was found in one place above all others."

Quill's eyes grew wide. "The Tree. Vald knew about the Eternity Tree."

"Yes. The Tree was the heart of the Everland, the pulsing center of the ancient life of the Folk. It tied the people to other worlds, to other ways of being, and gave them strength to withstand the mortal ravages of the world of Men. More than anything else, this was the single greatest source of power in all the Reach, perhaps in all of this Melded world itself. It would be all he needed to become Dreyd at last."

"But he didn't succeed," protested Padwacket. "By all reports, the Tree was destroyed, and he still didn't ascend."

"True, but the power of the Tree was rooted not just to the land—it was, to Vald's apparent surprise, also firmly rooted to the Folk themselves. As long as the Folk exist, the Tree's strength remains whole and thus inaccessible to the Dreydmaster and his purposes. For whatever reason, the travelers on the Darkening Road have not died under their torments but have, strangely enough, lately become even stronger. This confirms what we know about the *wyr*—it is the very essence and emanation of the flesh-bound *peoples*, not just of the elemental spirits of land, lake, and sky. The Everland is impoverished without the Tree and the bulk of the Folk, but pockets of the old country still maintain their strength, because scattered groups of Folk remain to honor the green world and give strength to the spirits abiding with them. As long as they endure and maintain those relations, those small bits of the Everland will endure as well."

"Forgive the bluntness of my question," Meggie said, uncharacteristically somber, "but if this is the case, why didn't Vald just slaughter all the Folk right in the Everland? Why drag all those thousands halfway across the Reach to dispose of them? Hardly an efficient use of resources."

Blackwick smiled. "What do you know of ancient history?"

The Woman shrugged. "Not so much. But I've read Tempest Sparks's *History of the Everland Folk and Their Legends and Hearth-Tales*." Denarra and Padwacket exchanged glances. They'd never seen a book in the matron's hand before, let alone such a rare and notorious volume. Meggie pointedly ignored their surprised looks.

"Then surely you remember the circumstances surrounding the Melding. In what part of this world did the Dreyd ascend?"

Meggie thought for a moment, and then she nodded in grim understanding. "Karkûr. They ascended in Karkûr, and in doing so turned it into a wasteland."

"Precisely," the old Ubbetuk said, taking another deep draught of his tea. Now that his hand was away from the banded trunk, whatever was inside began to move around again. Blackwick ignored it. "And for a thousand years, the Pit Fields of Karkûr have remained a ravaged blight. One would think that in all that time growing things would have found a way to reclaim the land, but they remain a rarity in Karkûr. The land is sick, and not simply because of the Melding of a thousand years past. It remains, like the Everland, a remnant of another world, but this one is blasted to its heart, and its poison seeps out to burn away all green life around it. It is a great Darkening, a pocket of shadow and death, the mirror-twin of the Everland, with a revenant oak at its venomous heart. The Veil Between Worlds is weakest there. Break the dam, unleash the power, and the Veil is sundered."

It took a while for Denarra to find her voice, and when she did, it was small and trembling. "So Vald drives the Folk to the Pit Fields, butchers them all, and uses their *wyr*-born essence to cross the Veil and join the Dreyd."

They sat in silence for a long time, all lost in their own nightmares. The sudden revelation and its implications were too terrible to fully comprehend. It seemed so impossible, but now that they could see the pattern, it made horrifying sense.

The box rattled, its iron bands straining hard against an unseen pressure.

Suddenly Quill looked at the Chancellor. "But if all this was hidden from us for so long, how did *you* come to know all this?"

His shoulders sagged. "The knowledge came slowly . . . and with no little difficulty." He sighed. "I am older than I appear, Tetawa. Indeed, I am older than any of my kind, and I have learned much over those many years. Above all else, I have learned that enemies come in many guises, both from within and from without, and the only way to survive is to be ever vigilant. The danger that threatens your people endangers mine as well—it threatens us all." A bitter smile crept across his wizened face. "Many years past, my people abandoned the greater teachings of the Deep Green and embraced instead the magics of iron and steel, machines and industry. But even in doing so, we did not turn away from the wisdom of the past. It continued among a small, select group of scholars and intellectuals who maintained that knowledge and integrated it into the new ways that were ensuring our people's survival. I am a guardian of those teachings. They give me strength today. And they give me other ways of knowing than some might expect." He glanced at the box.

Denarra and Quill backed away from the iron bindings. The Chancellor motioned for Meggie and Padwacket to help him remove the cover. When they pulled the heavy wooden plank away, Quill cried out in horror at the creature that lay within, its humanoid head and feathered body wrapped in blood-spattered metal bands. It was a Not-Raven, and its fanged maw gaped wide in fury as it thrashed wildly for escape.

"The cold-eyed Man will kill you all, yes, he will kill you!" the creature hissed and giggled through bleeding lips. "He will crush your bones and suck dry the marrow. You will weep, but, oh, death will come slowly. None escape. None ever escape."

Blackwick's face darkened. He raised his wrinkled hand over the box, and the Not-Raven let loose a shriek of half-heard curses before crouching into a quivering ball.

"You know me," the Chancellor said, his voice suddenly deep, ancient, and terrible as winter thunder, "and you know what I will ask. You have fed on your master's blood, and you know his thoughts. What do you see?" The creature squirmed and whined pitifully, as though it was fighting a devastating battle with itself. The old Ubbetuk's fingers curled slightly. The room grew cold. Denarra, Quill, and Merrimyn felt a frigid surge of power roll into the room.

"You know your master's mind. Tell me!" Blackwick growled. The Not-Raven twitched a bit, and a stream of black bile tricked from its mouth. In spite of herself, Quill felt a great swell of pity for the creature.

"The ascension is at hand, yes," it whispered at last, its voice broken and weak. Blackwick's fingers curled again, and the Not-Raven gasped, "The green witch, she is the source . . . she is the key. Within her is the power, oh yes, and when she dies, the master rises. He rises . . . he . . ." A low hiss escaped its mouth, and its head lolled to one side.

"We are not yet too late, but we are running short of time," Blackwick whispered as he slid back into his chair.

"You're a Wielder," Denarra said with amazement.

The Chancellor smiled weakly and shook his head. "No. The Wielders of the Ubbetuk died out long, long ago." His eyes grew hard. "You understand? There are *no* Wielders among us. None. I am simply an old politician with an interest in the arcane histories of my people."

Denarra nodded. The other Folk suffered greatly from the ignorance of their neighbors, and the Way of Deep Green was generally considered witchery among a good many Humans in the Reach. The Ubbetuk, though victims of other kinds of suspicion, were at least spared this one. If it was known that they possessed *wyr*-gifts in addition to their already distrusted mechanical genius, vague fear would become burning hatred, and there would be no safe place for the Ubbetuk in the Melded world.

They sat drinking their tea, no one willing to break the silence, until the bell at the front door began ringing. Blackwick smiled. "Ah, at last. I have taken the liberty of inviting some other guests to join us, now that the greater measure of our personal discussion is finished."

They heard a gasp from young Ellefina as she opened the door. Two familiar Men entered. One was of a middling height, with blond hair and somber brown eyes. The other Man moved with an easy authority. He was older, taller in stature and broader in the shoulder than his companion. His tight black curls and silver-streaked goatee were trimmed close to the dark skin, and his black eyes looked at the gawking group with grave respect. Though the taller Man hadn't been an active campaigner for many years, the warrior's regalia rested as easily on his frame as a second skin, far more comfortably than the fine silks he'd worn when Quill first met him.

Blackwick stood. "I am sure you all remember the Reachwarden, and the captain of his guard, Neidam?"

"*Former* Reachwarden," Qualla'am Kaer responded in the trade-tongue. "Or will be, soon enough, when news of this gets out."

Denarra shook her head, her face lighting with sudden joy. "What . . . how . . . what are you doing here?"

Kaer smiled apologetically. "I'd taken an oath as Reachwarden to preserve the Reach at any cost. As long as I was bound to that oath, that was my first and only duty. But some things aren't grey, and some costs are far too high, even under the bonds of duty. We're here to help, in some way, if you'll have us. And if you'll forgive my earlier cowardice."

It was the first time Quill had ever seen the Strangeling struck speechless. Denarra's mouth snapped open and shut, but there was no sound. At last, her voice returning, she jumped up with a whoop and threw her arms around the startled politician. "Forgive you?! Oh, you beautiful, gorgeous, glorious Man, you're entirely forgiven! Why, I'd even give birth to your firstborn child, if I actually had any interest in bearing one of the squalling little beasties!"

Amidst the laughter, the Chancellor patiently waved them all toward the door. "We must begin—Vald is nearing the end of his preparations, and you have many long miles to cover before he is finished. I have ordered all available airships in the region to prepare for any eventuality; my own ship is ready for you now."

Quill shook her head. "But we might be too late, even with the airships. There's no way we'll be able to get there in time." Her own mouth dropped open as the group turned to stare at her expectantly. "Oh, no . . . you don't think . . . I can't . . ."

Blackwick smiled strangely. "I was most intrigued by the story of your arrival in Chalimor. Are you willing to test those skills again?"

"I . . . I don't know if I can," the Dolltender whispered. Her body began to tremble. They had no idea what the smaller ceremony had already cost her; she could only imagine what another one would demand.

Denarra knelt down. "You can do this, Quill—I know you can. You were born to do this. These teachings were given to you for a reason, and I'll be right there with you." The Strangeling embraced her. "This is your chance to save our people."

Denarra didn't know. Quill hadn't told her about the blood-debt she'd already paid to save their lives from Vergis Thane. She thought back to their earlier argument, when she'd chided the Strangeling for keeping news of the Expulsion from her: "*That kind of secret is still a lie. It hides your heart from the people who deserve to know it.*" Now, at last, she understood why her friend had made the difficult choice to hold back the truth, at least for a little while. It wasn't unkindness—it was mercy, and love.

They were all looking at her, waiting. Her friends, who had already sacrificed so much. These new friends and allies, who were willing to give up their comfort, security, and possibly even their lives to help in this quest. Great deeds required great sacrifice, and not just from one, but from many. They were willing to give more. Could she do any less?

Quill's eyes glittered, and her face was very pale, but she stood tall and squared her shoulders. Turning to the Chancellor, she said, her voice trembling only a little, "All right; I'll do it." She stopped and smiled apologetically to Meggie. "But I think I'm going to need a *lot* more apples."

41

Wrongness

TRULY THE OLD WINTER WITCH, *Shobbok of the Ice-Pierced Heart, reigns supreme. Her malice is clear in the murderous blizzard that has raged for weeks and shows no sign of slowing. She's long been jealous of the Eld Green and its bounty, and now that the Veil Between Worlds has been sundered, her long-harbored resentment rises up in carnage as burning ice and blinding snow sweeps like a blanket over the lands of Folk and Men alike. Shobbok can feel each death as the inner fire sputters out, from the candle-flame of the songbird to the bonfire of the great ocean whale, and she laughs in triumph as the world falls before eternal winter. The wizened old spirit rides through the snows upon the back of a skeletal polar bear, accompanied by her pack of life-stealing skriker hounds, great black predators bearing the faces of those slain by their fangs and claws. They are all ravening hunters now, seeking out the last flickering fires of resistance, driven by a hunger that none can explain or defy. The world, at long last, is dying. And the Dreyd watch over all.*

I shouldn't be here. I should be as dead as the rest of the world, and yet I still stand before a blazing fire pit in the middle of a wyrwood grove. The howling winds still rage around the trees, and snow piles up ever higher, but there is safety among the lichen-crusted trunks and moss-draped limbs, perhaps the last of their kind in this world. I'm here for a reason, and only for a short time, because the branches are creaking under the strain of the screaming wind and snow. The storm is getting fiercer: Shobbok is coming.

I'm not alone. The fire is surrounded by she-Kyn, all dressed in long robes of soft owl feathers, their hair pulled back from their faces and sensory stalks, strings of abalone shells and copper disks hanging from their necks. Each wears a wooden mask like those that circled the guardian of the Eternity Tree. When I enter the circle, five of the she-Kyn remove their masks, and I look upon my proud aunt Vansaaya and gentle aunt Geth, who exchange a sad glance between them, their faces waxy in the yellow firelight. My diplomatic companions on the road to Eromar, sour-faced Imweshi and sweet young Athweid, nod curtly when they remove their masks. But it is the fifth who makes me tremble in mingled joy and grief: Unahi, auntie, friend, and guardian through the chaos of Awakening, teacher of thorn and thunder, the ways of Deep Green. Unahi smiles warmly, but she stands back, as though reluctant or unable to come near. She points her chin to the two last masked she-Kyn, and I rise.

Both are still masked, and they stand still as I come near. The first mask is painted red and black and is lined with a crackling mane of dried grass. Squares of bright copper cover where the eyes should be. The other she-Kyn wears a mask painted blue and white, with ragged black ribbons streaming down from the head and chin, and black-stone eyes that hide the face behind.

Something snaps overhead. I look up. The branches are covered with a multitude of motionless white owls who gaze down without fear or emotion. A blast of wind sends leaves raining down into the fire, and I hear something else through the noise of the storm, something that sends my heart beating in terror. Something is howling in the darkness beyond, a noise like mutilation incarnate, the voices of Men and Folk emerging from feral throats. The skriker howl.

The seven she-Kyn dance around the flames, slowly and with great dignity. They lift their voices in a song that I've experienced before, a language that I don't understand any more now than when I first heard it. It is the bloodsong of my Awakening, the war-chant that rose above the shattered trunk of the Eternity Tree, and yet something else. The dancers are trying to speak beyond words, beyond my waking mind, but the meaning is just out of reach, and I grit my teeth in frustration. Whatever they're singing this night, it isn't for me. Not yet.

The figure in the red-and-black mask steps out of the circle and stops in front of me. "Don't worry. There's still time," she says. The voice is strange. It has the ring of familiarity to it, but distant. The stranger lifts her hands and removes the mask. It is Lan'delar, my mother. Turquoise-blue eyes gaze into my own.

"You've grown so brave and beautiful, my daughter," Lan'delar says as her fingers slide a stray hair away from my face. "Such a strong, proud warrior."

The howls grow nearer, and with them the screaming laughter of Shobbok.

"Mother, what is it?" I ask, seeing the sadness in her eyes.

She doesn't respond. Instead, she moves toward the circle, and when she turns back to me, there is fear in her eyes. "There's one other whom you must meet, and you must be brave again. You mustn't turn away until you know what's coming. Only then will you understand, and only then will you be prepared."

A branch falls from the trees above and smashes into the flames, sending ashes and sparks into the air, where they are swallowed by the storm. Some of the owls above are growing restless; they flap their wings and snap their beaks in annoyance, throwing clumps of snow from the branches down on the dancers.

I want to grab my mother, Unahi, Geth, to hold them all in my arms and never lose them again. I want to stay here with them forever, in spite of the storm and all the horrors that are so swiftly approaching, but Lan'delar shakes her head and joins the dance as the last of the masked she-Kyn steps out to meet me.

The figure has a familiar stride. Her blue-and-white mask seems to waver strangely in the fading firelight. I know without any doubt that I've seen this she-Kyn before. The feeling troubles me more than the approaching skrikers or the terrible storm. I'm supposed to know something here, but it's still beyond my awareness.

Suddenly an owl bursts out of the darkness and swoops down toward us. I duck, but the other she-Kyn stands still, and the owl's talons strike out to catch the upper edge of the mask and lift it into the air. As the bird vanishes again in the night, blue-green light explodes from the figure's exposed face, and horror fills me as I finally recognize the figure and understand, at last, what is expected. Yet before I have a chance to even scream, a wave of black fur and glistening fangs rolls through the grove as the skriker hounds descend upon us. The seven dancers disappear beneath the wave of howling death, and both the firelight and the green glow vanish in swirling snow and blood.

The last thing I hear before falling is my voice raised at last in song.

The Wielder awoke with a jolt, sweat pouring down her skin. Except for her copper armbands and choker she was naked, and the early morning air was ice-cold on her skin. Her heart pounded painfully.

She took a few deep breaths and remembered that she was in Garyn's wagon, wrapped safely in the arms and legs of Daladir and Jitani, who both slept on undisturbed.

She lay between her lovers for a while longer, pleased that they'd both finally found restful comfort in slumber, but the dream was still so clear in her mind, and sleep was now far away. Perhaps a bit of movement in the fresh air would lift the shadows from her thoughts. With infinite care she slid from their tangled embrace, and pulled a woolen trade blanket over her shoulders before stepping from the wagon.

She knew instantly that something was terribly wrong.

The camp was deathly quiet. She heard nothing: no coughing, no rustling, no crying or soft whispers. Even the Men's horses made no noise. Tarsa could see sleeping bodies everywhere. They weren't dead; their chests moved up and down with breath, but they were so still and silent. Everywhere she looked lay Folk, Men, Beasts of all sorts, horses and war-dogs, even a few scavenging birds, all trapped in dreamless sleep. The air was strangely heavy, and it carried an odd sensation, as though a trace of the *wyr* had been drawn out and stretched beyond its limits, like a layer of ice spread too thinly over deep, deadly waters.

Taking a heavy breath, Tarsa closed her eyes and reached out into the air, but the feeling was elusive, and it slipped from her grasp. Whatever had done this, it was alien to the *wyr* as she knew it.

The Wielder was so focused that it took a couple of heartbeats for her to notice that not *all* sounds had stopped, as a single tread of soft footsteps approached her through the camp. She looked up and was stunned for a moment into silence.

Shakar.

The Shield's violet eyes examined the threadbare blanket wrapped around Tarsa's shoulders. "Apparently *all* the Old Ways endure," she sniffed in disdain. "Even with our people abused, degraded, and dying all around us, you still revel in the flesh. I should hardly be surprised."

The initial shock of the Shield's appearance faded. In the past Tarsa might have attacked with heedless abandon, but not this day. She was the keeper of the Heartwood of the Eternity Tree, more than either a warrior or a Wielder, and the *wyr* tempered her rage as it filled her with firm resolve. "Every step of the Darkening Road I've waited for this day, traitor," she said. "Every time I walked past one of our kith lying dead at the side of the road or soothed the cries of a sapling cast alone into the world I've thought about what I'd do when I met you. Your death won't bring our people joy, but it might give them comfort."

"You presume too much, Wielder. I did what was necessary, no matter how unpleasant . . . as I am doing now."

Tarsa's eyes narrowed. "What are you—?" she began, but fell back with a guttural scream as a blast of blinding agony consumed her senses, sending her writhing to the ground.

Denarra had seen many things in her lifetime, but this had to be the strangest, most impressive sight of all. She stood on the deck of the Chancellor's own wasp-headed airship. Knowing that this would be a momentous event worthy of a fashionable entrance, Denarra ravaged her dressing room, and the results were magnificent: she stood resplendent in her finest scarlet skirt, pleated at the flowing bottom and draped with pearls of many sizes and shapes. A tight-fitting, forest-green jacket with broad shoulders, long sleeves, and a wide, upturned collar offered both complement and contrast to the dress; it enhanced the tightly laced bodice that revealed just enough to border on scandalous. The protective iron-ward girdle, although rather drab in contrast to the shimmering silks and muslins of the rest of her attire, added a touch of earthy simplicity with its flecked brown and grey surface. The crowning touch, however, and the one of which Denarra was most proud, was the sweeping hat of a rich jade hue, with bold peacock feathers in the brim that lay at a jaunty angle over her dyed and curled hair. She was going into great danger that she very well might not survive, but she'd be doing it in style, and that knowledge eased her doubts considerably. Death was painful but short; bad taste lingered forever.

The ship hovered low above the city in the twilight before dawn, as did the two dozen other Dragons that dotted the skies around them, summoned by the Chancellor and fully provisioned for the journey to come. From her lofty position Denarra looked down at the open plaza on the ground below, where Quill was making her final preparations. The Reachwarden had ordered the Chalimite marshals to clear one of the city's smaller market squares for the massive ritual, likely one of the last commands he'd be able to make after the Assembly heard of his participation in this extralegal operation. Neidam was organizing the marshals in their tasks, helping them to keep curious bystanders away, a surprisingly difficult task given the early hour. Surrounded by Ubbetuk Bluecap guards and a wide circle of dolls, Quill paced back and forth nervously in preparation.

"She's pushing herself much too hard," Denarra whispered to no one in particular, but the Reachwarden stepped to her side and looked down.

"It's hard to believe that someone so small could accomplish such a great task." Kaer's tone wasn't mocking or condescending; his voice carried a depth of sympathy that Denarra still found rather surprising. He'd gone against popular opinion by supporting the Folk's claim to the Everland, and though he refused to embroil the Reach in a civil war by declaring Eromar's actions illegal, his willingness to risk censure and even possible impeachment by helping Blackwick and the others was both unexpected and impressive. With this single action, Qualla'am Kaer had committed political suicide, but perhaps it would give them the time they needed to stop Vald, or at least to be with their people when the end came.

Either way, it was a brave and honorable act, and it gave her a bit of hope for the possibility of understanding between Folk and Men. Not much hope, but some was better than none, for she'd become far too used to being disappointed by Men.

Reflecting on Kaer's sacrifice, Denarra bit off her initial snide response. "Darling, there's more fighting spirit inside that little Dolltender than in all the Men of the Reach combined. I don't doubt for a minute that she can do it. I just worry about its effects. She's only just discovered this rare and wondrous skill, and now she's been asked to do something that even great Wielders would find terribly difficult. The last gate-walk was bad enough. She'll do it, certainly, but . . ." Her voice trailed off, and Kaer didn't press the issue further.

There were many stories about Wielders who'd been consumed by their dabbling in the Spirit World, falling prey to madness or worse. Quill was strong, and the teachings she'd received were rooted in a deep wisdom and respect for the spirits, but many things could go wrong with a Wielding such as this, and the young Dolltender was largely untrained in the finer points of her inheritance.

Besides, Denarra wasn't so self-absorbed after the gate-walking experience that she hadn't noticed the way Quill rubbed the pain from her lower belly when she thought no one was looking, or the sad look in the *firra*'s eyes when she'd see laughing children chase each other in the cobblestone streets.

The Man and the Strangeling lapsed into silence. Denarra wanted to be down in the square with her friend, to share in the dangers of this moment. But the *wyr*-fed energies that would be pulsing through the ritual site would be both powerful and unpredictable, and the presence of other Wielders or Crafters might upset the delicate balance that Quill required to create this gate. If she failed to maintain her concentration, if she stumbled in the dance or forgot a word in the song, she might bring catastrophe upon them all.

Rather than risk such dangers, Denarra and Merrimyn had agreed to stay on the Chancellor's Dragon floating above the ceremony, watching from a reasonable distance, while the Bluecaps remained below both to protect the Dolltender and to hurry her onto a small skiff that would bring her to the Chancellor's galleon for the journey. Yet it was difficult for Denarra to do nothing but watch, and even the confident knowledge of her own elegant appearance did little to ease either her fear or her impatience.

Merrimyn joined the Strangeling and the Reachwarden at the railing as a Bluecap horn blared below. The ritual was beginning.

She'd left her gourd-shell rattle in Denarra's old traveling wagon on the night they fled Vergis Thane's attack, but Quill had managed to find a suitable replacement in one of the market stalls of Chalimor that morning. It didn't have as nice a sound as hers, as it was a composite of thin wood and dried seeds rather than the more musical gourd or turtle shell rattles, nor was it as cheerily painted, but it would suffice for today. Green Kishka approved, and of all the dolls she was perhaps the most unrelenting about the precise requirements of this particular ceremony.

Although the dolls were unhappy about the Tetawa's decision for reasons no one had to mention, they all agreed that the alternative was too terrible to consider. Their kind had been created by the Dolltenders of old to bring wise counsel and aid to the Tetawi. There had never been a time when that wisdom was needed so desperately. Yet in the morning, when Quill brought them to the open square near Denarra's house, they looked with dismay at the twenty-eight makeshift dolls that she and her friends had hurriedly thrown together the night before. Such figures were little more than mindless automatons without personality or even recognizable facial features on their air-browned apple heads. Cornsilk complained that these things were smelly and half-naked, while Kishka groused about the emptiness of their dried-pea eyes. Mulchworm simply pursed his lips and clicked his white bead teeth with frustration.

Carefully prepared with prayers, tobacco, and other precious medicinals, each painted on the forehead with a drop of Quill's own blood, the half-formed dolls would be touched by spirits, but they would be conduits only, not beings with thought and will of their own. It would be the three old dolls and the Dolltender herself who'd have to carry the biggest burden. Such a task would be difficult enough with a hundred of the true dolls. But there were only three, and that would have to do.

Quill looked around, and her optimism sank when she realized that so much depended on so many odd, ugly, unfinished mannequins. She'd always taken great pride in her doll-craft, and such shoddy work grieved her. Yet at the sound of the horn, she turned her mind to the task at hand.

She lifted her head and shook her rattle four times as she called out to Green Kishka across the circle. Kishka sang to Mulchworm, who stamped his corncob feet on the flagstones in response. Cornsilk took up the song, and as her high-pitched trill rose high, the half-made dolls stood jerkily to their feet, their corn-husk dresses crackling as they moved in a westerly circle.

"*When the dance begins, Spider-child,*" Cornsilk had told her, "*ye mustn't stop. Don't stop until the song is over, or the gate will close, and we'll all be lost. The dance must continue . . . no matter what happens. There will be pain, cub. Lots of pain. But don't stop dancing.*" It had seemed like such a simple thing then, but Quill now understood what Cornsilk meant, as a hot, heavy weight struck them, like the rising blast of a furnace, and the twisting ache began again in her lower abdomen. It was nothing like the last gate-dance. This time they were too ambitious, attempting something that they had neither the strength nor the ability to do. The air seemed to be sucked away, leaving Quill straining for breath as she lifted her feet in time with the rattle and rhythm of the dance. The pain pulsed in time with the beat, growing sharper with each step. Sweat poured down her face. She wanted to look around, to see if the Bluecaps were feeling the strain, but inattention could be worse than fatal here, so the Dolltender gritted her teeth against the heat and pain and swift exhaustion and followed the dolls in an ever-widening circle. And as they moved, a small globe of darkness opened in the air above them. Shadowy filaments streamed out from the shimmering mass, a celestial web stretched across the sky.

Shukka, shukka, shukka, shukka. Shukka, shukka, shukka, shukka. The half-formed dolls moved in unison, following the others without hesitation or delay, and the dancing circle grew wider still. The withering heat seemed to do nothing more than wrinkle the apple-flesh of the new dolls, but Kishka, Mulchworm, and Cornsilk felt the strain. Their faces grew crimped and pained, while bits of fabric and corn husk slipped to the stones as they moved. And still they danced.

Another horn blared below, and Denarra turned her attention to the massive, star-shimmering portal that began to open in the sky. The first of the Dragons slid delicately toward the gate to test its stability. The air buckled slightly, but the gate held, and the airship slid into the iridescent shadow, followed swiftly by others—three, then six, and more. The ceremony was almost over. It wouldn't take too long for the small armada to be through the gate and on their way to the Pit Fields of Karkûr and the terrible new dangers that awaited them.

The Strangeling looked down again and nearly swooned from the blistering heat that radiated upward. Quill and her three small dolls had stumbled out of the circle while the other dolls continued to dance. The gate above quivered for a moment but remained largely stable. A dozen airships had disappeared into the gate, and most of the others were moving toward it, filling the air with the sound of whirring gears and wheezing gas bellows and whistles.

Quill's tawny face had gone a ghastly yellow, and she was bent and sweating. She seemed to be on the edge of collapse as she picked up the old dolls in shaking hands and secured them in her belt-pouch.

Yet she managed to stagger toward a Bluecap, who handed her an iron-ward belt and led her gently but swiftly toward the waiting skiff.

As Quill and her escort turned, the small airship suddenly exploded in a blinding ball of flame, annihilating its Ubbetuk crew and sending bodies and debris flying high into the air. Quill and the Bluecap fell stunned to the ground, and a few of the dolls in the ceremonial circle vanished under the rain of flesh and rubble. The gate in the sky shuddered again, this time more violently. Alarm horns on the remaining Dragons began to wail, and everyone rushed to the railings, peering through the flames and smoke to see what was happening below.

That it was sabotage was certain. An accident was nearly impossible, as the Dragons were crafted with extraordinary care, and each possessed various mechanisms to isolate potential problems and prevent such a catastrophe. Ubbetuk sharpshooters with stout crossbows slid wicked bolts into place and waited for the smoke to clear. Whoever had destroyed the skiff wouldn't find the other ships such easy targets.

"The gate is weakening—we have to get her!" Merrimyn shouted over the chaos. Their own vessel was the closest to the ground, but it still floated more than a hundred feet above the market. Yet lowering the ship was impossible if they wanted to reach the increasingly unstable gate, as the gas-bladders required most of their fuel for lifting off the ground.

"If we try to land now, we'll never be able to make it to the gate before it collapses." Denarra looked around in desperation. "Over there," she cried, pointing to a rope ladder hanging from the inner edge of the large cast-iron railing. She and the Binder lifted it up and over and watched the lower edge trail nearly to the ground. The Strangeling grabbed her skirts in her hand and started climbing over the edge.

A hand on her shoulder stopped her. Qualla'am shook his head. "I'll do it. I'm faster, and you're needed here."

"What are you talking about?" Denarra shouted, furious at the delay.

The Man pointed to the ground. She looked down and covered her mouth to stifle a scream.

Vergis Thane emerged from one of the buildings on the edge of the square and moved toward the little Dolltender, who lay unconscious amidst the smoking rubble of the skiff.

The Reachwarden crawled over the edge of the ship and slid swiftly down the ladder.

42

Sacrifice

"FLESH-ADDLED CHILD," Shakar hissed as she walked toward the fallen Wielder. "Have you forgotten your history so soon?"

The torment faded, and Tarsa lifted a shaking hand to her forehead, expecting blood. She took a breath and pulled her hand away. Nothing. No blood, no bruise—only a deep pounding throb in her sensory stalks. Her whole body ached.

The Shield lifted her blue skirts to avoid stepping on an old he-Tetawa who lay sprawled and snoring on the ground, yet her violet gaze remained fixed on the Wielder, who struggled to stand against the steady, crushing pressure bearing down on her. "Have you never wondered why it was that your kind fell so swiftly in the Purging? Have you never wondered why your precious *wyr*-witchery was of no avail against the power of the Shields? The Wielders were trapped in the weaknesses of fragile flesh. We chose the higher path—that of the mind, pure, unyielding, untainted by lower desires. We bent our thoughts to our wills, shaping and honing them into tools . . . and weapons. Yours is the way of flesh, Wielder, of all things frail and transient. Mine is the path of eternity. The pleasures and pains of flesh are a distraction, a sad reminder of our earth-bound forms. There is so very much more to what we can be."

Tarsa glowered as she looked around for a weapon to defend herself; Dibadjiibé and her belt knife were still in the wagon. "I have no interest in the teachings of a traitor. The blood of thousands is on your head."

Shakar's eyes were cold. "Still singing that sad song, Wielder? Here—let me teach you another." A brittle smile crossed her lips.

But Tarsa was ready this time. The *wyr* surged through her body in response to Shakar's attack, and the mind-shattering blast dissipated. The Wielder staggered back, feeling the Heartwood recoil from the alien force. Whatever this poisonous power was, it didn't have its origin in the Deep Green. It continued to skitter like a thousand spiders around the edges of her *wyr*-shield, trying to find a weak spot to pierce.

"Impressive," Shakar said as she stalked around the young Wielder with the focused purpose of a hawk circling a wounded rabbit. "Most impressive. Not many Wielders have withstood the first strike without falling into gibbering madness; fewer still have had the wits to defend themselves for the second wave. But you are still very young, and flesh is weak. You cannot withstand me forever."

"True," Tarsa groaned. "But I won't need to." She dropped the barrier and, in the same heartbeat, released a whirlwind of her own, a surge of pure *wyr* that burned through Shakar's attack, catching the Shield with its full force, spinning her through the air to smash hard into the rocky ground. Shakar pulled herself up on one elbow, her breathing labored, her dirt-stained silks tangled and torn.

Yet the Wielder had made a mistake. The sudden surrender of so much of the Heartwood's strength broke down other defenses, and the overpowering voices rushed in again, inundating her senses as they did on the day the barge sank in the storm-ravaged waters of the Shard Ford. The song tore through her thoughts. The voices were desperate now, trying to force understanding upon her, but the cacophony engulfed all thought, all feeling but torment. Her sensory stalks thrashed wildly, and she fell screaming to her knees.

Shakar slowly stood and wiped the dirt and blood from her hands. The sleeping Folk began to stir, freed from the Shield's influence by Tarsa's defensive attack, but it hardly mattered now. She now had what she came for. Turning to the pain-wracked Wielder, Shakar brought her fingers to her temples and focused her will, stripping her mind of all emotion except for pure, undiluted rage. A pulsing cone of invisible fury bore down on the green-skinned she-Kyn, and Tarsa collapsed without a sound.

The Shield clapped her hands together, and a pale gelding trotted out of the rubble on the edge of the camp, heedless of the shouting, sleep-bleary Folk who scrambled to get out of his way. The Shield lifted her hands and watched dispassionately as Tarsa's limp body rose into the air and fell roughly over the saddle. Swinging up behind the Wielder, Shakar spurred the horse forward, a small smile creeping across her weary face as the alarm went up.

The Folk would awaken to the knowledge that their savage savior was gone. As always, the flesh collapsed before the power of a disciplined mind. And when at last all hope for the return of the primal folly of their wild ways was lost, the people would at last see the truth, and Shakar would return to lead them in patient wisdom and grace. Only when the Deep Green was finally erased from the memory of this Melded world would the Folk have a place among Men.

Something soft and wet touched the Shield's face. She held out a hand. Snow. Winter had come to the Pit Fields at last. This would make her task that much easier, as ice and cold sapped a defiant will even better than did hunger. There would be little to fear now.

She drove the horse toward the rising storm and disappeared into a blinding curtain of white.

Denarra screamed in frustration. She couldn't touch the elemental spirits with the iron-ward around her waist, but removing the belt would expose her to the Dragon's debilitating poison. She grabbed an empty crossbow from a nearby stand and tried to crank it back, but her agitation and lack of skill made the task impossible, so instead she lifted the weapon over her head, took aim, and threw it over the edge of the ship. It didn't come close to striking Thane.

A handful of Ubbetuk sharpshooters were more successful, however, and sent a barrage of missiles toward the Seeker, hoping to keep him from gaining on Qualla'am Kaer, who'd finally reached Quill. The Dolltender seemed to be coming to her senses, but her Bluecap escort lay unmoving, either dead or unconscious. The remaining half-dolls continued their dance, but their movement was growing as erratic as the gate between worlds. Their time was growing short.

In spite of the skill of the archers from above, their bolts met empty air, for they were no match for Thane. Nor were the surviving eight Bluecaps on the ground, who raised their weapons and fired at the man. Drawing on all the Dreydcraft defenses he knew, and fueled by long-tempered fury, Thane's sword was a cyclone of silver fire. As the bolts shattered into splinters and dust, the Man was among the Bluecaps, his dark cloak blurring his form like the mantle of Grim Death. One Ubbetuk charged with his sword held out like a spear. It was a foolish, desperate move. The Seeker brought his own blade down to block the attack. As the Ubbetuk staggered back from the impact, Thane's left hand disappeared into his belt and appeared again with a small dagger that he hurled into the Bluecap's belly. Rushing past the gurgling creature, Thane slid his boot under the Ubbetuk's fallen sword and kicked it into the air, grabbing the hilt with his empty hand and moving in on his other opponents with two blades now at the ready.

Thane closed in on the Bluecaps so quickly that those above had to hold back, afraid to strike their own. Unaware of their vulnerability, and refusing to be cowed by a single Man, three of the remaining Bluecaps stepped out to meet him, swords drawn, and moved in a small circle. They were strange, deadly dancers, darting around like silent hornets, stabbing outward and then retreating out of the reach of the Man's blades. With other opponents, such movements were unnerving, but Thane seemed more annoyed than intimidated. He lunged at the nearest one, who hopped away and blocked the sword. But Thane was faster than he looked. As one of the other fighters zipped in to take advantage of the Seeker's feint, Thane spun back around and brought his sword down hard on the Bluecap's extended wrist, neatly severing the hand. Ignoring the spurting blood, Thane ducked and rolled into the shrieking Ubbetuk, hurling him against his companions.

The Seeker was on his feet again in an instant, swords twirling, and he dispatched the fallen attackers with twin throat thrusts, leaving the lesser blade embedded in the neck of one of the dying soldiers. A bolt flashed through the air. It slowed down as it neared the Seeker, whose free hand flew up, and the Bluecap archer watched aghast as Thane caught the Craft-slowed bolt in midair, the force whipping him around as he sent it winging back at full speed, all in the same fluid movement. The archer didn't even have a chance to think before the bolt plunged into his open mouth. He was dead before he hit the paving stones.

The last three Bluecaps faced the Man, eyes desperately seeking escape. Although they were the elite warriors of the Ubbetuk Swarm, they'd never faced such an enemy. He seemed to be a born predator, or worse, for he had no fear. They forgot the steps of their deadly dance, and that lost memory was fatal. Thane reached under his cloak and pulled out a black-muzzled hand-musket. There was a flash of fire, a roar, and one of the Bluecaps lurched forward with a cry. The others turned and tried to flee, but Thane dashed in, sliding the point of his sword behind the knees of the first and smashing the other Bluecap on the head with the butt of the musket. Both fell and twisted in pain, trying in vain to avoid the blade that slashed across their flailing arms and through their throats, leaving them gasping in their own lifeblood.

The great galleon buckled in the air. The filaments stretching out of the gate began to unravel and weaken. One of the ship's crew cried out, "We've got to go—*now!*" The Dragon moved ponderously into the air toward the gate.

"Kaer's got her!" Denarra screamed. "Just a moment longer!"

The Reachwarden had watched Thane's efficient carnage with horrified fascination. Although widely considered an expert with the blade, the former soldier had never seen such swift and unemotional destruction, and the knot of fear at the pit of his stomach moved up and squeezed his heart. In one hand he held his sword free of its scabbard. He dragged Quill toward the ladder with the other, but he quickly realized that one of the two would have to go—though neither was excessive on its own, the weight of both would slow him too much, and he needed every possible advantage in these precious moments. He'd had the sword since his elevation to captain of the Republic Army, over thirty years now. It had served him well and saved his life a thousand times. But he couldn't defend himself against Thane and climb to the ship with the stunned Tetawa at the same time, and given the Seeker's skills and uncanny powers, even then Kaer wasn't sure the weapon would do him much good. He looked up just as Thane dispatched the last of the Bluecaps. The Seeker lifted his dripping knife and turned his single cold eye to Kaer, smiling with grisly satisfaction as he identified the Reachwarden's dilemma.

In the face of this menace, only one choice was possible, so Kaer tossed the injured Dolltender tightly over his left shoulder and ran at top speed toward the rope ladder rising swiftly off the ground. With a twinge of regret he flung the sword away to clang sharply on the cobblestones, launched himself forward, and caught the third rung of the ladder. Quill, dazed and nauseated but now conscious, reached out weakly and grabbed the rope.

They weren't alone. Ignoring the bolts that crashed into the flagstones around him, Thane dashed forward like a panther and threw himself at Kaer's legs, clutching tightly with one powerful arm. The Dragon thundered upward into the sky, slowly picking up speed as it flew ever higher above the city. Kaer kicked downward as hard as he could, but the Seeker's vice-like grip was unbreakable.

Thane ignored the Reachwarden. His eye was fixed on the Dolltender, whose own terrified gaze was locked on the long knife in Thane's free hand.

The gate was collapsing, and the air trembled and warped with the strain. The great Dragon groaned as a sudden blast of wind smashed into its side. Denarra clutched at the railing and watched the rope ladder spin out of control, its passengers straining desperately to hold onto their one small chance for survival, one that was growing more precarious with every passing moment. The ladder wasn't meant for this kind of strain. Already the rope was fraying against the airship's rough hull.

"We've got to get them to the deck before we enter the gate!" Merrimyn yelled.

Denarra shook her head. "Are you completely out of your senses? We can't bring Thane on this ship—he'll kill us all!"

"Then what are we going to do? We can't shoot him off and risk killing the others."

The ship shuddered again. They were almost at the gate, the last ship to pass through, but most of the elemental filaments had disappeared into black fire, and the great gate seemed to be vanishing even as they watched. A wave of bitterly cold wind rushed outward to envelop the ship.

Denarra stood still at the railing, her white-knuckled fingers wrapped tightly around the metal bar, her gaze fixed on the sunrise. Quickening in the east, the light of a new blue morning rose to life in bright contrast to the storm-ravaged gate that quivered ahead of them. She'd never seen a dawn quite so lovely before, with feathery clouds of lavender and coral pink glowing softly against the deep gold of the birthing sun. It seemed to be the first dawn the Strangeling had ever really experienced in all its wondrous possibility. She took a deep, ragged breath and let the Melded world's broken beauty wash over her. When she finally turned back to Merrimyn and the Ubbetuk crossbowmen, she had a smile on her face, but there were tears in her eyes.

"You won't have much time to get them up here after Thane is gone, so be ready." She began to unbuckle the iron-ward around her waist.

The Binder looked on in momentary confusion that gave way to dismayed understanding. "No . . . you can't . . ."

She reached out and pressed her fingers to his lips. "It's been a bold and grand adventure, darling, but a true lady always knows the best time for a graceful exit. I promised to get her to Chalimor; you'll have to help her get back home to her sweet Tobhi. Do this for me, my friend. Now, get ready . . . and thank you." Before Merrimyn could say anything else, Denarra ripped off the iron-ward and launched herself into the air.

"*NO!*" he wailed as she disappeared over the railing.

A burst of wind met the Strangeling on her way down, and although the iron-sickness threatened to overwhelm her senses, she was able to direct the wind toward the flailing ladder. Thane's attention was focused on his loosening hold on Kaer's leg, so he wasn't aware of the Wielder until her arms were wrapped around his throat and free arm. He gasped in pain and amazement, nearly losing his grasp as her knees smashed, hard, into the small of his back. Quill cried out and reached for her friend.

The moment of surprise was all the time Denarra needed to grab the steel blade from Thane's hand. The metal erupted in crackling mauve flame. The Strangeling's emerald gaze lingered on Quill's grief-ravaged features, and she flashed a merry smile. "Keep the fire, darling!" she shouted as she drove the burning knife with all her remaining strength through the Seeker's hand and into Kaer's upper calf. Thane screamed, and his hand shot open involuntarily as Kaer kicked backward with a bellow.

The smoking blade slipped out of the Reachwarden's leg. With Denarra still clinging to his back, the Seeker fell away from the ladder to disappear among the clouds, a brief flash of red silk and brown leather, as the great airship finally slipped into the gate and vanished with the rising sun.

43

Decay

<<IT IS TIME.>>

Forty-seven years, eight months, and nineteen days had passed since the Dreyd first unveiled themselves to Lojar Vald, who was then only a struggling young jurist in a lawless land. He had made a life of watching enemies stumble and vanish under their accumulated mistakes, allies grow tired and frail with the years, while the might of Eromar flourished under his firm guidance. And as his fidelity to the Dreyd grew, so did his strength, and so too did that of his people. There was no province in the Reach more feared or more imposing than Eromar; no one doubted the ability of the Dreydmaster to pursue his goals with unwavering commitment. Any doubts that once may have existed had been erased by the fall of the Everland—a military victory unsurpassed in the history of the Reach. No enemy could stand against Lojar Vald. No state dared impose its rule over the people or government of Eromar. They were one, the Man and the State, and as he ascended, so, too, would Eromar.

Yet worldly ambitions posed no appeal except as they could enhance the greater goal on Vald's mind, and now, at last, the two came together in a broken, barbarous land far from the timbered walls of Gorthac Hall. Soon the decades of personal deprivation, endless study, political maneuvering, and retributive justice would bear sweet fruit, and the Dreydmaster would leave this flawed mortal shell and join the new Immortals, free of the indignities of age and infirmity, free to experience all the delights enjoyed by absolute power. He and his name would live in triumph forever.

Vald surveyed the preparations with rising excitement. Hundreds of Eromar militia joined with the Dreydcaste Binders and Seekers on a great shattered pinnacle of red stone that jutted from Riekmere Swamp, a boggy, bowl-like valley that stretched for nearly six miles in each direction. Thousands of Unhumans of every unwholesome mixture milled around in the frigid morass, struggling to find dry footing on the sodden valley floor, along with a few hundred of their traitorous Human collaborators. Soldiers with muskets and cannons lined the sharp stone ridge surrounding the valley and kept the exhausted captives from escaping. The last large group of Unhumans would be arriving soon, and once they joined their kindred in the swamp they would find their exit blocked by well-armed mercenaries and slavers, all with experience in keeping these creatures in check. This final bit of rabble included the Unhumans that Vald had been most interested in seeing, for it was among their ranks that the most troublesome of their kind had been found.

She had been so arrogant in Gorthac Hall, never lowering her eyes respectfully as a proper Woman would have done, even daring to condescend to him—to *him!*—and going so far as to destroy half of the structure with her witchery. But she was no longer so proud and defiant. She and her people were broken. It was their fate to vanish with the day's last sunset, fading into the oblivion of memory at long last. And in their destruction would come the full redemption of Men.

<<All is readied, Vorgha. At long last, it is time to begin.>> The Dreydmaster turned to his attendant, who bowed his head reverently and stepped to the side. They walked together to the edge of the rocky plateau, Vald in front and Vorgha behind, where the Reaver could observe the events as they transpired.

A few hundred Men ringed the ridge valley, with groups clustered every quarter mile around massive copper-capped posts of cold iron driven into the stone. Chained to each post was the thrashing form of an Unhuman witch, brought from prisons and holding pens from around the Dreyd-dominated lands of the Reach; beside each of these stood a well-trained Binder with snaring-tome held ready. Long copper cables rose from the tops of the posts, stretched across the valley, and wrapped around spikes at the tip of a narrow tower, crudely erected of crisscrossing iron latticework at the apex of the central stone peak. It was here that the Veil Between Worlds would again be pierced, and it was here that the greatest of the Unhuman witches would have the honor of watching the new Melding take place. Once enough power was unleashed, Vald would move to the center of the pinnacle and finish the greatest Reaving the world had ever known. Dying, the witch would unleash her power, the Veil would be torn asunder, and he would step at last into immortality.

Vorgha lifted a small horn to his lips and sounded three piercing blats. Screams erupted from the witches at every post along the valley bowl as the Binders began their delicate tasks. The Dreydmaster turned toward the iron tower, his eyes gleaming with an almost childlike joy. <<Bring her to me,>> he called to his Manservant. <<Bring me the Spearbreaker. Bring me Tarsa'deshae.>>

"What happened?" Tobhi yelled as he rushed toward the wagon, his eyes still bleary from sleep. He'd been awakened by screams, followed by whispers that sent his heart racing. Grabbing his hat and pack, he ran to find his friends, but when Tarsa failed to emerge from the wagon with the others, his heart plummeted.

Jitani slipped into her boots, her face grave. "They took her, not long ago. They had a Shield with them."

Tobhi glanced at Daladir. "It was Shakar," the he-Kyn confirmed. "All the descriptions are the same. The whole camp was asleep; nobody knew she was here until just before she thundered away with Tarsa."

Jitani turned to the darkened west before kneeling to examine the remaining hoof tracks scattered through the camp. "She took her the same direction we're going. We're all a part of the same thing, one way or another. I just don't know why they're in such a hurry—we'll be there soon enough, before sunset if we push on as we've been doing."

"It's not Tarsa they want as much as what she carries, and Vald has much need of that," said Daladir.

"Well, then," Tobhi frowned and pulled his hat down securely on his head, "we'd best get her back."

"And what are we going to do about them? I don't think they'll let us just walk out of here." Jitani gestured toward a large group of soldiers standing nearby. The Men milled around nervously, clutching their weapons in their white-knuckled hands, and watched the agitated and long-brutalized Folk with increasing discomfort.

"They will die if they hurt you." A shadow fell across the three companions. Tobhi glanced up to see Biggiabba standing over them, a ragged cloak protecting her body from the worst of the sun's rays, her once-massive bulk worn down to a nearly skeletal thinness, her hair matted and dirt-crusted. Great oozing sores stretched across her grey skin, and the eyes that stared out at the world gleamed with an agony that bordered on madness.

For a moment Tobhi thought that Biggiabba would fall upon them in her delirium, but instead the Gvaerg matron bowed her head and croaked, "All dead. Sons, brothers, husbands, fathers. From wide-eyed pebble-child to worn-stone elder, Men killed them all, hundreds and hundreds. They attacked Delvholme. It was a peace-city, a place of sanctuary, and they burned the houses and destroyed the sacred caves. Our he-Gvaergs—they all died, every one. Drove stakes through their bodies, pinned them to the mountainside until the suns rose, then laughed as the sunlight burned them, boiled their blood, turned them to stone from within. The she-Gvaergs, they all tried to fight, tried to stop it, but the Men drove them back, cut them, pierced them, destroyed all hope of help." Her ravaged shoulders shook with suppressed sobs. "I should have been with them. I could have stopped the killing. No Man set foot in my people's mountains while the Gvaerg Wielders stood strong. I came to Sheynadwiin, and my people died. I failed them all."

"No," Tobhi whispered, resting his tiny hand on the Wielder's too-thin arm. "Ye en't to blame. Ye did the only thing ye knew to do. That's what we all did. There en't no shame in that. We en't to blame for the evil that was brought down on us by the greed and hate of these Men. That burden belongs to them, not us."

Biggiabba's eyes narrowed as she looked past the Tetawa to the crowd of soldiers. "Yes, of course—you are right. It was Men who brought this down on us. It will be Men who pay for their part in this evil."

Tobhi jumped back in alarm as the Wielder snarled, her mouth ringed with blood-specked froth. "*VENGEANCE!*" she roared with a voice that crashed like an earthquake in the rocky valley. "Death to Men!" Before anyone could stop her, she charged at the stunned soldiers, her massive fists sweeping Men and horses aside so quickly that the survivors' only response was to flee as the sounds of gurgling screams, cracking bones, and shredded flesh filled the air. For a moment Biggiabba was alone, and then other Folk joined her, their rage finally unleashed.

"Now!" Jitani hissed. She grabbed Tobhi's arm and jerked him toward the rocky ridge and motioned to Daladir, who watched the devastation with revulsion.

"Daladir, this will be our only chance—look!" The mercenary pointed to the far end of the camp, where another group of soldiers was galloping at full speed toward the uprising. "Dreyd-cursed fool!" she shouted. "Think of Tarsa!" At last the he-Kyn turned, his face pale and troubled, and rushed to the wagon. He emerged an instant later with Tarsa's wyrwood staff in one hand and Jitani's sword in the other, and followed his companions into the rocks at the edge of the camp. They rushed on, heedless of pursuit, until they breathlessly reached the top of the ridge and threw themselves over the edge and out of view.

"Do you think they—" Tobhi began, but his words were lost in a sudden chorus of musket-fire, followed by thin, wailing screams that went silent all too quickly.

They crouched together in somber silence. "Come on," Jitani whispered at last. "We can't help them now; we'd only die along with the rest. The only hope we have is to find Tarsa and the Heartwood, and quickly."

Tobhi wiped a dirty sleeve across his eyes and followed, with Daladir close behind.

"We've got to go back! We can't leave her!" Quill screamed, throwing herself at the railing again, heedless of the iron-sickness that pulsed through her body. Merrimyn tried to wrap the charmed talisman around her waist, but the Dolltender's struggles made the task impossible. Another seizure struck her, and she crashed to the deck in white-eyed agony, her hands curled into claws.

Qualla'am Kaer snatched the sash out of Merrimyn's hands, pinned Quill to the wooden planks with his right hand, and wound the iron-ward around the Tetawa's thrashing body, holding her down until it took effect.

Merrimyn looked down at the spreading scarlet pool under the Reachwarden's leg. He swallowed, the memory of the fight too close and painful to contemplate, and turned to one of the deckhands. "A poultice and some bandages—hurry, please." As the Ubbetuk rushed away, the young Binder turned back to Kaer, who now held the sobbing Dolltender in his arms and rocked her back and forth gently.

"We've got to find her," Quill whispered, her voice small and choked with deep sobs. "She's going to need our help . . . we've got to . . ." Exhausted, and pained beyond endurance, she slipped into a fitful sleep.

The old soldier looked up at the Binder, but neither Man spoke. When the ship's surgeon arrived to look at Kaer's injuries, Merrimyn sat with legs crossed on the deck, slid his snaring-tome and chain out of the way, took Quill's sleeping body into his own arms, and cried.

The flight of Dragons emerged from the darkness of the gate into the orange glow of the late-day sun. It was impossible to tell how long they'd been between worlds, and few could describe what that nether-realm had been like. For some it seemed like an endless night, with strange stars shining everywhere; for others, it was a grey mist that burned with ghostly hues and vanished as the eye tried to focus on them. Watching the alien sky brought only dizziness and confusion, so those on deck or inside the hold of each ship quickly turned their attention to mundane tasks, uncertain if they would ever emerge from the gate and, if they did, fearful of what awaited them.

The Chancellor was no different, although he watched from the comfort of his well-appointed apartments in Chalimor through one of the many viewing globes he used to keep track of the armada. A few moments of viewing were enough to send him reeling to his quarters, where he shrugged off assistance and slumped into a high-backed chair to settle his nerves with a goblet of silvered mead until the nausea passed and he could return to his scrying.

Such weakness infuriated the old Ubbetuk beyond words. He rarely succumbed to emotional displays, even in private, and his durability had by now become the stuff of legend. It was a carefully managed image, one that hid the flaring pain in his joints, the fading eyesight, and the numerous aches that made each morning's awakening more difficult than the last. It was the best defense for an aging politician with the chilly breath of mortality at the base of his neck. His reputation as a pillar of fortitude was enough to unnerve all but the most desperate enemies, and those few who remained to trouble him were generally dealt with in ways both decisive and subtle.

And yet, for all his wisdom and foresight, Blackwick had underestimated Vald's ambition, and this mistake had already proven quite costly, both to him and to the Swarm itself. A mortal-minded adversary always needed resources, and the Swarm's unsurpassed talents with advanced machinery and arms gave it economic leverage in every part of the Reach. No province had been a more enthusiastic trading ally than Eromar, but now, too late, Blackwick saw the fatal flaw in the bargain: Vald's allegiance stretched only as far as his celestial ambitions were served. Once enough Ubbetuk resources were in reach to pursue the central focus of his crusade quickly and efficiently, Vald had no further need of the Swarm, and any attempt by the Chancellor or the Whitecap Council to punish Eromar with trade sanctions or a harsh embargo had no effect. Without that threat, the only alternative was war.

The weary Ubbetuk leaned back and slid a thick fingernail against the rim of the glass, taking dour satisfaction from the high-pitched scraping sound that set his teeth on edge. War. It was always his last choice. To declare war was to admit defeat, for the inevitable catastrophe to all involved would demonstrate with painful certainty that there could be no true victory at the end. It would be a gruesome experience, with death and bloodshed unlike any seen since the last Melding.

He hadn't been entirely forthright with the others during their plans for the attack on Vald and his troops. True, Blackwick sincerely wanted to rescue the Folk from their torment, but there was another reason to participate, one that was far more immediately compelling. Lojar Vald had presumed to confiscate Ubbetuk airships and take their crews hostage. The Dragon fleet, although not the only

weapon in the mostly hidden arsenal of the Swarm, remained its economic, political, and military lifeblood. If Men presumed to claim
for themselves what had emerged from hundreds of years of Ubbetuk
artistry and genius, then the Swarm would never be free of danger.
This flight of Dragons came, not simply for liberation, but as a lesson to all Men, for all time: Blackwick would see the Dreydmaster's
power scattered like autumn leaves in a storm. From this day on,
Men would never doubt the power of the wrathful Swarm.

Indeed, it might be the start of a new era for the Ubbetuk, one in
which delicate diplomacy could give way to the irresistible certainty
of their industrial might.

If things went badly, and the flight of Dragons was destroyed by
anything less than another Melding, Blackwick would begin again,
secure now in Chalimor. He'd left a few airships in the city, just in
case—his long life was the result of leaving many alternatives open,
even when the odds were firmly in his favor.

If, on the other hand, Denarra's ambitious friends could help to
prevent Vald's ascension, so much the better, for both themselves and
the Swarm. He'd been sad to see the Strangeling's sacrifice but wasn't
surprised that the Binder and the Dolltender were continuing on.
They were certain in their purpose, and that was enough to get them
through all but the worst trials to come.

Yet the Ubbetuk had survived the first Melding. They would
most likely survive another.

The Chancellor held up his goblet and watched the glistening
liquid move across the crystal in soft, delicate swirls. The nausea was
passing; he was already feeling better. Standing with care, Blackwick
returned once again to the scrying room.

Only in her Awakening had Tarsa experienced pain like this, tongues
of blood-borne fire that twisted through her body from flesh to
bone and back again, jagged spirit blades that tore her apart from the
inside, leaving her broken nearly beyond healing. During that time,
seemingly so long ago, she'd simply surrendered to the hurt, unable
to claw her way out of the iron-veined pit to which she'd been exiled
by her townsfolk. Yet now, as the Heartwood pulsed like a drum

through her veins and those now-familiar voices sang out in response to the smothering crush of iron that surrounded her, a spark of defiance flickered to life, and she fought back. Though the words of the song were still unclear, the desperation in the voices was unmistakable: whatever the torment, she must survive.

To do so, the young she-Kyn would have to draw again on an earlier strength, the training of mind, body, and spirit that belonged to an ancient tradition every bit as old as that of the *wyr*-bound Wielders. Tarsa was a Wielder now, but she would always be a Redthorn warrior, and there was no place in that tradition for despair. A Redthorn fought out of duty and love—a love of the People, of home and life. The song filled her thoughts and vision, and she joined the chorus, her voice small and broken, but growing. The words seemed to lift her out of her flesh and the pain, drawing her from the haze that clutched at her spirit and into a shimmering radiance that beat with the pulse of primordial life and resonant awareness beyond comprehension.

Into the Deep Green.

And as the verdant glow enveloped her, she felt it burn away the taint of iron that coursed through her blood. She was left weak, but once again whole. Her body trembled uncontrollably. Even when she joined with the Heartwood after the fall of the Tree, she had never reached the Deep Green. Such knowledge was elusive and unknowable by those bound to the mortal realm. Even now, just heartbeats later, the certainty of the experience left her mind, and all that remained was a renewed vigor in her muscles and the faint but unmistakable scent of deep-woods flowers and moist soil that lingered in the air.

Tarsa's sensory stalks stroked her face, tenderly drawing her back to the waking world. She lifted her head from the dry stones with a low groan, catching her breath as she gazed into the flat, empty eyes of Lojar Vald, who stared at her with patient scorn, his black greatcoat fluttering like dark wings in the rising wind. Behind him in a hooded blue cloak stood Shakar, her head bowed and face shadowed by the cowl.

Rage surged through the Redthorn Wielder. She flung herself forward but screamed in frustration as the cold chains around her throat, wrists, and ankles dragged her back to the rocky earth.

"A savage to the last, Wielder?" Vald said in the trade-tongue, shaking his head in amazement. "And at such an auspicious moment. I should perhaps be thankful. Your consistent predictability has made this so much easier for us all." He clapped his hands, and a group of six heavily armed Men jerked on the chains. Together they wrapped the links around the wide base of an iron tower that stretched high in the air, its open scaffolding gleaming with a dull, bloody hue in the fading light of day. Dozens of stout copper cables stretched outward from the top of the structure, but Tarsa couldn't tell where those led, as the chain bearers pulled her to her knees and thus out of sight of anything but this wind-worn shelf of rock. They stepped away, and Shakar moved in with a small net of a strange shining metal in her hands. This she draped over the Wielder's head, and Tarsa's sensory stalks thrashed frantically under its blistering touch.

An agonized scream split the air from far beyond her view, and one of the copper cables hummed, its length rapidly vibrating. Another scream followed, and another, and soon all the wires above buzzed with wild energy. The she-Kyn watched in growing horror at the pulsating, irregular shadow that streaked across the first wire toward the tower. As it drew near, her skin tingled with familiarity. Tarsa's body buckled, and her own guttural cry joined the others as the mingled life-essence of the shattered Wielders was absorbed by the metal netting and drove down, ripping through flesh and spirit, rooting inward to tear the Heartwood from her thrashing body.

<<It is your turn now, my lady. Begin the extraction, and we will finish this final ceremony. Redemption is ours.>> Vald nodded to Shakar. <<Our time is at hand.>> The Shield lowered her hood. Her face was devoid of expression, but she trembled as she approached the screaming Wielder.

The Dreydmaster motioned to Vorgha, who lifted his small bugle and sounded three long calls. There was silence for a moment, and then the cannons roared, followed by the thunderous discharge of muskets firing into the defenseless Folk in the valley below.

"The Binders are killing them!" Daladir shouted to the others, who struggled up the rubble-strewn slope behind him. They'd rushed through broken canyons and across sharp, narrow cliffs that slashed their boots, knees, and hands until each limped and stumbled with more will than strength, trying desperately to move toward the shroud on the horizon without exposing themselves to discovery. Now they were here, close enough to witness the terrible events unfolding on the ridge beyond but overwhelmed by the sudden realization that they were hopelessly outnumbered. And there was still no sign of Tarsa.

The trio stood about a quarter mile behind the ridge and could see a massive promontory stretching out of the deep valley beyond. One of the iron posts that lined the ridge was well within their sight. There, chained tightly to the rust-streaked metal, crouched one of the deer-Folk Ferals, his battered face unrecognizable at this distance. They watched with spirit-sick revulsion as a thin, white-haired Woman with a massive book chained to her right wrist shouted something and lifted the open text high into the air. The Feral Wielder twisted in visible agony with each word. The Woman's voice soon vanished under the gibbering shriek that clawed its way from the Wielder's throat, and a shimmering shadow snaked up the side of the post and slid across the wire toward a tall spike of lacy scaffolding that jutted from the top of the massive tower of stone. The scream ended abruptly, and the Feral's body slumped in the chains.

Tobhi fell to his knees. What had become of their world? How could they possibly stop a whole nation of unnatural enemies like these who knew no limits in their ambitions? He'd once believed that good intentions and right actions were enough to have a long, love-filled life, even in frightening times. He lived by that philosophy, treated others with care, and tried to bring light to the lives of those around him. But it wasn't enough to stop the Darkening Road, and he didn't know how to make sense of the world again. Sometimes you could do everything right and cruelty would still reign in this life. Sometimes the only thing to do was push on, no matter how terrible the world might become, no matter how much one suffered, never depending on hope but never quite giving up on it, either.

Maybe not giving up was the only thing left at the end. But even that seemed useless now.

His heart a stone weight in his chest, Tobhi turned to check again that they weren't being followed. There seemed to be nothing behind them but ravaged stone and broken earth, but then a movement caught his attention, and his eyes followed a strange pattern of dappled shadows darkening the ground. As his gaze moved upward toward the source of those shadows, his mouth dropped open with a gasp.

"It can't be," he whispered in suddenly rekindled hope.

The sky was filled with Dragons.

44

Stone and Spear

THE FERAL WIELDER'S SCREAM was followed by dozens more, each one more terrible than the last. The two Kyn ran forward now, heedless of the danger, quickly closing the distance. The slicing of the stones on their wounded feet held no more concern for them, nor did the masses of Men who surrounded each tortured Wielder. Only one thing mattered now: doing something—anything—to stop this madness. The mercenary and the diplomat, side by side, joined by their love of their people . . . and of a green-skinned beauty who was lost, just beyond their reach. Jitani drew her wyrwood sword and started singing her war-chant. Daladir glanced at her for a moment, then lifted Tarsa's staff and joined in her song.

Suddenly, above the dying screams of the Wielders and the droning chants of the Binders, a familiar voice rising in a wail of torment filled their minds, and both Kyn fell to the earth. The voice was connected to them through their past healings and bondings, and for the space of a breath her agony was their own. Jitani and Daladir held their hands to their heads, trying to drive away the clutching dread. Although their stalk wrappings were still secure, the intensity of the scream penetrated these thin defenses.

"Tarsa," Jitani groaned, digging her hands through the rough soil, trying desperately to push herself back to her feet.

Daladir lifted himself to his elbows. "We're too late," he hissed through clenched teeth. "We're too far away."

A grinding roar shook the ground, and something darkened the sky as a cloud of blinding dust struck them. The dazed and coughing Kyn looked up to see a small Ubbetuk airship floating above them, its massive, moth-shaped wings flapping furiously beneath a billowing gas-bag. Tobhi stood on the deck, his long black hair whipping wildly in the wind.

"Ye want to try this again?" the Tetawa shouted to Daladir, waving his hat with glee.

Averyn pushed Garyn aside as musket-shot splashed in the frigid bog. The Governor swayed and toppled into the muck, narrowly avoiding another blast.

"Run toward the tower!" Averyn cried, jerking hir lover to his feet, but Garyn held back.

"Not there—look!" He pointed to a line of Men at the base of the rocky outcropping who were following the example of the soldiers on the ridge above. "They're everywhere, beloved. We're trapped." The air blazed with screams and the metallic tang of fresh blood and flashpowder. Death surrounded them. There was no place now to run or hide.

They'd traveled hundreds of miles and shared numerous loving years together, side by side. Love had found them easily and without ceremony: Averyn had been brought in by the Branch-mothers of Thornholt Town as a healer when Garyn, then Firstkyn of the town and representative to Sheynadwiin, suffered a crippling fall. The young zhe-Kyn, then just past hir adulthood rites, stayed with Garyn and gave him medicinals and deep stretches to ease the pain in his hip, taught him of joy and the peace of soft music, and, eventually, remained to teach him of other pleasures, too. And in spite of the years and qualities that separated them, they found strength in each other from then on, even in these days of darkness.

Averyn grabbed Garyn and kissed him deeply, tears streaming unchecked down hir cheeks. They said nothing; words were futile now. They simply held tight to each other, standing tall against the onslaught from above. As their people fell dead and wounded around them, they never let go, even after the musket balls tore into their own flesh and drove them, gasping, into the cold embrace of the swamp.

The sky was alive with cannon fire, and the Dragon tilted precariously to the side. Kaer pointed toward the ridge. "We've got to stop those cannons!"

Merrimyn scrambled back to his feet after being tossed down by the last explosion. Lurching to the edge, his hair askew and eyes wild, he cried out, "Binders—at least a hundred of them! They'll be worse than the soldiers!"

Nodding, Kaer turned to the ship's captain, an immaculately dressed Greencap. "Is this ship armed?"

"Of course it is!" the Ubbetuk said with a harsh laugh. "Do you think the Swarm would travel into hostile territory without adequate defenses?" He waved to some of his blue-capped crew, who moved to a series of arched doors in the lower side of the ship, below the portholes. Motioning to the Men, he turned to the observation railing with a strange glimmer in his eyes. "Watch closely," he said. "This will be a story to share for years to come. Witness for yourselves the power of the Dragons."

The sharp peal of bells and whistles split the air, and the airship shifted westward. Suddenly, one side of the airship seemed to fall away, and a series of carved metal tubes stretched slowly outward like monstrous mouths, their ends pointing toward one of the cannons below. Another whistle screeched, and the air exploded in a gout of liquid fire that roared with unerring precision toward the ridge, sweeping downward and incinerating everything in its path. The fiery torrent continued, on and on, blasting downward as the Dragon shifted to the north, following along the top of the ridge, unleashing its deadly barrage on the frantic Men beneath them. The fire burned long after the ship passed by, and Merrimyn watched in fascinated disgust as the militiamen and mercenaries tried hopelessly to free themselves of the clinging fire. They lasted scant seconds before collapsing in charred, smoking heaps.

In the sky around them, the rest of the Ubbetuk fleet unleashed its deadly cargo on Vald's soldiers, assiduously avoiding the release of any fire on the Folk who crouched, wounded and terrified, in the valley beyond. Some of the ships commandeered by Vald's soldiers moved to intercept the Swarm armada, but most drifted in the air, unmoving, as their Ubbetuk crews rose up against their Eromar captors.

For now, at least, the Swarm ruled the skies.

Quill, standing in a shadowed alcove on the other side of the airship, also observed the destruction of Eromar's militia. Though her belly was still tender and her legs unsteady, her insides had quit clenching so badly; now there was nothing but emptiness, a hollow ache to remind her of what she'd surrendered to be here at this terrible moment. Yet in spite of all the cruelty brought on her people by Vald and his kind, she couldn't look on the scene below without loathing and pity. She tasted thick bile on her tongue.

"So much death, so much pain. Will it ever end?" she whispered, looking toward the east, her thoughts winding back to a vanished friend far away. More had been lost than Quill had ever imagined, and there would be so much more to come.

"We're drenched in blood this day." She put her face in her hands. "Oh, Granny Jenna, Old Turtle, forgive me. Forgive us all."

Shakar focused her thoughts and wove them into Tarsa's struggling mind. She gasped. The suffering was extraordinary, worse than anything she'd ever experienced in her own weak and wounded flesh, and yet, impossibly, the Wielder still fought against the intrusion. Cocooning her senses from Tarsa's pain, the Shield marveled at Tarsa's strength. If it had been another time, a different world, they might have admired one another, maybe even been allies, if never friends. They shared a love of their people and an unwavering conviction of purpose. But in this world, they were destined to be on opposite sides of history. As difficult as their situation was, there could be only one survivor. In all things, it was the strong who endured, and the Deep Green had no place in the world of Men. It was another age now, and Shakar intended for her people to be a part of that age, even if they had to be dragged into it against their collective will. The last remaining barrier was represented by this raging, tattooed creature crouched and chained before her, a creature more Beast than Kyn. The Wielder's death, like that of her mentor, Unahi, would be a small price to pay for the survival of the Folk.

Like a rabid wolf infecting others with its poison, the *wyr*-witches had too long tainted their people. And although Shakar's duty was unpleasant, it was the necessary excision to ensure the health of all. There was only one cure for a diseased cur like this one.

More Wielders died on the surrounding ridge, and as each one's bound spirit smashed into Tarsa's thrashing body, Shakar found the resistance lowering. She could feel thin filaments of the Heartwood begin to spread outward and away from the weakening Wielder, desperate to hold on, yet helpless to resist the multiple attacks. The Shield redoubled her efforts as the last of the Binders released their snared powers. The wall began to crumble. The young Wielder pushed against Shakar's mind, but she was too weak, and the nearness of success gave Shakar a tremendous advantage. There would be no failure now.

A thin, tearing shriek rose up from Tarsa's throat as Shakar at last pulled the Heartwood free, and the Wielder collapsed amidst the pile of chains, her face ashen. Backing away from the young she-Kyn, Shakar looked upon the pulsing green radiance in her hands. Hundreds of slender tendrils stretched outward and caressed the Shield's trembling fingers, and the mass seemed to expand and contract with a life of its own. The emerald light stretched down her arms and flowed over her body. She staggered backward and turned to Vald.

<<Take it!>> she gasped, holding the *wyr*-power as far from her body as possible. She could feel the Heartwood moving through her, changing her, opening doors in her mind that she had thought locked forever. The masks were falling. Layers of certainty and pride fell away, and she feared to see what remained. <<Please, hurry!>>

The Dreydmaster smiled at Vorgha. At last. This was his destiny. He'd been born to rule Men, and now he would be reborn to rule worlds. The Not-Raven spies had told him the truth—the she-Kyn witch was the source of the power. And now, that power was his. He held his hands up to Vorgha, who took a small knife from his belt and cut a long, wicked gash in each of his master's palms.

Turning to Shakar, Vald reached out and took her hands in his own, smearing them with his blood. For a moment the Heartwood recoiled, its tendrils clinging desperately to the Shield's trembling arms, and then it was gone, slipping into the Man's bleeding flesh like water into parched earth.

Shakar stepped away, shaken and sick, and her gaze moved beyond Vald to the valley below, where cannons and musket blazed into the screaming Folk. Confusion clouded her eyes.

<<What are they doing?>> she said, her words slow, uncertain. <<They're killing—you must stop this, you must . . .>> She shook her head, as if to clear it of a nightmare grown too real in waking. Her eyes moved from the carnage below to the great iron scaffolding, following the copper wires to the chained and battered Wielder who lay gasping softly at its base.

<<Betrayed,>> she whispered evenly, as much to herself as to the Dreydmaster. <<This was never what I wanted.>> She began to tremble. <<Oh, Moon-Maiden, please—anything but this.>>

Vald ignored her. He stood staring at his hands. Suddenly his body stiffened and his head dropped back, his eyes wide and staring. He swayed slightly, balling his hands into fists and breathing heavily, his mouth working as if repeating words no one else could hear.

Unnerved at his master's uncharacteristic behavior, Vorgha reached out and touched the Dreydmaster's arm. <<Authority?>> he whispered. <<Are you—?>>

Vald's head spun around, and his mouth opened wide. Green fire burned from his eyes and mouth. <<Mortal filth, you dare touch the Dreyd? You are unworthy! *You are unclean!*>> A pale, clawed hand shot out and smashed through the servant's chest, spraying gore in a scarlet fountain across the dusty rocks.

Vorgha's body collapsed, and Vald dropped the Man's still-beating heart atop it with disdain. The Reaver's own form was growing, changing, becoming monstrous, magnificent. He roared in proud exultation as power rose up within his frail Human flesh, making it greater than even his most fevered dreams could have imagined.

His ascension was at hand.

He turned to the Shield who stood at the edge of the cliff, her lowered gaze still locked on the massacre in the valley. His bubbling voice dripped with malice. <<Now, Shakar, we finish the ceremony. This is the end.>>

The Shield turned, her violet eyes bright, her lips in a thin, taut line. <<That, at least, is true,>> she hissed, and her thoughts drove like a blazing spear into the Dreydmaster still-Human mind. He clawed at his head and fell back with a bubbling howl, even as the transformation continued unabated. <<But I am Shakar no longer. My name is Neranda.>>

One small band of Binders gathered on the ridge, unobserved by the fire-spouting Dragons and their armed crews above. Vald hadn't expected an airship armada, but he was sensible enough to keep some of the Dreydcaste hidden in case of unexpected problems. These Men and Women could feel the Dreydmaster begin his transformation. The new Melding was imminent, and their faithful souls might still be spared if they died in his service.

As one, they gathered in a circle with arms extended. Calling out an obscure Crafting invocation, trying to keep their voices strong in spite of the acrid smoke that filled the air and choked their words, each reached into the snaring-tome of his neighbor, chanting louder as they felt their own spirits unravel and join the tortured entities within. Their bodies sagged, dripping into the ground like sun-warmed wax, and with a final, screaming burst, their embodied forms changed, shifting from flesh to flame, great spinning rings of yellow fire that shot into the sky to consume a great Dragon galleon in its path. The airship exploded instantly, and burning debris fell to earth like white-hot rain.

Merrimyn rushed to the railing, Quill beside him, and watched helplessly as two of the smaller ships, their gas-bladders shredded by shrapnel, crashed with a roar into the swamp. Like all Binders, he could feel every Crafting in the area, and the power of this conjuration burned in his senses. The Binders who destroyed the first galleon were dead, but their success emboldened others, and another group moved into a circle to repeat the catastrophic Crafting of their fellows. And the Dragon they focused on was his own.

Before he knew what he was doing, Merrimyn opened his snaring-tome and held it wide. But rather than simply call upon the powers within its leathery pages, he sent his soul in search of the spirits of the Folk that flew on silent white wings through the fading light, calling them to his aid. He didn't seek to snare them or force them to his will. He had neither the desire nor the power to control them. He was neither a Wielder nor a Reaver—neither *wyr*-touched nor a Dreydlord—but his need was great, and he sent it spinning into the twilight.

Nothing happened. The air around the Dragon grew heavy, pensive, as though the great airship knew its fate and was powerless to stop it. And still the young Binder held his book aloft, tears of fear and frustration streaking his face, his soft voice muttering his plea to the anxious air.

And then the floodgates opened, and a wave of glowing white mist washed over him from behind, sweeping down across the deck of the airship to push the young Man hard against the railing, his open snaring-tome pointed at the circle of Binders below. Quill fell back with a shriek as innumerable spirits danced across Merrimyn's body, through his bones and muscles, their sightless eyes finding vision through his own as they became a river of half-formed phantoms, his willing flesh the channel for their ageless vengeance. The snaring-tome shot forward through the air, held back only by the taut chain still shackled to Merrimyn's bleeding wrist, and the spirit wave burst down upon the chanting Binders, a screaming, howling torrent, tearing at the Humans with their curses, cutting soul as easily as flesh. The Binders vanished under the flood, and their destructive Crafting dissolved, its lingering thread vanishing with the last despairing cry.

Quill crept forward to Merrimyn, who lay limply against the ship's railing, his right arm hanging over the side. His skin was cold and damp to the touch, but his eyes fluttered open when the Dolltender grew near, and his beaming smile lit the night.

"Free," he whispered, and slid unconscious to the deck. Quill stared at his arm. The snaring-tome was gone, as was his hand, the stump healed, skin smooth and clean as a new dawn.

"There!" Jitani nodded to the flurry of activity atop the small butte in the center of the swamp. They couldn't tell exactly what was happening, but a battle was taking place between a small figure in blue and a pale, Man-shaped creature that seemed to be growing larger and more terrible as they watched. She looked down. "Tarsa's got to be there somewhere. Maybe she's the one battling that . . . thing."

Tobhi shook his head. "That en't her. No, that's someone else." He squinted and frowned, his sharp eyes following the wires that stretched across the valley to the iron monolith. "She's there!" he shouted, pointing to the tower's base.

Daladir turned to the Ubbetuk captain. "Get us as close as possible!" The Goldcap nodded, and the airship roared downward, but it lurched abruptly as a sharp blast shook the hull. The mercenaries on the ledge below the tower raised their cannons again, and the ship shuddered again as some of the artillery found its mark, some narrowly missing the great wheezing gas-bladders that kept the ships aloft.

Daladir slid Dibadjiibé into the back of his belt and threw the ladder over the edge of the ship. "We're too close to Tarsa to use the Dragon-fire, so we'll have to do this ourselves before the ship is destroyed." His face darkened. "We can't all go after Tarsa. Some of us will have to stop those cannons, or they'll kill her even if we can find a way to get her free."

A flash of pain crossed Jitani's face, slowly giving way to firm resolve. "My sword is ready." She turned to Tobhi. "We'll keep them away from you both as long as we can. It might not be for very long."

Tobhi nodded. "I won't fail ye," he whispered in a quavering voice. "I promise."

Daladir laid a hand on the Tetawa's shoulder and smiled gently. "I know you won't, my friend. *Tsodoka*."

His stomach twisted in a knot of grief, Tobhi embraced them both and moved toward the ladder. Daladir motioned to the captain. The airship swept dangerously low, its upper wing nearly touching the tower. Taking a deep breath, the little Leafspeaker threw himself off the deck, followed closely by Jitani and Daladir. Muskets and cannons exploded from below, and the Dragon limped away, one of its gas-bags pierced and leaking.

Thunder boomed over the valley. A web of lightning streaked through the sky. A swirling hole of shadow split the twilight clouds, opening into a roaring pit of darkness and chaos that grew slowly wider.

For the first time in a thousand years, the Veil Between Worlds began to open.

45

Remembrance

BETRAYAL.

She had surrendered her position, her reputation, honor, and home, even her family, some of whom now faced the horrors of death below. For years she'd believed the assurances of truth and benevolence, accepted what seemed to be inevitability. The Humans she had known so often truly seemed to care about the Folk; why else would they have worked so hard, so tirelessly, if not for a sincere desire to bring the Folk out of the darkness of savagery? She'd watched the Kyn fall back before the onslaught of Humanity, and she'd embraced the ways of Men as the only reasonable alternative to the obliteration she foresaw—change was preferable to extinction. Her mind and body had been trained in the arcane ways of the Shields until it was a keen weapon, but she rarely used its greatest power, for she wanted her victory to rest on reason, not on coercion. Her path was clear, and righteous; it required nothing more. If the future belonged to Humanity, it was as Humans that they must live.

And in all those years, after all the pain and suffering, she'd never once doubted that the Kyn would endure, even if they were transformed beyond recognition. Life mattered more than pride. Men said that the vanishing of the Folk was destiny, inevitability, but there was nothing inevitable about the massacre in the valley. It was

the long-planned, deliberate decision of a mortal Man and his minions. They chose each step willingly.

As did she. And now, she made a different choice.

All these things passed from her mind into the thing that was
once Lojar Vald, and he roared with pain as her consciousness seared
through his own. Grief now fueled her white-hot rage. She paid no
attention to his ever more massive bulk, which now seemed more a
bloated, tentacled fungus than a Man, nor did she regard the Dragons
above raining fire on the Dreydmaster's troops, the militia's deadly
cannon shot in response. Her full attention was focused on Vald, to
his torment.

The Dreyd-creature crashed against the tower, and the great
copper cables snapped and spun back down into the valley. Neranda's
mind was honed to its deadliest now, and she wouldn't surrender. She
would break him without quarter or mercy. Vald would not make a
liar of her, not again.

She reached deeply into his seething center and sought the
Heartwood.

Tobhi held a shaking hand to the back of his head. Blood, but
not much. His hat was gone again, lost among the ruins. He'd
reached the tower just as that huge *thing* smashed into it, sending
debris down on him as he scrambled out of the way to avoid all the
big chunks but not quickly enough to avoid the smaller ones. He
breathed heavily, thankful that he still wore the iron-ward from the
airship. If not for that, the nearness of all this cold iron might have
killed him.

Keeping a close eye on the battle between the monstrosity and
the now-recognizable Shakar, Tobhi crept over to the pile of chains
to find Tarsa crumpled within. Panic seized him. He reached out and
pulled on one of the chains. Nothing. Moving closer, he tugged hard
on the chained shackle around Tarsa's throat. The Wielder's eyes shot
open in wild fear, and she struggled for breath.

Tobhi reached around to the back of the band. It had a rusty latch
that he unhooked with only a little effort. The shackle sprang open,
and Tarsa fell forward, coughing and choking.

Repeating the movement on the rest of the bindings, Tobhi quickly freed the she-Kyn, and she leaned heavily into his arms in exhausted relief. He tried to pull her away from the tower, but they were both weak and wounded, and it was all she could do to crawl away from the pile of chains.

A battle raged here on the hilltop, but screams and musket shots just beyond their view indicated another fierce fight, one with dear friends against dozens of well-armed adversaries. Tobhi tried to push the thought from his mind. He was here to get Tarsa to safety, and their chances for escape weren't much better here than they'd be in the valley.

He looked into the sky and gawked at the sight of the sundering Veil. Light seemed to die as it reached the great fissure, and a bone-cold wind flooded from the roaring darkness. The sky seemed to shift, as though the firmament itself was cracking under the strain of the ever-widening wound.

Tarsa lifted her head. She was alive. It was much more than she expected after her struggle with Shakar. But the true struggle was far from over.

"Help . . . me . . . stand," she whispered to Tobhi, each word catching painfully in her scream-shredded throat. She pushed with the little remaining strength in her legs as the Tetawa struggled upward. They breathed heavily from the strain. She tried to pull away from him, but he shook his head. "You can't stay here, Tobhi. It's going to be too dangerous."

He chuckled, wincing from the sudden pain in his wounded head. "Ye think so? Don't seem all that bad to me." He sobered. "I'll be by yer side through the rest of this journey, Tarsa. We started out together, and that's how we'll finish it, however it ends."

She smiled. "Then that's as it should be." Together they stumbled forward, Tarsa leaning on the exhausted Tetawa, as the mutating abomination thrashed around on the ground, its fleshy appendages whipping the stony ground with frenzied fury.

<<NO!>> Vald roared in a frothing voice that barely resembled Human speech. <<YOU CANNOT HAVE IT! IT IS MINE!>>

The Shield moved forward in torn and ravaged blue robes, her hands on her temples, sweat and blood streaming down her face, sensory stalks flailing wildly from the unyielding extension of her strength. The air crackled. She pushed on, heedless of her swiftly weakening state and her injuries, unaware of anything but her hated enemy. Vald had finally collapsed under her relentless attack. She staggered a bit, then stood straight as she brought her hands together with a swift cutting motion.

A crack of thunder shook the mountainside, and the Shield stood tall, a glowing orb of pulsing green resting lightly in her trembling hands.

Tarsa stumbled forward and faced the Shield. Neranda lowered her arms and gently cradled the Heartwood, no longer resisting its cleansing touch.

"I was honest with the world and never once surrendered to temptation," Neranda said, her voice weak. "None could have ever made the claim that I broke my word, or gave myself to any cause I believed to be less than worthy of honor. And in spite of it all, I have failed." Her lips tightened. "No one will remember me with anything but hatred and contempt. I am 'Shakar' now, to everyone. But I am no traitor. I . . . I never meant to be."

Tarsa was silent for long moments, her turquoise gaze unyielding. Finally, her face softened, and she nodded. Their war was over.

Neranda took a deep, shuddering breath of resignation. The power that had strengthened her against Vald's Dreydcraft had finally faded away. All that remained was heartsick desolation, and a weakness that went beyond physical exhaustion. She knew that she would not be returning from this terrible place.

"I do not ask you for forgiveness, Wielder. All I ask is that you remember me as I was—as I am, at this moment—even if no one else will do so." Her voice grew thick with emotion. "I do not want to be forgotten."

The Shield held the Heartwood out to the Wielder, but as Tarsa reached to accept it, a chalky grey tentacle wrapped around Neranda's waist, jerking her backward, the Heartwood still clinging to her hands. Vald's great writhing bulk rose high above her, his pallid, vaguely Man-shaped visage twisted in madness. His wide maw opened wide, putrid slime dripping from thousands of spear-like teeth.

<<*I hunger, little pain-giver. You will be the first!*>> Vald fell upon the Shield and the shining Heartwood, swallowing both in a single

swift movement, leaving behind only a burning pool of black ooze on the rocks. Neranda's cry of despair lingered in the air.

<<*You are next, witch!*>> His voice was the wet hiss of a thousand snakes, his form the contorted mass of a thousand nightmares given ravenous shape. His head slid upward, and a hideous grin crossed his lengthening face as steaming liquid dribbled down his chin. <<*And with you comes the end of an error left too long uncorrected. At long last, this world will be free of your kind. Men will rule supreme, and the Unhumans will be driven from the memory of a world that should never have been yours.*>>

The Veil Between Worlds gaped wider. Arching bursts of gold-green lightning radiated through the sky to smash into a few airships, hurling them to the earth.

Tarsa stood motionless and watched Vald roll toward her. The abomination's great body lurched forward on a wave of slime-coated tendrils that had once been legs. There was a strange, distant expression on her face. She could feel Tobhi tugging at her arm, but she ignored him.

She finally understood.

The *wyr*-formed voices had whispered to her for months, their language always just beyond her reach or understanding. From the earliest moments of her Awakening on that night in Red Cedar Town, when she'd watched the Stoneskin's body burn to ash and felt a new world of power and frightening possibility open up within her, the voices and their haunting songs had remained a maddening mystery, ever present but just beyond comprehension.

Yet now, at last, in Vald's triumphant words she'd found the answer.

The dream of my mother, Unahi, and the others, around the blazing fire in that icy, snow-blasted wyrwood grove. The last she-Kyn, the one with the blue-and-white mask of mourning. It's Neranda. And it's me. We're part of this world. This world is us.

Ours are the voices I've been waiting for.

"It was a memory song," she whispered to herself as the monstrous once-Man loomed above her, blue-black ichor falling in sizzling pools around her feet. "This is no Melded world. It has always been our own. *This* is the Eld Green, all of it. They wanted us to forget, to believe that we didn't belong here."

She looked up. "But I remember now. We will *all* remember." She raised her hands toward the sky, and the mountain shuddered, knocking Tobhi to the ground and sending Vald skittering backward. Bright-eyed eagles with burning plumage the color of rainbow fire swept out of the darkness above and fell upon the monstrous Dreyd-creature, their talons tearing into his still-mortal flesh, and the Redthorn Wielder began to sing in a language strange but beautiful, her voice growing stronger and more forceful.

She sang, and the world responded.

For the first time since the fall of Sheynadwiin and the start of the Darkening Road, Tobhi felt no fear. He heard the song in his blood, felt the rhythm flow through him like the very beat of his heart. It spoke to him in the voice of his ancestors, of the great Clan-Beasts and their proud legacy. He heard the voice of Buborru the Badger, knowledge-keeper of the Burrows family, and all the guardians of the Spirit World who had watched over their Tetawi kindred since time immemorial. The song drew Tobhi closer to them all and opened a world of understanding that the lore-leaves had only ever hinted at.

Lore-leaves. He'd almost forgotten them. It had been so long since he'd turned to the leaves for comfort or guidance. But he was a Leafspeaker, and he remembered his duty. The badger-snouted pouch trembled at his side, and he pulled open the clasp. As his own voice joined Tarsa's and the song grew in strength, the leaves came swirling out of the satchel, all aglow with a bright inner fire, dancing joyfully around him like playful dragonflies newly awakened to a lush green world. They wove a new story for the Leafspeaker, one that he'd never before read in their varied and shifting movements. And as the lore-leaves shared this great storyweaving, their ancient symbols burned cool blue on Tobhi's body, seventy-seven bold and painless honor markings that would hold the story in his flesh for the rest of his days. It was a story that renewed the world and realigned the cosmos.

Now he understood what Tarsa meant. The Thresholds had always seemed to be the last remnants of their lost world, but in truth the Folk had never left the Eld Green. The whole of this world—all the Reach and other lands claimed by Men—were the homelands of the Folk. Kaantor's ancient betrayal hadn't brought the world of the Folk into the world of Men. It had simply brought Men into the Eld Green, and they'd laid claim to it. And over the years, as the Folk fell to the tyranny of Men and the lands beyond their Thresholds grew harsh and hostile, many forgot the truth and came to believe the lies Men told to assure themselves of the right of conquest.

But the spirits remembered.

Averyn looked up, blood streaming into hir eyes, as the song reached them. Garyn lay motionless in hir arms, bleeding heavily from a dozen different wounds. One of Averyn's stalks had been torn open in the last barrage, and zhe could barely contain all the agony as zhe tried desperately to hold the Governor out of the filthy water and maintain some hold on hir own sanity. Others were screaming all around them. It was pure, unrelenting madness.

And then came the song. Zhe gasped as the words wove into hir deepest being. The screams faded, and all zhe heard was the slow, steady throb of hir heartbeat, or of a drum pounding its primal rhythm in the center of the earth. The zhe-Kyn, like all the zhe-Folk, was a between-worlder, neither male nor female, something other than both. The healer inhabited a space between and among the others, and such a position brought with it knowledge and a responsibility distinct to the zhe. Of all worlds and none.

It was what zhe was meant to bring to this moment.

As the song opened hir spirit and zhe began to understand what had so long been forgotten, Averyn added hir own voice to the chorus. Zhe didn't know what zhe was singing, but zhe knew that the words were right. And as zhe sang, the world changed.

Garyn shuddered and opened his eyes, the song already on his lips as he returned to consciousness. The screaming stopped, and others took up the chant, growing stronger with the words. Musket shot fell harmlessly into the mud. The cannons were stilled, and Men ran screaming as a figure emerged from the darkness and took shape from the zhe-Kyn's song, finding form and strength as others took up the rhythm. It grew larger as Averyn's voice grew more certain, its great rainbow wings stretching across the valley, lightning dancing across its antlers and moon-curved claws, its serpentine body blazing upward like a comet, triumph and fury bright in its dark ursine eyes. The strange shape of a winged and antlered rabbit flew fiercely at his side.

Guraadja roared in fury, a crackling thunderstorm boiling through the sky in his wake. Finally free from his ages-long prison, he and the other Anomalous rose up in the renewed world to strike at the enemies of the Folk.

Great cracks opened up in the earth. The demon Vald laughed, and slime sprayed outward. <<*Little green fool, is that all you can do? Sing on, sing on—it will do you little good. I can sing, too!*>> He lifted his head and bellowed, and from the torn Veil flapped a horde of chittering Not-Ravens. The firebirds joined Saazja and great Guraadja as they rushed to meet the foul creatures, and the air was soon filled with skyfire, feathers, and blood.

Vald lumbered forward, his glistening, hairless bulk shining in the light of the Dragon-fire that still burned around the rim of the valley. <<*Enough of this foolishness. I hunger still. Now, witch, you are mine!*>> He rolled toward her but stopped with an ear-piercing shriek as a wyrwood blade and the jagged end of a wyrwood staff plunged deeply into his flesh. Tarsa's heart soared as Jitani and Daladir pulled the weapons free of Vald's quivering bulk, Dibadjiibé's amber tip glowing fiercely, but before the monstrous creature could crush the Kyn warriors for their impertinence, the ground shifted beneath his weight, forcing him to once again face the Wielder.

He spun back to see Tarsa standing calmly beside the remnants of the iron tower, her voice and arms lifted high in remembrance and certainty.

Those she loved most were with her now. Tobhi, Jitani, Daladir. Unahi, Geth, Lan'delar. Living and spirit, they all strengthened her. The *wyr* flowed through the world again, other voices answered the call, and the Folk were renewed.

Hunger gnawed at Vald's belly. Neranda wasn't dead, not yet. She would be gone, and with her, the miserable Wielder who had caused him so much trouble. He needed only a little more strength to rise up and pass through the Veil. With a howl of triumph, he surged forward, a seething, flowing mass of slavering menace.

But the hunger inside him suddenly changed. It became something else, moving from an aching emptiness to a sharp, piercing pain that spread out, growing larger and more insistent.

Vald slid to a halt. He felt Neranda's flickering life-spark take up the green witch's song in the brief flash before it was extinguished. Now the words were everywhere: in his head, in his bones, in his quivering flesh. They seared him with an unimaginable pain, as though his very organs were aflame.

The torment inside moved up, then down, everywhere, and the Dreydlord felt something *move* deep inside.

His Dreyd-touched senses knew what was happening. And he knew that he'd failed.

There would be no ascension, not now, not ever.

So close to victory. So very close.

Green fire tore upward through his skin, shredding muscle and blood, twisting outward through pierced and broken bowels and the crackling shards of his smoking bones. He opened his gibbering maw wide to spew his bitter hate and fury on the Melded world, a poison to corrupt everything it touched, but his lungs vanished beneath the upward rush, and even the gurgle of blood gave way to blue-green radiance and the silvered rustling of leaves as the first branch shot from Vald's mouth into the open sky. More branches burst through his pulpy flesh, sending bile shooting in upward sprays until, as the massive creature convulsed from the pressure of the flowering Heartwood, Lojar Vald split apart, and the Eternity Tree emerged reborn from the shattered remains of the former Dreydmaster.

A high-pitched wail filled the night as the surviving Not-Ravens fled back through the Veil. The great rift between the worlds slowly faded, and another shape filled the heavens, a vision that none of the survivors below ever expected or even dared hope to see again.

The air was filled with the smell of fertile earth and wyrwood leaves, the primal flush of life incarnate. The firebirds wheeled in celebration, and Guraadja roared triumphantly in the sky above as the Greatmoon, Pearl-in-Darkness, watched over the Folk once more, his cool light shining down upon the remembered world.

46

Gathering Grounds

THE PROPER NAME OF THE NEW HOMELAND was Shemshéha—"The Place of the Good Red Earth" in the Tetawi tongue—but most of the survivors simply called it Folkhome. The naming was the first of many steps in the long, difficult task of healing both themselves and their wounded new homeland, which still bore the scars of a thousand years of devastation. They went slowly about the task of rebuilding their lives, making homes, towns, and settlements, discovering ways of understanding the spirits of new animals and plants and introducing the many remembered Beast and plant people who had traveled with the Folk on the Darkening Road, familiarizing themselves with the weather patterns and the flow of waters, connecting with the ghosts who still inhabited the wilder places of this new Everland. Although the reborn Eternity Tree—now known as the Forevergreen Tree— gave them strength, there was still deep grief, for there were none who hadn't lost at least one beloved friend or family member.

Some had lost far more. Nearly half the Folk of the Old Everland had died or disappeared on the Darkening Road. Families were shattered, many broken to the core. Some of the Seven Sister nations had suffered more than others: the Wyrnach were no more, and most of the he-Gvaergs had been murdered, impaled and turned to stone on the sun-bleached slopes of their old mountain-holds. But most

Branches, Clans, and even some of the Gvaerg Houses survived and opened themselves to new kith, and love expanded to embrace those left alone by the devastation.

Tobhi and Quill married quickly and opened their moundhouse to a trio of Road-made orphans, two Tetawi—Benji, the cub who'd stolen Tobhi's boots one awful morning on the Road, and Anja, who'd watched her mema and siblings vanish into surging waters on the sunken barge at Shard Ford—and a she-Gvaerg youngling named Brigga. Their adoption of the orphans into Quill's Spider Clan was a ceremony of great joy among the Tetawi. Life had changed them, but the Folk continued.

They struggled to build a homeland that would endure, but bitter divisions exploded into bloody feuds between rival groups. The Kyn Shields, although diminished, continued to exercise their influence, although now with more humility under the wise guidance of old Braachan, Tobhi's he-Kyn companion on much of the terrible journey, who had come to prominence in Neranda's disgrace. Rather than view the Celestial Path as the enemy of the Deep Green, Braachan taught that the two ways could coexist, each giving strength to the People, both dedicated to the growth and survival of all.

Yet many of the Greenwalking Folk still held the Shields accountable for their troubles, and a number of the latter died in midnight executions, with reprisal attacks following from some of the more intransigent Celestials of the old order. A few of the allied Humans who walked the Road were targets for violence as well—especially the Proselytors who believed that the Dreyd had put the Folk through this terrible trial for their own good—but as most Men and Women were adopted into Folk families and protected by their kinship connections, their lives were spared. Eladrys had been adopted into Willow Branch before the Expulsion, and she maintained her ties with her Kyn family, so she was protected by that relationship. Those who'd traveled with Tarsa and Quill—Merrimyn, Qualla'am Kaer, Oryn, and the rest—became part of either Cedar Branch among the Kyn or Spider Clan among the Tetawi in honor of their efforts.

But it was still a cruel, bloody time when the Folk turned on one another in their grief and pain. There were conflicts with some of the Jaaga, who were growing increasingly and fairly resentful of the Folk's intrusions into their hunting grounds. The brutal winter that followed Vald's destruction added to the tensions, and in its first few months Folkhome risked falling into chaos.

Yet calmer minds and more forgiving hearts prevailed. Now honored as the Keeper of the Forevergreen Tree, Tarsa said very little in the debates, but when she did speak, draped regally in her restored leaf and feather cloak of office and bearing Dibadjiibé, the worn wyrwood staff of her martyred aunt, her voice carried a weight far beyond her years. Garyn and Averyn joined Daladir, Molli Rose, and at least forty representatives from all groups of the Folk to begin the creation of the much-discussed confederation that would honor their individual traditions and yet give structure and security to the Sevenfold Nation. Garyn, though blinded by his injuries in the final conflict, was filled with a fiery energy that inspired others with its strength and continuing wisdom.

Through the long, cold winter, the assembly discussed, cajoled, argued, fought, and pleaded, from dawn until long after sunset every day, and by the first flowering of the new spring had given structure to the Free Folk Alliance of Shemshéha. The first Speaker of the new Alliance, elected unanimously by the council and affirmed by the population at large, was Molli Rose, the Tetawa matron who'd spoken so eloquently for the strength of the Folk at the old Sevenfold Council.

After much discussion, those Kyn who had walked the Darkening Road now called themselves the Free Kyn Nation of Folkhome, to distinguish their government from that of the remnant under Sinovian's leadership in the Old Everland. Their new capital was built close to the Tree in the valley, and they named it Dweshamaagamig, "the Place of the Flowering Tree," a peace-city and neutral ground, all the more blessed because it had been born from so much blood and violence.

Garyn continued his work as Governor of the Free Kyn with the blessing of all seven Branches. Many of the artifacts and ritual items he'd had hidden from the first wave of invasion in the Old Everland had been lost, but others gradually found their way to the new homeland, where they were quickly returned to their work of rooting the People in land and memory. Garyn's work ended in late winter, when he took ill after a sudden fall, and he died peacefully with his beloved Averyn at his side and many friends nearby.

The debate over Garyn's successor was a surprisingly contentious one, but Tarsa's nominee was the one who finally received the Branch-matrons' assent, and the reconstituted Kyn Assembly of Law had little choice but to support it: Averyn, the healer and longtime consort to Garyn, became Governor, and in so doing became the most politically prominent zhe-Kyn in living memory. Some of the Celestial Kyn argued against a zhe-Kyn as leader, fearing that the Human disdain for between-worlders would bleed into Folkhome's fragile political recognition and some of the negotiations with Chalimor over their independence from the Everland Kyn. But Averyn proved hirself a skillful leader and formidable opponent to those who would challenge Kyn sovereignty. Many underestimated hir strength, and those who'd once doubted hir ability gradually became some of hir staunchest defenders.

Garyn's peacemaking legacy lived on.

The surviving Wielders and their *wyr*-touched kindred gave guidance to the grieving and provided words of comfort for the dead as their kith struggled to recover from the nightmares of the past and present throughout those dark months. Though wounded and still frail, old Biggiabba's sharp mind had returned, and she gave much of her remaining strength to this healing work. And although the whispering boughs of the Forevergreen Tree were now empty of dark-eyed owls, the spirits of the lost were remembered that spring in the strange, small flowers that sprouted up around the new Tree and throughout Shemshéha. Seven pale white leaves radiated from the scarlet center of every blossom, each leaf tipped with a soft streak of gold. They grew alone or in thin clusters in shadowed undergrowth.

The sevenfold rose came to symbolize the new life of the Folk.

Spring in Folkhome was far different from the same season around Spindletop. In her old home ground, Quill could plant her garden just after the snows disappeared, but here, even with the snow long gone, the soil remained hard and frozen for weeks longer. The growing season would likely be shorter, the plants somewhat peculiar in comparison to those she was most familiar with. She didn't worry much about the quality of food, however, as the *wyr* that flowed from the Forevergreen Tree would ensure a bountiful harvest. It would just take some time to get used to the changes.

She was glad to finally be able to start her garden now. The reborn Tree was strong, but it couldn't make food out of nothing. If not for the Ubbetuk airships and the supplies they brought each week, the Folk might well have starved to death or fallen to illness or the bitter cold that rushed down from the frozen northlands known as the Lawless. Although she appreciated the Swarm's help, she couldn't help but be nervous about the Chancellor's intentions. The look on his face as he ripped information from the Not-Raven in Denarra's house chilled her even now, and she still had nightmares about the fire raining down from the Dragons. As they'd learned to their painful regret in the past year, there were few free gifts in this life. She wondered what the price would be for the Chancellor's generosity.

She shook the shadows from her thoughts and turned back to the task at hand. The garden wouldn't plant itself. For a moment Quill considered bringing one of the apple dolls outside for some advice, but she quickly reconsidered, as the dolls now generally spent their days in pleasant drowsiness, uninterested in mundane domestic tasks like these, unless they involved the new orchard that Tobhi was planting down in the valley as a wedding gift to his new bride. At night, though, the dolls often told stories to the cubs, with Green Kishka taking the lead on sharing the teachings of old. The dolls were far from young anymore—indeed, they'd all been given to Quill by her own mema, passed down from her granny—and their adventure and the loss of so many of their fellows had aged them a bit, but they had a new vitality now, especially now that there was a rapt, wide-eyed audience to listen. Young Benji, the oldest of their new cubs, vowed to be the first *fahr* Dolltender, and Quill thought he just might be right, particularly as Anja and Brigga seemed more inclined toward Tobhi's Leafspeaking. Continuity through change, transformation through tenacity. It was the guiding principle of their new life. Not everything had to remain the same to endure.

But it would be a while before she taught Benji to make the dolls. She hadn't had much time or, more honestly, much heart to begin again. It wasn't that she was unhappy, because she had a loving husband and children who filled her life with more joy than she'd ever known, no matter that they weren't born of her flesh. Tobhi was her spirit-mate, and theirs was a healing love. Yet she was different now. She'd seen more of life than she'd ever expected, and much of it was unimaginably cruel. Even now she woke sometimes with the eyes of the dead haunting her dreams.

Fortunately, however, there were other, kinder memories to think on, and friendly faces to welcome into her life and thoughts. Merrimyn lived nearby, sharing a house with dark, lovely Eladrys, who enjoyed teaching the onetime Binder the many joys he'd missed in the forced celibacy of his former life. Quill came to adore Tarsa and her fiery consort Jitani. And she could understand why Tobhi had such admiration for Daladir's quiet strength. The he-Kyn was rarely present, as he spent most of his time renewing diplomatic ties to the Reach in Chalimor. Qualla'am Kaer had been impeached and was largely disgraced in Chalimor, though he was now a hero to many Folk-allied Humans through the Reach for his brave defiance of the self-serving bigotry of Reach politicians. He had a home in Shemshéha, not far from their own new settlement of Turtletown. He couldn't return to Chalimor without risk of arrest, but he gave able guidance to Daladir and the other Alliance treaty and trade negotiators from afar. To all reports, they seemed to be making progress, though it was maddeningly slow going.

She'd long missed her vanished cousins Gishki and Medalla, but recent news gave hope that they might be part of another Tetawi town founded to the south of Shemshéha, where Men and Folk currently lived together in peace and for mutual benefit. But while she missed these friends, she mourned most for one whose tinkling laugh and emerald eyes left her world infinitely sadder for their absence.

She'd hoped for news from Chalimor, that maybe Padwacket or Meggie Mar would have heard something, but when Daladir went to the little brick and stucco house on one of his trips to the city, he found it abandoned, the garden overgrown, Denarra's prized peacocks gone. Only some of the furniture remained, hurriedly and only partially draped with dusty sheets. No one knew when the other inhabitants had vanished, but they hadn't been seen since the day of the Strangeling's long fall.

Quill wiped her eyes, leaving smudges of garden dirt on her face, then cleared her throat and looked up. Where were the she-cubs? They'd been clamoring to help all morning; now that she could actually use their assistance, they were nowhere to be seen. They'd likely be exploring with some of the other Turtletown cubs, while their quiet older brother spent his day helping Merrimyn and some of the *fahr* build a moundhouse for a newly arrived family. The settlement was small, named for the town of the same name in the Old Everland, with no more than forty families right now, built into a sheltered hollow at the eastern edge of the Valley of the Tree. They'd even started building up their own ceremonial mound; not too impressive thus far, but a worthy beginning. It was a leisurely walk from both the mound and her home to the Brown Lodge, the large, timbered gathering hall of the Tetawi Clans, where Tobhi served as official chronicler of Shemshéha and one of Molli Rose's most trusted advisors. The Dolltender had been offered a post in the Speaker's circle, but she much preferred to stay at home and give help to those who stopped by, as in the old days. For her, the hearth was the best place to change the world.

The scuffling of boots on dirt caught her attention, and Quill looked up to see her daughters, dainty Anja and massive, broad-shouldered Brigga, rush up the hill with eager grins on their faces. Skidding to a stop just before the freshly turned garden, the cubs nearly fell over one another in excitement.

"Mema, see what we found!" Anja said in a breathless rush. "Isn't it pretty?" She held up a long, slightly crumpled shape, waving it back and forth so wildly that Quill couldn't quite make out what it was. Brigga held one, too, but she handled hers with tender care, as if afraid that it would fly off into the air if she didn't treat it gently. She was younger than Anja but stood nearly three times the little *firra*'s height.

A flash of bright color caught Quill's eye, and she walked over to Brigga, who smiled and opened her arms to show her new discovery. The Dolltender swallowed a gasp, and tears sprang to her eyes as she took it in her trembling fingers. "Where did you find these, sweet cubs?"

"By river," Brigga giggled. "Come see!" They ran down the hillside with Quill on their heels. It was a short, well-worn path to the water's edge, and there Quill stood weeping silently among the cattails and reeds. She wasn't sure if it was tears of grief or joy that streaked down her cheeks.

Floating leisurely in the sluggish river, playfully iridescent in the light of the bright spring sun, were thousands of blue-green peacock feathers.

Cycle Seven
Forevergreen

Tobhi lifts the last leaf into place and steps away to watch the pattern develop. The symbols on his exposed flesh shine in bright blue response to the gold fire of the swirling shapes. The leaves weave together slowly, carefully, as though momentarily uncertain of the answer to his questions, but they finally quicken their movement to create a clear picture. His eyes glaze over, and he whispers quietly to himself until he understands what has been revealed, and then he places his hands against the blurring leaves until they slow down enough to be returned to their red cloth and the small leather satchel at his side. The images on his skin go dark, looking once again like the honor marks of old.

As many times as I've seen this, it's always an amazing sight. Who would imagine that there would be so much wisdom in these light, fluttering things? Who would believe that within each is the life-giving force of the world?

I'm sitting on a rock, not far away from Tobhi. Although I've tried to be quiet to avoid disturbing him, my swollen belly is making such sitting rather uncomfortable, and I'm relieved to finally be able to shift into a new position as the Leafspeaking finishes. "Well?" I ask, slowly massaging my sides.

Rubbing the blurriness from his eyes, Tobhi smiles. "She'll be a strong daughter, Tarsa—strong and healthy, just like her memas."

I let out a deep sigh and try to stand up, placing one hand against my lower back for support, pulling myself forward on Dibadjiibé with the other. The old staff continues to serve me with the same dependability it served Unahi, and I am grateful, but even with the assistance I'm still too unwieldy *to stand. "I had the same feeling, but I wanted to hear it from someone else. It's going to be another hard year ahead. And a lonely one."*

Tobhi takes my extended hand and leans back, pulling me to my feet. "Ye know ye're always welcome to stay with us. There's plenty of room. Merrimyn's got a place of his own now."

"I know," I say, walking slowly toward the rough path that leads to the top of the narrow peak. "But Jitani will be back soon from her visit with Sinovian in the Old Everland. She's hoping to make it home before the birth, and we'll need that time alone together. She's as nervous about being a mother as I am! We'll send for Quill and Biggiabba when it starts, and when four nights have passed you can come by to visit. Until then, it's just the mothers and aunties."

He nods and follows me up the thin trail, watching for any loose rocks that might cause us to tumble. I don't tell him that it's still sometimes hard for me to find comfort among others. A bit more solitude might help me make sense of all the ways I've changed. The Heartwood brought me closer to the wyr, *but it pulled me away from those around me, and it's been a longer journey of returning than I'd expected. I'm distant in ways that I still don't understand. But those who love me the most are patient, and that's reason enough to find my way back to them.*

We've been hiking since the day before, seeking the highest point in the area around the Valley of the Tree, and are finally approaching the summit of a red sandstone spur. We'll watch the sunrise and begin the ceremony today. Everyone thinks I should have waited until after the little seedling is born, but this is the right time to do it, and they don't fight, even if they do worry. Tobhi's is the only company I want, for both the Leafspeaking and his calming presence.

We don't see each other much these days, as the duties of our new life in Folkhome calls us to different tasks. I'm the guardian of the Tree and keeper of its teachings, and he's the lore-keeper of the new Council, almost giddy in love with sweet Quill and their new cubs. This is one opportunity to bring us closer together again. The last time we spent much time with each other was when we each spoke in the great Gathering of the Law, where the surviving Wielders came together to share the teachings of the Eld Green with the assembled Folk. It's an old tradition that was long abandoned in the lost Everland, but as with many old things, we're giving it a place of honor in our new homeplace. With so few of us remaining, we must do all we can to renew these sacred fires and make them relevant to the struggles of today.

Neither Daladir nor Jitani can make this journey with me. She should return in the next few days, and then we'll need to prepare the birthing room.

We hope that Sinovian will be able to visit soon. He and Tobhi will each give our daughter a name, as is the maternal uncles' duty and right; with two mothers and two such uncles, she will be doubly blessed. Daladir's new life is largely spent in Chalimor, as much by choice as circumstance. He's there now negotiating a new treaty with the Reach, and it's taking him longer than he'd hoped. Qualla'am and Blackwick are giving him good guidance, though, so he shouldn't be too long this time. We still see each other on occasion, and he'll meet his daughter when his other duties are done. Beyond that, nothing between us—the three of us—is settled or certain.

But those are thoughts for another time. I stop and look around, stretching the pain from my back. "We're here."

Spearbreaker was my warrior name, but I am Tarsa'meshkwé now, the Spearplanter. The spear stands tall in rich red soil, its roots deepening with time. I will be a warrior-Wielder for the growth of good things, a Greenthorn Guardian. Those blooding days I spent as a Redthorn are done.

My Tetawa brother and I stand side by side on the upper crest of a broad sandstone ridge that extends a few miles to the north of the Valley. Sharp towers of rock rise up high in all directions around us, but from this height we can see above most of them and look off to the eastern horizon, which slowly brightens with the approaching dawn.

We paint our faces red and white—war and peace, challenge and mercy in balance—and then I reach into the long leather pouch draped across my shoulder and pull out a tapered golden sphere as large as my hand. It's a wyrwood seedpod, the first one that has fallen from the Forevergreen Tree since its rebirth. It will be the start of Folkhome's renewal, Zhaia's gift to her tree-born descendants. Wide wyrwood forests filled these valleys before the rise of the Dreyd and the coming of Men, and although the land is broken and battered, it still holds the memory of those soaring trees and singing leaves.

My belly moves, reminding me of the importance of this ceremony. We've suffered much this past year. What remains of Red Cedar Town is far, far away. Unlike the great stories of quests and adventure that I loved so much in my younger days, there's no possibility of homecoming, no returning to those hills and the life I once knew. This must be our home now. Many beloved friends died or were lost on the way: Unahi and my aunts Vansaaya and Geth, kind Garyn, Quill's friend Denarra, and so many others. Sheynadwiin is now in ruins. We belong now to Shemshéha, far from the Everland that gave us life and for so long shared its strength with us.

The Redthorn warriors are still here, still the first to defend our homeland against intruders, but they're now joined by other Greenwalkers. We call ourselves the Greenthorn Guardians, a small but growing group of Folk dedicated to the teachings of the reborn Tree, its continued renewal, and its protection. We sing the songs and keep the dances. We plant the trees and restore the waters. We will heal this land, and when we're finished, we'll heal the rest of this wounded world. Seven young she-Folk are training in both Redthorn and Greenthorn traditions to be my assistants at the Tree—it will be ably protected, even when I've gone on, in my time, to the ghostlands.

There are now new gathering grounds, and even some of the Celestials have started to come to the grounds to keep the Tree alive. Of the Seven Sister Nations, only the Wyrnach aren't present at the Greenthorn grounds. Their arbor stands empty, in remembrance. There are Kyn, Tetawi, Ferals, and even some Gvaergs and Beast-Folk among the Greenthorns, as well as a few rare and honored Humans. Kinship is so much more than blood. It's a lesson we should never forget.

And we haven't forgotten. We've learned from the Ancestrals of the past, and keep their memories and legacies alive today. Now it is time to look to the future.

I sing and hold the seedpod to the rising sun. Tobhi joins his voice to mine and draws Quill's rattle from his belt, shaking it in time with the song, watching as the golden pod ever so slowly splits apart and thousands of small winged seeds, glimmering copper red, burst outward and float into the air.

"Our memory has returned," I say, watching the seeds scatter on the wind. "We won't forget again. We dance beneath the arbors, sing beneath the moon. The balance endures. Everywhere a seed takes root, the Deep Green will flourish, and so, too, will we. A healing is taking place at last. This is our home.

"We will change, as all things change, and our future will be no better or worse because of it. We will simply be. The Folk will continue. We'll lose some of what we are, and gain other things, other ways, but we'll endure, and so will the Green. That's the way of life in this Melded world of Folk and Men. It's our blessing and our curse. It's our great hope."

Tobhi and I stand together in joyful song, voices proud and clear, and watch the healing seeds rise high with the dawn. They dance on the breeze and swirl eastward, toward the sister suns.

The End

Glossary

Names and Other Stories

A

Academies. Human houses of higher learning. Most Academy curricula are separated into the following schools: Rationalism (Moral Sciences), Alchaemy (Natural and Elemental Sciences), Philosophy (Theological and Terrestrial Law), and Manufactory (Industrial Sciences). The Learnèd Academy in Chalimor is the largest and most celebrated of the Academies in the Reach.

Adelaide of the Veil. Mysterious singer and member of Bremen and Crowe's Medicine Show and Repertory of Thespian Delights.

Airships. The primary military and mercantile transportation vessels of the Ubbetuk Nation. These galleons draw elemental energies from the air for lift, causing dramatic atmospheric disruptions and great lightning storms that can be seen for many miles. Called Dragons by Humans; the preferred colloquial Ubbetuk name is Stormbringers. An Ubbetuk armada is known as a flight of Dragons.

Akjaadit. "The Hummingbird's Granddaughter." The Dragonfly in Tetawi teachings.

Alchaemy. The twin Human sciences of physical change, both bodily healing and elemental transmutation.

Allied Wilderlands. A southern province of the Reach. It is a loose confederation of independent townships inhabited by rugged and self-reliant Human miners and foresters who often trade with and marry among the Folk, and who have little use for either the Dreyd Creeds of Andaaka or the political posturing of the Reach-capital of Chalimor.

Ancestrals. The first of the Kyn to emerge from the Upper Place to the Eld Green; the primeval ancestors and progenitors of the Kyn Nation.

Andaaka. A southwestern province of the Reach best known as the home of Bashonak, the heart of Dreyd-worship in the Republic.

Anja Redbird Meadowgood. The adopted Tetawa daughter of Quill Meadowgood and Tobhi Burrows.

Anomalous. Spirit-beings formed from the strengths of miscellaneous creatures of the three planes of existence—the Upper Place of order (sky), the Lower Place of chaos (underworld), and the Middle Place of balance (earth)—and tasked with the duty of protecting the Eld Green and its peoples. The most powerful Anomalous are Guraadja, the great winged Bear-Snake, and his swift companion, the Stag-Rabbit Saazja.

Ascension. In Dreyd teachings, the promised rise of a dutiful and deserving Dreyd adherent to the ranks of the immortal Dreyd themselves. The only known true ascension was the Melding that first brought the Dreyd to godhood a thousand years past.

Ashanna dol'Graever. Newly married socialite from one of the First Families of Chalimor and acquaintance of Denarra Syrene.

Assembly of Law. The governing council of the unified Kyn Nation in the Old Everland, which replaced the Gathering, an earlier council-meet of the autonomous Kyn towns.

Athkashnuk. Wyrm Wielder present at the Sevenfold Council.

Athweid. Young Celestial she-Kyn diplomat to Eromar murdered by Vald before the Expulsion.

Averyn. Zhe-Kyn healer; consort and advisor to Garyn Mendiir.

Avialle. The River-Mother; a spirit-being of the Eld Green.

Awakening. The first emergence of *wyr*-powers in the life of a young Wielder, generally around the time of puberty. It is often a physically traumatic experience; if a Wielder is unguided in the transformation, the uncontrolled *wyr* can lead to madness and/or death.

Ayeddi'olaan. Cedar Branch matron of Red Cedar Town and deceased grandmother of Tarsa'deshae.

B

Barrow Hills. According to the Tetawa historian Tempest Sparks, and based on conversations with Tetawi and Wyrnach elders prior to the Expulsion, a region in the southern Everland where great standing stones and tombs mark the sacred burial ground of the once-great Wyrnach. As their numbers diminished, they gradually retreated from the region, taking the memory of its full significance with them. Tetawi in the region called the stone-haunted hills the Downlands, and treated it with both respect and some measure of fear. While other areas in the Everland were claimed by Human squatters, there were enough strange and frightening events in the Barrow Hills to prevent Human settlement. Its reputation has become far more sinister in the years since the Expulsion.

Bashonak. The capital city of the Dreydcaste in the Reach. It is a massive stone fortress at the edge of the Tuskwood in Andaaka, known as much for its rigidly authoritarian creeds as for the skilled military training of its adherents.

Battle of Downed Timber. The last battle of a war between the allied forces of the Everland and Eromar against brigands from the Lawless. Lojar Vald was a young man at the time of the battle, and his life was saved by a he-Kyn warrior, Damodhed, who later expressed regret for not letting a Lawless fighter kill the future Dreydmaster.

Battle of Five Axes. The last great battle between Humans and the Folk, where Human prospectors and their military protectors were driven from the Everland by a confederation of Folk warriors.

Béashaad. The capital province of the Reach, located on the eastern edge of the continent. Its inland region is a temperate mix of hills, farmlands, and wide prairies, while its coastal waters teem with marine life. The great metropolis of Chalimor is built on the eastern shores of Béashaad.

Beast-tribes. The various communities of animal and bird people who called the Old Everland home. Each group has its own chosen leaders, and those leaders often meet in council.

Beastwalkers. Tetawi *wyr*-workers gifted with the power to communicate with and sometimes take on the bodily form of animals.

Benji Woodlock Meadowgood. The adopted Tetawa son of Quill Meadowgood and Tobhi Burrows.

Betthia Vald. Long-suffering wife of Lojar Vald.

Between-Worlders. Folk who share characteristics of multiple genders. See *Zhe-Folk.*

Biggiabba. Gvaerg Matron and Wielder.

Binder. The second rank among the Dreydcaste. Binders draw the essence of spirits caught by Seekers into their snaring-tomes for use by Reavers.

Birchbark Hollow. A rugged valley in the Everland, at the eastern edge of the Meshiwiik Forest; home of the Brown Lodge and the Igwimish Mound, the central council house and ceremonial grounds of the western Tetawi.

Blackfly Fen. A dense and fetid swamp at the southern tip of the Everland, inhabited by furtive swamp-dwarfs known as Powries.

Blackwick. D'Yeshkha-Faalg III. The aged Chancellor of the Ubbetuk Swarm.

Blood Vow. A sacred Kyn oath of protection.

Blue Sage Valley. The homestead of Vergis Thane's ranching family in the Certainty Hills.

Bluecap. The military and defense rank of the Ubbetuk Swarm.

Braachan. Apple Branch he-Kyn elder and Shield.

Braek the Older. A he-Kyn Wielder and Greenwalker; father of Braek the Younger.

Braek the Younger. A he-Kyn Lawmaker of the Celestial Path; estranged son of Braek the Older.

Branch. One of the seven maternal clans of the Kyn. Each Branch is named for an ancestral tree-spirit and is known for its gifts in particular spheres of Kyn life: Willow, trade and diplomacy; Oak, leadership and philosophy; Ash, healing; Thorn, defense; Cedar, lore and the arts; Apple, horticulture; and Pine, mysticism and dream-guidance. According to the Tetawa historian Tempest Sparks, Apple Branch is named not for the sweet apples brought to the Everland from eastern Sarvannadad but rather refers to the tart mountain crabapple indigenous to the Kraagen Mountains. Sparks also notes that some Branches have more than one affiliation: Oak, Ash, and Cedar are constant, but Willow is sometimes replaced by Birch, Pine by Spruce or even Juniper, and Thorn by Sycamore or Elm; Maple, Walnut, and Butternut are regional variations of the more common Apple. Regardless of difference in name, the affiliations, rights, and obligations remain constant.

Branch-Mothers. The leading she-Kyn of a particular Branch. They determine Branch law and ensure proper behavior and ritual observance among their kith.

Bremen and Crowe's Medicine Show and Repertory of Thespian Delights. Traveling performance company and refuge for outcasts, eccentrics, and outlaws. Strange rumors have followed the Medicine Show and its uncanny founder for decades, as its appearances have often accompanied political and geological disruptions. Featured in both ghost stories and hearth-side hero tales, it follows no known calendar or route and cannot be found by those seeking it directly.

Brigga Marblemace Meadowgood. Adopted she-Gvaerg daughter of Quill Meadowgood and Tobhi Burrows.

Bright-Eye. The smaller of the sister suns of the Everland.

Brownbrick District. An area of Chalimor of growing economic and social importance. Not as fashionable as Rosewood Hill but far from the rough reputation of Mariners' Quay, Brownbrick is home of merchants, traders, and other ambitious professional families.

Brownies. A pejorative but widespread Human term for Tetawi.

Bryn. A young Moth Clan he-Tetawa of Spindletop.

Buborru. The chthonic Badger-spirit and wisdom-keeper of Tetawi teachings.

Burning Mouth. An iron-veined pit on the outskirts of Red Cedar Town used to imprison Wielders during the Purging.

C

Canopy Veil. The *wyr*-woven mystical barrier between the immortal Eld Green and the mortal world of Humanity.

Carinne. Binder and Dreydcaste administrator in the south Eromar city of Chimiak.

Celestial Path. The philosophical principles of Luran-worship, descended from Dreyd teachings brought by the Proselytors who accompanied the first Human traders into the Old Everland. The Path is characterized by a denial of the flesh and an emphasis on the power of the purified mind, a commitment to hierarchy and obedience, a rejection of the *wyr* and the relational values of the Way of Deep Green, and an embrace of the individualistic and commercial values of Humanity.

Celestials. Kyn followers of the Celestial Path. The Shields of Luran's Glory are the ritual and philosophical leaders of the Celestials.

Certainty Hills. A contested, arid region in Dûrûk, best known for its lush, grassy hills, which are popular among both the cattle of Human ranchers and the wild bison and antelope hunted by Jaaga-Folk.

Chaada. A young Moth Clan she-Tetawa of Spindletop.

Chacatl. A dark, bitter bean from the southlands of Pei-Tai-Pesh. When roasted, ground, and mixed with spices and honey, chacatl is a delectable and highly addictive after-meal refreshment. Though enjoyed to excess among the urbane Chalimites, chacatl is treated with ceremonial regard among the Human inhabitants of Pei-Tai-Pesh.

Chal Bay. The bright, fish-rich waters of the edge of Chalimor.

Chalimite. An inhabitant of Chalimor.

Chalimor. "Jewel of the Reach." The capital city of the Reach of Men, named for its location between the white shores of Chal Bay and the rugged slopes of Mount Imor; political, artistic, and cultural center of Humanity; home to the great Hall of Kings, the Reachwarden, and the Sovereign Republic Court.

Changeling. A Tetawa with the ability to shape-shift into the form of her Clan animal. The shape-changing Tetawi witches—Skeegers—are a cursed form of Changeling without the calming Clan influence.

Chanting-sash. A woven or braided belt, generally of wyrweave or sturdy linen, into which a Wielder sews or beads some of her more powerful prayers, stories, and medicinal formulas. The sash serves as a calming memory aid to help balance the Wielder's mind and emotions as she does her work.

Chestnut Grove. The Human name for the former community of Spindletop.

Clan. The primary social and political foundation of Tetawi life, with each structured through matrilineal authority and descent. All Clans are named for the animal spirit-being from which it descends and from which it derives its qualities; the spirit-being and its moral descendants are deeply honored by all members of that Clan. The most powerful are the Four Mother Clans of the First Fire: Raccoon, Spider, Kingfisher, and Trout. The Second Fire comprises Squirrel, Cricket, Snake, Peccary, Beetle, Rabbit, Lizard, Owl, Raven, Badger, Mouse, Snake, Bee, Dog, and Bat.

Clan herald. The animal spirit-being from which a Clan takes its name. For example, Chukkor'aa the Far-Spinner is the mother and herald of Spider Clan; Hraak the Keen-Eyed is the herald of Raven Clan.

Cloud-Galleon. See *Airship.*

Code of Confederation. The foundational political document of the Reach Republic. It defines both the governmental bodies and their respective powers. It is the highest law of the Republic, beyond even the Dreydcaste Creeds.

Colonel Bedzo. Orator and member of Bremen and Crowe's Medicine Show and Repertory of Thespian Delights.

Cornsilk. Apple-headed spirit doll of Quill Meadowgood.

Crafting. The Human use of occult ritual and elemental alchaemy to shape the fabric of reality.

Creeds. The ruling doctrines and dogmas of the Dreydcaste. Among the most popular among Human adherents is the Supremacy Creed, which is often interpreted as a justification for the subjugation of all non-Human life to the will and benefit of Humans.

Cropminders. Tetawi *wyr*-workers gifted with the power to communicate with domesticated plant life.

Crystal Court. The crystal-domed center atrium of the Hall of Kings.

Cub. Tetawi youngling.

D

Daladir Tre'shein. Ash Branch he-Kyn diplomat for the Old Everland; stationed for some time in Eromar City.

Damodhed. Uncle of Reiil Cethwir and noted warrior of the Battle of Downed Timber.

Dardath Vale. The ancient valley home of the Kyn city of Sheynadwiin in the heart of the Kraagen Mountains.

Darkening. A pocket of Decay within the mortal world.

Darkening Road. The death march of the Folk who were part of the forced Expulsion from the Old Everland.

Darveth Thane. Younger brother of Vergis Thane and spurned suitor of Denarra Syrene.

Decay. A chaotic elemental force that destroys all mortal things.

Deep Green. The ancient ceremonial, mystical, and kinship traditions of the Eld Green; maintained by the Wielders. Also known as the Old Ways.

Deermen. Deer-headed Ferals of the Kraagen Mountains.

Delvholme. The great underground capital of the Gvaerg Nation in the Old Everland. Built in the caldera of a long-extinct volcano, Delvholme was the grandest and most ancient settlement of the Gvaerg, a testament to Gvaerg adherence to Kunkattar's will. It was the site of horrific atrocities during the Expulsion, when the gates were breached by cannon fire and the he-Gvaerg were staked and exposed to the killing suns.

Denarra Syrene. "Wildflower, Last of Autumn." Eccentric Strangeling Wielder and adventurer. Born Ander Bandabee to Dreyd-sought fugitives—the Human Zoola-Dawn Bandabee and her Kyn mate, Walks-With-the-Winds—and resentfully raised by her mother's Dreyd-devoted brother in the remote trading settlement of Jawbone

Crossing, Denarra changed gender and name when she Awakened into her *wyr*-powers in late adolescence.

Desha'al Myyrd. Minor Celestial dignitary in the service of Pradu Styke.

Dibadjiibé. An enspirited wyrwood staff, topped by a large chink of veined amber with the Wielder's symbol encased within. Originally shaped by the Wyrnach *wyr*-worker Ikath'daarnaval, the staff was lost when Ikath disappeared in the early months of the Purging, after he had come to the assistance of the besieged Wielders in the northeastern Sunrise Forest of the Everland. Dibadjiibé disappeared for decades but ultimately made itself known to Unahi Sam'sheyda when she and Biggiabba drove a group of Human miners from the Kraagen Mountains. The staff was subsequently gifted to Unahi's niece Tarsa'deshae, and it accompanied her on her many adventures.

Dolltender. A Tetawa *wyr*-worker who draws on handmade dolls—usually with dried-apple heads and corn-husk bodies—for spiritual guidance.

Downbriar Town. A Stoneskin-ravaged Kyn town in the southern Everland.

Downlands. A more neutral name for the Barrow Hills of the southern Everland.

Dragon. The Human name given to a mechanized Ubbetuk airship.

Dreaming World. The nether-realm to which all beings travel in times of sleep, delirium, and unconsciousness, and from which some can draw wisdom and guidance. It is a strange and dangerous place for those unable to comprehend its distinct logic, which differs much from that of the Waking World.

Dreyd. An order of now-deified Human priests and sorcerers who overthrew the Old Immortals of Men and assumed their place, thus causing the cataclysmic Melding.

Dreydcaste. The rigidly authoritarian and Human-supremacist followers of the Dreyd. Their holy city and seat of power is Bashonak.

Dreydcraft. The alchaemical sorceries of the Dreydcaste.

Dreydlord. A very rare term for a Dreydmaster who has risen to the top ranks of the mortal Dreydcaste.

Dreydmaster. A leader of the Dreydcaste. There are generally no more than three Dreydmasters in the world at any single time, and each is largely autonomous, though the Dreydmaster of Bashonak is widely regarded as the authoritative voice among them and the one who issues binding creeds and dictates for the Dreydcaste as a whole.

Dreyd-Pledged. Followers of the Dreyd and their teachings.

Drohodu. "Grandfather of the Mosses." Spirit-being; green-skinned consort to Zhaia and father of the Kyn.

Dûrûk. The westernmost province of the Reach, characterized by broken and blasted lands at its eastern border, wind-swept prairies in the
center, and stormy coasts in the west. Its largest settlement—aside
from the tent-cities of the Jaaga-Folk—is the notorious Harudin Holt.

Dweshamaagamig. "Place of the Flowering Tree." The new capital and
peace-city of the Free Kyn in Folkhome.

Ε

Eaters of Old. The collective name for an ancient group of grotesque,
carnivorous beings best known for their uncontrollable hunger. The
Stoneskins are among the most powerful of the Eaters.

Edgewood. A dense pine and scrub oak forest to the south of the
Everland and within the territories of the Spindetop Hollow
Tetawi.

Edified. Those Folk who have accepted the teachings of the Dreyd
Proselytors. Distinguished from *Sanctified* by the degree of inspiration: the Edified are informed, but the Sanctified are truly
transformed.

Eladrys. Human knife-fighter and adoptee into Willow Branch who
chooses to walk the Darkening Road and remain with her friends
and family among the Folk rather than vow fealty to Eromar and
the Reach.

Eld Green. The lush, ancient world of the Folk before the arrival of
Men.

Eldarvian Woods. The largest forest in the Everland. Deep and shadow-
filled, this dense woodland is the home of the largest population of
wyrwood trees in the Reach and is thus vigorously protected by the
Folk.

Ellefina. Giggling young Human housekeeper in the employ of
Denarra Syrene.

Eromar. A heavily industrialized and militaristic province that abuts
the Everland on the north, east, and south. Eromar is the primary
political antagonist of the Folk of the Everland.

Eromar City. The capital city of Eromar, built on a bluff overlooking
the Orm River. It is the location of Gorthac Hall, the home of the
Dreydmaster Lojar Vald.

Essiana. Murdered she-Kyn fiddler and one of the Sisters of
Wandering Virtue.

Eternity Tree. The physical manifestation of Zhaia, the first mother of
the Kyn, the source of the *wyr* in the Everland, and the living covenant between the Folk and the land.

Everland. See *Old Everland.*

Everlights. Perpetual Wielder-shaped balls of soft-glowing *wyr*-fire.

Expulsion. The Eromar-led campaign to drive the Folk from the Old Everland.

F

Fa'alik. The zhe-Kyn lore-keeper of the Redthorns of Red Cedar Town.

Fahr. In the Tetawi tongue, the word for a male.

Fear-Take-the-Fire. A he-Kyn ambassador to Eromar who dies under mysterious circumstances.

Feaster. See *Eaters of Old.*

Ferals. Folk whose bodies resemble a union of Humans and Beasts, such as the birdlike Harpies, the antlered and hoofed Deermen, and the sly and furred Fox-Folk.

Fey-Folk. A slightly pejorative term among Humans for the Folk. "Fey" designates mystery or strangeness at best, evil difference at worst.

Fey-Witch. The common Dreyd term for Wielders and other *wyr*-workers.

Firra. In the Tetawi tongue, the word for a female.

First Families. The wealthiest, most elite, and most insular families among the upper echelons of Chalimor high society. Social station and propriety are paramount concerns among the First Families, for whom domestic subterfuge is a fine art.

First Magistrate. The chief jurist on the Sovereign Republic Court. Kell Brennard is the current First Magistrate.

Firstkyn. Town chieftains among the Kyn before the separate towns were unified into the Kyn Nation.

Flight of Dragons. The Ubbetuk airship armada.

Folk. The collective term for those peoples and nations originating from the Eld Green, including the Kyn, Tetawi, Gvaergs, Ferals, Beast-tribes, Wyrnach, Ubbetuk, and the distantly related Jaagas, among others. While such an encapsulating term acknowledges the shared post-Melding history of such peoples, it can also erase their significant cultural, geographic, ceremonial, and physical distinctiveness.

Folkhome. The common name for the new homeland of the Folk following the Expulsion.

Forevergreen Tree. The name given to the reborn Eternity Tree after the events of the Darkening Road.

Free Folk Alliance of Shemshéha. The name of the Folk confederation, which was formed to give a permanent structure to their shared concern while respecting and acknowledging each nation's sovereignty and independence. The Alliance is a permanent counterpart to the crisis-centered Sevenfold Council.

Free Folk. The defiant survivors of the Darkening Road in Folkhome.

Free Kyn Nation of Folkhome. The new name for the surviving government of the Kyn Nation of the Old Everland, used to distinguish them from the now-autonomous government of those Kyn who remained behind.

Friends of the Folk. A group of self-congratulatory Humans dedicated to saving the Folk from their supposed barbarism and backwardness through assimilation into Human values and Dreyd Creeds.

G

Gallery House. The home of the Kyn Governor in Sheynadwiin; located at the back of the Gallery of Song.

Gallery of Song. The central gathering chamber of the Kyn Assembly of Law and the Sevenfold Council in now-ravaged Sheynadwiin.

Garyn Mendiir. Pine Branch he-Kyn Governor of the Kyn Nation and Speaker of the Sevenfold Council.

Gate-walking. Travel between worlds through *wyr*-work. Such journeying requires long preparation and significant safeguards, for it demands much of the *wyr*-worker's skill and life-force to ensure its success.

Gathering. The ancient council-meet of the autonomous Kyn towns before unification. Replaced by the centralized Assembly of Law.

Gathering Grounds. The open-air ceremonial centers of the new Greenthorn Guardians and other followers of the Deep Green.

Geth. Cedar Branch she-Kyn of Red Cedar Town and deceased aunt of Tarsa'deshae. Died in the Human raid on Red Cedar Town.

Gishki. Spider Clan she-Tetawa of Spindletop and cousin of Quill Meadowgood.

Goblin Chancellor. See *Blackwick.*

Goblins. The common term used by Humans for the Ubbetuk; often perceived by the Ubbetuk as an insult, as it associates them with a mythological race of idiotic and carnivorous monsters common in Human folktales before the Melding.

Goldcap. Ubbetuk merchant or trader of high rank.

Goldmantle. Largest of the sister suns of the Everland.

Gorthac Hall. The sprawling, many-gabled estate of Lojar Vald in Eromar City.

Governor. The political leader of the unified Kyn Nation.

Granny Turtle (Jenna). Spirit-being and creator of the first Tetawi people.

Great Ascension. The Human name for the Melding; refers to the rise of the Dreyd over the Old Immortals of Men.

Great Way Road. Major east–west travel and trade route through the Reach of Men.

Greatmoon. See *Pearl-in-Darkness.*

Greatwyrm. Also known as Wyrm. A massive serpent with poisonous saliva, deer-like antlers, and panther-like legs, which makes its home in subterranean tunnels and deep swamps. Greatwyrms cannot fly, but they can run swiftly and swim well.

Green Kishka. Apple-headed spirit doll of Quill Meadowgood.

Greenthorn Guardians. Greenwalkers who work as the healing ceremonial counterparts to the more war-oriented Redthorns.

Greenwalker. An adherent of the Way of Deep Green.

Grugg. An elder Wielder of the Oak-Folk.

Guaandak. The Emperor Triumphant of the Marble House of Kunkattar of the Gvaerg Nation.

Guraadja. In Tetawi tradition, the Anomalous winged Bear-Snake and guardian of the Eld Green.

Gvaerg Nation. One of the Seven Sister Folk nations, the Gvaergs are rough-featured, largely hairless giants who live in vast cave cities beneath the earth. Their link to the *wyr* is through earth-borne spirits. Gvaerg society is rigidly divided into proud and pious Houses under the ancestral authority of aged patriarchs. The suns are deadly to these subterranean Folk, as their light turns he-Gvaergs to dead stone, but wyrweave wrappings can defend against that fate.

Gweggi. Ubbetuk groom and carriage driver.

H

Hak'aad. Celestial he-Kyn diplomat to Eromar and son of Imweshi.

Hall of Kings. The residence and forum of the Reachwarden in Chalimor. Though the leader of the Reach is now elected from the Assembly, the Hall retains its name from the old monarchies that had long ruled the territories claimed by the Republic.

Harpies. Called Kuth'kurathkash in their own language, the most powerful of the Feral peoples with the heads of wizened old Women and the bodies of massive eagles.

Harudin Holt. The westernmost city of the Reach, second in size and influence only to Chalimor. It is a tiered and sprawling city built on the limestone cliffs of the storm-shattered Reaving Coast, and is best known as a haven for pirates, mercenaries, criminals, and fortune-hunters. Though it is managed in the name of the Lord Mayor, the Three Guilds are the true power of Harudin Holt.

Heartwood. The stable *wyr* essence of the Eternity Tree.

Hickory. A sour-faced apple-head doll belonging to Quill Meadowgood.

High Hall. The seat of political and spiritual Dreyd authority in grim Bashonak.

High Houses. See *First Families*.

High Marching Town. A Stoneskin-ravaged Kyn town in the southern Everland.

High Timber. The thinning pine and aspen trees near timberline in the Kraagen Mountains.

'Hold. See *Threshold*.

House of States. The public forum and debate chamber of the Assembly of the Reach Republic.

Houses. The primary social and political foundation of Gvaerg life, with each being patrilineal in authority and descent. All Branches are named for a stone, mineral, or type of metal, which is deeply honored by all members of that House.

Humans. The collective term for those peoples and nations originating from the lands beyond the Eld Green, including such diverse populations as the theocratic Dreyd of Andaaka, the fiercely independent miners and foresters of the Allied Wilderlands, the republican aristocrats of Béashaad, and the defiant tribespeople and merchants of Sarvannadad. While such an encapsulating term acknowledges the shared post-Melding history of such peoples, it can also erase their significant cultural, political, and physical differences.

I

Illirius Pym. Chalimorean showman, smuggler, and black marketeer; acquaintance and frequent rival of Denarra Syrene. His true name is unknown, but he is far older and stranger than he appears, and his stratagems and ambitions extend well beyond shining Chalimor.

Imweshi. Celestial she-Kyn diplomat to Eromar and mother of Hak'aad; poisoned by Vald in Eromar.

Iron. Deadly poison to all Folk but Ubbetuk and Gvaergs. This virulent quality is well known to many Humans, and they use it to their advantage against many of the Folk, particularly the highly sensitive Kyn.

Iron-ward. An amulet created by the Gvaergs for their Folk kith to protect the latter from the toxic effects of iron.

Iseya. She-Kyn maidservant to Neranda Ak'shaar.

Ivida. Cedar Branch she-Kyn of Red Cedar Town and aunt of Tarsa'deshae.

Ixis. Harpy Mystic and Wielder.

J

Jaaga-Folk. One of the Folk peoples, descended from the Strangeling unions of Kyn and Humans. Though not one of the Seven Sister nations, the Jaagas consider themselves and are generally considered by other Folk to be kith of the Seven Sisters. They are a musical, largely nomadic, patrilineal people who inhabit the northwestern wilds of the Everland, as well as the sweeping grasslands of the Reach province of Dûrûk.

Jago Chaak. Tetawa toymaker and Skeeger changeling.

Jekobi. Raven Clan he-Tetawa of Birchbark Hollow, Leafspeaker, and father of Tobhi Burrows.

Jenna. See *Granny Turtle.*

Jippita the Whistler. In Tetawi tradition, the brave Cricket spirit.

Jitani Al'daar. Thorn Branch she-Kyn warrior and mercenary; sister of Sinovian.

Jorgi. Tetawa freedom fighter; brother of Jothan.

Jothan. Tetawa freedom fighter; brother of Jorgi.

Jubilee. The social event of the year in Chalimor, hosted by the Reachwarden himself in the Crystal Court of the Hall of Kings.

Jurist Temple. The stark stone chambers of the Sovereign Republic Court in Chalimor.

Jynni Thistledown. Badger Clan she-Tetawa of Birchbark Hollow, healer, and maternal aunt of Tobhi Burrows.

K

Kaantor. The Human Blood King of Karkûr and treacherous instigator of the Melding.

Kajia. A long-dead former lover of Tarsa'deshae.

Karkûr. A once lush and bountiful land ruled by Kaantor, now the desolate and poisoned devastation known as the Pit Fields.

Kateline Crossing. The narrow but unpredictable strait at Shard Ford that links the Great Kultul Sea and the Riven Sea between Eromar and Dûrûk.

Kei'shaad Mendiir. Pine Branch she-Kyn of Thornholt Town and mother of Garyn Mendiir.

Kell Brennard. Former Reachwarden; currently First Magistrate on the Sovereign Republic Court. During his term as third Reachwarden, Brennard advocated the incorporation of the Everland, its people, and its resources into the larger sovereignty of the Reach of Men.

Kidarri. She-Jaaga root-worker.

Kinnit. Acrobat and occasional lover of Denarra Syrene; member of Bremen and Crowe's Medicine Show and Repertory of Thespian Delights.

Kishkaxi. Harpy Brood Mother of the North Wind Aerie.

Kith. Family, relations. Depending on context, the term refers to either immediate, extended, or distant relationship through blood or transformative adoption.

Kitichi. In Tetawi tradition, the trickster Squirrel spirit.

Kiyda. Cedar Branch she-Kyn of Red Cedar Town and deceased aunt of Tarsa'deshae.

Klaus. Groom, hunter, and caretaker of Bremen and Crowe's Medicine Show and Repertory of Thespian Delights.

Kraagen Mountains. A massive mountain range bisecting the Everland from north to south.

Kunkattar. Spirit-being of stone; father of the Gvaerg peoples. Each Emperor Triumphant is considered by the pious Gvaergs to be the reincarnated embodiment of Kunkattar.

Kyn Nation. The most numerous and widely dispersed of the Seven Sister nations. The *wyr* of the Kyn is drawn from the green growing world and elemental forces of nature, although a growing number of Kyn follow the Celestial Path and ways separated from the *wyr*. Kyn have a heightened sensitivity to the spirits of nature through their serpentine sensory stalks. Their matrilineal branches are descended from the seven sacred trees of the Old Everland. Sheynadwiin, the great peace city of the Everland, was their political and cultural capital; it is now Dweshamaagamig in Folkhome.

L

Lan'delar Last-Born. Cedar Branch she-Kyn of Red Cedar Town and deceased mother of Tarsa'deshae.

Lartorsha. Dancer and member of Bremen and Crowe's Medicine Show and Repertory of Thespian Delights.

Lawless. The rugged, snow-swept region at the margin of the Reachwarden's influence. It is without a central government, although there are numerous small settlements scattered throughout the area that maintain their own laws and order. While home to many brigands, outlaws, and petty despots, it is also home to many fiercely independent people—Folk, Human, and Beast—who settle their own grievances and avoid conflict unless it is forced upon them.

Leafspeaker. A Tetawi *wyr*-worker who interprets the patterns of *wyr*-shaped leaves to communicate with the Spirit World and to preserve stories and teachings. The leaf-reading skills are the Tetawi expression of Kyn teachings, thus highlighting some of the cooperative links between the two peoples.

Leith Fynon. He-Kyn Celestial messenger in the service of the Sevenfold Council.

Lojar Vald. "The Iron Fist." Prefect of the state of Eromar and ambitious Dreydmaster.

Lore-leaves. Wyr-working tools used by Tetawi Leafspeakers. Each possesses a unique naming symbol, a personality, and a voice. For example, *Ek-shewi* and *Gwai'shewi* are the fawn and the doe respectively, and they often travel together in readings.

Lower Place. One of the three primary worlds of existence in the Eld Green and, to a lesser extent, the Melded world. It is a realm of chaos and shadow, though not necessarily evil.

Lower Rinj. High-quality smoking leaf with relaxing and slightly hallucinogenic qualities.

Lubik. Trout Clan elder *fahr;* pepa of Medalla and Gishki, uncle of Quill Meadowgood.

Luran. Moon-Maiden. The Celestial manifestation of the Human Dreyd entity Meynannine; revealer of the Celestial Path to the Kyn Shields. For most Folk, the Greatmoon of the Everland, Pearl-in-Darkness, is male; the virginal female representation is drawn from Human cosmology.

M

Makers. Ancient predecessors of the Wielders who first learned to harness the *wyr* currents of the Eld Green. Though powerful, the Makers became selfish and tyrannical, and they were overthrown by the Folk; those who survived taught their Wielding descendants to be humble, and to use their powers in service to the People. The Shields drew upon the old memories of the rebellion against the Makers in their instigation of the Purging.

Mandra. She-Kyn maidservant of Neranda Ak'shaar.

Mardisha Kathek (née don Haever). Chalimite socialite and general secretary of the Friends of the Folk.

Mariner's Quay. The dangerous docks district of Chalimor.

Mashamatti. Long-dead he-Kyn Wielder of Thistlewood, and grandfather of Unahi Sam'sheyda.

Medalla. Spider Clan she-Tetawa of Spindletop and cousin of Quill Meadowgood.

Medicinals. The herbs, roots, plants, bones, insect stingers, animal glands, and diverse other pharmacopoeia used by the Folk for healing and visioning.

Meerda. A Moth Clan she-Tetawa of Spindletop; mother of Bryn and Chaada.

Meggie Mar. Humorless and lovingly efficient housekeeper of Denarra Syrene.

Melding. The catastrophic union of the Eld Green and the mortal world of Humanity a thousand years past.

Mema. "Mother" or "auntie" in the Tetawi tongue; an inclusive term, used to identify the cub's primary female influence, not necessarily used only to refer to the *firra* who gave birth to the cub.

Merchant's Ward. See *Brownbrick District.*

Merrimyn Hurlbuck. Young Human Binder, fugitive from Eromar City, and rebel against the Dreydcaste Creeds.

Methieul. Youngest daughter of Lojar Vald.

Middle Place. The material world inhabited by Humans and Folk.

Mim. Shy daughter of the Oak-Folk Wielder, Grugg.

Moché. An extremely bitter drink made from dried and ground beans from the southern mountains of Ardûk-Shei. Used by Humans and increasing numbers of Folk to clarify the mind and energize the body, or as part of rituals of general social interaction.

Molli Rose. Tetawa Clanmother, Spirit-talker, and former leader of the confederated Tetawi settlements of the Old Everland. After the Expulsion, she serves as Speaker of the Free Folk Alliance of Shemshéha.

Mother Baraboo. Rotund leader and resident mystic of Bremen and Crowe's Medicine Show and Repertory of Thespian Delights. She was known by grander names and forms in the time of the Immortals of Old, but this is the guise she prefers in her current travels across the Reach.

Mother Malluk. In Tetawi tradition, the strong but unpredictable Peccary spirit.

Moundhouse. Stout Tetawi cabin with sharp eaves, cedar-tiled arched roof, interior and exterior carved support posts, and deep-set hearth. Moundhouses generally surround a ceremonial mound at the center of the settlement.

Mount Imor. The soaring, snow-covered peak that overlooks the Reach capital of Chalimor.

Mulchworm. Apple-headed spirit doll of Quill Meadowgood.

Mungo. Rabbit Clan he-Tetawa and father of Quill Meadowgood.

Myrkash the Unbroken. The great elk chieftain of the Everland Beast-tribes.

N

Namshéké. "Storm-in-Her-Eyes." The youngling name of Tarsa'deshae.

Neidam. Captain of the Reachwarden's guard.

Nenyi. Badger Clan she-Tetawa of Birchbark Hollow and mema of Tobhi Burrows.

Neranda Ak'shaar. "Violet Eyes, Daughter of the House of Shaar." Celestial she-Kyn of Pine Branch. Legislator and Shield. See *Shakar.*

New Immortals. Another name for the Dreyd.

Nightwasp. Ubbetuk mechanical summon insect.

Nine Oaks Town. A Stoneskin-ravaged Kyn town in the southern Everland.

Not-Raven. A malevolent ghost and flesh-eating spy. Originally from shadow-pockets beyond the Melded world, the Not-Ravens come from the Darkening lands of death and suffering beyond the Canopy Veil.

O

Oak-Folk. A small and furtive people of the Everland. They are spirit-bonded to ancient trees and spend their lives tending their home groves. Though shy, Oak-Folk can be fierce opponents when treated with disrespect.

Oath of Western Sanctuary. The euphemistic title given by Lojar Vald to the writ of Expulsion presented to the Everland Folk.

Oathsworn. Pejorative term given to the Kyn conspirators who signed the Oath of Western Sanctuary in defiance of the legitimate Folk leaders of the Sevenfold Council.

Oda'hea. She-Kyn leader of the Red Cedar Town Redthorns, killed in the defense of that community during the Expulsion.

Oinara. "Strange New World." The Human name for the Melded world, derived from a word in the now-defunct dialect of Pei-Tai-Pesh.

Old Everland. The ravaged remnants of the Everland after the Expulsion. Though most of the Folk were forced from their homeland, some pockets of resistance remain; a large number of the Kyn, Tetawi, and rebel Humans are led by the Redthorn warrior Sinovian.

Old Immortals (of Men). The gods of Humanity who were overthrown by the Dreyd during the catastrophic Melding. Though displaced and significantly diminished, it is rumored that the Old Immortals did not die and have long plotted their return to ascendancy.

Old Ways. The teachings and traditions of the Eld Green that pre-dominated among the Kyn before the rise of the Shields.

Old Windle Road. An ancient travel route that bisected the Reach of Men before the Melding. After the Melding shattered the continent and an inland sea opened up in its path, the Windle was replaced by the Great Way Road to the south.

One Moon Path. A euphemism for the Celestial Path, which holds a single moon as the supreme representation of Luran's remote beauty and purity.

Ore-Runner. Deceased infant son of Biggiabba.

Oryn of Deldmaar. A Human trader who chooses to walk the Darkening Road and remain with his friends among the Folk rather than vow fealty to Eromar and the Reach.

P

Padwacket. Weed-addled valet and loyal friend to Denarra Syrene.

Peace-City. A site of sanctuary, where violence and physical conflict are forbidden and where all are given refuge. The Kyn capital of Sheynadwiin was the oldest peace-city in the Everland; its successor in Folkhome is Dweshamaagamig.

Pearl-in-Darkness. The Greatmoon of the Everland. He is sole survivor of a trio of celestial night-spirits of the Eld Green; his brothers were shattered in the Melding, but their broken bodies remain in the form of a sparkling silver ring that surrounds the world in both night and day. Pearl-in-Darkness emerges from his grief to show his face to the Everland every twenty-eight days; for most of that time, he is in various stages of mourning for his lost brothers.

Pepa. "Father" or "uncle" in the Tetawi tongue, affirming more of an emotional attachment of respect and kinship rather than a lineal relationship.

Peredir. The mortal world of Men before the Melding.

Perwit. He-Tetawa captain of the Spindletop militia.

Petyr. The Human name given to Pishkewah, a Tetawa *fahr* in the employ of Mardisha Kathek.

Pit Fields (of Karkûr). The blighted epicenter of the devastating Melding.

Pixi. A Chalimite poet of Jaaga heritage and friend of Denarra Syrene.

Pox. A blistering, feverish illness that originated in Human lands and has caused successive waves of death among the Folk, especially the Kyn. Death from the pox is slow and excruciating.

Pradu Styke. He-Kyn Celestial captain and opportunist.

Proselytors. Dreydcaste adherents dedicated to the transformation of the world through the teaching of the Creeds to the "unsanctified," by reason if possible, by force if necessary.

Puckerlips. Apple-headed doll belonging to Quill Meadowgood.

Purging. The decimation of the Wielders by fear-maddened Kyn during the last great pox epidemic. Up to two-thirds of Wielders were killed during the three-year campaign of terror, during which time the Shields rose to power.

Purifiers. Dreydcaste defenders of orthodoxy through torture. Often found in the company of Questioners.

Q

Qualla'am Kaer. The fifth and current Human Reachwarden and former soldier for the Reach Republic.

Questioners. Dreydcaste defenders of Dreyd orthodoxy through rigorous interrogation techniques. Often found in the company of Purifiers.

Quill Meadowgood. She-Tetawa of Spider Clan. Dolltender and *wyr*-worker.

R

Ramyd Thalsson. Human merchant and father of Garyn Mendiir.

Reach (of Men). Also known as the Reach Republic. The primary political and economic power in the Melded world, dominated by Humans and their ambitions.

Reach Assembly. The parliamentary decision-making body of the Reach Republic.

Reach-tongue. The common Mannish tongue in the Reach. While many variant and mutually intelligible dialects exist, the dominant dialect is known to linguistic philosophers and historians as Imperial Sarvendene, the language of ancient Sarvannadad.

Reachwarden. The elected leader of the Reach Republic, chosen for a five-year term by a majority of parliamentary representatives.

Reachwarden's Jubilee. See *Jubilee.*

Realignment. According to Celestial doctrine, the final cleansing of the Melded world of all corruption and impurity. Only rigid adherence to the ways of the Celestial Path will provide safety during this tumultuous future event.

Reaver. The highest rank among the Dreydcaste. Reavers use alchaemical formulae and Crafting to control the spirits captured by Binders.

Red Cedar Town. A Kyn town in the southern Everland destroyed prior to the Expulsion; sapling home of Tarsa'deshae.

Redthorn Warrior. Greenwalking warriors dedicated to the Old Ways and the vigorous defense of the Folk.

Reiil Cethwir. He-Kyn diplomat to Eromar.

Riekmere Swamp. A fetid marsh at the heart of the Pit Fields of Karkûr.

Rijjik. A term in the Gvaerg language to designate one who is either ritually unclean or an unbeliever in the dictates of Kunkattar, the Sovereign Stone and Ore-Father of the Gvaerg people.

Riven Sea. The stormier of two freshwater seas intersecting the Reach of Men.

Rosewood Hill. The gated and gardened district of the First Families of Chalimor.

Ryggin. A Wielder of the Fox-Folk Ferals.

Ryn. Murdered he-Tetawa scout in the employ of Sylas Gwydd.

S

Saazja the Dreamer. In Tetawi tradition, the Anomalous flying Stag-Rabbit and companion to Guraadja.

Sadish. Only surviving son of Lojar Vald.

Sanctified. Those Folk who have been transformed by the Dreyd Creeds. See also *Edified.*

Sapling. Kyn adolescent, ranging in age between youngling sprout and adult.

Sarvannadad. A wide territory to the north of the Reach; though largely friendly in matters of trade, Sarvannadad is as yet independent of the Republic's political authority, and it zealously guards its sovereignty. Once a great, continent-spanning empire, the nation was shattered in the Melding, and the Reach of Men rose to power in the ensuing years. People of Sarvannadad are known as shrewd political adversaries, but they are also widely feared, as their continuing imperial ambitions are no less expansive than those of the Reach, and they have had much longer trade with the Ubbetuk Swarm for war technologies.

Sathi'in. Cedar Branch she-Kyn of Red Cedar Town and aunt of Tarsa'deshae.

Seedling. Kyn youngling, ranging in age between infant sprout and adolescent sapling.

Seeker. The lower rank of the Dreydcaste. Seekers wander through the Reach in search of Folk Wielders and Human witches, whom they bring to Dreydholds for the use of Binders and Reavers.

Sensory Stalks. Fleshy head-tendrils that give the Kyn a deeper sensitivity to the elemental and emotional world around them. He-Kyn have one on each temple; she-Kyn have two on each side; zhe-Kyn generally have three, two on one side and one on the other.

Setharian Kills-Two-Men. Oak Branch he-Kyn of Red Cedar Town; father of Tarsa'deshae.

Sethis Du'lorr. Speaker of the Wyrnach at the Sevenfold Council. Last of the Wyrnach to die on the Darkening Road.

Settlements. Tetawi community sites.

Seven Sister nations. The Kyn, Tetawi, Gvaergs, Ubbetuk, Wyrnach, Ferals, and Beast-tribes, representing most of the Everland Folk.

Sevenfold Council. A political assembly of Folk leaders, called only at times of great importance to all the Folk. Succeeded in Folkhome by the permanent Free Folk Alliance.

Sevenfold Rose. A red and white flower with seven petals, previously unknown, that began to bloom after the Folk arrived in their new homeland.

Shakar. "Traitor" in the old Kyn tongue, and a name given to Neranda Ak'shaar after she signed the Oath of Western Sanctuary.

Sheda. Eldest daughter of Lojar Vald.

Shemshéha. "The Place of the Good Red Earth." The proper name for Folkhome, the new homeland of the majority of the removed Folk. From the Tetawi tongue.

Sheynadwiin. The ancient peace-city and capital of the Kyn Nation in the Old Everland, destroyed in the Expulsion.

Shield (of Luran's Glory). The spiritual, political, and economic leaders of the Celestial Path.

Shobbok. The Winter Witch of the Ice-Pierced Heart; a spirit-being of the Eld Green.

Shudwagga. High-ranking member of the Consulting Council of the Ubbetuk Swarm.

Sinovian Al'daar. He-Kyn Redthorn warrior and resistance fighter; brother of Jitani Al'daar.

Sister Suns. The two celestial spirits of the daytime: Goldmantle, the bronze elder sister, is calmer and larger than Bright-Eyes, who burns white-hot with the fires of youth.

Sisters of Wandering Virtue. The name chosen by Denarra Syrene, Jitani Al'daar, and their friend Essiana on their youthful adventures through the Reach.

Skeeger. Cannibalistic Tetawi changeling.

Skriker. A predatory spirit-hound under Shobbok's thrall. Those killed by a skriker become one after death, and the face of each hound resembles that of its mortal self.

Smudge. Ill-tempered mule deer mount of Tobhi Burrows killed in the siege of Sheynadwiin.

Snake-Head. An insulting term used to refer to the Kyn. It refers to their thick, vaguely serpentine sensory stalks.

Sovereign Republic Court. The foremost legal authority in the Reach Republic.

Spindletop. A small Tetawi settlement in the Terrapin Hills of the southern Everland and home of Quill Meadowgood.

Spirit World. The hidden realm of elemental beings, the dead, and spirits of the Green world.

Spirit-weaver. A neutral Human term for Wielders; *witch* is the more negative version.

Sprout. Kyn infant.

Stoneskin. A fierce carnivorous creature with an unquenchable appetite. Named for the layer of protective stones embedded in its flesh.

Storm-Born Twins (Skyfire and Thunder). In shared Folk tradition, descendants of great Guraadja; two powerful and much-respected transformer spirits of the ancient times.

Stormbringer. The preferred Ubbetuk term for their airships, named for the storms that surround each airship when in flight.

Stormdrake. A massive winged and lightning-spitting serpent that inhabits the upper sky.

Story-leaves. See *Lore-leaves.*

Strangeling. A descendant of a he-Kyn/female Human union. If born into a Branch, the descendant is understood as a Kyn; if born out of a Branch (that is, if the youngling's father is non-Kyn), the descendant is generally defined as a Strangeling. The Jaagas are a distinct people born of Strangeling unions and now known by their own name for themselves.

Strivix. "The Unseen." The great and fearsome Owl of Tetawi teachings.

Supremacy Creed. See *Creeds.*

Swarm. The collective Ubbetuk Nation.

Sylas Gwydd. A respected Human trader who lives in Sheynadwiin.

T

Tangletop Forest. A dense wood at the southeastern edge of the Everland.

Tarsa'deshae. "The Spear, She Breaks It," or "She-Breaks-the-Spear." She-Kyn of Cedar Branch. Redthorn Warrior and Wielder; adopted sister of Tobhi Burrows and niece of Unahi. Later Tarsa'meshkwé: "The Spear, She Plants It," or "She-Roots-the-Spear," in honor of her duties as keeper of the Forevergreen Tree.

Tempest Sparks. Self-taught Tetawa historian and author of the great genealogical and documentary tome, *History of the Everland Folk and Their Legends and Hearth-Tales,* among other books. Sparks's unapologetic privileging of Folk perspectives and diverse scholarly protocols put him at odds with the leading Human historians of the time, who either dismissed or attacked his work. In spite of these challenges, he remains the best and most accurate chronicler of Folk customs, laws, stories, and relationships of the Expulsion period and the difficult years following the founding of Folkhome.

Terrapin Hills. The rocky hill country around Spindletop at the eastern rim of the Edgewood.

Tetawi Nation. One of the Seven Sister nations. The Tetawi are an honest and forthright people, short and brown-skinned. Their social and political lives are centered in their matrilineal Clans, each of which is descended from a spirit animal of the Eld Green. They make their homes in squat moundhouses, generally in rough hill country or in forested areas. Their connection to the *wyr* is through empathy with the Beast-Folk; due to this, Tetawi are the greatest healers amongst the Folk.

Thanael Tibb-Wooster. A devoted Dreyd Proselytor to the Folk before and during the Expulsion. When his settling house was confiscated by the Eromar militia, Tibb-Wooster walked the Darkening Road

with his charges and continued his work after the establishment
of Folkhome. His vocal opposition to the Old Ways of the Folk
and active political maneuvering against the elected governments
made him widely unpopular. His departure from Folkhome back to
Chalimor—it is unknown whether the move was voluntary—was,
in the end, mourned by few.

Theedeet the Whisperer. In Tetawi tradition, the dreamy Moth spirit.

Thistlewood. A small pine forest in the southeastern Everland.

Thornholt Town. The second-largest Kyn city in the Everland, located
in the southern Eldarvian Woods.

Threshold. A pocket of the Eld Green that survived the Melding. The
Everland is the largest 'Hold in the Reach.

Tobhi (Etobhi) Burrows. He-Tetawa of Badger Clan. Leafspeaker, scribe,
translator, and lore-keeper. Adopted brother of Tarsa'deshae.

Towns. Kyn community sites.

Trade-tongue. The shared economic, cultural, and political language of
the Folk.

Tree-born. See *Kyn Nation*.

Trump-the-peg. A strategy game popular among Humans, played with
multicolored pegs on a long wooden board.

Tsijehu. An ancient cedar tree that once stood in the center of Red
Cedar Town.

Turtletown. A Tetawi settlement in Folkhome, named in memory of a
settlement of the same name in the Old Everland.

U

Ubbetuk Nation. One of the Seven Sister nations of the Folk, and
the one most estranged from the ways of the *wyr*. Immune to the
poisonous effects of iron, the Ubbetuk have used their fascination
with machines and industrial experimentation to create technologies of rare and sometimes terrifying capability. Among their
greatest achievements are the Stormbringer airships and the floating sky-cities to which many of the population have retreated in
the wake of anti-Folk persecution in the Reach. The Ubbetuk are
a worldly and unfailingly courteous people to whom adherence
to political protocol, cultural etiquette, and proper social rank are
the mark of moral excellence. Collectively known as "the Swarm"
and symbolized by the fierce wasp, their leadership is a hierarchical
gerontocracy led by the Whitecap Council under the guidance of
the aged Chancellor.

Unahi Sam'sheyda. Cedar Branch elder she-Kyn Wielder of
  Thistlewood. Aunt of Tarsa'deshae. Killed by Neranda/Shakar in
  the assault on the Eternity Tree.
Unhumans. The pejorative term used by Humans for the Folk.
Unsanctified. In Dreyd teachings, the name for those Folk who have
  not yet submitted to the authority of the Creeds.
Upper Place. One of the three primary worlds of existence in the Eld
  Green and, to a lesser extent, the Melded world. It is a realm of
  order and light, though not necessarily good.
Uru Three-Claw. A Wielder of the bear-faced Ferals of the Kraagen
  Mountains.

V

Vansaaya. Cedar Branch she-Kyn of Red Cedar Town and eldest
  aunt of Tarsa'deshae. Sickened on the Darkening Road and died in
  Dweshamaagamig.
Veil (Between Worlds). See *Canopy Veil.*
Verdant Grange. A large trading post in the Certainty Hills of Dûrûk.
Vergis Thane. Unassuming one-eyed Seeker of the Dreydcaste and
  patient vengeance-taker.
Victory Peak. A mountain considered sacred by the Tetawi of
  Birchbark Hollow; home to Molli Rose.
Vorgha. Trusted attendant of Lojar Vald.

W

Waking World (also *Waking Time*). The world of awareness in the waking hours of life.
Warrior's Lock. A symbolic gesture of endurance and disregard for
  physical harm among Redthorn Kyn, the lock is a braided strip of
  hair down the center of the head; the rest of the hair is painfully
  shaved away. In an exercise of strength, the warrior is forbidden
  from binding her, his, or hir sensory stalks against the pain.
Way of Deep Green. See *Deep Green.*
Wears-Stones-for-Skin. Stoneskin that ravaged the Kyn towns of
  Downbriar, High Marching, and Nine Oaks.
Weltspore. Toxic hallucinogenic fungus sometimes used in
  assassinations.
White Chamber. The Reachwarden's private offices in the Hall of Kings.
Whitecap Council. Members of the Ruling Council of the Ubbetuk
  Swarm.

Whitecaps. Members of the Ruling Council of the Ubbetuk Swarm.

Wielder. Greenwalkers and *wyr*-workers of the Kyn.

Wielders' Circle. The Grand Council of Folk *wyr*-workers in Sheynadwiin.

Wild One. A pejorative Celestial term for a Greenwalker.

Wildwater. Large, raging river that flows through the Kraagen Mountains.

Witchery. The use of *wyr* or other medicine skills toward selfish and generally destructive aims.

Wyr. The life source of the Everland, formed from the living voices and embodied memories of the ancestors, the spirits of the Eld Green, and the life-spark of the Folk themselves. It is the elemental life-song of creation, drawing upon and giving sustenance to all remnants of the Eld Green, strengthened by attentive care and weakened by neglect. Its embodied manifestation is the Eternity (now Forevergreen) Tree. According to the Tetawa historian Tempest Sparks, the word *wyr* is actually a much-corrupted form of the original Wyrnach term *dweidwiir*, roughly translated as "all that is, which, when spoken, becomes."

Wyrm. See *Greatwyrm.*

Wyrnach. The eldest of the Seven Sister nations, the Wyrnach are also known as the "Spider-Folk" for their eight limbs and multiple eyes. They are a rare and reclusive people, standing well over eight feet high, and are well known among the Folk for their *wyr*-fed powers of divination. Of all the Folk, the Wyrnach have the deepest links to the *wyr*, and their seeming extinction during the Expulsion was a grievous blow to followers of the Deep Green. Though there have been stories of Wyrnach remnants in the Old Everland, these may be hopeful rumors only.

Wyr-ward. A device of Human Crafting that addles the mind and blocks the access of Wielders to the *wyr*, thus leaving them vulnerable and confused.

Wyrweave. Light and strong fabric made of the inner fibers of the wyrwood tree.

Wyrwood. A type of tree that grows only in 'Holds, the wyrwood is a vital resource to the Folk. Its leaves and naturally shed outer bark, when stripped and pounded into flexible fibers, can be used for durable wyrweave fabric, clothing, and armor; its red roots and fallen branches can be shaped by Wielders into both armor and weapons, as can its rarely accessed heartwood; and its golden sap is both nourishing and medicinal. The tree roots of living wyrwood draw poisons out of the surrounding soil, thus purifying both earth and water. Its lofty canopy provides housing for many Folk, as do the massive trunks of the more ancient trees. In many ways, the wyrwood tree provides the daily link between the Folk and the *wyr*-currents of their homeland.

Wyr-worker. Those Folk gifted with the strength and talent to draw upon and guide the *wyr* toward particular aims or goals.

Y

Yelseth Kathek. Boorish but wealthy husband of Mardisha Kathek.

Z

Zhaia. Tree-Mother. The ancient spirit of the green world from whom the seven Kyn Branches are descended. She is first and eldest, the elemental personification of the Deep Green.

Zhe-Kyn. A third gender among the Kyn that shares some of the qualities of both the she-Kyn and the he-Kyn. Zhe-Kyn are border crossers between genders, and they often excel at healing, which requires sensitivity to the different challenges of the often distinct male and female social worlds. See *Between-Worlders.*

Biography

DANIEL HEATH JUSTICE is a Colorado-born Canadian citizen of the Cherokee Nation. He lives with his husband, mother-in-law, and two dogs in a log house near the shores of Georgian Bay in Huronia/Wendake, the traditional homelands of the Huron-Wendat confederation. A scholar as well as a fantasy writer, Daniel teaches in the Department of English and Aboriginal Studies Program at the University of Toronto. More information about his creative and scholarly work can be found at www.danielheathjustice.com.

ML 12/2018